STONEHEART VALLEY

CLARK PETERSON AND BILL WEBB

ADDITIONAL MATERIAL BY ERICA BALSLEY, GREG A. VAUGHAN, AND SKEETER GREEN

Developers

Ken Cliffe and Skeeter Green

Editors

Ed McKeogh James Redmon, Erica Balsley,
and Skeeter Green

Electronic File Conversion

Karen McDonald (God-Empress of the Universe),
Jai Erwin, and Skeeter Green

Art Director

Richard Thomas with Matt Milberger and
Clark Peterson

Layout and Book Design

Charles A. Wright

Interior Artists

Michael Bielaczyc, Paul Bielaczyc, Andrew DeFelice,
Steve Ellis, John Massé, MKUltra Studios, Jason Sholtis

Front Cover Art

Artem Shukayev

Cartography

Conan Venus and Robert Altbauer

Front & Back Cover Design

Charles A. Wright

Original Playtesters

C.J. Land, David Peterson, John Ackerman, Mike Weber, Chip Schweiger, Joe Weimortz, Gene Cotton, John Birk, Mike Nisco, Christopher Laurent, Conrad Claus, Timothy Laurent, Karl Harden, Nicolas Laurent, Ken Hommel, Ken Chan, Dale Haines, John Murdoch, Ian Thompson, J.P. Johnston, Louis Roberts, Karl Johnson, Roger and Marc Cram, Jesse Briggs, Sean Jones, Jennifer Chalfan and "Betty", and Scar the Cat plus Jeffrey Klingbeil, Angelina Mohr, Steve Vogel, John Sostarich, Art Braune, Chris Sladowski, Yanda Bushfield, Todd Rooks and the rest of the GenCon 2001 Demo Team.

Special Thanks

Stephan Wieck and everyone at White Wolf. Ryan Dancey at Wizards of the Coast for pioneering the D20 license, bringing our favorite game back to life and providing third-party publishers the ability to support the game we all love. Eric Rowe and Dustin Right at the Wizard's Attic for helping us get off the ground. Jason Klank, Kyle Charon, Hyrum Savage, Mac Golden, Brad Thompson, John Bacon, Alec Burkhardt, Tim Duggar and everyone on the D20/OGL lists. Skeeter Green would like to say a special thanks to all the fans who clamored for this update. This book wouldn't have happened without the tireless support of the Necromancer Games fans from the messageboards (everyone who posted in the "Tomb of Abysthor Errata" thread; Duke Omote, brvheart, DestyNova1, magoo, peteasman, and mostly eyelessgame, hats off to you!)

Table of Contents

FROG GOD GAMES IS

CEO
Bill Webb

Creative Director: Swords & Wizardry
Matthew J. Finch

Creative Director: Pathfinder
Greg A. Vaughan

V. P. of Marketing & Sales
Rachel Ventura

Art Director
Charles A. Wright

Just Ran Out of Gum
Skeeter "I am smiling" Green

Foreword

A Word from the Paladin

What's the Stoneheart Valley?!?

Some long-time fans of **Frog God Games** and **Necromancer Games** before are well familiar with the Tomb of Abysthor, Fairhill, and the environs described in this adventure. And, if you are one, you are likely asking yourself what exactly is this Stoneheart Valley that we speak of. Sure there are valleys in the region of Bard's Gate. There's the Lyre Valley north of the city and the Valley of the Shrines that leads to the entrance of Abysthor's tomb, but Fairhill lies along the Tradeway between Reme and Bard's Gate, and no valley was ever mentioned in regards to it.

To you good folk we say, "Bravo, true fans!" and "Hang with us for a minute here while we explain." Your observations are correct, and if you have been with us a long time, then you're probably familiar with the fan-made map by The Lone Goldfish that provided our first real glimpse of an attempt to link together some of sites presented in various adventures in the early days of the company. Of course, it shows no geographic feature called the Stoneheart Valley, nor does the later attempt to canonize and expand upon that map in *K6: Shades of Gray* by **Necromancer Games**. Rest assured, we are well aware of this and have taken it into account in the naming of this adventure. And since you're such great fans and sticklers for details, I'm going to give you some spoilers. So stop reading this if you don't want to know.

Still here? Okay, you asked for it; here goes:

It's been no great secret that we've been talking about creating the official **Frog God Games** campaign setting (to include the material from **Necromancer Games** as well, of course), and you've probably even heard that it's going to be called *The Lost Lands*—hence the title of this book. Well, everything in *The Lost Lands* starts with The Lone Goldfish map and grows from there. You'll notice that there was no scale on The Lone Goldfish map, which is good because *The Lost Lands* are big...way bigger than the scale on the *K6* map would indicate. We'll still incorporate the *Shades of Gray* map into the final product, but it's going to require some modification and scaling to make it fit. Another thing you'll notice is that The Lone Goldfish map only covers a narrow stretch of territory running from Reme to Freegate—the Stoneheart Mountains look like an itty-bitty little range, and there's basically nothing south of Bard's Gate.

So here's our philosophy in the development of *The Lost Lands* (you've probably already seen it posted elsewhere, but I'll repeat here for anyone that came late). *The Lost Lands* will directly incorporate *every* book released by **Necromancer Games** and **Frog God Games**...yes, all of them...with a couple exceptions as outlined here:

We can't include the **Judges Guild** books; **Judges Guild** owns that Intellectual Property, and the *Wilderlands of High Fantasy* setting is complete in its own right. If you want to plop it down in your **Frog God Games** campaign world, that's fine, but we won't be writing it directly into the setting.

Though Bill and Clark were involved in the some of the early **Sword & Sorcery Studios** titles—particularly the *Creature Collections*—that material will not be incorporated into the setting either. The *Scarred Lands* is its own entity and property and will not be incorporated for the same reason given above.

Robert J. Kuntz's *Maze of Zayene* series will not be included. That's part of Robert's game world that he let **Necromancer Games** play around in, but it will not appear within *The Lost Lands*.

Morten Braten's *Ancient Kingdoms: Mesopotamia* is geographic Earth, so it will not be directly included, but all of Morten's stuff is fantastic, and we will certainly be indirectly incorporating it as much as possible.

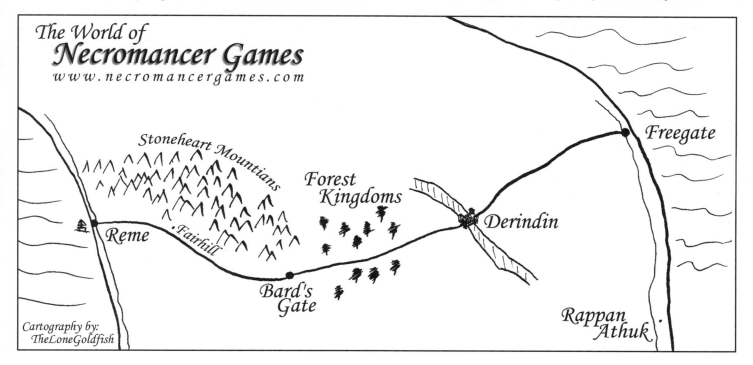

The World of
Necromancer Games
w w w . n e c r o m a n c e r g a m e s . c o m

Stoneheart Mountians

Freegate

Forest
Kingdoms

Derindin

Reme

Fairhill

Bard's
Gate

Rappan
Athuk

*Cartography by:
TheLoneGoldfish*

THE LOST LANDS: STONEHEART VALLEY

Gary Gygax's Necropolis is set in the Earth analog of Khemit. We will be incorporating it as part of the world so you can run that adventure seamlessly.

John Stater's **Hex Crawl Chronicles** are set in their own self-encompassed world that John is fleshing out himself, so those adventures from **Frog God Games** will not be directly incorporated into **The Lost Lands** either (though look for some future indirect connections with his own opus campaign, the **Land of Nod**).

What does that leave? Well…everything else published by the Frog God or the Necromancer. It will all be included and, though there may be a necessary tweak here and there to make it all fit, it will be faithful to its original intent…Barakus, the Gray Citadel, Darkmoon? It's all there, and it will also include newcomers like the Razor Coast, the Northlands, and Richard Pett's forthcoming **The Blight** city setting. It'll all be in there.

So what should you expect from the Lost Lands? Well, like I said, it's big…really big. As I mentioned, we took The Lone Goldfish map and started from there. We took the Stoneheart Mountains to be true to their name and made them a geographic lynchpin—the range is huge and is considered the "backbone" of the world. Everything spreads out from there with Bard's Gate and the Stoneheart Valley holding a central location.

Oh, that's right, we were talking about the Stoneheart Valley earlier. The Stoneheart Valley encompasses the area of the central Tradeway including Fairhill to the west and the foothills all the way to Bard's Gate to the east. It's really more of a gap or basin in the range between the main body of the mountains and their southern terminus than a true valley. As a result, only the northern portion of the Stoneheart Valley is seen on the maps in the adventures included herein or on The Lone Goldfish map.

With the fact that we're building a world around the one whose framework we already have in mind, now I'll give you one more spoiler if you're still game. Though the work itself is still in progress, what follows is the introduction to the forthcoming **The Lost Lands** campaign setting. Enjoy.

— **Greg A. Vaughan**
April 26, 2013

"There have been many names for our world: Kala, Eorthe, Midgard, Erce the Mother. The Khemitians call it Geb; the ancient Hyperboreans,—who were giants among men, conquerors and builders—called it Boros after their homeland under the Pole Star. The Daanites, the last remnant of that ancient and noble race by their own reckoning, call it Lloegyr, which in their tongue means the Lost Lands and, I suppose, in a way that's really what it is…lands that once felt the tread of civilization's true grandeur and now exist as but a shadow of that former glory. But for most it has no real name at all; it is just the earth we live on, and toil upon, and call home, and to whose embrace we one day return.

These Lost Lands exist on three known continental landmasses, with two great oceans beyond which none have ever explored. The Tempest Meridians, a line of storms and rough seas where navigational techniques fail and ships founder that exists in each direction across the seas from the known continents, bar safe passage and hold their secrets close. He that braves the oceans Uthaf or Oceanus to successfully chart the Tartaren Passage to that green sea of darkness beyond will surely know much renown and be remembered in history as the greatest of explorers.

The center of modern civilization as we know it resides on the largest continent, Akados, seat of the former Borean Monarchy of the Foerdewaith (now our fractured Kingdoms of Foere) and long-lost home of the ancient Hyperborean Empire, that glorious bastion of civilization that was and is no more. To the north lies the frozen polar continent of Boros from which the Hyperboreans first descended to bring their learning to the world and where, perhaps, they returned when their time of ascendance ended. To the east, across the Gulf of Huun, lies the second-largest continent, Libynos, where the Triple Kingdom of Khemit, the Ammuyad Caliphate, and the city-states of the Crusader Coast hold sway, though the dark interior of endless jungle and svelte knows many other cultures barely glimpsed in the west.

The blessed light of Rana, the Sun, holds court in the firmament during the hours of the day, rising in the east and setting in the west, and the night sky of Lloegyr serves as the abode for the moons Narrah, the Pale Sister, and smaller Sybil, the Dark Sister, as they weave their intertwining course sunwise through the darkness. A multitude of stars add their jeweled illumination to the Sisters, the brightest of which is Oliarus, the winking Pole Star that hovers above the northern homeland of the Hyperboreans, ever awaiting their return. Other stars of note that travel across the night sky are Mulvais the Red Star, Cyril the Blue Chariot, and Xharos the Black Star, though the astrologers of ancient Hyperborea tell us that these are actually planets like our own world, spinning in emptiness thousands of leagues away, as preposterous as that may sound. Their ancient scrolls also hint that there may be other worlds unseen even farther away. Better to leave such fancies to god-touched fools and the mad.

Time in these Lost Lands is guided by the dance of our moon Sisters as they transit the Thirteen Houses of the Zodiac. Each year is comprised of thirteen moons, each of which consists of four weeks, composed of seven days, for a total of 364 days a year. The hours of the day number 24 after the blessed Tesseract. The seasons rely upon the dance of these moons to guide them in at the proper hour and recede in the presence of the new season as it arrives. All beings on Lloegyr revere the twin Sisters in some form or fashion as the key to life upon the earth…"

—*from* Illuminatus Geographica *by Master Scrivener Drembrar of Bard's Gate*

THE WIZARD'S AMULET

Introduction

The Wizard's Amulet is a short, introductory adventure for six newly created good-aligned 1st-level characters. The adventure revolves around Corian, a fledgling Sorcerer. While an apprentice, Corian discovered a letter written by a wizard named Eralion, who it is said some years ago attempted to become a lich — and failed. Accompanying the letter was a mysterious amulet with strange markings. Joined by newfound companions, Corian set off in search of Eralion's keep and his supposedly unguarded treasure. But Corian is not alone in desiring to unlock the mystery of Eralion's fate. Darker, more evil forces have designs on the secrets reputedly hidden with Eralion — forces willing to stop at nothing to obtain…*The Wizard's Amulet*.

This adventure is designed to be used "out of the box," meaning you can run it right away with little preparation time. *The Wizard's Amulet* is the perfect adventure for new GMs who want to try their hand at running their first adventure. Just follow the steps outlined in the section entitled **Using this Adventure** and you should be playing your first game within fifteen minutes!

The adventure itself covers several programmed encounters that Corian and his comrades face on the road from Reme to Fairhill, the purported location of Eralion's keep. The adventure culminates in an ambush by Corian's nemesis Vortigern who tries to capture Eralion's amulet by force. The adventure uses an **Act and Scene** format to facilitate ease of use with little preparation. Veteran GMs should feel free to flesh out the adventure and include events on the road not covered in this module.

Using this Adventure

This adventure requires the *Pathfinder Roleplaying Game Core Rulebook*. We presume you as the GM have spent some time familiarizing yourself with the rules. We presume you have called over a bunch of your friends and ordered some pizza. We also presume you have secured a good table as well as paper, pencils and all those funny dice we gamers love so much. You should also have a dry erase board or some other way to draw up the "battle map" for any encounters your character will face. A big pad of paper will do in a pinch. If you have lead figures or some other way to represent the characters we suggest you use them. We recommend that you print a hard copy of this adventure for your reference and copies of the pre-generated characters for your players' use. Now sit back, relax, break out the chips and dip (since the pizza is probably gone) and follow these steps. You should be playing within 15 minutes!

First, read the sections entitled **Notes for the GM** and **Adventure Background** to yourself, spending a few minutes becoming familiar with the plot line and the main non-player characters. Also, read **Corian's Supplemental Information** found at the very end of this module.

Second, pass out the pre-generated characters. (See the section entitled **Pre-generated Characters** at the end of this book.) You can do this one of two ways: you can either pick which six characters you want your players to play and let the players divide those six as they wish. Or you can show them all of the pre-generated characters and let them choose which six to play.

You **must** include **Corian**, the sorcerer, in the party. You also should include Galdar, the cleric, in the party, though he is not essential.

If you decide to choose the six characters yourself, we recommend that in addition to Corian and Galdar you include at least two of the primary **fighters** as well as either Helman, Phelps, or Flarian the bard because of the importance of having a character with stealth skills. Playtesting demonstrates that this party composition gives the best chance of success. You should use no more than seven or eight total characters — with six being the optimal number. If you add more characters you may have to increase the number of monsters encountered to keep the combat challenging. If you have fewer than six characters or if your players choose primarily non-combat characters, then you will have to reduce the difficulty of the encounters. Notes are provided to cover these situations.

Once the players have **selected** which characters they will play, you should give the player who is playing Corian a copy of **Corian's Supplemental Information**, found at the very end of this module. Make sure to keep the information private, since the contents are to be revealed at Corian's discretion.

Third, have the characters familiarize themselves with their characters. The person playing Corian should pay particular attention to his or her back-story and to the letter from Eralion.

Fourth, read the section entitled **Player's Introduction** to yourself so you understand it and then read it aloud to your players.

Fifth, once you have read the **Player's Introduction** aloud, turn to the section titled **Running the Adventure** and play out the acts and scenes of the adventure in the order provided. You are officially under way.

Sixth, at the end of the night use the section entitled **Concluding the Adventure** to wrap things up.

There you have it — fifteen minutes and you should already be adventuring!

Character Selection

Make sure someone plays Corian; encourage someone to play Galdar; don't hand out **Corian's Supplemental Information** until after the players have selected their characters.

Make sure at least two of your players select combat oriented characters. There is going to be plenty of fighting in this adventure and the party will need to be able to handle it.

Generally you should stay out of the character selection process, but if two players want to play the same character resolve it the old fashioned way: roll for it! The one rolling higher on a d20 gets to play the character.

If you want more information about continuing the story started by this adventure, about the system or about **Frog God Games** and our products, sections addressing these topics can be found at the very end of this module.

As a final matter, remember the **Frog God Games** "golden rule": *use what you want, discard or change the rest*. We have presented this adventure in a strict step-by-step format to make it easy to get that first game going without any hassle. But if you want to change some things around, go right ahead. In fact, we hope ambitious GMs will use this adventure as a campaign seed. Feel free to flesh out the city of Reme and to roleplay Corian's discharge from his apprenticeship and his investigation into Eralion and the amulet. Go ahead and play out the meeting between the various characters. Draw up an overland map and handle all the travel rather than just the programmed encounters provided by this adventure. Maybe even throw in a few non-player characters of your own. It's your world. Your players are just playing in it.

Notes for the GM

This section is primarily aimed at newer GMs, though reading the tips in this section may remind veteran GMs of how they learned these same lessons through much experience. Your players' characters will be mighty wizards, devout clerics, stout fighters and cunning rogues. But you are in a sense above even the greatest of these, for you are the shaper of the world in which your players adventure. It is your job to breathe life into these written words and make for your players a fictional reality into which they can immerse themselves.

Though players cannot function without a GM, it is also true that a GM cannot function without players. Thus, the best advice for a new GM is this: always remember that your adventures should be like cooperative stories written by both you and your players. You must work together for everyone to have fun. That doesn't mean you should break rules to make your players happy. What it does mean is that, like an enlightened ruler, you should adjudicate your games with fairness and graciousness. Your power should be unquestioned not because it is frequently exercised but rather because it is not. You should never be "out to get" your players. If your adventures are challenging and you run them fairly you will be heralded as a great GM.

You have many hats to wear as the GM. First and foremost, as already mentioned, you are the fair arbiter of the rules. But you are also the person who plays all the monsters and non-player characters (NPCs) that the players encounter. Where the players play one (or at most two) characters, you will play many: the person met at the inn or on the road, the vile orc, the mischievous leprechaun, the evil cleric, the friendly wizard, the power-mad king and all the gods. You are, in short, everything except the player characters. When you are the thief, be cunning and dishonest, when the orc, cruel and chaotic, when the paladin, noble and chivalrous, when the town guard, loyal and stern. Inject as much of your own personality into your roles as possible. Always remember, however, to be fair both to the characters and to yourself. As one of the best GMs to ever run a game once said: "When playing a monster or an NPC, temper your actions with disinterest in the final outcome and play only from the viewpoint of that particular monster or NPC." Being a GM is challenging — requiring more skill than that of the best player — but it is equally rewarding. Learn to wear all of your hats well, and to be fair while doing so, and your players will enjoy themselves immensely.

To assist you, we have provided "side boxes" — material in the margins which are specific GM notes deserving of special attention. Here you will find important things to remember, monster tactics, trap summaries, highlights of rule changes in the new edition and other material of specific use to you as the GM. We hope these notes make running this adventure as easy as possible.

We have also provided "boxed text" — pieces of narrative to be read directly to your players to describe key encounter areas and events. Normally, we believe that GMs should describe encounters in their own words. However, since this adventure is designed to be used "out of the box" with little preparation time by novice GMs, we decided to include the boxed text. You should, of course, use your own words if you desire.

Also, because this adventure module is designed for people using the new edition of the game rules for the first time (both novice and veteran GMs) we have provided a large amount of step-by-step material to help you make sure you are using the new rules properly.

One final note: Do not let disputes swallow the gaming session. Since this adventure is designed to be one of your first adventures under the new rules, there is a greater chance that you or your players will not be entirely familiar with all the new rule changes. If a dispute arises, listen briefly to the party's complaint. If you can remedy their problem without unnecessarily bending the rules then do so. The point of the game is for everyone to have fun. If you intend to rule against the party, explain to them that after the session you can all discuss the matter at length but that you need to make a decision now and continue play. Then make the decision. Remember that your decision for that session is final. Continue with play. If, after discussion following the session, you determine that your decision was incorrect then you should do your best to remedy the faulty ruling. Either let the players replay the particular encounter or, if a character was killed, allow that character to return to life. Rules exist for a reason. They must be enforced, but not at the cost of damaging friendships and ruining everyone's fun. A good GM needs to be firm in his or her rulings but at the same time not afraid to admit he or she was wrong and correct that wrong. Remember, as GM you are a fair judge, not an opponent.

But most of all have fun.

Adventure Background

Long ago, **Eralion** was a good and kind wizard. He was devoted to his patron deity, a god of law and righteousness. As the shadow of his death grew long and he began to sense his own mortality, Eralion's heart darkened and his desire for power and fear of death became greater than his devotion to his god. He turned his attention to ways to lengthen his fading life. He learned the rumor of the fabled Mushroom of Youth in the dungeon of *Rappan Athuk*, the legendary Dungeon of Graves, but he lacked the courage to enter those deadly halls. He researched *wish* spells, but he did not have the power to master such mighty magics, being himself a mage of only meager power.

Finally, in his darkest moment, Eralion turned to **Orcus**, the Demon-lord of the Undead, imploring the dread demon for the secret of unlife — the secret of becoming a **lich**. Orcus knew that Eralion lacked the power to complete the necessary rituals to become a lich, as Eralion had barely managed the use of a scroll to contact him in the depths of the Abyss in his Palace of Bones. Orcus smiled a cruel smile as he promised the secret of lichdom to Eralion. But there was a price. Orcus required Eralion to give to him his shadow. "A trifling thing," Orcus whispered to Eralion from the Abyss. "Something you will not need after the ritual which I shall give to you. For the darkness will be your home as you live for untold ages."

In his pride, Eralion believed the demon-lord. He learned the ritual Orcus provided to him. He made one final trip to the city of Reme to purchase several items necessary for the phylactery required by the ritual. While there, he delivered a letter to his friend **Feriblan the Mad**, with whom he had discussed the prospect of lichdom — though only as a scholarly matter. Feriblan, known for his absent-mindedness, never read the letter, but instead promptly misplaced it and its companion silk-wrapped item.

Eralion returned to his keep and locked himself in his workroom. He began his ritual, guarded by zombies given to him by Orcus — sent more to make sure Eralion went through with the ritual than to offer him aid. As he uttered false words of power and consumed the transforming potion he realized the demon's treachery. He felt his life essence slip away — transferring in part to his own shadow, which he had sold to the Demon Prince. Eralion found himself Orcus' unwitting servant, trapped in his own keep. And there he would have stayed, forgotten to the world, had it not been for the actions of a lowly apprentice.

Some twenty years later, a young wizard's apprentice named **Corian** learned of Eralion accidentally. During his final days under his uncle's tutelage, Corian and his master had traveled to the library of Feriblan the Mad in the city of Reme. Corian was never pleased to visit Feriblan, for while there he was always forced to have contact with **Vortigern**, Feriblan's apprentice, and his loathsome raven familiar — **Talon**. Luckily for Corian, this day he managed to avoid Vortigern. While perusing mundane documents in an outer sitting room as his master and Feriblan studied ancient scrolls, Corian nervously fiddled with a clasp on the back of a small reading stand. Quite to his surprise, a secret compartment opened which contained a small, bound piece of parchment and an item wrapped in silk cloth. Checking to see that his actions were unobserved, Corian slipped both items into the folds of his robe. The parchment proved to be the letter Eralion had left for Feriblan on his last visit before his ritual, and the item wrapped in the silk cloth an amulet of some unknown design.

The *Sorcerer's* Amulet?

Corian is a sorcerer with the arcane bloodline. That means that he has the arcane bond class ability like a wizard. To keep things simple, we've written Corian with the bonded item version of the arcane bond. That way a new player doesn't have to keep up with a second character sheet for his familiar. Because he has a bonded item, Corian casts his spells with the aid of a special ring, staff, wand, weapon… or *amulet*.

An interesting twist for this adventure and Corian's background would be to have his bonded item be Eralion's amulet! When Corian touched it for the first time, he felt a charge of arcane energy pass through him and the bond was forged. His powers as a sorcerer were truly awakened in that moment. What does this bode for the young sorcerer? Does this bond also link him with the powers of Orcus? Does the Demon Lord of the Undead have special plans for Corian? Who knows? It's your game and what this ultimately means is up to you!

Note that after Vortigern steals the amulet, Corien will be at a distinct disadvantage in spellcasting. The concentration DC to cast spells without a bonded object is 21 (DC 20 + spell level). Corian must add his level (1st), plus his ability score modifier (Cha 17 = +3), to a 1d20 roll and get a 21 or more to cast a spell. So, roll 1d20, plus 4 (ability modifier plus level); Corian needs to roll a 17 or better every time he wants to cast a spell. That's a tall order! Make sure the player using Corian is aware of this; no one is happy playing a certain type of character and then having the rug pulled out from under them!

Corian's actions, however, did not go unnoticed. Vortigern was fast becoming a wizard of some power. It was whispered that had the old wizard Feriblan not been mad, he would have discharged Vortigern from his apprenticeship long ago. It was believed — correctly — that Vortigern had learned all the skills of an apprentice and was remaining with Feriblan under the guise of an apprentice in order to have continued access to Feriblan's legendary library. Among the many musty volumes and forbidden tomes, Vortigern discovered a tract describing how to call forth an imp from the lower planes. Sacrificing the familiar that Feriblan had called for him, Vortigern summoned the small, devilish creature in secret to act as his familiar. The imp took the form of Vortigern's prior familiar — a raven — to prevent suspicion. It was this imp who, while in raven form, saw Corian take the amulet and parchment. Talon reported what he saw to his master, though neither knew the significance of the letter and the amulet at that time.

Freed from his apprenticeship, Corian returned to Feriblan. Taking the risk of asking a direct question of the addled wizard, Corian learned that Eralion was nowhere near powerful enough to become a lich. "Eralion! A lich?!" the old wizard exclaimed. "He was no apprentice, my son, but neither was he a mage with the mastery of the eldritch powers necessary for such a dangerous undertaking! If you have heard such rumors, boy, I shall put them to rest. The magics required for such a transition were far beyond his grasp." Once on the topic of his old friend, Feriblan spoke at length, though in a disjointed fashion. He told Corian of Eralion's keep near the village of Fairhill. Feriblan made reference to a staff that Eralion possessed which apparently had magical powers. He also mentioned that Eralion had never returned several valuable magical tracts and spell books. Corian left the old wizard determined to find this tower and the items it contained — for if Eralion was not a lich, the items should be there for the taking!

Once again, Corian's actions did not go unobserved.

Vortigern commanded his imp familiar Talon to watch the old mage and Corian as they met together. And so it was that Talon overheard their conversation. Once informed by Talon, Vortigern guessed the connection between Corian's visit and the purloined letter and item. To solidify his suspicion, Vortigern commanded Talon to consult his devilish patron — Dispater — who confirmed that the amulet Corian possessed was somehow a link to Eralion's sanctuary within his keep.

Readying himself with the necessary equipment for travel to Fairhill, Corian visited a local tavern — the *Starving Stirge*. There he posted a notice seeking the aid of able-bodied adventurers willing to join him in an expedition to a wizard's tower. Promising an equal division of all gold recovered; he soon gathered a group of comrades-at-arms eager for adventure and glory. Corian was also joined by Galdar, a priest, who was instructed in a vision from his god to seek out Corian and to follow where the amulet led him. Someone or something, it appeared, had angered the God of Retribution. Corian was glad for his company.

But Corian was reluctant to give the full story to his new friends, having on more than one occasion seen Talon, the familiar of Vortigern, peering into his chamber window in raven form. Corian, worried that his theft of the amulet and letter had been seen by the wicked bird, did not wish to risk further discovery while still in Reme. The party set out from Reme some four days prior to the start of this adventure, with light hearts and heavy packs — only Corian nursing the nagging fear that Vortigern and his loathsome bird somehow knew of his goal.

Their hearts would not have been so light had they known of Vortigern's plotting, for Vortigern had not been idle. While Corian gathered his allies, Vortigern assembled several magical items and two unsavory companions. Delayed with his magical preparations, Vortigern and his henchmen set out from Reme two days behind Corian and his band, intent on recovering the amulet at any cost. And that is where our story begins…

If you choose not to locate this adventure in your own world, the following description of the area will help you describe the setting to your players. Reme is a large port city on the eastern coast of an Inland Sea. The tradeway — a merchant road — runs directly east from Reme to the city of Bard's Gate and on towards the forest kingdoms of the east. North of the tradeway, and running parallel to it, lay the Stoneheart Mountains. South of the tradeway, and also parallel to it, is the river Greywash. The vale between the river and the mountains through which the tradeway runs is verdant green and dotted with pine forests, though the forests have mostly been cleared back from the road. Fairhill lies just north of the tradeway about 8 days march from Reme, approximately half way from Reme to Bard's Gate. Hawks and falcons are a common sight, as are larger eagles. The vale is plentiful with game.

Player's Introduction

Read the following text to your players:

You have traveled four days from Reme with your newfound companions. Rain and cloudy weather have marred your travels since you left, slowing your pace and forcing you to keep off the main road and travel under the eaves of the light woods to the north of the tradeway. It seems odd at this time of year to have such strange weather. Sunshine can be seen on the far horizon, and you all have a feeling that something is amiss, as if a dark cloud is following you from Reme. Each of you thinks back to the *Starving Stirge* — the inn where you formed your fellowship. You shift your packs, which seem even heavier in the rain, and recall Corian's notice: *"Seeking Fellow Adventurers,"* it read. *"Companions to share in glory and gold and adventures unnumbered."* As you look down at your muddy boots, you think to yourself that you would gladly trade Corian's promises of gold for dry clothes and a warm fire.

Running the Adventure

Now that you have read the **Player's Introduction**, proceed through the adventure presented below in **Act and Scene** format. Each scene begins with a section of boxed text to be read to your players. It then contains information for you to use to run the particular scene.

Act I: A Safe Haven

The First Watch

> Weary from the long walk, you finally find a nice sheltered area and build your campfire. One of your scouts makes a quick catch of a small brace of conies and soon the smell of roasting rabbit wafts through the air. Each of you feels as if you can finally relax, rest your sore feet and change into dry clothing. It appears your luck may be changing.

The party makes their camp to get out of the rain. Draw up a map of a small clearing against the base of a hill, amidst a grove of trees. The small clearing is about 20 feet in diameter. The hillside is steep and gives protection from the wind and rain, and the light trees give some protection from the rain as well. Stress that the characters should take off their armor and stow their weapons to keep them dry. Make a point of mentioning rust and the problems of **sleeping in armor**. Ask the players what they do with their other equipment. Figure out where they build their fire — if they build it in the open of the clearing, they have trouble keeping it lit. The better location would be either against the hillside or by one of the trees under cover from the rain. Regardless of what your players decide to do, draw a map of the camp. Ask the party if they set a watch and if so in what order the characters stand watch. Make them arrange their characters on the map — where they sleep, etc. Once this is determined, darkness begins to fall, leading to the next scene.

Act and Scene Format

Now all you have to do is proceed through the adventure scene by scene. Veteran GMs should feel free to flesh out actions between scenes as they see fit.

A Voice in the Darkness

Wait!

Before you read the boxed text, determine which encounter you are going to use — the leucrotta or the stirges.

Read the subsection entitled **Encounter Modification**, below, and determine what monster your players encounter. Then determine who has the first watch. If you decide not to use the leucrotta, read the boxed text provided under **Encounter Modification**. If you choose to use the leucrotta, then the person on watch has the following encounter:

> Darkness falls, and the fire begins to die down. As the characters not standing watch drift off to sleep, a child's voice can be heard, crying in the darkness. Taking a brand from the fire, [the person on watch] leaves the fireside to investigate, when suddenly he is attacked from the rear by a hideous stag-like creature with the head of a badger, large, yellowish-gray fangs and demonic red glowing eyes. The beast smells of rotting corpses. Twenty feet away is another, much larger than the first, crying in the voice that you thought was the child's. You are stunned that such a beautiful and innocent sound could come from so demonic looking a beast.

Encounter Modification: If you are a new GM and running the leucrotta encounter seems too complicated, then replace the leucrotta with **3 stirges**. Note, however, that 3 stirges are more dangerous than one young leucrotta. Obviously, since the leucrotta are no longer involved, the player on watch is not lured away from the fire. Instead, the stirges come flying in with a horrible buzzing, concentrating their attacks on the character on watch. If the players encounter stirges they do not encounter the leucrotta and if they encountered the leucrotta they don't encounter the stirges. One encounter is enough for 1st-level characters! If you decide to use the stirges, read the following to your players:

> With a horrible buzzing, three strange flying insects the size of large rats with bat wings, grasping claws and hideous mosquito-like snouts swarm all around you. You shout to wake your comrades as the grotesque monstrosities are upon you — seeking your warm flesh with their evil beaks.

We are going to presume for the following description that you have chosen the leucrotta encounter. If you haven't, turn to the end of this section for information on running the stirge encounter.

Running the Leucrotta Encounter

OK, so here it is. The first encounter. If you are a new GM, this is probably your first time refereeing a combat. So you might be a little concerned about running the encounter properly. Even if you aren't a new GM, the recent edition of the rules is probably new to you. For these reasons, we have provided a substantial amount of detail on how to run this encounter step-by-step, so that novices and experts alike feel comfortable running the encounter under the new rules.

The person lured away from the camp has been drawn ten feet into the woods surrounding the clearing in which the party has made camp and there has been attacked by a young **leucrotta**. The mother leucrotta is making the noise of the crying child, drawing the character on watch right by where the baby leucrotta is hiding, ready to spring. As the character passes by its hiding place the young leucrotta jumps out of the darkness to strike. Though the boxed text makes it seem as if the character has been surprised by the leucrotta, that has yet to be determined.

Determining Surprise

The player ambushed rolls a Perception check. The leucrotta rolls a Stealth check. Unless the character ambushed rolls higher, he is surprised. Until a combatant acts, he is "flat footed" and loses his Dex bonus to AC. Any combatant that can act during the surprise round is limited to a single action. See the *Pathfinder Roleplaying Games Core Rulebook*, "Surprise."

Starting Combat: The first thing you need to do is determine if the character lured into the woods is aware of the leucrotta prior to the attack. If he is not aware of the leucrotta then it gets a free round to act, known as the **surprise round**. Have the character roll to see if he has spotted the leucrotta as he passed by it. To see if he spotted the monster, the character has to roll against his Perception skill. His Perception check is an opposed roll. To know if he makes the Perception check, you first have to know how well the leucrotta is hiding. Roll 1d20 for the leucrotta and add his +8 bonus for his Stealth skill. If the character rolls a higher modified number on his Perception check than the leucrotta did on his Stealth check then the character sees the leucrotta before it attacks and he is not surprised. If he fails his roll then he is surprised and the leucrotta gets a free surprise round. You do not have to roll for the other leucrotta (the mother) because she does not enter combat initially.

Surprise round: If the character is surprised then the young leucrotta gets a free surprise round. In that round, the young leucrotta makes a 5 ft. step out of hiding and attack the character from the rear with its bite. This is a single action, since the leucrotta has been readying, waiting for the character to walk by. Remember, that during the surprise round, all surprised characters are flat footed and do not receive their Dex bonus to their AC. In addition, persons (and monsters) acting during the surprise round can only take a single action. And don't forget that the leucrotta's bite is armor piercing — see its listed special attack. Because the attack in the surprise round is from behind, the armor piercing bite affects the target's armor, not his shield.

Initiative: After the Surprise round or if the character is aware of the leucrotta you need to roll **initiative**. All combatants aware of each other must roll 1d20, adding their initiative bonus if any. The higher roll moves and attacks first. If there is a tie, the combatant with the higher total Initiative Bonus moves first. Record the order of initiative. Persons who subsequently enter combat roll initiative and are added to this ranking. Remember, a person remains flat footed (without their Dex bonus to AC) until they have actually acted. So if the character lured into the woods loses initiative he remains flat footed until he acts.

What the Young Leucrotta Will Do: If the character is not surprised, the leucrotta still takes the action described above — do a 5 ft. move and attack. The leucrotta then, next round, turns around and retreat at full movement, using its double-kick retreat special attack. It still hasn't mastered this attack technique, so its rear kick is a secondary attack (already reflected in the monster stat block for the young leucrotta). If the young leucrotta won initiative, then remember that the victim is still flat footed. After this initial attack and retreat, the young leucrotta makes a full movement to move around behind the character to try to attack him again. However, since it is still young, the baby leucrotta has not yet learned the

importance of focusing its attack on one victim. If it encounters another person it forgets about the initial victim and launches an attack against the new target. If there are other persons nearby then they are just as likely to be attacked. You should randomize the victims of the young leucrotta's attacks.

What the Mother Leucrotta Will Do: The other, larger leucrotta is the young beast's mother, who stands and watches the fight, while the baby moves in, bites and leaps out kicking. The mother is interested in seeing whether or not the youngster is properly using the hunting techniques she has taught him. She remains some 20 feet away watching his actions. The mother only joins in if the baby is killed outright or if she is attacked. If the baby has been killed she does not cease her attacks until she is killed or until every member of the party is dead.

Ending the Combat: If the baby takes a cumulative total of 6 hit points of damage or more, the pair retreats into the night. Also, if more than three persons show up to fight against the young leucrotta, the mother calls out in their foul language and the two retreat. Finally, if the fight is going poorly for the party, the GM in his or her discretion can decide that the beasts have had enough practice and have them retreat (mercifully). If any of these occur, the GM should have the mother tease the party for the next two nights, but not really attack them. They continually hear a baby crying off in the distance or a wounded animal in pain.

The Leucrottas

MOTHER LEUCROTTA   **CR 3**
XP 800
CE Large magical beast
Pathfinder Roleplaying Game Bestiary 2 "Leucrotta"
Init +6; **Senses** darkvision 60 ft., low-light vision; **Perception** +4

AC 14, touch 11, flat-footed 12 (+2 Dex, +3 natural, −1 size)
hp 39 (6d10+6)
Fort +6; **Ref** +7; **Will** +1

Speed 40 ft.
Melee bite +7 (1d8+2) or double-kick +7 (1d6+3 plus trip)
Space 10 ft.; **Reach** 5 ft.
Special Attacks armor piercing bite, double-kick retreat

Str 14, **Dex** 14, **Con** 12, **Int** 8, **Wis** 9, **Cha** 8
Base Atk +6; **CMB** +9; **CMD** 21 (25 vs. trip)
Feats Improved Initiative, Run, Skill Focus (bluff)
Skills Bluff +4 (+14 to imitate voices), Perception +4, Stealth +3; **Racial Modifiers** +10 to Bluff to imitate voices
Languages Leucrotta
SQ mimic voice

Armor Piercing Bite (Ex) The bony ridges that a leucrotta has for teeth can chew through metal or wood. In addition to inflicting damage on the character attacked, the leucrotta's bite deals damage to the character's armor or shield (GM's choice). If the damaged caused by cumulative leucrotta bites exceeds half the hit points of the shield or armor, it gains the broken condition. If the armor or shield is reduced to 0 hp it is utterly destroyed. See the *Pathfinder Roleplaying Games Core Rulebook*, "Breaking Items" for the hardness and hit points of armor and shields.
Double-Kick Retreat (Ex) When a leucrotta turns to flee it instinctively kicks with both of its rear legs. This attack is a free action which must be followed by a double move away from its target. This movement provokes attacks of opportunity. Only one attack and damage roll is made for both legs, and the leucrotta adds 1.5 times its Strength bonus to the damage. This attack also counts as a **trip attack** in that the person kicked can be knocked over.
Mimic Voice (Ex) A leucrotta can mimic the voice of a man, woman, child, or a domestic animal in pain. This is often

---

Escape Hatch

If the combat is going poorly for the players (more than one character is seriously wounded or one character is unconscious), and the baby leucrotta is still alive, then the mother and the baby retreat, having had enough practice for one night.

Playing the Leucrotta

Jump in and bite; don't forget the bite is armor piercing; then retreat and use the double-kick retreat; people kicked may be knocked over as with a trip attack; then run away and circle around the character for another attack two rounds later. Lather, rinse, repeat.

Trip Attack

When the leucrotta successfully hits with its double-kick retreat, it immediately makes a trip attack to knock its opponent down, in addition to the damage inflicted with the kick. Ouch! Roll 1d20 + the leucrotta's CMB; if that roll exceeds the target's CMD, the target is knocked prone. If the target has more than two legs, add +2 to the DC of the combat maneuver attack roll for each additional leg it has. Some creatures — such as oozes, creatures without legs, and flying creatures — cannot be tripped.

used to lure a victim into attack range. To mimic a voice the leucrotta must make a Bluff check opposed by the Perception check of any listeners.

YOUNG LEUCROTTA   CR 1
XP 400
CE Medium magical beast
Pathfinder Roleplaying Game Bestiary 2 "Leucrotta", "Young"
Init +8; **Senses** darkvision 60 ft., low-light vision; **Perception** +3

AC 15, touch 14, flat-footed 11 (+4 Dex, +1 natural)
hp 13 (3d10–3)
Fort +2; **Ref** +7; **Will** +0

Speed 30 ft.
Melee bite +3 (1d6) or double-kick –2 (1d4 plus trip)
Special Attacks armor piercing bite, double-kick retreat

Str 10, **Dex** 18, **Con** 8, **Int** 8, **Wis** 9, **Cha** 8
Base Atk +3; **CMB** +3; **CMD** 17 (21 vs. trip)
Feats Improved Initiative, Run
Skills Bluff +0 (+10 to imitate voices), Perception +3, Stealth +8; **Racial Modifiers** +10 to Bluff to imitate voices
Languages Leucrotta
SQ mimic voice

Armor Piercing Bite (Ex) The bony ridges that a leucrotta has for teeth can chew through metal or wood. In addition to inflicting damage on the character attacked, the leucrotta's bite deals damage to the character's armor or shield (GM's choice). If the damaged caused by cumulative leucrotta bites exceeds half the hit points of the shield or armor, it gains the broken condition. If the armor or shield is reduced to 0 hp it is utterly destroyed. See the *Pathfinder Roleplaying Games Core Rulebook*, "Breaking Items" for the hardness and hit points of armor and shields.

Double-Kick Retreat (Ex) When a leucrotta turns to flee it instinctively kicks with both of its rear legs. This attack is a free action which must be followed by a double move away from its target. This movement provokes attacks of opportunity. Only one attack and damage roll is made for both legs, and the leucrotta adds 1.5 times its Strength bonus to the damage. This attack also counts as a **trip attack** in that the person kicked can be knocked over. The young leucrotta has not yet mastered this ability, so it is considered to be a secondary attack.

Mimic Voice (Ex) A leucrotta can mimic the voice of a man, woman, child, or a domestic animal in pain. This is often used to lure a victim into attack range. To mimic a voice the leucrotta must make a Bluff check opposed by the Perception check of any listeners.

A leucrotta is a horrible, unbearably ugly beast. It has the body of a stag, the head of a badger and a leonine tail. It has bony, yellow-gray ridges for teeth and burning, feral red eyes. Their bodies are tan, darkening to black at the head. The stench of rotting corpses surrounds the beast and its breath reeks of the grave. A full-sized male can reach seven feet tall at the shoulder, though they average six feet. Other animals shun this foul creature.

Leucrotta are very intelligent and speak their own evil language. They are wicked and malicious. Because of their mountain goat-like surefootedness, leucrotta normally make their lair in treacherous, rocky crags accessible only to them.

Running the Stirge Encounter

The stirges are not particularly quiet. The character on watch can make a DC 13 Perception check. If successful, he is aware of the stirges' approach and is not surprised. The stirges concentrate on one victim until they drain enough blood to sate their thirst, at which time they detach themselves and fly away at one-half their speed — bloated from their recent feast. If an attached stirge sustains a hit and takes damage — even if not enough to kill it — that stirge detaches itself and fly away seeking less resistant prey elsewhere. See the **Running the Leucrotta Encounter** section above for information on initiative and surprise and surprise rounds and other general advice.

STIRGES (3)   CR 1/2
XP 200
N Tiny magical beast
Pathfinder Roleplaying Game Bestiary "Stirge"
Init +4; **Senses** darkvision 60 ft., low-light vision, scent; **Perception** +1

AC 16, touch 16, flat-footed 12 (+4 Dex, +2 size)
hp 5 (1d10)
Fort +2; **Ref** +6; **Will** +1

Speed 10 ft., fly 40 ft. (average)
Melee touch +7 (attach)
Space 2–1/2 ft.; **Reach** 0 ft.
Special Attacks blood drain

Str 3, **Dex** 19, **Con** 10, **Int** 1, **Wis** 12, **Cha** 6
Base Atk +1; **CMB** +3 (+11 to grapple when attached); **CMD** 9 (17 vs. trip)
Feats Weapon Finesse
Skills Fly +8, Stealth +16
SQ diseased

Attach (Ex) When a stirge hits with a **touch attack**, its barbed legs latch onto the target, anchoring it in place. An attached stirge is effectively grappling its prey. The stirge loses its Dexterity bonus to AC and has an AC of 12, but holds on with great tenacity and inserts its proboscis into the grappled target's flesh. A stirge has a +8 racial bonus to maintain its grapple on a foe once it is attached. An attached stirge can be struck with a weapon or grappled itself—if its prey manages to win a grapple check or Escape Artist check against it, the stirge is removed.

Blood Drain (Ex) A stirge drains blood at the end of its turn if it is attached to a foe, inflicting 1 point of **Constitution damage**. Once a stirge has dealt 4 points of Constitution damage, it detaches and flies off to digest the meal. If its victim dies before the stirge's appetite has been sated, the stirge detaches and seeks a new target.

Diseased (Ex) Due to the stagnant swamps in which they live and their contact with the blood of numerous creatures, stirges are harbingers of disease. Any creature subjected to a stirge's blood drain attack has a 10% chance of being exposed to filth fever, blinding sickness, or a similar disease. Once this check is made, the victim can no longer be infected by this particular stirge, though attacks by different stirges are resolved normally and may result in multiple illnesses.

GM Tips

You should get into the habit of drawing up the night's campsite on the battle map even if you know there won't be an encounter. Otherwise, players quickly figure out that you only draw the map when there is an encounter. Keep them on their toes. Don't ignore drawing up the map just because you know there is nothing special about this hill.

Touch Attack

A touch attack ignores the armor and shield bonuses of the target, though the target retains their Dexterity bonus and any magical bonus. A stirge's attacks are touch attacks.

Ability Damage

Some attacks such as poison or stirge bites do temporary damage to an attribute. Every 2 points of Constitution damage reduces the character's current hit points by an amount equal to his level. It also reduces his Fort save total by 1. A character reduced to 0 Constitution from such damage dies. Brutal! Fortunately, one point of Constitution is regained each night of rest, so try to get some sleep.

The Smiling Skull

> You have driven off the beasts, though some of you are wounded. You know that you must get out of this wilderness soon. You travel for two more days, and finally you believe the beast's haunting childlike cry is behind you. At last, the weather starts to clear, and as you stop for a water break along a stream, you see a strange rock formation atop a hill to the west. You can't be sure, but from your current angle it looks as if the rocks have been placed purposefully. You venture closer and discover that someone has arranged large rocks on the top of the hill in the shape of a grinning human skull.

This is a red herring, and has nothing to do with this adventure. In fact, it is an homage to a classic old adventure, which had just such an arrangement of stones on the hill in which a certain tomb was located. The

party may wish to waste a lot of time and energy here, but there is nothing to find. One of the rocks, however, has been enchanted with a *magic aura* spell, detecting as moderate abjuration magic if the party casts a *detect magic* spell.

Act II:
A Bird in the Hand

A Pleasant Camp

> Today's travels were a pleasant change from the previous four days. You even found some fresh blueberries and two of your group downed a small deer. You make camp in the open, near a copse of trees, and bask in the warmth of the late afternoon sun with full bellies dry clothes. You figure your party is still four days travel from Fairhill.

At this point, draw up a camp on the battle map. Feel free to modify the clearing map provided for the previous encounter. Talk about a proposed watch order, as if you are going to proceed to spending the night. Once those matters are all settled, continue on to the next scene.

Corian's Tale

> As the sun drops below the horizon and the fire dims, Corian asks you all to gather. You have been waiting for Corian to explain more of his purpose behind the formation of your group, wondering at his true motives. Before tonight, he has always rebuffed your questions, saying that he will speak further when you are far from prying eyes and ears in Reme. It appears that time has come.

This scene is entirely for the players, and you should stay out of it as much as possible. Let the player who is playing Corian tell as much or as little of Corian's back-story as he or she wishes. Encourage the player to speak to the group contemporaneously rather than simply reading from the provided background sheet. But remember that this is probably the first major block of role playing in this adventure and that it is being done with pre-generated characters, not characters the players made themselves, so the Corian player has less of a connection than usual with his or her character. Let the other players ask questions of Corian. The length of this scene should be dictated entirely by the interaction of the players. Just sit back and watch. You should only intervene if the Corian character makes an obvious mistake. But even in that situation, don't correct it immediately — the player may be having Corian lie on purpose. Let them bring the scene to a conclusion — not you. Just as they seem to be coming to a comfortable conclusion, shift immediately to the next scene.

Talon

> Just before Corian finishes speaking, one of you notices that you are not the only listeners. About fifteen feet away is the largest raven you have ever seen, and its eyes glow with red fire. You jump up, frightened, as the raven flies off into the night with a shriek. This must be Talon, the familiar of Corian's nemesis, Vortigern. You fear that your enemies are near at hand.

There is no way the PCs can kill Talon now, and he automatically gets away in the round it takes the characters to grab their weapons. He turns invisible and flies away at full speed. Play up the fear of the impending attack which never comes and make them hear plenty of "things that go bump in the night" for the rest of the night (2–3 noises disturb the watch). Vortigern, however, remains a day behind the group and does not appear until **Act III**. He sent Talon ahead to scout… successfully, it seems.

The characters may be frightened into traveling at night — which is unwise. If they do, halfway through the night they are attacked by **3 stirges**. The stirges are completely unrelated to Vortigern and Talon and are a random encounter. The party does have this encounter if they remain in their camp through the night. Use the stirge statistics from the alternate encounter described in the **Encounter Modification** section of the **Voice in the Darkness** scene, above.

STIRGES (3)	CR 1/2
XP 200	

hp 5 (*Pathfinder Roleplaying Game Bestiary* "Stirge")

Act III: Vortigern's Trap

The Farmhouse

You have traveled two days and nights since the demonic bird disturbed your camp, drawing within two days travel of Fairhill. Finally, you feel as though your enemies have lost your trail. You see a farmhouse off in the fields, near the woods, and you decide to see if the farmer will let you rest in his barn for the night. As you approach the small dwelling, you notice that something is terribly wrong. The farmer — or what is left of him — lies in the front yard of the home, half eaten and missing one arm. His wife, and three small children lie in various contorted positions, the smallest boy completely disemboweled. Blood covers the hay in the yard, and a chicken pecks at the corpse of a young girl lying in front of the barn.

You need to **draw this map**. Depict a simple farm dwelling with one door and several windows, as well as a barn, with an open front and small three-foot high wooden-fenced pen enclosing the front area. The gate in the wooden fence is open allowing the animals out of the barn and pen. The farmer's body lies in front of his home. His wife's body and two of their children lie just inside the door to the farmhouse. Their young daughter's body is inside the animal pen in front of the barn.

GM Tip

There is a really cool picture of the farmhouse included. You should show it to your characters as they approach. Hey, we give you this art for a reason. Use it!

Draw This Map

Use the farmhouse picture and the description here to help you. Make sure that off to one side of the farmhouse (we suggest off to the left, a little to the back) you place a copse of trees about 60 feet away — this is where Vortigern is hiding to set up his ambush.

Examination of the bodies by a healer or any fighter familiar with combat wounds easily determines that they were all killed with swords or axes and that the murderers were enthusiastic in their work. If a healer or cleric with healing powers makes a successful DC 15 Heal check, that character discovers that two of the children have dagger-like wounds that

drip a strange poison. Allow any character with the Heal skill to make a DC 23 check to evaluate the poison. If they make the roll, tell them it appears to be poison from some magical creature. If the roll is failed, tell them they have never seen such poison before.

Searching the House: The house and barn have several animals running around: 4 pigs, 30 chickens, and a draft horse. In the trees a few hundred feet away — in the opposite direction of Vortigern — are 3 cows. There is little of value in the house, but an old short sword hanging above the fireplace is in fact a *+1 short sword*, though it has no outward appearance of being magical. A hidden compartment in the bed (DC 20 Perception check unless they specifically search the bed, then DC 15) contains 22 silver and 45 copper pieces. Two lanterns and numerous other dry goods are about as well. If the party buries or consecrates the bodies, they do have to fight zombies when Vortigern springs his trap (see **Ambush!**, below). If they wish to search or bury bodies, let them do so. As soon as they either make camp at the farm or leave the farm to make camp somewhere else, proceed to the next scene immediately. Don't let the party get set up inside the house. The encounter with Vortigern is at hand…

Ambush!

All right, here it is — the grand finale. But before we begin the fight itself, a little background is in order.

Vortigern's Plan: Vortigern orchestrated this encounter to get the amulet from Corian. He has underestimated the party and believes he can simply take the amulet by force. Vortigern and his thugs have been following behind the characters for some time. Using Talon as a scout, Vortigern learned the party's direction of travel. Projecting the party's path, Talon scouted and found this farmhouse. Vortigern and his thugs came here and slaughtered the farmers, figuring that would draw Corian and his comrades to investigate — setting the perfect trap. Using a *scroll of animate dead* stolen from Feriblan's library, he animated the farmer and his family as zombies and ordered them to literally "play dead" until the trap was spring. The "code word" that would cause the zombies to rise up was the final word of the verbal components of Vortigern's *summon monster III* spell.

So far the plan has worked exactly as Vortigern envisioned. Vortigern plans to summon additional undead to surround the characters while he and his thugs hide in the nearby trees and fire missiles and spells at them. He then intends to send Talon to retrieve the amulet from Corian. In preparation for this encounter Vortigern cast a number of spells on himself. He is protected by the following spells: *mage armor*, *protection from arrows*, *resistance*, and *shield*. See his description for more details.

Starting the Encounter:

Watch what your players do around the farmhouse. When it seems like a good time to spring the trap, read the following text:

As you move about the farm, Corian suddenly hears a familiar voice. He looks over and sees Vortigern and two large men with bows drawn, just inside the cover of the surrounding woods some 60 feet away. Vortigern has his familiar — the devil-eyed raven — perched on his shoulder and he is reading a scroll. As Vortigern finishes reading the scroll, the raven transforms into a small, devilish, winged creature and with a hideous shriek flies off Vortigern's shoulder and immediately goes invisible. Instantly, the ground comes alive.

Skeletal hands claw through the ground and begin to encircle the party.

Read the following only if the farmer's bodies were not buried and if you are not using the *Easy* difficulty setting:

The corpses of the dead farmers also rise and move slowly towards you.

Ambush!

Once the characters start to make camp, or start to bury the bodies of the farmers, you need to think about having Vortigern spring his trap as detailed in the next scene. Take a break (it will put your players at false ease), read the next section and decide what you want to do.

Encounter Difficulty: Now that you know the basics of Vortigern's plan, you have to decide how difficult you want the combat to be.

Difficult: This level of difficulty should be used only if your players are veterans and if they are relatively uninjured going into the combat. Now is a good time to remember the GM advice we gave you at the beginning of the adventure — don't be out to get your players. Only use this level of difficulty if your players can handle it. If you decide on using this level of difficulty:

Vortigern springs the trap at the most strategically advantageous time — just as the characters are burying the farmers' bodies (which veterans will certainly do).

Vortigern leans towards attacking after dark if the players are still outside, since all his allies have darkvision.

Vortigern knows the whereabouts of every character because Talon, who has been flying around invisible, is telling him this information telepathically. This lets Vortigern summon a ring of fiendish skeletons around the characters and allows the farmer-zombies to rise up within the circle.

The thugs fire right into the circle of skeletons, since they are resistant to piercing weapons. The party has to deal with zombies inside their group, skeletons circling them, thugs firing arrows at them and Vortigern casting offensive spells at Corian, trying to kill him.

Vortigern uses all his offensive spells against Corian, starting with *magic missiles* and leading up to *acid arrow*. Vortigern saves his *flare* spells for use on any characters that charge his location.

Vortigern also commands Talon to use his stinger on Corian and to pry the amulet from him once he is dead.

This is probably the most true to what Vortigern would do in this situation. It is also probably going to result in one or two dead characters. Don't worry. If you continue on to *The Crucible of Freya*, Shandril the priestess can raise them from the dead. Though there might be a small price…

Average: This is the default level of difficulty and the one that you should use unless your players are veterans. You may even use this level of difficulty if your players are veterans but several of the characters are injured. The general set up is the same as above, with the same number of foes, except:

Don't send Talon out to use his stinger on Corian. Send Talon out invisibly to retrieve the amulet.

Have Vortigern use his *magic missiles* on Corian, but have him reserve his *acid arrow* for his own protection if someone charges him. He uses *flare* on other fighters.

At this difficulty, Vortigern has not been using Talon as an invisible spy, so he might not know the location of all the characters. He, therefore, might not spring the trap at the best strategic time — meaning that all the characters may not be inside the circle of summoned skeletons.

Easy: If your players are all new or if they have some experience but several of the characters are injured, you should use this level of difficulty. At this level of difficulty:

Vortigern only has one thug with him.

Vortigern doesn't cast any offensive spells at Corian.

Vortigern sends Talon out to steal the amulet, but Talon is visible.

Vortigern has not gotten all the characters within the ring of summoned skeletons

There are only 4 skeletons, not 5.

Vortigern did not animate the farmer and his family as zombies.

If someone charges Vortigern's location, the thug with Vortigern flees rather than defends him.

Vortigern's CR

As an NPC with 3 levels in a PC class, Vortigern's CR would normally be 2. He stole some powerful magic scrolls and *dust of disappearance* from Feriblan, and thus has gear far more valuable than is normal for a 3rd level character. Because of his exceptional gear, Vortigern is treated as being 1 level higher for the purposes of determining his CR.

Vortigern and his Allies

VORTIGERN   CR 3
XP 800
Male human necromancer 3
LE Medium humanoid (human)
Init +1; **Perception** +2

AC 11, touch 11, flat-footed 10 (+1 Dex)
hp 19 (3d6+3)
Fort +2; **Ref** +2; **Will** +3

Speed 30 ft.
Melee dagger +1 (1d4)
Necromancer Spell-Like Abilities (CL 3rd; melee touch +1, ranged touch +2):
6/day—*grave touch* (1 round)
Spells Prepared (CL 3rd; melee +1, ranged +2):
2nd—*acid arrow*, *ghoul touch* (DC 15), *protection from arrows*
1st—*cause fear* (DC 14), *mage armor*, *magic missile*, *shield*
0 (at will)—*bleed* (DC 13), *flare* (DC 13), *read magic*, *resistance*
Specialist School Necromancy **Opposition Schools** Illusion, Transmutation

---

Str 10, **Dex** 13, **Con** 12, **Int** 16, **Wis** 10, **Cha** 12
Base Atk +1; **CMB** +1; **CMD** 12
Feats Alertness (when Talon is within reach)[B], Brew Potion, Command Undead (6/day, DC 12), Improved Familiar, Scribe Scroll[B], Spell Mastery (*mage armor*, *magic missile*, *shield*)
Skills Craft (alchemy) +9, Diplomacy +3, Intimidate +4, Knowledge (arcana) +9, Knowledge (planes) +8, Perception +2, Spellcraft +9
Languages Abyssal, Common, Infernal, Orc
SQ arcane bond (talon), arcane familiar nearby, deliver touch spells through familiar, empathic link with familiar, grave touch (6/day), opposition schools (illusion, transmutation), share spells with familiar, specialized schools (necromancy)
Combat Gear *dust of disappearance*, *potion of cure light wounds*, *scroll of animate dead*, *scroll of summon monster III*; **Other Gear** dagger

---

TALON THE IMP FAMILIAR   CR—
XP—
LE tiny outsider (devil, evil, extraplanar, lawful)
Pathfinder Roleplaying Game Bestiary "Devil, Imp"
Init +3; **Senses** darkvision 60 ft.; **Perception** +7

AC 19, touch 16, flat-footed 15 (+3 Dex, +1 dodge, +3 natural, +2 size)
hp 9 (3d10); fast healing 2
Fort +1; **Ref** +6; **Will** +4

Improved Familiar

Talon's existence as Vortigern's familiar is an example of how you, the GM, can alter the rules to suit your story.

Ordinarily, Vortigern, a 3rd level wizard, could not gain Talon as a familiar using the Improved Familiar feat.

Strictly by the rules, a wizard with Improved Familiar would have to be 7th level before he could have an imp familiar. Vortigern is different. He made a special pact, forever linking his soul to Talon in the service of the lords of Hell.

Talon gains all of the special abilities of the familiar of a 3rd level wizard, and Vortigern gets the service of a minor devil that would normally not be available to him.

To help balance out this slight change of the rules for Vortigern's benefit, there is a terrible drawback: if Talon is killed, Vortigern immediately suffers 2 permanent negative levels. See the *Pathfinder Roleplaying Games Core Rulebook*, "Energy Drain and Negative Levels."

If Talon is killed, Vortigern takes a –2 penalty on all ability checks, attack rolls, combat maneuver checks, Combat Maneuver Defense, saving throws, and skill checks. In addition, he reduces its current and total hit points by 10. He is also treated as 2 levels lower for the purpose of level-dependent variables (such as spellcasting). He does not lose any prepared spells or slots as a result of negative levels.

Thus, the death of Talon seriously cripples Vortigern.

DR 5/good or silver; **Immune** fire, poison; **Resist** acid 10, cold 10

Speed 20 ft., flight 50 ft. (perfect)
Melee sting +8 (1d4 plus poison)

Space 2 1/2 ft.; **Reach** 0 ft.
Spell-Like Abilities (CL 6th):
Constant—*detect good, detect magic*
At will—*invisibility* (self only)
1/day—*augury, suggestion* (DC 15)
1/week—*commune* (6 questions, CL 12th)

Str 10, **Dex** 17, **Con** 10, **Int** 13, **Wis** 12, **Cha** 14
Base Atk +3; **CMB** +4; **CMD** 15
Feats Dodge, Weapon Finesse
Skills Acrobatics +9 (+5 jump), Bluff +8, Diplomacy +4, Fly +21, Intimidate +5, Knowledge (arcana) +7, Knowledge (planes) +7, Perception +7, Spellcraft +7, Stealth +11
Languages Common, Infernal
SQ change shape (boar, giant spider, rat, or raven), improved evasion

Poison (Ex) Sting—injury; save Fort DC 13; frequency 1/round for 6 rounds; effect 1d2 Dex; cure 1 save. The save DC is Constitution-based, and includes a +2 racial bonus.

GRENAG AND SLAAROC   **CR 1/3**
XP 135
Male half-orc warrior 1
CE Medium humanoid (human, orc)
Init +1; **Senses** darkvision 60 ft.; **Perception** −1

AC 15, touch 11, flat-footed 14 (+3 armor, +1 Dex, +1 shield)
hp 6 (1d10)
Fort +2, **Ref** +1, **Will** −1
Defensive Abilities orc ferocity

Speed 30 ft.
Melee battleaxe +5 (1d8+3/x3) or longsword +4 (1d8+3/19–20/x2)
Ranged shortbow +2 (1d6/x3)

Str 16, **Dex** 12, **Con** 11, **Int** 9, **Wis** 9, **Cha** 8
Base Atk +1; **CMB** +4; **CMD** 15
Feats Weapon Focus (battleaxe)
Skills Climb +1, Intimidate +5, Swim +1
Languages Common, Orc
Gear studded leather armor, light steel shield, battleaxe, longsword, shortbow, 20 arrows, 14 gp, 6 sp

FIENDISH HUMAN SKELETONS (5)   **CR 1/3**
XP 135
NE Medium undead
(*Pathfinder Roleplaying Game Bestiary* "Skeleton," "Fiendish")
Init +6; **Senses** darkvision 60 ft.; **Perception** +0

AC 14, touch 12, flat-footed 12 (+2 Dex, +2 natural)
hp 4 (1d8)
Fort +0, **Ref** +2, **Will** +2
DR 5/bludgeoning; **Immune** cold, undead traits; **SR** 5

Speed 30 ft.
Melee 2 claws +2 (1d4+2)
Special Attacks smite good (1/day, +1 damage vs. good creatures)

Str 15, **Dex** 14, **Con** —, **Int** —, **Wis** 10, **Cha** 10
Base Atk +0; **CMB** +2; **CMD** 14
Feats Improved Initiative[B]

HUMAN ZOMBIES (2)   **CR 1/2**
XP 200
NE Medium undead
Pathfinder Roleplaying Game Bestiary "Zombie"

Init +0; **Senses** darkvision 60 ft.; **Perception** +0

AC 12, touch 10, flat-footed 12 (+2 natural)
hp 12 (2d8+3)
Fort +0; **Ref** +0; **Will** +3
DR 5/slashing; **Immune** undead traits

Speed 30 ft.
Melee slam +4 (1d6+4)

Str 17, **Dex** 10, **Con** —, **Int** —, **Wis** 10, **Cha** 10
Base Atk +1; **CMB** +4; **CMD** 14
Feats Toughness
SQ staggered

HUMAN ZOMBIE CHILDREN (3)   **CR 1/3**
XP 135
NE Small undead
(*Pathfinder Roleplaying Game Bestiary* "Zombie")
Init +1; **Senses** darkvision 60 ft.; **Perception** +0

AC 13, touch 12, flat-footed 12 (+1 Dex, +1 natural, +1 size)
hp 12 (2d8+3)
Fort +0; **Ref** +1; **Will** +3
DR 5/slashing; **Immune** undead traits

Speed 30 ft.
Melee slam +3 (1d3+1)

Str 13, **Dex** 12, **Con** —, **Int** —, **Wis** 10, **Cha** 10
Base Atk +1; **CMB** +1; **CMD** 12
Feats Toughness
SQ staggered

Summary of Tactics:
Before we spell out the combat step-by-step, here is a summary of what the various combatants do.

Vortigern: Vortigern uses his spells from a distance, focusing first on taking out Corian, as detailed in the difficulty level you selected. He uses the trees on the fringe of the farm as cover, which gives him +4 to his AC. As mentioned above, Vortigern has prepared himself with several spells prior to the encounter — see his stat block for details. He should be nearly impossible to hit from distance. If the battle goes against him, he uses his *dust of disappearance* to escape. In addition, if Talon recovers the amulet, Vortigern and Talon flees, using his *dust of disappearance*. See the section entitled **Escape?** below.

Difficulty Level

This encounter can kill characters. So before you run it, you need to pick the difficulty level. The default level of difficulty is *Average*. Don't use the *Difficult* level without good reason.

The Crucible of Freya

For more information on *The Crucible of Freya* see the section entitled **Continuing the Story**, below.

Vortigern's Thug(s): Vortigern's thugs are an NPC class known as warriors, which are essentially lesser fighters. Neither of Vortigern's thugs engages the party in hand to hand combat unless directly attacked. They prefer to fire their missile weapons into combat, letting the summoned undead handle melee. Vortigern and his thugs take advantage of the natural cover provided by the grove of trees. If any members of the party break through the ring of undead and charge Vortigern's location, the two thugs drop their bows and engage any such characters to prevent them from reaching Vortigern. They foolishly protect Vortigern with their lives. He, of course, would not hesitate to leave them behind to save his own skin.

The Undead: The summoned skeletons emerge from the earth in a ring around the player characters, encircling them. If the party is in the process of burying the farmers when Vortigern animates them, they rise as zombies and the party attack inside of the ring of skeletons (unless you are running the encounter as *Easy*, in which case there are no zombies.) The skeletons and zombies (if present) attack the characters mindlessly. Remember that the zombies are not present if the characters buried and consecrated the bodies of the farmers prior to Vortigern launching his trap. Of course, Vortigern would most likely have sprung his trap before letting that happen…

Talon: Vortigern telepathically commands Talon to attempt to steal the amulet from Corian — or whoever else obviously possesses it. If you are running the encounter as *Easy* then Talon is visible, otherwise he uses his invisibility. Talon must roll against a DC of 16 to steal the amulet if it is exposed. Once he has successfully grasped an exposed amulet he flies away with it. If the amulet is tossed to the ground or to another character Talon chases after the amulet since retrieval of the amulet is his primary goal. If you are running the encounter as *Difficult*, Talon tries to kill Corian with his stinger if he can't find the amulet. But even at *Difficult*, if Talon sees the amulet go somewhere else, he chases after it. Aside from stinging (if you are running the encounter as *Difficult*) or trying to snatch the amulet, Talon does not fight directly unless wounded or cornered because Vortigern has commanded him not to. If frustrated in his attempt to obtain the amulet and injured in combat, Talon flees to Vortigern. He does not want to risk being killed — that would damage Vortigern and would result in his imprisonment in Hell for 66 years before he would be allowed to serve as a familiar again, and he likes his current job here on the Material Plane. If Talon does get the amulet, he goes invisible and returns to Vortigern. The two flee. See the section entitled **Escape?** below.

Running the Combat

You got a taste of running combat with the leucrotta/stirge encounter. But now things get tricky — multiple opponents, missile fire and NPC spell casters. If you can run this encounter then you have definitely graduated from the novice GM ranks. It's our job to help you do it. So here are step-by-step instructions on running this encounter. Even experienced GMs should appreciate having this encounter spelled out.

Determining Surprise: At this point, the characters can make a Perception check at DC 20 (includes distance, cover and other relevant modifiers). If any character makes either skill check, then they may act during the surprise round. If this happens, roll initiative for all combatants that are aware of each other.

Surprise Round: Vortigern more than likely surprises the party. He and his thugs are hiding in the trees some 60 feet away from the farmhouse. They are out of sight until Vortigern springs the trap. Talon is either flying around invisible (*Difficult* level) or is outside of the trees watching the characters. Once the characters are outside the farmhouse in a group, Talon telepathically tells Vortigern. He motions to the thugs to get into position. Vortigern then reads his special *scroll of summon monster III*. This *scroll*, which Vortigern also purloined from Feriblan's library, contains an unusual necromantic version of the spell and summons 5 fiendish skeletons. As Vortigern utters the last word in the verbal component, the zombie farmers stand up as well. (The zombies can't attack this round because, as zombies, they can only take one action per round; all they can do is stand up.) Vortigern and the thugs stay inside the cover provided by the fringe of trees.

During the surprise round, Vortigern finishes reading his *scroll*, and the skeletons and zombies (if appropriate) rise from the ground. The skeletons appear on Vortigern's initiative and can attack in the same round in which they are summoned. The thug(s) take one bow shot each into the melee. Talon shrieks, goes invisible and flies towards Corian at double his movement. If (by some miracle) a member of the party is able to act in the surprise round then he or she can move out of the forming ring of

skeletons without provoking an attack of opportunity.

First Regular Round of Combat: All persons now should be aware of their opponents (unless there is some character inside the farmhouse). Make sure everyone who hasn't done so yet rolls initiative, including the monsters. Make the initiative list in order of initiative from top to bottom. This round, Vortigern casts a *magic missile* at Corian (unless you are using the *Easy* level of difficulty, in which case he just watches). The thugs reload, stay behind the trees and fire another round into melee. The skeletons and zombies attack. If any characters try to run past the skeletons or zombies they open themselves up to attacks of opportunity, even if the skeletons or zombies have already attacked!

Subsequent Rounds of Combat: Here is what the combatants do.

The Undead: The skeletons continue to stay in a circle around the characters, attacking them. They take attacks of opportunity on any that pass by them — always taking the first attack of opportunity. They are too mindless to delay their attacks of opportunity. They remain for 5 rounds before vanishing back to Hell (5 rounds is the duration of a 5th-level *summon monster III* spell). The zombies continue to attack until they are destroyed.

The Thugs: The thugs continue to reload and fire bow shots at the characters. If any character has broken free from the circle of skeletons, they focus their shots on those characters. If a character moves within 30 feet of their location, they drop their bows and draw their weapons. They remain in front of Vortigern and protect him.

Vortigern: Vortigern fires another *magic missile* at Corian, unless he is being charged then he casts *flare* at the person charging him. If a person gets close enough to engage in melee with his two thugs, Vortigern steps back into the woods, out of view of the ring of skeletons. If things get tough, he uses his *dust of disappearance*. He does not flee until Talon recovers the amulet, Talon is injured and forced to retreat or his thugs are killed. Then he flees. See the section entitled **Escape?** below.

Talon: Talon finishes his movement to Corian and tries to obtain the amulet. If Corian isn't wearing it openly, Talon uses his innate ability to *detect magic* on Corian to see if he has it. If he doesn't find the amulet on Corian he stings him if you are playing the *Difficult* level. Otherwise, he uses his *detect magic* ability to locate who has the magical item. Of course, if another member of the party has a magical item, Talon is not able to differentiate which one has the amulet in particular. He checks all of the persons who are carrying magical items. Talon tries to take the amulet from them if he can see it. Regardless of difficulty level, if someone other than Corian has the amulet and they have the amulet hidden on their person so that Talon can't get it, Talon stings that person. This means if he detects that two people have magical items hidden on their person, he stings both of them. He then searches their corpse(s) to retrieve the amulet. Talon always immediately goes invisible after attacking unless you are playing the encounter at the *Easy* level of difficulty. If he is injured, Talon flees back to Vortigern. Vortigern is more concerned with keeping Talon alive than finding the amulet at the price of Talon.

Killing Talon: Remember that if Talon is killed, Vortigern gains 2 permanent negative levels. Note that this is different from the standard familiar rules because Talon is not your normal familiar.

Ending the Combat

Basically, you just have to play this out until one of four things happens: everyone in the party dies, all of the bad guys are killed (which would be quite an accomplishment), Vortigern and Talon get away with the amulet, or Vortigern and Talon get away without the amulet. Once any of these conditions occur, go to the next section entitled **Escape?** Everyone agrees that the first ending (the party dies) is not very fun. So how do we avoid that result without using some cheesy "bolt from the blue" to save the party? Easy — use an "escape hatch."

Escape Hatch: OK, so what if things are really going poorly for the party? Here are a few suggestions:

If it has been several rounds of combat, you could have Vortigern's *summon monster III* spell expire early (the party doesn't know this isn't the normal spell duration) and have the skeletons fall to the ground in pieces — leaving just Vortigern, Talon, the thugs, and the zombies (if you were using them).

GM Tips

Firing into Melee

Normally, if you shoot into melee you do so at a –4 to avoid hitting your allies. The thugs don't suffer that minus because they don't care about hitting the skeletons or zombies. It's nice not to have a conscience! You may, however, treat the skeletons as cover for the characters.

Attacks of Opportunity

Attacks of opportunity occur when a person moves through the threatened area of another combatant. Even if the combatant has already attacked, they get an attack on the person moving through their threatened area. However, unless a feat allows for more (such as Combat Reflexes), a combatant only gets one attack of opportunity per round even though several persons may move through their threatened area. See the **Actions in Combat** section of the *Pathfinder Roleplaying Games Core Rulebook*.

Resistance and Fast Healing

Remember that Talon has damage reduction 5 against all but silver or good-aligned weapons. He also automatically heals 2 hit points per round from his fast healing.

Spell Resistance

Because they are fiendish, the skeletons have SR (Spell Resistance) 5. To penetrate a target's spell resistance, the spell caster must make a roll of 1d20 plus caster level that is equal to or greater than the subject's Spell Resistance DC — it's like a magical Armor Class. Make it and the spell gets through. Miss it and the spell is wasted.

Initiative for Monsters

Don't just make one initiative roll for all the bad guys. You should make one roll for each group of monsters: one for Vortigern, one for Talon, and one roll for both Thugs (since they have the same modifier). The skeletons and zombies act on Vortigern's initiative count.

Cover

Cover provides a bonus to AC. See the **Combat Modifiers** section of the *Pathfinder Roleplaying Games Core Rulebook*. In this case, Vortigern and the thugs get the benefit of cover and get a +4 to AC because they are firing from behind trees.

Escape Hatch

If things are really going poorly for the characters, consider using an "escape hatch." See below for escape hatch ideas.

You could have Vortigern's thugs flee because they are cowards at heart. After all, the hardest thing about being a bad guy is that "good help is hard to find."

If you're using the zombies, you could have them start to attack the skeletons or turn to go after Vortigern and the thugs; the zombie farmers retained just enough of their memories of life to rebel against their new evil master! Make a die roll behind your GM screen and look disappointed, as if the fact that the undead might fight each other is actually some legitimate part of the spell effect.

We don't mean for you to use these escape hatches just because it looks like Vortigern and Talon are about to escape with the amulet — that's OK. That just leads to more adventure. Escape hatches are for situations where it looks like the party is about to get wiped out. Here is a good rule of thumb: if two or more characters are dead use an escape hatch. Or, in this particular adventure, if Corian dies use an escape hatch.

If you do decide to use an escape hatch, whatever you do — and this is a key GM skill — don't let on that you are saving the party. That's just between us. Don't worry, everyone has done it. But remember these two important rules: first, give them a full and fair opportunity to win on their own — meaning, don't use the escape hatch too early. And second, don't do this often. Your players need to understand that death is a consequence of adventure. You can't let your players come to expect that you will always save their bacon. A dead character isn't the end of the world. In fact, in this case, a dead character is incentive for the party to get to Fairhill as soon as possible… which leads right to *The Crucible of Freya*.

Escape?

If Talon manages to snatch the amulet, read the following:

> Vortigern's devilish familiar seizes the amulet and with a shriek flies off, becoming invisible. Vortigern, too, ducks back into the surrounding woods escaping from your sight. You search everywhere, but you cannot seem to locate the evil apprentice. Yet his laughter is all around you.

If the tide of battle turns against Vortigern and Talon and they have the opportunity to escape without the amulet, read the following:

> Sensing defeat, Vortigern yells a command to Talon, his devilish familiar. Leaving his henchmen to finish the battle, Talon and Vortigern disappear into thin air. You search everywhere, but you cannot seem to locate the evil apprentice. For the time being you have prevented Vortigern from obtaining the amulet.

In either case, Talon uses his innate *invisibility* and Vortigern uses his *dust of disappearance* to render himself invisible. Neither stays to harass the party. They immediately flee the area. If they have the amulet, they proceed towards Fairhill, though they do not enter the village. They have abandoned their henchmen, but should the thugs manage to survive, Vortigern and Talon links up with them. Vortigern has Talon use his ability to contact Dispater to learn the location of Eralion's keep. With this information, they head towards the keep. If Vortigern and Talon are forced to flee without the amulet they head towards Fairhill. These events are detailed further in the next adventure module, *The Crucible of Freya*. Proceed to the section entitled **Concluding the Adventure**, below.

If the party vanquishes Vortigern and Talon and his evil minions, which should be a tale well worth retelling, you should congratulate the party and read the following:

> Your foes are defeated. Talon, Vortigern's devilish familiar, writhes and smokes as he dissolves into a stinking mass of slime. The hired thugs, routed or slain, shall trouble you no more. And the foul undead conjured by Vortigern have found their final rest at the end of your blade. This farmhouse, previously a scene of slaughter, is now a scene of vengeance.

Obviously, your players will want to search the bodies. They find all the items listed on the **Gear** line of the various foes' stat blocks. Once they do so, proceed to **Concluding the Adventure**.

Concluding the Adventure

Following the final encounter with Vortigern, regardless of the ending, read the following text to your players:

> Corian's worst fear has come to pass. But now your encounter with Vortigern and his minions is over. It has become too dark to look for other lodging, so you light the fire in the fireplace of the farmhouse and bar the door. You clean the blood from your blade and tend to your wounds as well as those of your comrades. You set watch, and each of you says a silent prayer to your respective gods that the spirits of your foes find their rest and trouble you no further this night. You eventually drift off to sleep, but your sleep is fitful — filled with Talon's devilish screams. You wake to the sound of rain and gray skies. The sun, even hidden behind the clouds, is a welcome sight.

If any of the party was slain in the encounter with Vortigern, remind them that Fairhill is two days away. Suggest that perhaps there is someone there who can aid them and that possibly the party could trade something or pledge their service in return for having their friend restored to life.

Awarding Experience

Finally, after you handle any healing and any other record keeping, you can determine experience for the night's session. The new edition of the rules handles the computation of experience differently. It uses a "Challenge Rating" or CR system for each monster. Here is a scene-by-scene breakdown of experience:

First Watch: If the party made a good camp and were smart about their preparations, let them split 50 xp.

A Voice in the Darkness: If the party encountered the young leucrotta and drove him off without having to fight the mother, award 400 xp plus 400 xp for avoiding the mother for a total of 800 xp. If the party had to fight the young leucrotta *and* the mother, then award 1,200 xp (the monsters' CRs are 3 and 1, which works out to a CR 4 encounter!) to be divided equally between the party. If you had to use an escape hatch, subtract 200 xp. If the party only encountered the stirges, their value is 600 xp (3 stirges at 200 xp each).

The Smiling Skull: Award 50 xp to be split between the party for searching around the hill and finding the rock with the *magic aura*.

Corian's Tale: This award is for good roleplaying. Give anyone who did a good job 25 xp. If Corian did well, give that player 50 xp.

Farmhouse: Making a roll to identify the poison is worth 25 xp. Evaluating the cuts on the farmers gets 10 xp. Deciding to bury and sanctify the bodies gets 25 xp per person involved in doing so; 50 xp for a good-aligned cleric.

Ambush!: Actually making your Perception check to avoid being ambushed is worth 25 xp to any character who made the roll. Calculating experience for the main combat is tricky. The total CR for Vortigern and the thugs is CR 4; that's an epic challenge for four 1st level characters according to the guidelines for determining CR. Increase the CR to 5 if you used the *Difficult* level. If you used the *Easy* difficulty level, then reduce the CR to 3. Note that no extra experience is given for Talon or the skeletons and zombies because Vortigern summoned them and thus they are included in his CR value. Thus, the final xp value is as follows for the final encounter: Difficult — 1,600 xp, Average — 1,200 xp, Easy — 800 xp.

Escape?: If Vortigern and Talon escape with the amulet, subtract 400 total xp. If they escape without the amulet, subtract 200 total xp. If you had to use an escape hatch to save the party, subtract 200 total xp. If the party manages to kill both Vortigern and Talon, award an additional 300 total xp.

With the dawn, Fairhill awaits two days march ahead. What will your characters find there? What will become of *The Wizard's Amulet*? What secrets lay buried with Eralion?

Continuing the Story

The story line started in this adventure can be completed in *The Crucible of Freya*. In *The Crucible of Freya* the characters finally arrive in Fairhill and learn rumors of Eralion's nearby ruined keep. The village of Fairhill is fully described and mapped, including details of all its important NPCs. The characters quickly become involved in assisting Shandril, a local priestess of Freya, in recovering a stolen holy item which eventually leads them to Eralion's keep. Of course, Corian's amulet unlocks the secret to the keep. The ruined keep is mapped as are the levels beneath it where Eralion resides — tricked by Orcus into his horrid fate. If Vortigern escaped the final encounter in this adventure, The Crucible of Freya provides ideas on using Vortigern as a continuing antagonist for the party — as he travels to Fairhill himself to seek Eralion's keep, possibly running afoul of the party a second time. Unlike this adventure, which was tightly scripted and linear to accomplish the goal of playing without much preparation, *The Crucible of Freya* can be run either as a tight story continuing this adventure or it can be used as a sourcebook for GMs to run their own adventures in Fairhill.

Of course, you are free to develop the story started here without following up with *The Crucible of Freya*. Eralion's lair can be placed in any keep or tower near some small out of the way village in your own campaign world. Eralion would not have set up shop in a highly visible area — he sought privacy. Place a secret door somewhere in the tower or keep that is enchanted so that only Eralion or a person who possesses the amulet can open it. You should detail a small wizard's lair, which is now haunted by Eralion. Perhaps the rumors are wrong. Perhaps Eralion did succeed in becoming a lich but is somehow trapped in his lair — the limiting enchantment on the secret door no longer allowing him to pass since he is no longer truly Eralion, nor is he a lich. Perhaps he has some task for the party. Or perhaps he wishes to undo what he has done. A party of first-level characters encountering a lich and being asked by him for aid would certainly make an interesting adventure. Or maybe he is some other twisted form of undead. You are free to draw this up on your own. Or you can check out *The Crucible of Freya*, where we have already done it all for you (and more).

THE CRUCIBLE OF FREYA

Introduction

A challenging adventure for four to six characters of 1st or 2nd level, *The Crucible of Freya* is an excellent beginning to any new fantasy campaign. The adventure begins with the players' arrival in the village of Fairhill, but quickly involves them in a quest to recover a stolen holy item recently taken in an orc raid. In hot pursuit of the thieving orc band, the characters discover the orcs have taken up residence in a ruined keep nearby. Once there, the party learns that even more sinister forces are at work: the keep's original owner may still wield some influence over his now-ruined abode.

Adventure Background

The village of Fairhill has long been a peaceful town, located off the tradeway between two major cities-the merchant town of Bard's Gate to the east and the Grand Duchy's port city of Reme to the west. Fairhill's fields are fertile and its populace happy, due in large part to the blessings of Freya-the goddess of love and fertility-who is the patron deity of Fairhill. The temple to Freya is the focal point for the citizens of the village, and **Shandril**, the village priestess, is a devoted follower of her fair goddess. Under Shandril's inspired guidance, the village fields yield great quantities of grain, the cattle produce milk and calves in abundance and married couples live in joyous harmony with numerous children. As a result of its location, Fairhill has become a favorite layover on the tradeway between Reme and Bard's Gate.

In recent weeks, trouble has come to Fairhill. A small band of marauding orcs began raiding the outskirts of the village and the surrounding farmland at night. There is a darker force at work behind the orc raids. **Tavik**, an evil priest of the demon-lord Orcus, has been commanded to desecrate the temple of Freya in Fairhill. Tavik's plan (and the central motivating plot point for this adventure) hinges on his orc minions stealing the *Crucible of Freya*. The *Crucible* is necessary to one of the most important rituals in the village-the blessing of the new wheat harvest, which is only a few days away. By stealing the *Crucible* and interfering with the ritual, Tavik intends to blight the normally bountiful harvest.

However, Tavik and his evil creatures are not the only minions of Orcus near Fairhill. There is a presence that is darker still, if of less immediate threat. The keep in which Tavik and his orcs have taken up residence was once the retreat of **Eralion**, a reclusive mage of some local repute. Years ago, as the shadow of his death grew long and he began to sense his own mortality, Eralion's heart darkened. He turned his attention to lengthening his fading life. He heard the rumor of the fabled Mushroom of Youth in the dungeon of Rappan Athuk, the legendary Dungeon of Graves, but he lacked the courage to enter those deadly halls. He researched *wish* spells, but lacked the power to master such mighty sorceries, being only a wizard of modest power.

Finally, in his darkest hour, Eralion turned to Orcus, the demon-lord of the undead, and implored the dread demon for the secret of unlife-the secret of becoming a lich. Orcus knew that Eralion lacked the power to complete the necessary ritual to become a lich, as Eralion had barely managed the use of a scroll to contact him in the depths of the Abyss in his Palace of Bones. Orcus smiled cruelly as he promised the secret of lichdom to Eralion. But there was a price. Orcus required Eralion to surrender his shadow. "A trifling," Orcus whispered to Eralion from the Abyss. "Something you will not need after performing the ritual which I shall give to you. For the darkness will be your home as you live for untold ages."

In his desperation, Eralion believed the demon-lord. He learned the ritual Orcus provided to him. But as he uttered false words of power and consumed the transforming potion, he realized too late the demon's treachery. He felt his life essence slip away-transferring in part to his own shadow, which he had sold to the demon-lord. Eralion found himself Orcus' unwitting servant. Now, trapped in the prison built by his own pride, his mind long shattered by an all-consuming hate, Eralion hides from the light and curses his unlife.

Soon after the characters arrive at Fairhill, Tavik executes his plan. His orcs raid the village and steal the *Crucible of Freya*, killing several town guards in the process and setting fire to the temple. Shandril realizes that the characters are the only means of recovering the *Crucible*, and she implores them to assist her and her deity. Their quest inevitably leads them to the ruined keep and to a showdown with the marauding orcs. The characters should be able to cleanse the keep of its infestation and, hopefully, uncover the evil designs of Tavik, who can be an ongoing antagonist for the characters. The characters may unearth Eralion's lair and encounter him in the foul form he now wears. At the conclusion of this adventure, the characters should have increased in level, made several friends as well as a powerful enemy in Tavik, liberated some gold, acquired a *+1 sword* and possibly even recovered *Eralion's staff* and spell books.

Module Overview

Though *The Crucible of Freya* can be used on its own, the plot in **Part Two** is a direct continuation of the story of Corian the Sorcerer, as told in *The Wizard's Amulet*. We strongly recommend you use it as a lead-in to this adventure.

This module is presented in several parts. **Part One**, entitled "Areas of Adventure," details each relevant area in and around Fairhill-the village of Fairhill itself, the wilderness surrounding Fairhill, several monster lairs and the ruined keep, including the chambers beneath it where Eralion waits, imprisoned. **Part Two**, entitled "**The Crucible**," presents a specific story line: the theft of the *Crucible of Freya* by the orcs and the players' quest to retrieve it — leading them to the ruined keep. This story is presented in Act and Scene format, similar to that of a play to make it easier for less-experienced Game Masters (GMs) to run the adventure. **Part Three**, entitled "**Supplemental Information**," includes additional story ideas, tips on how to continue the adventure and links to other **Frog God Games** modules and supplements.

Notes for the GM

This module is designed for beginning players and GMs, and it requires the use of the *Pathfinder Roleplaying Game Core Rulebook* and the *Pathfinder Roleplaying Game Bestiary*. Additional books from the *Pathfinder Roleplaying Game* are also referenced, but can be substituted or ignored as you like. Prior to play, you should familiarize yourself with the entirety of this module, in particular **Part One**, which details all of the areas of adventure. Spend some time getting to know Shandril, Arlen, Baran, Lauriel, and most of all Tavik — the evil priest of Orcus. The more familiarity you have with the main characters, the richer the adventure experience will be for both you and your players. If you are a new GM, study the chapters of the *Pathfinder Roleplaying Game Core Rulebook* concerning running adventures for some useful advice.

This adventure is very difficult and may result in the death of a player character (PC) unless they are clever and play well. Due to this, a number of non-player characters (NPCs) are provided along the way to allow for PC replacement. The level of difficulty is reduced if you focus on running the primary adventure in Part Two and leave the optional material, such as the other monster lairs, for future adventuring. At **Frog God Games**, we believe that the most fulfilling game experiences come from difficult adventures. They provide bragging rights and long-winded stories for years to come. Recovering the *Crucible*, defeating Tavik and his minions and encountering Eralion should provide your players with just such opportunities.

Modifying the Adventure

As with all **Frog God Games** products, this adventure is designed to be easily adapted to any campaign setting. Reme and Bard's Gate can be replaced with any two major cities in your campaign world that are joined by a road that travels through the wilderness. Fairhill can be placed as a village along this road, as long as there is a small forest nearby where the ruined keep can be located. You should also feel free to substitute the deities used in this adventure. Freya can be replaced with any good-aligned deity. However, the replacement deity should be a deity of lesser importance in your pantheon and should not be a deity to which any of the player characters are devoted. Orcus can be replaced with any evil god-but the evil god you choose should be related to the undead to keep the feel of the adventure intact. You may modify encounters, but we encourage you not to reduce the difficulty of the encounters without much forethought. They are difficult on purpose. Some of these areas and encounters are places to which your players can return when they achieve higher levels.

How to Begin

If you have used *The Wizard's Amulet*, then this adventure begins as your brave heroes travel to the village of Fairhill to rest and lick their wounds following their fight with Vortigern. At the conclusion of *The Wizard's Amulet*, there were three possible outcomes, each of which affects this adventure:

If Vortigern was slain and the party still has Corian's amulet, you may ignore any reference to Vortigern in this module.

If Vortigern escaped but the party still has Corian's amulet, then Vortigern and his familiar, Talon, are in Fairhill, staying at the *Cask and Flagon* under the name "Feriblan." Vortigern's two henchmen, if alive, are also with him, staying in the room at the inn, keeping out of sight.

If Vortigern escaped with Corian's amulet, he and his cohorts head directly to the ruined keep, where they befriend Tavik and the orcs. Vortigern and Tavik have not yet learned the use of the amulet since they have not yet discovered the hidden trap door in the floor of the southwest tower.

If you have not used *The Wizard's Amulet* as a lead-in to this adventure, you will need to invent a reason why your players' characters are headed to Fairhill. Maybe the characters are headed to the famous dungeon of Rappan Athuk to test their mettle and stopped at Fairhill along the way. They may be here because a cleric in the party wants to pay her respects at the temple of Freya. They may have a message to deliver to Arlen the magistrate from someone in Bard's Gate. They may have had a previous encounter with Lannet during which he stole something of value from them, and they have trailed him to Fairhill. Or, most likely, they heard the tale of Eralion and his now-ruined keep, and they wanted to seek it out. In particular, spellcasters in the party might view the keep as a possible treasure trove of spell books. If you use this last hook, you should allow the party to start with two of the rumors about Eralion's keep from the rumor section below. Also, you must provide one of the characters with a *scroll of knock* to enable them to open the portal to the lower portions of the keep. Without such a scroll, the party will have no way to bypass the *arcane locked* door leading to Eralion's sanctum. Of course, if you have not used *The Wizard's Amulet*, you should ignore any reference to Vortigern, Talon, Vortigern's henchmen Grenag and Slaaroc, Corian and Corian's amulet contained in this module.

Areas of Adventure

Wilderness Areas Around Fairhill

Fairhill lies some 10 miles north of the tradeway, about 8 days' march east from the port city of Reme, approximately halfway between Reme and Bard's Gate. North of the tradeway and parallel to it range the Stoneheart Mountains. South of the tradeway is the river Graywash. The tradeway follows the northern bank of the river as it winds its course from Reme, past Bard's Gate to the forest kingdoms beyond. The Graywash River serves as a political boundary, as it has few fordable sections. South of the river, most settlements are simple farming and fishing communities. It is feared these plains will one day be the battleground between the Grand Duchy and the warlike, expansionist nations to the south.

The vale between the river and the mountains through which the tradeway runs is verdant green and dotted with pine forests and lesser woodlands, though the forests have been cleared back from the road. Hawks and falcons are a common sight, as are larger eagles. The vale contains plentiful game. Several small towns and villages dot the countryside. Lake Crimmormere and Crimmor village lie on the northern path further east of Fairhill between Reme and Bard's Gate. Small farms are common sights as you draw near to any of the villages.

The tradeway is well patrolled by both bandits and the Grand Duke's sheriffs who hunt them. It is also well traveled by merchants and adventurers in search of fortune and glory. It has also recently seen a number of orc raiding parties, causing much concern to merchants and villagers alike. Never before have orcs been present in such number, nor have they been bold enough to dare a daytime raid on the main road. The road itself is raised and made of hard-packed dirt. In some stretches it is even paved with smooth stones. Occasionally there are way stations to the side of the tradeway-large stockades made of logs with large gates in which merchants can corral their wagons and rest for the night with some security.

The half-day's march from the tradeway to the village of Fairhill runs along a small but well-traveled dirt road through lightly rolling hills and fertile grasslands, sloping gently upward toward the foothills of the Stoneheart Mountains.

Also north of the river is the Stoneheart Forest, a dense forest barely penetrated by the tradeway. The forest itself is dark and oppressive. It is unusually wet, the ground damp. Large spider webs can be seen from the tradeway, glistening with dew. Those making a DC 10 Perception check notice that the forest is strangely devoid of the noise of birds or small game. The forest is called Stirge Wood by some because of its large population of these foul creatures. It is believed that somewhere in the forest there is a vast cave where the creatures breed. Local legends insist that an evil wizard has made his lair there and has somehow brought the creatures under his sway. If a party is in the forest at night, they automatically have an encounter with **2d6 stirges**, in addition to any other random encounters rolled for the night. See the **Appendix** for stirge statistics. Because of the large stirge population, there are few bandits in the forest, though there are other humanoids such as bugbears and ogres. There are also a large number of monstrous spiders that feed on the stirges. Any party traveling for more than one hour in the forest will encounter **2d4 giant spiders**. See the **Appendix** for spider statistics.

Shown on the **Wilderness Map** are four additional areas of interest. These encounter areas are monster lairs, detailed as areas **A** through **D**, below. They can be used as additional sub-adventures for the party based on adventure hooks gained from roleplaying in the village itself or they can be used to add a little "roll playing" to your role-playing session as you see fit. The other towns and villages depicted on the map, as well as Crimmormere, are not detailed here and may be expanded upon by you.

Wandering Monsters

Check for encounters once per hour. If an encounter occurs, roll 1d6 on the table below. The following noncumulative modifiers apply: more than one mile off the main merchant road: + 2; in the forest: +4; in the foothills: +6. Plus, add a cumulative +2 if the encounter occurs at night. Special groups and their various reactions are detailed below.

TOTAL ROLL	ENCOUNTER
1	**Merchant caravan**
2	**2d6 villagers**, heading to/from Fairhill
3	**2d4 common orcs** and **1 orc leader**
4	**Sheriff's patrol**
5	**2d4 brigands** and **1 brigand leader**
6	**Small cavalry patrol**
7	**1d10 gnolls**
8	**1d6** (+2 if at night) **stirges**
9	**1 owlbear.** This is not the owlbear from Area C
10	**1 ogre** with **2d4 goblins**
11	**1 troll.** This is not **Karigror** the troll from Area A
12	**1d3 worgs** with **1d8 wolves**
13	**Girbolg the ettin**, from **Area 8**
14	The **male manticore**, from **Area D**

Brigands: Brigands size up the party, and if the party appears weak or if the brigands outnumber the party by two-to-one or more, they attack. Normally, brigands ambush travelers using missile weapons.

BRIGANDS   CR 2
XP 600
Male or female human rogue (thug) 3 (*Pathfinder Roleplaying Game Advanced Player's Guide* "Thug")
NE Medium humanoid (human)
Init +1; **Perception** +6

AC 15, touch 12, flat-footed 13 (+3 armor, +1 Dex, +1 dodge)
hp 16 (3d8 plus 3)
Defensive Abilities evasion
Fort +1; **Ref** +4; **Will** +1
Defensive Abilities evasion

Speed 30 ft.
Melee rapier +3 (1d6/18–20) or dagger +3 (1d4/19–20)
Ranged shortbow +3 (1d6/x3)
Special Attacks brutal beating, frightening, rogue talent (slow reactions), sneak attack +2d6

Str 10, **Dex** 13, **Con** 11, **Int** 10, **Wis** 11, **Cha** 8
Base Atk +2; **CMB** +2; **CMD** 14
Feats Dodge, Mobility, Weapon Finesse
Skills Acrobatics +6, Appraise +6, Bluff +5, Climb +4, Disable Device +4, Escape Artist +6, Intimidate +5, Knowledge (local) +4, Perception +6, Sleight of Hand +6, Stealth +6
Languages Common
Gear studded leather armor, rapier, dagger, shortbow, 40 arrows, 1d4 sp, 2d4 cp

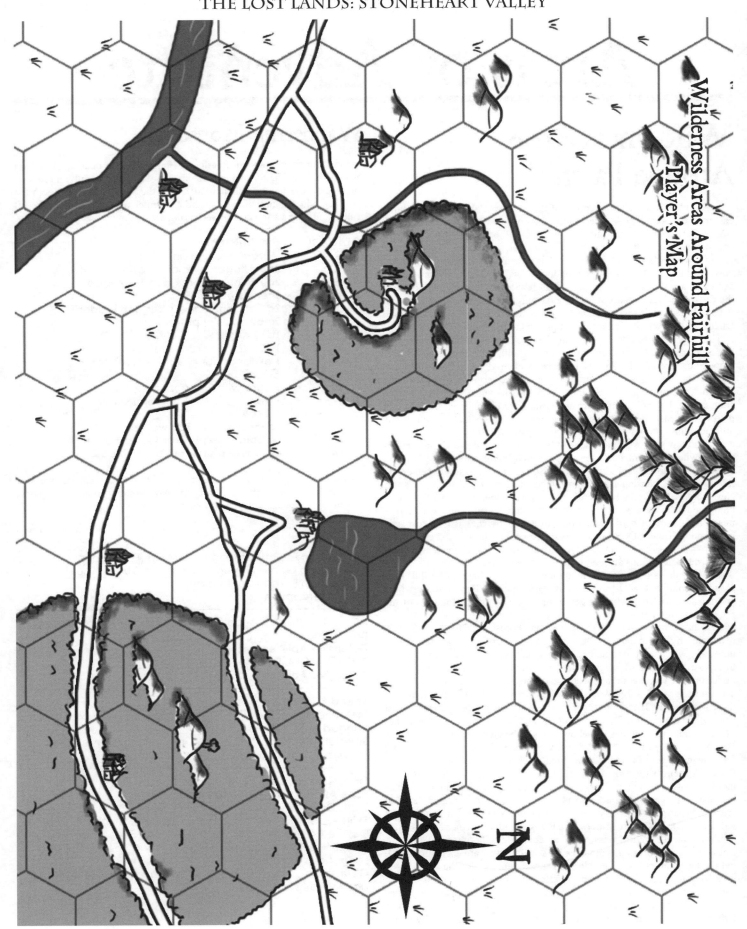

Wilderness Areas Around Fairhill
Player's Map

BRIGAND LEADER — CR 4
XP 1,200
Male or female human rogue (thug) 5 (*Pathfinder Roleplaying Game Advanced Player's Guide* "Thug")
NE Medium humanoid (human)
Init +6; **Perception** +8

AC 16, touch 13, flat-footed 13 (+3 armor, +2 Dex, +1 dodge)
hp 35 (5d8+5 plus 5)
Fort +2; **Ref** +6; **Will** +1
Defensive Abilities evasion, uncanny dodge

Speed 30 ft.
Melee rapier +5 (1d6/18–20) or dagger +5 (1d4/19–20)
Ranged shortbow +5 (1d6/x3)
Special Attacks brutal beating, frightening, rogue talent (bleeding attack), rogue talent (slow reactions), sneak attack +3d6

Str 10, **Dex** 14, **Con** 12, **Int** 11, **Wis** 11, **Cha** 10
Base Atk +3; **CMB** +3; **CMD** 16
Feats Dodge, Improved Initiative, Mobility, Weapon Finesse
Skills Acrobatics +7 (+3 jump), Appraise +8, Bluff +8, Climb +2, Diplomacy +4, Disable Device +3, Escape Artist +6, Intimidate +8, Knowledge (local) +5, Linguistics +4, Perception +8, Sleight of Hand +4, Stealth +6, Swim +1
Languages Common, Goblin
Combat Gear *potion of cure moderate wounds*; **Other Gear** masterwork studded leather armor, rapier, dagger, shortbow, 10 *+1 arrows*, 40 arrows, 1d4 gp, 2d4 sp.

Cavalry Patrol: A cavalry patrol consists of **six mounted Waymarch Cavalrymen** and **one Waymarch Cavalry Leader**. Unlike the sheriff's patrol, which patrols the tradeway, these small cavalry units ride across the countryside because of an increased hostile military presence to the south. They only travel through the forest if speed is needed; otherwise they stay strictly to the tradeway. They consider their military duty above the needs of helping adventurers, only offering aid in an extreme case (a DC 20 Diplomacy check or person in life-threatening peril). They will not escort the party under any circumstances, stating that their duty lies elsewhere.

CAVALRYMAN (6) — CR 3
XP 800
hp 34 (see **Sheriff's Patrol, Knight**, below)

CAVALRY LEADER — CR 3
XP 800
hp 36 (see **Sheriff's Patrol, Sheriff**, below)

WARHORSES (7) — CR 2
XP 600
hp 24 (see **Foot Patrol**, below)

GNOLLS — CR 1
XP 400
hp 11 (*Pathfinder Roleplaying Game Bestiary* "Gnoll")

GOBLINS — CR 1/3
XP 135
hp 6 (*Pathfinder Roleplaying Game Bestiary* "Goblin")

Merchant Caravan: The caravan comprises 1d8 wagons or carts and pack animals as well as **1d4 guards** per cart or wagon. There are **1d3 merchants** per cart as well. Though the merchants are on guard and want little to do with adventurers, a successful DC 15 Diplomacy check encourages the merchants to tell the characters of the recent orc raids in the area and to offer information about Fairhill in general. They do not otherwise offer any aid to the party.

CARAVAN GUARD — CR 1
XP 400
Male or female human fighter 2
N Medium humanoid (human)
Init +5; **Perception** +4

AC 16, touch 12, flat-footed 14 (+3 armor, +1 Dex, +1 dodge, +1 shield)
hp 16 (2d10+2 plus 2)
Fort +4; **Ref** +1; **Will** +0; +1 vs. fear
Defensive Abilities bravery +1

Speed 30 ft.
Melee longspear +4 (1d8+1/x3) or short sword +3 (1d6+1/19–20)
Ranged light crossbow +3 (1d8/19–20)
Space 5 ft.; **Reach** 5 ft. (10 ft. with longspear)

Str 12, **Dex** 13, **Con** 12, **Int** 10, **Wis** 10, **Cha** 10
Base Atk +2; **CMB** +3; **CMD** 15
Feats Alertness, Dodge, Improved Initiative, Weapon Focus (longspear)
Skills Handle Animal +4, Intimidate +4, Knowledge (local) +2, Perception +4, Sense Motive +2
Languages Common
Gear studded leather armor, buckler, longspear, short sword, light crossbow, 20 bolts, 1d12 gp, 2d12 sp, 3d12 cp.

MERCHANT — CR 2
XP 600
Male or female human expert 4
N Medium humanoid (human)
Init +0; **Perception** +9

AC 12, touch 10, flat-footed 12 (+2 armor)
hp 22 (4d8 plus 4)
Fort +1; **Ref** +1; **Will** +4

Speed 30 ft.
Melee mwk dagger +3 (1d4–1/19–20)
Ranged light crossbow +3 (1d8/19–20)

Str 8, **Dex** 10, **Con** 11, **Int** 12, **Wis** 11, **Cha** 13
Base Atk +3; **CMB** +2; **CMD** 12
Feats Alertness, Skill Focus (Appraise), Skill Focus (Sense Motive)
Skills Appraise +11, Bluff +8, Diplomacy +8, Handle Animal +8, Linguistics +8, Perception +9, Profession (merchant) +7, Sense Motive +12
Languages Common, Dwarven, Elven, Gnome, Goblin, Halfling
Combat Gear 1d4 of the following potions (roll 1d6): (1) *cat's grace*, (2) *eagle's splendor*, (3) *invisibility*, (4) *cure light wounds*, (5) *cure moderate wounds*, (6) *longstrider*; **Other Gear** masterwork leather armor, masterwork dagger, light crossbow, 10 bolts, 2d10 gp; additional coffer of coins hidden in wagon, total value of approximately 10 x total HD of all NPCs in caravan.

OGRE — CR 3
XP 800
hp 30 (*Pathfinder Roleplaying Game Bestiary* "Ogre")

ORCS — CR 1/3
XP 135
hp 6 (*Pathfinder Roleplaying Game Bestiary* "Orc")

ORC LEADER · CR 2
XP 600
Male half-orc barbarian 3
CE Medium humanoid (human, orc)
Init +1; **Senses** darkvision 60 ft.; **Perception** +6

AC 14, touch 11, flat-footed 13 (+3 armor, +1 Dex)
hp 40 (3d12+12 plus 3)
Fort +7; **Ref** +2; **Will** +1
Defensive Abilities ferocity, trap sense, uncanny dodge

Speed 40 ft.
Melee mwk greataxe +9 (1d12+7/x3)
Special Attacks rage (12 rounds/day), rage power (intimidating glare)

Str 21, **Dex** 13, **Con** 18, **Int** 8, **Wis** 10, **Cha** 12
Base Atk +3; **CMB** +8; **CMD** 19
Feats Intimidating Prowess, Power Attack
Skills Acrobatics +1 (+5 jump), Climb +9, Intimidate +14, Perception +6, Survival +4, Swim +9
Languages Common, Orc
SQ fast movement +10
Combat Gear potion of cure light wounds; **Other Gear** masterwork studded leather armor, masterwork greataxe, 249 gp, 9 sp

OWLBEAR · CR 4
XP 1,200
hp 47 (Pathfinder Roleplaying Game Bestiary "Owlbear")

Sheriff's Patrol: The Grand Duke's well-trained sheriff's patrol the tradeway and the lands in the vale between the river and the mountains. A normal patrol consists of **eight Waymarch Footmen, two Waymarch Knights** and a **Waymarch Sheriff** who leads the patrol. Sheriffs are wary of travelers unless openly aligned with a good deity. With a successful DC 15 Diplomacy check, the patrol can be convinced to escort a party in need. Otherwise they warn characters to be wary of orcs and brigands and be on their way.

FOOTMAN (8) · CR 1
XP 400
Male human fighter 2
LN Medium humanoid (human)
Init +5; **Perception** +2

AC 15, touch 11, flat-footed 14 (+3 armor, +1 Dex, +1 shield)
hp 19 (2d10+2 plus 2)
Fort +4; **Ref** +1; **Will** +0; +1 vs. fear
Defensive Abilities bravery +1

Speed 30 ft.
Melee longspear +4 (1d8+1/x3) or longsword +3 (1d8+1/19–20)
Ranged light crossbow +3 (1d8/19–20)
Space 5 ft.; **Reach** 5 ft. (10 ft. with longspear)

Str 12, **Dex** 12, **Con** 12, **Int** 10, **Wis** 10, **Cha** 10
Base Atk +2; **CMB** +3; **CMD** 14
Feats Improved Initiative, Quick-Draw, Run, Weapon Focus (longspear)
Skills Intimidate +5, Perception +4, Sense Motive +2
Languages Common
Gear studded leather armor, buckler, longspear, longsword, light crossbow, 20 bolts, 2d12 gp.

KNIGHTS (2) · CR 3
XP 800
Male or female human fighter 4
LN Medium humanoid (human)
Init +6; **Perception** +5

AC 20, touch 12, flat-footed 18 (+6 armor, +2 Dex, +2 shield)
hp 34 (4d10+8 plus 4)
Fort +6; **Ref** +3; **Will** +2; +3 vs. fear
Defensive Abilities bravery +1

Speed 20 ft. (base 30 ft.)
Melee lance +8 (1d8+3/x3) or longsword +8 (1d8+3/19–20)
Space 5 ft., **Reach** 5 ft. (10 ft. with lance)

Str 16, **Dex** 14, **Con** 14, **Int** 10, **Wis** 12, **Cha** 12
Base Atk +4; **CMB** +7; **CMD** 19
Feats Improved Initiative, Mounted Combat, Ride-By Attack, Spirited Charge, Weapon Focus (lance), Weapon Focus (longsword)
Skills Handle Animal +8, Perception +5, Ride +9
Languages Common
Gear chainmail, heavy wood shield, lance, longsword, 2d10 gp, 40+2d10 sp.

SHERIFF · CR 3
XP 800
Male human aristocrat 2/fighter 3
LN Medium humanoid (human)
Init +6; **Perception** +10

AC 17, touch 13, flat-footed 14 (+3 armor, +2 Dex, +1 dodge, +1 shield)
hp 36 (2d8+2 plus 3d10+3 plus 2)
Fort +4; **Ref** +3; **Will** +5; +6 vs. fear
Defensive Abilities bravery +1

Speed 30 ft.
Melee longsword +6 (1d8+1/19–20)

Str 12, **Dex** 14, **Con** 12, **Int** 14, **Wis** 12, **Cha** 14
Base Atk +4; **CMB** +5; **CMD** 18
Feats Alertness, Combat Expertise, Dodge, Improved Initiative, Mounted Combat, Skill Focus (Diplomacy)
Skills Diplomacy +13, Handle Animal +10, Knowledge (local) +10, Perception +10, Ride +10, Sense Motive +11
Languages Common, Giant, Goblin
Combat Gear 2 potions of cure serious wounds; **Other Gear** masterwork chain shirt, masterwork light steel shield, masterwork longsword, surcoat bearing the insignia of their ruler, writ of authority, five 20 gp gems, 2d10 gp, 2d10 sp.

WARHORSES (3) · CR 2
XP 600
N Large animal
Init +4; **Senses** low-light vision, scent; **Perception** +8

AC 18, touch 13, flat-footed 14 (+3 armor, +4 Dex, +2 natural, −1 size)
hp 24 (2d8+10)
Fort +8; **Ref** +7; **Will** +3

Speed 50 ft.
Melee 2 hooves +6 (1d4+5)
Space 10 ft., **Reach** 5 ft.

Str 20, **Dex** 18, **Con** 21, **Int** 2, **Wis** 17, **Cha** 11
Base Atk +1; **CMB** +7; **CMD** 21 (25 vs. trip)
Feats Endurance, Run[B]

Skills Perception +8
Gear studded leather barding, saddle, saddlebags, bedroll and food for itself and its rider for one week.

Trained for Combat (Ex) The warhorse treats its hoof attacks as primary attacks. It knows the tricks attack, come, defend, down, guard, and heel.

STIRGES   CR 1/2
XP 200
hp 5 (*Pathfinder Roleplaying Game Bestiary* "Stirge")

TROLL   CR 5
XP 1,600
hp 63 (*Pathfinder Roleplaying Game Bestiary* "Troll")

Villagers: If encountered in the morning, the **villagers** (Male and female human Com1; hp 3) are leaving Fairhill; if encountered in the evening, they are returning to Fairhill. Normally a friendly lot, these villagers are cautious around adventurers because of the recent problems. A successful DC 12 Diplomacy check allows the villagers to tell the party of the recent orc trouble and of the family that was raped and mutilated on the road leading from the village to the tradeway just days ago. Further questioning reveals that the villagers believe that a vampire in an old ruined keep is the cause of the mutilations. They invoke the protection of Freya and encourage the party to seek shelter indoors and the safety of a fire when night falls. The villagers can be convinced to offer aid to the party if the need is dire, including taking the party to a farmhouse or house in the village.

WOLF   CR 1
XP 400
hp 13 (*Pathfinder Roleplaying Game Bestiary* "Wolf")

WORG   CR 2
XP 600
hp 26 (*Pathfinder Roleplaying Game Bestiary* "Worg")

Monster Lairs

These descriptions detail the lairs marked on the wilderness map. Care should be exercised in using these encounters, as many are very difficult. They should be used as follow-ups to wandering monster encounters, as part of the story line based on interactions with the folk of Fairhill or after the main adventure has been completed. However, if the characters are foolish enough to blunder around in the wilderness and run into these lairs, their gruesome deaths become cautionary tales for the local children.

Area A: The Lair of Karigror the Troll (CR 5)

> You come upon a small grove of trees with a bubbling brook along its side. A few yards away, you see a small pool of water with fish jumping and insects skimming along the pool's surface... you also notice a large number of human bones in the stream. As you look around some more, you see a cave entrance on the hillside about 20 feet up. Two men in chainmail hang upside down from a pole balanced against a tree limb, their throats cut. It is obvious to you that someone (or *something*) is aging meat for dinner.

This cave is the lair of **Karigror the Troll**. A few rounds after the party sees the bodies or if it investigates the cave, Karigror appears at the cave mouth and jumps down the slope landing a few feet from his pool. He stands there and looks menacingly at the party, holding his axe in one hand and a human femur in the other. Karigror will likely slaughter an entire low-level party without breaking a sweat. If your party is foolish enough to explore where it shouldn't be exploring, it meets guys like Karigror.

KARIGROR THE TROLL   CR 5
XP 1,600
hp 63 (*Pathfinder Roleplaying Game Bestiary* "Troll")

If the group does not immediately attack or flee, Karigror demands tribute in broken Common for "Stealin' me water." You should play up Karigror's personality and make the party think he is big, mean, green and scary-which he should be to them. Have him crunch on the femur and suck some marrow out of the bone while they are talking with him, then have him discard the bone and begin to finger the edge of his axe. If the party flees, Karigror gives a roar and chases them, but he is only doing this to keep up appearances. He has no intention of chasing down the party though with his speed, he could.

Tactics: Karigror is quite happy to let the party go free if they pay him a ransom of at least 100 gp, as his pantry is already full and he is rather tired from his last fight. If the party attacks him, keep in mind that Karigror is old and wise and makes good use of the pool of water should the party try to bum him. If he is seriously wounded in battle (less than 10 hp left), he jumps up and hides in his cave, pushing into place a large boulder to block the entrance, requiring a DC 26 Strength check to dislodge. Up to three characters can add their Strength bonus to the roll.

Lair and Treasure: If the party actually defeats Karigror, his lair consists of three small caves. The first contains bones and rotten armor left over from previous meals. The second is his sleeping quarters and has piles of leaves as bedding. Beneath the leaves are 320 gp, 560 sp and 652 cp. The third chamber is his larder. This room holds the two-week-old bodies of four men. Two have intact armor (chain and leather), and two

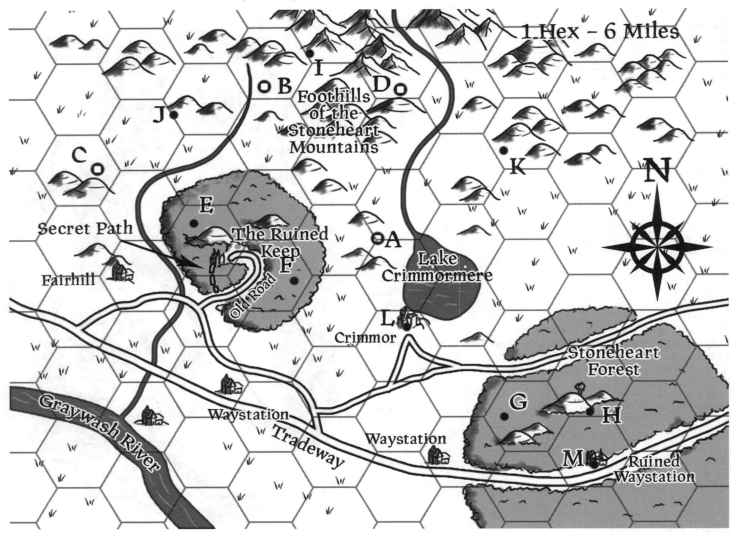

1 Hex = 6 Miles

polearms are also usable. Beneath one particularly well-aged morsel is a metal kite shield, apparently used as a serving tray. On a dismembered hand is a gold and sapphire ring worth 500 gp.

Area B: The Lair of Girbolg the Ettin (CR 6)

> You find a stony path leading from the woods up a hill. On top of the hill, you see a large round tower in a state of disrepair, with several fallen stone blocks. As you approach the tower, you hear a beautiful female voice singing a love song accompanied by a harp being played rather badly.

This is the home of **Girbolg the Ettin**. The party automatically surprises Girbolg in the act of playing the aforementioned harp. Girbolg was a normal, run-of-the mill chaotic-evil ettin until he put on a magical helmet that he took off of a dead adventurer. This helmet — a *helm of opposite alignment* — turned Girbolg's right head lawful good, leaving Girbolg's left head chaotic-evil and leaving Girbolg one very confused ettin. On one of his previous raids, he'd captured a small group of humans, including **Arialle**, the daughter of the village blacksmith, who is in fact a young bard. Girbolg has eaten all of the captives except Arialle, sparing her because of her beautiful voice. She is currently chained to a large rock, singing while Girbolg plays the harp (badly).

Girbolg has a 50% chance of having either his left or right head in charge at any given moment. When the party arrives, make a roll to see if good-Girbolg or bad-Girbolg is in charge. If good-Girbolg is in charge, he is friendly unless he or Arialle is attacked. He asks the party to join the music

(he is playing the harp) and is especially impressed if a bard is present. If bad-Girbolg is in charge, he attacks. If the party runs, he will not pursue, instead making sure that Arialle remains with him. He kills (and later eats) anyone he catches. Arialle is very frightened, and she desperately wants to go home. If the party finds Girbolg in a "good" mood, they can talk him into releasing Arialle with some degree of difficulty (promises to come by and play music, etc.).

If the party forces the issue or does not bargain properly, there is a 90% chance that bad-Girbolg takes over and attacks. Otherwise, good-Girbolg cries and pleads for Arialle not to leave. If he is in a "bad" mood, the party will have to kill him (not likely) or distract him long enough to make an escape. He will not pursue the party more than 200 yards from his tower, but don't let them know that. If the party rescues Arialle, award the party 200 XP in addition to the XP for defeating Girbolg. Arialle's father makes the party a suit of custom light or medium armor as a reward once they return to Fairhill.

GIRBOLG THE ETTIN CR 6
XP 2,400
hp 65 (*Pathfinder Roleplaying Game Bestiary* "Ettin")

Language: Thanks to Arialle, Girbolg has learned a limited number of words in Common. Speaking to Girbolg in Common requires a DC 10 Linguistics check.

Possessions: Filthy hide armor, 2 large spiked clubs (one in each hand), 3 large spears, Arialle's masterwork harp, 3d12 gp in a small sack with several large rocks and a leather thong threaded through 13 human vertebrae.

Tactics: Though ettins have a low intelligence, they are cunning fighters, ambushing their victims rather than charging into combat. Once the battle is joined, ettins fight furiously until all enemies are dead or the battle turns against them. Ettins do not retreat easily, doing so only if victory is impossible.

Arialle's Locked Chain: 1 in. thick; Hardness 10; hp 5; Break (DC 26); Disable Device (DC 20).

ARIALLE   CR 1
XP 400
Female human bard 2
CG Medium humanoid (human)
Init +6; **Perception** +5

AC 12, touch 12, flat-footed 10 (+2 Dex)
hp 13 (2d8)
Fort +0; **Ref** +5; **Will** +3; +4 vs. bardic performance, sonic, and language-dependent effects

Speed 30 ft.
Special Attacks bardic performance 7 rounds/day (countersong, distraction, fascinate [DC 12], inspire courage +1)
Spells Known (CL 2nd):
1st (3/day)—*cure light wounds, sleep* (DC 12), *ventriloquism* (DC 12),
0 (at will)—*dancing lights, daze* (DC 11), *ghost sound* (DC 11), *lullaby* (DC 11), *prestidigitation* (DC 11)

Str 9, **Dex** 14, **Con** 10, **Int** 13, **Wis** 10, **Cha** 13
Base Atk +1; **CMB** +0; **CMD** 12
Feats Improved Initiative, Skill Focus (Perform [sing])
Skills Appraise +5, Bluff +9, Diplomacy +5, Knowledge (local) +6, Linguistics +5, Perception +5, Perform (sing) +9, Perform (string instruments) +6, Profession (merchant) +5, Sense Motive +9, Sleight of Hand +6, Spellcraft +6, Survival +1, Swim +0, Use Magic Device +5
Languages Common, Elven, Ettin
SQ bardic knowledge, versatile performance abilities (singing), well versed
Gear Arialle is currently unarmed and wearing only simple peasant clothes. Her sole possession is the masterwork harp described above, which Girbolg is currently de-tuning.

Treasure: In addition to the masterwork harp (crafted by the legendary Fathilir of Bard's Gate and bearing his runic signature) worth 1,000 gp to any connoisseur, Girbolg has amassed a hoard of 1,100 gp, 14,600 sp and 8,400 cp. Lost in the rubble of the tower interior — in an area about 20 yards from where Girbolg makes his lair — is a *ring of wizardry I*, which can only be found if a large amount of rubble is moved and a *detect magic* spell is cast.

Area C: The lair of the Owlbear (CR 4)

> As you walk through the forest, the terrain gets rocky and dry. You move to the side of the path, and a horrible smell burns your nostrils. You hear a thrashing, crunching sound a few feet away. A tree falls, and as the dust settles, you are confronted by a huge, bear-like creature with red, glowing eyes and a beak like a bird's, only filled with dozens of sharp teeth, each as long as a human finger. Blood soaks the chest of the beast, and you see the remains of its previous victim, a deer. The monster charges you!

This creature is the **owlbear** that has been raiding some local farms. So far, it has killed only cattle and sheep, but it is just a matter of time until it gets a taste for humans. The farmers who have asked the party for help have had a number of livestock bitten in half and would be very happy to have the culprit killed. If the owlbear is killed after the group is asked to help, award a 200 XP story award. The farmers try to marry off their daughters or throw a party to reward the characters.

OWLBEAR   CR 4
XP 1,200
hp 47 (*Pathfinder Roleplaying Game Bestiary* "Owlbear")

Lair and Treasure: The lair of the owlbear is about 500 feet through the woods from where this encounter occurs. It is very easy to track back to its lair due to the swath of destruction it leaves in its wake — a DC 8 Survival check is all that's required to track it. The lair is an abandoned house in the woods. The occupants are long dead or moved away, and no readily apparent treasure can be found. Just a few feet away are a cluster of old graves. If they are dug up, a necklace worth 500 gp can be found within a coffin. Each good-aligned PC doing so should lose 200 XP.

Area D: The Manticore Lair (CR 5 - male only, 7 - female and cubs, or 8 - whole family)

There are three ways your party can encounter the manticores. First, if they are exploring the foothills to the north of the village at night, they may encounter the manticore as a wandering monster. If so, read the boxed text below. Second, if they enter the area of the wilderness map marked "**D**," whether day or night, there is a 20% chance (1 or 2 on 1d10) that they encounter the male manticore as described below. Third, they may make it to the manticore lair directly. If so, proceed to the second set of boxed text below and read that to your group.

> You crest a hilltop and look out over the surrounding countryside. You can see all the way west to the ocean from here, and you imagine you can smell the crisp air of an ocean breeze. The way is rocky, but it is vastly better than moving through the underbrush of the forest below. Suddenly, you hear a whooshing of wings, and as if materializing from thin air, a great beast is upon you! It looks like a giant flying lion, but has a man's head and a spiked tail!

This is the male manticore, fetching a PC for its children to use for hunting practice. Its intent is not to kill anyone, but instead to capture one PC and return to its nest.

MALE MANTICORE   **CR 5**
XP 1,600
hp 57 (*Pathfinder Roleplaying Game Bestiary* "Manticore")

Tactics: The manticore swoops in instead of shooting tail spikes. In combat, it strikes for non-lethal damage. PCs knocked unconscious are carried away, only to wake up an hour later in the manticore's lair. Remember that characters heal nonlethal damage at the rate of 1 hit point per hour per character level. If the male manticore takes over half of its hit points, it flies up and shoots four volleys of tail spikes before leaving in search of easier game. If the male can lower the party to less than two PCs with tail spikes, it resumes its attack/capture attempt. It will be able to grab an unconscious opponent and fly off (two rounds of missile fire from the PCs can stop it) unless it takes over 10 points of damage, in which case it drops the PC carried (4d6 damage from the fall to the PC) and continues as above.

If the manticore manages to fly away with a PC, the party can easily see it fly to a hilltop lair about 2 miles away. The group can travel to the lair in about 1 hour. When they arrive, the cave entrance is unguarded. Read the following text to them:

> You reach a strange cave entrance that sits some 20 feet up a steep hillside. There is a small ledge in front of the cave mouth. Even from this distance, the cave smells of great cat urine and human blood. Dozens of bones of all shapes and sizes litter the stones in front of the cave and the ground beneath — a grisly warning to all who approach.

If any PC was captured and returned by the male manticore to the lair, read the following text to that player:

> You awaken in a dark cave, and as your eyes adjust, you can see daylight a few dozen yards away. Your weapons are missing. You see another of the large creatures and two smaller versions. The large one has a distinctively female face, beautiful in a way, but made ugly by its protruding fangs and horrid scowl. The two smaller beasts move towards you.

This is the manticore lair. The male is only present if he was reduced to less than half his hit points during the initial fight. If he was not, he is off in search of another victim (not the PC group). The captive has had all of his weapons removed (though the manticores are 90% likely to miss a small item like a dagger or a *wand*). Inventive PC captives can pick up a bone (treat as club) or tail spike (treat as dagger) to defend themselves. Only the baby manticores attack, unless they are both killed in which case the mother retaliates (at +2 to hit and damage). Unless the male is present, the rescue party surprises the mother from behind as she blocks the captive's escape and watches the kids have fun. If the male is present, it is watching the entrance.

The captive is about 80 feet from the cave entrance, and the female manticore sits 50 feet away, about 30 feet from the entrance. In the back of the cave (to the left of the captive) are all of the captured PCs' weapons, as well as the treasure hoard of the monsters.

FEMALE MANTICORE   **CR 5**
XP 1,600
hp 57 (*Pathfinder Roleplaying Game Bestiary* "Manticore")

MANTICORE CUBS (2)   **CR 3**
XP 800
LE Medium magical beast
(*Pathfinder Roleplaying Game Bestiary* "Manticore")
Init +3; **Senses** darkvision 60 ft., low-light vision; **Perception** +9

AC 17, touch 13, flat-footed 14 (+3 Dex, +4 natural)

hp 15 (2d10+4)
Fort +5; **Ref** +6; **Will** +1

Speed 30 ft., fly 40 ft. (clumsy)
Melee bite +3 (1d6+1) and 2 claws +3 (1d6+1)
Ranged 4 spikes +6 (1d4+1)

Str 12, **Dex** 17, **Con** 14, **Int** 7, **Wis** 12, **Cha** 9
Base Atk +2; **CMB** +3; **CMD** 16 (20 vs. trip)
Feats Weapon Focus (spikes)
Skills Fly −1, Perception +9, Survival +1 (+5 tracking); **Racial Modifiers** +4 Perception, +4 Survival when tracking
Languages Common

Spikes (Ex) With a snap of its tail, a manticore cub can loose a volley of four spikes as a standard action (make an attack roll for each spike). This attack has a range of 90 feet with no range increment. All targets must be within 15 feet of each other. The creature can launch only 12 spikes in any 24-hour period.

Treasure: One suit of human-sized half-plate mail armor and a matching suit of chain barding for a war-horse, pierced in numerous places from manticore spikes, requiring at least one week of work by an armorer to repair at a cost of 200 gp. Piles of torn and stripped human clothing. Detect magic reveals a *cloak of protection +2*. Assorted coins and gems in a pile total 123 gp, 245 sp and 111 cp. There are four 50 gp garnets and one 1,000 gp ruby among the coins. It requires a DC 15 Perception check to find the gems. A battered but still usable traveling spell book containing the spells *fly*, *blink*, *detect invisibility*, and *protection from arrows*. A locked iron box, nicked with scratches and bite marks, with a fine-quality lock contains a *manual of quickness of action +1* and two non-magical masterwork daggers.

Locked Iron Box: 1/2 in. thick; Hardness 10; hp 15; Break (DC 26); Disable Device (DC 22).

If the mother and babies are slain while the male is away, the male returns with a victim (from one of the local farms) in about 2 hours. The male is no more wounded than whatever damage the PCs caused, drops the farmer and flies into a berserk rage when he sees his dead family. The male attacks at +2 on all dice rolls at that time. Rescue of the farmer nets the party a 200 XP story award in addition to any combat award for the manticore and a great deal of fame for the party!

Area E: The Old Crone (CR 5)

This location is the cave home of **Gethrame the Crone**. The cave entrance is well hidden behind bushes and brambles, set into a hillside. The cave itself is small, containing two linked chambers. The first holds Gethrame's *magic bowl* and a low table and various other creature comforts, including a small fire pit. The rear chamber contains her bed area. Gethrame was long ago the lover of Eralion. Shandril banished her from Fairhill many years ago and cursed her with blindness for using her *magic bowl* to scry on the holy rituals of Freya. Blind, Gethrame fled into the wilderness. Eralion found his love in a cave and she beseeched him to help her to see again. He did so, creating a *magical staff of lesser arcane eye* that allowed her sight. Creating the *staff*, however, required as a material component: the eyes of a wererat shaman. Gethrame used the *staff* to continue to scry with her *bowl* from her cave. She saw Eralion's future and warned him of the dark fate that would eventually befall him. He ignored her warnings.

Eventually, Eralion abandoned Gethrame. Heart broken, she has lived alone in her cave for many years. Unbeknownst to her, a ranger named **Herl**, who secretly loves her, has kept watch over her all these years. Though once beautiful, Gethrame is now a woman of faded beauty and old age with an air of tragedy about her. Recently, her *staff* that allows her magical sight was stolen by wererats. Her cave is a shambles from her blind stumbling. She wails loudly, bemoaning her cruel fate. Only the unknown presence of Herl has kept her from harm from passing creatures.

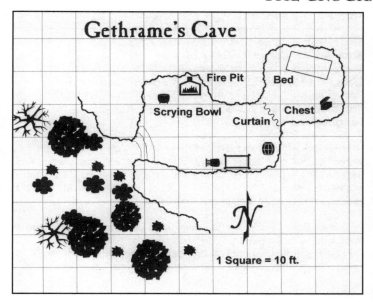

Gethrame's Cave

Fire Pit
Bed
Scrying Bowl
Chest
Curtain

N

1 Square = 10 ft.

GETHRAME THE CRONE   **CR 5**
XP 1,600
Female human adept 7
N Medium humanoid (human)
Init +0; **Perception** +4 (non-sight related)

AC 10, touch 10, flat-footed 10
hp 31 (7d6+7)
Fort +3; **Ref** +2; **Will** +7
Weakness blind

Speed 30 ft.
Melee quarterstaff +3 (1d6)
Spells Prepared (CL 7th; melee touch +3, ranged touch +3):
2nd—*animal trance* (DC 14), *darkness, invisibility*
1st—*cause fear* (DC 13), *command* (DC 13), *obscuring mist, sleep* (DC 13)
0 (3/day)—*detect magic, ghost sound* (DC 12), *mending*

Str 10, **Dex** 10, **Con** 12, **Int** 14, **Wis** 14, **Cha** 12
Base Atk +3; **CMB** +3; **CMD** 13
Feats Empower Spell, Enlarge Spell, Heighten Spell, Skill Focus (Knowledge [arcana]), Skill Focus (Use Magic Device)
Skills Appraise +3, Diplomacy +2, Heal +8, Intimidate +2, Knowledge (arcana) +15, Knowledge (nature) +9, Knowledge (religion) +9, Perception +4, Sense Motive +6, Spellcraft +10, Stealth +4, Survival +8, Use Magic Device +11
Languages Common, Elven, Sylvan
Other Gear *magical bowl of scrying*, allowing the user to cast *scrying* 1/day

HERL   **CR 3**
XP 800
Male half-elf ranger 4
N Medium humanoid (elf, human)
Init +4; **Senses** low-light vision; **Perception** +9

AC 19, touch 15, flat-footed 14 (+3 armor, +4 Dex, +1 dodge, +1 shield)
hp 30 (4d10+4)
Fort +5; **Ref** +8; **Will** +2; +2 vs. enchantment
Immune sleep

Speed 30 ft.
Melee mwk handaxe +7 (1d6+2/x3)

Ranged mwk composite longbow +9 (1d8+1/x3) and throwing axe +6 (1d6+2)
Special Attacks favored enemy (animals +2)
Spells Prepared (CL 1st):
1st—*charm animal* (DC 12)

Str 14, **Dex** 18, **Con** 12, **Int** 10, **Wis** 13, **Cha** 10
Base Atk +4; **CMB** +6; **CMD** 21
Feats Dodge, Endurance, Mobility, Point Blank Shot, Skill Focus (trapper)
Skills Bluff +0 (+2 vs. animals), Climb +9, Craft (traps) +7, Handle Animal +6, Heal +7, Knowledge (geography) +3 (+5 vs. animals, +5 while in forest terrain), Knowledge (nature) +3 (+5 vs. animals), Perception +9 (+11 vs. animals, +11 while in forest terrain), Profession (trapper) +9, Ride +8, Sense Motive +1 (+3 vs. animals), Stealth +10 (+12 while in forest terrain), Survival +7 (+9 vs. animals, +9 while in forest terrain, +9 to track), Swim +6 (+10 to resist nonlethal damage from exhaustion)
Languages Common
SQ combat styles (archery), elf blood, favored terrain (forest +2), hunter's bonds (companions), track, wild empathy
Combat Gear healer's kit; **Other Gear** masterwork studded leather armor, masterwork buckler, masterwork composite longbow (Str +1), 20 arrows, masterwork handaxe, 2 throwing axes, masterwork artisan's tools (Craft [traps]), climber's kit

Area F: The Twisted Tree and the Rat-Man Warren (CR Varies, 4–12)

A coven of wererats live at this location beneath a twisted and evil tree. The entrance to their warren is through the hollowed trunk of the tree itself, which leads down a set of stairs carved into the roots of the tree into a series of caves. Locating the entrance to the wererat warren will prove difficult, though it can be located with a successful DC 25 Perception check. Most likely, the PCs locate the entrance to the wererat lair by running afoul of its evil guardian: the **twisted tree**.

THE TWISTED TREE   **CR 4**
XP 1,200
NE Large plant
Init +0; **Senses** low-light vision; **Perception** +9

AC 20, touch 9, flat-footed 20 (+11 natural, −1 size)
hp 45 (6d8+18)
Fort +8; **Ref** +2; **Will** +5
DR 5/slashing; **Immune** plant traits
Weaknesses vulnerability to fire

Speed 0 ft.
Melee 2 slams +9 (1d8+5)

Space 10 ft.; **Reach** 10 ft.

Str 21, **Dex** 10, **Con** 16, **Int** 12, **Wis** 16, **Cha** 13
Base Atk +4; **CMB** +10; **CMD** 20
Feats Improved Sunder, Power Attack, Weapon Focus (slam)
Skills Bluff +5, Intimidate +5, Knowledge (nature) +5, Perception +9, Sense Motive +5, Stealth +0 (+16 in forests);
Racial Modifiers +16 Stealth in forests
Languages Treant

Description: The "twisted tree" was once a treant sapling. It was warped and twisted by the evil power of the rat folk shamans and their dark goddess. It now serves as the guardian of their warren. It has knotted and twisted bark and branches and its leaves are a deep sickly green. It appears to be afflicted with some type of wood rot.

Tactics: The twisted tree attacks any that attempt to enter the hole in its trunk leading to the warrens of the wererats. Any person passing through the opening in the trunk draws an attack of opportunity from one of the limbs of the evil tree. It uses its lengthy reach to attack any passers-by.

Wererat Warren: Once past the tree, the underground lair is filled with the tree's twisted roots, which hang down from the ceiling, sometimes forming pillar-like root columns. Any of the wererat witches can manipulate the dangling roots of the tree, once per day

Rat-man Warrens

Witches' Nest

Nest

Nest

Nest

Nest

Witches' Nest

Glaathaa's Nest

Outline of Evil Tree Above

▨	Root Stairs
◉	Root Pillar
•	Large Root From Above
✊	Glaathaa's Chest
🌿	Nest
✪	Wererat Guard

1 square = 10 ft.

as an *entangle* spell affecting all non-wererats. There are several cave rooms to the underground lair. A total of **14 wererat, 4 wererat witches** and **Glaathaa, the shaman leader**, live in the caves. There is a 25% chance that 1d8 wererats are away from the nest at any time, accompanied by 1d2 wererat witches. There is always a guard stationed at each of the two points marked on the map of the warrens. Each room marked "Nest" is the lair of 3 wererats. In each nest can be found 2d8 gp and 2d20 sp. Each room marked "**Witches' Nest**" is the lair of 2 wererat witches. In each of their nests can be found 2d20 gp and 2d100 sp. The room marked "**Glaathaa's Nest**" is her personal lair. Her nest is much larger and is not made of the normal straw and cloth. Her nest is made of shreds of fine cloth, portions of tapestries, bones, animal hides and a blanket of animal and humanoid hair. In a **small locked chest** in her lair can be found a *wand of ghoul touch* (12 charges), an *elixir of swimming*, a *potion of cure moderate wounds*, a golden yellow topaz worth 500 gp and 3 vials of unholy water. It also contains an ivory scroll case that holds a non-magical scroll written in Aklo detailing all the spells they know, requiring *read magic* and *comprehend languages* to read. These particular wererats are the descendants of the tribe nearly eradicated by Eralion when he killed their shaman leader and used her eyes to create Gethrame's *staff of limited arcane eye*. They have, by communing with their evil goddess, recently learned the location of Gethrame's cave and stolen her *staff*. Glaathaa currently possesses the *staff*.

Small locked chest 1 in. thick; Hardness 5; hp 1; Break DC 17; Disable Device DC 20

WERERATS (14)   CR 2
XP 600
hp 18 (*Pathfinder Roleplaying Game Bestiary* "Lycanthrope, Wererat")

WERERAT WITCH (4)   CR 4
XP 1,200
Female wererat witch 4 (*Pathfinder Roleplaying Game Bestiary* "Lycanthrope, Wererat", *Pathfinder Roleplaying Game Advanced Player's Guide* "Witch")
CE Medium humanoid (human, shapechanger)
Init +6; **Senses** low-light vision, scent; **Perception** +5

AC 12, touch 12, flat-footed 10 (+2 Dex)
hp 26 (4d6+8)
Fort +3; **Ref** +3; **Will** +7

Speed 30 ft.
Melee dagger +2 (1d4/19–20)
Special Attacks hexes (evil eye [DC 13], slumber [DC 13])
Spells Prepared (CL 4th; melee touch +2, ranged touch +4):
2nd—*hold person* (DC 13), *invisibility*ᴮ, *web*
1st—*cause fear, chill touch, mage armor, ray of enfeeblement* (DC 12), *ventriloquism*ᴮ
0 (at will)—*dancing lights, light, read magic, resistance*
Patron Deception

Str 10, **Dex** 14, **Con** 15, **Int** 13, **Wis** 12, **Cha** 8
Base Atk +2; **CMB** +2; **CMD** 14
Feats Accursed Hex#, Improved Initiative, Iron Will
Skills Climb +1, Diplomacy –1 (+3 to change attitude vs. animals related to lycanthropic form), Handle Animal +1, Heal +6, Knowledge (arcana) +6, Knowledge (nature) +6, Perception +5, Spellcraft +7, Use Magic Device +6
Languages Aklo, Common
SQ +2 to fortitude saves, change forms, deliver touch spells through familiar, empathic link with familiar, hexes (coven), lycanthropic empathy, patron spells (deception), share spells with familiar
Gear dagger, crimson robes, spell component pouch, 2d8 gp
#*Pathfinder Roleplaying Game Ultimate Magic*

RAT FAMILIARS   CR—
XP—
N Tiny magical beast (animal)
Init +2; **Senses** low-light vision, scent; **Perception** +8

AC 16, touch 14, flat-footed 14 (+2 Dex, +2 natural, +2 size)
hp 13 (1d8)
Fort +2; **Ref** +4; **Will** +5

Speed 15 ft., climb 15 ft, swim 15 ft.
Melee bite +6 (1d3–4)
Space 2 ft.; **Reach** 0 ft.

Str 2, **Dex** 15, **Con** 11, **Int** 9, **Wis** 13, **Cha** 2
Base Atk +2; **CMB** +2; **CMD** 8 (12 vs. trip)
Feats Weapon Finesse
Skills Acrobatics +2 (–6 jump), Climb +14, Fly +6, Handle Animal –2, Heal +3, Perception +8, Spellcraft +2, Stealth +18, Swim +10, Use Magic Device +0

GLAATHAA   CR 7
Female wererat witch 7 (*Pathfinder Roleplaying Game Bestiary* "Lycanthrope, Wererat", *Pathfinder Roleplaying Game Advanced Player's Guide* "Witch")
CE Medium humanoid (human, shapechanger)
Init +6; **Senses** low-light vision, scent; **Perception** +5

AC 12, touch 12, flat-footed 10 (+2 Dex)
hp 51 (7d6+21)
Fort +5; **Ref** +4; **Will** +8

Speed 30 ft.
Melee mwk dagger +4 (1d4/19–20)
Special Attacks hexes (charm [DC 15], evil eye [DC 15], slumber [DC 15])
Spells Prepared (CL 7th; melee touch +3, ranged touch +5):
4th—*phantasmal killer* (DC 18)
3rd—*bestow curse* (DC 15), *blink*ᴮ, *vampiric touch* (DC 15)
2nd—*cure moderate wounds, daze monster* (DC 14), *hold person* (DC 14), *invisibility*ᴮ, *spectral hand*
1st—*hypnotism* (DC 13), *inflict light wounds* (DC 13), *mage armor, ray of enfeeblement* (DC 13), *sleep* (DC 13), *ventriloquism*ᴮ (DC 15)
0 (at will)—*dancing lights, light, read magic, resistance*
Patron Deception

Str 10, **Dex** 15, **Con** 16, **Int** 15, **Wis** 12, **Cha** 8
Base Atk +3; **CMB** +3; **CMD** 15
Feats Accursed Hex, Greater Spell Focus (Illusion), Improved Initiative, Iron Will, Spell Focus (Illusion)
Skills Climb +1, Diplomacy –1 (+3 to change attitude vs. animals related to lycanthropic form), Escape Artist +7, Handle Animal +5, Heal +7, Knowledge (arcana) +10, Knowledge (nature) +10, Perception +5, Spellcraft +11, Use Magic Device +9
Languages Aklo, Common, Draconic
SQ arcane familiar nearby, change forms, deliver touch spells through familiar, empathic link with familiar, hexes (coven), lycanthropic empathy, patron spells (deception), share spells with familiar, speak with animals, speak with familiar
Gear masterwork dagger, crimson robes, spell component pouch, 4d8 gp, 2 gems worth 25 gp, *staff of lesser arcane eye*, which allows the holder of the staff to have an *arcane eye* (as per the spell) in effect at will, though the eye is permanently mounted to the end of the *staff* and cannot move around. Her other treasure is kept in the chest in her lair.

RAT FAMILIAR   CR —
XP—
N Tiny magical beast (animal)
Init +2; **Senses** low-light vision, scent; **Perception** +8

AC 18, touch 14, flat-footed 16 (+2 Dex, +4 natural, +2 size)
hp 25 (1d8)
Fort +2; **Ref** +4; **Will** +6

Speed 15 ft., climb 15 ft, swim 15 ft.
Melee bite +7 (1d3–4)
Space 2 ft.; **Reach** 0 ft.

Str 2, **Dex** 15, **Con** 11, **Int** 9, **Wis** 13, **Cha** 2
Base Atk +3; **CMB** +3; **CMD** 9 (13 vs. trip)
Feats Weapon Finesse
Skills Acrobatics +2 (–6 jump), Climb +14, Escape Artist +7, Fly +6, Handle Animal +2, Heal +4, Perception +8, Spellcraft +5, Stealth +18, Swim +10, Use Magic Device +3

Tactics: The guards give a squeak and use their ranged weapons, drawing melee weapons to defend any witches if they are engaged. The wererats fight to the death to prevent harm to the witches. The spellcasters use magic from a distance. The witches also use their power to call on the roots of the evil tree above as an *entangle* spell (unless it has been slain). Glaathaa casts *mage armor* early in combat and uses *phantasmal killer* where appropriate. If pressed, she uses *invisibility* and flees. She will also parley with the PCs if it is for her gain. She will not, however, willingly relinquish the *staff*—claiming that it is hers by blood right, since her predecessor died for its creation.

Area G: The Spider Lair (CR 5)

The PCs could be searching for the missing adventurers as a result of a rumor heard in Fairhill or they could simply stumble upon this lair as they travel through the Stoneheart Mountain Forest, possibly looking for the source of the stirge menace. This location is a nest of **5 Medium monstrous spiders**. As the PCs arrive, one of the spiders is attacking a trapped squirrel. What the PCs don't know is that four others are about to attack them. Allow anyone who looks up a Perception check opposed by each spider's Stealth check to notice the spiders descending on them (don't forget the spiders get a +8 to Stealth when descending on their web strands). Anyone who does not look up is automatically caught flat-footed. Note that these spiders are more poisonous than the normal monstrous spider of the same size. Dozens of egg sacs are present in the webbing overhead.

GIANT SPIDERS (5)   CR 1
XP 400
hp 16 (*Pathfinder Roleplaying Game Bestiary* "Spider, Giant")

Tactics: The spiders spread out and attack multiple opponents (including animals if present). The spiders shoot webs, and then bite an opponent until he falls from the poison. They then wrap them in webs. Any opponents webbed are left alone until all opponents are subdued. Medium opponents webbed can make a DC 13 Strength check to escape, as they are too big to be effectively webbed.

Treasure: Spun into the webs are the corpses of a group of adventurers. Three recently slain bodies, drained of all fluids, reside in the webs. One was a female fighter, still wearing her chainmail and has a dagger on her belt. All other equipment is lost in the woods, and cannot be located. The second body was rogue who still clutches his masterwork short sword in his left hand. In a pouch on his belt are a set of masterwork thieves' tools, 4 gems worth 10 gp each, and 22sp. He wears leather armor. The final body was a wizard, wearing only his robe. Tucked inside his robe is a leather scroll case containing a scroll of 3 spells (CL 5th; *charm person*, *shield*, *mirror image*). His pouch is still on his belt and contains 22gp, a 100 gp pearl and a vial of *holy water*. If the webs are burned, there is a 40% chance that the *scroll* is destroyed and a 25% chance that the masterwork thieves' tools are destroyed.

Area H: The Stirge Caverns (CR Varies, 10–12)

This is the location of a cave complex under a hill in the Stoneheart Mountain Forest, know to the locals as "Stirge Wood." The complex is filled with stirges, and is the home to **Yandarral**, a twisted and half-mad elf mage/druid, who resides there with his "pets." He has crafted a strange baton that allows him to control the stirges. He is not so much evil as fanatical. He hates the development of Fairhill and other local villages (such as Crimmor), seeing them as a blight on the natural landscape. He has lost connection with reality to a degree, and has taken on some of the traits of his charges. He plans to use his stirges to eliminate the villages. He sends "advance parties" of **2d6 stirges** to periodically assault the various villages. He plans to send all of his stirges to swarm and attack the occupants of Crimmor within the coming months.

Entrance and Caverns: The entrance to the cave complex is difficult to find (DC 20 Perception check) unless it is searched for at dawn or dusk when stirges can be seen coming and going in large numbers. The entrance slopes down steeply for some 40 feet and then opens into the entrance cavern. This cavern always contains at least **12 stirges**. Numerous passages lead away from this initial chamber, twisting their way to many other rooms, each containing **2d6 stirges**. After 1d4+4 of these rooms have been encountered, the PCs reach the chamber of Yandarral. His spartan cave contains a few creature comforts such as a cot, a lantern and a low desk as well as **10 stirges**. He also has several ornamental cages in which he keeps his current favorite stirges. In the past, he has used *stone shape* to craft seats, a cubby-hole set into the far wall where he makes his bed, and other useful pieces of furniture from the stone of his cavern.

YANDARRAL
CR 10

XP 9,600

Male elf druid 5/sorcerer 6

CN Medium humanoid (elf)

Init +3; **Senses** low-light vision; **Perception** +11

AC 13, touch 13, flat-footed 10 (+3 Dex)

hp 54 (5d8+6d6 plus 3)

Fort +6; **Ref** +6; **Will** +15; +2 vs. enchantments, poison and sleep, +4 vs. spell-like and supernatural abilities of Fey and against effects that target plants

Immune magic sleep; **Resist** elven immunities, photosynthesis

---

Speed 30 ft.

Melee +1 quarterstaff +5/+0 (1d6−1)

Ranged mwk sling +10/+5 (1d4−2)

Spell-Like Abilities (CL 6th)

6/day—tanglevine (CMB +9)

7/day—lightning arc

Spells Known (CL 6th; melee touch +4, ranged touch +9):

3rd (4/day)—fireball (DC 16)

2nd (6/day)—acid arrow, barkskin[B], blindness/deafness (DC 15)

1st (7/day)—burning hands (DC 14), entangle[B] (DC 14), magic missile, shield, silent image (DC 14)

0 (at will)—acid splash, dancing light, detect magic, light, mage hand, mending, read magic

Bloodline Verdant*

Spells Prepared (CL 5th):

3rd—cure moderate wounds, gaseous form[D], summon nature's ally III

2nd—heat metal (DC 16), resist energy, summon swarm, wind wall[D]

1st—calm animals (DC 15), charm animal (DC 15), goodberry, obscuring mist[D], pass without trace

0 (at will)—create water, detect poison, light, read magic

D Domain spells **Domain** Air

Str 6, **Dex** 17, **Con** 10, **Int** 9, **Wis** 18, **Cha** 17

Base Atk +6; **CMB** +4; **CMD** 17

Feats Brew Potion, Craft Wondrous Item, Eschew Materials[B], Iron Will, Scribe Scroll, Skill Focus (Knowledge [arcana]), Skill Focus (Knowledge [nature])

Skills Climb +2, Diplomacy +4, Fly +7, Handle Animal +7, Knowledge (arcana) +10, Knowledge (geography) +4, Knowledge (local) +1, Knowledge (nature) +12, Perception +11, Spellcraft +3 (+5 to determine the properties of a magic item), Stealth +4, Survival +11

Languages Common, Druidic, Elven

SQ elven magic, nature bond abilities (air), resist nature's lure, spontaneous casting, trackless step, wild empathy (+8), wild shape (1/day, animal), woodland stride

Gear +1 quarterstaff, masterwork sling, 20 sling bullets, baton of stirge control (see below).

*Pathfinder Roleplaying Game Advanced Player's Guide

Description: Yandarral wears no armor, only a tattered and stirge-dung stained smock over a much neglected robe. He appears absent-minded and slightly mad. He is melancholy and mildly depressed.

STIRGES (60)
CR 1/2

XP 200

hp 5 (Pathfinder Roleplaying Game Bestiary "Stirge")

Baton of Stirge Control

Aura strong enchantment; **CL** 15th

Slot none; **Price** 18,000 gp; **Weight** 1 lb.

DESCRIPTION

Created by Yandarral to control the stirges of the forest and turn them on the "civilized" world, this 2 foot baton is fashioned from dark, twisted oak. It originally had 50 charges, which now have been mostly used. Only 10 remain. All of the stirges in the cave are under its control, as are any stirges bred from those under the control of the wielder of the rod. Any stirges controlled by the wielder of the rod may be controlled as per a mass charm monster spell.

The baton was created by Yandarral at the height of his madness, and the method he used to create the rod should not normally possible for a wizard of his level; whatever method for its creation is completely lost and must be independently rediscovered.

CONSTRUCTION

Requirements Craft Wondrous Item, mass charm monster, the blood of 10 stirges; **Cost** 9,000 gp

Treasure: In a **small chest** in his cavern, Yandarral keeps 329 gp, 22 pp

Small chest 1 in. thick; Hardness 5; hp 1; Break DC 17; Disable Device DC 20

Area I: Winter Wolves (CR 13)

This location is the lair of a den of winter wolves. The den consists of **3 large male** and **5 large female** winter wolves, as well as the **alpha-male leader** of the pack. There are also **5 smaller female winter wolves** that ordinarily will not fight unless the **8 cubs** are threatened. During colder winters, the wolves range down from their lair. The lair can be found easily with a successful DC 12 Perception check.

Lair: Their lair consists of three ice-caves. The three large males and several of the large females occupy the front cavern. The other females and the young occupy the second cavern and the alpha-male has the rear cavern. Carcasses of other animals can be found outside the lair, and some furs line the alpha-male's chamber as well as the pups' den.

Treasure: The main treasure is probably the animal pelts of the wolves themselves, each being worth from 500 to 1,000 gp. In the lair of the alpha-male is a collection of 1,580 gp and 3,668 sp.

Area J: The Grove of the Moon

This grove is the meeting place of a coven of druids. The grove appears at first glance to be nothing more than a simple clearing. But further observation shows that the plants have arranged themselves in particular position: the thorny briar bushes provide a defensive ring, the trees immediately surrounding the grove have shaped their branches into convenient arches above the grove as well as into seats and ledges where small items can be placed. In the center of the grove is the stump of an ancient tree. Its base is carved with Sylvan and Druidic runes and its top has been carved into a basin, which, when filled with pure rain water, can be used as a scrying device by the Druids (see below).The grove is considered hallowed ground and is used for various rituals. The druids of the grove are a loose band. Each druid lives in their own separate lair, not detailed here. They serve nature and the balance and are dedicated to harmony. There is no strict requirements for membership, other than alignment, and their number fluctuates as various druids come and go serving their own visions of the balance. The group finds the perfect blend of organized worship and individual action. They embrace newcomers who are like-minded and will not hesitate to use their powers if they can be convinced that nature and the balance will be benefited by doing so.

The druids are led by **Illarda, the Priestess of the Moon.** This particular sect of druids worships **Narrah,** a female incarnation of the moon, as their goddess of Nature. For this reason, they follow the natural movement of the moon closely and many important rituals revolve around the rising and setting of the moon as well as its phases. The trees surrounding the grove open at night to allow moonlight into the grove. When the moon's reflection is captured in the basin of rain water collected in the tree stump it is used as a scrying device. Ripples in the waters of the basin capturing the moon's image are interpreted as per an *augury* spell. With their connection to the moon, the grove is protected by a group of **5 good-aligned worgs.** The druids of the grove prefer wolf form for their *wild shape*. The druids detailed below are the permanent members of this group and none of them will join the party as a PC, though they may be convinced to assist the party as NPCs, or train any PC druids. They will typically also be joined by 1d10 additional druids (Drd1–Drd4). These additional "non-permanent" members may join the party as PCs.

WINTER WOLF (13)　　　　　　　　　　**CR 5**
XP 1,600
hp 57 (*Pathfinder Roleplaying Game Bestiary* "Worg, Winter Wolf")

WINTER WOLF ALPHA　　　　　　　　**CR 8**
XP 4,800
Male winter wolf (*Pathfinder Roleplaying Game Bestiary* "Worg, Winter Wolf")
NE Large magical beast (cold)
Init +5; **Senses** darkvision 60 ft., low-light vision, scent; **Perception** +14

AC 17, touch 10, flat-footed 16 (+1 Dex, -1 size, +7 natural)
hp 85 (9d10+36)
Fort +10; **Ref** +7; **Will** +5
Immune cold
Weakness vulnerability to fire

Speed 50 ft.
Melee bite +14 (1d8+7 plus 1d6 cold plus trip)
Space 10 ft.; **Reach** 5 ft.
Special Attacks breath weapon (every 1d4 rounds, 15-ft. cone, 6d6 cold damage, DC 17 Reflex save for half)

Str 20, **Dex** 13, **Con** 18, **Int** 11, **Wis** 14, **Cha** 10
Base Atk +9; **CMB** +15; **CMD** 26 (30 vs. trip)
Feats Alertness, Improved Initiative, Run, Skill Focus (Perception), Weapon Focus (Bite)
Skills Acrobatics +1 (+5 to jump with a running start, +9 jump), Knowledge (nature) +4, Perception +14, Sense Motive +4, Stealth +8 (+14 in snow), Survival +10; **Racial Modifiers** +6 Stealth in snow
Languages Common, Giant

ILLARDA, PRIESTESS OF THE MOON　　**CR 7**
XP 3,200
Female elf druid 8
N Medium humanoid (elf)
Init +6; **Senses** low-light vision; **Perception** +13

AC 21, touch 14, flat-footed 19 (+5 armor, +2 deflection, +2 Dex, +2 shield)
hp 44 (8d8 plus 5)
Fort +6; **Ref** +6; **Will** +9; +2 vs. enchantments, +4 vs. spell-like and supernatural abilities of Fey and against effects that target plants
Immune sleep

Speed 20 ft.
Melee +1 darkwood shortspear +10/+5 (1d6+4/x2)
Spell-Like Abilities (CL 8th):
6/day—*lightning arc*
Spells Prepared (CL 8th; melee touch +9, ranged touch +8):
4th—*air walk*ᴰ, *moonstruck* (DC 17), *summon nature's ally IV*
3rd—*call lightning* (DC 16), *dominate animal* (DC 16),

gaseous form^D, *quench, summon nature's ally III*
2nd—*animal messenger, gust of wind* (DC 15), *lesser restoration, stone call, wind wall*^D
1st—*calm animals* (DC 14), *charm animal* (DC 14), *faerie fire, obscuring mist*^D, *pass without trace, summon nature's ally I*
0 (at will)—*detect magic, flare* (DC 13), *know direction, resistance*
D Domain spells **Domain** Air

Str 17, **Dex** 14, **Con** 10, **Int** 9, **Wis** 17, **Cha** 11
Base Atk +6; **CMB** +9; **CMD** 23
Feats Combat Casting, Improved Initiative, Lightning Reflexes, Natural Spell
Skills Acrobatics +0 (–4 jump), Climb +1, Handle Animal +8, Heal +7, Knowledge (nature) +9, Perception +13, Ride +0, Sense Motive +9, Spellcraft +3 (+5 to determine the properties of a magic item), Stealth +1, Survival +10, Swim +5
Languages Aquan, Common, Draconic, Druidic, Elven, Sylvan
SQ elven magic, nature bond abilities (wolf), resist nature's lure, trackless step, wild empathy (+8), wild shape (3/day, animal, elemental, plant), woodland stride
Combat Gear *feather token* (fan), *potion of haste, potion of shield of faith +2, wand of cure moderate wounds,* antitoxin, thunderstone (2); **Other Gear** *+1 hide armor, +1 darkwood light wooden shield, +1 darkwood shortspear, dust of dryness,* fishing net, holly and mistletoe, silk rope, spell component pouch, gold torc, 43 gp, 100 gp of valuables

KERIK   CR 5
XP 1,600
Male human druid 6
CN Medium humanoid (human)
Init +1; **Perception** +9

AC 13, touch 11, flat-footed 12 (+2 armor, +1 Dex)
hp 25 (6d8–6)
Fort +4; **Ref** +3; **Will** +8; +4 vs. spell-like and supernatural abilities of Fey and against effects that target plants
Resist acid 10

Speed 30 ft.
Melee sickle +4 (1d6)
Domain Spell-Like Abilities (CL 6th; ranged touch +5)
6/day—*acid dart* (1d6+3)
Spells Prepared (CL 6; melee touch +4, ranged touch +5):
3rd—*call lightning* (DC 16), *dominate animal* (DC 16), *gaseous form, stone shape*^D
2nd—*animal messenger, soften earth and stone*^D, *stone call, summon nature's ally II, summon swarm*
1st—*charm animal* (DC 14), *magic stone*^D, *obscuring mist, pass without trace, summon nature's ally I*
0 (at will)—*flare* (DC 13), *light, stabilize, virtue*
D Domain Spell **Domain** Earth

Str 11, **Dex** 13, **Con** 8, **Int** 11, **Wis** 16, **Cha** 18
Base Atk +4; **CMB** +4; **CMD** 15
Feats Alertness, Augment Summoning, Skill Focus (Knowledge [nature]), Spell Focus (Conjuration)
Skills Diplomacy +10, Handle Animal +13, Heal +7, Knowledge (nature) +13, Perception +9, Sense Motive +10, Spellcraft +4, Stealth +3, Survival +14, Swim +5
Languages Common, Druidic
SQ nature bond abilities (earth), resist nature's lure, trackless step, wild empathy (+10), wild shape (2/day, animal, elemental), woodland stride
Combat Gear *scroll of cure light wounds;* **Other Gear** leather armor, sickle, holly and mistletoe, 89 gp

VALANTHE   CR 4
XP 1,200
Female half-elf druid 5
N Medium humanoid (elf, human)
Init +2; **Senses** low-light vision; **Perception** +11

AC 20, touch 13, flat-footed 17 (+5 armor, +2 Dex, +1 dodge, +2 shield)
hp 31 (5d8+5)
Fort +6; **Ref** +6; **Will** +9; +2 vs. enchantments; +4 vs. Fey and plant-targeted effects

Speed 20 ft.
Melee quarterstaff +2 (1d6–1) or sickle +2 (1d6–1)
Ranged mwk sling +6 (1d4–1)
Domain Spell-Like Abilities (CL 5th; ranged touch +5)
7/day—*acid dart* (1d6+2)
Druid Spells Prepared (CL 5th; melee touch +2, ranged touch +5)
3rd—*spike growth* x2, *stone shape*^D
2nd—*barkskin, bear's endurance, soften earth and stone*^D, *summon swarm*
1st—*cure light wounds, magic stone*^D, *obscuring mist, shillelagh, speak with animals*
0th (at will)—*create water, guidance, know direction, light*
D Domain Spell **Domain** Earth

Str 8, **Dex** 14, **Con** 13, **Int** 12, **Wis** 18, **Cha** 10
Base Atk +3; **CMB** +2; **CMD** 15
Feats Dodge, Lightning Reflexes, Natural Spell, Skill Focus (Survival)
Skills Climb +1, Fly +4, Handle Animal +6, Heal +10, Knowledge (dungeoneering) +6, Knowledge (nature) +11, Perception +11, Spellcraft +7, Survival +15
Languages Common, Druidic, Elven, Undercommon
SQ elf blood, nature bond (Earth domain), nature sense, trackless step, wild empathy (+5), wild shape (1/day, animal), woodland stride
Combat Gear *wand of cure light wounds,* 3 vials alchemist's fire; **Other Gear** *+1 hide armor,* heavy wooden shield, quarterstaff, sickle, masterwork sling, 20 bullets, *cloak of resistance +1,* backpack, healer's kit, holly and mistletoe, 50 ft. silk rope, spell component pouch, 91 gp

SORDRIA   CR 2
XP 600
Female gnome druid 3
CN Small humanoid (gnome)
Init +2; **Senses** low-light vision; **Perception** +8

AC 18, touch 13, flat-footed 16 (+3 armor, +2 Dex, +2 shield, +1 size)
hp 24 (3d8+6 plus 1)
Fort +5; **Ref** +3; **Will** +5; +2 vs. illusions
Defensive Abilities defensive training

Speed 20 ft.
Melee sickle +1 (1d4–2)
Special Attacks hatred
Spell-Like Abilities (CL 3rd; melee touch +1, ranged touch +5):
1/day—*dancing lights, ghost sound, prestidigitation, speak with animals*
Domain Spell-Like Abilities (CL 3rd)
6/day—*lightning arc*
Spells Prepared (CL 3rd; melee touch +1, ranged touch +5):
2nd—*flaming sphere* (DC 14), *summon swarm, wind wall*^D
1st—*cure light wounds* x2, *obscuring mist*^D, *speak with animals*
0 (at will)—*flare* (DC 12), *light, stabilize, virtue*

D Domain Spell **Domain** Air

Str 6, **Dex** 14, **Con** 15, **Int** 10, **Wis** 15, **Cha** 14
Base Atk +2; **CMB** –1; **CMD** 11
Feats Augment Summoning, Spell Focus (conjuration)
Skills Acrobatics +1 (–3 jump), Climb –3, Escape Artist +1, Fly +3, Handle Animal +7, Heal +6, Knowledge (nature) +6, Perception +8, Ride +1, Spellcraft +6, Stealth +8, Survival +10
Languages Common, Druidic, Gnome, Sylvan
SQ illusion resistance, nature bond abilities (air), trackless step, wild empathy (+5), woodland stride
Combat Gear 3 scrolls of cure light wounds, scroll of spider climb, tanglefoot bag (2); **Other Gear** +1 leather armor, masterwork heavy wooden shield, sickle, holly and mistletoe, spell component pouch, 95 gp

FARGOL   CR 2
XP 600
Male half-orc druid 3
CN Medium humanoid (human, orc)
Init +0; **Senses** darkvision 60 ft.; **Perception** +7

AC 12, touch 10, flat-footed 12 (+2 armor)
hp 21 (3d8+3 plus 1)
Fort +4; **Ref** +1; **Will** +6
Defensive Abilities ferocity

Speed 30 ft.
Melee sickle +4 (1d6+2)
Domain Spell-Like Abilities (CL 3rd):
6/day—lightning arc (1d6+1)
Spells Prepared (CL 3rd; melee touch +4, ranged touch +2):
2nd—summon nature's ally II, summon swarm, wind wall^D
1st—detect animals or plants, entangle (DC 14), obscuring mist^D, speak with animals
0 (at will)—flare (DC 13), light, stabilize, virtue
D Domain Spell **Domain** Air

Str 14, **Dex** 10, **Con** 13, **Int** 8, **Wis** 17, **Cha** 11
Base Atk +2; **CMB** +4; **CMD** 14
Feats Augment Summoning, Spell Focus (Conjuration)
Skills Handle Animal +5, Heal +7, Intimidate +2, Knowledge (nature) +5, Perception +7, Spellcraft +3, Stealth +2, Survival +11
Languages Common, Druidic, Orc
SQ nature bond abilities (air), trackless step, wild empathy (+3), woodland stride
Combat Gear scroll of cure light wounds; **Other Gear** leather armor, sickle, holly and mistletoe, 89 gp

GAURDIAN WORGS (5)   CR 2
XP 600
hp 26 (Pathfinder Roleplaying Game Bestiary "Worg", with the following changes: alignment NG)

Area K: The Monastery of the Standing Stone

The Monastery of the Standing Stone was founded long ago around a large stone in a grove of trees by a group of monks who found serenity in the alignment of the stone in relation to the trees and the surrounding mountains. A small, simple garden has since been planted around the stone. It is a place of meditation. **Master Kala of the Yellow Robe** is the leader of the monastery and she carries on the traditions of those masters who have gone before her. The monastery currently consists of several low buildings of wood and stone (a mix of the surrounding mountains and forest) in a rough circle surrounding the garden and the standing stone. Trees have grown up within the compound and mix harmoniously with it. The whole place possesses a clean, simple, ascetic beauty. One of the largest buildings is the dirt-floored dojo where the monks practice the mental and physical rigors of their discipline. Similarly, hidden in a set of nearby caves, are the graves of the honored ancestors and prior members of the monastery. Much reverence is given to the honored dead.

The only inhabitants at the monastery are the monks and any visitors. All monastery duties are shared by the brother monks, including cooking, cleaning and tending the garden and grounds. There is an intricate and detailed list of rotating duties that each of the monks must perform. The monks of the monastery are a bit distant, due to their penchant for meditation, though they are not an unfriendly lot. They are receptive to visitors, making available to them all the simple creature comforts the monastery provides and treating them as guests of honor. Kala, the master of the yellow robe, greets all visitors without pleasure but with honor. Kala believes and teaches the suppression of emotion, as have all the masters of the monastery before her. She teaches that honor and duty and the fulfillment of those principles, are the ultimate expression of a living creature. One is measured by his or her faithful fulfillment of these principles, not the outcome of his or her actions.

Kala has assigned **Hord**, a young monk, to oversee all visitors. PCs visiting the monastery will have most of their interactions with him. He sees to all their needs. He carries his shortbow with him at all times.

Known as the master of the yellow robe, Kala is a short, thin woman of indeterminate age and few words. She wears a thin, flexible robe of yellow silk, bright as the sun, tied off with a white sash. The robe is emblazoned on the front left breast and the back with a stylized representation of a stone and a tree. It is obviously of finest craftsmanship. Kala is a master at working with silk and she crafted the robe before it was enchanted. Kala is also one of the few monks expert at using the sansetsukon in combat—an exotic two-handed martial arts weapon made of three lengths of wooden staff joined by chain links. The weapon has great defensive capabilities and provides a +1 AC bonus.

The other members of the monastery are detailed below. Each is proficient with and has access to all normal, monk weapons, so specific weapons are not detailed (except for Hord's shortbow). None possess any magic items. None will leave the monastery to join the party as PCs, though some may be convinced to accompany the party as an NPC for a brief time, with Kala's permission.

MASTER KALA OF THE YELLOW ROBE   CR 9
XP 6,400
Female human monk 10
LN Medium humanoid (human)
Init +5; **Perception** +15

AC 22, touch 18, flat-footed 20 (+2 armor, +1 Dex, +1 dodge, +2 monk, +2 natural, +4 Wis)
hp 63 (10d8+10 plus 5)
Fort +11; **Ref** +11; **Will** +14; +2 vs. enchantment
Defensive Abilities evasion, improved evasion; **Immune** disease

---

Speed 60 ft.
Melee sansetsukon +11/+6 (1d10+6/19–20) or +1 dagger +12/+7 (1d4+5/19–20) or +1 keen kama +12/+7 (1d6+5/19–20) or unarmed strike +11/+6 (1d10+4)
Ranged +1 dagger +9/+4 (1d4+5/19–20)
Special Attacks flurry of blows +8/+8/+3/+3, ki strike (cold iron/silver, lawful, magic), stunning fist 10/day (DC 19, stun, fatigue, sicken)

Str 18, **Dex** 12, **Con** 12, **Int** 10, **Wis** 18, **Cha** 16
Base Atk +7; **CMB** +14 (+16 to trip); **CMD** 29 (31 vs. trip)
Feats Alertness, Dodge, Extra Ki, Improved Initiative, Improved Trip, Improved Unarmed Strike, Lunge, Martial Weapon Proficiency (sansetsukon), Medusa's Wrath, Power Attack, Scorpion Style, Stunning Fist
Skills Acrobatics +11 (+23 jump, +21 to jump), Climb +12, Diplomacy +9, Heal +10, Knowledge (history) +8, Perception +15, Sense Motive +17, Stealth +10, Survival +9, Swim +8

Monastery of the Standing Stone

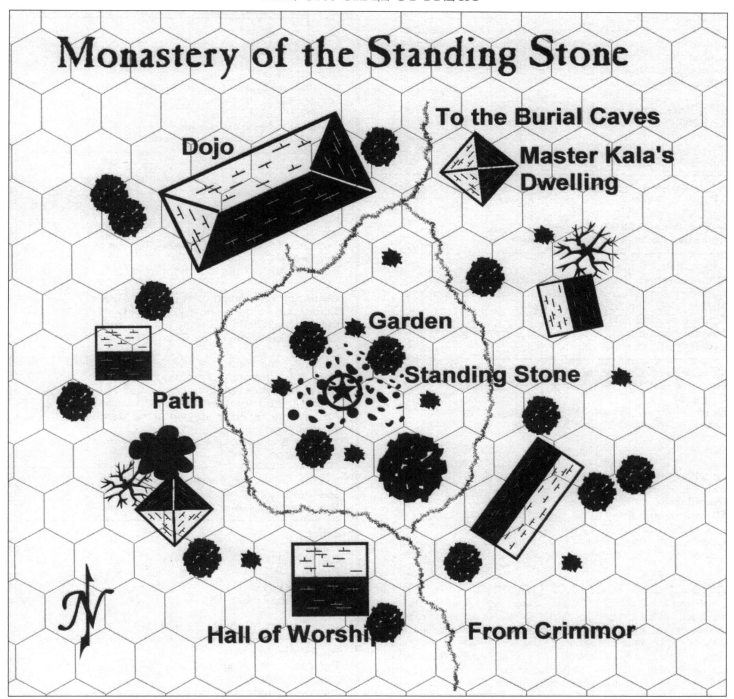

Dojo

To the Burial Caves

Master Kala's Dwelling

Garden

Standing Stone

Path

Hall of Worship

From Crimmor

Languages Common
SQ fast movement (+30 ft.), high jump, ki defense, ki pool, maneuver training, purity of body, slow fall 50 ft., wholeness of body
Combat Gear *potion of barkskin +2, potion of cure moderate wounds, potion of see invisibility;* **Other Gear** *sansetsukon#, 2 +1 daggers, 2 +1 keen kama, belt of giant strength +2, bracers of armor +2, +2 robe of blinding*, masterwork manacles, 195 gp
* The *robe of blinding* is a magical kimono with the *blinding* special quality normally associated with magic shields.
#*Pathfinder Roleplaying Game Ultimate Combat*

HORD   CR 1/2
XP 200
Male human monk 1

LN Medium humanoid (human)
Init +3; **Perception** +6

AC 16, touch 16, flat-footed 12 (+3 Dex, +1 dodge, +2 Wis)
hp 6 (1d8 plus 1)
Fort +2; **Ref** +5; **Will** +4

Speed 30 ft.
Melee unarmed strike +3 (1d6+1)
Ranged mwk composite short bow +3 (1d8+1/x3)
Special Attacks flurry of blows −1/−1, stunning fist 1/day (DC 12, stun)

Str 12, **Dex** 16, **Con** 10, **Int** 13, **Wis** 15, **Cha** 8
Base Atk +0; **CMB** +1; **CMD** 17
Feats Combat Reflexes, Dodge, Improved Unarmed Strike,

Weapon Finesse
Skills Acrobatics +7, Knowledge (history) +5, Knowledge (religion) +5, Perception +6, Sense Motive +6, Stealth +7
Languages Common, Dwarven
Gear robes, masterwork composite shortbow [Str +1], 40 yellow-fletched arrows.

STANDING STONE MONK   CR 4
XP 1,200
Male human monk 5
N Medium humanoid (human)
Init +5; **Perception** +11

AC 16, touch 16, flat-footed 14 (+1 Dex, +1 dodge, +1 monk, +3 Wis)
hp 31 (5d8 plus 5)
Fort +5; **Ref** +5; **Will** +7; +2 vs. enchantment
Defensive Abilities evasion; **Immune** disease

Speed 40 ft.
Melee kama +6 (1d6+3) or nunchaku +6 (1d6+3) or quarterstaff +6 (1d6+4) or sai +6 (1d4+3) or siangham +6 (1d6+3) or unarmed strike +6 (1d8+3)
Ranged shuriken +4 (1d2+3)
Special Attacks flurry of blows +3/+3, ki strike (magic), stunning fist 5/day (DC 15, stun, fatigue)

Str 16, **Dex** 13, **Con** 12, **Int** 10, **Wis** 16, **Cha** 10
Base Atk +3; **CMB** +8 (+10 to grapple); **CMD** 22 (24 vs. Grapple)
Feats Combat Reflexes, Dodge, Improved Grapple, Improved Initiative, Improved Unarmed Strike, Power, Scorpion Style, Stunning Fist
Skills Acrobatics +7 (+11 jump, +12 to jump), Climb +8, Diplomacy +1, Escape Artist +5, Knowledge (history) +4, Knowledge (nature) +1, Knowledge (religion) +8, Perception +11, Sense Motive +11, Stealth +9, Survival +4
Languages Common
SQ fast movement (+10 ft.), high jump, ki defense, ki pool, maneuver training, purity of body, slow fall 20 ft
Gear yellow robes, (one or two of the following weapons) kama, nunchaku, quarterstaff, sai, 5 shuriken, siangham

Area L: The Village of Crimmor

Crimmor is a small village, slightly smaller than Fairhill. It was once a rather prosperous fishing village and a gathering place for merchants on their way from Bard's Gate to Reme. It is run by a merchant's guild, though in recent years an informal thieves' guild has become the true base of power. Originally, the lake near Crimmor, Lake Crimmormere, was a source of a rare type of fresh water fish—a type of largemouth bass famed for its flavor and its ability to be dried and preserved. In the last 10 years, however, these fish have all but disappeared. In truth, the fish have been mostly devoured by a band of fresh water locathah that have made their underwater lair in the north end of the lake. Rumors abound in Crimmor about strange creatures that have been spotted by fishermen. They are only seen in the water at night and are considered by locals to be the ghosts of Crimmor fishermen who died in boating accidents on the lake. Now, with the ascendancy of Fairhill, the lack of fish and the corruption in the guilds, Crimmor has declined, and is rarely visited, except by the traveling merchants who know of Stipish's prowess in repairing wagons. The lack of fish, however, is not Crimmor's most pressing concern. Every night, the village is beset by **2d6 stirges** sent as scouts by Yandarral from the Stirge Caves (see **Area H**). Yandarral is planning a major attack against Crimmor in the near future.

GM's Note: The stat block for Crimmor below uses the Settlement rules from the *Pathfinder Roleplaying Game GameMastery Guide*. If you don't have that book, it's ok. The Settlement rules add a bit more flavor, but aren't essential to running encounters in the town.

Crimmor

LE small town
Corruption +5; **Crime** +2; **Economy** +2; **Law** −5; **Lore** +0; **Society** +0
Qualities insular, notorious
Disadvantages impoverished
Danger +10

Government secret syndicate (The town is run by a merchant's guild, headed by the aristocratic merchant Flendon. This is actually a front for a small thieves' guild, headed by Wistus. Flendon is beholden to Wistus.)
Population 226 (170 humans, 30 half-elves, 11 elves, 6 dwarves, 4 halflings, 3 gnomes, 2 half-orcs)
Notable NPCs
Flendon, Aristocratic Merchant (N male human aristocrat 2)
Wistus, Thieves' Guildmaster (CN male half-elf rogue 4)
Sjordia, the Bard (CG female half-elf bard 2)
Kenthus, the Cleric (LG male human cleric 3 of Mitra)
Corlar, the Captain of the Guard (LN male human fighter 1)
Iindriarog, the Witch (CN female half-orc adept 2)
Florg, the Fisherman (N male gnome commoner 7)
Stipish, the wheelwright (LN male human expert 4)
Hen, a Retired Warrior (NG female human warrior 4)
An Adventuring Party, staying at the Merchant's Wagon (fighter 3, rogue 2, sorcerer 2)
Xon, the Bouncer at the Merchant's Wagon (N female half-orc barbarian 1)

Base Value 800 gp; **Purchase Limit** 5,000 gp; **Spellcasting** 4th
Minor Items 2d4; **Medium Items** 1d3; **Major Items** —

Others:
Bard 1 (1)
Cleric 1 (2)
Fighter 1 (1)
Guild Thieves (2 rogue 2, 4 rogue 1)
Guildsmen (2 expert 2, 5 expert 1)
Sorcerer 1 (2)
Town Guards (2 warrior 2, 9 warrior 1)

Paces of Note:
The Merchant's Wagon, a local tavern and inn that has seen better days
Iindriarog's Tent, a hut on the outskirts of town where the adept sells trinkets of local witchcraft (most having to do with fishing) though of no real power
The Blessed Net, a tavern for local fisherman that is now a rather depressing and dilapidated watering hole
The Guildhall, where the guildsmen meet
Crimmor Market, an open market where merchants can trade their wares
The Docks, from which fishermen still put out their small boats and cast their nets in the lake only to return empty handed
Stipish's Shop, though the town may be run down, **Stipish** (Craft [wood] +7) is still the best at making and repairing wheels for carts and wagons and his shop is usually busy.

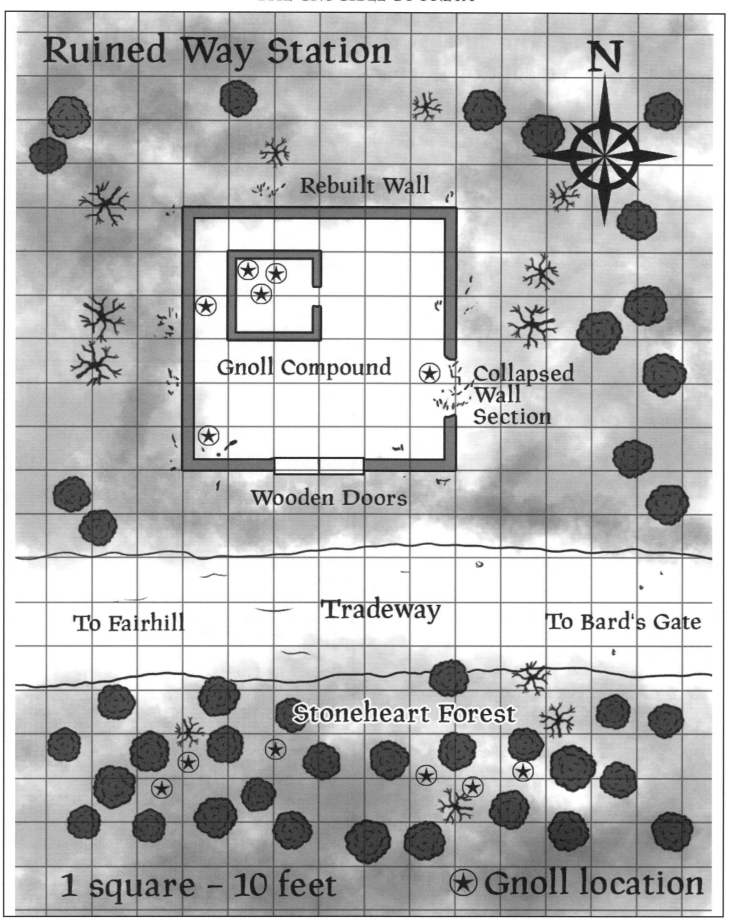

Ruined Way Station

N

Rebuilt Wall

Gnoll Compound

Collapsed Wall Section

Wooden Doors

Tradeway

To Fairhill

To Bard's Gate

Stoneheart Forest

1 square – 10 feet

⭐ Gnoll location

STIRGE   CR 1/2
XP 200
hp 5 (*Pathfinder Roleplaying Game Bestiary* "Stirge")

Area M: Ruined Way Station (CR 8)

As with all such way stations, this is a 60 foot by 60 foot compound with a 15 foot high wooden palisade wall and a 20 foot wide set of wooden double doors set within the wall. The compound itself does not have a roof. This particular station has been mostly burned down and occupied by a band of marauding gnolls. Though most way stations do not have interior structures, the gnolls have built a small inner 20 foot by 20 foot compound of wood with a makeshift roof. A total of **11 gnolls** and their **gnoll leader** occupy the compound: 6 gnolls within the compound and the remaining gnolls (including the leader) wait outside in the surrounding forest. They are hopeful that official forces will come to attack. They have been paid by agents of the nations to the south to lure and attack Waymarch troops. They flee rather than fight to the death if battle goes against them. These gnolls are allied with the tribe in the foothills of the Valley of Shrines (see the *Tomb of Abysthor*, **Wilderness Area 8**), and are expanding the gnoll area of influence.

GNOLLS (11)   CR 1
XP 400
hp 11 (*Pathfinder Roleplaying Game Bestiary* "Gnoll")

GNOLL LEADER   CR 3
XP 800
Male gnoll fighter 3 (*Pathfinder Roleplaying Game Bestiary* "Gnoll")
CE Medium humanoid (gnoll)
Init +0; **Senses** darkvision 60 ft.; **Perception** +3

AC 13, touch 10, flat-footed 13 (+2 armor, +1 natural)
hp 17 (2d8+2 plus 3d10+3 plus 3)
Fort +7; **Ref** +1; **Will** +1; +2 vs. fear
Defensive Abilities bravery +1

Speed 30 ft.
Melee battleaxe +6 (1d8+2/x3) or spear +7 (1d8+3/x3)
Ranged longbow +4 (1d8/x3)

Str 15, **Dex** 10, **Con** 13, **Int** 8, **Wis** 11, **Cha** 8
Base Atk +4; **CMB** +6; **CMD** 16
Feats Point Blank Shot, Power Attack, Precise Shot, Run, Weapon Focus (spear)
Skills Acrobatics +0 (+4 to jump with a running start), Intimidate +3, Perception +3, Survival +4
Languages Gnoll
Gear leather armor, heavy wooden shield, battleaxe, spear, longbow, 15 arrows, 3d4 sp

Treasure: Inside the compound, the gnolls have a **small wooden chest** containing 1,000gp—their pay-off money to start trouble.

Small wooden chest 1 in. thick; Hardness 5; hp 1;Break DC 17; Open Lock DC 20.

The Village of Fairhill

The village of Fairhill rests on the largest of several gently sloping hills about 10 miles from the tradeway. Four-hundred and twenty souls inhabit the village and surrounding farmland. The village is governed by Arlen, the village magistrate. The town has a general alignment of neutral good, though individuals of all moral codes live here under the protection and goodwill provided by the temple of Freya. Though numerous other shrines are present, Freya is the patron deity of Fairhill and her temple is the most prominent. Thus, the true "leader" of Fairhill is Shandril, the priestess of Freya. She disdains that role, however, and openly supports Arlen as magistrate. There is little political strife in Fairhill, as Arlen, Shandril, Captain Baran and the tavern owners all work together. Fairhill is a peaceful town and has not had any real troubles with bandits or monsters. That is, until recently…

For the past several weeks, orcs have appeared of the outer farms and roads of Fairhill. A village family was raped and mutilated on the road leading from the village to the tradeway just days before the players arrive. Rumors of a vampire in an old ruined keep are running rampant, and the peace that the villagers once enjoyed is seemingly at an end.

GM's Note: The stat block for Fairhill below uses the Settlement rules from the *Pathfinder Roleplaying Game GameMastery Guide*. If you don't have that book, it's ok. The Settlement rules add a bit more flavor to Fairhill, but aren't essential to running encounters in the town.

Fairhill

NG village
Corruption −1; **Crime** −2; **Economy** −4; **Law** −4; **Lore** +0; **Society** −4
Qualities insular, strategic location
Danger +20; **Disadvantages** hunted
Note Once the PCs have completed this module and dealt with the owlbears and the manticores, Fairhill loses its hunted disadvantage. Increase its Economy, Law, and Society modifiers by +4 each, reduce its Danger to +0, and increase the Base Value to 550 gp.

Government autocracy
Population 420 (331 humans, 19 dwarves, 33 elves, 4 gnomes, 9 half-orcs, 24 halflings)
Notable NPCs
Arlen, Magistrate (NG male human fighter 3)
Baran, Captain of the Guard (NG male human fighter 5)
Lauriel, Baran's Lieutenant (LG female elf fighter 2)
Shandril, the Priestess of Freya (NG female elf fighter 1/cleric 5)
Tamen, Proprietor of the *Cask and Flagon* (N male human commoner 5)
Glarian, Proprietor of the *Drunken Cockatrice* (NG female half-elf commoner 2)
Yoril the Blacksmith (male human expert 6)
Notes: local militia, warrior 2 (x25); expert 1 (x11); bard 1 (x2); fighter 2 (x3); wizard 1 (1); rogue 1 (x6); commoner 1 (x365).

Base Value 450 gp; **Purchase Limit** 2,500 gp;
Spellcasting 3rd
Minor Items 2d4; **Medium Items** 1d4; **Major Items** —

The village militia is composed of 25 well-trained guards, led by Baran, the captain of the guard, and Lauriel, his lieutenant. Arlen, himself a grizzled old veteran of many dungeon crawls, is the nominal leader of the militia, though Captain Baran is its true leader. During the day, there is always at least one group of four guards making a circuit around the perimeter of the village and another similar group stationed in the central market (**Area 8**). At night the guards light a number of fires that ring the village perimeter. Through the course of the night, there are always a minimum of two patrols of five guards each that carry torches and travel a circuit from fire to fire making sure they stay lit and keeping watch for orcs or other evil creatures. In addition, there are always at least three guards stationed at each of the two guardhouses (**Area 7**), as well as three guards stationed at the top of the Tower of the Guard (**Area 1**). Arlen and Baran have proposed building a wall around the village, but Shandril is reluctant to do so, trusting instead in Freya's protection.

Rumors in Fairhill

While in Fairhill, the party may hear any number of local tales and legends either through information gathered via the Diplomacy skill or through roleplaying. The sample rumors below are listed by the DC for

Rumors of the Fairhill Environs

DC 8 (General): "Adventurers! Hah! Probably end up like that lot that went into Stirge Wood a while back looking for spider treasure. Haven't heard from them since. Good riddance, I say. The wizard that was with them was an arrogant fool!"

DC 8 (General): "Have you seen that new group of adventurers headed by that ranger, Nathiel? He sure is handsome! What heroes they seem to be!"

DC 8 (General): "These orc raids have been growing more and more frequent. Bah! It's as if we live next to Rappan Athuk or some other den of evil!"

DC 8 (General): "I heard merchants talking. They said someone has destroyed the old way station on the Tradeway through Stirge Wood [the local name for the Stoneheart Forest]. The Duke's men will have to do something about that or the merchants won't be able to get here from Bard's Gate."

DC 8 (General): "It's horrible! I hear they found the whole family by the road, mutilated. And the women and children… they were… I can't speak of it!"

DC 8 (General): Heard from merchants: "The road from Bard's Gate to Reme is getting downright dangerous. I've heard tales of orc attacks. And someone has burnt down the old way station in the Stoneheart Forest [also known as Stirge Wood]. Now you have to be mad to travel that road at night."

DC 8: "Eralion? Wasn't he the wizard who built that old keep off in the forest? They say it's ruined now. I wouldn't go near it. 'Happy is the village whose wizards are all ashes,' I say."

DC 8 (General): "Stirge Wood [the local name for the Stoneheart Forest]! Hah! You wouldn't catch me dead in that place. And dead is what you'll be if you go there. Full of spiders and stirges, it is! Nasty!"

DC 10 (General): "Eralion's Keep? Everyone knows that a vampire lives within those ruined walls. What else can explain the shadowy figure people see at night? I would advise you to stay away from that accursed place!"

DC 10 (General): "Shandril has been here for a long time — as long as I can remember. Without her, this village would have disappeared long ago. Praise be to Freya."

DC 10 (General): "Looks like a hard winter. They say winter wolves have been seen in the northern hills between the two rivers."

DC 10 (General): Heard from merchants: "We were beset by a group of gnolls in Stirge Wood [the local name for the Stoneheart Forest]. Seems they've taken up residence in the burnt way station. We left with our lives but not our purses. And they took three of our horses!"

DC 10 (General): "The Monastery of the Standing stone is run by the Master of the Yellow Robe, a fierce warrior!"

DC 12: "The wizard Eralion? He's been dead these last 20 years or so. His keep is in ruins now. Someone said he used to worship Thyr, but how can that be when his keep was built by demons and held together by magic? You won't catch me going near some ruined wizard's castle."

DC 12 (General): "There is a grove of druids to the northwest. I hear they are led by a group of evil shapshifters. They are strange and

they worship the moon."

DC 12 (General): "So, you fancy yourselves adventurers, do you? You're probably friends of that halfling, Lannet. You tell him he owes me for those beers."

DC 12 (General): "I heard that the folks in Crimmor are having more trouble with stirges. Of course, they live so close to that evil forest no one should be surprised."

DC 12 (General): "That monk, Hord, was recently in town from the monastery getting supplies. A stirge flew nearby and in the blink of an eye Hord strung his shortbow and shot the beast at over 100 yards! It was quite a shot!"

DC 14: "I heard tell that Baran lost his hand to swamp trolls years ago and that even Shandril couldn't heal him."

DC 14: "Have you heard the story of Fendrin? He lost his wife and children to some evil beast. A manticore I heard it called, though I've never seen it. He's probably over at the Cockatrice now, drowning his sorrows."

DC 14: "The druids of the grove? I hear they are led by a high priestess named Illarda."

DC 16: "Rat-men? I hear they live in the eastern portion of the same forest where that old wizard built his keep."

DC 16 (General): "Adventurers are you? Huh! Some villagers went missing recently. They fancied themselves adventurers. Never saw them again, did we? One of them was the blacksmith's girl, Arialle."

DC 18: "You know, they say that Arlen used to be a great adventurer and that he even served in the Lyreguard [an elite military unit] at Bard's Gate."

DC 18: "I wouldn't cross Shandril. They say that when she first came to Fairhill she drove out an old witch who tried to kill her. They say Shandril blinded her. Some say she still lives in the forest near to Eralion's keep."

DC 18: "Master Kala is the leader of the monks at the monastery. She is very wise. Her yellow robe is magical!"

DC 20: "Some say Shandril is more than she seems. I think she might have used some strange magic on Arlen. He always seems to do what she wants. I don't trust her."

DC 18 (General): "They say that the stirges that have been attacking Crimmor are bred from a giant stirge as big as a dragon."

DC 20: "Illarda, the high priestess of the druids to the north, is a werewolf."

DC 20: "I heard that some years ago a group of Rangers tracked some rat-men back to their lair below an evil tree. But they couldn't defeat the tree so they were never able to eradicate those evil menaces."

DC 22: "A wizard and a bird? You know, now that you mention it, I did see someone matching that description. I remember that bird. There was something not right about it. My dog barked at it and then hid behind my legs. I think I saw them at the Cask and Flagon."

DC 22: "I heard tell that long ago Eralion was in love with both Shandril and some witch and Shandril cursed the both of them! They say the old witch still lives in a cave near his keep and mourns for her lost love."

FAIRHILL

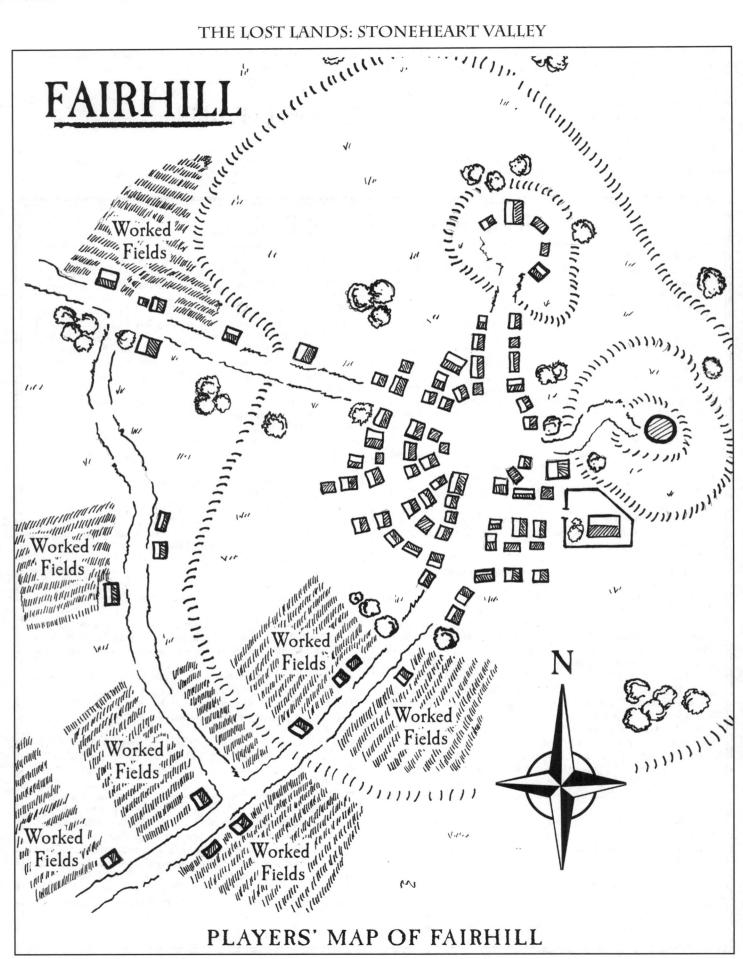

PLAYERS' MAP OF FAIRHILL

Worked Fields

Worked Fields

Worked Fields

Worked Fields

Worked Fields

Worked Fields

N

the Diplomacy check to gather information. A successful check provides one rumor at the closest DC at or below the check roll. Rumors marked "General" can be learned without specific questioning. The rumors about particular NPCs can only be obtained by specifically asking about those persons. Certain locations in town provide modifiers to a character's Diplomacy check. There is a reason why inns and taverns full of adventurers are good places to hear local legends. When a character stumbles upon a rumor, don't just read it; use it as an opportunity for roleplaying.

Locations in Fairhill

1. Tower of the Guard

This stone building is the watchtower where the garrison monitors folks approaching the town. During the day, **Baran**, **Lauriel** and **12 town guards** are stationed here. The tower has three upper levels. The first floor contains the barracks/mess hall. The second floor contains Baran's chambers, where he lives in Spartan simplicity. The third floor contains a storage room, holding extra spears, arrows, longbows, shields, swords and shirts of mail sufficient to outfit 12 men. All the doors in this tower are **iron-reinforced doors** that can be barred and locked.

Iron-reinforced doors: 2 in. thick; Hardness 5; hp 20; Break DC 25 [+2 if barred]; Disable Device DC 22.

Baran, Lauriel and the sergeant of the watch (the most senior guard on duty in the tower) all have keys to the doors. The roof has a signal fire and is crenellated. There are always a minimum of three town guards on the roof at any time. An old spear-firing **ballista** (3d8, 19–20/x3, range 120 ft., 2 rounds to reload) is mounted on the roof and 36 spears are stored in a barrel next to it. Next to the ballista is a large bell that those on watch can use as an alarm for the town.

Beneath the first level, accessible by a hidden stair, is the dungeon, which has four individual cells and a watch station for a jailer. Diplomacy checks to gather information at the tower are made at –4.

2. Magistrate's House

Arlen lives in this enclosed dwelling with a small garden. It is one of the few stone buildings in the village. His house, though opulent by Fairhill standards, is far from luxurious. It offers all the amenities one might find in an average house in a city such as Bard's Gate or Reme — which is uncommon in a village of this size. Inside the house, Arlen has well-crafted furniture brought by him from Bard's Gate. Arlen is a very gracious host, frequently inviting visiting persons to dine with him. His wife, **Ginia** (NG human female Com4; hp 14), and his daughter, **Sirya** (NG human female Com1; hp 5; Dex 15, Cha 14; Stealth +2), share Arlen's gracious demeanor. Sirya fancies herself a rogue and is intrigued by any adventurers. Arlen is less-than-enthusiastic about her recent obsession. In his inner room, he has a locked chest containing 4 *potions of cure serious wounds* and 3,000 gp in gems, as well as 529 gp and 303 sp.

Locked Chest: 1 in. thick; Hardness 5; hp 1; Break DC 17; Disable Device DC 20.

3. Noble's House

Similar in design to Arlen's house, this house is slightly smaller. Normally used by the relatives of the magistrate, passing nobles or characters of importance, this building is currently empty. Arlen has the key to the front door. Unbeknownst to anyone, the last traveling dignitary to stay here had recently pilfered a valuable gem (1,000 gp) from his home city. Fearful that someone knew of his theft, he decided to abandon the gem and hid it in a nook in the top desk drawer in the house (DC 25 Perception to find). If the characters complete the adventure detailed in **Part Two** of this module, Arlen may allow them to stay in this house whenever they visit Fairhill, so long as he is magistrate.

Front Door: 1 in. thick; Hardness 5; hp 1 0; Break DC 18; Disable Device DC 20

4. Temple of Freya

Normally, **Shandril** is here. This wooden building with its peaked roof is an open one-room shrine with a stone altar at the north wall. The altar is decorated with a carving of the head of a stag. The silver *Crucible of Freya* rests upon the altar. It is used to sacrifice wine or wheat from the harvest or to bless a person or creature with fertility. When Shandril is not present, the *Crucible* rests here unguarded — no one in town would dare touch it.

The Crucible of Freya

Aura moderate abjuration and transmutation; **CL** 20th
Slot none; **Weight** 1/2 lb.

DESCRIPTION

This silver bowl appears far too decorative and fragile to be used to melt or burn anything placed inside of it. It is finely worked and traced with the same strange runes that appear on Shandril's sword, *Valkyria*. Despite its fine appearance, the bowl itself is magical so that the user, when invoking Freya, is protected as if under a *protection from energy (fire)* spell (CL 20th, 3/day). Once per week, the *Crucible* may be filled with fresh rainwater and, if blessed by a priestess of Freya, the water becomes holy water. In addition, once per week, when a female consumes the above detailed holy water from the *Crucible* and is simultaneously blessed by a priestess of Freya, she is blessed with fertility and can successfully conceive offspring regardless of age.

DESTRUCTION

If the *crucible* is placed on an evil alter, filled with unholy water, and a *dispel good* spell is cast upon it, all its magical powers are lost.

---

5. Shandril's House

Though Shandril has been given a house indicative of her status in the village, she lives here grudgingly. She much prefers to stay in the temple. The house is furnished with only the most essential wooden furniture, though she has a very large wood-framed bed covered with numerous animal furs (worth 50 gp each). A chest (unlocked) at the foot of the bed holds articles of clothing.

6. Shrines to Other Gods

Each is a small covered shrine with small statues of the other gods worshipped locally, such as Mitra, Muir, Thyr and Telophus. At any time, **2d6 worshipers** (Com1, hp 2) can be found here in various phases of worship. In addition, there may be **1d4 priests** (Clr1–3) of any of the above deities paying respects to their respective gods. Only **Kath**, a cleric of Bowbe, lives in Fairhill on a permanent basis (see below). The other priests are traveling clerics. Interestingly, there are no druidic shrines in the village, nor is there a shrine to Darach-Albith, or Dwerfater. If questioned about this, Shandril replies simply: "It is the will of Freya."

7. Guardhouses

Stationed in each of these stone buildings are **3 guards**. The guardhouses have stout wooden doors and contain a rack of short spears, shields and short swords as well as several barrels of arrows. Diplomacy checks to gather information are made here at a –2.

Wooden Doors: 2 in. thick; Hardness 5; hp 20; Break DC 23.

FAIRHILL

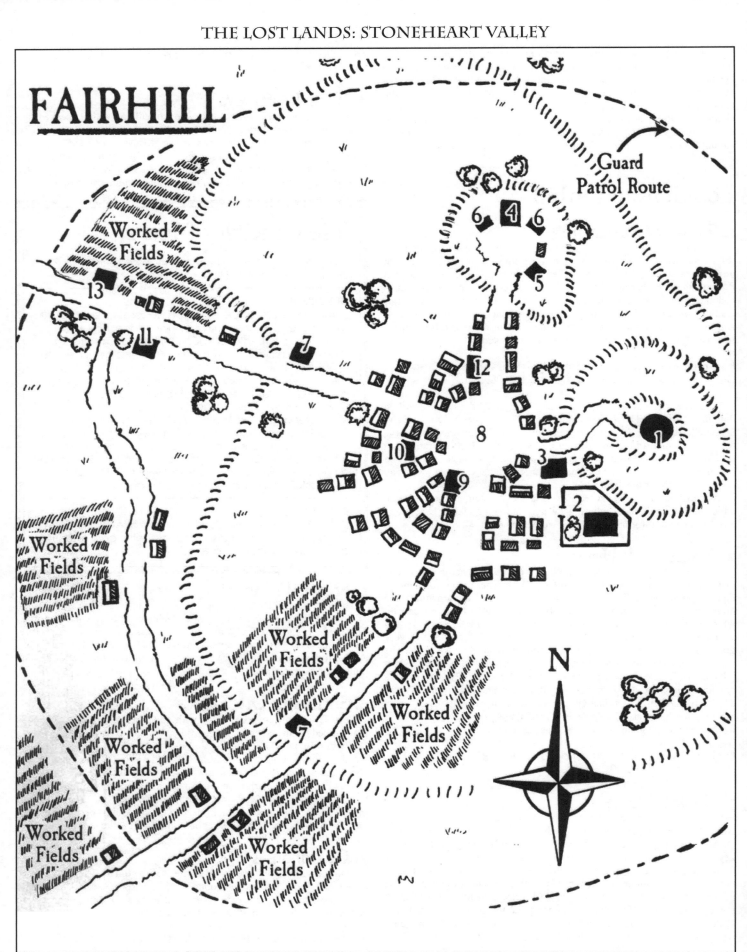

Guard
Patrol Route

Worked
Fields

13

11

6 4 6

5

7

12

2

8

10

3

9

1

2

Worked
Fields

Worked
Fields

Worked
Fields

Worked
Fields

Worked
Fields

N

8. Central Market

Here, fanners and merchants gather at the great tables under their tents in the sun and sell all manner of goods. Anything in the **Equipment** chapter of the *Pathfinder Roleplaying Games Core Rulebook* costing 450 gp or less (550 gp or less once Fairhill loses its hunted disadvantage) is usually available here. The loose assemblage of merchants and farmers is overseen by the town guard (**4 guards** are here at any time) and by Arlen himself — the merchant life of the village being a primary concern of his. Breach of the peace in the central market is not tolerated and will win the violator a week in one of the dungeon cells in the tower of the guard until the matter can be decided by Arlen and Shandril.

9. The Drunken Cockatrice Inn

Run by **Glarian**, a female half-elf (NG female half-elf Coml; hp 6; Profession [innkeeper] + 5). The bar is clean, the ale fresh, the hearth-fire roaring, the food well-cooked and the rooms reasonably priced. The inn has three stories, reached by beautifully crafted wooden-railed stairs, and a total of 12 rooms to rent. Rooms cost 2 gp per night, meals 2 sp — a bargain considering Glarian's cooking is famous as far away as Bard's Gate. **Fendrin** can usually be found here, drunk. He will tell his sad tale to anyone who will listen. See his description below. Diplomacy checks to gather information here are made at +2.

10. The Cask and Flagon

Cheaper and less clean than the *Cockatrice*, this inn is run by **Tamen** (N male human Com5; hp 18; Profession [innkeeper] + 1), an elderly human who used to adventure long ago but who no longer possesses any of his prior skills. The inn itself is poorly maintained and consists of a large common room with a fireplace, a large kitchen and a storage room in the rear. The food is substantially worse than the *Cockatrice*. The common room has four booths along one wall with curtains that can be drawn for privacy. Tamen's four dogs normally sleep on the floor of the common room and beg at customers' feet for table scraps at meal times. To the side of the room, a set of railed stairs allows access to the upper level where the eight individual rooms are located. Each room is locked and only the lodger has the key — even Tamen does not keep a spare. Three of the rooms are currently rented. Tamen charges 1 gp per night for a room and 1 sp per meal.

Lannet the thief currently boards here because it's cheap, but he eats at the *Cockatrice*. If **Vortigern** is in Fairhill, he is staying here under the assumed name of "Feriblan." Diplomacy checks to gather information are made here at a +3. If questioned, Tamen may recall Vortigern and Talon (a DC 15 Intelligence check) and tell the party that such a person is staying here in one of the upstairs rooms.

11. The Tavern of the Three Kegs

This tavern also stables horses for travelers at 1 gp per horse per day, plus 2 sp per day for feeding. The ale here is local product and is outstanding, though expensive (1 sp per pint). A surly, fat halfling named **Perik** (CN male halfling Com3; hp 8; Cha 7; Profession [barkeep] +2, Craft [beer] +10) runs the tavern. Perik wants nothing to do with his patrons, simply taking their money and dispensing their ale. The tavern does not have any rooms for rent since Perik prefers horses to people. Luckily his main waitress, **Dalia** (NG halfling female Com1; hp 3; Cha 17; Profession [waitress] +5) more than makes up for Perik's lack of charm. Diplomacy checks to gather information here are at +2.

12. Smithy

This smithy is run by **Voril** (LN human male Exp6; hp 21; Craft [armor] +4, Craft [metal] +5, Craft [weapons] +5, Profession [blacksmith] +6). Voril desperately misses his daughter, Arialle, who has not returned from a recent adventuring expedition. She is currently the captive of the confused ettin, Girbolg. (See **Wilderness Area B**, above.) He is a competent smith and with enough time can craft or repair medium or light armor. Heavy armor is beyond his ability, though he will offer to craft a personalized

suit of light or medium armor for anyone who rescues his daughter. Voril is suffering greatly from her absence, and he has not made anything in his forge for weeks. His depression causes him to take four times as long to make any requested item.

13. Fendrin's Farm

This simple dwelling is **Fendrin's** farm. He is currently at the *Drunken Cockatrice*, mourning the death of his wife and son. See his description, below. The house is unlocked; the door stands open. There is little of value inside, though hidden in a drawer of a small chest near the unmade bed are several pieces of jewelry (a necklace, ring and broach, 25 gp each) belonging to Fendrin's now-dead wife. Next to the bed stands Fendrin's poor-quality short sword with no scabbard. The fields behind Fendrin's house remain unplowed.

Major NPCs in Fairhill

There are a number of important non-player characters in Fairhill that are central to any story set in the village. Become familiar with them.

Arlen

Arlen is a stern but fair man. He is 45 years old, and his hair and beard are dark, with a hint of gray above the temples and a small streak of gray in his short beard. Arlen has a proud and confident demeanor. He carries a three-foot rod of hard, dark wood covered by bands of iron with him at all times, and it functions as a *+1 light mace*. He carries it as a badge of his office as magistrate. In combat he girds himself with his trusty short sword, which, though non magical, has been with him since his days in the Lyreguard in Bard's Gate. His dark eyes seem to pierce whomever he holds in his gaze, making it difficult to lie directly to him. Arlen's preference for robes, his dark hair, dose-cropped dark beard, steely gaze and ever-present rod convey to those who don't know him the impression that he must be a mage. He is not. He has had many occupations. He was once a captain of the Lyreguard of Bard's Gate. He was an adventurer and explored the Stoneheart Mountain dungeon. Rumors say he has been to the famous dungeon of Rappan Athuk, but if the place is ever mentioned in his presence he goes pale and refuses to speak of it. He was a 7th level fighter, but gained four permanent negative levels due to undead attacks in Rappan Athuk, which led him to give up adventuring and settle down in Fairhill. For more details on these locations, see the **Necromancer Games** supplement *Bard's Gate* and the **Frog God Games** dungeon modules *The Tomb of Abysthor* (later in this book) and *Rappan Athuk*.

ARLEN   **CR 2**
XP 600
Male human fighter 3
NG Medium humanoid (human)
Init +1; **Perception** +7

AC 19, touch 12, flat-footed 18 (+6 armor, +1 deflection, +1 Dex, +1 shield)
hp 25 (3d10+3 plus 2)
Fort +4; **Ref** +2; **Will** +3; +4 vs. fear
Defensive Abilities bravery +1

Speed 30 ft.
Melee *+1 light mace* +7 (1d6+3) or short sword +5 (1d6+2/19–20)

Str 15, **Dex** 12, **Con** 12, **Int** 13, **Wis** 14, **Cha** 14
Base Atk +3; **CMB** +5; **CMD** 17
Feats Alertness, Combat Expertise, Power Attack, Skill Focus (Sense Motive), Weapon Focus (light mace)
Skills Climb +3, Diplomacy +5, Perception +7, Ride –4, Sense Motive +10, Stealth –4, Survival +6
Languages Common, Elven

Combat Gear *potion of cure light wounds;* **Other Gear** chainmail, light steel shield, *+1 light mace,* short sword, *ring of protection +1,* robes, 3 gp

Shandril

Shandril is unique in many ways. Aside from her captivating beauty, she is one of very few elves who are clerics of a non-elven deity. Shandril is tall for an elven female. She wears her long hair in braids, also unusual for an elf, in the style of a Valkyrie — a warrior maiden of Freya. Though she prefers a simple tunic and, in colder weather, her cape of winter-wolf fur, when the situation dictates, she will don her shining scale mail, shield and silver helm. When so arrayed, she is an imposing figure. She is kind and gentle, yet firm in her opinions and her devotion to her goddess. She has no desire for political power, though she has a considerable amount of it as a result of her standing in the village. She is a friend of Arlen. The two of them consult on important issues.

As with many people who are now in Fairhill, Shandril was once an adventurer. As a young elven warrior, she found the sword, *Valkyria,* which she liberated from a spider's hoard. Upon drawing the sword, she was visited by a vision of the goddess herself. Filled with the ecstasy of that visitation, Shandril pledged herself from that day forward to be Freya's devoted priestess. Abandoning her homeland, Shandril ventured north, through many lands, doing Freya's will until she came to the rolling hills south of the Stoneheart Mountains. There she found the small merchant village of Fairhill. At Freya's direction, she founded the temple in the goddess' honor in her new home. That was some 90 years ago. Under Shandril's guidance and with the blessing of Freya, Fairhill has become a fertile, prosperous and peaceful village. Shandril also has been blessed by her goddess with an item of great significance — the *Crucible of Freya.* With the *Crucible,* Shandril makes burnt offerings of new shoots of wheat and newly picked grapes to invoke the blessing of Freya for the fertility of the land. She also uses the *Crucible* to make holy water and to bless the residents with fertility and love.

SHANDRIL   CR 5
XP 1,600
Female elf cleric 5/fighter 1
NG Medium humanoid (elf)
Init +7; **Senses** low-light vision; **Perception** +12
Aura Good

AC 20, touch 13, flat-footed 17 (+5 armor, +3 Dex, +2 shield)
hp 46 (1d10+1 plus 5d8+5 plus 5)
Fort +7; **Ref** +4; **Will** +7; +2 vs. enchantments
Immune sleep

Speed 20 ft.
Melee *Valkyria* +6 (1d8+2/19–20) or longspear +5 (1d8+1/ x3)
Ranged composite longbow +7 (1d8+1/x3)
Special Attacks channel positive energy 8/day (3d6, DC 15)
Domain Spell-Like Abilities (CR 5th):
6/day—battle rage, rebuke death
Spells Prepared (CL 5th; melee touch +5, ranged touch +7):
3rd—*magic vestment*ᴮ, *prayer, searing light*
2nd— *augury, consecrate, spiritual weapon*ᴮ, *zone of truth* (DC 15)
1st— *bless, divine favor, magic weapon*ᴮ, *protection from evil, shield of faith*
0 (at will)—*detect poison, guidance, light, resistance*
D Domain spell **Domains** Healing, War

Str 13, **Dex** 17, **Con** 13, **Int** 14, **Wis** 16, **Cha** 17
Base Atk +4; **CMB** +5; **CMD** 18
Feats Alertness, Combat Expertise, Extra Channel, Improved Initiative
Skills Diplomacy +7, Handle Animal +7, Heal +12, Knowledge (local) +3, Knowledge (religion) +7, Perception +12, Ride +1, Sense Motive +10, Spellcraft +6 (+8 to determine the properties of a magic item), Survival +7
Languages Celestial, Common, Elven, Sylvan
SQ elven magic
Combat Gear *potion of cure light wounds,* scroll (*cure serious wounds* [x3], *heal, raise dead*), 8 vials holy water;
Other Gear scale mail, heavy steel shield, *Valkyria* (see the **Appendix**), longspear, composite longbow, 20 arrows, leather tunic, cape of winter-wolf fur, silver holy symbol of Freya, the *Crucible of Freya,* ceremonial garb, 25 gp, 102 sp.

Baran

Baran, the captain of the guard, is a stern man. He keeps his reddish-brown hair pulled back from his face. His full mustache hides a scar above his mouth. Baran's most immediately noticeable feature, aside from his demeanor, is the fact that he has no right hand. His right arm ends in a grisly stump of scar tissue. He lost his hand fighting swamp trolls in the fens to the far south, and the pain of the wound has never left him. After years of mercenary service, he found himself in Fairhill. There he found a place of peace and safety; respite from his years of pain. He befriended Shandril who was unable to heal his arm — too much time had passed since the injury. He won the trust of Shandril and Arlen and 10 years ago was appointed the captain of the guard. The safety and security of the town are his primary concerns. He will sacrifice anything to keep Fairhill safe. The recent troubles have caused him great anguish. He feels personally responsible for the safety of the village, and every villager who is harmed affects him as if he himself had been stricken.

BARAN THE ONE-HANDED,
CAPTAIN OF THE TOWN GUARD   CR 4
XP 1,200
Male human fighter 5
NG Medium humanoid (human)
Init +6; **Perception** +5

AC 17, touch 13, flat-footed 14 (+4 armor, +2 Dex, +1 dodge)
hp 48 (5d10+10 plus 5)
Fort +6; **Ref** +3; **Will** +1; +2 vs. fear
Defensive Abilities bravery +1

Speed 30 ft.
Melee *+2 bastard sword* +12 (1d10+8/19–20)
Ranged light crossbow +7 (1d8/19–20)
Special Attacks weapon training abilities (heavy blades +1)

Str 16, **Dex** 14, **Con** 14, **Int** 10, **Wis** 10, **Cha** 12
Base Atk +5; **CMB** +8; **CMD** 21
Feats Combat Reflexes, Dodge, Exotic Weapon Proficiency (bastard sword), Improved Initiative, Step Up, Weapon Focus (bastard sword), Weapon Specialization (bastard sword)
Skills Climb +7, Diplomacy +2, Perception +5, Ride +6, Sense Motive +2, Survival +8
Languages Common
Gear *+1 studded leather armor, +2 bastard sword,* light crossbow, 20 bolts, dark green cloak with *Crucible* device

Lauriel

Lauriel, Baran's lieutenant, is slight of build, though she is made of stem stuff. She is fiercely loyal to Baran because he saved her from certain death at the hands of an ogre several years ago. She is grim and determined, unafraid to express her opinion when not in the presence of her superiors. Her piercing eyes shine with an inner strength. She is also dedicated to Shandril, whom she views as a role model. She is considering becoming a paladin of Freya (which she will, in fact, do when she gains her next level of experience). If she sees Shandril give her magic sword to any member of the party, she will protect the sword and its wielder at all costs as if they were Shandril herself. She will harbor a secret jealousy — feeling that she should have been given the honor of wielding Shandril's sword.

LAURIEL, BARAN'S LIEUTENANT   CR 1
XP 400
Female elf fighter 2
LG Medium humanoid (elf)
Init +7; **Senses** low-light vision; **Perception** +5

AC 18, touch 13, flat-footed 15 (+4 armor, +3 Dex, +1 shield)
hp 21 (2d10+2 plus 2)
Fort +4; **Ref** +3; **Will** +1; +2 vs. enchantments, +2 vs. fear
Defensive Abilities bravery +1; **Immune** sleep

Speed 20 ft.
Melee longsword +4 (1d8+1/19–20) or shortspear +3 (1d6+1)
Ranged longbow +5 (1d8/x3)

Str 13, **Dex** 16, **Con** 13, **Int** 12, **Wis** 12, **Cha** 12
Base Atk +2; **CMB** +3; **CMD** 16
Feats Combat Reflexes, Improved Initiative, Weapon Focus (longsword)
Skills Acrobatics +0 (–4 jump), Climb –2, Escape Artist +0, Fly +0, Heal +2, Perception +5, Ride +4, Stealth +2, Swim –2
Languages Common, Elven, Orc
SQ elven magic
Gear chain shirt, light steel shield, short spear, longsword, longbow, 40 arrows, adventurer's pack, 50 ft. silk rope, small sack with 12 gp and 29 sp, light green cloak with *Crucible* device

Town Guards

For a rural village, the guards of Fairhill are of exceptional quality and organization. Baran has trained them well. The guards are of any race, though most often human and half-elven. They can be either male or female. They wear a green surcoat with a small silver bowl device worked on the left breast over their chain shirts, and they carry wooden shields that bear no device. They are to the last person loyal to Baran and Arlen.

TOWN GUARD   CR 1
XP 400
Male or female human fighter 2
N Medium humanoid (human)
Init +5; **Perception** +4

AC 16, touch 11, flat-footed 15 (+4 armor, +1 Dex, +1 shield)
hp 20 (2d10+4 plus 1)
Fort +5; **Ref** +1; **Will** +1; +2 vs. fear
Defensive Abilities bravery +1

Speed 30 ft.
Melee shortspear +5 (1d6+3) or short sword +5 (1d6+3/19–20)
Ranged shortbow +3 (1d6/x3)

Str 17, **Dex** 13, **Con** 14, **Int** 10, **Wis** 12, **Cha** 8
Base Atk +2; **CMB** +5; **CMD** 16
Feats Alertness, Improved Initiative, Point Blank Shot, Precise Shot
Skills Acrobatics –2, Climb +0, Handle Animal +5, Intimidate +3, Perception +4, Profession (soldier) +5, Ride +5, Sense Motive +3, Stealth -2, Survival +5, Swim +0
Languages Common
Gear chain shirt, heavy wooden shield, short spear, short sword, shortbow, green surcoat with *Crucible* device, small sack with 2d4 gp.

Kath, Cleric of Bowbe

Kath is a large man, great of girth, with a booming voice and a friendly demeanor. He has extremely large hands and has a habit of wearing his spiked gauntlets at all times, even during prayer and at meals. Bowbe is exuberant and greets friends with great enthusiasm. Unfortunately, because of his spiked gauntlets, characters failing a DC 8 Reflex save take 1d2 piercing damage when Kath locks them in one of his affectionate bear-hug greetings and slaps their backs. Kath, of course, does not realize the damage he causes and cocks his head in confusion when his friends on occasion avoid his hugs. Kath means well, but he is rather dimwitted. Though dim, he is an incredibly lucky person. He has bumbled his way into any success he has ever had. Shandril has befriended Kath and is very patient with his meager understanding of his own deity. Kath does whatever Shandril asks and is always the first to volunteer to face any peril. He may volunteer to aid the party if they are in need, though he will not remain as a permanent member.

KATH   CR 1
XP 400
Male human cleric 2
CN Medium humanoid (human)
Init +0; **Perception** +1
Aura chaotic

AC 15, touch 10, flat-footed 15 (+5 armor)
hp 17 (2d8+2 plus 2)
Fort +4; **Ref** +0; **Will** +4

Speed 20 ft.
Melee spiked gauntlet +4 (1d4+3) or greatsword +4 (2d6+4/19–20)
Special Attacks channel positive energy 3/day (1d6, DC 11)
Spell-Like Abilities (CL 2nd)
4/day—*battle rage, strength surge*
Spells Prepared (CL 2nd; melee touch +4, ranged touch +1):
1st—*bless, command* (DC 12), *divine favor, enlarge person*ᴰ (DC 12)
0 (at will)—*detect magic, guidance, purify food and drink* (DC 11), *virtue*
D Domain Spell **Domains** Strength, War

Str 16, **Dex** 10, **Con** 12, **Int** 7, **Wis** 12, **Cha** 10
Base Atk +1; **CMB** +4; **CMD** 14
Feats Improved Unarmed Strike, Power Attack
Skills Climb –1, Heal +5, Knowledge (religion) +3, Sense Motive +5, Stealth –4
Languages Common
Gear scale armor, greatsword, spiked gauntlets, wooden holy symbol of Bowbe, 2 gp

Lannet

Lannet is your stereotypical halfling thief: nosy and unable to resist his larcenous impulses, particularly as they relate to shiny objects and gems. His pickpocketing is innocent, and Lannet, if confronted, returns any item to its owner with a smile and a wink. Like more traditional halflings, Lannet is slightly chubby with a ruddy complexion. His face has an ever-present smile beneath his green eyes and curly brown hair. He wears leather armor and a gray cloak of obviously fine quality, which is in fact a *cloak of elvenkind*. What sets Lannet apart is his inquisitiveness and his *cloak*. Though most halflings have rather short attention spans, if Lannet finds something that interests him, a person or an item, he obsessively tries to learn everything about that person or thing. If Vortigern and Talon are in town, Lannet becomes interested in Talon and uses his cloak to spy on the two as much as possible. Lannet also takes an interest in the party when they arrive in Fairhill. He uses his cloak and follows them when they set off on adventure, which can be a blessing if you as GM need an unlooked-for dagger throw to get the characters out of a jam.

LANNET, THE MUCH-TOO-INQUISITIVE THIEF   CR 2
XP 600
Male halfling rogue 3
N Small humanoid (halfling)
Init +3; **Perception** +7

AC 17, touch 15, flat-footed 13 (+2 armor, +3 Dex, +1 dodge,

+1 size)
hp 18 (3d8+3)
Fort +3; Ref +7; Will +1; +3 vs. fear
Defensive Abilities evasion, trap sense (+1)

Speed 20 ft.
Melee mwk dagger +4 (1d3/19–20)
Ranged mwk hand crossbow +7 (1d3/19–20) or mwk shortbow +7 (1d4)
Special Attacks sneak attack +2d6

Str 10, Dex 17, Con 13, Int 13, Wis 8, Cha 15
Base Atk +2; CMB +1; CMD 15
Feats Dodge, Mobility
Skills Acrobatics +11 (+7 jump), Appraise +5, Bluff +8, Climb +6, Diplomacy +6, Disable Device +8, Disguise +7, Escape Artist +9, Fly +5, Perception +7 (+8 to locate traps), Sense Motive +4, Sleight of Hand +9, Stealth +18, Use Magic Device +7
Languages Common, Elven, Halfling
SQ fearless, rogue talents (fast stealth), trapfinding +1
Combat Gear potion of cure serious wounds; Other Gear masterwork leather armor, 4 masterwork daggers, masterwork hand crossbow, 20 bolts, masterwork shortbow, 20 arrows, cloak of elvenkind, 36 gp, 12 sp, 5 50 gp gems, masterwork thieves tools, any items Lannet has filched from others.

Dwarves of the Shattered Axe

This band of novice adventurers is heading from Reme to Bard's Gate, or so they claim. The dwarves got sidetracked in Fairhill. They are staying at the Cask and Flagon where they imbibe large amounts of ale until all hours of the morning. They get the name of their adventuring band from the device on Durgis' shield-an axe with a broken haft. At first glance, they do not appear to be seasoned warriors.

Durgis

Durgis is a pompous, self-important dwarf who acts as if he is a 15th level fighter. He refers to his axe as "Grodek" and says he recovered it from the hoard of a troll some years back. He claims it is a magical and intelligent weapon. Anyone can see (with a DC 10 Appraise check) that it is in fact a weapon of common craftsmanship at best. He claims to have been to the dungeon of Rappan Athuk and to have found piles of gold there. When asked why he doesn't retire given his claimed wealth, he responds brusquely, "Adventurin' is in me blood, boy. But then a wee whelp such as yourself wouldn't understand an adventurer's life." He hitches up his belt and refuses to speak any further. For more information on Rappan Athuk, see the **Frog God Games** dungeon module *Rappan Athuk*.

Unless offended as previously described or his veracity challenged in some other way, he will tell his false tales all night long (particularly if someone else is buying the ale), each tale getting more grandiose and unbelievable. Many of his tales will be factually impossible, such as his tale of how he allegedly turned a gorgon's gaze against itself, thus turning it to stone (which, of course, is not how a gorgon's petrification power works). He claims to have traveled with numerous characters of legend. A bard or mage can make an opposed Knowledge (history) check against Durgis' Bluff check to notice that Durgis' stories are based on well-known tales (though none of which mention his involvement) but that he has gotten several of the facts wrong. Despite his boasting, Durgis is a coward at heart. At the first sign of trouble, he will feign a hangover or claim that "such a task is beneath a man of my skills."

DURGIS   CR 1/2
XP 200
Male dwarf fighter 1
N Medium humanoid (dwarf)
Init +0; Senses darkvision 60 ft.; Perception –1

AC 18, touch 10, flat-footed 18 (+5 armor, +3 shield)

hp 13 (1d10+2 plus 1)
Fort +4; Ref +0; Will –1; +2 vs. poison, spells, and spell-like abilities
Defensive Abilities defensive training

Speed 20 ft.
Melee dwarven waraxe +3 (1d10+1/x3)
Special Attacks hatred

Str 12, Dex 10, Con 14, Int 8, Wis 8, Cha 15
Base Atk +1; CMB +2; CMD 12 (12 vs. bull rush and trip)
Feats Shield Focus, Weapon Focus (dwarven waraxe)
Skills Acrobatics –6 (–10 to jump), Appraise –1 (+1 to determine the price of nonmagic items with precious metals or gemstones), Bluff +3, Perception –1 (+1 to notice unusual stonework, such as traps and hidden doors in stone walls or floors), Stealth –6, Swim –5
Languages Common, Dwarven
SQ greed, hardy, slow and steady, stability, stonecunning +2
Gear scale mail, heavy wooden shield, dwarven waraxe, 24 gp, 41 sp, 2 10 gp gems

Trel, Burl and Gar

Durgis' companions, **Trel, Burl and Gar**, have been browbeaten by Durgis into submitting to his pretend authority. They generally restrict themselves to saying "Yes, Durgis," or "Right you are, Durgis." They travel with Durgis because they actually believe Durgis is as experienced an adventurer as he claims to be. When Durgis tells his tall tales, the three stare at him in awe of his fictional prowess. They have more courage than Durgis, if less intelligence, and if Durgis is insulted they will stand and draw their weapons against whoever would be bold enough to insult such a "great and legendary adventurer." As long as Durgis is around, they would never consider leaving his company to join up with the player characters.

TREL, BURL and GAR   CR 1/2
XP 200
Male dwarf fighter 1
N Medium humanoid (dwarf)
Init +3; Senses darkvision 60 ft.; Perception –3

AC 18, touch 13, flat-footed 15 (+3 armor, +2 shield, +3 Dex)
hp 15 (1d10+4 plus 1)
Fort +6; Ref +3; Will –3; +2 vs. poison, spells, and spell-like abilities
Defensive Abilities defensive training

Speed 20 ft.
Melee battleaxe +5 (1d8+3/x3)
Ranged heavy crossbow +4 (1d10/19–20)
Special Attacks hatred

Str 16, Dex 16, Con 18, Int 5, Wis 5, Cha 8
Base Atk +1; CMB +4; CMD 17 (17 vs. bull rush and trip)
Feats Power Attack, Weapon Focus (battleaxe)
Skills Acrobatics +0 (–4 jump), Appraise –3 (–1 to determine the price of non-magic items with precious metals or gemstones), Climb +4, Perception –3 (–1 to notice unusual stonework, such as traps and hidden doors in stone walls or floors)
Languages Common, Dwarven
SQ greed, hardy, slow and steady, stability, stonecunning +2
Gear studded leather armor, heavy wooden shield, battleaxe, heavy crossbow, 20 bolts, 8 gp, 29 sp

Lasha

Lasha set out some four months ago from the Monastery of the Standing Stone to wander the world and grow in wisdom. She has befriended Shandril and is discussing with her the distinctions between the monk and the priest. She admires Shandril's devotion and her wisdom. Lasha, believing there is something to learn from the teachings of all deities, desires to spend a month or more in Fairhill, discussing religious matters with Shandril and spending time in quiet meditation. If asked to join the party, she meditates on the topic before giving her response. She sits for two days in undisturbed thought and then agrees if the party is friendly to Shandril. She fights with a unique two-weapon style in addition to her unarmed tactics. Lasha has shaved her head bald, wears no jewelry and keeps no possessions other than her staff, her two kama, her robe and a small pouch. She is polite and always measures her response before she answers any question. She has a habit of bowing slowly and low to anyone at greeting and departure.

LASHA   **CR 1**
XP 400
Female human monk 2
LN Medium humanoid (human)
Init +2; **Perception** +8

AC 16, touch 16, flat-footed 13 (+2 Dex, +1 dodge, +3 Wis)
hp 19 (2d8+4)
Fort +5; **Ref** +5; **Will** +6
Defensive Abilities evasion

Speed 30 ft.
Melee kama +3 (1d6+1) or quarterstaff +2 (1d6+1) or unarmed strike +3 (1d6+1)
Special Attacks flurry of blows +0/+0, stunning fist 2/ day (stun, DC 14)

Str 13, **Dex** 15, **Con** 14, **Int** 12, **Wis** 16, **Cha** 13
Base Atk +1; **CMB** +2 (+4 to grapple); **CMD** 18 (20 vs. grapple)
Feats Dodge, Improved Grapple, Improved Unarmed Strike, Mobility, Stunning Fist, Weapon Finesse
Skills Acrobatics +6, Climb +5, Escape Artist +6, Heal +4, Knowledge (nature) +3, Knowledge (religion) +6, Perception +8, Sense Motive +7, Stealth +6
Languages Common, Draconic
Gear 2 kamas, quarterstaff, monk's robe, 6 gp

Fendrin

Fendrin (N human male Com1; hp 3; Melee –1 [1d6–1, short sword]) is a local farmer whose property has fallen into disrepair. His fields lie fallow and unplowed — the plow rusting in the rows. He drowns his sorrows in ale at the *Drunken Cockatrice*. Fendrin came to this sad state some six months ago when his wife and son were captured by the male manticore (see **Monster Lair, area D**, above). Fendrin shot at the beast with his shortbow as it flew off with his family. He managed to hit his wife with one arrow, killing her. The manticore then dropped his son, who fell to his death. At the time Fendrin figured death was preferable to whatever fate awaited them at the manticore's lair. Now, however, he laments his decision, believing he should have tried to rescue them. He is reluctant to tell his tale, but if talk of the party venturing to kill the manticore is raised, a grim fire ignites in his eyes, and he insists on accompanying the party to take vengeance on the monster. If he ever sights the beast, he charges it with maniacal frenzy without thought to his own safety or the safety of the party. Fendrin has a poor-quality short sword that he is not skilled at using. He has a shortbow and 20 arrows. He is similarly unskilled with his bow, and it was a miracle he was able to hit his wife in the grasp of the flying manticore.

The Ruined Keep

The now-ruined keep sits on a low mound within a small forest near Fairhill, the dark trees encroaching on its broken walls. The keep was constructed by the mage Eralion some 90 years ago (about the time Shandril arrived in Fairhill) using scrolls and elementals, not demons as mentioned in local rumors. Though Eralion did later turn to darkness, he was not originally an evil mage. In fact, when the keep was built, he erected a chapel to his patron deity, Thyr.

As the darkness grew within him, Eralion abandoned his god. The chapel remained hallowed until Tavik arrived. With Eralion's death, the magics holding the keep together weakened, and it deteriorated. Some years ago, the keep was a haven for bandits. They never learned of the evil that dwelled beneath them. A small unit of Waymarch forces rooted out the bandits and did much damage to the already decrepit structure. The keep lay abandoned until several months ago, when Tavik arrived with his cadre of orcs. At Tavik's direction, the orcs set about fortifying the keep. They filled some of the major cracks in the otherwise intact towers. They installed a "back door" in one of these cracks, using an iron door from the destroyed gate in the internal wall. They raised a dirt palisade in the exposed portions of the exterior curtain wall, sharpening large logs and setting them at intervals along the palisade. They repaired the scorpion and moved it to the top of the chapel tower.

Above Ground

The walls of the keep are crenellated to a height of 18 feet. The top of the wall behind the crenellations is 12 feet high. The towers are three stories high, and their roofs are crenellated as well. The gatehouse is two stories tall with a crenelated roof. Unless otherwise noted, all doors in the keep are iron-reinforced oak doors (2 in. thick; Hardness 5; hp 30; Break DC 25) that can be barred from the inside. The floors between levels are made of thick wooden planks and beams. Many are rotted. In total, the keep is home to **Tavik (Area 8)**, **Nagrod the orc chieftain (Area 9)**, **Grosh the ogre (Area 9**, second level), **2 orc sentries (Area 8**, bell tower) and **18 orc warriors** (4 at **Area 8**, 6 on guard duty around the palisade and 8 off duty in **Area 9**), as well as **Kren** and his **6 orcs**.

1. The Main Path and the Gatehouse

Eralion never had much contact with the neighboring village of Fairhill, going so far as to clear a road giving him access to the forded river east of Fairhill and the road south to the tradeway. That road, however, has now been almost fully overgrown. Neither the current occupants nor the prior bandits made any use of the road. In fact, they considered the direct approach it provided a defensive liability and were happy for the hindrance of the overgrowth. The keep's gatehouse is intact, but the inner and outer portcullises have permanently rusted shut, making them effectively impassable. The orcs, therefore, do not guard the gatehouse. They have gone into the gatehouse through the door on the second floor, which opens out onto the north curtain wall, and removed any items of value to store them elsewhere.

Ground Floor: This level consists of the main passage through the gatehouse, closed on either end with the rusted portcullises. The chambers to either side of the main passage have arrow slits allowing hidden soldiers to fire arrows at any intruders. These rooms are abandoned. They are accessed either by a trap door from the second floor or by large doors on the south wall leading into the main courtyard of the keep.

Rusted portcullises: 2 in. thick; Hardness 10; hp 60; Break DC 30; Lift DC 35.

Second Floor: This level consists of one large room. Unlike other buildings, the floor of the gatehouse is stone. In the center of this room above the main passage are "murder holes," allowing defenders to pour

hot oil or other liquids on intruders below. Also in this large room are two winches — one for both the front and rear portcullises blocking the first-floor passageway. Both are stuck and unusable. In fact, as an added measure of security, the orcs disabled the winches and broke the chains. Access to this level can be had through **two barred trap doors** in the floor that lead down to the first level. Also, this large room has two doors, each opening onto the curtain wall on either side of the gatehouse.

Barred trap doors: 2 in. thick; Hardness 5; hp 10; Break DC 25; can be opened without a Break check by persons on the second floor.

2. The Secret Forest Path

This is the path used by the orc raiding parties. It ends at the "back door" of the keep. The path itself is even more heavily overgrown than the main path. Following the secret path to the keep requires three successful DC 10 Survival checks, with each check constituting one hour of time. The total time to reach the keep depends on how well the party can follow the path. Characters exiting the secret path can make a DC 15 Perception check to notice the orc sentry in the bell tower. See **Act III**, below.

3. The Northwest Tower and the "Back Door"

Ground Level: The northwest tower, which is missing a portion of its roof and second floor, is known as the "**back door**." The orcs filled the crack in the tower with stones from the destroyed walls and installed a large external iron door that they took from another part of the keep. It is locked with a large iron padlock. The key to the lock is given to the leader

of whatever raiding party has set out from the keep. It can be picked, but the lock is of surprisingly high quality. If the party has encountered and defeated Kren and his raiding party, they should have the key to the door in their possession and can easily use it to unlock the door. The orcs keep the lock and the hinges surprisingly well-oiled. Inside the tower, in the very center, is a colony of **green slime**. There is a well-defined path around the outside of the room that avoids the slime, which is obvious (DC 10 Perception check) to anyone who looks. The orcs also sometimes "mine" the green slime, filling small ceramic pots with the stuff to use as wicked projectiles. The orcs also use torches to burn a path around the slime and to keep it away from the iron door. The duty of mining or clearing the slime is given to any orcs who displease Tavik. More than one orc has lost a hand doing this. A set of stone stairs leads to the second floor. The wooden floor on the level above is rotted and has a large hole in it, as does the roof.

The Back Door, locked, iron-reinforced oak door: 2 in. thick; Hardness 6; hp 25; Break DC 25; Disable Device DC 26.

GREEN SLIME   CR 4
XP 1,200 (*Pathfinder Roleplaying Game Bestiary* "Hazard")
This dungeon peril is a dangerous variety of normal slime. Green slime devours flesh and organic materials on contact and is even capable of dissolving metal. Bright green, wet, and sticky, it clings to walls, floors, and ceilings in patches, reproducing as it consumes organic matter. It drops from walls and ceilings when it detects movement (and possible food) below.

THE RUINED KEEP

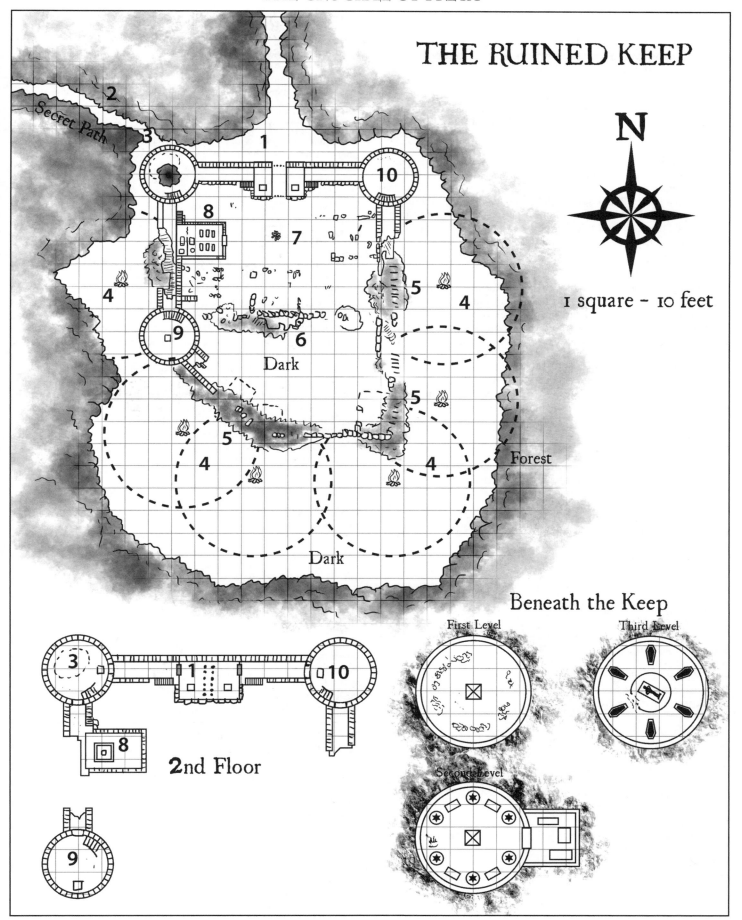

2

Secret Path

3

1

10

8

7

N

5

4

4

1 square – 10 feet

9

6

Dark

5

5

4

4

5

Forest

4

Dark

Beneath the Keep

First Level

Third Level

3

1

10

8

2nd Floor

9

Second Level

A single 5 ft. square of green slime deals 1d6 points of Constitution damage per round while it devours flesh. On the first round of contact, the slime can be scraped off a creature (destroying the scraping device), but after that it must be frozen, burned, or cut away (dealing damage to the victim as well). Anything that deals cold or fire damage, sunlight, or a *remove disease* spell destroys a patch of green slime. Against wood or metal, green slime deals 2d6 points of damage per round, ignoring metal's hardness but not that of wood. It does not harm stone.

Second Level: The second level has a rotted floor with a large opening to the first level below. The roof above is also destroyed. The floor collapses under almost any pressure. Anyone walking on the floor must succeed on a DC 15 Reflex save or fall to the floor below, suffering 2d6 damage and falling into the green slime. A person can safely stay against the wall and move along it to either of the two doors that open onto the curtain wall of the keep.

4. Watch Fires

Normally, there are no watch fires around the keep. However, if the orcs fear attack, they build watch fires at the locations indicated on the map. See **Act III** for more details about the orcs' levels of alertness. These fires make it very difficult for the party to sneak into the keep at night. Stealth checks (at −2, orc Perception checks at +2) must be made for all players attempting to cross the watch-fire area. If the party is wise, they wait for the fires to die down (about 4 hours). The lazy orcs do not go out to stoke the fires, and if the party does wait, the orc sentries are unlikely to notice anyone crossing the watch-fire area (+2 to character Stealth checks, −2 to orc Perception checks under these circumstances).

5. Palisade

The palisade is made of dirt and rocks and is sloped on the inner side. It drops sharply on the outer side, which is also set at intervals with sharpened logs to repel charging attacks and to provide cover for defending orcs. A total of **6 orc palisade guards** stand watch at the palisade at any given time. Unlike the other orcs, these orcs use longspears and bows to take advantage of the cover provided by the palisade and spikes. Climbing the external wall of the palisade requires a DC 10 Climb check.

ORC PALISADE GUARDS (6)   CR 1/3
XP 135
Male orc warrior 1 (*Pathfinder Roleplaying Game Bestiary* "Orc")
CE Medium humanoid (orc)
Init +0; **Senses** darkvision 60 ft.; **Perception** −1

___

AC 13, touch 10, flat-footed 13 (+3 armor)
hp 7 (1d10+1)
Fort +2; **Ref** +0; **Will** −1
Defensive Abilities ferocity
Weakness light sensitivity

___

Speed 30 ft.
Melee longspear +3 (1d8+3/×3) and short sword +3 (1d6+2/19–20)
Ranged shortbow +1 (1d6/×3)

___

Str 14, **Dex** 10, **Con** 10, **Int** 8, **Wis** 8, **Cha** 8
Base Atk +1; **CMB** +3; **CMD** 13
Feats Point Blank Shot
Skills Acrobatics −1, Climb +1, Intimidate +3, Stealth −1, Survival +0, Swim +1
Languages Orc
Gear studded leather armor, short sword, longspear, shortbow, 20 arrows

6. The Outer Courtyard

The outer courtyard sees the most orc activity, since it is adjacent to the southwest tower where Nagrod the chieftain resides and where the off-duty orcs sleep. At night, however, it is abandoned and dark by Tavik's order to better allow watching orcs to spot possible intruders. Six of the above-described orcs stand watch at the palisade in the outer courtyard.

7. The Inner Courtyard

The inner courtyard is much quieter, as it connects to Tavik's abode. The inner courtyard has only two of the above-described orcs standing watch at the palisade on the west wall of the keep. Inside the inner courtyard are the remains of several wooden structures. These buildings were burnt to the ground when the Waymarch forces drove out the brigands. There is also a well here that remains serviceable.

8. The Chapel (CR 3, CR 5 if Tavik is also present)

Ground Level: This building was once a chapel to Thyr, god of justice. At any given time, **4 orc warriors** sleep among the ruined pews of the desecrated chapel, as does **1 orc sentry** who keeps lookout in the bell tower above. The chapel itself consists of one main room with an altar, behind which is a small sanctum, divided from the main room by a curtain. The sanctum was once the chamber of the resident priest. It is now the home of Tavik, the evil priest of Orcus. The walls of the chapel are covered with evil runes and orc feces. The angelic statue of a celestial servant of Thyr remains unmarred, but only because Tavik wants Thyr, through the statue, to witness the desecration of his temple. The altar itself has been smeared with blood, and Tavik has placed a *candle of defiling* upon it, which acts as a *desecration* and *bane* spell for all of Tavik's enemies as long as the candle burns. The tapestries and pews, which were once of fine quality, have been destroyed and are currently used as soiled bedding by the orcs who sleep here. If any person invokes Thyr while in this defiled shrine and calls for justice, Thyr places the equivalent of a *prayer* spell on that person and his or her allies for the duration of the combat.

ORC WARRIORS (4)   CR 1/3
XP 135
Male orc warrior 1 (*Pathfinder Roleplaying Game Bestiary* "Orc")
CE Medium humanoid (orc)
Init +0; **Senses** darkvision 60 ft.; **Perception** −1

___

AC 15, touch 10, flat-footed 15 (+5 armor)
hp 7 (1d10+1)
Fort +2; **Ref** +0; **Will** −1
Defensive Abilities ferocity
Weakness light sensitivity

___

Speed 20 ft.
Melee greataxe +4 (1d12+3/×3)
Ranged shortbow +1 (1d6/×3)

___

Str 14, **Dex** 10, **Con** 10, **Int** 8, **Wis** 8, **Cha** 8
Base Atk +1; **CMB** +3; **CMD** 13
Feats Weapon Focus (greataxe)
Skills Acrobatics −4 (−8 jump), Climb −2, Escape Artist −4, Stealth −4, Survival +0
Languages Orc
Combat Gear 2 flasks of oil; **Other Gear** scale mail, greataxe, shortbow, 20 arrows, belt pouch, flint and steel, 2 torches, 1d6 gp, 2d8 sp

ORC SENTRY   CR 1/3
XP 135
Male orc warrior 1 (*Pathfinder Roleplaying Game Bestiary* "Orc")

CE Medium humanoid (orc)
Init +0; **Senses** darkvision 60 ft.; **Perception** –1

AC 13, touch 10, flat-footed 13 (+3 armor)
hp 7 (1d10+1)
Fort +2; **Ref** +0; **Will** –1
Defensive Abilities ferocity
Weakness light sensitivity

Speed 30 ft.
Melee short sword +3 (1d6+2/19–20)
Ranged light ballista +1 (3d8/19–20)

Str 14, **Dex** 10, **Con** 10, **Int** 8, **Wis** 8, **Cha** 8
Base Atk +1; **CMB** +3; **CMD** 13
Feats Exotic Weapon Proficiency (light ballista)
Skills Acrobatics –1 (–5 jump), Climb +1, Intimidate +3,
Stealth –1, Survival +0, Swim +1
Languages Orc
Combat Gear 2 flasks of oil; **Other Gear** studded leather
armor, 5 light ballista bolts, short sword, belt pouch, flint and
steel, 2 torches

Tavik resides in the priest quarters, where he keeps his prayer book and
evil items dedicated to Orcus. If the party played through *The Wizard's
Amulet* and Vortigern and Talon stole the amulet from Corian, then
Vortigern and Talon are present here as well. Vortigern and Talon sleep in
this room during the night and are active and awake during the day. Tavik
sleeps here during a majority of the day and is active at night. The two
evil spellcasters have developed an unholy alliance in an attempt to gain
power from the mage's keep. They continually argue about the relative
worth of Law and Chaos. They have not yet determined how to use the
amulet.

TAVIK   **CR 3**
XP 800
Male half-orc cleric of Orcus 4
CE Medium humanoid (human, orc)
Init +1; **Senses** darkvision 60 ft.; **Perception** +3
Aura evil

AC 19, touch 11, flat-footed 18 (+6 armor, +1 Dex, +2 shield)
hp 29 (4d8+4)
Fort +5; **Ref** +2; **Will** +6
Defensive Abilities ferocity

Speed 20 ft.
Melee +1 unholy spiked heavy mace +8 (1d8+4)
Special Attacks channel negative energy 4/day (2d6, DC
13), destructive smite (+2, 5/day)
Domain Spell-Like Abilities (CL 4th; melee touch +6):
5/day—bleeding touch (2 rounds)
Spells Prepared (CL 4th; melee touch +6, ranged touch +4):
2nd—bull's strength, death knell^D (DC 14), hold person (DC
14, x2)
1st—bane (DC 13), cause fear^D (DC 13), doom (DC 13),
protection from good, silence
0 (at will)—bleed (DC 12), guidance, resistance, virtue
D Domain Spell **Domains** Death, Destruction

Str 16, **Dex** 12, **Con** 12, **Int** 12, **Wis** 15, **Cha** 12
Base Atk +3; **CMB** +6; **CMD** 17
Feats Power Attack, Weapon Focus (heavy mace)
Skills Acrobatics –4 (–8 jump), Climb –2, Diplomacy +7, Heal
+6, Intimidate +6, Knowledge (religion) +8, Perception +3,
Sense Motive +6, Spellcraft +5, Stealth –4, Survival +4
Languages Abyssal, Common, Orc
Combat Gear 2 potions of cure serious wounds, 6
vials unholy water; **Other Gear** masterwork chainmail,

Candle of Defiling

Aura faint evocation; **CL** 5th
Slot none; **Price** 2,500 gp; **Weight** 1/2 lb.

DESCRIPTION

This black tallow candle is designed to be placed
on altars of good deities by evil priests, thus defiling
the altars. The candle burns with a wicked, flickering
light, dripping a viscous, red ichor that stains any
substance as if with blood. While the candle burns, it
acts as if both *desecrate* and *bane* spells have been
cast. The candle burns for 12 hours. It may be snuffed
out and re-lit. The candle lights at the will of its owner
by speaking the name of his or her evil deity. The
speaker must be no more than 60 feet away to light
the candle in this manner. One hour of burning the
candle on a good-aligned altar is sufficient to require
that the altar be re-sanctified.

CONSTRUCTION

Requirements Craft Wondrous Item, *desecrate*, *bane*;
Cost: 1,250 gp

masterwork heavy steel shield, +1 unholy spiked heavy
mace, restorative ointment, key ring, special holy
symbol of Orcus. **Note:** The party will not recover any of
these items if Tavik is slain because the refuge spell cast
on his holy symbol transports his corpse and these items
to the temple of Orcus (see **Tactics**, below, for more
details).

Tactics: Tavik is anxiously awaiting news from his raiding party. If he
hears a commotion outside, such as an attack, he calls up to the sentries to
determine the nature of the attack. He is overconfident about the strength
of his force. He has seen nothing from Fairhill that causes him to fear that
his keep will be assaulted. He believes his orcs and his ogre are more than
a match for any invaders. Thus, if he hears combat, he enters into any
melee, believing he can bring even greater glory to his evil demon god.

If encountered in the chapel, he immediately invokes Orcus, lighting the *candle of defiling* as he wades into combat.

If battle turns against him, he flees to the northeast tower (Area 10) and hides with the spiders. If he appears to be in mortal danger or if he is brought to 5 or fewer hit points, he uses his unholy symbol to return himself to the temple of Orcus in the Stoneheart Mountain dungeon, detailed in the module *The Tomb of Abysthor*. Unbeknownst to Tavik, if he is slain, an alternate casting of the *refuge* spell is triggered, transporting his corpse to the same temple to be raised from the dead (after sufficient torment by Orcus in his Palace of Bones in the Abyss). If slain by the party, Tavik (after being raised) attempts to hunt down and kill the party.

Treasure: Tavik has an unlocked small chest containing 831 sp and 51 gp, as well as a 50 gp brooch. He carries most of his important treasure on him.

Bell Tower: The chapel also has a wrought-iron circular staircase in the back of the main room next to the altar that leads up to a trap door and beyond it to the bell tower, which provides an excellent vantage point over most of the keep and the surrounding forest. There is **1 orc sentry** permanently stationed here, and another **orc** sleeps below. The sentry has a horn that he can blow in case of trouble, and he mans a **scorpion** — a large, mounted, siege crossbow that is trained in the direction of the main courtyard to the south. The orcs have removed the bell from the tower so that they can use the scorpion. There are 12 steel spears specially made to be fired from the scorpion, which can be brought to bear and fired in 2 combat rounds once an enemy is sighted. The orcs cannot bring the scorpion into a firing line on persons approaching the "back door" of the keep or the gatehouse. They can target anyone in the outer courtyard or the field to the south of the keep. The spear ends are coated in a pitch that can be ignited by the sentries if they have a lit torch, which they usually do not. After the sentries light a torch, it takes an additional round to ignite the spears prior to firing them. It takes two rounds to reload the scorpion.

ORC SENTRY   CR 1/3
XP 135
Male orc warrior 1 (*Pathfinder Roleplaying Game Bestiary* "Orc")
CE Medium Humanoid (orc)
Init +0; **Senses** darkvision 60 ft.; **Perception** −1

AC 13, touch 10, flat-footed 13 (+3 armor)
hp 7 (1d10+1)
Fort +2; **Ref** +0; **Will** −1
Defensive Abilities ferocity
Weakness light sensitivity

Speed 30 ft.
Melee *+1 dagger* +4 (1d4+3/19–20), short sword +3 (1d6+2/19–20)

Str 14, **Dex** 10, **Con** 10, **Int** 8, **Wis** 8, **Cha** 8
Base Atk +1; **CMB** +3; **CMD** 13
Feats Exotic Weapon Proficiency (light ballista)
Skills Acrobatics −1, Climb +1, Intimidate +3, Stealth −1, Swim +1
Languages Orc
Combat Gear 2 flasks of oil; **Other Gear** studded leather armor, *+1 dagger*, short sword, belt pouch, flint and steel, 2 torches, signal horn, 8 sp, 21 cp

ORC WARRIOR   CR 1/3
XP 135
hp 7 (see **Area 8**)

9. The Southwest Tower

Ground Level: The first floor of this tower houses **Nagrod, the orc chieftain**, and **8 orc warriors. Grenag** and **Slaaroc**, Vortigern's evil henchmen, are also here if Vortigern is here and if they survived *The Wizard's Amulet*. (Their statistics reprinted here, if needed) The floor of this level of the tower is strewn with once-fine rugs stolen from a caravan headed to Fairhill. They are now soiled, having been used as sleeping blankets by the orcs.

NAGROD, THE ORC CHIEFTAIN   CR 1
XP 400
Male orc barbarian 2 (*Pathfinder Roleplaying Game Bestiary* "Orc")
CE Medium humanoid (orc)
Init +2; **Senses** darkvision 60 ft.; **Perception** +4

AC 18, touch 12, flat-footed 16 (+6 armor, +2 Dex)
hp 26 (2d12+6 plus 1)
Fort +6; **Ref** +2; **Will** −1
Defensive Abilities ferocity, uncanny dodge
Weakness light sensitivity

Speed 30 ft.
Melee orc double axe +4 (1d8+4/1d8+2/x3)
Special Attacks rage (9 rounds/day), rage powers (powerful blow +1)

Str 18, **Dex** 15, **Con** 16, **Int** 8, **Wis** 8, **Cha** 8
Base Atk +2; **CMB** +6; **CMD** 18
Feats Two-weapon Fighting
Skills Acrobatics +2, Climb +0, Intimidate +4, Knowledge (nature) +3, Perception +4, Stealth −2, Survival +3, Swim +0
Languages Orc
SQ fast movement +10
Gear breastplate, orc double axe, key to the "back door", 2 25 gp amethysts, 347 sp

ORC WARRIORS (8)   CR 1/3
XP 135
hp 7 (see **Area 8**)

Beneath the center of the soiled rugs and under a large board that the orcs have placed covering it, there is a **secret trap door** in the floor that leads to the rooms below. It is crafted into the flagstone floor. Unless the rugs are moved, it is impossible to find the door. If the rugs are moved, the door can be found with a DC 20 Perception check. The trap door is not locked and, once found, can be freely opened. However, because the rugs are so soiled with orc urine, anyone moving them must succeed on a DC 15 Fortitude save or be nauseated for 1d4 rounds.

Treasure: Though most of the rugs (22) are so soiled as to be beyond recovery, three can be saved and (after much cleaning) are worth 300 gp each. Again, Fortitude saves are required for each rug cleaned.

The Upper Level: The second floor of the tower is the home of **Grosh the Ogre**. He keeps no treasure of his own other than a leather thong on which hang 12 human skulls. He comes downstairs immediately if he hears any sign of melee in the area. His two-handed spiked club is a fearsome weapon.

GROSH THE OGRE   CR 2
XP 800
hp 30 (*Pathfinder Roleplaying Game Bestiary* "Ogre")

10. The Northeast Tower (CR 4, CR 6 if Tavik is also present)

The **door** to the northeast tower is locked from the outside. It contains **2 unusually intelligent giant spiders**. The ground floor is filled with debris — broken furniture and torn tapestries. Stone stairs lead to the second level. The floor of the second level is completely rotted. Anyone walking on the floor above falls through the floor to the level below, suffering 2d6 points of damage. A DC 30 Reflex save is allowed for the character to grab the edge of the floor rather than fall. The orcs have thrown all the broken wooden items from the keep into this room. The orcs are deathly afraid of the spiders. They have killed three, but two still remain. Their plan was to set the wooden items on fire, but Tavik forbade it because he does not want a large fire to reveal their presence. Characters who enter this room may think of the same idea. All they need do is throw a lit torch into the room and shut the door. The spiders quickly die. Of course, the entire tower goes up in flames as all the upper floors catch fire.

Tower Door: 2 in. thick; Hardness 5; hp 30; Break DC 25, Disable Device DC 18.

UNUSUALLY INTELLIGENT GIANT SPIDERS   **CR 2**
XP 600
NE Medium magical beast (*Pathfinder Roleplaying Game Bestiary* "Spider, Giant")
Init +7; **Senses** darkvision 60 ft., low-light vision, tremorsense; **Perception** +8

AC 14, touch 13, flat-footed 11 (+3 Dex, +1 natural)
hp 22 (3d10+3 plus 3)
Fort +4; **Ref** +6; **Will** +1

Speed 30 ft., climb 30 ft.
Melee bite +3 (1d6 plus poison)
Special Attacks web 8/day (3 hp, DC 12)

Str 11, **Dex** 17, **Con** 12, **Int** 3, **Wis** 10, **Cha** 2
Base Atk +3; **CMB** +3; **CMD** 16 (28 vs. trip)
Feats Improved Initiative, Toughness
Skills Climb +24, Perception +8, Stealth +11 (+15 in webs), Swim +4

Poison (Ex) Bite—injury; *save* Fort DC 14; *frequency* 1/round for 4 rounds; *effect* 1d2 Strength damage; *cure* 1 save. The poison save includes a +2 racial bonus.

Treasure: Two *potions of cure moderate wounds* can be found in the webs of the spiders and among the debris (a DC 18 Perception check to discover).

Notes: If Tavik is hiding here, he remains hidden until the spiders attack the party, after which he joins the attack. The spiders do not attack Tavik, their wicked intelligence recognizing him as a fellow creature of evil.

Beneath the Keep

The following rooms can be reached only by finding the trap door in the southwest tower. All rooms are 40 feet in diameter. Each, except the last, has a trapdoor set in the center of the floor. There are no stairs between the levels. (Eralion used *feather fall, jump, rope trick, fly, dimension door* or other magic to move up and down between levels.)

GM Tip: Right about now, your characters should be getting a little scared about what could be down below. Here is a way to increase the tension: Roll dice when you don't need to as if you are checking for something. Couple this with questions directed at specific characters, such as, "What is your Fortitude save?" or "What is your Perception skill?" Then roll a d20 in secret and make a face of concern.

Lower Tower Level 1 — The Battered Room

You enter the dark, musty chamber beneath the orcs' den and see a swath of destruction. Everything smells like orc, or maybe ogre — you can't be sure. Broken pieces of once fine furniture lay strewn about, and shredded tapestries lay scattered as if by the wind. A single trap door is set in the center of the floor, and the area around it is strangely free of debris, as if someone cleared all the trash away from it purposefully.

Once someone in the party descends into the room and examines the trap door, read the following text:

The trap door is nailed shut with silvery nails, and a number of what appear to be silver pieces are wedged into the cracks, forming a nearly complete silver square around the perimeter of the door itself. Several runes are etched into the door.

This room contains broken furniture, shredded tapestries and broken items of unknown use. There is nothing of value here. The trap door to the next level has been nailed shut by silver nails. The orcs (or someone) have driven what appear to be wedges of silver — made out of coins or other objects — into the trap door to try to keep it shut from this side!

Any character can notice this if they make a successful DC 8 Perception roll. Any cleric should know that silver is a traditional ward against the undead. Now would be an appropriate time to remind the party of the rumor that there is a vampire in the keep. If you are running this adventure as an extension of *The Wizard's Amulet*, you might point out that though rumor has it that Eralion failed to become a lich, that doesn't mean he simply died. This should add to the scare factor and give some credence to the "vampire in the keep" rumor. The inscription on the trap door is identical to that etched on the amulet Corian found accompanying the letter from Eralion; characters who played through *The Wizard's Amulet* or who have seen the letter immediately recognize the runes.

The trap door is protected by an *arcane lock* spell (CL 9th). It detects as magical. It requires either a *knock* spell to open, or if this adventure is being run as an extension of *The Wizard's Amulet*, anyone possessing Corian's amulet, which accompanied Eralion's letter, can open this door by producing the amulet and waving it above the door.

Lower Tower Level 2 — The Wizard's Workroom (CR 4)

A faint gust of stale air rushes out as the door seal is broken. Dry, stale air fills your nostrils with the smell of a charnel house as you peer down into the darkness. The room below appears to be some sort of laboratory, with candles, tubes, and various pieces of glassware strewn about on a series of tables. Statues ring the room.

Once any member of the party has descended into the room, read the following text:

Your torchlight seems somehow dimmer here and creates dancing shadows against the walls. You notice that the room is ringed with a series of man-sized statues of knights in mail and full helms.

Around the wall, sitting as stationary statues, are **6 zombies**. The zombies are dressed in chainmail and wear full helms, giving no indication while stationary (other than the horrible stench) that they are undead. The zombies animate and attack two rounds after the party enters the room. Have a few worms jump from the eye-slots of the zombies' helms onto the PCs. The worms are harmless, but increase the terror factor.

ZOMBIES IN CHAINMAIL (6)   CR 1/3
XP 135
NE Medium undead (*Pathfinder Roleplaying Game Bestiary* "Zombie, Medium")
Init −1; **Senses** darkvision 60 ft.; **Perception** +0

AC 17, touch 9, flat-footed 17 (+6 armor, −1 Dex, +2 natural)
hp 13 (2d8 plus 4)
Fort +0; **Ref** −1; **Will** +3
DR 5/slashing; **Immune** undead traits

Speed 20 ft.
Melee slam −3 (1d6+1)

Str 12, **Dex** 8, **Con** —, **Int** —, **Wis** 10, **Cha** 10
Base Atk +1; **CMB** +2; **CMD** 11
Feats Toughness
Skills Climb −4, Stealth −6
SQ staggered
Gear chainmail

There is a **trap door** in the center of the room. The trap door leads to **Level 3**, below. There is a **door** on the east side of this room that leads to a small chamber that has not been disturbed. It contains a bed, a brazier with incense and other creature comforts of a mage.

Eastern Door: 1 in. thick; Hardness 5; hp 10; Break DC 20; Disable Device DC 20

Treasure: On a bedside table in this side chamber are several magical books with spells in them. One prominent volume holds nine first-level wizard spells and five second-level wizard spells. There is also a volume on zombie creation, which includes a copy of the spell *animate dead*.

Lower Tower Level 3 — The Crypt (CR 5)

> The trap door opens with an eerie creak. You peer into the darkness and see some kind of crypt. Six small stone sarcophagi line the walls at regular intervals, and on a raised dais of blackest stone, in the very center of the room, rests an ornately carved stone coffin covered with hieroglyphs and symbols. A skeletal corpse lies on the stone coffin, one arm drooped over the edge grasping a staff. Shards of a once-ornate flask lie on the ground in front of the coffin, and several loose paper sit beside it.

This room contains seven stone sarcophagi: six around the perimeter of the room and one on a raised dais in the center of the room. The six crypts contain the remains of six humans used by Eralion in his final ritual. All were entombed alive, and if the crypts are opened (DC 35 Strength check to open, up to four characters can add their Strength bonuses) scratch marks can be seen where the poor victims tried to claw their way out. If someone examines the corpse and the runes on the dais, read the following:

> As your torchlight flickers against the runes, you can tell that the writings are of a most ancient script, yet appear to be freshly carved. The corpse is dressed in the fine robes of a mage. He holds his staff in a death grip. A cold wind seems to blow here, and you feel a chill run down your spine.

On the dais in front of the main crypt there is a broken flask of fine make that contained what Orcus told Eralion was the potion that would transform him into a lich. The potion was instead a very lethal poison. There appears to be some residual sticky substance inside the flask. The papers detect as evil, if checked, and contain writing in Draconic that is indecipherable. The residual substance on the flagon is poison (ingested; *save* Fort DC 20; *onset* 1 round; *frequency* 1/minute; *effect* 2d6 Con

damage; *cure* 2 saves). On the main sarcophagus rests the corpse of Eralion, dressed in ornamental robes, covered in blood-smeared runes and wearing a false phylactery. In his right hand, which drapes over the side of the stone bed, Eralion's corpse grasps his staff (DC 12 Strength check to pry it from his grasp). This room is the home of Eralion, who, transformed by Orcus' treachery, is now a shadow. He has never previously had visitors to his lair. His shattered mind believes the characters may be his old friend, Feriblan, finally come to visit him. The characters can make a DC 15 Perception check; if successful, they hear what they believe to be the whispered question "Feriblan?"

Once Eralion realizes the intruders are not his old friend, Eralion attacks. Eralion was, long ago, the mage of this keep. His failed attempt at lichdom, as a result of treachery by Orcus, turned him into a vile shadow. He was, at his peak, a 9th level wizard. He retains some small bit of his prior arcane knowledge, though it has been twisted by his evil fate. Though there is no reasoning with Eralion initially, if a character makes a successful DC 18 Bluff check and convinces Eralion that he is in fact Feriblan, then Eralion will materialize, opening himself up for attack. If he is not attacked, he will attempt to speak with the characters, but his broken mind prevents intelligent communication. At this point, if the characters ask Eralion if they can help him, a portion of Eralion's consciousness returns. He says, simply, "Chapel." If the characters restore the chapel above by having the altar re-consecrated and if they open all the trap doors so that Eralion may leave his resting place, he travels to the chapel and ask forgiveness of Thyr. His deity, however, is the god of justice. With a holy flash, Eralion is judged and destroyed; his soul sent to the Abyss for eternal torment, with the players left to wonder which is worse: unlife as an undead or eternal torment in Orcus' Palace of Bones. What did you expect, a happy ending?

ERALION CR 5
XP 1,600
Male shadow necromancer 3 (*Pathfinder Roleplaying Game Bestiary* "Shadow")
CE Medium undead (incorporeal)
Init +2; **Senses** darkvision 60 ft.; **Perception** +9

AC 16, touch 14, flat-footed 13 (+2 armor, +1 deflection, +2 Dex, +1 dodge)
hp 35 (3d8+3 plus 3d6+3 plus 3)
Fort +3; **Ref** +4; **Will** +7
Defensive Abilities channel resistance +2, incorporeal; **Immune** undead traits

Speed 0 ft., fly 40 ft. (good)
Melee touch +3 (1d6 Str damage)
Special Attacks
Spell-Like Abilities (CL 3rd; melee touch +3):
5/day—*grave touch*
Spells Prepared (CL 3rd; melee touch +3, ranged +5):
2nd—*darkness, spectral hand, spectral hand*^B
1st—*chill touch* x2 (DC 13), *chill touch*^B (DC 13), *true strike*
0 (at will)—*ghost sound* (DC 12), *mage hand, touch of fatigue* (DC 12)
Arcane School Necromancy **Prohibited School** Conjuration, Illusion

Str —, **Dex** 14, **Con** —, **Int** 14, **Wis** 12, **Cha** 13
Base Atk +3; **CMB** +5; **CMD** 19
Feats Command Undead (5/day, DC 12), Dodge, Scribe Scroll^B, Skill Focus (Perception), Spell Mastery (*chill touch, spectral hand*)
Skills Fly +13, Knowledge (arcana) +11, Knowledge (geography) +9, Knowledge (planes) +7, Knowledge (religion) +8, Linguistics +6, Perception +9, Spellcraft +10, Stealth +8 (+12 in dim light, −4 in bright light); **Racial Modifiers** +4 stealth in dim light, −4 in bright light
Languages Common, Draconic, Shae
SQ arcane bond (object [obsidian ring]), create spawn, strength damage
Gear *Eralion's staff, incorporeal bracers of armor +2, incorporeal obsidian ring* (125 gp value)

Elixir of Longevity

Prerequisite: Alchemist 14
Benefit: Once per day, an alchemist can brew an elixir of longevity. This special concoction costs 20,000 gp to create and takes 1 hour of work. An elixir of longevity, when administered by the alchemist who brewed it, doubles the natural lifespan of the imbiber, extending all age categories proportionally. There are no provisions against meeting a violent end.

Tactics: Eralion hates light and seeks to extinguish it, attacking anyone holding a light source. He enjoys sneaking up behind his victim from the shadows and draining their strength by touching but not damaging them, so that his touch goes unnoticed — with only the victim's growing weariness as an indication of his attack. Tell any person struck in this fashion that they are feeling weary, ready for sleep, and the weariness is getting worse. Remember that in indirect light, such as torchlight, Eralion is virtually undetectable. The only way to locate Eralion is to either be attacked directly by him or to count the shadows on the floor (Intelligence check DC 20 to think of this tactic, if the players don't figure it out on their own). Once he is discovered, Eralion begins to use his touch spells to damage his victims in addition to draining Strength. Once he is attacked, he cannot be reasoned with. The only way to distract him into speaking with the party is by bluffing him, as described above, and then trying to reason with him.

Treasure: In the hands of Eralion's corpse is the best weapon to defeat his shadow: *Eralion's staff* casts *daylight* 3 times per day, upon uttering the name "Eralion." In addition, once per day it allows the wielder to cast *feather fall* upon uttering the name "Gethrame." Both spells are cast as if by a 9th level caster. It takes the *identify* spell to discover these command words, as there are no clues or indicators on the staff itself. Also in his sarcophagus are 276 gp, 2,007 sp, 1,567 cp, eight gems of 25 gp value and six pieces of jewelry valued at 150 gp total. Also present on Eralion's corpse is the masterwork ceremonial dagger used in the failed ritual for lichdom. There is an *elixir of longevity* and a *scroll of invisibility sphere* inside the sarcophagus (same chance to open as others above). Additionally, if Eralion is slain, his *bracers of armor +2* and obsidian ring (125 gp value) become corporeal, if extremely cold.

The Crucible

This part details the adventure, starting with the characters' arrival in Fairhill and ending with their assault on the ruined keep. It makes use of the material detailed in **Part One**. The following section is presented in Act and Scene format to make it run smoothly and dramatically. Of course, this is just one of many stories that could be told using the information provided in **Part One**.

Prologue

GM Tip: It is always a good idea to start a game session with a little action. In this case, the early excitement is an encounter with an orc raiding band — introducing the party to what will become their main foe throughout this module, though they don't know it yet. Before you get to the action, you should do a few things. First, make sure the characters have reviewed their character sheets. If they have any questions, resolve them now. Ask any spell users which spells they memorized during the previous night's rest. Resolve any other miscellaneous issues such as healing and equipment. Finally, have your characters indicate a general marching order. Once you have accomplished these housekeeping matters, proceed to "**A Little Excitement**." Your players will certainly have more than a little excitement.

A Little Excitement

There are two slightly different introductions depending on whether or not your players have played through *The Wizard's Amulet*. If they have, read both of the following text boxes. If they have not, do not read the first text box:

> It has been two nights since the encounter with Vortigern and his devilish familiar, Talon. You still bear the wounds of the battle. Many of your group nurse lingering injuries, both physical and mental, not the least of which are the nightmarish images that plague Corian in his dreams. You recall vividly the bodies of the innocent farmers, the clawed hands of the skeletons as they rose from the earth, summoned by Vortigern, and the hellish shriek as Talon revealed his true form.

> Weary from your long journey and many experiences, your party makes its way along the path towards the villages of Fairhill, searching for a warm fire and a safe bed — a place to brush the dirt of the road from your boots. The road you travel gradually slopes upward as you leave the tradeway behind, heading towards the foothills of the Stoneheart Mountains. The rolling hills are covered with green grass and spring flowers, lifting your spirits. You believe that you should arrive in Fairhill within two hours.

Have the characters make a DC 20 Perception check. If any of the characters succeed, read the following text:

> As you travel the road to Fairhill, your natural instincts — heightened by your recent adventures — cause you to scan the hills for possible areas of ambush. Your instincts prove to be good ones. You spot three humanoids with bows hiding slightly behind the crest of a nearby hill, their backs to the afternoon sun, making it hard to discern their exact nature. You find just enough time to shout a warning and dive to the ground as the volley of arrows hisses towards you.

If the characters all fail the Perception check, read the following text.

> The all-too-familiar hiss of an arrow cutting through the air pulls you from your daze. You count one… two… three of them! You hardly have time to wonder how you could have let your instincts be dulled by the thought of a soft bed as you asses your current situation and look around to see which of your companions have been injured.

The attackers are **3 orcs**, sent by Tavik to harass villagers and merchants. This group of orcs recently stole food from a nearby farmhouse and, following their feast, took up a position on this hill. As taught by Tavik, they try to ambush with the sun behind them so they are hard to see.

ORCS (3)   **CR 1/3**
XP 135
Male orc warrior 1 (*Pathfinder Roleplaying Game Bestiary* "Orc")
CE Medium humanoid (orc)
Init +0; **Senses** darkvision 60 ft.; **Perception** –1

AC 14, touch 10, flat-footed 14 (+3 armor, +1 shield)
hp 7 (1d10+1)
Fort +2; **Ref** +0; **Will** –1
Defensive Abilities ferocity
Weakness light sensitivity

Speed 30 ft.
Melee battleaxe +3 (1d8+2/x3)
Ranged shortbow +1 (1d6/x3)

Str 14, **Dex** 10, **Con** 10, **Int** 8, **Wis** 8, **Cha** 8
Base Atk +1; **CMB** +3; **CMD** 13
Feats Weapon Focus (battleaxe)
Skills Acrobatics –2, Climb +0, Intimidate +3, Stealth –2
Languages Orc
Combat Gear 2 flasks of oil; **Other Gear** studded leather armor, light wooden shield, battleaxe, shortbow, 20 arrows, belt pouch, flint and steel, 2 torches, 2d6 sp, 3d10 cp

Tactics: These orcs are new recruits and are not yet coordinated enough to know to concentrate their fire on one target. Pick their targets within the party randomly. As long as the party stays prone (+4 AC vs. missile fire!) the orcs continue to fire at them for six rounds. Seeing that they are outnumbered by the party, once six rounds have passed or if the party charges the hill where the orcs are hiding, the orcs run for some nearby woods, having had enough target practice for one day. If they try, the party can easily track the orcs into the nearby woods with a DC 9 Survival check. Because the party cannot catch the orcs before they get into the woods, they must make a new Survival check at DC 9 once in the woods to relocate the tracks. The orcs figure they are safe once they make it to the woods, so they slow down. If the party succeeds on a DC 9 Survival check, they can overtake the orcs. The orcs make a desperate stand using their axes. If caught, they can be interrogated and quickly reveal that their base is the ruined keep nearby and that their leader is a half-orc named Tavik.

Arrival in Fairhill

When the characters arrive they most likely pass one of the guard stations at **Areas 7**. When they do, read the following text:

> As you approach the village proper, passing the outlying farmhouses, you are stopped by an imposing man with a grim expression. He is arrayed in well- used studded leather armor, his reddish-brown hair pulled back away from his face and his heavy green cloak swept back. A female elf in mail and two town guards holding spears and shield, wearing green surcoats with a small sliver bowl emblazoned on the left breast, accompany him. The man lifts his left hand, motioning you to stop. You notice that his right arm ends in a cruel scar and that he has no right hand, certainly lost in some horrible manner. In a well-worn scabbard, a bastard sword, its elongated pommel sticking out prominently, rests against his hip. He calls to your party in a commanding voice, "Announce yourselves and state your purpose."

The man is **Baran**, described in **Part One** above, and with him is his lieutenant, **Lauriel**, and **2 town guards**. Baran questions the party about their purpose and generally is suspicious of them. He only relents in his questioning if he notes a cleric of a known good deity among the party. He is brusque and short, acting as if the party was the sole source of his irritation. He curtly directs them to the *Three Kegs* where they can stable their horses if they have any. He also orders them to the Temple of Freya, where all visitors are expected to pay homage.

Lauriel stands by silently. She would never challenge Baran's authority, even though she disagrees with his treatment of the adventurers. If the characters cause problems, she is the first to draw steel and call for the guard. If such a problem arises, four additional guards with spears and shields arrive in four rounds.

The Temple of Freya

At some point, the characters will surely make their way to the Temple of Freya. If they explore the town first, proceed to "**Around Town**," below. But once at the temple, read the following text:

> You approach what must surely be the Temple of Freya. It is a simple wooden structure, with a peaked roof. Its front has no door and is open to the outside. Inside the one-room shrine is a stone altar in which is carved the head of a stag. A female elf of stunning beauty stands before the altar, wearing a tunic and a long cloak of winter wolf fur. In her hands she holds a shining silver bowl, worked with strange runes. Before you can stop her, she plunges her entire arm and the bowl into the flaming brazier next to the altar. She beings to intone words in a strange language.

The party enters as Shandril is finishing a small sacrifice of grain to Freya. Anyone foolish enough to interrupt her gains her disfavor. If they wait patiently, she finishes the small ritual and greets the party. If asked, she explains what the *Crucible* is and how it is used to bring fertility and prosperity to the village. She gladly discusses her faith with any other clerics. After a short time, she tells the party that she must continue with her devotions and returns to her prayers.

If the players request healing, Shandril gladly casts one *cure light wounds* on any injured individual, up to her spell limit. If the characters wish a companion raised from the dead, Shandril only agrees under the most serious of circumstances, especially if the person's help is essential to successfully recover the *Crucible* once it is stolen.

Around Town

This scene is rather freeform. Let your characters explore Fairhill. They can visit the central market and the various inns. They may want to secure a room before they do anything else. A DC 8 Diplomacy check lets them discover the basics about Fairhill: Arlen is the magistrate, Baran is the captain of the guard, the *Drunken Cockatrice* has the best food, the *Cask and Flagon* is cheaper and more boisterous and the *Three Kegs* doesn't have rooms but serves the best ale.

You may wish to have them meet Lannet, Fendrin or possibly Durgis and his dwarves. Perhaps Arlen takes an interest in them. Maybe they meet Lasha in meditation. If you want to get the action going, you can proceed to **Act I** the very first night the characters arrive at Fair hill. However, there is no rush. This scene can be as long or as short as you want it to be — from a few hours to a few days. This is where you expand on the roleplaying possibilities offered by Fairhill. If Vortigern and Talon are in Fairhill, you may wish to have them make an attempt on the characters' lives. Or you could spend a whole session having the characters locate and finally deal with Vortigern and Talon. The only thing that should happen is that the characters be given the chance to learn a few rumors.

Act I:
The Crucible Stolen

At the Inn

The party has probably checked into the *Drunken Cockatrice* or the *Cask and Flagon*. After their meal, read the following text:

> As the meal draws to a close, all seems in order. Your prior adventures behind you, you and your companions sit in the common room enjoying the warm fire and the cold ale. Talk begins to turn, as it always does, to legends of past exploits and to tales of wonder from distant lands, with each of you thinking that one day, folks may well be telling your story in a place such as this.

If they have not already met **Lannet**, you should introduce him to the characters. Have some fun roleplaying him. He becomes curious about the party. Let the party members tell tales if they wish. Repeat the rumor about the town recently being subjected to raids by marauding orcs and that several of the town guard have been killed. Make sure to repeat the

vampire rumor as well. Then, just as they are comfortable, spring the next scene on them.

Alarm!

> The loud peal of the town bell cuts through the din of the inn's common room. You hear sounds of battle from outside, and you see the flickering of strange lights through the window. As you grab your weapons and run outside, you immediately notice that the Temple of Freya is ablaze and there is a skirmish between a cadre of town guards and a group of humanoids. You can see that several town guards lie dead of injured. From the periphery, you notice Shandril and Arlen rushing towards you. The flames engulf the Temple fully and light the village with a hellish glow. With shout, the humanoids lob what appear to be flaming torches at the guards and flee to the east, shrieking in their foul tongue.

There is no way to cover the ground between the characters' current location and the temple in time to catch the humanoids. And even if the characters are so inclined, Shandril and Arlen call to them, asking for their aid. Shandril announces that the Temple of Freya has just been looted by orcs and that three town guardsmen were killed in the skirmish. Arlen and

Shandril take control of the situation and try in vain to put out the fire.

Seeing the party as Fairhill's only dependable allies, now that the town guard is absorbed in the tasks of restoring order and fortifying the town from future attacks, Shandril implores the party to help recover one of the stolen items — the magical *Crucible* sacred to Freya, necessary for the blessing of the harvest. Baran reluctantly agrees with Shandril's plan, looking the characters up and down disapprovingly. If the characters volunteer to help, read the following text:

> Shandril smiles. "Freya bless you for your courage," she says. She removes from her waist a sword in a very plain, unadorned leather scabbard. The handle is made of horn. It does not look like it would make a good combat weapon. Shandril presents the sword reverently. "Take this, if you will carry it," she says. "Promise to recover the *Crucible* and bring justice to those who have defile the temple of my goddess.

What Shandril offers is her sword, *Valkyria*. The recipient and all the party members must pledge to recover and return the *Crucible* and to bring the orcs to justice. If the sword is refused (because of its meager appearance), she smiles and replaces it on her hip. In any event, she blesses the party and provides them with *2 potions of cure moderate wounds*. If the sword is accepted, she also asks the recipient to swear that he or she will return the sword.

Baran tells the party that the raiding creatures were orcs and that he believes the orcs have occupied a ruined keep to the northeast. Baran is reluctant to send his forces after the orcs because he believes this foray may be a ruse to draw the guards away and thus leave the town exposed and unguarded. Arlen thanks the party and tells them that they are free to keep anything they recover from the orcs, aside from the *Crucible*. Arlen orders several guards to bring horses for the party. Baran reluctantly sends three of his guards to lead the party to the keep and to guard the horses. Lauriel, a female elf, one of the town guards appointed by Baran to accompany the party, is openly suspicious of the characters. She was, however, the first to volunteer to go with them. The other two guards sent with the party are named **Jerinor** and **Hathol**. If you feel that your characters are too underpowered to handle the keep, Lasha and/or Kath might volunteer to accompany the party. Lannet hides and then sneaks out after the party, using his magic cloak to follow along unobtrusively.

JERINOR AND HATHOL   CR 1/2
XP 200
Male human warrior 2
LG Medium humanoid (human)
Init +1; **Perception** +4

AC 16, touch 11, flat-footed 15 (+4 armor, +1 Dex, +1 shield)
hp 16 (2d10+2)
Fort +4; **Ref** +1; **Will** +0

Speed 30 ft.
Melee longsword +3 (1d8+1/19–20) or shortspear +4 (1d6+1)
Ranged shortbow +3 (1d6/x3)

Str 12, **Dex** 12, **Con** 12, **Int** 10, **Wis** 10, **Cha** 10
Base Atk +2; **CMB** +3; **CMD** 14
Feats Alertness, Weapon Focus (Shortspear)
Skills Acrobatics −1, Climb +2, Handle Animal +4, Perception +4, Ride +2, Sense Motive +2, Stealth −2, Swim −2
Languages Common
Gear chain shirt, light steel shield, longsword, shortbow, shortspear, 20 arrows, green surcoat with *crucible* symbol, small sack with 2d4 gp, bedroll, 7 days rations.

Act II: Hot Pursuit

The Chase

The first step in reaching the keep is to head east to the river where it can be forded. Though there is no real chance of catching the orcs at the ford even on horseback, make it dramatic.

GM Tip: A good way to raise the tension of a scene is to have the characters roll dice, even if it is irrelevant. What you have to do is make the die-rolling seem relevant. In this case, let the leader of the party roll a d20. You roll a d20 also. The higher the better. If you want, you can let the characters with tracking or some other relevant skill make DC 10 skill checks to get a + 2 on their d20 roll. Do this five or six times, telling the players that the rolls are to see if the characters are gaining on the orcs. Record the results after each roll on the game board, as if the number of wins has something to do with how far apart the party is from the orcs. Of course it doesn't, but the players don't need to know that. If they rolled well in the meaningless die-rolling above, make it seem as if they must be right on the heels of the orcs. If they rolled poorly, make it seem like they might be losing the trail.

Regardless of the die rolls, the players make it to the ford without

catching up to the orcs. Once across the river, the party must make a DC 13 Survival check. If successful, they pick up the orcs' trail. The trail leads to a fork in the road and past it along the road into the nearby forest.

Decision in the Forest

Once in the forest, have the characters make a DC 12 Perception check. If none of the party members succeeds at the roll, Lauriel does. Either Lauriel or the party member who made the Perception check notices that another path seems to break off from the main road and head off north into the forest. Lauriel says she does not remember seeing this path before. This path is the "secret path" on the wilderness map that leads to the ruined keep.

If the characters make successful DC 12 Perception checks to search the area, they find a small leather pouch containing several small items taken from the shrine — their prey, it seems, took this secret path. A successful DC 8 Survival check (the ground is softer here, and tracks are easier to find in the leaf litter) also confirms that the orcs went this way. The tracks seem very fresh and acting quickly the party may be able to overtake the orcs.

Regardless of this information, Lauriel proposes to lead the party east and to the north entrance of the keep, following the old road. She is forceful in suggesting this route. She argues that the secret path certainly heads to the keep, but that the old road can better accommodate horses and they can thus make better time. Plus, she fears an ambush on the secret path. Don't blurt these reasons out all at once, use them one by one in response to arguments from the characters.

Tell the party that she is correct. It would be difficult to take horses along the secret path. However, if no party member thinks of it, remind the person who accepted the sword that they pledged to recover the *Crucible* and that if they do not follow the orcs they may not be able to overtake them before they get to the keep. Then who can say if they will be able to recover the *Crucible* or not?

Following the Secret Path: If the party persists, Lauriel reluctantly agrees and suggests that Jerinor lead the horses out of the forest and stay with them at the edge of the forest. Lauriel and Hathol accompany the party onward to make sure it takes actions consistent with the wishes of the village. Unbeknownst to anyone, Lannet, shrouded in his *cloak of elvenkind*, is following. He does not make his presence known until later. The party travels along the secret path, through heavy undergrowth. Have them attempt DC 8 Survival checks. Each check represents one hour of time spent trying to follow the path. At any point, a successful check confirms that the characters are gaining on the orcs and that the orcs have slowed their pace. Proceed to the next scene: "**Encountering the Raiding Party.**"

Following the Road: If the party relents and agrees with Lauriel, they follow the old road east as it wraps around to the north of the keep. About two miles from where the secret path split from the road, the old road becomes overgrown and difficult to pass. Horses may be ridden, but only single file and only at a slow walk. It takes six hours to travel the old road to the keep. If at this point the characters decide to turn back and take the secret path they can still catch the raiding party. If they push onward, when they come within one mile of the keep on the old road, the forest encroaches on the road even further. Riders must dismount and walk their horses. Needless to say, the raiding party arrives at the keep before the characters do. This, however, is not as bad as it seems since the orcs celebrate the theft of the *Crucible* and many get drunk, making an assault on the keep easier. See **Act III**, "**Assault on the Keep.**"

GM Tip: Players love action, but good adventures always contain roleplaying opportunities. This scene is a chance for you to play up the conflict with Lauriel and get your players to do a little roleplaying. See how the characters react to Lauriel's stubbornness. Who is the leader of the party? How do they treat Lauriel? Do people follow their alignment strictures in their actions and words? Do they follow the teachings of their deities if they are priests?

Encountering the Raiding Party (CR 3)

> The sound of orc voices grows louder as you draw neared to the raiding party. You are now only a few dozen yards behind the orcs, and you can clearly hear their wicked songs of celebration. The overgrowth shrouds them from your view. Lauriel turns and makes the signal for silence, then circles her hand above her head, signaling everyone to rally to her to plan your attack. Hathol smiles, knowing the orcs are unaware that their death is at hand!

The orcs are loud and boisterous from their successful raid, believing in their foolishness that they have not been followed. They are happier than usual because raiding the temple was an important task given to Kren by Tavik. Kren hopes this success may help him unseat Nagrod as the leader of the orc band. Kren carries the *Crucible*.

Because of the noise the orcs are making, allow the players to dictate the encounter, including moving ahead of the orcs and setting an ambush. If the characters don't think of an ambush, Lauriel recommends it. The path is five feet wide, and the orcs are traveling in a single-file line, with Kren traveling at its head. He holds the *Crucible* aloft, often spitting in it. If the characters stage an ambush, all the characters get a free surprise action before the orcs can act. The orcs do not get to roll to prevent surprise. If any of the characters loudly invoke the name of Freya as they attack, the orcs suffer a −1 morale penalty to their attack rolls for three rounds, stricken with fear.

KREN, ORC SUB-LIEUTENANT   CR 1
XP 400
Male orc warrior 3
CE Medium humanoid (orc)
Init +2; **Senses** darkvision 60 ft.; **Perception** +3

AC 16, touch 12, flat-footed 14 (+4 armor, +2 Dex)
hp 28 (3d10+9 plus 3)
Fort +6; **Ref** +3; **Will** +2
Defensive Abilities ferocity
Weakness light sensitivity

Speed 20 ft.
Melee greataxe +7 (1d12+4/x3)

Str 16, **Dex** 14, **Con** 16, **Int** 9, **Wis** 12, **Cha** 10
Base Atk +3; **CMB** +6; b 18
Feats Power Attack, Weapon Focus (greataxe)
Skills Acrobatics −1 (−5 jump), Climb +0, Escape Artist −1, Intimidate +4, Perception +3, Stealth −1, Swim +0
Languages Common, Orc
Gear hide armor, greataxe, *the Crucible of Freya*, large iron key, sack tied on his belt containing a 100 gp pearl, 18 gp, 33 sp

---

ORC WARRIORS (6)   CR 1/3
XP 135
Male orc warrior 1 (*Pathfinder Roleplaying Game Bestiary* "Orc")
CE Medium humanoid (orc)
Init +0; **Senses** darkvision 60 ft.; **Perception** −1

AC 15, touch 10, flat-footed 15 (+5 armor)
hp 7 (1d10+1)
Fort +2; **Ref** +0; **Will** −1
Defensive Abilities ferocity
Weakness light sensitivity

Speed 20 ft.

Melee greataxe +4 (1d12+3/x3)
Ranged shortbow +1 (1d6/x3)

Str 14, **Dex** 10, **Con** 10, **Int** 8, **Wis** 8, **Cha** 8
Base Atk +1; **CMB** +3; **CMD** 13
Feats Weapon Focus (greataxe)
Skills Acrobatics −4 (−8 jump), Climb −2, Escape Artist −4, Stealth −4, Survival +0
Languages Orc
Other Gear scale mail, greataxe, shortbow, 20 arrows, belt pouch, 1d4 gp, 1d8 sp

Lannet: Lannet stays some distance from the party when they launch their attack. He only appears if the party is in dire need, then provides a crucial sneak attack or thrown dagger. If you don't have to reveal his presence, don't.

To Press on or Turn Back . . .

Once the *Crucible* is recovered, the characters have another decision to make. Lauriel wants to return to Fairhill immediately and deliver the *Crucible* to Shandril. The party should realize that now may be its best opportunity to attack the keep. Certainly there must be more orcs at the keep than this small raiding party. If the raiding party never comes home the other orcs will know something is wrong. They may increase their defenses. They may even march on Fairhill. Remind the recipient of Shandril's sword that he or she pledged to bring those responsible to justice. Wouldn't all the orcs truly be responsible for these acts and thus need to be brought to justice? You may prod the characters to think that at the very least they should scout the rest of the trail to see if it leads to the keep and, if so, reconnoiter the keep to gather information on their foes while the orcs are unaware.

Again, bring the conflict to a head. Lauriel feels great loyalty to Shandril and is very insistent about returning the *Crucible*. If the recipient of Shandril's sword speaks, Lauriel suggests that she should have been given the sword and that the character is not worthy to bear it. Lauriel insists that she carry the *Crucible* back to Fairhill. If pressed on the issue, Lauriel agrees that they can scout the keep but not attack it until the *Crucible* is returned.

If the party decides to return to Fairhill: Shandril is pleased by their

THE CRUCIBLE OF FREYA

prompt return of the *Crucible*. If the person entrusted with Shandril's sword attempts to return it, Shandril tells him or her that she feels there is yet work to be done on behalf of the goddess and that the character should keep the sword for the time being. Both Arlen and Baran, however, question the characters after Lauriel gives her report. Baran is clearly disappointed that the party did not press on to the keep and worries that the orcs will take revenge on the village. Arlen agrees and asks the characters to volunteer to return to the keep once they are healthy at a minimum to determine the size of the orc force. If the characters scouted the keep but returned to Fairhill without attacking, Baran and Arlen both ask the characters to launch an attack quickly — tonight if possible. Shandril and Kath assist in returning the party to full health with healing spells.

Allow the characters to earn experience. See the *Pathfinder Roleplaying Game Core Rulebook*. In addition to the experience from the above encounters, the characters earn a 200 XP story award for returning the *Crucible* to Shandril. Characters who earn sufficient XP to increase in level may do so at this juncture even if they receive healing by spell and head back to the keep right away. Once the characters set off for the keep, proceed to **Act III**.

If the party decides to press on: The secret path is heavily overgrown and horses cannot pass. Negotiating the path requires two additional successful DC 10 Survival checks to reach the keep from the spot where the party ambushed Kren and his orcs. If the party did not return to Fairhill, it reaches the keep before the orcs realize the raiding party is missing. Proceed to **Act III**.

Act III: Assault on the Keep

Running the assault on the keep is by far the most difficult part of this adventure because there are so many variables. This section should assist you. You must first determine the circumstances controlling the orcs' level of alertness so that you will know what plusses or minuses might apply to the guards. Then you must determine the direction from which the party approaches the keep so that you can give it a proper description. You must next assess the manner of the party's entry into the keep. Finally, specific notes are provided for handling the assault. Each of these are dealt with in turn.

The Orcs' Level of Alertness

The level of alertness of the creatures in the keep depends mostly on external events, each of which is described below.

The orc raiding party has not yet gone missing: This situation occurs if the party encounters Kren and the orcs, defeats them and quickly pushes on to the keep without returning to Fairhill. In this situation, the keep is at its lowest level of alertness since it does not yet know that the raiding party has been defeated. All creatures are at their normal locations as indicated in **Part One**. None of the creatures has any bonuses or minuses to his alertness. They take no special actions. They await the return of Kren and his orcs. This situation is best for the party, particularly if it waits for Nagrod and his orcs to be dispatched (see below) and it ambushes that group as well, thus thinning the ranks of the orcs significantly.

The orc raiding party does not return: If the raiding party does not return for several hours, Tavik decides the raid has failed, which surprises him. Tavik then commands **Nagrod** and **4 orc warriors** to follow the secret path back to the village to learn what has happened to the raiding party. Since the "back door" is locked, Nagrod and the orcs exit over the northernmost palisade in the southwestern wall, just below the southwest tower. They travel up the edge of the keep to the "back door" and head away, down the secret path. If the characters have not yet entered the keep (because they have been busy reconnoitering the entire keep), the characters can ambush this group of orcs just as they did Kren's group. However, if they spring their ambush too close to the keep so that the

battle can be heard there or if any of the orcs escape, the keep immediately goes on full alert. If Nagrod does not return by morning, Tavik places the keep on full alert.

If the characters have already snuck into the keep through the "back door" when Nagrod and his orcs make their way to the secret path, they will notice that the padlock on the back door is open, because the characters cannot lock it behind them. However, Nagrod attributes it to Kren's sloppiness and simply locks the padlock. Nagrod has his own key to the "back door". This may prevent retreat by the characters, since there is no way to open the padlock on the "back door" from the inside. When Tavik dispatches Nagrod and his four orcs, he does not take any further defensive precautions because the thought has not yet occurred to him that anyone from Fairhill could be bold enough to bring the battle to him.

The orc raiding party returns with the *Crucible*, and the characters attack the keep that night: If the characters followed the old road and were unable to overtake Kren and the raiding party (or were unable to overtake the raiding party for any other reason), then the orcs return to the keep victorious, their prize in hand, to the gleeful shouts of their comrades. Tavik takes custody of the *Crucible*. He places it on the desecrated altar and defiles it by placing the *candle of defiling* inside of the *Crucible* and lighting it. Until the *Crucible* is properly cleansed of the staining filth created by the candle, none of its powers can be used.

The orcs open several kegs of ale and drink themselves into a stupor. In this situation, add Kren and his orcs to those normally present on the first floor of the southwest tower. Tavik is annoyed at his orcs' celebration, but he still believes that there is no real chance of any repercussion for his theft of the *Crucible*. If the party attacks the night of the celebration, all the orcs (including the guards) are at –2 to Perception checks. Due to the noise from the keep, all Stealth checks are at +2. In addition, there is a 30% chance that at any given time a posted guard will be away from his post. This does not apply to the sentries in the bell tower of the chapel. Though this situation provides some strategic advantages, the keep is at its fullest strength with the return of Kren and his orcs.

The orc raiding party returns with the *Crucible*, and the characters attack at dawn the next morning: This may prove to be the most advantageous situation for the characters, though as stated above, the orcs at the keep are at their greatest number. After their celebration, the orcs are severely hung-over. There is a 50% chance that any guard is asleep at his post. In addition, because it is now daytime, all the orcs are at –1 on their Perception checks and attack rolls. Also, the orcs who are normally "sleeping" and could wake up if the alarm sounds are now treated as "passed out." They must be woken up by another person, and they take an extra 5 rounds to respond to any alarm. This drunkenness does not apply to the sentries in the bell tower of the chapel. Kren and his orcs are passed out in the southwest tower. In the southwest tower, only Nagrod and Grosh the ogre are not passed out. Instead, they are simply "sleeping." Obviously, neither Tavik nor Vortigern (if he is present) are passed out.

The raiding party returns with the *Crucible*, but the characters do not attack the keep for a day or more: In this situation, Tavik has the *Crucible* with him in the chapel as above. Kren and his orcs are in the southwest tower. All other orcs are in their normal locations. Because Tavik believes someone may come to scout the keep, he posts two of Kren's orcs on the roof of the gatehouse. This is possibly the worst situation for the characters. The orcs are at full strength, more guards are posted and there are no situational modifiers in favor of the characters. Your players should have their characters make peace with their respective deities if they attempt to assault the keep under these circumstances.

Full alert: If a day or more has passed and the raiding party has not returned or if any of the other conditions causing full alert described above are met, Tavik puts the keep on full alert. The watch fires are lit at night. All guards gain a +1 to their Perception checks as they have been ordered to be attentive or they will be beaten and whipped (and possibly eaten) by Grosh the ogre. Noise is suppressed in the keep, and the ale casks are sealed on pain of death by Tavik. Tavik does not sleep for several days, keeping ever-vigilant. He uses divination magic to gain information. If Vortigern and Talon are present, they use Talon's ability to contact Dispater to gain information about the raiding party. Two extra guards patrol the perimeter of the keep's exterior, and a permanent guard is stationed at the top of the gatehouse. Take these extra orcs from the ones normally sleeping in the southwest tower. Nagrod personally patrols the outer courtyard at night. Two extra guards in addition to those just mentioned are posted at the door from the northwest tower into the inner courtyard. Approaching the keep under these conditions, without having previously thinned out the ranks of orcs, is tantamount to suicide. But what a story if the characters pull it off!

Approaching the Keep

There are three ways to approach the keep: by the secret forest path from the west, by the main path from the north leading to the gatehouse or through the woods from the south or east. If the party approaches at night when the keep is on full alert, read the following in addition to any text below:

> As you near the edge of the forest, you see a hellish glow coming from the area ahead of you. As you reach the clearing containing the keep, you notice that it is ringed with watch fires.

If the party approaches by the secret path, read the following:

> Suddenly, the forest opens before you, revealing the crumbled battlements of a ruined keep. Immediately in front of you is one of the large stone towers of the keep. The tower has a partially collapsed roof and a crack runs down its length. The crack has been filled with stones, and a large iron door has been set into the filled crack. An iron padlock seals the door. Above the crumbling curtain wall, you can see the remains of what must have been the steeple of a chapel. It is difficult to see much more from your vantage point, since the forest has grown up to the very walls of the keep.

Remember, characters can make a DC 15 Perception check to notice the orc sentry in the bell tower. If the characters do not make an excessive amount of noise, the sentry will not look in their direction unless the keep is on full alert. The sentry is used to hearing the returning orc parties before he sees them so he does not keep a sharp lookout on the secret path.

If the characters approach from the main road, read the following text:

> The brambles and branches clear, revealing a mostly intact curtain wall and gatehouse. The large, rusted portcullis of the gatehouse stands closed. The air is still. You see no one. The forest, it seems, has grown right up to the very walls of the keep. It is clear that the path you are on and the gatehouse before you have not been used for some time. The curtain wall and the encircling forest prevent you from seeing more of the keep from where you stand. The courtyard beyond the gatehouse is dark.

If the party approaches from the south or east, read the following text:

> You come to the edge of the forest, which opens to the south side of the keep. There is a wide stretch of open ground between the edge of the forest and the keep. Here, the curtain wall of the keep is almost entirely ruined. The denizens of the keep have erected a palisade of dirt with what appears to be sharpened logs set along its length filling the gaps in the ruined wall. You can see that both to the northwest and northeast the trees grow more closely to the walls of the keep. Several paces from you, you notice the corpse of an elf impaled against a tree by a large steel spear driven fully through the corpse's torso. Only something like a ballista could cause such a grisly death. It is disheartening, but the orcs in the keep might have such a weapon.

The party may decide to do a reconnaissance of the entire keep, having one or more of its number circle around the keep under the cover of the surrounding forest. If so, read each of the above pieces of boxed text as the characters pass the relevant locations. Have characters doing so make a Stealth check (with a +6 circumstance bonus due to the cover of the forest) as they pass each of the locations. Given the level of alertness of the keep as determined above, roll an opposed Perception check for the guards against the rolls made by the scouting characters. If the raiding party returned with the *Crucible*, read the following in addition to any text above:

> An overwhelming din comes from within the keep — the shouts and screams of the orcs celebrating their capture of the *Crucible of Freya*. A low, evil light comes from the inner courtyard of the keep.

Means of Entry

There are a number of ways to get into the keep, from the sneaky to the suicidal. They are detailed below:

The Back Door: The best way to enter the keep is through the "back door" using Kren's key. There are never guards posted outside of this door. The only danger is the **green slime** (which is why the orcs don't post a guard).

Over the Wall: The ruined walls can be scaled with a DC 10 Climb check. Due to the rubble and debris, a DC 14 Stealth check must be made with each Climb check or rocks are disturbed, possibly drawing attention to the climber. If there is a guard in the area, that guard can make a Perception check opposed by the failed Stealth result. If the Stealth check is successful, the guard does not get to roll a Perception check. Of course, if climbing a wall brings a person in the line of sight of a guard, that guard gets to make a Perception check (DC to be determined by the GM under the circumstances). Once on top of a ruined wall, the character must make an Acrobatics check to balance —DC 5–10 depending on the amount of wall remaining — or fall. Actually, the best wall to climb is the north wall flanking the gatehouse because that wall is normally not watched and it is not ruined, so it does not require a Stealth check. The north wall requires a successful DC 20 Climb check to scale.

The "Umbra": If the watch fires are lit, observant characters (Perception check DC 15) detect several shadowy areas where the firelight does not fully overlap. In these sections, any Stealth checks by characters are made at +4.

Sneak Past the Guards: A near suicidal proposition unless the guards are asleep from a hangover, this tactic may nevertheless be attempted. This requires a Stealth check, opposed by the guard's Perception skills. The modifiers based on alertness level apply as described above.

Frontal Assault: Characters bent on a heroic but swift death should choose this option. Covering the open ground between the forest and the keep exposes characters to numerous Perception checks by the orcs at the palisades, in addition to subjecting them to bow fire from those same orcs. Also, the sentry in the bell tower can bring the scorpion to bear on anyone crossing the open field or in the outer courtyard, as the elf impaled to the tree clearly demonstrated.

Running the Assault

As long as the characters maintain stealth, they can move about the keep as they wish. The best possible scenario is that an archer in the party kills the sentry in the bell tower or a spellcaster in the party puts him to sleep. Once combat breaks out anywhere within the keep, however, the rest of the orcs will most likely be alerted. The only way to avoid this is by sneak attacks that result in silent kills or combat under magical *silence*.

Once alerted, the sentry in the bell tower sounds the horn. When that happens, all sleeping orcs wake up in 2 rounds, exit their respective sleeping quarters and head to the sound of battle. Posted guards are told not to leave their posts, but since they are orcs, there is a 50% chance that any posted guard will leave his post and head toward the sound of melee. Nagrod emerges from the tower with his axe, spoiling for a fight. The melee will eventually draw all the orcs in the keep except for those disciplined enough to keep to their post. If the sentry in the bell tower lives, he fires the scorpion at any intruders.

If the sentry is killed so that there is no one to sound the horn, the only orcs alerted by the noise of combat are those close to the battle. The other orcs figure that if the danger is serious, the horn would sound. In this situation, the nearby orcs begin to arrive five rounds after they hear the battle. They are surprised to see intruders, believing that the sound of battle was from the long-anticipated showdown between Nagrod and Kren.

Regardless of whether or not the horn sounds, any sound of battle brings Tavik from the chapel to investigate. It also draws Grosh the ogre. Tavik gleefully enters melee, confident in his own abilities. However, as with most evil characters, Tavik is fond of "leading from the rear," ordering his orcs to attack the most capable-seeming opponent, while he picks on weaklings or good clerics. See the notes by his statistics above for more details regarding Tavik's tactics. Grosh wades into combat with no thought of defense, preferring to use charge attacks.

If Tavik is slain or if both Nagrod and Grosh the ogre are slain and the other orcs learn of this (i.e., the orcs witness their deaths or the party brandishes their heads), the orcs suffer a –2 morale penalty to all attack rolls. If all three are slain, the orcs drop their weapons and flee the ruins, never to return.

If Vortigern is present, he and Talon hang back from the melee. Vortigern knows all too well about the characters and believes that they may try to assault the keep. He has not shared this information with Tavik. Vortigern casts *protection* spells on his person and sends Talon up to the bell tower to see what is happening outside. Vortigern remains in the chapel receiving information from Talon until he sees that the battle has swung clearly in favor of one party or another. If in favor of the orcs, he emerges and casts a token *magic missile* at one of the intruders. If in favor of the party, he tries to make his escape (since he still has the amulet).

The Blessing of Thyr: Thyr shows his favor to any who serve justice on Tavik and the orcs. If his name is invoked during combat, he places all of the party under the equivalent of a *bless* spell. This lasts for the duration of the melee. This is in addition to any benefit of invoking his name in the chapel.

Lannet: Don't forget that Lannet has silently followed the party. He may provide a crucial sneak attack or dagger throw if needed to get the party out of trouble.

Repeated Forays

The characters may attack the keep and be forced to withdraw due to injuries before they have fully cleansed the keep of the orc infestation. Tavik can fortify his position by conscripting up to four more common orcs to take the place of any orcs that have fallen in combat. If Nagrod and Grosh are slain and Tavik has lost more than 12 orcs, he withdraws from the keep, reluctantly returning as a failure to the temple of Orcus in the Stoneheart Mountain dungeon. If ever reduced to less than 4 orcs or if the tide of battle turns horribly against him, Tavik flees.

If he has more than 10 orcs, Tavik orders two orcs to walk a patrol around the keep at all times. In addition, he posts two orcs at the end of the secret path. He posts four more orcs inside the outer courtyard as guards at the palisade. The guards are on full alert. If he has fewer than 10 orcs and if Vortigern is present, Tavik and his forces withdraw to the chapel, since he and Vortigern are convinced that the amulet somehow opens a secret chamber in the chapel. If Vortigern is not present, Tavik and his forces withdraw to the southwest tower.

Regardless, after an attack by the players, Tavik orders his orcs to mine some **green slime**. From this point on, all orcs have two ceramic jars containing green slime with them. They use these jars as projectiles. Anyone struck with a jar is affected by the green slime as if they touched it. The orcs also repair any damage to their fortification if they have the time, replacing sharpened logs and rebuilding the palisade.

Beneath the Keep . . .

Once the orc infestation is removed, the players may wish to explore the rooms beneath the keep. Use the material detailed in **Part One** to handle such exploration. Make sure to keep the tension level high. Eralion the shadow awaits!

Act IV: Return to Fairhill

Characters returning with the *Crucible* are hailed as champions. Shandril and Arlen are very pleased. Baran even smiles. If they return with the *Crucible* and have cleansed the keep, they are treated as heroes of legend. Arlen allows them to stay in the noble's house as if they were visiting dignitaries whenever they are in Fairhill. Glarian offers to hold a feast in their honor. Obviously, Shandril and Kath heal any injured party members, and Shandril uses her *scroll* to *raise* any one party member killed during the quest. Even Lauriel puts aside her jealousy and joins in praising the characters.

A local bard composes a song about their exploits. It contains a few glaring exaggerations, such as a part where the characters drive the vampire from the keep. If questioned about why he added the part about the vampire, the bard responds that he knows it is not true but he wanted to put to rest an old myth that was scaring the local children.

Concluding the Adventure

Returning the *Crucible* earns the party a 200 XP story bonus, as mentioned above. Returning the sword gives a 50 XP bonus to the wielder. Cleansing the above-ground portion of the keep and ridding the area of the orc raiders nets an additional 600 XP beyond the XP value of the combat with the denizens of the keep. Delving further and defeating Eralion, thus cleansing the entire keep, nets an additional 75 XP. Removing the desecration from the chapel of Thyr yields another 100 XP for the party and an additional 50 XP for any priest in the party who does so.

Tavik and Vortigern

Tavik (and Vortigern, if he was present) should have survived the adventure. Both travel on to Bard's Gate, where Vortigern hopes to learn additional information about the amulet. Tavik then heads from Bard's Gate to the temple of Orcus in the Stoneheart Mountain dungeon. If slain, Tavik returns to Fairhill once raised and uses new minions to learn the whereabouts of the party. Both attempt to take their revenge on the party. They should serve as antagonists for many more adventures.

A Bonus

In appreciation for their faithful service and loyal return of the sword, Shandril bequeaths her sword to the character who wielded it during the adventure if he or she has a Charisma of 12 or more, saying "Take this as a blessing from the bounty of the great goddess, Freya. It has done great service in your hands, and I feel it will do even greater service still."

Supplemental Information

Additional Story Ideas

The following items can be dropped into the main story at the discretion of the GM. Some are side quests, and some involve more extended roleplaying opportunities.

Vortigern's Revenge

If this adventure is being run as a continuation of *The Wizard's Amulet* and Vortigern escaped without the amulet, he is in Fairhill staying at the *Cask and Flagon*. A number of adventures could be run centered on Vortigern and Talon spying on the party and attempting to take their revenge or steal the amulet. Possibly Talon wanders the town invisibly, spying on the party. He might be shot down by the sharp-eyed Lauriel, who takes the unconscious imp to Shandril who attempts to learn its purpose. The characters are summoned and questioned. Or possibly Talon commits a crime while invisible and frames the party for it. They then needs to prove their innocence.

Lannet

Who better than a halfling thief to provide roleplaying opportunities? Have Lannet steal an item from the party. Or have Lannet seek out the party to provide him protection from someone who is after him for stealing a valuable item that he subsequently lost.

Missing Villagers

Make sure the characters hear the rumor of the missing "adventurers." Have them meet Voril and learn that his daughter, Arialle, a fledgling bard, is one of the missing young adventurers. He informs the party of the general direction in which the adventurers were traveling, pointing them toward the area of Girbolg's lair.

Fendrin's Tale

Surely the characters hear the sad tale of Fendrin. If the players successfully return with the *Crucible*, Fendrin resolves that they will be able to help him take revenge on the manticore. He does not take "no" for an answer. In fact, with all their notoriety, the villagers expect the party to aid Fendrin. After all, they drove the vampire out of the keep.

Sirya Runs Away

The town is in an uproar. Sirya, Arlen's daughter, has disappeared. She shows up either hidden in the party's room at the inn, begging to be taken along as an adventurer, or possibly she tags along behind the party when they set off after the *Crucible*. A wicked alternative is that Talon murders her and hides her body in the party's room at the inn, framing it for her murder.

Continuing the Adventure

There are a number of ways the adventure contained in this module can be continued.

Eralion's Request

This option requires modifying the information in this module. Rather than being reduced to a vile undead with a nearly shattered mind, in this alternative Eralion retains his former personality. If the characters descend into his lair, he asks them to help him restore his mortality. He sends them on an errand to somewhere dangerous to recover an item of your choosing that he requires to undo Orcus' evil curse. Possibly, he asks them to head to the Stoneheart Mountain dungeon to kill one of the evil priests responsible for providing him with the poisoned potion. See the dungeon module *The Tomb of Abysthor* (later in this book), which details that dungeon.

Arlen's Letter

If the characters successfully complete this adventure, they have won the undying friendship of Arlen, the magistrate. He tells the party of his youth as a captain of the Lyreguard in Bard's Gate and gives the party a letter, addressed to Imril, the current captain of the Lyreguard, recommending the party as trustworthy. This letter has great significance if the party heads on to Bard's Gate, as detailed in the **Necromancer Games** supplement, *Bard's Gate*. Arlen encourages the party to travel there. He says, with nostalgia, that the characters remind him of himself when he was young.

Tavik's Revenge

As mentioned above, Tavik should develop into a campaign-long nemesis. He sets into motion several nefarious agents of Orcus to exact his revenge on the party, including a famous assassin from Bard's Gate — **Noria Verilath**.

Additioanl Options

Some additional side quests that the PCs can undertake.

Arlen's Errand
(CR Varies, due to extended overland travel)

Arlen requests that the PCs travel to the Monastery of the Standing Stone and deliver a letter to Kala, the Master of the Yellow Robe. The letter is in fact a divine scroll of 3 spells that Kala asked Arlen to procure for her. Arlen does not want Shandril to know that he commissioned the scroll from a passing cleric as he does not want to hurt her feelings. So he informs the party that Shandril is not to know of their journey, telling them that the "letter" concerns her. Of course, it does not. Arlen's caution may however lead to an aura of mystery around the task. Use the wandering monster tables for overland travel, but be kind to the PCs and do not throw overly powerful monsters at them if they are being cautious. This errand will most likely take the PCs to Crimmor as well.

Lannet Gets Into (more) Trouble
(CR 3, 6 if linked to the spiders)

Once again, Lannet has pissed someone off. This time, Lannet lifted an important gem from a passing merchant. The merchant did not realize the theft until he arrived in Bard's Gate and went to deliver the gem to Duloth—the head of the black market in that city. The merchant has sent some "**agents**," headed by the rogue **Zalatha**, to Fairhill to recover the gem or kill Lannet (or both). It is possible that they will spare Lannet if he can return the jewel. The GM may decide that Lannet still has the jewel or has hidden it somewhere. Or the GM could link this adventure with the spider quest and have the gem be the item Lannet sold to the wizard, whose body is now in the spiderwebs at **Area G**. If this is done, the adventure becomes more difficult. In addition to its normal value as a precious stone, the gem—a fire opal—allows its possessor to cast either *dancing lights* or *color spray* once per day. It has a total of 20 charges and either use of the gem uses a charge. Use this encounter as a chance to roleplay and barter for Lannet's life, rather than a straight out fight.

ZALATHA   CR 2
XP 600
Male human rogue 3
LE Medium humanoid (human)
Init +8; **Perception** +9

AC 16, touch 13, flat-footed 13 (+3 armor, +3 Dex)
hp 26 (3d8+6 plus 3)
Fort +3; **Ref** +9; **Will** +4
Defensive Abilities evasion, trap sense

Speed 20 ft.
Melee dagger +6 (1d4–2/19–20) or short sword +6 (1d6–2/19–20)
Ranged light crossbow +6 (1d8/19–20)
Special Attacks rogue talents (finesse rogue), sneak attack +2d6

Str 7, **Dex** 18, **Con** 15, **Int** 11, **Wis** 16, **Cha** 11
Base Atk +2; **CMB** +0; **CMD** 13
Feats Improved Initiative, Lightning Reflexes, Point Blank Shot, Weapon Finesse
Skills Acrobatics +7 (+3 jump), Bluff +6, Climb +1, Disable Device +10, Escape Artist +1, Fly +1, Knowledge (local) +6, Perception +9 (+10 to locate traps), Ride +1, Sense Motive +9, Sleight of Hand +7, Stealth +7, Swim -5
Languages Common
SQ trapfinding +1
Combat Gear *potion of cure light wounds, potion of invisibility*; **Other Gear** studded leather armor, 2 daggers, short sword, light crossbow, 20 bolts, masterwork thieves' tools, 5 tindertwigs

TRANDA   CR 1/2
XP 200
Male half-orc warrior 2
NE Medium humanoid (human, orc)
Init +2; **Senses** darkvision 60 ft.; **Perception** +3

AC 17, touch 12, flat-footed 15 (+5 armor, +2 Dex)
hp 16 (2d10+2 plus 2)
Fort +4; **Ref** +2; **Will** +2
Defensive Abilities ferocity

Speed 20 ft.
Melee handaxe +6 (1d6+4/x3) and longspear +6 (1d8+6/x3)

Str 19, **Dex** 15, **Con** 12, **Int** 10, **Wis** 15, **Cha** 13
Base Atk +2; **CMB** +6; **CMD** 18
Feats Power Attack
Skills Acrobatics –2 (–6 jump), Climb +0, Intimidate +7, Perception +3, Ride +2, Stealth –1, Swim +0; **Racial Modifiers** +2 Intimidate
Languages Common, Orc
Combat Gear *potion of cure light wounds*; **Other Gear** scale mail, 3 handaxes, longspear, nag horse, 25 gp

GORAR   CR 1/2
XP 200
Male dwarf warrior 2
CN Medium humanoid (dwarf)
Init +1; **Senses** darkvision 60 ft.; **Perception** +0

AC 16, touch 11, flat-footed 15 (+5 armor, +1 Dex)

hp 20 (2d10+6 plus 2)
Fort +6; **Ref** +1; **Will** –1; +2 vs. poison, spells, and spell-like abilities
Defensive Abilities defensive training

Speed 20 ft.
Melee warhammer +5 (1d8+3/x3)
Ranged light hammer +5 (1d4+3)
Special Attacks hatred

Str 16, **Dex** 13, **Con** 16, **Int** 12, **Wis** 9, **Cha** 11
Base Atk +2; **CMB** +5; **CMD** 16 (16 vs. bull rush, trip)
Feats Power Attack
Skills Acrobatics –3 (–7 jump), Appraise +2 (+4 to determine the price of nonmagic items with precious metals or gemstones), Climb –1, Intimidate +4, Knowledge (nature) +2, Perception +0 (+2 to notice unusual stonework, such as traps and hidden doors in stone walls or floors), Ride +1, Stealth –2
Languages Common, Dwarven
SQ greed, hardy, slow and steady, stability, stonecunning +2
Combat Gear *potion of cure light wounds*; **Other Gear** scale mail, heavy steel shield, warhammer, 3 light hammer, 20 gp

BRUUBRAH   CR 1/2
XP 200
Male half-orc warrior 2
CE Medium humanoid (human, orc)
Init +2; **Senses** darkvision 60 ft.; **Perception** +0

AC 16, touch 12, flat-footed 14 (+4 armor, +2 Dex)
hp 20 (2d10+6 plus 2)
Fort +6; **Ref** +2; **Will** +0
Defensive Abilities ferocity

Speed 20 ft.
Melee greatsword +5 (2d6+4/19–20)

Str 17, **Dex** 14, **Con** 16, **Int** 7, **Wis** 10, **Cha** 9
Base Atk +2; **CMB** +5; **CMD** 17
Feats Power Attack
Skills Acrobatics –1 (–5 jump), Climb +0, Intimidate +5, Ride +3, Stealth –1, Swim +0; **Racial Modifiers** +2 Intimidate
Languages Orc
Combat Gear *potion of cure light wounds*; **Other Gear** hide armor, greatsword, 15 gp

Eralion's Journal (CR Varies, 3–9)

If they PCs recovered the tomes from Eralion's workroom (**Lower Tower, Level 2**) they no doubt spend some time reading them and learning new spells. Among those tomes they find a journal. It appears to have been written when Eralion was much younger.

Contents of the Journal: In addition to the customary wizardly notes, the journal tells of Eralion's acquaintance with Feriblan in Reme. It describes several journey she undertook as a young wizard, including a trip to Bard's Gate to have a staff created by Velior, a famous elven craftsman. There are many references to his god, Thyr, and details of his faith. It further tells how he came to live in Fairhill and his love for a human woman named Gethrame who is described as a priestess, though the god she worships is not named. It details how Shandril cast Gethrame out of Fairhill and blinded her with a curse. Eralion describes his anger about that event and he rails against his god, asking how a just god could allow such a thing to happen to his love. The journal tells that this rift with Shandril is what motivated Eralion to move from Fairhill and build his own keep. The PC reading the journal also gets the feeling that this event may be what led Eralion's heart to turn to darkness. The journal begins to detail the building of the keep and his anger over the loss of his love, who ran off screaming into the wilderness. Still, Eralion makes reference to Thyr, though with less zeal than earlier entries. His despair is prevalent in these subsequent entries, which grow less frequent. Then, a long entry, written in an elated tone, where he details finally locating Gethrame in a cave to the northwest of his keep. At her request, Eralion crafts for her a staff that allows her "great powers of sight" despite the incurable blindness inflicted upon her by Shandril. Eralion notes that he had to create the staff for his love, "despite the cost or consequences." The details of the creation of the staff are not given. The tone of the journal then darkens and in a later entry Eralion refers to some "foolish soothsaying," apparently casting aspersions on Gethrame's powers. Eralion then forsakes Gethrame, writing that he was forced to leave her, stating that he "could not stand to see what she had become or to hear her foolish ramblings." His last words on the topic are: "I leave her to her fate." The rest of the journal is mostly mundane, though written in an angry and pompous tone. It makes veiled reference to his desire to "live on with greater power," though it does not detail his plans, as if he is keeping secrets from his own journal. The PC reading the journal is left with the feeling that it is a chronicle not only of Eralion's life but also of his slow descent into evil and madness.

Information In Town: The PCs should be intrigued by the story of Gethrame. Certainly, learning the story behind one of the command words to Eralion's staff should interest them. The fact that she also has a staff created by Eralion allowing "great sight" might make them curious as well. If the PCs ask in town about Gethrame they may learn some of the rumors detailed above, though she is known as "the witch," not as Gethrame. Arlen knows nothing of the tale. Shandril knows it well, though she does not speak of it in detail, other than to say that Gethrame opposed the will of Freya and had to be punished. Shandril appears remorseful and states that she wished Gethrame had not forced her hand. She speaks no further of the matter. She does not know where Gethrame lives now, or if she lives at all.

Herl: If the PCs do ask around about Gethrame, they are contacted by Herl, an old half-elf. He pulls the characters aside and says that the name of Gethrame is known to him. He relates that he once loved that woman, some 90 years ago, before Eralion. But her favor did not rest on him. She scorned him in favor of Eralion. He watched and did nothing as Shandril cast Gethrame from Fairhill. He tells the party that Shandril caught Gethrame using some type of magical item to observe Shandril and the secret rituals of Freya. For that, Gethrame was blinded and cast out. Herl tells that he secretly helped Gethrame, using his powers over animals to have them lead her to a cave, when she fled in her madness. He tells that he has watched over her for the last 90 years, protecting her cave but never daring to enter or reveal his help, since he knows she does not love him. He confirms that indeed Eralion did visit Gethrame numerous times. He did not remain near her cave when Eralion came, fearing discovery of his secret vigil. On his last visit to her cave he noticed things were not as they normally were, as if there had been a disturbance within. He could hear her raising her voice in despair. He has heard that the PCs destroyed the "vampire" that lived within the keep, and, believing that to be Eralion, worries that their actions have upset Gethrame. He asks the PCs to help her and agrees to lead the characters to her cave in the woods (**Area E**). Herl cannot bring himself to aid her directly. Even if the PCs do not ask about Gethrame, the GM could still have Herl approach the PCs because he feels the destruction of Eralion has caused some distress to his love and he wishes them to make things right or help her do so.

HERL CR 3
XP 800
hp 30 (see **Area E** for details)

If the PCs, at Herl's urging, speak to Gethrame, she agrees to heal the party (if needed) and hints that she knows about Vortigern, the amulet and the story of Eralion. She also knows other local information that she will trade with the PCs. Feel free to substitute an important piece of knowledge that fits with your game world. But to gain this information the PCs must perform a service for her. She explains that her staff, which provides her with *arcane sight*, has been stolen by strange rat creatures. If the party agrees to recover the staff she will heal them. And if they return with it, she tells them the full story of Eralion which, hopefully, you have still kept secret from your players. She may also impart any

other important piece of information as you wish. This should send the characters after the rat-men (at **Area F**). They can find their warren with some difficulty, as detailed above. The rat-men fight to retain the staff but will parley with the PCs if forced. They reveal the true history of the staff. This should put the PCs in an ethical quandary. Gethrame will fulfill her bargain if the staff is returned. If she is told of the true origin of the staff she is distraught and requires the PCs to return the staff back to the rat-men. If good aligned characters butcher the rat-men without question or quarter there may be alignment penalties. This can be used as an interesting morality play and as an insight into the moral decline of Eralion.

Scaling this Adventure: You can make the adventure easier or harder (thus the sliding CR, above) depending on several factors. You can reduce the number of wererats to 6, with 2 witches and their leader. Or, you can have the PCs not fight the wererats at all, having them immediately encounter Glaathaa once they get inside the warren and have Glaathaa relate the origin of the staff before the fight. You can have Glaathaa say that she was told in a vision that the PCs would come seeking the staff. This reduces the CR and turns the adventure into more of a moral quandary than a fight. In fact, this is a good approach to take with low-level PCs who possibly couldn't handle the fight and who could use some good moral problem solving rather than hack and slash adventuring.

The Gnoll Bandits (CR 8)

A group of gnoll bandits have attacked and taken over the way station within the Stoneheart Forest, marked as the **Ruined Way Station** on the **Wilderness Map** and detailed above at **Area M**.

Adventure Hook: While the characters are in Fairhill, staying in the Noble's House (**Area 3** in Fairhill) as a result of their help to the village, a company of the Grand Duke of Westmarch's Sheriffs arrives in town, led by **Sir Erlinar**, accompanied by an impressive mounted **knight** and **6 footmen**. Sir Erlinar speaks with Arlen and, invoking the powers of the Grand Duke, indicates that he requires some men to aid them in retaking the way station and some craftsmen to begin work on logs and a gate to repair the burnt stockade.

Hopefully, the PCs volunteer to help. Certainly the populace of the village expects them to do so. If not, the Duke's men conscript eight of the town's militia. The group (again, hopefully including the PCs) then heads out to the ruined way station (**Area M**) to deal with the gnolls.

SIR ERLINAR CR 3
XP 800
hp 36 (see **Wandering Monsters**, above)

WAYMARCH KNIGHT CR 3
XP 800
hp 34 (see **Wandering Monsters**, above)

WAYMARCH FOOTMAN (6) CR 1
XP 400
hp 19 (see **Wandering Monsters**, above)

The Missing Adventurers (CR 5)

Rumors abound in Fairhill about a missing group of adventurers—a fighter, a rogue, a mage and a dwarven paladin—who set out to explore Stirge Wood and have not returned. The PCs may decide, for whatever reason, to look for them, possibly hoping to loot their bodies. Or it could be that the wizard is rumored to have an item that Lannet needs to get himself out of a jam. Perhaps Lannet stole an item and sold it to the party's wizard and now needs to get it back to its rightful owner. So the PCs have to hunt down the wizard to save Lannet's hide. If so, make sure to include an appropriate item at **Area G**, where the bodies are located. It also takes them into Stirge Wood (the local name for the Stoneheart Forest), which is a dangerous place. Follow the instructions in *The Crucible of Freya* for any forays into Stirge Wood.

The Druids' Request (CR 4)

The druids from the Grove of the Moon have recently come under attack by a **crazed owlbear**. They cannot seem to divine what has made the creature so enraged. They reluctantly resolved that it must be killed. They have heard of the presence of the PCs (and their success in the keep) and have sent a druid to Fairhill to request the PCs to come to the grove and there to ask them to kill the beast. For every night that the PCs camp within 2 miles of the grove, there is a 1 in 6 chance that they either encounter the owlbear or they find its tracks and can follow those (DC 10 Survival check to track) to its current location. This crazed owlbear is in fact the mate of the owlbear (at **Area C**) and if the crazed creature is slain, the other owlbear may track the PCs.

OWLBEAR   **CR 4**
XP 1,200
hp 47 (*Pathfinder Roleplaying Game Bestiary* "Owlbear")

Valkyria's Quest (CR 5)

If one of the PCs grasps *Valkyria*, sees a vision of Freya and is invited to worship Freya (as detailed in the *Valkyria* description in the **Appendix**), Freya may send the PC on a quest to prove his or her worth. Or, if the PC decides to take a level of experience next time he or she goes up a level as a cleric of Freya, Freya may require the PC to complete a quest. In either event, Freya (who hates spiders) sends the PCs to eradicate a den of spiders (the spiders at **Area G**). Valkyria, through divine connection to Freya, points the way to the spiders like a divining rod points to water if the PC grasps the sword, holds it out in front of her, speaks the words "Freya guide me" and closes her eyes. This quest takes the PCs into the Stoneheart Forest and includes all the perils of entering those woods.

Rival Adventuring Party (CR 6)

Another adventuring party has come to town, led by their charismatic ranger, **Nathiel**. They may compete with your PCs for some of the fame and fortune. Perhaps setting up an interesting rivalry.

NATHIEL   **CR 1**
XP 400
Male half-elf ranger 2
CN Medium humanoid (elf, human)
Init +3; **Senses** low-light vision; **Perception** +9

AC 15, touch 13, flat-footed 12 (+2 armor, +3 Dex)
hp 16 (2d10)
Fort +3; **Ref** +6; **Will** +2; +2 vs. enchantments
Immune sleep

Speed 30 ft.
Melee shortsword +1 (1d6+1/19–20) and shortsword +1 (1d6+1/19–20)
Special Attacks combat styles (two-weapon combat), favored enemy (goblinoids +2)

Str 12, **Dex** 16, **Con** 10, **Int** 13, **Wis** 14, **Cha** 18
Base Atk +2; **CMB** +3; **CMD** 16
Feats Skill Focus (Knowledge [nature]), Two-Weapon Defense, Two-Weapon Fighting
Skills Acrobatics +4, Bluff +4 (+6 vs. goblinoids), Climb +5, Handle Animal +8, Heal +6, Knowledge (geography) +6 (+8 vs. goblinoids), Knowledge (nature) +9 (+11 vs. goblinoids), Perception +9 (+11 vs. goblinoids), Sense Motive +3 (+5 vs. goblinoids), Stealth +8, Survival +7 (+9 vs. goblinoids, +8 to track), Swim +5; **Racial Modifiers** +2 Perception
Languages Common, Dwarven, Elven
SQ elf blood, track, wild empathy
Combat Gear *potion of cure light wounds*; **Other Gear** masterwork leather armor, 2 short swords, 2 belt pouches, flint and steel, backpack, bedroll, 3 days rations, waterskin

JARRA   **CR 2**
XP 600
Female human sorcerer 3
LN Medium humanoid (human)
Init +2; **Perception** +3

AC 13, touch 13, flat-footed 11 (+1 deflection, +2 Dex)
hp 20 (3d6+3 plus 3)
Fort +2; **Ref** +3; **Will** +4

Speed 30 ft.
Melee mwk quarterstaff +1 (1d6–1)
Ranged mwk light crossbow +4 (1d8/19–20)
Spells Known (CL 3rd; melee touch +0, ranged touch +3):
1st (6/day)—*charm person* (DC 14), *identify*[B], *mage armor*, *magic missile*
0 (at will)— *detect magic*, *disrupt undead*, *light*, *mage hand*, *read magic*
Bloodline Arcane

Str 8, **Dex** 15, **Con** 12, **Int** 14, **Wis** 12, **Cha** 16
Base Atk +1; **CMB** +0; **CMD** 13
Feats Alertness, Eschew Materials[B], Scribe Scroll, Skill Focus (Use Magic Device)
Skills Craft (alchemy) +8, Knowledge (arcana) +8, Knowledge (local) +4, Linguistics +3, Perception +3, Sense Motive +3, Spellcraft +8, Use Magic Device +12
Languages Common, Draconic, Elven, Orc
SQ arcane bond (masterwork quarterstaff), metamagic adept (1/day)
Gear masterwork quarterstaff, masterwork light crossbow, 20 bolts, *ring of protection +1*, spell component pouch, backpack, bedroll, 5 days rations, 37 gp

GARIELA   **CR 2**
XP 600
Female elf barbarian 1/bard 1/rogue 1
NE Medium humanoid (elf)
Init +2; **Senses** low-light vision; **Perception** +9

AC 15, touch 12, flat-footed 13 (+3 armor, +2 Dex)
hp 17 (1d12–2 plus 1d8–2 plus 1d8–2 plus 3)
Fort +0; **Ref** +6; **Will** +3; +2 vs. enchantments
Immune sleep

Speed 40 ft.
Melee longsword +4 (1d8+3/19–20)
Special Attacks bardic performance 5 rounds/day (countersong, distraction, fascinate [1 targets, DC 11], inspire courage +1, rage (4 rounds/day), sneak attack +1d6
Spells Known (CL 1st; melee touch +4, ranged touch +3):
1st (2/day)—*charm person* (DC 12), *comprehend languages*
0 (at will)— *dancing lights*, *ghost sound* (DC 11), *lullaby* (DC 11), *open/close* (DC 11)

Str 17, **Dex** 15, **Con** 7, **Int** 14, **Wis** 12, **Cha** 13
Base Atk +1; **CMB** +4; **CMD** 16
Feats Skill Focus (Perform [sing]), Toughness
Skills Acrobatics +2 (+6 jump), Bluff +6, Diplomacy +7, Disguise +5, Knowledge (arcana) +8, Linguistics +6, Perception +9 (+10 to locate traps), Perform (sing) +10, Perform (string instruments) +7, Sense Motive +6, Sleight of Hand +6, Spellcraft +6 (+8 to determine the properties of a magic item), Stealth +8; **Racial Modifiers** +2 Perception
Languages Common, Draconic, Elven, Gnome
SQ bardic knowledge, elven magic, fast movement, trapfinding +1
Gear masterwork studded leather armor, longsword, masterwork harp, backpack, bedroll, 50 ft silk rope, hammer,

6 spikes, flint and steel, 4 torches, 2 days rations, waterskin, 15 gp

DARKRAL
XP 600
CR 2

Male elf monk 1/sorcerer 2
LN Medium humanoid (elf)
Init +5; **Senses** low-light vision; **Perception** +8

AC 18, touch 18, flat-footed 12 (+5 Dex, +1 dodge, +2 Wis)
hp 20 (1d8 plus 2d6 plus 5)
Fort +2; **Ref** +7; **Will** +7; +2 vs. enchantments
Immune sleep

Speed 30 ft.
Melee mwk nunchaku +3 (1d6+1) or unarmed strike +2 (1d6+1)
Ranged mwk longbow +7 (1d8/x3)
Special Attacks flurry of blows –1/–1, stunning fist (stun, DC 13)
Bloodline Spell-Like Abilities (CL 2nd; melee touch +2)
6/day—*touch of destiny* (+1)
Spells Known (CL 2nd; melee touch +2, ranged touch +6):
1st (5/day)—*mage armor, protection from chaos*
0 (at will)—*detect magic, disrupt undead, mage hand, read magic, resistance*
Bloodline Destined

Str 13, **Dex** 20, **Con** 10, **Int** 13, **Wis** 15, **Cha** 16
Base Atk +1; **CMB** +2; **CMD** 20
Feats Dodge, Eschew Materials, Improved Unarmed Strike, Mobility, Stunning Fist, Toughness
Skills Acrobatics +9, Diplomacy +4, Escape Artist +9, Knowledge (arcana) +5, Knowledge (history) +5, Knowledge (religion) +5, Perception +8, Sense Motive +6, Spellcraft +5 (+7 to determine the properties of a magic item), Stealth +9, Swim +5; Racial Modifiers +2 Perception
Languages Common, Draconic, Elven
SQ elven magic
Combat Gear *scroll of dispel magic*; **Other Gear** masterwork nunchaku, masterwork longbow, 20 arrows, backpack, wool blanket, 3 days rations, waterskin, spell component pouch, 4 gp

KORUNGRA
CR 2

Male half-orc cleric 1/rogue 2
CN Medium humanoid (human, orc)
Init +2; **Senses** darkvision 60 ft.; **Perception** +6
Aura evil

AC 16, touch 13, flat-footed 13 (+2 armor, +2 Dex, +1 dodge, +1 shield)
hp 24 (1d8+2 plus 2d8+4)
Fort +4; **Ref** +5; Will +4
Defensive Abilities evasion, ferocity

Speed 30 ft.
Melee mwk dagger +4 (1d4+2/19-20) or mwk light mace +4 (1d6+2)
Ranged light crossbow +3 (1d8/19-20)
Special Attacks channel positive energy 3/day (1d6, DC 10), sneak attack +1d6
Domain Spell-Like Abilities (CL 1st; melee touch +3):
5/day—*copycat* (1 round), *touch of darkness* (1 round)
Spells Prepared (CL 1st; melee touch +3, ranged touch +3):
1st (2/day)—*disguise self, obscuring mist*ᴮ, *sanctuary* (DC 13)
0 (at will)—*detect magic, read magic, resistance*
D Domain Spell **Domains** Darkness, Trickery

Str 15, **Dex** 15, **Con** 15, **Int** 10, **Wis** 15, **Cha** 11
Base Atk +1; **CMB** +3; **CMD** 16

Feats Blind-Fightᴮ, Dodge, Mobility
Skills Acrobatics +7, Bluff +4, Climb +5, Disable Device +5, Disguise +4, Escape Artist +6, Fly +1, Intimidate +6, Knowledge (local) +4, Knowledge (religion) +5, Linguistics +4, Perception +6 (+7 to locate traps), Ride +1, Sense Motive +6, Sleight of Hand +5, Stealth +6, Swim +1; **Racial Modifiers** +2 Intimidate
Languages Common, Giant, Orc
SQ rogue talents (quick disable), trapfinding +1
Combat Gear 3 *scrolls of cure light wounds*; **Other Gear** masterwork leather armor, light steel shield, masterwork light mace, masterwork dagger, light crossbow, 15 bolts, masterwork thieves' tools, wooden holy symbol, backpack, 50 ft silk rope, grappling hook, hammer, 5 spikes, bedroll, 5 days rations, mirror.

The Dignitary's Agents (CR 5)

The visiting politician who abandoned the gem in the Noble's house (**Area 3** in Fairhill), has sent several agents to Fairhill to retrieve the gem. This could get interesting if the PCs are currently staying in the house as a reward for their success with the ruined keep.

FLET
XP 800
CR 3

Male halfling rogue 4
CN Small humanoid (halfling)
Init +8; **Perception** +11

AC 18, touch 15, flat-footed 14 (+3 armor, +4 Dex, +1 size)
hp 27 (4d8+4)
Fort +3; **Ref** +9; **Will** +4; +2 vs. fear
Defensive Abilities evasion, trap sense, uncanny dodge

Speed 25 ft.
Melee mwk rapier +9 (1d4/18–20)
Ranged shortbow +8 (1d4/x3)
Special Attacks sneak attack +2d6, rogue talents (combat trick [weapon finesse])

Str 10, **Dex** 19, **Con** 12, **Int** 13, **Wis** 14, **Cha** 13
Base Atk +3; **CMB** +2; **CMD** 16
Feats Fleet, Improved Initiative, Weapon Finesse
Skills Acrobatics +13 (+9 jump), Appraise +8, Bluff +5, Climb +6, Disable Device +11, Disguise +5, Escape Artist +11, Fly +6, Intimidate +6, Knowledge (local) +8, Linguistics +5, Perception +11 (+13 to locate traps), Sense Motive +6, Sleight of Hand +11, Stealth +15, Use Magic Device +5; **Racial Modifiers** +2 Acrobatics, +2 Climb, +2 Perception
Languages Common, Halfling
SQ fearless, rogue talents (fast stealth), trapfinding +2
Combat Gear *potion of cure moderatewounds*, *potion of glibness, wand of summon monster I* (10 charges); **Other Gear** masterwork studded leather armor, masterwork rapier, shortbow, 15 arrows, masterwork thieves' tools, 36 pp, 300 gp, 12 sp, 5 gems (valued at 8, 20, 50, 60 and 110 gp)

VORGYA
XP 600
CR 2

Female half-elf rogue 3
CN Medium humanoid (elf, human)
Init +7; **Senses** low-light vision; **Perception** +13

AC 15, touch 13, flat-footed 12 (+2 armor, +3 Dex)
hp 27 (3d8+9)
Fort +4; **Ref** +6; **Will** +3; +2 vs. enchantments
Defensive Abilities evasion, trap sense; **Immune** sleep

Speed 35 ft.

Melee dagger +5 (1d4/19–20) or punching dagger +5 (1d4/x3)
Ranged light crossbow +5 (1d8/19–20)
Special Attacks rogue talents (combat trick [weapon finesse]), sneak attack +2d6

Str 10, **Dex** 17, **Con** 17, **Int** 11, **Wis** 14, **Cha** 9
Base Atk +2; **CMB** +2; **CMD** 15
Feats Fleet, Improved Initiative, Skill Focus (Perception), Weapon Finesse
Skills Acrobatics +9, Appraise +4, Bluff +3, Climb +4, Disable Device +8, Disguise +3, Escape Artist +9, Intimidate +3, Knowledge (local) +4, Linguistics +4, Perception +13 (+14 to locate traps), Sense Motive +6, Sleight of Hand +9, Stealth +9, Use Magic Device +3; **Racial Modifiers** +2 Perception
Languages Common, Elven
SQ elf blood, trapfinding +1
Gear leather armor, dagger, punching dagger, light crossbow, 20 bolts, masterwork thieves' tools, 216 gp, 4 gems (valued at 8, 10, 12 and 40gp).

The agents will stop at nothing to obtain the gem. However, they do not necessarily use violent means. They could, if foiled, pay the party for the gem. They will pay up to 750 gp.

Creating a New Cloak (CR Varies, 7–10+)

Shandril's cape of winter wolf fur was in the shrine when it was set on fire by the orcs. She wants to make a new one. She requests the characters obtain a pelt for her. However, since the animals are sacred to Freya, the party must capture one and sacrifice it. She cautions them that any damage to the creature ruins the pelt—it must be captured without injury. The animal must be *blessed*, sprinkled with holy water and then sacrificed after a proper ritual at the new moon. The body of the wolf must be preserved (possibly by magic) and returned to Shandril where she can complete the skinning of the animal. Shandril provides a *scroll of bless* and 2 vials of holy water to the party. She indicates that winter wolves are rumored to be found in the hills between the two rivers. She points out the general area on their map: the hex containing the foothills of the Stoneheart Mountains (the hex containing **Area I**), the foothills directly to the south of that hex, and the hexes containing **Areas B** and **D**.

Once the PCs arrive in the hex containing the winter wolves, they have a 1 in 10 chance per hour of encountering **1d4+1 winter wolves**. In addition, any PCs with the Track feat can make a DC 15 Perception check to find winter wolf tracks leading to their lair, detailed at **Area I**.

Experience Award: Successfully completing this task by returning a perfect pelt earns the PCs full XP for the wolf captured as well as any wolves defeated. Plus, grant them a 1,000 XP story award. If they return with anything less than a perfect pelt they do not gain the story award and only earn half XP for the captured wolf. If, by some miracle, the PCs capture the alpha male winter wolf, increase the story award to 2,000 XP in addition to the XP value for the wolves. Though, killing winter wolves might trouble the druids at **Area J**…

WINTER WOLF   CR 5
XP 1,600
hp 57 (*Pathfinder Roleplaying Game Bestiary* "Worg, Winter Wolf")

The Stirge Menace (CR Varies, up to 9+)

An emissary from Crimmor has heard of the valor of the party and beseeches their aid against their new problem—a rash of stirge attacks! This leads to the PCs traveling to Crimmor and eventually finding the stirge lair—a cave complex filled with stirges, where a twisted and half-mad elf mage/druid resides (**Area H**). This adventure could almost become a mini campaign in its own right, thwarting the machinations of the master of stirges as he sends his creatures out to plague Crimmor. Possibly, the PCs are in Crimmor when the village is attacked by **48 stirges** and they fight heroically as 20 or more commoners die in the process. Perhaps the best way to run this encounter is to break the stirges into 4 groups of 12 stirges each. Each dozen stirges is a CR 6 encounter. Then the PCs have to trek into the forest to fight even more stirges in their caves. But while they are there, a large group of stirges is attacking Fairhill. The PCs must then retrieve the *baton of stirge control* and restore order, possibly even having to kill the deranged wizard in the process.

STIRGES   CR 1/2
XP 200
hp 5 (*Pathfinder Roleplaying Game Bestiary* "Stirge")

THE TOMB OF ABYSTHOR

Introduction

North of the city of Bard's Gate, in the hills of the Stoneheart Mountains, lie the ruins of twin shrines dedicated to Thyr and Muir — the God of Justice and the Goddess of Virtue and Paladinhood. Near the ruined shrines lies a series of catacombs used as burial halls for the followers of Thyr and Muir. Long abandoned, these catacombs are now home to various evil creatures. The complex has come to be known as the Stoneheart Mountain Dungeon.

This module details the entire Stoneheart Mountain Dungeon and is designed to challenge characters of 2nd to 8th level (with the deepest areas suitable for even higher level characters).

As with all **Frog God Games** products, the dungeon and the wilderness area surrounding it can be transplanted easily into any existing campaign. The specific gods used herein — Thyr and Muir — can be replaced by any other pair of lawful good deities related to paladins, or even merged and replaced with one lawful good deity. The Valley of the Shrines can be placed in the foothills a short distance away from any city in your campaign that has an accompanying temple dedicated to the lawful good gods. The gods you choose, however, should be minor deities in your campaign so that the themes of decay and decline can be maintained. Orcus, the evil demon-prince, can be replaced with any evil god prevalent in your campaign that has a connection with undead. Don't replace Tsathogga unless your campaign just happens to have another demon frog god.

History

In ages past, two vast temples to Thyr and Muir were erected in Bard's Gate at the founding of that great city that still stands today. The priestly followers of these noble gods erected smaller duplicates of the twin temples in a small, secluded valley to the north of the city, adjacent to a lake of crystalline clarity. This valley became known as the Valley of the Shrines. In the nearby hills they also carved burial halls to house their fallen heroes and worshipers. For years the worship of Thyr and Muir thrived, producing heroes and paladins of legend, some of whom are entombed in the burial halls.

But new gods came, replacing the older gods. And the worship of Thyr and Muir in the secluded valley — both demanding deities — waned in favor of the more liberal gods of song, craft and commerce in the city of Bard's Gate. Unable to maintain both the twin temples in Bard's Gate and the complex in the Valley of the Shrines, the priests of Thyr and Muir sealed the northern shrines in the valley and returned their worship to the temples in the city. Abandoned, the burial halls still remained sacred places, and small groups of pilgrims continued to make treks to the sealed temples to pay respect to their fallen predecessors and to peer into the crystalline lake.

As the years passed, the shrines in the northern valley increasingly fell to disuse and ruin. Only a handful of devoted priests, led by the high priest Abysthor, were left to continue the elaborate rituals of their gods. Even the great twin temples in Bard's Gate began to deteriorate. Despite Abysthor's devotion, his temple and the worship of his gods in general waned. In his final years, Abysthor spent many hours in the main temple in Bard's Gate

The Levels of the Stoneheart Mountain Dungeon

Entrance Level: The Burial Halls of Thyr and Muir
Level 1: The Upper Caves
Level 2: The Lesser Tombs and Dark Natasha's Lair
Level 2A: Balcoth's Lair and the Priest Barracks
Level 3: The Greater Burial Chambers
Level 4: The New Temple of Orcus
Level 5: The Great Cavern and the Temple of the Frog
Level 5A: Tomb, Blood and Stone
Level 6: The Deep Caverns

in communion with his deity. Declaring he had received a great vision, he traveled alone — aged and infirm — to the Valley of the Shrines, claiming he would return soon and that the glory of Thyr and Muir would be restored. Abysthor never returned. Some said he had gone there to die and had done so alone because no other priest could cast the spells necessary to consecrate him properly. Many groups of priests followed after him, though none could brave the corruption that had infested the burial halls since they had been abandoned.

Abysthor's failed quest was taken as a sign of decline. It has been some twenty years since Abysthor disappeared. Only a handful of priests remain in the temples in Bard's Gate, their cavernous temples falling to disuse, bereft of worshipers.

For the GM

The physical ruin of the shrines and burial halls in the Valley of the Shrines is by far the least of the corruption of the once-holy sanctuaries. In the great caves beneath the burial halls, the tsathar, inhuman priests of the foul god Tsathogga, long ago raised a temple to their hideous demon-frog god. More vile still, a contingent of priests of Orcus — the evil demon-god of the undead — recently came some ten years ago from the legendary dungeon of Rappan Athuk to corrupt the burial halls and exploit the location as a base of operations for further expansion of their evil cult. The followers of the two evil gods have reached an uneasy truce. Both, however, seek a power even darker still — the power of a legendary Black Monolith rumored to be hidden somewhere in these caverns, sealed away long ago by an ancient power.

In addition to these priests of evil, others inside the dungeon have their own agendas. "Dark Natasha," a renegade drow sorceress, seeks refuge from the sun and a place to practice her demonic conjurations. Balcoth, an undead mage from another plane, has also taken up residence in the dungeon. Neither of these two has yet joined the priests of Orcus.

Beneath all of this lies a power that none of the present or prior occupants — save one — has yet discovered: a *Chamber of Earth Blood* that holds the power of the Stoneheart Mountains themselves. Abysthor was told of this chamber by Thyr and instructed that its power could be used to purge the halls of evil and restore the temples to their former glory. Abysthor discovered this chamber when he descended into the depths of the caverns beneath the burial halls. In the gloom and evil of the great cavern beneath the halls, Abysthor encountered the vile tsathar and their high priest, Lokaug. Abysthor learned of the Black Monolith from Thyr, and of Lokaug's desire to find it and tap its power for his own evil ends. In the depths of the dungeon Abysthor built for himself a final resting place. But he knew he had one last task to complete — he needed to prevent either Lokaug or the priests of Orcus from accessing the Black Monolith. Dutifully, Abysthor warded his tomb against evil. Grasping his staff, he set out to find the legendary monolith. But Abysthor's strength failed him. He was ensnared by the dark magic of the monolith and now lies trapped in the lowest chambers of the dungeon — his prepared burial hall empty. He did, however, successfully thwart Lokaug and the priests of Orcus from discovering either the *earth blood* or the Black Monolith. But his wards will not stand forever…

A GM might wonder why all these groups would build their temples at this location. It is not uncommon for holy sites to be built unknowingly on sites that held power in antiquity. Such is the case here, as a brief timeline explains. The area where the dungeon is now located is the location of the earth spirit of these mountains (see **Level 2, Area 6**), which exudes a subtle but powerful aura of magic. In addition, many centuries ago, the earth god created the *Chamber of Earth's Blood* (**Level 5A, Area 13**) and his priests warded it. They disappeared. Next to arrive were the priests of Thyr and Muir who, sensing the power in the mountains, chose this site for their burial halls. Long after that — and unknown to either group — Lokaug and his tsathar were drawn here by the same earth power and erected their foul temple on **Level 5**. The tsathar had no contact with the burial halls above them and no knowledge of the *Chamber of Earth's Blood*. Then, as the power of Thyr and Muir waned, evil arose. Deific demonic forces placed the Black Monolith here, hopeful that their evil servants and followers would find it and use it as a *gate* to allow access to this plane. Lokaug became aware of this evil presence, though he could not locate it. Orcus commanded his priests to search for the monolith, and so some ten years ago Koraashag arrived with his contingent and built the evil temple to Orcus on **Level 4** and corrupted the burial halls. Thus, what began as a source of earth power has over the ages drawn many groups.

Dungeon Politics

The dungeon, in addition to being a collection of evil creatures, is a dynamic setting. The priests of Tsathogga run their vile temple — the Temple of the Frog. They seek the Black Monolith and have the best access to the level in which the monolith is located. The priests of Orcus are rather new to the dungeon and have come here from the famed dungeon of Rappan Athuk to attempt to locate the Black Monolith as well. Thus, the two evil groups — though not openly in conflict — both seek the same thing. The priests of Orcus are trying to find a "back way" to the level that contains the monolith, and thus have constructed some barracks on **Level 2A** in addition to their temple on **Level 4**.

The leaders of the two groups of priests — Lokaug, the high priest of Tsathogga, and Koraashag, the high priest of Orcus — have established a détente of sorts, though each secretly searches for the monolith, hoping the other does not find it first. In addition to their desire to locate the monolith, the priests of Orcus have grand plans of expansion and covet the use the upper levels and their newly created Font of Bones to lead an undead army against Bard's Gate — to once and for all destroy the temples of Thyr and Muir.

Add to this mix Balcoth and Dark Natasha — two powerful individuals with their own goals and desires — and it is clear that the dungeon denizens are at a tense standoff. All intelligent residents are affiliated in some fashion with the main groups. Either group (including Balcoth and Natasha as well) may enlist the PCs' aid against one of the other factions.

Use this Machiavellian environment to spice up a traditional dungeon crawl with cunning plans, elaborate subterfuges and chances for roleplaying.

Using a Dungeon

Dungeons are classic settings for heroic swords and sorcery adventuring. Turning your party loose in a dungeon to explore it and cleanse it of evil (and treasure) is a time-honored tradition. Certainly the Stoneheart Mountain Dungeon is loaded with evil and treasure sufficient to satisfy the lusts of any bold adventurer.

Dungeons, however, do not need to be tied to "hack and slash" adventuring. Instead, the best use of a dungeon is as a dramatic setting for storytelling. Rather than have your players simply bash in door after door looking for monsters and loot, design a purpose for the party to delve into the dungeon. Give them a quest or a goal to give them direction and a sense of accomplishment. It keeps their dungeon adventuring focused and keeps the tension high — there is a risk of failing to accomplish their mission.

There are a number of such story ideas for the Stoneheart Mountain Dungeon, from less to more difficult: recovering the holy tracts from the chambers beneath the shrine of Thyr, liberating a magic weapon from the stores beneath the shrine of Muir, retrieving the *Stone of Tircople* and the *Chalice of Elanir,* recovering the fabled *axe of blood* or even destroying the Black Monolith and freeing Abysthor himself. There are appropriate tasks for parties of all alignments and levels.

Standard Dungeon Features

Unless otherwise noted, the ruined temples and the Stoneheart Mountain Dungeon share the following features:

Dungeon Walls and Ceilings: The dungeon can be divided into carved sections and cavern sections. In the carved sections, passages are smoothly carved and run 8 to 12 feet in height. Interior masonry walls are generally 1 to 2 feet thick (hardness 8; hp 90–120 per 10-ft. section; Break DC 35). The rooms in carved sections average 10 to 15 feet in height. Larger rooms may be 20 feet high. Walls in the cavern sections are rough and somewhat slick from mineral deposits. The passages in cavern sections range from 6 to 10 feet in height, varying with the width of the passage. Rooms in cavern sections vary widely in height, normally being a minimum of 8 feet high, though larger rooms are as high as they are wide, or higher. All cavern sections have stalactites and stalagmites, some of which are joined into columns.

Climbing: Climbing a wall in a carved section is DC 20, unless otherwise specified. Climbing a wall in a cavern section is DC 15, unless otherwise specified.

Doors: All doors in the dungeon are locked and made of iron-reinforced wood. They tend to swing shut 1d4 rounds after they are opened.

Iron Reinforced Wooden Doors: 2 in. thick; hardness 5; hp 20; Break DC 23; Disable Device DC 25.

Secret Doors: All secret doors are made of stone and must be opened by a hidden latch to the right of the secret door. A counterweight opens the doors when the latch is pulled, and the same counterweight closes the door two rounds after it is opened.

Stone Secret Doors: 4 in. thick; hardness 8; hp 60; Break DC 30; Perception DC 20.

Stone Sarcophagi: Some rooms contain stone sarcophagi. Unless indicated otherwise, they have the following characteristics:

Stone Sarcophagus: 4 in. thick; hardness 8; hp 60; Break DC 30; DC 20 Str check to lift the lid.

Noise: Except for the levels occupied by humanoids (**Levels 2A, 4** and **5**), most of the dungeon is very quiet. Noise echoes throughout the level. Though the sounds are disorienting to the players, the denizens of the dungeon have grown used to identifying the location of such noises. All denizens of the dungeon gain a +2 circumstance bonus on Perception checks to hear noises, except on **Level 4** and the tsathar-occupied portions of **Level 5**, both of which have far too much commotion to allow such a modifier.

Lighting: Cavern sections are unlit, since they are mostly occupied by creatures with darkvision. The only exception is **Level 5**, which is dimly lit by the strange phosphorescence of the lake and the evil glow of the statue of Tsathogga. Carved sections all include sconces and torch holders. Normally these are empty or the torches unlit unless the area is occupied by humanoids (such as portions of **Level 2A** and all of **Level 4**). In that case, the torches are lit. **Level 4**, in addition, is lit with a hellish glow from the braziers of the temple of Orcus.

Monsters and Statistics

Full details of new monsters can be found in the **Appendices**. Standard monsters are given in an abbreviated stat block, with citation for where more information can be found.

A Note on Wandering Monsters: This module provides wandering monster tables. These tables are meant as a guide for possible encounters, reflecting the frequency and type of creatures that can be found roaming a level or an area. You should not allow a random table to dictate your game session. If you feel the result indicated is too challenging for your particular group, feel free to discard or reroll the result, or simply decide that the creatures watch the players rather than attack. The tables are provided as an aid, not as a requirement.

The Wilderness Areas

The **Wilderness Map** depicts the Valley of the Shrines, which lies in the foothills of the Stoneheart Mountains to the northwest of the city of Bard's Gate, as well as the wilderness area surrounding the Valley.

The vale north of Bard's Gate and the Valley of the Shrine is verdant green, dotted with birch and pine. The foothills of the Stoneheart Mountains in this region are rough, with sharp exposed rock. The mountains themselves are rougher still, making travel difficult. Because the region is so lush, even the foothill areas that are not marked as forested are wooded with pine and birch. It rains frequently and water is plentiful in the area surrounding the Valley. In the colder months, snow caps the tips of the Stoneheart Mountains. The nearby forest at the northwest end of the Valley has long been known as the Forest of the Faithful, since it contains the Burial Halls of Thyr and Muir. Now, however, it has fallen under the corruption brought by the priests of Orcus.

Acolytes and Lesser Priest of Orcus: This group consists of **3 acolytes** and **1 lesser priest of Orcus**. They are either heading to or returning from further desecrating the shrines in the valley.

Priests of Orcus and Font of Bones Skeletons: This group is on a significant mission from the evil temple of Orcus on **Level 4** of the dungeon, either making contact with the orc bands in the surrounding area or parlaying with the lesser gibbering orb at **Area 11**.

ACOLYTE OF ORCUS   **CR 2**
XP 600
hp 17 (see **Level 4**, **Area 1**)

ETTIN   **CR 6**
XP 2,400
hp 65 (*Pathfinder Roleplaying Game Bestiary* "Ettin")

FONT SKELETONS   **CR 1**
XP 400
hp 11 (see the **Appendix**)

GHAST (ADVANCED GHOUL)   **CR 2**
XP 600
hp 17 (see **Level 2**, **Area 21**)

GHOUL   **CR 1**
XP 400
hp 13 (*Pathfinder Roleplaying Game Bestiary* "Ghoul")

GOBLIN   **CR 1/3**
XP 135
hp 6 (see the *Pathfinder Roleplaying Game Bestiary* "Goblin")

GOBLIN LEADER   **CR 3**
XP 800
Male goblin rogue 4 (*Pathfinder Roleplaying Game Bestiary* "Goblin")
NE Small humanoid (goblinoid)
Init +5; **Senses** darkvision 60 ft.; **Perception** +9

AC 19, touch 16, flat-footed 14 (+3 armor, +5 Dex, +1 size)
hp 29 (4d8+4 plus 4)
Fort +2; **Ref** +9; **Will** +1
Defensive Abilities evasion, trap sense +1, uncanny dodge

Speed 30 ft.

Wandering Monsters

When the PCs travel in the area depicted in the Wilderness Map, check for a wandering monster every 3 hours or every time the party enters a different hex on the wilderness map. An encounter occurs on 1–4 on 1d20.

Roll the result on the following table on 1d6 with the following cumulative modifiers:

+1 in the northwest hex of the Valley of the Shrines (which contains part of the forest), +1 in a hill or foothill hex, +2 in a low mountain hex, +3 in a mountain hex, +2 in a forested hex, +2 if at night.

1D6 (+ MODIFIERS)	RESULT
1	**Special**. See below
2	**2d4 goblins**, 50% chance they are led by **1 goblin leader**
3	**2d4 stirges** (2d8 at night)
4	A group of **2 acolytes of Orcus** led by a **lesser priest of Orcus**
5	**2d6 wolves**. If at night they are accompanied by **1d2+1 worgs**
6	**2d4 ghouls**, if more than 4 ghouls there is a 25% chance they are accompanied by **1d2 ghasts**
7	**2d6 giant spiders**
8	**Brundle the OneEyed Troll**. See **Area 7**, below
9	**2 priests of Orcus** from the dungeon accompanied by **1d8+4 font skeletons**
10	**1d2 manticores**
11	An **ettin**
12	**1d3 wyverns**
13	The **lesser gibbering orb**. See **Area 11**, below

Special: The characters possibly encounter another adventuring party or a band of mercenaries; or possibly they have a sighting of Imril (the Captain of the Lyreguard from *Bard's Gate*) and a few of his elite guard on griffons flying overhead or possibly a sighting of what might be a wyvern or a black dragon.

Melee mwk dagger +10 (1d3+1/19–20)
Ranged mwk shortbow +10 (1d4/x3)
Special Attacks sneak attack +2d6, rogue talents (finesse rogue)

Str 12, **Dex** 20, **Con** 13, **Int** 8, **Wis** 10, **Cha** 10
Base Atk +3; **CMB** +7; **CMD** 18
Feats Agile Maneuvers, Alertness, Weapon Finesse[B]
Skills Acrobatics +12, Bluff +6, Climb +6, Disable Device +12, Escape Artist +10, Perception +9, Ride +9, Sense Motive +9, Stealth +20; **Racial Modifiers** +4 Ride, +4 Stealth
Languages Goblin
SQ rogue talents (fast stealth), trapfinding (+2)
Combat Gear *potion of cure light wounds, potion of*

invisibility; **Other Gear** masterwork studded leather, masterwork dagger, masterwork shortbow, 40 arrows, 1d4 sp, 2d4 cp

LESSER PRIESTS OF ORCUS   CR 4
XP 1,200
hp 55 (see **Level 4**, **Area 2**)

MANTICORES   CR 5
XP 1,600
hp 57 (*Pathfinder Roleplaying Game Bestiary* "Manticore")

PRIESTS OF ORCUS   CR 5
XP 1,600
hp 39 (see **Level 4**, **Area 8**)

SPIDERS, GIANT   CR 1
XP 400
hp 16 (*Pathfinder Roleplaying Game Bestiary* "Spider, Giant")

STIRGE   CR 1/2
XP 200
hp 5 (*Pathfinder Roleplaying Game Bestiary* "Stirge")

WOLF   CR 1
XP 400
hp 13 (*Pathfinder Roleplaying Game Bestiary* "Wolf")

WORG   CR 2
XP 600
hp 26 (*Pathfinder Roleplaying Game Bestiary* "Worg")

WYVERN   CR 6
XP 2,400
hp 73 (*Pathfinder Roleplaying Game Bestiary* "Wyvern")

Encounter Areas

The following areas are indicated on the Wilderness Map.

1. Ancient Path

This path winds its way from the floor of the vale north of Bard's Gate through the foothills up to the Valley of the Shrines. At points the path is steep and consists of stone stairs cut into the side of the hills. This path was made to facilitate pilgrims or groups of worshipers from Bard's Gate reaching the shrines. It is now rarely traveled and the beginning of the path from the vale below is difficult to find, requiring a DC 15 Perception check to find the two weathered white marble obelisks that mark the start of the path. Even today, a feeling of calm blankets those who travel the ancient path to the valley of the shrines, as if Thyr and Muir yet watch over those who would travel to their holy place. At the end of the path — at the entrance to the Valley of the Shrines — is another pair of weathered obelisks of white marble.

2. Shrines to Thyr and Muir (CR Varies, 2–6)

Near the dark lake stand the two Romanesque temples to Thyr and Muir, which were blackened and desecrated some 10 years ago when the temple of Orcus was established in the Stoneheart Mountain Dungeon. The shrine to Muir sits to the west of the shrine to Thyr. Both shrines face towards the center of the lake.

Each shrine shares the same layout — a stone slab foundation with a large central room, ringed by mighty pillars supporting a gently sloping inverted V-shaped stone roof. Thus, one map depicts the interior for each of the two shrines (as well as the rooms beneath, which are also identical in layout). The front of each shrine was once worked with bas relief images of their respective deities as well as with priests and warriors of legend. Inside of each shrine originally stood a great statue of the god to which the shrine is dedicated, standing some 20 feet tall, in front of which is a large stone altar.

Both shrines have since suffered neglect and defilement. Having been abandoned long ago, their roofs are mostly collapsed and many of the pillars are crumbled and broken. Both have been blasted by magical evil fire and their once white walls are now blackened. The standing pillars and the interior rooms of both shrines are covered with evil writings and smears of humanoid feces and blood. The small interior fonts for holy water have been chipped and broken (or left intact and foully corrupted) and the great statues of Thyr and Muir have been defaced and broken. Any lawful good person inside or near either shrine and able to witness the depths to which they have fallen suffer a –1 morale penalty to all rolls. The interior of each shrine is treated as if under the effects of a *desecrate* spell. There is a 50% chance that each shrine contains **2d4 font skeletons**. These skeletons are called "font skeletons" because they were created by the Font of Bones at **Area 6** of the **Entrance Level** of the dungeon. They serve the will of the priests of Orcus.

FONT SKELETONS   **CR 1**
XP 400
hp 11 (see the **Appendix**)

Cleansing the Shrines: Cleaning the filth and removing the runes in either shrine takes over 100 man hours of work in addition to 100 vials of *holy water* and 12 *consecrate* spells. If the PCs attempt to cleanse either of the shrines before destroying the temple of Orcus on **Level 4** of the dungeon, a group of **4 acolytes of Orcus, 2 lesser priests of Orcus a priest of Orcus** and **2d10 font skeletons** are dispatched to prevent the clean-up operation. Cleansing either shrine nets a 1,000 XP story award, 2,000 XP for both.

Inside the Shrine of Thyr (CR Varies, 4 or 6)

Inside the shrine of Thyr the statue of the seated Thyr the Lawgiver has been beheaded. The head is nowhere to be found. The rod of kingship he once held in his right hand is destroyed and the chalice of peace once held in his left hand is now a broken and unrecognizable lump of stone.

The statue of Thyr covers stairs down to secret rooms below. Barely discernible on the base of the great statue amid the evil runes and filth is a line of runes written in Celestial. On the base of the statue of Thyr are inscribed the words: "As you obey the commands of Thyr so does this figure obey your COMMAND." If a lawful good cleric casts a *command* spell and commands the statue to "open," or "move," the statue of Thyr shifts, revealing the stairs to the secret rooms below.

Trap: A total of three *glyphs of warding* have been placed in the shrine of Thyr — one is located at the base of the statue of Thyr and the other two located randomly on the walls of the shrine. The *glyphs* are triggered by any good-aligned character passing over, touching or reading the *glyph*.

GLYPH OF WARDING (BLAST) TRAP   **CR 4**
XP 1,200
Type magical; **Perception** DC 28; **Disable Device** DC 28

Trigger spell; **Reset** none

Effect spell effect (*glyph of warding* [blast], CL 5th, 2d8 fire, DC 15 Reflex save half damage); multiple targets (all targets within 5 ft.); may be identified (with *read magic*) without triggering it with a successful DC 13 Spellcraft check.

Beneath the Shrine of Thyr

The main room (**A**) is a central study chamber, with chairs, tables and book stands. Among the books are several journals and lesser holy tracts valuable to priests of Thyr or to historians (DC 15 Appraise check reveals 100 gp value).

The Secret Doors: The secret doors in the central study chamber are easy to locate (DC 8 Perception). Each door bears writing in Celestial. The door to **Room B** reads: "Passage comes with the blessing of Thyr." The door to room C reads: "Intone praises to Thyr, brother, and you may enter." The door to **Room D** reads: "Devout prayer is the pathway to knowledge." The doors can be opened by any good-aligned cleric casting *bless*, *chant* (reprinted from **Rappan Athuk**, see the **Appendix**) and *prayer* respectively on the doors to Rooms B, C and D. The doors open freely from the inside allowing passage back out to **Room A**. If the PCs manage to bypass the doors without damaging them, award them experience point bonus equal to a CR 4 encounter.

The Secret Rooms (B-D): Each secret room contains several cots as well as tables and chairs used long ago by the priests of the shrine for study and contemplation. Each secret room also contains several small chests with vestments and various minor religious items. In addition to these standard features, each secret room contains a number of unique items.

Room B contains 3 *divine scrolls*, each containing 5 divine spells: *cure light wounds* (x2), *bless*, *chant** and *prayer*. The room also contains 20 vials of holy water.

Chant* is detailed in the **Appendix.

Room C contains a large cache of 11 *divine scrolls*, each containing one spell: 3 *bless*, 3 *cure light wounds*, 3 *protection from evil* and 2 *prayer*. The room also contains 5 *potions of cure light wounds*.

Room D contains greater holy texts, worth 500 gp to priests of Thyr or historians. It also contains a cache of 14 *divine scrolls*, each containing one spell: 2 *magic weapon*, 2 *divine favor*, 2 *shield other*, 2 *augury*, 2 *cure serious wounds*, 2 *remove paralysis* and 2 *dispel magic*. In addition, in an unlocked chest, is a *+1 light mace*. These items were left behind by the priests when they sealed the shrines long ago in the event that they may one day be needed. Lawful good characters may use these items in need but should not be allowed to greedily take all of them.

Inside the Shrine of Muir (CR Varies, 4–6)

Inside the shrine of Muir the statue of the Lady of Paladins has been beheaded. The head lies on its side next to the base of the statue. It has been chipped away so that its features are unrecognizable and is covered with evil runes. The blade of her upraised sword has been broken off at the hilt. The shield of truth she bears has been defaced with a symbol of Orcus.

The statue of Muir, as with the statue of Thyr, covers stairs down to secret rooms below. On the base of the statue of Muir are inscribed the following words in Celestial: "Speak, O warrior stouthearted and true, the triune virtues of our Valorous Lady." If a lawful good character speaks the words "Truth, Honor and Courage," which are the tenets of Muir, the statue of Muir shifts, revealing the stairs to the secret rooms below. Non-worshippers may attempt a DC 20 Knowledge (religion) check to see if they know the tenets of Muir. PCs failing the roll ordinarily will not know the tenets of Muir unless they have previously acquired that knowledge in Bard's Gate.

Trap: A total of five *glyphs* are located in the shrine of Muir (one on the decapitated head of the statue, one on the front of the statue's shield, one at the base of the statue and the other two located randomly on the walls of the shrine). The *glyphs* are triggered by any good-aligned character passing over, touching or reading the *glyph*.

GLYPH OF WARDING (BLAST) TRAP   **CR 4**
XP 1,200
Type magical; **Perception** DC 28; **Disable Device** DC 28

Trigger spell; **Reset** none

Effect spell effect (*glyph of warding* [blast], CL 5th, 2d8 fire, DC 15 Reflex save half damage); multiple targets (all targets within 5 ft.); may be identified (with *read magic*) without triggering it with a successful DC 13 Spellcraft check.

Beneath the Shrine of Muir

The main room (**A**) beneath the Shrine of Muir is lined with four tapestries depicting Muir with her upraised sword (as depicted in the statue in the shrine above), Muir battling demons, Karith the Paladin slaying a dragon with his holy sword and a group of questing Justicars (high paladins of Muir). These tapestries are very valuable (DC 12 Appraise check indicates value of 500 gp each), though it would be sacrilege for any paladin or good-aligned cleric to disturb them.

The Secret Doors: As with the rooms beneath the shrine of Thyr, the secret doors in the central chamber are easy to locate (DC 8 Perception). Each door bears an inscription in Celestial. The door to **Room B** reads: "Invoke the divine favor of our goddess and speak the name of the virtue that is her shield." The door to **Room C** reads: "Call upon the power of our goddess to make your weapon as hers and speak the name of the virtue that is her sword." The door to room D reads: "Pray to our goddess that through your self-sacrifice you may protect others and speak the name of the virtue that is her armor." The doors can be opened by any lawful good character that casts the proper spell and speaks the proper word. The door to **B** requires the opener cast a *divine favor* spell and speak the word "Truth." The door to **C** requires the opener cast a *magic weapon* spell on his weapon and speak the word "Courage." The door to **D** requires the opener cast a *shield other* spell and speak the word "Honor." Note that paladins may use the scrolls from beneath the shrine of Thyr to cast the proper spells to open these doors.

If the PCs manage to bypass the doors without damaging them, award them experience point bonus equal to a CR 4 encounter.

The Secret Rooms (B-D): Room B contains numerous cots, as if the room once housed many warriors. Also in the room, neatly stacked, are 12 longspears, 12 short swords in scabbards and 12 light wooden shields.

Room C similarly includes a large number of cots as well as 12 longswords in scabbards, 12 light steel shields and 12 suits of studded leather armor.

Room D contains only a few cots. It also contains four suits of chainmail, four heavy steel shields, four full helms, four surcoats bearing the device of Muir (the red upturned sword), and, set aside on their own, laid over a large trunk, a *+1 longsword* and a suit of *+1 chainmail*. Inside the unlocked trunk are 2 *divine scrolls*, each containing 5 divine spells: *cure light wounds* (x2), *bless*, *chant** and *prayer*.

*Chant is detailed in the **Appendix**.

Any lawful good character touching the magic sword or armor is visited by an apparition of the great paladin Karith, who commands the character to don the armor and take up the sword in the name of Muir and recover the *Stone* and *Chalice* on the 2nd level of the dungeon (**Level 2, Area 2C**) and return them to the main Temple of Muir in Bard's Gate. Any non-good aligned character wearing the magic chainmail suffers a –4 penalty on initiative checks. In the hands of any non-good aligned character, the magic sword is treated as a cursed *–2 longsword*.

3. The "Crystal Lake" (CR Varies, 0–5)

Once a lake of crystalline clarity, the lake is now fouled with the excrement from the breeding pits of the Temple of the Frog in the caverns

below the burial halls. Muck rings the lake and reeds clog its shores. Anyone spending time on the shore of the lake amidst the reeds has a 1–5 on 1d20 chance of encountering **1d6 giant frogs** — insignificant tadpoles that escaped from the breeding pits and now make their home in the lake. In the depths of the lake (inaccessible without magical means) is an underwater passage that leads to the pools in the breeding pits of the Temple of the Frog at **Level 5, Area 4** of the dungeon.

GIANT FROGS   CR 1
XP 400
hp 15 (*Pathfinder Roleplaying Game Bestiary* "Frog, Giant")

4. Underground River Passage

The crystal lake at **Area 3** flows into a smaller river that eventually runs into a narrow canyon channel and falls through a crevasse into an underground passage. It emerges from a cave opening to the southwest. Running the entire distance of the underground river channel, next to and slightly above the water level, are a set of ancient stone stairs carved from the surrounding rock. They are extremely slick and require a DC 8 Reflex save every hour they are traveled. Those failing the save fall into the underground river and may drown. This treacherous path is another way to access the Valley of the Shrines. It is also rumored that along this path is a secret door leading to more tombs.

5. Path to the Burial Halls (CR Varies, 0–6)

As the PCs near the edge of the woods on the west side of the valley, they may detect that there is a break in the uniform wall of trees (DC 16 Perception check). This break is the beginning of the path to the entrance to the Burial Halls. It is flanked by two stone monoliths, similar to the ones flanking the ancient path at **Area 1**. The path and the twin obelisks, however, are overgrown and covered by trees and shrubs. The PCs may also find the path by skirting the edge of the wood. If they do so, allow

them to retry the check with a +2 bonus. Once the path is detected, it is strangely clear and easy to follow. It leads to **Area 6**.

As the PCs travel the path, check for an encounter every hour. On a 1–8 on 1d20 the PCs encounter **2d4 giant spiders**. This check is made in addition to any normal wandering monster checks since the forest is filled with the evil vermin.

GIANT SPIDERS   CR 1
XP 400
hp 16 (*Pathfinder Roleplaying Game Bestiary* "Spider, Giant")

6. Entrance to the Burial Halls and the Stoneheart Mountain Dungeon

The path ends in a small clearing surrounding an indentation into the side of the mountain. Set in that indentation is the entrance to the Burial Halls. Refer to the **Entrance Level, Area 1**, for more details.

7. Lair of Brundle the One-Eyed Troll (CR 5)

In a small cave a few miles east of the entrance to the Burial Halls is the lair of **Brundle the one-eyed troll**. His lair contains the hides of several bears and deer and a number of human and elven skulls. At the far end of the lair is a medium chest that is neither locked nor trapped. It contains 583 gp, 1,248 sp, four 100 gp gems, a golden chalice worth 50 gp, which was once a holy artifact from the temple of Thyr that Brundle got from killing an evil Priest of Orcus, a *potion of cure serious wounds*, a *necklace of fireballs* (IV) and a *+2 dagger*.

BRUNDLE THE ONE-EYED TROLL   CR 5
XP 1,600
hp 63 (*Pathfinder Roleplaying Game Bestiary* "Troll")

Tactics: Brundle was brash in his younger years, before an eager paladin with a flaming sword slashed his left eye, earning him his name. Rending that one was very enjoyable. Now he is older and wiser and he prefers to ambush his victims, attacking from concealment with hit-and-run tactics. He has learned the danger of fire and is overly wary of it, retreating if he sees his victims produce fire or acid.

8. Gnoll Village (CR Varies)

At this location is an above-ground village of gnolls containing **100–200 male gnolls**, in addition to females and young. There are additionally **10 sergeant gnolls** and **1 leader gnoll**. These forces will one day be brought to bear against Bard's Gate. PCs should be able to avoid these settlements, at worst encountering a small patrol of **2d4 gnolls**.

GNOLLS   CR 1
XP 400
hp 11 (*Pathfinder Roleplaying Game Bestiary* "Gnoll")

GNOLL SERGEANTS (10)   CR 3
XP 800
Male gnoll fighter 3 (*Pathfinder Roleplaying Game Bestiary* "Gnoll")
CE Medium humanoid (gnoll)
Init +0; **Senses** darkvision 60 ft.; **Perception** +3

AC 13, touch 10, flat-footed 13 (+2 armor, +1 natural)

hp 17 (3d10+2d8+8)
Fort +7; **Ref** +1; **Will** +1; +2 vs. fear
Defensive Abilities bravery +1

Speed 30 ft.
Melee battleaxe +6 (1d8+2/x3) or spear +7 (1d8+3/x3)
Ranged longbow +4 (1d8/x3)

Str 15, **Dex** 10, **Con** 13, **Int** 8, **Wis** 11, **Cha** 8
Base Atk +4; **CMB** +6; **CMD** 16
Feats Point Blank Shot, Power Attack, Precise Shot, Run, Weapon Focus (spear)
Skills Acrobatics +0 (+4 to jump with a running start), Intimidate +3, Perception +3, Survival +4
Languages Gnoll
Gear leather armor, heavy wooden shield, battleaxe, spear, longbow, 15 arrows, 3d4 sp

---

GNOLL LEADER	CR 5

XP 1,600
Male gnoll ranger 5 (*Pathfinder Roleplaying Game Bestiary* "Gnoll")
CE Medium humanoid (gnoll)
Init +3; **Senses** darkvision 60 ft.; **Perception** +10

AC 19, touch 13, flat-footed 16 (+5 armor, +3 Dex, +1 natural)
hp 45 (5d10+5 plus 2d8+2 plus 5)
Fort +8; **Ref** +7; **Will** +1

Speed 30 ft.
Melee short sword +8/+3 (1d6+2/19-20)
Ranged composite longbow +9/+4 (1d8+2/x3)
Special Attacks combat styles (archery), favored enemies (elves +2, humans +4)
Spells Prepared (CL 2nd):
1st—*entangle* (DC 11)

Str 15, **Dex** 16, **Con** 13, **Int** 8, **Wis** 11, **Cha** 13
Base Atk +6; **CMB** +8; **CMD** 21
Feats Deadly Aim, Endurance, Point Blank Shot, Precise Shot, Rapid Shot, Run
Skills Acrobatics +2 (+6 to jump with a running start), Bluff +1 (+3 vs. elves, +5 vs. humans), Climb +6, Escape Artist +3, Fly +2, Handle Animal +5, Intimidate +5, Knowledge (nature) +3 (+5 vs. elves, +7 vs. humans), Perception +10 (+12 vs. elves, +14 vs. humans, +12 while in mountainous terrain), Ride +2, Sense Motive +0 (+2 vs. elves, +4 vs. humans), Stealth +12 (+14 while in mountainous terrain), Survival +10 (+12 vs. elves, +14 vs. humans, +12 while in mountainous terrain, +12 to track), Swim +1
Languages Gnoll
SQ favored terrain (mountainous +2), hunter's bonds (companions), track, wild empathy
Gear +1 chain shirt, composite longbow [Str +2], 20 arrows, short sword, 2d6 gp

9. Entrance to the Under Realms

This dark cave leads steadily downward. It has no major side chambers or other passages. Hundreds and hundreds of feet below it joins up with a major passage of the Under Realms. The only significant feature of the downward path occurs when the passage intersects an underground river. The passage opens into a larger cavern at that point. The river plummets 100 feet below from an opening in the wall of the cavern. A stone stairway, slippery from the spray of the falls, parallels the waterfall and descends to the cave floor below where the downward passage continues. The cave has several side passages and chambers and is possibly the lair of a powerful monster.

10. Abandoned Mines (CR Varies)

These caves, once worked by miners from Bard's Gate, are now the home of **Calthraxus the black dragon**. Calthraxus is beginning to call to his lair other evil creatures to reside there with him. He has allowed several **trolls** and a group of **45 black orcs** to take up residence in the upper levels. Calthraxus' hoard is small, as he has eaten most of the gems.

CALTHRAXUS	CR 10

XP 9,600
Male young adult black dragon (*Pathfinder Roleplaying Game Bestiary* "Chromatic Dragon, Black")
CE Large dragon (water)
Init +5; **Senses** blindsense, darkvision 120 ft., dragon senses, low-light vision; **Perception** +21

AC 25, touch 10, flat-footed 24 (+1 Dex, +15 natural, –1 size)
hp 126 (12d12+48)
Fort +12; **Ref** +9; **Will** +10
DR 5/magic; **Immune** acid, paralysis, sleep; **SR** 21

Speed 60 ft., fly 200 ft. (poor), swim 60 ft.
Melee bite +18 (2d6+9), 2 claws +17 (1d8+6), tail slap +12 (1d8+9/x2), 2 wings +12 (1d6+3)
Space 10 ft.; **Reach** 5 ft.
Special Attacks breath weapon (80-ft. line, 10d6 acid, DC 21)
Spell-Like Abilities (CL 12th):
Constant—*speak with reptiles*
At will—*darkness* (50 ft. radius)
Spells Known (CL 1st; ranged touch +12):
1st (4/day)—*mage armor, ray of enfeeblement* (DC 12)
0 (at will)—*acid splash, bleed* (DC 11), *disrupt undead, message, read magic*

Str 23, **Dex** 12, **Con** 19, **Int** 12, **Wis** 15, **Cha** 12
Base Atk +12; **CMB** +19; **CMD** 30 (34 vs. trip)
Feats Alertness, Improved Initiative, Power Attack, Skill Focus (Stealth), Vital Strike, Weapon Focus (Bite)
Skills Acrobatics +1 (+13 jump), Fly +10, Handle Animal +13, Intimidate +16, Knowledge (arcana) +10, Perception +21, Sense Motive +4, Spellcraft +10, Stealth +18, Swim +29; **Racial Modifiers** +8 Swim
Languages Common, Draconic
SQ swamp stride, water breathing

Speak with Reptiles (Sp) A young or older black dragon gains the constant spell-like ability to speak with reptiles. This functions as *speak with animals*, **but only with reptilian animals.**
Swamp Stride (Ex) A very young or older black dragon can move through bogs and quicksand without penalty at its normal speed.
Water Breathing (Ex) A black dragon can breathe underwater indefinitely and can freely use its breath weapon, spells, and other abilities while submerged.

BLACK ORC	CR 1/3

XP 135
hp 8 (*The Tome of Horrors Complete* 464)

TROLL	CR 5

XP 1,600
HP 63 (*Pathfinder Roleplaying Game Bestiary* "Troll")

1 Hex - 6 Miles

11. The Lesser Gibbering Orb's Lair (CR 11)

Here, in a deep, twisting cave, **Xarrr'x the lesser gibbering orb** makes his lair. In recent weeks, the priests of Orcus have sent a delegation to speak with him in an attempt to form an alliance.

GIBBERING ORB, LESSER   CR 11
XP 12,800
hp 91 (*The Tome of Horrors 4* "Gibbering Orb, Lesser")

Treasure: In his lair, Xarrr'x has 3,000 gp, 4,000 sp, *5 potions* (*bull's strength, glibness, invisibility, detect scrying,* and *spectral hand*), a *wand of magic missiles* (29 charges), a *+2 longsword of dancing,* a *helm of underwater action* and one dose of *universal solvent,* in addition to a large amount of mundane weapons and armor, from his various victims.

12. Worm Holes
(CR Varies, 0 or 8+)

These massive sinkholes dot the landscape in a haphazard fashion. The truth of the geologic anomalies is that they are the air-holes for a swarm of purple worms that have travelled through the Stonehearts for a number of years. The tunnels are quite smoothly burrowed; however they are increasingly unstable after many years. There is a 1–2 chance on 1d20 that a tunnel will **collapse** while it is being investigated.

CAVE-IN / COLLAPSE CR 8
XP 4,800 (See the *Pathfinder Roleplaying Game Core Rulebook*)

Rivulets of water cascade down the steeper tunnels, sometime creating underground waterfalls and sizable ponds. Various Under Realm inhabitants investigate these "skylights", as they are quite rare to the underground denizens.

The holes are extensive; it is possible an entire campaign could be run using nothing but these enormous tunnels. It is possible (GMs discretion) that these tunnels may reach all the way east to the vast underground of the Cyclopean Deeps (see the *Cyclopean Deeps* from **Frog God Games**), but none have explored them that extensively.

There is a 1–3 chance on 1d10 that while spelunking in any worm hole, explorers run afoul of a **purple worm** meandering throw the tunnels. The worm attacks on sight.

PURPLE WORM CR 12
XP 19,200
hp 200 (*Pathfinder Roleplaying Game Bestiary* "Purple Worm")

13. Orc Camp

This small encampment of black orcs is a forward position for Calthraxus (**Area 10**) and his intent to fortify his position against the gnolls to the northeast (**Area 8**). The orcs are not hostile, and are simply a sentry position, watching the Ancient Path and making forays to the Crystal Lake (**Area 3**) under cover of night to judge how far the gnolls are roaming.If the orcs are attacked, the use a fighting withdrawal tactic to avoid casualties as much as possible.

BLACK ORCS (12) CR 1/3
XP 135
hp 8 (*The Tome of Horrors Complete* 464)

Entrance Level: The Burial Halls

This main level is the uppermost level of the ancient burial halls of Thyr and Muir. It contains the minor crypts and the old worship rooms once used by visiting clerics to pay respects to the dead. It was also once used as a viewing area for final rites on bodies being interred in the lower catacombs. The most significant feature on this level was the Font of the Ancients — a fountain of holy water. With the coming of the priests of Orcus this level has been defiled. They recently finished placing an exceedingly powerful rune on the fountain at **Area 6**, converting it into a horrible cursed item of evil — the Font of Bones — a fountain that can create an army of skeletons. Skeletons created from this evil fountain are more powerful than normal and are called font skeletons (see the **Font Skeleton** sidebar). The priests of Tsathogga rarely venture this close to the surface and are unaware of the activities of the priests of Orcus on this level.

ACOLYTE OF ORCUS   **CR 2**
XP 600
hp 23 (see **Level 2**, **Area 26**)

DIRE RATS   **CR 1/3**
XP 135
hp 5 (*Pathfinder Roleplaying Game Bestiary* "Rat, Dire")

FONT SKELETONS   **CR 1**
XP 400
hp 11 (see the **Font Skeleton** sidebar at the start of this chapter)

Font Skeleton

FONT SKELETON	**CR 1**

XP 400
NE Medium undead (see the **Appendix**)
Init +5; **Senses** darkvision 60 ft.; **Perception** +0

AC 15, touch 11, flat-footed 14 (+1 Dex, +3 natural, +1 shield)
hp 15 (2d8+2)
Fort +1; **Ref** +1; **Will** +3
Defensive Abilities channel resistance +4; **DR** 5/ bludgeoning; **Immune** cold, undead traits

Speed 30 ft.
Melee longsword +2 (1d8+1) or 2 claws +2 (1d4+1)

Str 12, **Dex** 12, **Con** —, **Int** —, **Wis** 10, **Cha** 12
Base Atk +1; **CMB** +2; **CMD** 13
Feats Improved Initiative[B]
Combat Gear longsword, light wooden shield

GHOUL   CR 1
XP 400
hp 13 (*Pathfinder Roleplaying Game Bestiary* "Ghoul")

1. Entrance (CR Varies, 6+)

The entrance to the burial halls is flanked by what were once two white marble monoliths worked with silver-inlayed glyphs and holy symbols of Thyr and Muir. Those monoliths still stand but have been desecrated and blackened by fire. The top has been knocked off each of the monoliths, and the inlaid symbols have been rudely chipped away. The entranceway itself was once made of white marble and covered with symbols of Thyr and Muir. It, too, has been defiled and now bears evil symbols written in charcoal or blood. The archway opens to a small room beyond with a hallway leading north.

The runes and symbols appear to have been placed recently. A DC 12 Knowledge (religion) check reveals the evil symbols on the archway to be linked to the demon-god Orcus. They are part of the plan by the priests to control the entrance to the dungeon for use in later assaults on Bard's Gate and the surrounding wilderness. Nearly invisible among the evil symbols is a **trap.**

Trap: One of the symbols is a *glyph of warding*. The *glyph* is traced on the front side of the capstone of the archway and is triggered by any good character passing beneath. In addition, triggering the *glyph* causes the Font of Bones at **Area 6** to generate **1d4+1 font skeletons** and dispatch them to this area (see **Area 6**, below). Characters earn XP for both traps by defeating either one, regardless of whether or not the other one is also sprung.

GLYPH OF WARDING (BLAST) TRAP   CR 4
XP 1,200
Type magical; **Perception** DC 28; **Disable Device** DC 28
___
Trigger spell; **Reset** none
Effect spell effect (*glyph of warding* [blast], CL 5th, 2d8 fire, DC 15 Reflex save half damage); multiple targets (all targets within 5 ft.); may be identified (with *read magic*) without triggering it with a successful DC 13 Spellcraft check; triggers the skeleton-summoning trap

SKELETON-SUMMONING TRAP   CR 4
XP 1,200
Type magical; **Perception** 28; **Disable Device** 28
___
Trigger spell; **Reset** none
Effect spell (*summon monster III*, CL 8th, summons **1d4+1 font skeletons**).

FONT SKELETONS (1d4+1)   CR 1
XP 400
hp 11 (see the **Font Skeleton** sidebar at the start of this chapter)

Modification: If good-aligned characters make a successful foray into the dungeon against the priests of Orcus (or if your party is of 5th or higher level), the priests of Orcus replace any discharged *glyphs* with *glyphs* that trigger *bestow curse* (–4 on attack rolls, checks and saves permanently until removed).

2. Entrance Room

This room must have once been an antechamber to the burial halls. A pair of strange stone protrusions, which in ages past must have been basins for holy water, flank the inside of the archway. They are smashed and desecrated. Tattered shreds of ancient tapestries depicting Thyr and Muir hang on the walls. More filth and foul symbols of evil cover the walls. None are magical.

Entrance Level

Difficulty Level: 2 for most of the level, 4 at the Font of Bones and 12 at **Area 10**.
Entrances: Main entrance only.
Exits: A poorly hidden secret door hides a passage to **Level 1**. A magically guarded secret door in the rear of the level leads to the evil temple on **Level 4**. Rat tunnels also lead to **Level 1**.
Wandering Monsters: There are few wandering monsters on this level. Roll a wandering monster check on 1d20 once per hour (–1 to the roll if it is night outside):

1D20	RESULT
1	1d3 ghouls
2	2d6 dire rats
3	1d6+1 font skeletons (see the **Font Skeleton** sidebar)
4	3 acolytes of Orcus, 50% chance accompanied by **2d4 font skeletons**
5–20	No encounter

Detections: PCs checking for magic or evil should be given the following information. They detect evil to the north of the entrance centered around the Font of Bones at **Area 6**. Past the Font of Bones, general evil can be detected with faint good toward **8A** and extreme evil to the north at **Areas 9A** and **10**. Strong necromantic magic emanates from the Font of Bones and can be detected easily 60 feet away.
Continuous Effects: Due to the evil symbols, the entire level is treated as if under the effects of a *desecrate* spell. An *unhallow* spell is centered on the Font of Bones at **Area 6**. The only way to remove this effect is to physically cleanse each room with holy water (requiring no less than one thousand man hours and one thousand vials of holy water!) followed by casting a *consecrate* spell in every cleaned room. Doing so nets a 3,000 XP story bonus. This does not destroy the evil of the Font of Bones, however, which must be handled separately. Both of these effects are at a CL 20th.
Standard Features: All of the rooms on this level are made of worked stone of extraordinary craftsmanship, recently marred by the priests of Orcus in their attempt to control this level. The walls of this level were once carved with the sacred eagle and lion of Thyr and the falcon of Muir, as well as their respective holy symbols. Those have all been marred or desecrated in some way. The beautifully worked white marble has also been desecrated or marred. The whole level is covered with foul runes and symbols of Orcus. Each room contains numerous symbols of evil associated with the demon-god Orcus and drawn in a paste of what appears to be charcoal and blood.

3. Priest's Room

Yet another defiled room, this chamber was once the room of the priest overseeing the burial halls, who would greet those entering the halls. His simple cot and plain table have long been destroyed. Nothing remains here but filth and vile runes of evil. The ancient book kept by the priest, bearing the names of all who visited the halls, was taken and burned long ago.

4. Secret Door (CR Varies, 7+)

The secret door itself is rather easy to find (DC 12 Perception check) because of its obvious seam, though the mechanism to open it is not (DC 20 Perception check). The opening mechanism is a small stone to the right of the door on the west wall that presses in and opens the door. Several of the runes on the surface of the door appear to overlap the outline of the secret door. A DC 8 Intelligence check reveals that opening the secret door would most likely violate the integrity of the symbols. Two of the symbols are magical **traps.**

Stone Secret Door with *Fire Trap* and *Summoning Rune*: 4 in. thick; hardness 8; hp 60; Break DC 28; Perception (DC 12 door, DC 20 opening mechanism); opening triggers *fire trap* spell and summons skeletons.

Disturbing the second sigil, which is highly unusual in appearance, causes the Font of Bones in **Area 6** to create **1d4+1 font skeletons** and send them toward the door (see **Area 6,** below). Both symbols can be removed normally, such as with an *erase* spell. Physically disturbing either rune (such as by opening the secret door) triggers them. The *summoning* rune is a strange and alien rune taught to the priests of Orcus by the rune-mage Balcoth on **Level 2A.** Characters earn XP for both traps by defeating either one, regardless of whether or not the other one is also sprung.

FIRE TRAP CR 5
XP 1,600
Type magical; **Perception** DC 29; **Disable Device** DC 29

Trigger spell; **Reset** none
Effect spell effects (*fire trap,* CL 8th, 1d4+8 fire, DC 16 Reflex save half damage); multiple targets (all creatures within a 5-ft. radius); triggers the skeleton-summoning trap

SKELETON-SUMMONING TRAP CR 4
XP 1,200
Type magical; **Perception** 28; **Disable Device** 28

Trigger spell; **Reset** none
Effect spell (*summon monster III,* CL 8th, summons **1d4+1 font skeletons**).

FONT SKELETONS (1d4+1) CR 1
XP 400
hp 11 (see the **Font Skeleton** sidebar at the start of this chapter)

5. Trap and Stairs Down (CR 2)

Beyond the secret door is a passage that curves to the north. On the south wall, just inside the door, is a small metal lever. The lever sits in a slot carved in the stone wall and is in the "up" position. The lever controls the locking mechanism for the **trap.**

Trap: In the "up" position, the lock is disabled and the pit opens when 50 or more pounds of weight are applied to its cover. A person falling into the pit falls 30 feet and takes 3d6 points of damage. The cover of the pit resets itself after two rounds, trapping anyone inside of the pit until it is opened again. In the "down" position, the lock is engaged and the pit may be crossed safety. In any case, moving the lever causes a metallic grinding noise. Beyond the pit are stairs down to **Level 1.**

30-FOOT DEEP PIT TRAP CR 2
XP 600
Type mechanical; **Perception** DC 20; **Disable Device** DC 20

Trigger location; **Reset** manual; **Bypass** lever

Effect 30-ft.-deep pit (3d6 falling damage); DC 20 Reflex avoids; multiple targets (all targets in a 10-ft.-square area)

6. Main Burial Hall — "The Font of Bones" (CR Varies, 4+)

This great hall contains over twenty stone sarcophagi and was once the main burial room. The holy symbols within the room have been desecrated and defiled. In the center of the room is something that is an abomination to behold: a fountain of what once was white marble, now stained crimson, filled with blood and bones. A glowing red rune, radiating pure evil, has been rudely carved into the once-pure fountain base. Gouts of blood bubble a spurt grotesquely from the top of the fountain, spattering the floor around the font with red ichor. The pall of evil hangs heavy here.

The sarcophagi are now all empty, their contents pillaged and piled in the Font of Bones. The room radiates *doom* (–2 penalty on attack rolls, ability checks, skill checks and saving throws for all good-aligned creatures) as well as *desecrate.* Presence in the room of any good-aligned character causes **4 font skeletons** to animate every other round within the font and move out to attack. There is no limit to the number of skeletons that may be generated this way; the skeletons continue to animate as long as any good-aligned character remains in the room. After 10 rounds, the Font begins to produce skeletons every round. If any good-aligned characters remain in the room after 20 rounds (2 minutes), the Font pauses for 1 round, then *summons* 1 **vrock demon** to the room, in addition to producing 2 skeletons. This continues every round a good-aligned character remains in the main burial hall. The Font stops producing creatures as soon as no good-aligned PCs are in the room, restarting the cycle from where it left off should they re-enter. After 24 hours of no good-aligned PCs in the room, the Font resets to begin the cycle anew. The glowing rune on the font is a *rune of undeath,* learned by the priests of Orcus from Balcoth, the undead rune mage on **Level 2A.** It cannot be removed unless the font is restored, as described below.

The Font of Bones: In the center of the room is the major feature of the room: a large fountain-like holy water font with a wide basin collecting the spilling water, similar to the fountains set in the plaza of a great city. Once a source of goodness, known as the Font of the Ancients, it is now filled with blood and piled deep with the desecrated bones of the faithful. This horrible artifact of evil was created by the priests of Orcus in mockery of the reverence of the followers of Thyr and Muir for their buried ancestors. It was created by a month-long ritual, and its power is tied to the evil temple of Orcus on **Level 4.** If that temple is destroyed and *consecrate, hallow* and *holy word* are subsequently cast on the font, it will be restored to its former goodness, providing unlimited holy water that additionally acts as *delay poison* and *lesser restoration.* Doing so nets the PCs a 6,000 XP story award. Strong necromantic magic emanates from the Font of Bones and can be detected easily 60 feet away.

FONT SKELETONS (4) CR 1
XP 400
hp 15 (see the **Font Skeleton** sidebar at the start of this chapter)

Notes on Continuous Effects: When resolving combat attacks against font skeletons in the main hall, the *desecrate* spell grants the font skeletons a +6 profane bonus on their channel resistance, a +2 profane bonus to hit, damage rolls, and saving throws, and +2 hp per HD (increased hp accounted for in their statblock; all Font skeletons in this adventure gain these extra hp). The *unhallow* effect triggers a *magic circle against good* spell, which grants a +2 deflection bonus and +2 resistance bonus to saves vs. Good opponents. Additionally, the *unhallow* effect triggers a *doom* spell; Good-aligned PCs that fail their DC 16 Will save are shaken, suffering a –2 penalty on attack rolls, ability checks, skill checks and saving throws.

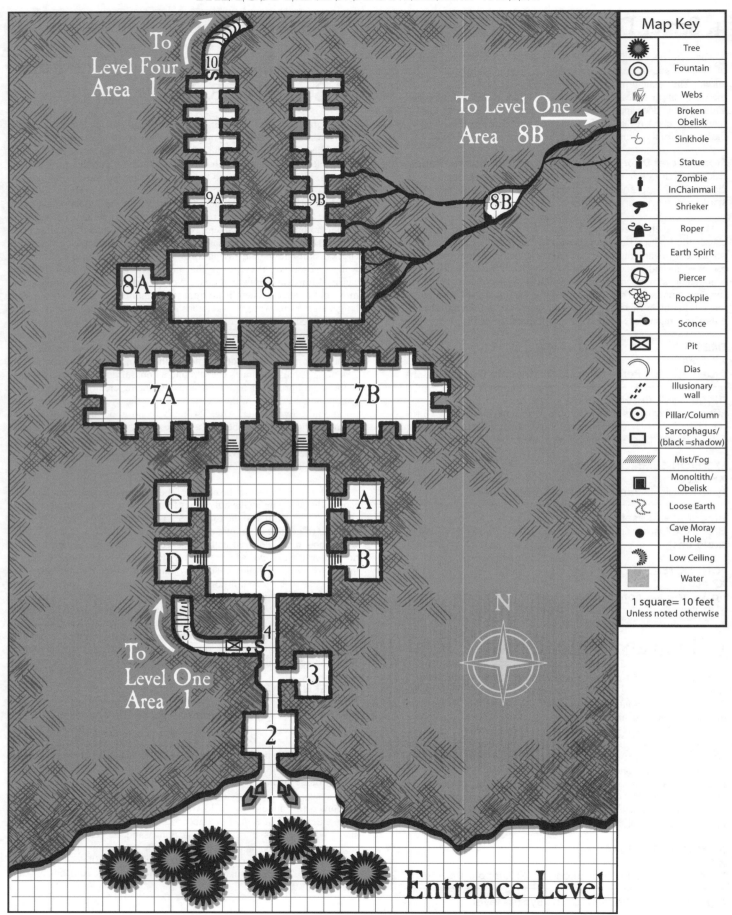

6A–D: Side Rooms (CR Varies, 4+)

Each of these rooms up small stairs from the main room contains slightly more elaborate sarcophagi. Each is empty. Presence of good-aligned characters in these rooms triggers the creation of an additional **4 font skeletons** every other round.

FONT SKELETONS (4)   CR 1
XP 400
hp 11 (see the **Font Skeleton** sidebar at the start of this chapter)

7A–B: Greater Crypts

These recessed crypts were once the burial place of more important clerics of Thyr and Muir. They, too, are empty; their bones now corrupted and piled in the font at **Area 6**.

8. Lesser Crypts (CR Varies, 1–5)

This room is filled with smaller stone coffins. All are empty, except for **3d6 dire rats** that have made nests here. There are large rat tunnels in the east wall, though no opening is more than 2 feet high. A Medium character could scurry through on his or her belly or hands and knees with difficulty.

A Small character could crouch or travel normally on hands and knees.

DIRE RATS   CR 1/3
XP 135
hp 5 (*Pathfinder Roleplaying Game Bestiary* "Rat, Dire")

8A. Priests' Tombs

This small side room holds four sarcophagi of ancient priests of Thyr. The room is under a *protection from evil* spell due to the enchanted stone sarcophagi and has not been *desecrated*. The aura of good is quickly apparent to any good-aligned creatures that enter, in stark contrast to the rest of the level. No monsters enter this room, including font skeletons. Font skeletons are not generated while the PCs are in this room. The remains of the priests are intact. They may not be disturbed by creatures of good alignment without suffering alignment conflict. PCs may rest here without fear.

8B. Rat's Nest (CR Varies, 4–7)

There are **3d6+6 dire rats** here. Beyond the nest continuing to the east are more rat tunnels, which eventually connect with the rat tunnels at **Level 1, Areas 6** or **8B**.

DIRE RATS   CR 1/3
XP 135
hp 5 (*Pathfinder Roleplaying Game Bestiary* "Rat, Dire")

Treasure: In the midst of a large pile of heavily soiled cloth and leather items are 128 gp, 387 sp and 1,091 cp, as well as 6 gems (25 gp each). There are also four daggers, one of which is a masterwork kukri. Also here is a *ring of resistance +1* (as a *cloak of resistance +1*, except it takes up a ring slot instead of a cloak slot). The PCs must succeed on a Perception check (DC 7 for the weapons, 18 for the coins, gems and ring) to locate the items.

9A–B. Hallway of Lesser Crypts (CR Varies, 1–4)

These two passage are lined on either side with inset crypts, all of which are empty — their contents having been added to the Font of Bones. At the end of passage **9A**, a glowing red, pulsing light can be seen, as if from an evil light source. If the PCs head toward it, proceed to **Area 10** below. Passage **9B** includes dire rat tunnels that link up with **8B** and eventually lead to **Level 1**. There is a 50% chance that there are **2d6 dire rats** in the tunnels from **9B**.

DIRE RATS   **CR 1/3**
XP 135
hp 5 (*Pathfinder Roleplaying Game Bestiary* "Rat, Dire")

10. Secret Door and *Geas* (CR 12)

As PCs approach within 30 feet of the end of the hall, they observe the source of the evil, red pulsing glow: a large red rune inscribed on the end of the hallway. They can't quite make out the details of the rune at this distance. If any good-aligned PCs approach any closer and look at the rune, they trigger the **trap**. The rune covers a secret door.

GM Note: This is an *extraordinarily dangerous trap*. Allow low-level characters to feel an aura of evil so strong that good-aligned characters must succeed on a DC 15 Will save or refuse to enter this hall due to the intensity of the evil. Do your best to discourage them from traveling to the end of the passageway. Of course, if they do not heed the warning, their deaths are at hand.

Trap: The rune at the end of the hallway, which glows with an evil, red pulsing glow, is a magical trap that casts a peculiar version of the *lesser geas* spell that affects multiple targets (and is effectively a 6th-level spell). The *lesser geas* is triggered by any good-aligned character coming within 10 feet of the trap, or by anyone touching or reading the strange rune. Failure to save against the *lesser geas* imparts the compulsion in the character to go to the temple of Orcus and pledge allegiance to the Demon Lord of the Undead. Triggering the trap also *gates* in the guardian of the door, **Urriligishool the Gatekeeper Demon** (a hezrou demon). This **trap** was placed by a high priest of Orcus from Rappan Athuk who helped establish the temple on **Level 4**. Characters earn XP for both traps by defeating either one, regardless of whether or not the other one is also sprung.

LESSER GEAS TRAP   **CR 8**
XP 3,200
Type magical; **Perception** DC 31; **Disable Device** DC 31

Trigger spell; **Reset** none
Effect spell (as *lesser geas*, CL 13th, DC 21 Will save to resist); multiple targets (all targets within 30 ft.); triggers the *gate* trap.

GATE TRAP   **CR 11***
XP 3,200
Type magical; **Perception** DC 31; **Disable Device** DC 31

Trigger spell; **Reset** none

Effect spell (*gate*, CL 17th, calls forth Urriligishool the Gatekeeper)

URRILIGISHOOL THE GATEKEEPER, HEZROU DEMON   **CR 11***
XP 3,200
hp 145 (*Pathfinder Roleplaying Game Bestiary* "Demon, Hezrou")

*Note: Reward the PCs for defeating a CR 11 creature only once if they encounter the *gate* trap. If they disable the trap, they get XP for that. If they fail to disable the trap and summon Urriligishool, they get XP for fighting him.

Tactics: If all persons present are evil, the demon opens the secret door and admits them to the temple below. He attacks any who are not evil, casting *chaos hammer* and *unholy blight* and *teleporting* back and forth amongst the party. If a PC fails to resist the *lesser geas*, Urriligishool does not slay him, but instead joins offers to show him the way to the temple to carry out his quest. He then leads the persuaded character to the temple below. There, the PC must swear a solemn oath to serve Orcus. This act lifts the *lesser geas* — and changes the character's alignment to chaotic evil. Urriligishool is rewarded with the convert's soul once the character dedicates himself to Orcus. Any cleric or paladin who agrees to convert is further rewarded — by Orcus himself — three levels of experience, several magic items and eternal life as a powerful undead (vampire or lich). A paladin who accepts the offer must exchange his paladin levels for anti-paladin levels on a one-for-one basis. (See the *Pathfinder Roleplaying Game Advanced Player's Guide* for more information on the anti-paladin class.)

Secret Door: The passage ends in a wall that is in fact a secret door. The door is covered with a powerful limiting magic and, short of a *limited wish* (which suspends the restriction for 1 hour), *wish* or *miracle*, it may be opened only by the demon, Urriligishool the Gatekeeper. If Urriligishool is slain, the door may be opened normally. This door was added by the evil priests of Orcus and hides a passage down to the evil temple on **Level 4**.

Stone Secret Door: 4 in. thick; hardness 8; hp 60; Break (impossible); Perception DC 20; covered with *symbol of pain* (see above). May be opened only by the demon or if the demon is slain.

Level 1: The Upper Caves

This level was once the exclusive home of Gorbash the ogre. The priests of Tsathogga never cared much about the levels near the surface and allowed him to create his lair here, though they have placed some of their lesser frog servants here to watch the passage to the lower caverns. Recently, the priests of Orcus installed Draeligor on this level in an attempt to gain control of the entrance to the dungeon as part of their future plan to use the dungeon as a base of operations for assaults on Bard's Gate. Gorbash and Draeligor have an uneasy truce. Unlike the entrance level, this level is not covered with evil runes of Orcus.

BAT SWARM   CR 2
XP 600
hp 13 (*Pathfinder Roleplaying Game Bestiary* "Bat, Swarm")

DIRE RAT   CR 1/3
XP 135
hp 5 (*Pathfinder Roleplaying Game Bestiary* "Rat, Dire")

FONT SKELETON   CR 1
XP 400
hp 11 (see the **Appendix**)

SHADOW   CR 3
XP 800
hp 19 (*Pathfinder Roleplaying Game Bestiary* "Shadow")

STIRGE   CR 1/2
XP 200
hp 5 (*Pathfinder Roleplaying Game Bestiary* "Stirge")

1. Entrance Cave and Iron Portal (CR 2)

The stairs come to an end and open into a small cavern. A large iron door is set into the cave wall on the far side of the cavern. The door is covered with strange runes similar to those on the level above. The wall has sconces for torches, all empty. A small pool of dark water fills one part of the room. PCs must skirt this pool to reach the far door. The air here is still.

In the pool, hidden beneath the surface of the dark water, are **2 giant frogs** — the least of the monstrosities bred in the dark pits of the Temple of the Frog in the caverns far below. They can be seen with a successful DC 20 Perception check. They have no treasure.

GIANT FROGS (2)   CR 1
XP 400
hp 15 (*Pathfinder Roleplaying Game Bestiary* "Frog, Giant")

Tactics: The giant frogs do not molest a large party, though one may attempt to use its tongue to seize a single character of Small size if that character is some distance from the main party, such as a scout or a rear guard. The pool leads to a small cave where the frogs make their lair.

Iron Door: The large iron door on the far end of the room is carved with strange runes. None of them is magical. A successful DC 15 Knowledge (religion) check reveals that some were once holy symbols of Thyr and Muir that have now been covered with symbols of the cult of Orcus. The door is not trapped. Any priest of Orcus (not including Acolytes or Lesser Priests) has a key to this door. The lock is somewhat rusted, allowing for an easier than usual chance to break in the door. Doing so prevents the

Level 1: The Upper Caves

Difficulty Level: 2–3.
Entrances: The three Sinkholes from the surface (**Area 2**), the cave access (**Area 1**).
Exits: Cave hole to **Level 2**, Stairs to **Levels 3, 4** and **5**. No water passages.
Wandering Monsters: Once past the door at **Area 1**, roll a wandering monster check on 1d20 once per 30 minutes or after the party makes any significant noise. Subtract 1 from the check if the party is in or to the east of the singing corridor.

1D20	RESULT
1	1d3 font skeletons
2	3d4 dire rats
3	1d6 stirges
4	Gorbash the Ogre: See **Area 15**, below. If he is encountered, play him intelligently. He would most probably lead the party to **Area 11**, and then to his rock pile setup. Note that Gorbash does not normally go into **Area 17** or beyond or **Area 9** or beyond.
5	1d4 bat swarms
6	Screaming Gust of Wind: Torches go out 50% of the time, lanterns 20% of the time. Papers are disrupted, communication is difficult and spell casting requires a DC 12 Concentration check.
7	1 shadow
8–20	No encounter

Standard Features: In the carved areas and the areas where the worshipers of Thyr and Muir were buried (including caverns), the walls have been worked with lions, eagles and falcons as well as holy symbols of Thyr and Muir, though the latter have been marred or destroyed. The craftsmanship is exquisite.
Light: This level is dimly lit from sinkholes or other cracks to the surface.

door from being locked in the future.

Locked Iron Door: 2 in. thick; hardness 10; hp 60; Break DC 20; Disable Device DC 20.

2. Sinkhole Above (CR Varies, 0 or CR 2 - bats, or CR 1–4 - stirges)

The floor and walls of these areas are covered with bat guano. Faint rays of light hit the floor, as the sinkhole allows access to the surface. The bats and stirges in the cave complex use these holes as a means of entry and exit.

There is a chance of an encounter here aside from any wandering monster encounters. Roll 1d20 any time the PCs enter these areas: 1–2: a **bat swarm**; 3–4: **2d4 stirges**, 5–20: no encounter.

BAT SWARM CR 2
XP 600
hp 13 (*Pathfinder Roleplaying Game Bestiary* "Bat, Swarm")

STIRGES CR 1/2
XP 200
hp 5 (*Pathfinder Roleplaying Game Bestiary* "Stirge")

3. The Large Cavern

The tight passage opens into a much larger cavern. Passages lead off in several directions. The far southwestern side of the cavern apparently ends in a ledge, leading to darkness. Immediately to the right is a 10-foot depression containing loose earth, blocking access to a passage beyond. Strangely, the cavern lacks stalactites and stalagmites.

Though large, the main cavern is empty. Its ceiling is some 30 feet above the floor. If a *detect evil* spell is in operation, it indicates the presence of evil toward the ledge in the southwest corner of the cavern. The ledge rises 10 feet from the floor of the cavern to **Area 7**. The depression at **Area 4** is 10 feet below the level of the cavern floor. The passage to **Area 6** is difficult to spot until the PCs are within 20 feet of the opening.

4. The Collapsed Section (CR 3)

The floor in this area has collapsed 10 feet below the level of the main cavern. Its floor is soft earth, and there are bones of several giant rats littered about. Ten feet under this soft earth is an **ankheg**, which waits for its meals to descend into the pit and cause vibrations that tell it to come and eat. Also within this depression is a hole in the wall of the cliff made by the collapsed portion of the floor, which leads to a passage that slopes down to **Level 2**.

ANKHEG CR 3
XP 800
hp 28 (*Pathfinder Roleplaying Game Bestiary* "Ankheg")

Treasure: If the PCs spend several minutes sifting through the soft earth and bones in the floor of the depression and make a successful Perception check for each of the following items (DC 18 for each of the weapons, DC 22 for the coins and gems), they locate 25 gp, a *+1 keen throwing axe,* a masterwork dagger, a mace, and five large pieces of malachite worth 25 gp each.

5. Dead End (CR Varies, 1–4)

Stairs descend 20 feet to an apparent dead-end passage. There is a 1–3 on 1d20 chance that **2d6 dire rats** are here. There is a small rat tunnel (DC 15 Perception check to notice) leading to the Entrance Level, Area 8B.

DIRE RATS CR 1/3
XP 135
hp 5 (*Pathfinder Roleplaying Game Bestiary* "Rat, Dire")

6. The Fungus Cavern (CR Varies, 0–3)

The walls of this cavern, due to dampness and air from the sinkhole, are covered with a barely luminescent green moss. Several (3d6) mushrooms of abnormal size also are in this room, but they are not magical. There is a 1–3 on 1d20 chance that **2d4 dire rats** are here feasting on the fungus and mushrooms. Several of the rat tunnels lead to the **Entrance Level**, **Areas 8B** and **9B**.

DIRE RATS CR 1/3
XP 135
hp 5 (*Pathfinder Roleplaying Game Bestiary* "Rat, Dire")

7. The Burial Room (CR 1)

In this man-carved alcove are four rotted coffins. They contain **1 skeleton** each, which wield scimitars and animate when any coffin is disturbed, or if a force of good comes within 15 feet of the coffins. These skeletons all wear *amulets of protection from good*, which provide +2 channel resistance in addition to the benefits of a *protection from good* spell.

SKELETONS (4) CR 1/3
XP 135
Male human skeleton (*Pathfinder Roleplaying Game Bestiary* "Skeleton, Medium")
NE Medium undead
Init +6; **Senses** darkvision 60 ft.; **Perception** +0

AC 16, touch 12, flat-footed 14 (+2 armor, +2 Dex, +2 natural); +2 vs. Good creatures
hp 4 (1d8)
Fort +0; **Ref** +2; **Will** +2; +2 vs. Good creatures
Defensive Abilities channel resistance +2; **DR** 5/bludgeoning; **Immune** cold, undead traits

Speed 30 ft.
Melee scimitar +2 (1d6+2) or 2 claws +2 (1d4+2)

Str 15, **Dex** 14, **Con** —, **Int** —, **Wis** 10, **Cha** 10

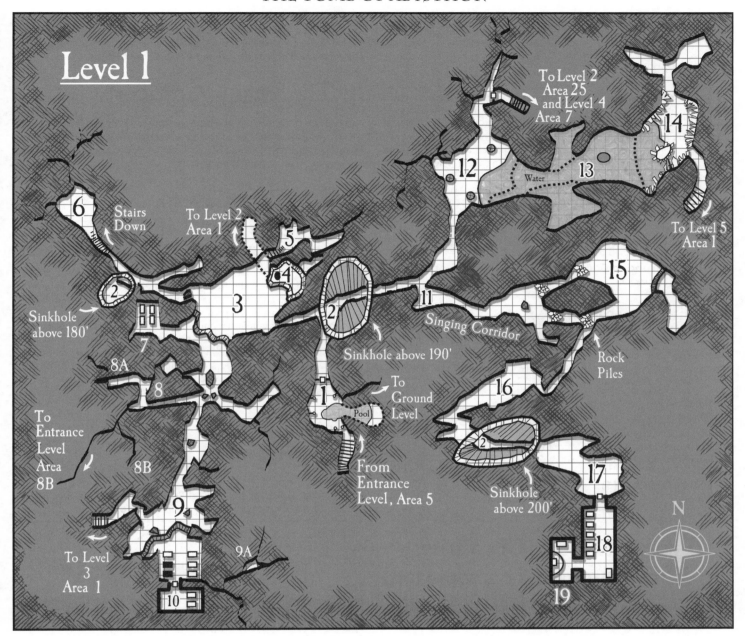

Base Atk +0; **CMB** +2; **CMD** 14 (16 vs. Good)
Feats Improved Initiative
Skills Acrobatics –2, Climb –2, Escape Artist –2, Stealth –2
Gear broken chain shirt, scimitar, *amulet of protection from good*

Treasure: In the coffins are a total of 26 gp and 134 sp.

8. The Rat Caves

These passages are all no more than 4 feet in height, and the rat tunnels themselves are from 2 to 3 feet in high.

8A. The Nest (CR 6)

There are a total of **28 dire rats** here of various sizes. The nest is made of rotted clothing, straw and fungus.

DIRE RATS (28)   CR 1/3
XP 135

hp 5 (*Pathfinder Roleplaying Game Bestiary* "Rat, Dire")

Treasure: Several shiny pieces of metal are in the nest, and one is a *ring of sustenance*. There are also a kukri and a punch dagger, both of which are non-magical, as well as several non-magical rings of both silver and gold (six valued at 5 gp each and three valued at 10 gp each), and a small jade statuette of a serpent worth 20 gp. The characters searching need to make Perception checks (DC 7 for the daggers and statue and 18 for the rings and gems) to locate the various items.

8B. The Hidden Nest (CR 4)

Reaching this nest requires the PC to crawl through rat tunnels; on the way he or she meets **12 dire rats**.

DIRE RATS (12)   CR 1/3
XP 135

hp 5 (*Pathfinder Roleplaying Game Bestiary* "Rat, Dire")

Treasure: The nest here is mostly made of shredded cloth, and within it is a total of 12 gp, 64 sp and 129 cp. There are also five 1 sp rings, one *ring of climbing* and a masterwork longsword in a bejeweled scabbard worth 100 gp. The characters searching need to make Perception checks

(DC 7 for the sword, 10 for the coins and 18 for the rings) to locate the various items.

9. Cavern

The passage opens up to reveal a strangely-shaped cavern with a depression at the far end that leads to an obviously man-made alcove. A wooden door is set in the far man-made wall. The alcove is filled with what appear to be wooden coffins, though they have rotted and decayed.

The main cavern itself is unpopulated, as is the depression to the south, which descends 10 feet below the floor of the main cavern. The depression contains a man-made alcove filled with six rotted and destroyed coffins. They are unoccupied. However, the **shadows** from **Area 10** may be present. If so, they occupy the two sarcophagi marked on the map. See **Area 10** for more details. The small passage to the west contains stairs down to **Level 3, Area 1**. A wooden door in the south wall leads to **Area 10**. The door is locked with a poor-quality lock and is rather old.

Old Locked Wooden Door: 1 in. thick; hardness 5; hp 10; Break DC 12; Disable Device DC 15.

9A. Dire Rat Shadows (CR 5)

The shadows at **Area 10** captured a pack of dire rats that lived in the nest to the east of their room and turned them into **5 dire rat shadows.** These rather strange undead befuddle anyone familiar with the power of normal shadows, which usually create only human shadows. They have no treasure. The shadows took it all.

Tactics: These dire shadow rats swarm in their incorporeal state and attack once with an incorporeal Strength-draining bite. They then become corporeal and attack with their bite that causes disease as well as Strength drain (a powerful attack). They serve the whim of the shadows and attack until slain or commanded to retreat.

DIRE SHADOW RATS (5)   **CR 1**
XP 400
hp 4 (*The Tome of Horrors Complete* 504)

10. The Back Room (CR Varies, 5 or 7 if they summon the shadow rats)

These coffins are the normal home of **2 shadows.** They are most likely encountered at **Area 9**, however. See "Tactics," below.

SHADOWS (2)   **CR 3**
XP 800
hp 19 (*Pathfinder Roleplaying Game Bestiary* "Shadow")

Tactics: The shadows that reside here will most likely not be in their coffins. The light from the approaching party's torches disturbs them, and they move to wait for the party in the corners of the alcove in **Area 9** to come upon the party from behind. Once the PCs draw near, they summon their servitor **dire shadow rats** that they have created from **Area 9A**. The shadows then attack with their touch attacks, draining Strength. If discovered and successfully attacked, they use their incorporeal form to pass through the walls and escape their attackers. They never materialize or enter melee (aside from their touch attacks).

GM Note: Use your discretion with this encounter. If your PCs are of too low a level or are not schooled in the concept of running to fight another day, you may decide not to have the shadows summon the dire rat shadows.

Treasure: Coffin 1 contains silver jewelry amounting to 45 gp, as well as 28 gp, 18 pp, fourteen 25 gp gems, three *potions of cure light wounds*

and a masterwork dagger. Coffin 2 contains 183 sp, two silver rings valued at 2 gp each, a gold statuette of a nude woman of exquisite craftsmanship valued at 300 gp, a *potion of delay poison*, a *potion of glibness* and a *scroll of 2 arcane spells* (*web* and *ice storm*, CL 7th for both).

11. The Singing Corridor

At this corridor, due to the wind between the sinkholes, there is a great whistling, and the party is affected by a blast of wind as if **Wandering Monster Table** result #6 had been rolled. Perception checks are at –4 due to the loud noise masking other sounds.

12. The Pool Cavern (CR Varies, 7 or 8 if giant poisonous frogs are present)

The dripping of the water from the stalactites into the pool can be heard echoing down the corridor before this room is entered. This room is very wet, and a thin patina of water covers the whole room. Any fast movement in the room (such as combat) requires a DC 12 Reflex save or the character slips and falls. At the three "X"s are the denizens of this room: **3 piercers.** There is, however, no treasure in this room since the piercers do not care about it and the other monsters in the dungeon scavenge it off the floor. There is also a 1–4 chance on 1d20 that **1d3 giant poisonous frogs** from **Area 13** are lurking in the portion of the pool that intrudes into this room.

PIERCERS (3)   **CR 2**
XP 600 (*The Tome of Horrors Complete* 760)

GIANT POISONOUS FROGS   **CR 3**
XP 800
N Large animal
(*Pathfinder Roleplaying Game Bestiary* "Frog, Dire")
Init +6; **Senses** low-light vision, scent; **Perception** +6

AC 19, touch 11, flat-footed 17 (+2 Dex, +8 natural, –1 size)
hp 50 (4d8+28)
Fort +11; **Ref** +8; **Will** +2

Speed 40 ft., swim 40 ft.
Melee bite +8 (1d8+6 plus grab and poison) or tongue +8 touch (grab)
Space 10 ft.; **Reach** 10 ft. (20 ft. with tongue)
Special Attacks pull (tongue, 10 feet), swallow whole (1d8+6 bludgeoning damage, AC 12, 2 hp), tongue

Str 23, **Dex** 15, **Con** 24, **Int** 1, **Wis** 12, **Cha** 10
Base Atk +3; **CMB** +10 (+14 grapple); **CMD** 22 (26 vs. trip)
Feats Improved Initiative, Lightning Reflexes
Skills Acrobatics +11 (+15 jumping), Perception +6, Stealth +2, Swim +14; **Racial Modifiers** +4 Acrobatics (+8 jumping), +4 Stealth

Poison (Ex) Injury—bite; *save* Fort DC 19; *frequency* 1/round for 6 rounds; *effect* 1d2 Con damage; *cure* 1 save. The save DC is Constitution-based

Door and Stairs: Here, a door bars passage down to **Level 4**. The large bronze door has a silver lock. The lock can be picked only (Disable Device DC 30) after the door itself has had a *knock* or *dispel magic* cast on it. Otherwise, one needs one of the several silver keys that the priests of the temple possess to open this door.

13. Water Passage (CR 7)

Only a very strong swimmer could make this swim through the narrow underwater passage without magical aid, let alone without light, since the water is very dark. In the northern area of the water passage, under an inch of silt on the bottom, are a suit of Medium masterwork half-plate armor (that can be restored with a DC 15 Craft (armorsmithing) check and 200 gp worth of material) and a *ring of protection +1*. The pool itself is occupied by **6 giant poisonous frogs**. These frogs were placed here by the priests of Tsathogga and are killing machines bred in the pits of the Temple of the Frog in the caverns below.

GIANT POISONOUS FROGS (6)   **CR 2**
XP 600
hp 15 (see **Level 1, Area 12**)

Tactics: The poisonous frogs viciously attack any persons swimming through the passage. They always pair up when attacking, with at least two frogs attacking each victim, allowing a flanking bonus.

14. The Crystal Cavern (CR 4)

This room has its walls covered by highly reflective crystals of an unusual size. Any light source brought into the room causes shimmering colors and strange and blinding prismatic special effects. The crystals themselves are quite hard and not easy to break. They have little value individually, other than to be used as curios on pendants by superstitious commoners.

Alcoves: In these side alcoves north of the main room are **2 giant poisonous frogs**.

GIANT POISONOUS FROGS (2)   **CR 2**
XP 600
hp 15 (see **Level 1, Area 12**)

Stairs: The stairs from this room lead down to the Great Cavern and the Temple of the Frog on **Level 5**.

15. Gorbash's Lair (CR 5)

In this large cave, filled with skins and bones and garbage, is **Gorbash the ogre**. Gorbash is rather bright (unlike his brother Ambro, who resides in the dungeon of Rappan Athuk) and has consumed several parties of adventurers, earning the experience that raised him to 6 Hit Dice. Gorbash does not like undead, though he has an uneasy truce with Draeligor the wight — purchased by the magic maul given to him by the priests of Orcus on **Level 4**. For now the evil priests are content to purchase Gorbash's loyalty. He does not ordinarily travel into **Area 17** (or beyond). Nor does he go into **Areas 9** or **10**. In fact, he generally does not even travel down the corridor to **Area 16** unless he is forced to, as described below. Instead, Gorbash waits for his meals to come to him, as described under "**Tactics**," below. He can occasionally be caught roaming the halls of this level, hunting for dire rats, which are his favorite food (when adventurers are unavailable).

GORBASH   **CR 5**
XP 1,600
Male ogre barbarian 3 (*Pathfinder Roleplaying Game Bestiary* "Ogre")
CE Large humanoid (giant)
Init –1; **Senses** darkvision 60 ft., low-light vision; **Perception** +6

AC 17, touch 8, flat-footed 17 (+4 armor, –1 Dex, +5 natural, –1 size)

hp 66 (3d12+9 plus 4d8+12 plus 9)
Fort +10; **Ref** +1; **Will** +4
Defensive Abilities trap sense, uncanny dodge

Speed 35 ft.
Melee *maul of the titans* +14/+9 (2d8+12)
Ranged javelin +7/+2 (1d8+6)
Space 10 ft.; **Reach** 10 ft.
Special Attacks rage (11 rounds/day), rage power (knockback)

Str 22, **Dex** 9, **Con** 16, **Int** 9, **Wis** 10, **Cha** 7
Base Atk +6; **CMB** +13; **CMD** 22
Feats Intimidating Prowess, Iron Will, Toughness, Vital Strike
Skills Acrobatics –4, Climb +10, Escape Artist –4, Intimidate +11, Perception +6, Ride –4, Stealth –8, Survival +4, Swim +7
Languages Giant
SQ fast movement +10
Gear hide armor, *maul of the titans*, 4 javelins, 3d6 sp, 1d4 gp

Tactics: His favorite tactic is to wait by the big column that divides the entrance into his room into a north and a south passage. He has learned that torchlight means a meal is on its way. At the points on the map marked "rock piles," he has piled a small rock wall low enough for an 8-foot, 6-inch ogre to jump over easily but high enough to require smaller characters to climb (DC 10 Climb check). Since the rocks are an obstacle to PCs, Gorbash waits and looks to see where any approaching light is coming from. This delay allows him to get a good fix on the party. He then waits for the light to start moving again — telling him that the party is past the first of the two rock walls. Gorbash then circles around the other path and comes on the party from behind — hopefully while they are between the two rock walls. If the party is few in number, he tries to sweep right through it. If the party is large, he kills the rear character (and maybe one more) and then goes back around the other way while the PCs struggle with the rock walls. If combat goes against him, Gorbash tries to flee to **Areas 18** and **19**, where he calls on the aid of Draeligor. He is loath to do so, however, since such an act would establish Draeligor as the leader of this level. If summoned to Gorbash's aid, Draeligor brings four of his skeletons.

Small Cave: There is a small cave at the far east end of Gorbash's cave. The entrance to this cave is some 15 feet off the ground. It can be reached with a DC 10 Climb check.

Treasure: In this cave is Gorbash's treasure. It consists of five sacks, a small wooden chest and a pile of clothing, weapons and armor.

The five sacks respectively contain the following.
Sack 1: 2,063 sp
Sack 2: 45 sp, 350 gp
Sack 3: 1,067 gp
Sack 4: Eight 50 gp gems, three necklaces (worth 10 gp each), a silver bracelet (5 gp) and a small jade statuette (25 gp)
Sack 5: Two brass candleholders (8 gp), a fine mirror (25 gp), a silver chalice (10 gp), seventeen assorted earrings (1 gp total), five gold rings (worth 2 gp each), a *ring of jumping* and a silver holy symbol of Mitra (10 gp)

Locked Wooden Chest (small): 1 in. thick; hardness 5; hp 1; Break DC 17; Disable Device DC 20.

The small wooden chest is locked and contains three *potions* (*water breathing, heroism,* and *poison*). Gorbash once opened the chest and tasted the poison potion and decided it was icky, so he let it be.

In a pile in the rear of the cave Gorbash has collected 6 longswords, 2 maces, 3 short swords, 8 daggers, 2 throwing axes, a greatsword, a masterwork composite longbow [Str +1] made by a famous half-elf bowyer in Bard's Gate, a light crossbow, a dwarven waraxe, a greataxe and a *+1 frog bane trident*. In a pile he has various cloaks and other items of clothing, a suit of Small leather armor, a suit of Small chainmail, three sets of Medium chainmail, a suit of Medium studded leather, three light steel shields, and two tower shields. All of the armor and shields have the broken condition, and require some degree of repair from obvious combat damage (GM to determine — from 5% to 50% of the value of the armor). The weapons, though, are in good condition, except for the light crossbow, which is without its string or goat's foot lever.

16. Cavern

This cavern is empty save for four half-burned-out torches lying on the floor and a broken holy water vial near the far wall.

17. Worked Cavern

This cave is empty and deathly still. The south wall has obviously been worked and has a door in the center of it that is wooden with iron bands. It is not locked, but it requires forcing, as the wood of the door has expanded due to the dampness of the dungeon. Two discarded longswords lie on the floor, one of which is heavily notched.

Stuck Iron-Banded Wooden Door: 1 in. thick; hardness 5; hp 20; Break DC 15.

18. Crypt (CR 2)

This room of carved stone contains six stone sarcophagi. Each holds a skeleton in chainmail with a scimitar. Once a force of good enters the room, the **6 skeletons** animate. Their proximity to the evil shrine at 19 as well as their *amulets* give them channel resistance (+4).

SKELETONS (6)   CR 1/3
XP 135
Male human skeleton (*Pathfinder Roleplaying Game Bestiary* "Skeleton, Medium")
NE Medium Undead
Init +6; **Senses** darkvision 60 ft.; **Perception** +0

AC 16, touch 12, flat-footed 14 (+2 armor, +2 Dex, +2 natural); +2 vs. Good creatures
hp 4 (1d8)
Fort +0; **Ref** +2; **Will** +2; +2 vs. Good creatures
Defensive Abilities channel resistance +4; DR 5/bludgeoning; **Immune** cold, undead traits

Speed 30 ft.
Melee scimitar +2 (1d6+2) or 2 claws +2 (1d4+2)

Str 15, **Dex** 14, **Con** —, **Int** —, **Wis** 10, **Cha** 10
Base Atk +0; **CMB** +2; **CMD** 14 (16 vs. Good)
Feats Improved Initiative
Skills Acrobatics –2, Climb –2, Escape Artist –2, Stealth –2
Gear broken chain shirt, scimitar, *amulet of protection from good*, 2 15 gp rubies

Treasure: Each of the skeletons has a 15 gp ruby in each of its eye sockets (twelve in all), which glow while the creatures live their unlife. Each skeleton also wears an *amulet of protection from good*, which provides +2 turn resistance in addition to the benefits of a *protection from good* spell while worn. When the skeletons are destroyed, the gems cease to glow. There is a 75% chance that combat in this room draws Draeligor, the denizen of **Area 19**, into this room.

19. The Shrine of Darkness (CR 4)

This room contains a dais of black stone carved in a demonic likeness (DC 12 Knowledge [religion] check reveals it to be Orcus) and spattered with blood. The room is permanently shadowed. Even strong light provides no more than flickering illumination, effectively negating normal light sources to 10 feet of illumination. In this evil room all undead gain channel resistance (+4). Further, merely being in this room causes good characters to make a DC 12 Will save or take a –1 morale penalty and 1d3 points of Strength damage from the negative energy emanating from the altar.

The stone sarcophagus in this room is the resting place of the evil undead guardian of this horrible shrine of darkness — **Draeligor the wight.** Draeligor came to this dungeon with the priests of Orcus from Rappan Athuk. He was stationed here to gain control over the first level of the dungeon. He wears magical banded mail emblazoned with an obscene magical rune of Orcus that causes fear. Because Draeligor has so much additional power from the evil shrine in this room, he is CR 4 here. If he is encountered in any other room, he is only CR 3.

DRAELIGOR THE WIGHT   CR 3 (or CR 4)
XP 800 (or 1,200)
Male wight warrior 2 (*Pathfinder Roleplaying Game Bestiary* "Wight")
LE Medium undead
Init +1; **Senses** darkvision 60 ft.; **Perception** +12

AC 23, touch 11, flat-footed 22 (+8 armor, +1 Dex, +4 natural)
hp 44 (2d10+4 plus 4d8+8)
Fort +6; **Ref** +2; **Will** +5
Defensive abilities channel resistance +4; **Immune** undead traits

Speed 20 ft.
Melee slam +6 (1d4+1 plus energy drain)
Special Attacks energy drain (1 level, DC 14)

Str 12, **Dex** 12, **Con** —, **Int** 11, **Wis** 13, **Cha** 15
Base Atk +4; **CMB** +5; **CMD** 16
Feats Blind-Fight, Skill Focus (Perception), Weapon Focus (claw)
Skills Acrobatics –4 (–8 jump), Climb –4, Intimidate +10, Knowledge (religion) +7, Perception +12, Stealth +13
Languages Common
SQ create spawn, resurrection vulnerability
Gear +1 banded mail of fear (armor possesses 6 charges of cause fear; when invoked as a free action, all in 30-ft. radius must make DC 14 Will save or be stricken as per the fear spell), six vials of unholy water (2d4 damage to good-aligned outsiders and paladins).

Create Spawn (Su) Any humanoid creature that is slain by a wight becomes a wight itself in only 1d4 rounds. Spawn so created are less powerful than typical wights, and suffer a –2 penalty on all d20 rolls and checks, as well as –2 hp per HD. Spawn are under the command of the wight that created them and remain enslaved until its death, at which point they lose their spawn penalties and become full-fledged and free-willed wights. They do not possess any of the abilities they had in life.

Resurrection Vulnerability (Su) A raise dead or similar spell cast on a wight destroys it (Will negates). Using the spell in this way does not require a material component.

Tactics: Draeligor prefers to remain in his shrine unless drawn by the sound of combat in **Area 18**. He immediately uses a charge from his armor of fear and wades in to attack any persons not stricken by fear. He attacks priests first, using his energy drain power. Even if the tide of battle turns against him, Draeligor does not flee. Death of his corporeal form is nothing compared to the torment he would suffer at the hands of Orcus for abandoning the shrine he was entrusted to guard.

Treasure: In his crypt, Draeligor has 21,476 cp, 1,612 sp, 222 gp, 50 pp, four small 100 gp diamonds and three golden statues of Orcus valued at 50 gp each, as well as a +1 buckler and 20 +1 arrows.

Experience: In addition to XP for the combat encounter, destroying the shrine by cleansing it with holy water and consecrating it nets a 900 XP group story award and good-aligned clerics and paladins an additional 200 XP individual award.

Level 2: The Lesser Caves And Dark Natasha's Lair

This strange level is home to a diverse set of occupants. It contains one of the hidden burial halls of Thyr and Muir. Dark Natasha makes her home on this level in the rooms beyond the strange mist she created to shroud approach to her lair. Stirges fill the northern caves and are a deadly nuisance throughout the level. The priests of Orcus have temporary barracks here near the stairs down to their temple. Though he does not live on this level, Balcoth (from **Level 2A**) is a constant threat. Balcoth and Dark Natasha are at a standoff, having reached an agreement that neither is to enter the other's domain. Neither Balcoth nor Dark Natasha has yet joined with the priests of Orcus, though the evil priests are courting them. Otyughs wander the entire level and are a continuous menace, particularly to low-level adventurers.

ACOLYTE OF ORCUS   CR 2
XP 600
hp 23 (see **Level 2**, **Area 26**)

DIRE BATS   CR 2
XP 600
hp 22 (*Pathfinder Roleplaying Game Bestiary* "Bat, Dire")

GHOUL   CR 1
XP 400
hp 13 (*Pathfinder Roleplaying Game Bestiary* "Ghoul")

LESSER PRIESTS OF ORCUS   CR 4
XP 1,200
hp 55 (see **Level 2A**, **Area 14**)

Level 2: The Lesser Caves and Dark Natasha's Lair

Difficulty Level: 4.
Entrances: Cave passage from **Level 1, Area 4**.
Exits: Overhead intersecting passage that leads to **Level 2A** (Balcoth's Lair), Stairs to **Level 3** and hidden stairs to **Level 4**.
Wandering Monsters: The level is divided into several areas for purposes of wandering monsters:
Areas 1 and 5–8: Check once per 30 minutes on 1d20:

ROLL 1D20	RESULT
1	**2d6 stirges.** If a lightly armored character is killed in combat with a stirge horde, eight to ten stirges combine to carry the character back to **Area 3A**.
2	**1d4 otyughs**
3	**2d4 dire bats**
4–20	No encounter

Areas 2–4: Follow the "Stirge Check" guides given in **Area 3**. All random encounters here are **stirges**. If a lightly armored character is killed in combat with a stirge horde, 8 to 10 stirges combine to carry the character back to **Area 3A**.
Areas 9–15: These areas do not have random encounters since no monsters enter the mist that Natasha has created. Natasha herself is not always in one set location.
Areas 16–21: These areas are very densely populated. Check once per 30 minutes on 1d20:

ROLL 1D20	RESULT
1–4	**2d6 stirges.** If a lightly armored character is killed in combat with a stirge horde, eight to ten stirges combine to carry the character back to **Area 3A**.

5	**Balcoth.** In his insubstantial form, Balcoth is roaming this level, testing out the limits of Natasha's watchfulness. He observes the party but does not attack unless he is attacked. He is never found in or beyond **Area 9** (the purple haze). See **Level 2A**, **Area 7**, for details.
6	**1 manticore**
7	**Dark Natasha.** She is most likely *invisible*. She spies on the party. From this point on she is alerted to their presence. She does not attack them immediately. See **Area 12** for details.
8	**1d4 otyughs**
9–20	No encounter

Area 24–25: Roll 1d20 when any such room is entered:

ROLL 1D20	RESULT
1	**A delegation of priests (1 lesser priest** and **1d4 acolytes of Orcus)** either heading to or coming from the graves at **21** or Balcoth on **Level 2A**.
2	**Acolyte workers (1d6 acolytes of Orcus** led by a **lesser priest)** defacing holy runes and spreading filth.
3	**1d4 ghouls**
4–20	No encounter

Standard Features: The cavern sections are unlit. The worked sections have torch holders every 20 to 30 feet — simple iron rings in which torches can be set.
Continuous Effects: All spell effects on this level are at CL 9th unless otherwise noted. **Areas 2, 2A–C, 4** and **4A** are covered by a *hallow* spell. **Area 9** is filled with the *magical mist* created by Dark Natasha.

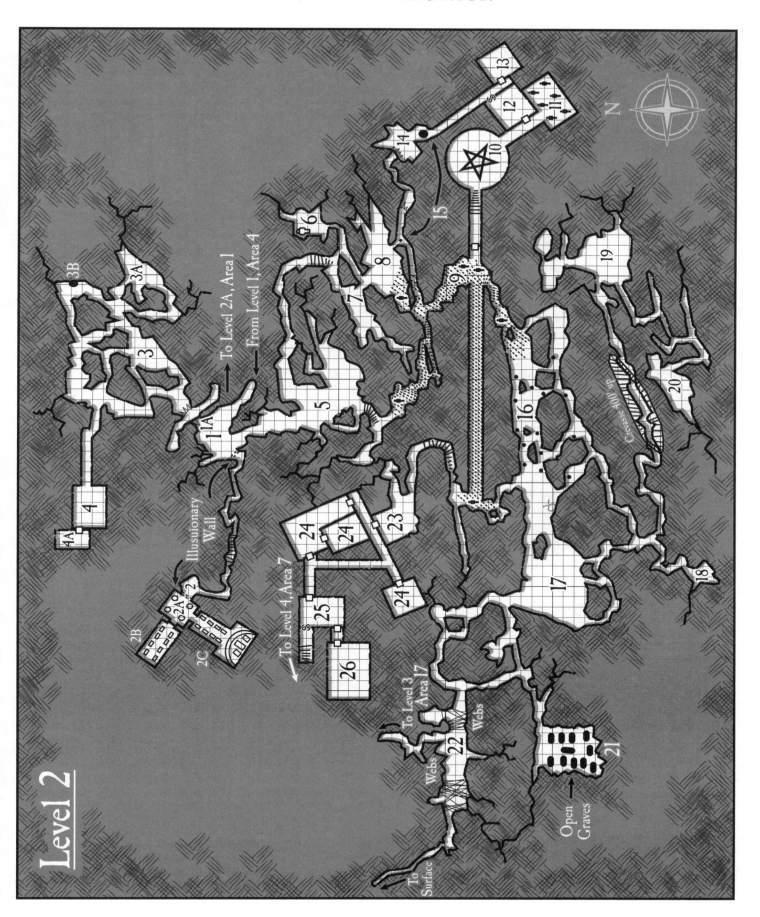

Level 2

MANTICORES   **CR 5**
XP 1,600
hp 57 (*Pathfinder Roleplaying Game Bestiary* "Manticore")

OTYUGHS   **CR 4**
XP 1,200
hp 39 (*Pathfinder Roleplaying Game Bestiary* "Otyugh")

STIRGE   **CR 1/2**
XP 200
hp 5 (*Pathfinder Roleplaying Game Bestiary* "Stirge")

1. Entrance Cavern (CR Varies, by wandering monster)

This large, vaulted cavern smells faintly of offal and decay. The ceiling is over 60 feet above the cavern floor. A passage leads off to the south. Obvious on the northern wall is an opening some 30 feet above the cave floor (see **Area 1A**, below). It appears that passages lead off from that opening in either direction.

Wandering Monsters: As the PCs enter, immediately roll on the **wandering monster** table, as the sound of approaching footsteps and light has a chance to draw a monster.

Illusory Wall: The passage leading to **Area 2** has been covered with an *illusory wall* spell to appear as part of the surrounding stone wall. A DC 16 Will save is allowed to disbelieve the illusion if the *illusory wall* is interacted with. See Illusions in the *Pathfinder Roleplaying Game Core Rulebook* and the *illusory wall* spell description for more details.

Detections: The *illusory wall* radiates moderate illusion magic, if detected.

1A. Passage above to Balcoth's Lair

Here, the passage is blocked by a ledge that rises to 30 feet above the floor (the ceiling is 50 feet above) and bisects the passage. On either side of the ledge, 30 feet above the ground, are openings that lead to **Level 2A — Balcoth's Lair**. See **Level 2A, Area 1**. This passage also effectively keeps monsters out of the area to the north, except for the major denizen: stirges.

To pass over the ledge to **Areas 3** and **4** beyond, characters (and monsters) must climb (or fly) up the south side of the ledge and then go down the north face, which on that side is 40 feet above the floor of the cavern, requiring a DC 12 Climb check.

Detections: Detections: Magic (divination and abjuration) can be detected emanating from the magical runes Balcoth has placed on the ledge above. See **Level 2A, Area 1**, for more details.

2. The Hidden Cave And the Sanctuary

This area, accessed by a narrow path behind the *illusory wall,* appears to be nothing but a small cave. The west wall, however, is also covered with an *illusory wall* spell. A DC 16 Will save is allowed to disbelieve the illusion if the *illusory wall* is interacted with. See Illusions in the *Pathfinder Roleplaying Game Core Rulebook* and the *illusory wall* spell description for more details.

Even if the *illusory wall* is not detected, this area is under the effects of a *hallow* spell (see **Area 2C**). Good-aligned creatures feel the presence of the protection this spell provides and feel safe here.

Detections: The *illusory wall* radiates moderate illusion magic, if

detected. Evocation magic from the *hallow* spell can also be detected.

2A. Anteroom

This room of white stone was carved long before this complex was corrupted by minions of evil and has remained pure ever since. The four white pillars are graven with holy runes. In the northeast wall is a silver basin filled with the equivalent of ten vials of holy water. This water replenishes itself at the rate of one vial per day.

This room is also covered by the *hallow* spell (see **Area 2C**).

2B. Hall of Warriors

This room is filled with eight standing stone sarcophagi (see **Standard Features**) that contain the corpses of valiant warriors who have fallen in the service of Thyr and Muir. PCs can make a DC 22 Knowledge (history or religion) check to recognize the names of these lesser knights of legend. GMs are free to create these names as befits their campaign.

Each corpse wears a suit of armor of differing types (four wear chainmail, one wears scale, one wears banded, one wears splint and the last wears a breastplate), and each bears a shield (four are heavy steel, two are tower, one is a light steel and one a heavy wooden) and a weapon (two are longswords, three are bastard swords, one is a greatsword, one a heavy mace and one a longspear). The armor, shields and weapons may be of special make. Roll 1d20 individually:

ROLL 1D20	RESULT
1	*+1* and *light emitting* if a weapon
2	masterwork and *keen* if a weapon
3–4	masterwork
5–20	normal

Each wears a circlet of silver worth 50 gp.
This room, too, is under the effects of the *hallow* spell (see **Area 2C**).

Experience: Absent a quest or some other deific justification, any good-aligned character disturbing these sarcophagi or their contents loses 500 XP. Any lawful good–aligned character loses 1,000 XP, must do *atonement* prior to advancing in level and is *quested* to return any items taken.

2C. The Tomb of Alaric

This tomb is lined with eight stone sarcophagi (see **Standard Features**) of heroes as is the tomb described above (see **Area 2B**). However, at the far end of the tomb on a raised dais is the tomb of Alaric the Paladin, who lived during the time of the great reign of the Third High Lord, before the corruption and downfall.

Inside of this stone sarcophagus (see **Standard Features**) is the perfectly preserved corpse of Alaric himself, dressed in *+2 full plate* and holding his *+3 bastard sword*. Both of these items are restricted to use by lawful good persons, or the user finds that he or she becomes *armor of arrow attraction* and a *–1 bastard sword*. Alaric also wears a circlet of pure gold worth 1,000 gp.

The *Chalice* and the *Stone*: To his right and left side are small altars, both covered with a small silk cloth. Behind his tomb is a large holy symbol of Muir. On the altar to the right is a silver chalice. On the altar to the left is what appears to be a broken chunk of carved marble.

The silver chalice is the *Chalice of Elanir*, a holy chalice that radiates good. Any liquid poured into it becomes pure wine of a fine quality, fit to drink (regardless of its previous magical qualities, poison content or impurities — excepting only *earth blood*, which it will not change). Filling the chalice with holy water and then consuming the entire contents acts as a *cure serious wounds* spell, operating in this manner once per day.

The broken piece of marble is the *Stone of Tircople*. This holy artifact is a piece of the altar stone of the now ruined and desecrated great temple in the ruined holy city of Tircople. The holder of the stone gains a permanent *protection from evil*.

The two may be used in combination. If the *Chalice* is placed upon the *Stone* and the *Chalice* filled with two vials of holy water and the whole

is consecrated with a *bless* spell and then consumed, whoever drinks receives the effects of a *cure disease* spell in addition to the *cure serious wounds* effect above. The *Stone* and *Chalice* can operate together in this manner once per week, and only if the *cure serious wounds* power has not been used on the day in question.

Both the *Stone* and the *Chalice* have an effective CL 12th.

Obtaining the *Chalice* and *Stone*: If proper respect is given to the tomb, and if a cleric or paladin of Thyr or Muir worships at the tomb as is befitting ceremony, the character is visited and instructed that he or she is worthy and has been chosen to carry the *Stone* and the *Chalice* from the tomb to further the will of his or her deity.

Hallow: This tomb is the focus of the *hallow* spell, which also protects **Areas 2, 2A** and **2B**. Long ago, the priests of Thyr and Muir placed a *hallow* spell on this tomb, along with an accompanying *bless* spell. The *bless* spell has long since worn off and has not been renewed.

Experience: This tomb should not be troubled or desecrated in any way by any good-aligned character. Absent a quest or some other deific justification, any good-aligned character disturbing these sarcophagi or their contents loses 500 XP. Any lawful good-aligned character loses 1,000 XP, must do *atonement* prior to advancing in level and is *quested* to return any items taken. However, proper care by good-aligned characters nets them a 100 XP bonus; lawful good characters (or clerics or paladins of other religions) earn a 200 XP bonus. Being chosen to bear the *Chalice* and *Stone* from the tomb is worth an additional 500 XP individual award.

3. The Stirge Caverns (CR Varies, 7+)

GM Note: This section is ***very dangerous***. Discourage low-level characters from entering. An attack by a small group of stirges with the threat of many more in the caves beyond should do the trick.

These caves are filled with stirges. There are at least **24 stirges** here in these several caves at all times. This number does not reflect the total number of stirges that inhabits the cavern, as many are flying outside and around the various levels. Stirges are vital elements of the dungeon food chain, and destroying this complex of caves (with several *fireballs* or the like) causes a meteoric rise in the rat and bat populations until the stirges can be replaced by the **stirge demon** (see **Area 3B**, below).

STIRGES (24+)　　　　　　　　　　　　　　　　　　**CR 1/2**
XP 200
hp 5 (*Pathfinder Roleplaying Game Bestiary* "Stirge")

Stirge Check: Upon entering **Area 3** by coming over the ledge to **2A**, roll 1d6 every minute. On a 1–3, **2d6 stirges** show up and attack. Continue this process as long as the characters remain north of the ledge to **2A**. Remember to continue checking every minute, even when combat is joined.

3A. The Main Lair (CR Varies, 1–4)

This is where stirge hatchlings from the stirge demon are brought by the stirge drones and nursed. Young stirges are disgusting, misshapen larvae that are a sickly pinkish white in color. Currently twelve of the foul hatchlings are here. They are helpless. They are attended by **2d4 stirges** at all times.

STIRGES (2d4)	CR 1/2
XP 200	

hp 5 (*Pathfinder Roleplaying Game Bestiary* "Stirge")

Treasure: Also in this room is the following treasure: 2,365 cp, 1,704 sp, 4,339 gp, six gems worth 50 gp each, twelve pieces of jewelry worth 25 gp each, a *keen kukri*, a *+1 quarterstaff of striking**, a set of *+1 leather shadow armor*, a *scroll of 3 arcane spells* (*rain of frogs*#, *boiling blood*# and *web shelter*#, all CL 5th) and two *potions: cure serious wounds* and *heroism*.

*The *striking* special ability of the quarterstaff is detailed in the **Appendix**.

#*Pathfinder Roleplaying Game Ultimate Magic*

3B. Lair of the Stirge Demon (CR 10+)

At the far end of the stirge cave is a small hole, about 2 feet in diameter. It reeks of offal and of the abyss. It radiates demonic-level evil.

GM Note: You should discourage all but high-level PCs (8th level plus) from exploring this hole.

Beyond the hole is a twisting passage about 2 feet in diameter that heads practically straight down over 100 feet. At the terminus of this long passage is a set of small caverns, not depicted on the map, attended by **12 stirges**, is the **stirge demon**. The stirge demon lays the larval stirges that are then taken by the stirge drones up to **Area 3A**, where they hatch. The dungeon will never fully be rid of stirges until this demon is destroyed.

STIRGES (12)	CR 1/2
XP 200	

hp 5 (*Pathfinder Roleplaying Game Bestiary* "Stirge")

STIRGE DEMON	CR 10

hp 92 (*The Tome of Horrors Complete* 175)

4. Undisturbed Tomb — Anteroom (CR 1)

Due to the number of stirges that have since made their home here, this tomb has never been disturbed or corrupted by the evil minions of Orcus. The room marked "4" proper is the anteroom to the tomb. It has several moldy tapestries hanging from the walls.

Stirge Check: Once the party begins down the passage toward **Area 4**, the "Stirge Check" mentioned above in **Area 3** happens only once every 5 minutes. This continues as long as the players remain in **Areas 4** and **4A**.

Door and Pit Trap: The door to **4A** is a large wooden door with a lock (see **Standard Features**). It is trapped with a pit in front of the door that opens along with the door. The pit is 25 feet deep and is filled with gooey mold that is not harmful.

PIT TRAP	CR 1
XP 400	

Type mechanical; **Perception** DC 20; **Disable Device** DC 20

Trigger location; **Reset** manual
Effect 25-ft.-deep pit (2d6 falling damage); DC 20 Reflex avoids; multiple targets (all targets in a 10-ft.-square area)

Detections: The tomb beyond the door detects as good.

4A. The Tomb

Within this tomb are four stone sarcophagi. Each contains the corpse of a warrior. Two of them are dressed in masterwork chainmail and hold masterwork bastard swords, and the other two are dressed in masterwork half plate and hold masterwork great swords. The weapons and armor are in fine condition. The two-handed swords are of fabulous workmanship. They are fine weapons made by the old master weaponsmiths. They are also rather impressive as antique works of skill. Some of the crafting techniques have been lost and the items are of special value to craftsmen.

Protection from Evil: This tomb is under the permanent effects of a *magic circle against evil*. All good-aligned characters instinctively feel that this is a safe place.

Experience: Absent a quest or some other deific justification, any good-aligned character disturbing these sarcophagi or their contents loses 500 XP. Any lawful good–aligned character loses 1,000 XP, must do *atonement* prior to advancing in level, and is *quested* to return any items taken.

5. Large Cavern (CR Varies, 7 or see below)

In this large cavern, which gives off a rather foul odor of dung, are **3 otyughs**.

GM Note: Otyughs can be very dangerous. If you feel your characters are either too low level or are unacquainted with the concept of running away from an encounter, feel free to reduce the number of creatures to two (CR 6) or even one (CR 4). Reduce the CR of the encounter accordingly.

OTYUGHS (3)	CR 4
XP 1,200	

hp 39 (*Pathfinder Roleplaying Game Bestiary* "Otyugh")

Treasure: In a pile of offal in the most easterly spur of the room (DC 20 Perception, only if specifically searched) are the following: 3,561 cp, 2,450 sp, 687 gp, a *potion of alter self* and a *–1 cursed longsword* placed here by Balcoth (see **Level 2A**) as a cruel joke.

6. The Cavern of the Stone Enigma

In this cavern is a large, humanlike head standing 8 feet tall. It has a blank stare and a closed mouth, but one gets the distinct feeling that it is on the verge of speaking one very powerful word. The statue radiates neither good nor evil, but it does radiate magic — a dim flicker of magic, deep within and distant. The radiation of magic is due to the fact that the root of this statue reaches down into a pool of *earth blood* (see **Level 5A**), and the power courses through the statue. Mortal weapons or spells may not harm the statue. The original builders of the complex unearthed it long ago.

This statue is an earth spirit. In fact, it is the spirit of the Stoneheart Mountains. It spoke the word that made these mountains when the earth god commanded it, and it will one day speak the word that shall destroy them. It is said that a spirit such as this exists within every formation of earth that is a distinct entity: mountain ranges, gorges, hills, cliffs, and so on. Further, it is said that these spirits, if found, may be made to reveal the words that they can speak — words of great power. It is rumored that when Margon and Alycthron raised the Wizard's Wall and changed the face of the land, they did so only because the combined power of their wizard's staves was able to extract one of these great words from the earth spirit of that region.

If one stays in the chamber for a sufficient period of time and examines the face, it becomes obvious that for some reason it grieves. Possibly for the word it must one day pronounce; possibly for the corruption of the earth that it embodies by the foul minions of Orcus and Tsathogga and their shrines; possibly because it wishes to speak that word that lingers on its lips now, but knows it cannot or possibly because of some fate man cannot fathom. The statue should fill the characters with a sense of awe of the powers above their pitiful magic, of the powers that exist in the very earth itself, of the life that is in all things.

7. Cavern

This cavern is empty.

8. Cavern (CR 1/2)

This cavern is also of little interest, except that its southwest exit is shrouded in the purplish mist that Natasha has placed here to guard her lair. Also, as indicated by the circled "X" on the map, one of her **zombie guards** is located here. The zombie is an incredibly poor guard, but its position here is almost certainly going to generate considerable noise when a party approaches, tipping off Natasha.

ZOMBIE IN CHAINMAIL   **CR 1/2**
XP 200
NE Medium undead (*Pathfinder Roleplaying Game Bestiary* "Zombie")
Init –1; **Senses** darkvision 60 ft.; **Perception** +0

AC 17, touch 9, flat-footed 17 (+6 armor, –1 Dex, +2 natural)
hp 13 (2d8 plus 4)
Fort +0; **Ref** –1; **Will** +3
DR 5/slashing; **Immune** undead traits

Speed 20 ft.
Melee halberd –6 (1d10+3/x3) and slam –7 (1d6+3)

Str 15, **Dex** 8, **Con** —, **Int** —, **Wis** 10, **Cha** 10
Base Atk +1; **CMB** +3; **CMD** 12
Feats Toughness
Skills Acrobatics –6 (–10 jump), Climb –3, Ride –6, Stealth –6, Swim –3

SQ staggered
Gear chainmail, halberd

Staggered (Ex) Zombies have poor reflexes and can only perform a single move action or standard action each round (it has the staggered condition.) A zombie can move up to its speed and attack in the same round as a charge action.

Note: See the description of the purple haze below for its effects and the concealment it provides to the zombies stationed within the mist.

9. The Purple Haze (CR Varies, 3 or 12 if Dark Natasha is present)

Natasha created this mist through a strange and intricate ritual that she herself only partially understands. The formula for this ritual can be found in her spell tomes. The moist, purplish mist feels wet and cold. Vision is limited to 5 feet in the best of light conditions, such as light from a *daylight* spell or darkvision. Torchlight allows only sputtering light that often cannot illuminate the hand at the end of a human's outstretched arm. Natasha and her zombie minions are immune to the mist's effect on vision, seeing through it as if it were not there. The mist cannot be moved with any wind-based spells. It can be dispelled if two successful *dispel magic* rolls are made, treating the mist as created by a 20th-level sorcerer.

Within the mist, at the spots designated on the map with a circled "X," Natasha has posted her guards: **6 zombies in chainmail.** There is a 1–4 on 1d20 chance that **Dark Natasha** (see **Area 12**) is present in the mist, keeping watch for Balcoth.

Concealment: The mist provides total concealment to those inside of it (50% miss chance on all attacks against those concealed). Remember that Natasha and the zombies are immune to the mist's effect on vision, and so their attacks do not suffer the miss chance.

ZOMBIES IN CHAINMAIL (6)   **CR 1/2**
XP 200
hp 13 (see **Area 8**, above)

Note: Remember to apply the miss chance on all attack rolls against the zombie due to the mist.

Zombie Tactics: The zombies stay within the mist. They use their pole arms to attack outside the mist, but they themselves do not leave it. Natasha can give them simple commands, such as "attack" or "return," which cause them to return to **Area 10**.

Natasha's Tactics: If Natasha has ample warning or is alerted to the presence of intruders, she wanders inside the mist to see if it is Balcoth approaching. If it is, she slips back into **Area 10**. If it is not, she harasses any intruders with spells from the mist and then retreats to **Area 10**.

Iron Door: Also located within the mist is a large iron door that is not physically locked, but is *arcane locked* and warded with an *alarm* spell that goes off quietly in **Areas 10**, **12** and **13**. The password for the door is "Balcoth." Since it is Balcoth she is primarily protecting against, Natasha finds her selection of his name as a password quite amusing. She does, however, consider him a serious adversary, though now they are at a standoff.

Arcane Locked **Iron Door:** 2 in. thick; hardness 10; hp 60; Break DC 38; Disable Device DC 35 (if *arcane lock* is dispelled). The password "Balcoth" suspends the *lock* and allows one person to pass.

10. The Room of Protection

This circular chamber is 60 feet in diameter and 35 feet high. Created long ago to house priests servicing this level of the burial halls, the room has a pentagram of magical protection, which operates as an inward facing *magic circle against evil* in the center of the room, and a *magic circle against evil* around the perimeter of the room. These circles are carved into the floor and are permanent. Natasha has chosen not to attempt to remove them, as they serve to keep Balcoth (and his summoned minions) from entering this room, though the symbols cause her discomfort.

Tactics: Natasha generally retreats to this room to prepare for battle. Natasha likes to hide up in the shadows of the room's ceiling (using *spider climb*) when adventurers enter, and rain spells down onto them after summoning her guards from the next room to come and melee the intruders. She then flees *invisibly*.

11. Guard Room (CR 3)

This barren room contains more of Natasha's **zombies in chainmail**, which come at her command.

ZOMBIES IN CHAINMAIL (6)   **CR 1/2**
XP 200
hp 13 (see **Area 8**, above)

12. Natasha's Room (CR 12, if Natasha is present)

This chamber is lavishly decorated with silks and satins, velvet curtains and pillows, a warm fire of coals from a bronze brazier, a divan and a large bed, a wardrobe full of sumptuous robes of various silken textures and rich furs, and a very large full-length silver mirror. Natasha is a sensuous creature who enjoys the vanity and comforts that her power and beauty bring her. From the brazier, a trail of musky incense rises, giving the whole room a very sexual feel. Above the bed, the canopy is hung with a gossamer resembling a spider's web. On her small table is a golden idol of the demon spider goddess (worth 300 gp). This is Dark Natasha's shrine. She does not keep her treasure in this room.

DARK NATASHA   **CR 12**
XP 19,200
Female drow cleric 5/mystic theurge 3/sorcerer 5 (*Pathfinder Roleplaying Game Bestiary* "Drow")
CE Medium humanoid (elf)
Init +7; **Senses** darkvision 120 ft., low-light vision; **Perception** +11
Aura evil

AC 23, touch 16, flat-footed 20 (+5 armor, +3 deflection, +3 Dex, +2 natural)
hp 99 (5d8+15 plus 8d6+24)
Fort +9; **Ref** +6; **Will** +14; +2 vs. enchantments
Immune sleep; **SR** 19
Weakness light blindness

Speed 30 ft.
Melee +2 *unholy light mace* +11/+6 (1d6+4)
Ranged hand crossbow +9/+4 (1d4 plus drow poison/19–20)
Special Attacks channel negative energy 9/day (3d6, DC 18)
Spell-Like Abilities (CL 13th):
1/day—*dancing lights, darkness, faerie fire*
Bloodline Spell-Like Ability (CL 13th):

9/day—*tremor* (CMB 11)
Domain Spell-Like Ability (CL 13th; melee touch +8):
7/day—*bleeding touch* (2 rounds)
Arcane Spells Known (CL 8th; melee touch +8, ranged touch +9):
4th (4/day)—*charm monster* (DC 20)
3rd (6/day)—*displacement, protection from energy*
2nd (8/day)—*alter self, darkvision*[B], *invisibility, see invisibility*
1st (8/day)—*alarm, expeditious excavation*[#B] (DC 17), *erase, magic missile, ray of enfeeblement* (DC 17), *silent image* (DC 17)
0 (at will)—*detect magic, flare* (DC 16), *ghost sound* (DC 16), *mage hand, open/close, ray of frost, read magic, touch of fatigue* (DC 16)
Bloodline Deep Earth[#]
Divine Spells Prepared (CL 8th; melee touch +8, ranged touch +9):
4th—*death ward*[D], *divine power, freedom of movement, spell immunity*
3rd—*animate dead, bestow curse* (DC 17), *deeper darkness, dispel magic, poison*[D] (DC 17)
2nd—*align weapon, hold person* (DC 16) x2, *silence* (DC 16), *summon swarm*[D]
1st—*command* (DC 15), *cure light wounds, divine favor, doom* (DC 15), *protection from good, spider climb*[D]
0 (at will)—*bleed* (DC 14), *create water, read magic, resistance*

[D] Domain Spell **Domains** Death, Vermin*

Str 14, **Dex** 16, **Con** 17, **Int** 17, **Wis** 18, **Cha** 22
Base Atk +6; **CMB** +8; **CMD** 24
Feats Blind-Fight, Deep Sight, Enlarge Spell, Eschew Materials, Improved Initiative, Silent Spell, Skill Focus (Knowledge [religion]), Weapon Finesse
Skills Climb +7, Diplomacy +10, Escape Artist +4, Fly +7, Intimidate +16, Knowledge (arcana) +13, Knowledge (dungeoneering) +11, Knowledge (history) +10, Knowledge (local) +7, Knowledge (planes) +14, Knowledge (religion) +18, Perception +11 (+13 to notice unusual stonework, such as traps and hidden doors in stone walls or floors), Sense Motive +10, Spellcraft +14, Stealth +8, Use Magic Device +11
Languages Abyssal, Common, Drow Sign Language, Elven, Undercommon
SQ combined spells (2nd), poison use, stonecunning +2
Combat Gear 3 *potions of cure serious wounds, potion of fly, potion of haste, potion of heroism*, 3 *scrolls of dread bolt*** (CL 8th); **Other Gear** +3 *leather armor*, +2 *unholy spiked light mace of venom* (as *dagger of venom*), hand crossbow, 10 bolts, *amulet of natural armor* +2, *cloak of elvenkind, ring of protection* +3, *ring of spectral hand* (7 charges, see **Appendix**).

Poison Use (Ex) Drow are skilled in the use of poison and never risk accidentally poisoning themselves. Drow favor an insidious toxin that causes its victims to lapse into unconsciousness—this poison allows drow to capture slaves with great ease.

Drow Poison—*injury; save* Fort DC 13; *frequency* 1/minute for 2 minutes; *initial effect* unconsciousness for 1 minute; *secondary effect* unconsciousness for 2d4 hours; *cure* 1 save.
#*Pathfinder Roleplaying Game Advanced Player's Guide*
*see the **Appendix**
**Pathfinder Roleplaying Game Ultimate Magic*

Natasha's Tactics: Natasha attacks the party directly only if it seems to present an immediate threat. Even then, she attacks with her zombie minions, supporting them with spells such as *poison* and *hold person* as well as her channel energy power in conjunction with her *ring of spectral hand*. She is most concerned with shifting the balance of power against Balcoth, and to that end she may engage the PCs with promises of magic items if they agree to exterminate him. She has no intent to live up to her end of the bargain. Instead, she follows behind the PCs *invisibly* to either finish off the party or Balcoth, depending on who is left standing.

If events go against her, Natasha has been known to return to this room and pretend to be the trapped concubine of the wizard that the "valiant party has obviously driven off." Now the characters can "rescue" her and reap their rewards, which she is willing to give. Of course she slays the party when given the opportunity.

Secret Door: The secret door is hidden behind a velvet curtain and is *arcane locked.* It is opened by touching first the stone to the right of the door and then the stone to the left. It makes for an excellent getaway hatch.

Escape Route: If Natasha escapes using this secret door, she heads north through **Area 14**, past the *illusory wall* at **Area 15** and down to **Area 9**, where she reenters the mist and heads west and south, bypassing **Areas 16** and **17** and then heading up to **Area 22**, where she takes the stairs down to **Level 3**, then up the stairs on **Level 3** to **Level 1**, passing the shadows and **Area 4** and going out to the surface. There, she heads to the entrance to the Under Realms labeled on the **Wilderness Map**.

13. Natasha's Study (CR 5)

This room is far less lavish. It contains several tables, bookshelves and a desk. It also has a cask of both water and wine and a large barrel holding iron rations (which Natasha covers with a *silent image* to appear as gourmet meals). There are three chests in the room. The tables are covered with spell components for all the spells that Natasha knows as well as other odd chemicals and unguents and several neat stacks of parchment holding Natasha's current notes and thoughts.

Trapped Chests: Each chest is **trapped** with poison needles covered in potent spider poison.

Locked Wooden Chest: 1 in. thick; hardness 5; hp 10; Break DC 18; Disable Device DC 24.

POISON NEEDLE TRAP   CR 2
XP 600
Type mechanical; **Perception** DC 20; **Disable Device** DC 20

Trigger touch; **Reset** repair; **Bypass** lock (Disable Device DC 30)
Effect Attack +10 melee (1 plus Medium spider venom)

The chests hold:
Chest 1: 12,407 sp.
Chest 2: 4,562 cp, 3,875 gp and four *potions (cure serious wounds, fly, invisibility* and *spider climb)*. Natasha normally does not carry these potions with her, holding them in reserve for special need.
Chest 3: Fine silks and furs worth 800 gp total, several necklaces, rings and other female jewelry worth 500 gp total.

14. The Back Room

This small cavern has a cask of wine and a cask of water as well as a sleeping bag in a backpack. The pack also contains 50 feet of rope, iron spikes, two small sacks, two vials of unholy water, and flint and steel in a tinderbox. This is Natasha's special hideout room.

15. Alarm-Trapped *Illusory Walls*

The two locations marked as "15" on the map are both locations where Natasha has covered a boulder-filled passage with an *illusory wall* spell to make the passage appear to be part of the surrounding wall. A DC 16 Will save is allowed to disbelieve the illusion if the *illusory wall* is interacted with. See Illusions in the *Pathfinder Roleplaying Game Core Rulebook* and the *illusory wall* spell description for more details.

Alarm: Also, both locations are covered with *alarm* spells. They go off with a small chime in **Areas 10, 11, 12** and **13**.

Detections: The *illusory walls* radiate moderate illusion magic, if detected.

16. The Gauntlet (CR 10)

This place is the home of **14 cave morays,** which live in holes or fissures in the cave walls. The holes are noted on the level map. They lunge out and strike at anything that passes. A DC 15 Perception check allows PCs within 15 feet of a hole to notice it. Roll for each hole.

CAVE MORAYS (14)   CR 2
XP 600
hp 19 (*The Tome of Horrors Complete* 99)

Experience: Remember that consciously avoiding these creatures can be worth XP as well. We propose that you award 500 XP for traveling the southern route — which only goes by four holes, as opposed to the main passage, which goes by nine holes. Use your discretion in this matter. Players should not get additional XP for blindly stumbling on the proper path. Award this bonus only if they consciously choose the wiser path.

17. Mold Cavern (CR Varies, 0–5)

This large cavern is rather damp. It is covered with fungi of various types, including large mushrooms. They are neither special nor harmful. There is a 45% chance of **1d3 piercers** being in this room.

PIERCERS   CR 2
XP 600 (*The Tome of Horrors Complete* 760)

18. Dripping Cave (CR Varies, 0–2)

This small cave has a large stalactite in the center of it, which slowly drips water onto the floor. There is a small pool of water beneath the formation. It is good, fresh water, and there is a 25% chance that **1d6 dire rats** are here.

DIRE RATS   CR 1/3
XP 135
hp 5 (*Pathfinder Roleplaying Game Bestiary* "Rat, Dire")

19. The Manticores (CR 7)

This room is the play area for **2 manticores.** It is a large cavern with a very high ceiling (nearly 75 feet), facilitating use of the creatures arching volleys of tail darts. They live primarily off of the rats that drink at the pool at **18,** or wandering spiders. In fact, one is often waiting by the intersection leading to **Area 18.** They also occasionally leave the dungeon by half-clawing and half-flying up the crevasse on the map near their lair that leads to a secluded section of the surrounding mountains. There, they hunt other creatures.

MANTICORES (2)   CR 5
XP 1,600
hp 57 (*Pathfinder Roleplaying Game Bestiary* "Manticore")

Lair: In the small alcove to the north of the main room, in a bed of straw, is the lair of the **2 manticores.** It smells of urine and rat corpses.

Treasure: In the eastern spur of the northern alcove, in a pile on the ground, is the treasure the monsters have collected: 3,872 cp, 2,976 sp, 2,812 gp, a *+3 longsword,* an *elixir of fire breath,* a *wand of magic missile* (23 charges) and a scroll of 5 arcane spells (*control water, black tentacles, lightning bolt, stone shape* and *cone of cold,* all CL 9th).

20. Rats (CR Varies, 1–3)

In this large cave, and in the unmapped tunnels that lead from it, live a colony of dire rats. There are **2d8 dire rats** here when the characters enter.

DIRE RATS   CR 1/3
XP 135
hp 5 (*Pathfinder Roleplaying Game Bestiary* "Rat, Dire")

21. The Graves (CR 8)

This room once held graves of the faithful of Thyr and Muir, but they have since been unearthed — leaving foul-smelling open pits — and the contents turned into vile undead. In this room there are **12 ghouls,** and their leader, who is a **ghast.** The priests of Orcus took all of their treasure.

GHOULS (12)   CR 1
XP 400
hp 13 (*Pathfinder Roleplaying Game Bestiary* "Ghoul")

GHAST (ADVANCED GHOUL)   CR 2
XP 600
CE Medium undead
(*Pathfinder Roleplaying Game Bestiary* "Ghoul"; see the
Appendix)
Init +4; **Senses** darkvision 60 ft.; **Perception** +7
Aura stench (10-foot radius, Fort DC 15 negates, sickened for 1d6+4 minutes)

AC 18, touch 14, flat-footed 14 (+4 Dex, +4 natural)
hp 17 (2d8+8)
Fort +4; **Ref** +4; **Will** +7
Defensive Abilities channel resistance +2; **Immune** undead traits

Speed 30 ft.
Melee bite +5 (1d6+3) and 2 claws +5 (1d6+3 plus paralysis)
Special Attacks paralysis (1d4+1 rounds, DC 15, elves are *not* immune to this effect)

Str 17, **Dex** 19, **Con** —, **Int** 17, **Wis** 18, **Cha** 18
Base Atk +1; **CMB** +4; **CMD** 18

Feats Weapon Finesse
Skills Acrobatics +6, Climb +8, Intimidate +9, Perception +9, Sense Motive +9, Stealth +9, Swim +5
Languages Common

Disease (Su) *Ghoul Fever:* Bite—injury; *save* Fort DC 15 ; *onset* 1 day; *frequency* 1/day; *effect* 1d3 Con and 1d3 Dex damage; *cure* 2 consecutive saves. The save DC is Charisma-based. A humanoid that dies of ghoul fever rises as a ghoul at the next midnight. A humanoid who becomes a ghoul in this way retains none of the abilities it possessed in life. It is not under the control of any other ghouls, but it hungers for the flesh of the living and behaves like a normal ghoul in all respects. A humanoid of 4 Hit Dice or more rises as a ghast.

22. The Spider Room (CR 6)

This cave is the home of **7 giant spiders.** Natasha has taken all of their treasure.

GIANT SPIDERS (7)   CR 1
XP 400
hp 16 (*Pathfinder Roleplaying Game Bestiary* "Spider, Giant")

Webs: Note that the spiders have spun webs in this room as detailed in the *Pathfinder Roleplaying Game Bestiary.* These sheets of sticky webbing can be seen with a DC 20 Perception check; otherwise the approaching creature stumbles into the web and is trapped as though by a successful web attack.

Webs: hp 6; Break DC 16; Escape Artist DC 12; Spot DC 20; damage reduction 5/— .

23. The Fresco Room (CR 5)

This room, though empty, has three sides of worked stone that were carved with frescos and decorations honoring the dead that were buried beyond the door. Those carvings have since been destroyed and defaced by the priests of Orcus. The door itself is a large iron door. It has a heavy lock and must be picked. The evil priests have also added a deadly poison needle trap.

Locked Iron Door: 2 in. thick; hardness 10; hp 60; Break DC 28; Disable Device DC 20.

POISON NEEDLE TRAP   CR 5
XP 1,600
Type mechanical; **Perception** DC 20; **Disable Device** DC 20

Trigger touch; **Reset** repair; **Bypass** lock (Disable Device DC 30)
Effect Attack +20 melee (1 plus shadow essence poison)

24. Empty Rooms

Each room is filled with cheap wooden coffins that have been destroyed. Their contents are now vile undead in the service of Orcus. All of the rooms show signs of having been recently occupied by humanoids — bedrolls, litter, scraps of somewhat fresh food, empty water skins and so on, even if the room does not currently have occupants.

Roll on the **wandering monster** table for **Area 24** when any of the rooms marked "**24**" are entered.

25. Secret Door Room

This room is like the others before it, except that it contains a **secret door to Level 4** (Perception DC 20 to locate). The secret door is opened by a small catch in the seam of the north and south wall. Like in **Area 24**, check for a **wandering monster** here as well.

26. Priests of Orcus (CR 8)

This room is the sleeping quarters for **Barzag**, the Master of Acolytes, as well as **4 acolytes minions**. Barzag is in charge of defiling these graves and the ones in **Area 21**. As can be seen, his task is nearly complete. The room holds their bedrolls as well as various and sundry supplies.

BARZAG, PRIEST OF ORCUS   **CR 5**
XP 1,600
Male orc disciple of Orcus 6 (*Pathfinder Roleplaying Game Bestiary* "Orc"; see the **Appendix**)
CE Medium humanoid (orc)
Init –1; **Senses** darkvision 60 ft.; **Perception** +5
Aura evil

AC 18, touch 9, flat-footed 18 (+7 armor, –1 Dex, +2 shield)
hp 42 (6d8+6 plus 6)
Fort +7; **Ref** +2; **Will** +10
Defensive Abilities ferocity
Weakness light sensitivity

Speed 20 ft.
Melee mwk heavy mace +8 (1d8+2)
Special Attacks channel negative energy 6/day (3d6, DC 14)
Spells Prepared (CL 6th; melee touch +6, ranged touch +3):
3rd—*animate dead*ᴰ, *blindness/deafness* (DC 17), *invisibility purge*, *prayer*
2nd—*align weapon*, *bear's endurance*, *ghoul touch*ᴰ (DC 16), *hold person* (DC 16), *spiritual weapon*
1st—*bane* (DC 15), *cause fear*ᴰ (DC 15), *divine favor*, *entropic shield*, *obscuring mist*
0 (at will)—*bleed* (DC 14), *detect magic*, *detect poison*, *guidance*
D Domain Spell **Domain** Undead˙

Str 14, **Dex** 8, **Con** 12, **Int** 10, **Wis** 18, **Cha** 13
Base Atk +4; **CMB** +6; **CMD** 15
Feats Combat Casting, Command Undead (DC 14), Extra Channel, Weapon Focus (heavy mace)
Skills Heal +8, Knowledge (arcana) +4, Knowledge (planes) +5, Knowledge (religion) +7, Linguistics +4, Perception +5, Spellcraft +5, Stealth –5
Languages Abyssal, Common, Orc
SQ death's kiss (3 rounds, 7/day), see in darkness, undead lord's proxy, variant channeling (undeath#)
Combat Gear *potion of cure serious wounds*; **Other Gear** *+1 breastplate*, masterwork heavy steel shield, masterwork heavy mace, *cloak of resistance +1*, iron holy symbol of Orcus

See in Darkness (Ex) The holiest of rites to Orcus are performed in total darkness. At 1st level the Disciple of Orcus gains darkvision 60 ft. The range increases to 90 ft. at 6th level. At 8th level the Disciple of Orcus can also see in magical darkness. If the Disciple of Orcus already possesses darkvision its range increases by +30 ft. at 1st and 6th levels.
Undead Lord's Proxy (Su) Undead recognize the Disciple of Orcus as a conduit to the Demon Lord. At 3rd level Disciples add +2 to the DC to resist channeled energy when used to command undead.
Undeath Variant Channeling (Su) *Heal*—This works like a standard channel (not halved). *Harm*—The healing effect is enhanced (+50%) for undead creatures and those with negative energy affinity.
˙*Pathfinder Roleplaying Game Advanced Player's Guide*
#*Pathfinder Roleplaying Game Ultimate Magic*

ACOLYTE OF ORCUS (4)   **CR 2**
XP 600
Male orc disciple of Orcus 3 (*Pathfinder Roleplaying Game Bestiary* "Orc"; see the **Appendix**)
CE Medium humanoid (orc)
Init +0; **Senses** darkvision 60 ft.; **Perception** +6
Aura evil

AC 17, touch 10, flat-footed 17 (+5 armor, +2 shield)
hp 23 (3d8+3 plus 3)
Fort +4; **Ref** +1; **Will** +6
Defensive Abilities ferocity
Weakness light sensitivity

Speed 20 ft.
Melee mwk light mace +5 (1d6+2)
Special Attacks channel negative energy 4/day (2d6, DC 10)
Spells Prepared (CL 3rd; melee touch +4, ranged touch +2):
2nd—*aid*, *darkness*, *ghoul touch*ᴰ (DC 15)
1st—*cause fear*ᴰ (DC 14), *endure elements*, *magic weapon*, *summon monster I*
0 (at will)—*create water*, *detect magic*, *read magic*, *virtue*
D Domain Spell **Domain** Undead˙

Str 14, **Dex** 10, **Con** 13, **Int** 12, **Wis** 17, **Cha** 8
Base Atk +2; **CMB** +4; **CMD** 14
Feats Alignment Channel (Good), Command Undead (DC 10), Extra Channel
Skills Acrobatics –4 (–8 jump), Climb –2, Knowledge (planes) +6, Knowledge (religion) +6, Perception +6, Spellcraft +6, Stealth –4
Languages Abyssal, Common, Orc
SQ death's kiss (1 round, 6/day), see in darkness, undead lord's proxy, variant channeling (undeath#)
Combat Gear *potion of cure light wounds*, *wand of inflict light wounds* (CL 3rd); **Other Gear** masterwork scale mail, masterwork heavy wooden shield, masterwork light mace, wooden holy symbol of Orcus, 2d4 sp

See in Darkness (Ex) The holiest of rites to Orcus are performed in total darkness. At 1st level the Disciple of Orcus gains darkvision 60 ft. The range increases to 90 ft. at 6th level. At 8th level the Disciple of Orcus can also see in magical darkness. If the Disciple of Orcus already possesses darkvision its range increases by +30 ft. at 1st and 6th levels.
Undead Lord's Proxy (Su) Undead recognize the Disciple of Orcus as a conduit to the Demon Lord. At 3rd level Disciples add +2 to the DC to resist channeled energy when used to command undead.
Undeath Variant Channeling (Su) *Heal*—This works like a standard channel (not halved). *Harm*—The healing effect is enhanced (+50%) for undead creatures and those with negative energy affinity.
˙ *Pathfinder Roleplaying Game Advanced Player's Guide*
#*Pathfinder Roleplaying Game Ultimate Magic*

Level 2A: Balcoth's Lair And the Priest Barracks

Level 2A: Balcoth's Lair And the Priest Barracks

Difficulty Level: 6 (9 if Balcoth or the Delegation is encountered)

Entrance: Passage opening dropping to **Level 2** below.

Exits: Stairs to **Level 6** behind a secret door in the newly constructed priest barracks.

Wandering Monsters: Once onto the passageway area at 1 from **Level 2**, check every 30 minutes on the following table:

ROLL 1D20	RESULT
1	**2d4 stirges** (past **Area 2**, treat as no encounter, since stirges don't make it past the webs)
2	The **phase spider** (see **Area 2**)
3	**"Rusty" the rust monster** (see **Area 4**)
4	**Balcoth** (see **Area 7**). **Note:** Balcoth is most likely aware of the party. He generally chooses to watch it and to retreat to his lair if it appears to notice him.
5	The sound of very large footsteps in the distance
6	**1d2 psionic chokers** (see **Area 6**)
7	A **delegation of priests** of Orcus (3 lesser priests sent by the priests on **Level 4** as emissaries to Balcoth)
8–20	No encounter

This relatively small level contains the lair of Balcoth — a wizard from another dimension who practices strange magic and has transformed himself into a wraith. He has surrounded himself with a great many magical protections as well as a charmed rust monster and a group of psionic chokers. Also on this level is a delegation of priests of Orcus who are attempting both to persuade Balcoth to join their cause and to use this level as a means of entering **Level 6** and thus level **5A** — where they hope to find the Black Monolith. Balcoth also seeks the Black Monolith for his own reasons. The tsathar priests of Tsathogga do not venture to this level and are unaware of the activities of the priests of Orcus here. Dark Natasha, aware of Balcoth's magical traps through hard experience, does not venture onto this level.

LESSER PRIESTS OF ORCUS　　　　　　　　　　**CR 4**
XP 1,200
hp 55 (see **Level 4, Area 2**)

STIRGE　　　　　　　　　　　　　　　　　　　**CR 1/2**
XP 200
hp 5 (*Pathfinder Roleplaying Game Bestiary* "Stirge")

1. Ledge (CR Varies, 0–4)

This ledge has slopes down on the north and south sides that lead to **Level 2** (with the ledge being 30 feet above the floor on the south and 40 feet above on the north). Both sides are very steep. The ceiling, 20 feet above the ledge, also serves as the ceiling for **Level 2, Area 1**.

Runes: Balcoth has placed a *rune of fire* (10d6), a *rune of darkness* and a *rune of seeing* here (see the **Sidebar** for more information on these unique spells). Balcoth has also placed an *alarm* spell here, which alerts him to the presence of individuals on the ledge. Like *glyphs*, the runes are very difficult to spot (DC 27 Perception check). See the **Sidebar** for more details. If Balcoth is actively using the

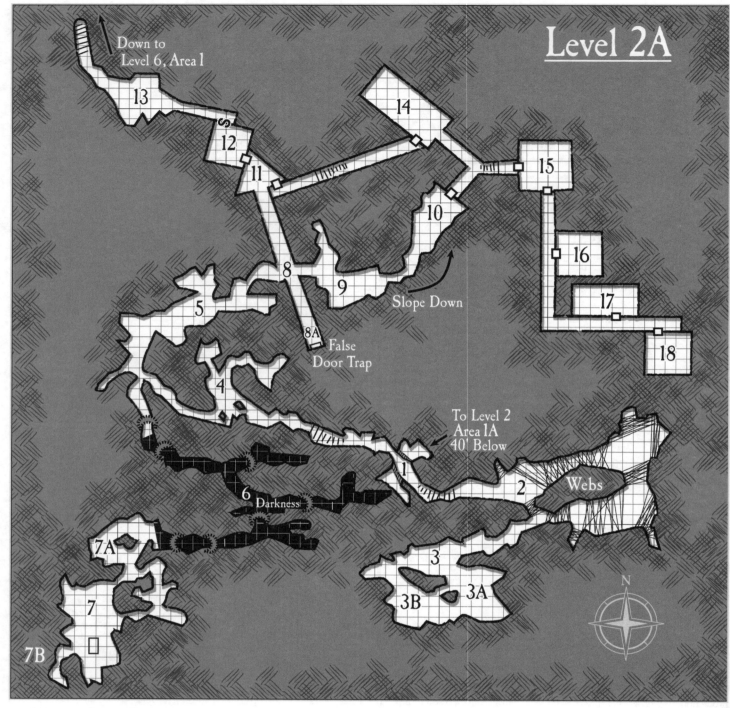

Level 2A

Down to Level 6, Area 1

13

12

14

11

S

8

10

5

9

Slope Down

8A — False Door Trap

15

16

17

18

4

To Level 2 Area 1A 40' Below

1

6 — Darkness

2 — Webs

7A

3

7

3B — 3A

7B

N

rune of seeing to spy on the PCs, all characters with Intelligence 12 or more can make a DC 20 Intelligence check to notice the scrying through the *rune.*

Balcoth's Tactics: Once the *alarm* spell sounds, Balcoth activates his *circle of seeing* and views the ledge through the *rune of seeing* placed there (see **Area 7** for more details on the *circle*). If there are several intruders, he activates the *rune of fire,* which explodes for 10d6 points of damage. He then sends Rusty the rust monster (see **Area 4**) and/or several psionic chokers (see **Area 6**) to dispatch the intruders.

Detections: The runes, though not visible, detect as faint divination and abjuration magic.

"Stirge Check": In addition to any wandering monster checks, roll 1d6 every minute PCs remain on the ledge. On a 1–3, **2d6 stirges** show up and attack. Remember to continue checking every minute, even when combat is joined.

STIRGE CR 1/2
XP 200
hp 5 (*Pathfinder Roleplaying Game Bestiary* "Stirge")

2. Caves of Webs

These caves are high ceilinged. If ample light is in the room, it can easily be seen that the ceiling is covered in webs. Also both the entrances to the two eastern-most caves are closed off with webs. However, there is no spider here. This is his stirge trap. The spider lives in **Area 3**.

Webs: The phase spider has spun webs in these caves as detailed in the *Pathfinder Roleplaying Game Bestiary.* These sheets of sticky webbing can be seen with a DC 20 Perception check; otherwise the approaching creature stumbles into the web and is trapped as though by a successful

Rune Trap Spells

Rune of Darkness

School abjuration; **Level** sorcerer/wizard 2
Casting Time 1 minute or 10 minutes (see text)
Components V, S, M (charcoal, and see below)
Range touch
Area up to 30 ft. radius sphere
Duration until discharged or up to 1 year, see text
Saving Throw none; **Spell Resistance** yes

When triggered, the rune causes a globe of impenetrable darkness to come into being, as per a *deeper darkness* spell. The rune affects an area up to 30 ft. radius. The caster may affect a lesser area if he wishes. Once triggered, the darkness lasts for 1 hour/level. The caster may specify a lesser duration if he wishes.

To make the rune physically permanent (though not magically permanent) requires 25 gp worth of silver inlay mixed with the dust of a 50 gp sapphire and a Craft (stonemasonry) check at DC 10 to carve the intricate patterns of the rune, requiring 10 minutes to complete. Failure means all components are lost and the carving must be attempted again.

Rune of Fire

School abjuration [fire]; **Level:** sorcerer/wizard 3
Casting Time 1 minute or 10 minutes (see text)
Components V, S, M (charcoal, and see below)
Range touch
Area up to 30 ft. diameter sphere spread
Duration until discharged or up to 1 year
Saving Throw reflex half; **Spell Resistance** yes

When triggered, the *rune of fire* explodes for up to 1d6 fire damage per caster level (maximum 10d6). If the caster wishes to set the rune to do less damage than his level, he may do so. The rune explodes in an area up to 30 ft. in diameter. The caster may provide for a lesser area if he wishes.

To make the rune physically permanent (though not magically permanent) requires 50 gp worth of silver inlay mixed with the dust of a 150 gp sapphire and requires a Craft (stonemasonry) check at DC 12 to carve the intricate patterns of the rune, requiring 10 minutes to complete. Failure means all components are lost and the carving must be attempted again.

Rune of Seeing

School divination; **Level** sorcerer/wizard 3
Casting Time: 1 minutes or 20 minutes (see text)
Components V, S, M (charcoal or sulfur, and see below)
Range see text

Target 1 rune
Duration 1 hour/level
Saving Throw none; **Spell Resistance:** no

When this spell is cast, the caster etches or traces the outline of a strange and complex rune in charcoal or sulfur paste on the desired surface. When the spell is completed, the rune fades into the surface and becomes nearly invisible. As a standard action until the end of the spell, the caster may switch his sensory input between his current surroundings and the area surrounding the rune. Changing his sensory focus to the rune requires a concentration check (DC 10). If successful, the caster views the area where the rune was traced as if he were standing on it. The caster can turn 360 degrees in place, and he has full use of all of his senses. Any magical enhancements to his senses remain in effect, including such spells as *comprehend languages*, *darkvision*, *read magic*, *see invisible* and *tongues*. The caster cannot use any detection magic through the circle, even if it was cast on his person prior to using the circle, nor may he use magic to affect anything he or she sees or hears through the circle. However, the caster may be affected by certain sensory-damaging or -influencing spells while he is scrying through the rune. For example, he might be affected by a troglodyte's odor if such a creature were within smelling distance of the rune. The caster may also cast this spell without placing a new rune. To do so, the caster rolls a concentration check (DC 10 + 1) for each day since he contacted his last rune) and attempts to reestablish a link to the most recent rune of seeing he has placed, provided that rune was a silver etched, permanent rune. A successful check treats the prior rune as if it had just been drawn. A failed check means the spell is wasted and that prior rune can never be re-contacted. The distance from the *runes of seeing* to the caster is not a factor, and the rune may even be on another plane of existence. This spell may also be used in conjunction with the *circle of seeing* and *greater circle of seeing* spells. The casting time for this spell depends on whether the rune is being drawn anew or whether a previously placed, permanent rune is being empowered. Drawing a new rune takes 1 minute. Empowering a previously placed, permanent rune takes 20 full minutes.

Magical runes such as this one are hard to detect. When the rune is active, that is when the caster is seeing through it, it becomes a magical sensor. Any creature nearby with an Intelligence of 12 or higher may make a DC 25 Perception check to notice the sensor. *Detect scrying* will also detect an active rune of seeing. Runes that are located can be identified with *read magic* and a successful Spellcraft check (DC 13). A *rune of seeing* that has been located may be *erased* or *dispelled*. If the rune is disabled, *erased* or *dispelled*, the spell ends and such a rune can never be re-used in subsequent castings. If this happens, the caster knows that his spell was cancelled in this manner.

To make the rune physically permanent (though not magically permanent) requires 250 gp worth of silver inlay and requires a Craft (stonemasonry) check at DC 12 to carve the intricate patterns of the rune. Failure means all components are lost and the carving must be attempted again.

These spells originally appeared in **Relics and Rituals** by *Sword and Sorcery Studios*

web attack. These webs are gooey and do not burn easily or quickly.

Webs: hp 12; Break DC 32; Escape DC 26; Spot DC 20; damage reduction (5/ –), resistance to fire 10. Note that the phase spider normally uses *ethereal jaunt* to pass through his own webs.

3. The Spider (CR 5)

Out of phase in **Area 3**, near the tunnel entrance, lurks the **phase spider** that has made the webs in **Area 2**. On occasion he can be found in **Area 2** feasting on trapped stirges. The priests of Orcus have bargained with him, offering him fresh food (humans captured from the surrounding villages) in exchange for allowing them unmolested passage on this level. This particular spider is rather intelligent and slightly evil.

PHASE SPIDER
XP 1,600
hp 51 (*Pathfinder Roleplaying Game Bestiary* "Phase Spider")

CR 5

3A. Treasure

Here the spider keeps the older bones and corpses of his kills. As a result of that collection, he has amassed some treasure, consisting of 2,376 cp, 4,207 sp, 292 pp, 2,081 gp, two pearls (worth 100 gp each), two non-magical rings of gold (25 gp each), a silver necklace (25 sp), a *+1 keen scimitar* and a *ring of blinking*.

3B. Food

This cave has several decalcified corpses and a few fresh ones. There is also a pile of clothing nearby. Within it is a *robe of eyes* (DC 18 Perception check).

4. Rusty's House (CR 3)

This is the normal home of **Rusty, the charmed rust monster.** If he has not been previously encountered or moved by the will of Balcoth, he can be found here. Rusty lives here in a pile of cloth strips. Rusty wears a strange hardened leather collar carved with runes that was created by Balcoth. Any creature that is not a humanoid or monstrous humanoid that wears the collar comes under the mental control of Balcoth as if under a *dominate monster* spell. Normally prone to leaping and bounding like an enthusiastic puppy, Rusty is instead subdued and depressed due to the leather collar he wears that subjects him to the evil will of Balcoth.

RUSTY, THE CHARMED RUST MONSTER
XP 800
hp 27 (*Pathfinder Roleplaying Game Bestiary* "Rust Monster")

CR 3

Note: Removing Rusty's collar frees him from Balcoth's control. He immediately flees the level.

5. Cave of Spikes (CR Varies, 0–3)

This cavern is full of stalactites and stalagmites of a very large size. Though players may become paranoid, there are no piercers in here. However, there is a 1–5 on 1d20 chance that one or both of the **psionic chokers** are here, playing amongst the stalactites (see **Area 6** for details).

6. The Dark, Constricted Passages (CR 5)

These tight passages are bathed in magical darkness (see below) and often have areas that constrict down to 4 feet in diameter (marked by dashed lines on the map). The sections that are not so constricted have high ceilings — some 15 to 20 feet high. The tall sections are filled with stalactites and stalagmites. If the passage constriction, stalactites and darkness were not bad enough, these passages are the hunting grounds of **2 psionic chokers** (unless previously encountered in **Area 5**) who have made a pact with Balcoth to guard him. He uses his *rune of seeing* to help locate food for them.

PSIONIC CHOKERS (2)
XP 800
CE Small aberration (*Pathfinder Roleplaying Game Bestiary* "Choker"; see the **Appendix**)

CR 3

Init +6; **Senses** darkvision 60 ft.; **Perception** +1

AC 17, touch 13, flat-footed 15 (+2 Dex, +4 natural, +1 size)
hp 16 (3d8+3)
Fort +2; **Ref** +3; **Will** +4

Speed 20 ft., climb 10 ft.
Melee 2 tentacles +6 (1d4+3 plus grab)
Space 5 ft.; **Reach** 10 ft.
Special Attacks constrict (1d4+3), grab (Large), psionic assault, strangle

Str 16, **Dex** 14, **Con** 13, **Int** 4, **Wis** 13, **Cha** 14
Base Atk +2; **CMB** +4 (+8 to grapple); **CMD** 16
Feats Improved Initiative, Skill Focus (Stealth)
Skills Climb +16, Stealth +13
Languages Undercommon
SQ quickness

Psionic Assault (Su) At will as a standard action, a psionic choker can unleash a stunning blast in a 15 ft. cone. Any creature within the area of effect must succeed at a DC 15 Will save or be stunned for 1d3 rounds. An opponent that succeeds on the saving throw is immune to that same creature's psionic assault for 24 hours. Psionic chokers are immune to this ability.
Quickness (Su) A choker is supernaturally quick. It can take an extra move action during its turn each round.
Strangle (Ex) Chokers have an unerring talent for seizing their victims by the neck. A creature that is grappled by a choker cannot speak or cast spells with verbal components.

Greater Rune of Darkness (CL 10th): At the location of the number 6 on the map is a *greater rune of darkness* permanently inscribed on the ceiling. Balcoth placed this rune using a *scroll* as a means of warding his lair. He does not know how to cast this spell himself. The effect of the magical darkness covers the area marked on the map with impenetrable darkness as if by a *deeper darkness* spell. Balcoth and the psionic chokers are immune to the darkness effect, having been specifically named when the *greater rune* was placed. Normal light brought into the darkness is extinguished. Magical *daylight* temporarily negates the darkness within its sphere of illumination, allowing normal light to function.

6A. The Psionic Choker's Lair (CR Varies, 0 or 5)

If not previously encountered, the psionic chokers are here. They have a pile of treasure that consists of 4,829 gp and a *+2 defending keen longsword*.

7. Balcoth's Lair (CR 14)

GM Note: Balcoth is a wizard specializing in runes and knows many powerful new spells detailed in the **Sidebar.** Familiarity with those spells is imperative for running this encounter.

This dank, wet and unnaturally dark cavern is the haunt of the wraith-wizard Balcoth. His resting place, an ornate stone sarcophagus, is in the south end of the room. Around his sarcophagus is a *permanent magic circle against good.* Behind Balcoth's sarcophagus is his permanently inscribed *circle of seeing* (see the **Sidebar** for details).

About the room, amid the smell of putrid decay, are various rotted trappings of a wizard: divans and bookshelves with rotted tracts; a table in the south corner with several glass and stone jars holding various liquids, powders and unguents; colored chalks; bees wax; candles; sulfur and various carving and inscribing tools, as well as all of the spell components to cast each spell he knows several times.

Runes: Balcoth has placed a number of runes around this room. He can trigger any of them with a *trigger rune* spell. At the entrance to the cavern he has also placed two *runes of darkness* and four *runes of fire* (5d6 each). He has also placed a *rune of poison* near his sarcophagus. He can discharge these with the *trigger rune* spell (see the spell description for details). In addition, he placed the runes that are found on the entrance ledge to this level at **Area 1**. Balcoth has been working on placing other runes — particularly *runes of seeing* keyed to his *circle* — but Dark Natasha keeps erasing them. Balcoth is researching several other *rune* spells, including *rune of control* (allowing a *dominate person* or *dominate monster* effect) and several types of *runes of protection*. He has as yet, not mastered them, but if he were to gain additional resources…

BALCOTH
CR 14

XP 38,400
Wraith sorcerer 10 (*Pathfinder Roleplaying Game Bestiary* "Wraith")
LE Medium undead (incorporeal)
Init +7; **Senses** darkvision 60 ft., lifesense 60 ft.; **Perception** +12
Aura unnatural aura

AC 17, touch 17, flat-footed 14 (+4 deflection, +3 Dex)
hp 119 (5d8+20 plus 10d6+40
Fort +8; **Ref** +7; **Will** +15
Defensive Abilities channel resistance +4, incorporeal;
Immune undead traits
Weaknesses sunlight powerlessness

Speed fly 60 ft. (good)
Melee incorporeal touch +11 (1d6 negative energy plus 1d6 Con drain)
Special Attacks create spawn
Spells Known (CL 10th; melee touch +11, ranged touch +11):
5th (3/day)—*magic jar* (DC 19)
4th (6/day)—*circle of seeing***, *dimension door*B, *ice storm*, *rune of poison*** (DC 19)
3rd (7/day)—*dispel magic*B, *fireball* (DC 17), *rune of fire*** (DC 18), *rune of seeing***
2nd (7/day)—*acid arrow*, *false life*, *invisibility*B, *rune of darkness***, *touch of idiocy*
1st (7/day)—*alarm*, *identify*B *magic missile*, *ray of enfeeblement* (DC 15), *shield*, *trigger rune***
0 (at will)—*detect magic*, *mage hand*, *open/close*, *read magic*
Bloodline Arcane

Str —, **Dex** 16, **Con** —, **Int** 18, **Wis** 18, **Cha** 19
Base Atk +8; **CMB** +11; **CMD** 28
Feats Alertness, Blind-Fight, Combat Reflexes, Eschew MaterialsB, Improved Channel Resistance#, Improved Counterspell, Improved Initiative, Resistance to Positive Energy* x2, Spell Focus (Abjuration)
Skills Appraise +10, Bluff +10, Craft (stonemasonry) +16, Diplomacy +10, Escape Artist +4, Fly +15, Intimidate +17, Knowledge (arcana) +20, Knowledge (planes) +13, Linguistics +11, Perception +12, Sense Motive +13, Spellcraft +22, Stealth +12, Use Magic Device +20
Languages Abyssal, Aklo, Common, Daemonic, Dreamspeak, Dwarven, Elven, Giant, Infernal, Orc, Terran, Undercommon
SQ arcane bond (*brooch of shielding*), manifest, metamagic adept (2/day)
Gear *brooch of shielding* (16 charges, that operates whether he is corporeal or incorporeal)

Create Spawn (Su) A humanoid slain by a wraith becomes a wraith in 1d4 rounds. These spawn are less powerful than typical wraiths, and suffer a –2 penalty on all d20 rolls and checks, receive –2 hp per HD, and only drain 1d2 points of Constitution on a touch. Spawn are under the command of the wraith that created them until its death, at which point they lose their spawn penalties and become free-willed wraiths. They do not possess any of the abilities they had in life.

Constitution Drain (Su) Creatures hit by a wraith's touch attack must succeed on a DC 16 Fortitude save or take 1d6 points of Constitution drain. On each successful attack, the wraith gains 5 temporary hit points. The save DC is Charisma-based.

Lifesense (Su) A wraith notices and locates living creatures within 60 feet, just as if it possessed the blindsight ability.

Manifest (Su) Unlike most wraiths, Balcoth can become corporeal. Shifting his state from incorporeal to corporeal or back again is a move action. Balcoth must be corporeal to cast spells.

Sunlight Powerlessness (Ex) A wraith caught in sunlight cannot attack and is staggered.

New Spells

Circle of Seeing

School divination; **Level** sorcerer/wizard 4
Casting Time 1 hour or 1 minute (see text)
Components V, S, M (charcoal, sulfur, blood, see below)
Range see text
Target several linked *runes of seeing* (see text)
Duration 1 hour/level (D)
Saving Throw none; **Spell Resistance** no

This spell creates a temporary magical circle linked to other *runes of seeing* that have been created by the same caster. The linked *runes of seeing* must have been placed prior to the casting of this spell, and they must be designated when the spell is cast. The caster may designate a number of *runes of seeing* that he can view up to his Intelligence modifier. The distance of the *runes of seeing* from the circle is not a factor. The runes may even be on other planes of existence. When the caster stands within the circle, he can view the location of any of the linked *rune of seeing* as if he or she were actually standing at the location of the rune. Like *rune of seeing*, switching between different viewpoints requires a standard action from the caster, and changing views to any vantage point of a rune requires a successful Concentration check (DC 10). *Circle of seeing* then functions identically to viewing and area through a *rune of seeing* (see that spell description) with the exception that the caster may also cast *trigger rune* on any previously placed rune in sight of the caster while he is scrying. When used thus, the rune of seeing flares briefly but visibly when *trigger rune* is cast.

The casting time for the spell depends on whether the circle is being drawn anew or whether a previously placed, permanent circle is being empowered (see material components, below). Drawing a new circle takes one hour. Empowering a previously placed, permanent circle takes one minute. Neither of these casting times includes the time necessary to gather and prepare the necessary material components.

The basic runes and patterns of the circle must be drawn in charcoal and sulfur or inscribed in silver. One pint of the caster's blood (or the blood of a sacrificed intelligent victim) must then be mixed with an ounce of powdered dragon bone or tooth or the powdered bone of an outsider (costing a minimum of 250 gp per ounce). The resulting paste must then be used to trace the most important runes with a brush of the finest hair (worth a minimum of 50 gp). A permanently inscribed circle must be made of inlaid silver at a cost of no less than 2,500 gp. The creator of a permanently inscribed circle must make a successful Craft (stonemasonry) check (DC 16) to carve the intricate design when the circle is created. Failure means that all components are lost and that the carving must be attempted again.

Circle of Seeing, Greater

School divination; **Level:** sorcerer/wizard 8
Casting Time 10 minutes or 2 hours (see text)
Components V, S, M
Range See text
Target several linked *runes of seeing*
Duration 1 hour/level
Saving Throw none; **Spell Resistance** No

This spell functions as does a circle of seeing, except that it allows the caster to cast any spell of 4th level or less through the circle to the location of the viewed *rune of seeing*. Like *circle of seeing*, any spell cast through a *rune of seeing* connected to a *greater circle of seeing* makes that rune flare visibly during the channeled spell's casting time. Spellcasters present at the location of the rune may attempt to counterspell any spell cast through the rune. However, their Spellcraft checks to identify the spell being cast has a +10 DC circumstance penalty, since casters at the location of the rune cannot see the caster who is using the rune as a conduit. Range and similar effects of a spell cast through the greater circle are computed as if the caster were standing on the *rune of seeing* he is currently viewing. No spells with a range of touch may be cast through the *greater circle*. In addition, unlike the *circle of seeing*, all detection spells in effect on the caster function through the circle into the viewed location. This powerful spell takes 2 hours to cast if the circle is being created anew or 10 minutes to cast if a previously placed, permanent circle is being empowered. Casting a spell through the *greater circle of seeing* requires a Concentration check against DC 22 + the spell level being cast. Failure means the spell intended to be cast through the circle fails and the spell is wasted. A natural roll of 1 on this check results in the caster being stricken as per a *confusion* spell (CL 15th). No save or spell resistance is allowed against this *confusion* effect. No such roll is required to cast the *trigger rune* spell through the greater circle of seeing.

The same as for the *circle of seeing* (see above), except that four times the quantity of bone is required and four times the gold piece value is needed to permanently inscribe the circle. Drawing the complex and alien pattern of the *greater circle of seeing* requires an area of no less than 20 feet by 20 feet, and requires a DC 20 Craft (stonemasonry) check.

Rune of Poison

School abjuration; **Level** sorcerer/wizard 4
Casting Time 10 minutes or 1 minute (see text)
Components V, S, M (silver and sapphire dust, and see below)
Range touch
Area up to 20-ft. diameter sphere spread
Duration until discharged or up to 1 year
Saving Throw fortitude negates; **Spell Resistance** yes

When triggered, this rune causes all creatures within the area of effect to be stricken as if by a *poison* spell. This poison deals 1d3 Constitution damage per round for 6 rounds. Poisoned creatures can make a Fortitude save each round to negate the damage and end the affliction. The rune affects an area up to 20 feet in diameter. The caster may provide for a lesser area if he wishes. The area does not remain poisonous after the rune is triggered.

To make the rune physically permanent (though not magically permanent) requires 250 gp worth of silver inlay mixed with the dust of a 500 gp sapphire and requires a Craft (stonemasonry) check at DC 16 to carve the intricate patterns of the rune. Failure means all components are lost and the carving must be attempted again.

Trigger Rune

School transmutation; **Level:** sorcerer/wizard 1
Casting Time 1 action
Components V, S
Range long (400 ft. + 40 ft./level)
Target 1 rune
Duration instantaneous
Saving Throw none; **Spell Resistance** No

When casting this spell, the caster picks any one rune that he has placed previously and that is the listed trigger rune range. The selected rune is triggered immediately. The caster does not need to see the rune he wishes to trigger, unless he is casting the spell through one of the *circles of seeing*.

These spells originally appeared in **Relics and Rituals** by *Sword and Sorcery Studios*.

Unnatural Aura (Su) Animals do not willingly approach within 30 feet of a wraith, unless a master makes a DC 25 Handle Animal, Ride, or wild empathy check.
*The Tome of Horrors Complete
**see the sidebar for details
#see **Rappan Athuk** for details

Background: Balcoth is a wizard from a far-off plane who specializes in rune magic. By an arcane and evil ritual Balcoth long ago turned himself into a wraith. Balcoth is evil because of his undead nature, but above all he seeks knowledge and will barter with the players for information. Some years ago he learned of a monolith of power here under these mountains and he came to these halls to look for it. He believes he has located it, though he cannot approach it because of the wards. He might employ the PCs to gain access to the monolith. Were he to join with the priests of Orcus, the balance of power in the dungeon would shift in their favor. He is reluctant to join with them because he is suspicious of them attempting to control him. Remember that though he is undead, he is not a servant of Orcus. He also distrusts the tsathar and their vile god. He is opposed to Natasha because when he manifested and attempted to speak to her to form an alliance she was repulsed by him, rebuffed him and attacked him. They are currently locked in a standoff, with both parties wary of the other though taking no direct action against one another. Balcoth may employ the PCs to assault or spy on Natasha.

Tactics: Balcoth is ordinarily aware of any intruders on this level that enter the level by way of the ledge at **Area 1**. He uses his *circle* to view the ledge through the *rune of seeing*. Thus, he should be familiar with any foes that come against him. He normally lurks in the shadows and sends Rusty against any fighters in the party. He requests the aid of the psionic chokers to attack the party. If intruders enter his lair, he detonates his *rune of darkness*, *rune of fire* and *rune of poison*. He then casts *shield* and goes incorporeal and uses his energy drain ability. If the circumstances require it, he uses *magic jar* to overcome a fighter to melee the other PCs. If this fails he escapes in incorporeal form. He prefers to remain in the area of his sarcophagus.

7A. The Cave of Chains

This small cave is full of jingling, wet chains. Some are on the wall and end in manacles. Others are dangling from the ceiling and end in meat hooks. All are covered with either dried or fresh blood. Hanging from one hook is a dead and partially flayed and dismembered halfling. Many skeletons litter the floor. This is a favorite waiting place for Balcoth when he is expecting a group of victims. He often lurks here.

7B. Treasure and Books

Treasure: Balcoth keeps all of his spell books here in a large bookcase. There are twenty-one volumes in all — including one huge volume that is set to the side on its own table. There is also a wooden chest present.

Books: Each set of books is written in a strange and alien language, requiring magical aid to read. They require a DC 20 Linguistics check to decipher, in addition to magical means (*read magic* and *comprehend languages*).

Three small tomes bound in black leather with bronze catches, written in cramped script, contain all 0-level and 1st-level spells from the *Pathfinder Roleplaying Game Core Rulebook*.

Another two large books covered in thick brown leather with stained parchment contain twenty random 2nd-level spells. This is an excellent resource for GMs to introduce spells from other sources than the *Pathfinder Roleplaying Game Core Rulebook*.

Three books made of solid bronze covers with thin metallic plates for pages, the words stamped in an alien language, detail eight 3rd-level spells.

Four more tomes of various sizes, each bound in what appears to be the hide of a strange animal and dyed white, detail a total of six 4th-level spells.

A huge volume covered in red hide and written with broad brush strokes on thick wooden boards contains three 5th-level spells (including *permanency*). This book weighs over 200 pounds and, because of its size, requires four persons to lift and carry. This volume is not in the bookcase but is instead on a large table to the side of the bookcase.

Six tracts — one each detailing the spells *trigger rune*, *rune of seeing*, *rune of darkness*, *rune of fire* and *rune of poison* plus a volume detailing Balcoth's work on inventing other rune spells — are more properly described as six groups of notes, drawings and diagrams each held together by a bronze clip and contained in a tube of some type of otherworldly horn and topped with a silver-fitted cap. Each of these silver caps is trapped with a *fire trap* (CL 9th). The *fire trap* detonates if the word "Berarja" is not spoken as the caps are removed.

A small and cramped book of vellum pages, bound in unadorned black hide, contains the spell *circle of seeing* as detailed in the sidebar. The book is written in strange black and red ink that seems to shift and swirl as the words are read. Reading this book requires the viewer to make a DC 12 Will save or lose 1 point of Wisdom permanently due to the alien and chaotic nature of the ideas contained in the book. The pages (and cover) of this book are trapped with a coating of non-magical contact poison (black lotus extract)

Black Lotus Extract *Type* poison (contact); *Save* Fortitude DC 20; *Onset* 1 minute; *Frequency* 1/round for 6 rounds; *Effect* 1d6 Con damage; *Cure* 2 consecutive saves

The final volume is a tome of blue leather, beautifully bound in gold and wrapped in an exquisite red silk cloth. The book is a *tome of clear thought +1*. Balcoth has not read this book.

These tomes — particularly the ones on *rune* magic — are nearly priceless and are a good way to introduce spells from outside sources to your players.

Chest: Also here is a locked chest with a poison needle trap that contains: a *potion of resist elements*, a *potion of haste*, 6,540 cp, 3,590 sp, 120 pp, 3,805 gp, four gems worth 100 gp each and a pair of diamond earrings worth 300 gp.

Locked Wooden Chest: 1 in. thick; hardness 5; hp 10; Break DC 18; Disable Device DC 20.

POISON NEEDLE TRAP   CR 5
XP 1,600
Type mechanical; **Perception** DC 20; **Disable Device** DC 20

Trigger touch; **Reset** repair; **Bypass** lock (Disable Device DC 30)
Effect Attack +20 melee (1 plus shadow essence poison)

8. The Remains

At this spot, there was a battle between Balcoth and a party of adventurers. The intersection is scorched and burned as if by a *fireball* explosion. There are some charred skeletons and globs of metal and wood cinders that were once weapons. There is, however, nothing important here, as this area has been picked clean.

8A. The Old False Door Gag (CR 5)

When the party reaches the end of this corridor and the door is touched, the 10-foot-square slab in the ceiling drops on all in front of the door.

FALLING BLOCK TRAP   CR 5
XP 1,600
Type mechanical; **Perception** DC 20; **Disable Device** DC 20

Trigger location; **Reset** manual
Effect Atk +15 melee (6d6); multiple targets (all targets in a 10-ft. square)

9. The Empty Cave

This cave is empty, though water can be heard dripping from the many stalactites and stalagmites in the southern half of the room. The eastern passage slopes steeply downward to **Area 10**.

10. Worked Cavern and Hidden *Glyph* (CR 4)

This cavern is nondescript, save that the east face has been worked smooth and is set with a large door. On the lintel above the door on the east side of the door is traced a *glyph of warding*. It inflicts damage as per an *inflict serious wounds* spell to any person of good alignment that passes beneath it in either direction.

Note: Persons approaching from the west cannot see the *glyph* since it is carved on the east side of the door.

GLYPH OF WARDING
(*INFLICT SERIOUS WOUNDS*) TRAP   CR 4
XP 1,200
Type magical; **Perception** DC 28; **Disable Device** DC 28

Trigger spell; **Reset** none
Effect spell effect (*glyph of warding* [*inflict serious wounds*], CL 5th, 3d8+5 damage, DC 14 Will save half damage); The *glyph* may be identified (with *read magic*) without triggering it with a successful DC 13 Spellcraft check.

11. Triangle Room (CR 4)

This room is empty save for two doors. The south door is normal and has a *glyph of warding* as in **Area 10** on the lintel above the door on the south side.

GLYPH OF WARDING
(*INFLICT SERIOUS WOUNDS*) TRAP   CR 4
XP 1,200
Type magical; **Perception** DC 28; **Disable Device** DC 28

Trigger spell; **Reset** none
Effect spell effect (*glyph of warding* [*inflict serious wounds*], CL 5th, 3d8+5 damage, DC 14 Will save half damage);. The *glyph* may be identified (with *read magic*) without triggering it with a successful DC 13 Spellcraft check.

12. Secret Door Room

This room is not only empty, it is immaculately clean. It is devoid of all dust, dampness, cobwebs and odor associated with dungeons. The door to **Area 13** is covered with an *illusory wall* spell, preventing the easy location of the secret door. A DC 16 Will save is allowed to disbelieve the illusion if the *illusory wall* is interacted with. See Illusions in the *Pathfinder Roleplaying Game Core Rulebook* and the *illusory wall* spell description for more details. Unless the *illusion* is bypassed, the door cannot be located.

13. The Room of Sigils and Stairs

This partially-worked cavern is covered with odd and meaningless sigils. There is a *magic aura* spell on each and every one (there are 3,593 in all). They cover the floor, walls and ceiling (and there are illusory

symbols suspended in midair as well), and there is no way to cross the room without stepping on at least a few hundred. The stairs lead down to the great bottom level: **Level 6**.

14. The Delegation (CR 11)

This room is the temporary lair of 6 priests from the temple on **Level 4**. They are here as emissaries to Balcoth, in attempt to align him with the followers of Orcus. Three of the priests are wandering around the level and will not be encountered here (see the **Wandering Monster Tables**), however, **Staurauth** and **2 lesser priests** will be here.

The room contains several mats and a bed, as well as several backpacks that the priests have filled with food and equipment to reach Balcoth. Also, though they have no treasure, Staurauth has a great silver key that opens the door on **Level 1, Area 12** that leads to **Level 4**. The key detects as magic.

Staurauth is second in command to Koraashag (found on **Level 4**), and he has personal ambitions of power. He hopes to make an alliance with Balcoth and overthrow Koraashag to become leader of the evil priests. He is a fearsome fighter and uses his channel energy power, prior to wading into combat with his wicked mace..

STAURAUTH   CR 9
XP 6,400
Male half-orc disciple of Orcus 6/necromancer 4 (see the **Appendix**)
CE Medium humanoid (human, orc)
Init +2; **Senses** darkvision 120 ft.; **Perception** +6
Aura evil

AC 22, touch 12, flat-footed 20 (+7 armor, +2 Dex, +3 shield)
hp 84 (6d8+18 plus 4d6+12 plus 10)
Fort +9; **Ref** +5; **Will** +13
Defensive Abilities ferocity

Speed 20 ft.
Melee Melee +1 *unholy wounding heavy mace* +12/+7 (1d8+6)
Special Attacks channel negative energy 6/day (3d6, DC 16)
Necromancer Spell-Like Abilities (CL 4th; melee touch +10, ranged touch +8):
6/day—*grave touch*
Arcane Spells Prepared (CL 4th; melee touch +10, ranged touch +8):
2nd—*ghoul touch* (DC 17), *scorching ray* x2, *spectral hand*^B
1st—*chill touch* (DC 16), *magic missile*, *magic missile*, *ray of enfeeblement*^B (DC 16), *charm person* (DC 14)
0 (at will)—*resistance*, *touch of fatigue* (DC 15), *mage hand*, *disrupt undead*
Arcane School Necromancy **Opposition Schools** Divination, Illusion
Divine Spells Prepared (CL 6th; melee touch +10, ranged touch +8):
3rd—*animate dead*^D, *blindness/deafness* (DC 19), *dispel magic*, *glyph of warding* (DC 17)
2nd— *augury*, *bull's strength*, *ghoul touch*^D (DC 18), *hold person* (DC 16), *silence* (DC 16)
1st—*bless*, *cause fear*^D (DC 17), *command* (DC 15), *cure light wounds*, *protection from good*
0 (at will)—*create water*, *detect magic*, *guidance*, *read magic*
D Domain **Domains** Undead*

Str 20, **Dex** 14, **Con** 16, **Int** 16, **Wis** 19, **Cha** 13
Base Atk +6; **CMB** +11; **CMD** 23
Feats Command Undead (6/day, DC 15), Extra Channel, Greater Spell Focus (necromancy), Improved Channel, Scribe Scroll, Spell Focus (necromancy), Toughness

Skills Bluff +2, Climb +1, Diplomacy +10, Intimidate +10, Knowledge (arcana) +11, Knowledge (planes) +12, Knowledge (Rappan Athuk) +16, Knowledge (religion) +16, Perception +6, Sense Motive +10, Spellcraft +12, Stealth –2, Swim +1
Languages Abyssal, Common, Draconic, Goblin, Orc
SQ arcane bond (*+1 unholy, wounding heavy mace*), death's kiss (3 rounds, 7/day), see in darkness, undead lord's proxy, variant channeling (undeath#)
Combat Gear *potion of owl's wisdom, scroll of 3 spells* (*spiritual weapon, water walk, invisibility*), *scroll of 3 spells* (*summon monster II, locate object, web*), *wand of cure moderate wounds, wand of magic missile*; **Other Gear** *+1 breastplate, +1 heavy steel shield, +1 unholy, wounding heavy mace*, iron unholy symbol of Orcus, 10 gems worth 100 gp each

See in Darkness (Ex) The holiest of rites to Orcus are performed in total darkness. At 1st level the Disciple of Orcus gains darkvision 60 ft. The range increases to 90 ft. at 6th level. At 8th level the Disciple of Orcus can also see in magical darkness. If the Disciple of Orcus already possesses darkvision its range increases by +30 ft. at 1st and 6th levels.
Undead Lord's Proxy (Su) Undead recognize the Disciple of Orcus as a conduit to the Demon Lord. At 3rd level Disciples add +2 to the DC to resist channeled energy when used to command undead.
Undeath Variant Channeling (Su) *Heal*—This works like a standard channel (not halved). *Harm*—The healing effect is enhanced (+50%) for undead creatures and those with negative energy affinity.
*Pathfinder Roleplaying Game Advanced Player's Guide
#Pathfinder Roleplaying Game Ultimate Magic

LESSER PRIESTS OF ORCUS (2)　　　　　　　**CR 4**
XP 1,200
Male human disciple of Orcus 5 (see the **Appendix**)
CE Medium humanoid (human)
Init +2; **Senses** darkvision 60 ft.; **Perception** +6
Aura evil

AC 20, touch 12, flat-footed 18 (+6 armor, +2 Dex, +2 shield)
hp 55 (5d8+15 plus 5)
Fort +7; **Ref** +3; **Will** +7

Speed 20 ft.
Melee *+1 unholy morningstar* +8 (1d8+4)
Special Attacks channel negative energy 8/day (3d6, DC 15)
Spells Prepared (CL 5th; melee touch +6, ranged touch +5):
3rd—*animate dead*ᴰ, *bestow curse* (DC 16), *blindness/deafness* (DC 16)
2nd—*bull's strength, ghoul touch*ᴰ (DC 15), *hold person* (DC 15), *silence* (DC 15)
1st—*bane* (DC 14), *cause fear*ᴰ (DC 14), *command* (DC 14), *cure light wounds, protection from good*
0 (at will)—*detect magic, guidance, light, resistance*
D Domain **Domains** Undead*

Str 16, **Dex** 14, **Con** 16, **Int** 16, **Wis** 17, **Cha** 16
Base Atk +3; **CMB** +6; **CMD** 18
Feats Combat Casting, Command Undead (DC 15), Extra Channel, Selective Channeling, Weapon Focus (morningstar)
Skills Appraise +7, Diplomacy +7, Heal +11, Knowledge (arcana) +11, Knowledge (dungeoneering) +4, Knowledge (engineering) +4, Knowledge (history) +7, Knowledge (planes) +7, Knowledge (religion) +11, Perception +6, Sense Motive +7, Spellcraft +11, Stealth –4
Languages Abyssal, Common, Goblin, Undercommon
SQ death's kiss (2 rounds, 6/day), undead lord's proxy, variant channeling (undeath#)
Gear masterwork chainmail, heavy steel shield, *+1 unholy morningstar*, wooden unholy symbol of Orcus, 2 vials of unholy water

See in Darkness (Ex) The holiest of rites to Orcus are performed in total darkness. At 1st level the Disciple of Orcus gains darkvision 60 ft. The range increases to 90 ft. at 6th level. At 8th level the Disciple of Orcus can also see in magical darkness. If the Disciple of Orcus already possesses darkvision its range increases by +30 ft. at 1st and 6th levels.
Undead Lord's Proxy (Su) Undead recognize the Disciple of Orcus as a conduit to the Demon Lord. At 3rd level Disciples add +2 to the DC to resist channeled energy when used to command undead.
Undeath Variant Channeling (Su) *Heal*—This works like a standard channel (not halved). *Harm*—The healing effect is enhanced (+50%) for undead creatures and those with negative energy affinity.
*Pathfinder Roleplaying Game Advanced Player's Guide
#Pathfinder Roleplaying Game Ultimate Magic

Tactics: The priests attack any good-aligned creatures without mercy. However, if things go against the priests, Staurauth flees. Also, if the priests are aware of a good party approaching, they assist Balcoth in defeating it, and possibly vice versa. If pressed, they may parley with the PCs, surrendering some of their armor and lesser items to spare their own lives.

15–18. The Unused Rooms (CR Varies, 2–4)

These rooms all have locked doors. All are empty. The rooms are still rough and unfinished. This section was planned to be a new set of burial rooms, but the work was never completed. Each room contains rotted crates and barrels of spoiled food (there is a 1–4 on 1d20 chance of having **burrowing grubs** in the molding food) and water, as well as wine that has turned to vinegar, which was to sustain the builders. In addition, rotted piles of timber and stone working tools are also present. There is a chance (GM to determine) that **1d3 acolytes of Orcus** can be found meditating in any of these empty rooms.

ACOLYTE OF ORCUS　　　　　　　**CR 2**
XP 600
hp 23 (see **Level 2, Area 26**)

Level 3: The Greater Burial Chambers

This level consists of two things: the major burial areas of Thyr and Muir and a set of monster lairs. Unless noted otherwise, monsters are not always in their lairs. This is very much a wandering monster level, as there is a large amount of monster activity here. Also, throughout the level are statues of creatures that the basilisk that resides on this level has turned to stone (see the **Sidebar**).

ANKHEG   CR 3
XP 800
hp 28 (*Pathfinder Roleplaying Game Bestiary* "Ankheg")

BASILISK   CR 5
XP 1,600
hp 52 (*Pathfinder Roleplaying Game Bestiary* "Basilisk")

MOBATS (1d6)   CR 3
XP 800
hp 34 (*The Tome of Horrors Complete* 53)

OTYUGHS   CR 4
XP 1,200
hp 39 (*Pathfinder Roleplaying Game Bestiary* "Otyugh")

PSIONIC CHOKER   CR 3
XP 800
hp 16 (see **Level 2A, Area 6**)

STIRGE   CR 1/2
XP 200
hp 5 (*Pathfinder Roleplaying Game Bestiary* "Stirge")

1. The Huge Entry Cavern (CR Varies, 3–8)

This gigantic cavern is in parts over 130 feet wide. Also, it is over 100 feet high. There are, however, very few stalactites or stalagmites in this room; it is very open. There are spots of bat droppings on the floor in more than the usual concentrations. That is because of the monsters that dwell in **1A**. When a party enters this room, **1d6 mobats** from **1A** come to examine their new meal.

Stone Statue: The first of the stone statues (see the **Sidebar**) is present in this room.

MOBATS   CR 3
XP 800
hp 34 (*The Tome of Horrors Complete* 53)

1A. Mobat Lair (CR Varies, 0–10)

Here, hanging upside down, are **2d6 mobats**. Light disturbs them. On a 1–4 on 1d20 they fly away; otherwise they attack. They have no treasure.

MOBATS   CR 3
XP 800
hp 34 (*The Tome of Horrors Complete* 53)

Level 3: The Greater Burial Chambers

Difficulty: 5
Entrances: Stairs from **Level 1**, stairs from **Level 2**
Exits: None
Wandering Monsters: Lots. Once every 15 minutes or any time the PCs make substantial noise or ignite a new source of light, roll 1d20 on the following table:

ROLL 1D20	RESULT
1	1d4 mobats
2	1d2 psionic chokers
3	2d4 stirges
4	1 ankheg
5	The **basilisk**
6	1d4 otyughs
7–20	No encounter

Shielding: Areas **12**, **13** and **14** are encompassed by a lead box worked into the stone of the place so that the demon at **Area 14** cannot *teleport* too far away. This lead lining interferes with *teleportation* and other types of magical transportation.

---

2. Cave Morays (CR 10)

Like the level above it, this level also has a gauntlet of **18 cave morays**. This time the gauntlet is in two places — the north passage being the most deadly. There are eighteen in all, five in the north passage and thirteen in the south. They feed on mobats, stirges and regular bats, and the occasional evil priest or adventurer. They have no treasure.

CAVE MORAYS (18)   CR 2
XP 600
hp 19 (*The Tome of Horrors Complete* 99)

Experience: Remember that consciously avoiding these creatures can be worth XP as well. Use your discretion in this matter.

3. The Obelisks and the Brazen Portals

Set into the northern worked face of this cavern are two large brass portals, flanked by two large white marble obelisks. The brass doors are worked with celestial figures and the images of Thyr and Muir. The obelisks are inlaid with gold and silver runes and glyphs holy to Thyr and Muir. The portals and the obelisks have not been defiled.

Obelisks: The obelisks radiate good, law, and magic. They are

116

Stone Statues

There are a number of statues throughout the level, as indicated on the map by uppercase letters. These figures can be revived with a *stone to flesh* spell, presuming the creatures restored in this fashion make an appropriate saving throw. If this is done, the GM must determine appropriate statistics and equipment. The statues are as follows:

A	A human adventurer (fighter 4) holding a lantern and a sword, with a startled look on his face, facing the door to the south
B	A dwarf (barbarian 5) with an axe at his feet in the process of shielding his eyes
C	A psionic choker
D	8 dire rats
E	An elf mage (wizard 3) with a staff raised
F	A halfling thief (rogue 4) in creep mode, with a dagger out and his cloak pulled tight around him
G	2 charging human fighters (fighter 2) both with swords and shields raised, but not raised high enough
H	A basilisk — someone got lucky
I	A human cleric (cleric 5 Thyr) holding up a holy symbol of Thyr, but trying (in vain) to avert his eyes
J	An evil priest (cleric 4 Orcus) with a look of fear on his face in the act of fleeing, but foolishly looking over his shoulder
K	A human fighter (fighter 5) with a mirror in one hand and a sword in the other, wearing *+2 chain mail* that was, amazingly, not turned to stone. This fighter had the right idea, he just didn't count on the second basilisk. Chipping away the stone or turning the statue to mud allows the armor to be retrieved.
L	A Large giant spider
M	A half-elf female ranger (ranger 4) lying on her back with a look of terror on her face trying to scurry backward
N	An elf bowman (fighter 5) in firing position
O	A human mage (sorcerer 6) with his back pressed to the wall

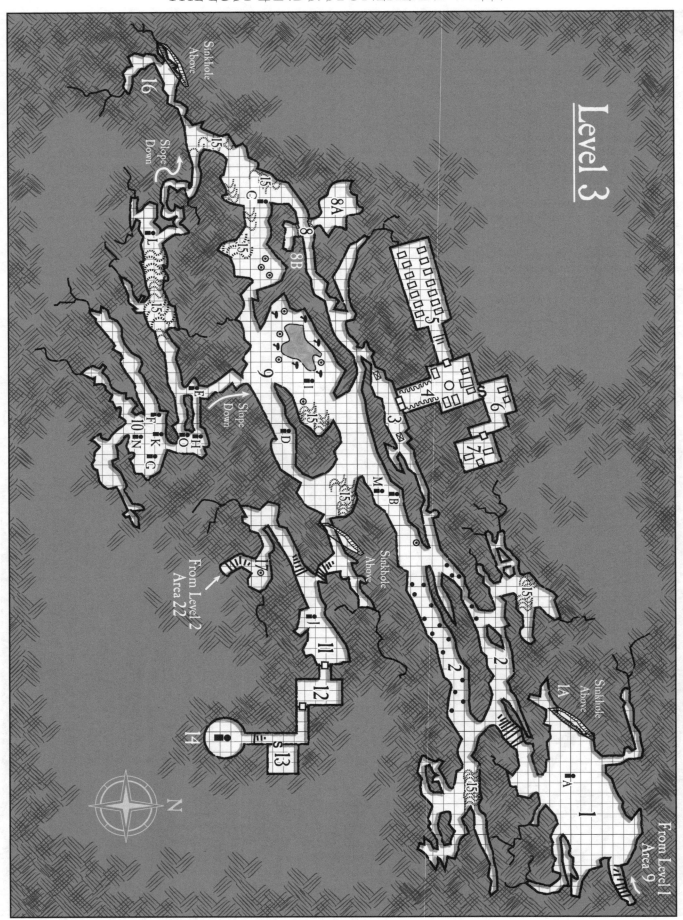

enchanted with a *forbiddance* spell so that only lawful good-aligned followers of Thyr or Muir may pass without suffering damage. All others are met as if with a *wall of force*.

Brass Doors: The doors themselves have no handle, lock or hinges. As a result of a ritual enchantment, the doors can be opened only by a lawful good-aligned follower of Thyr or Muir who casts *bless* upon the doors and then utters a *command* that they open. The doors, too, are covered with a *forbiddance* spell, limiting them to lawful good–aligned characters.

Rat Tunnel: The only way to bypass these protections is to use the rat tunnel to the west from the cavern that leads to **Area 5**.

Experience: Opening the door earns the character a 200 XP individual award.

4. The Inner Sanctum and Final Resting Place of Flail the Great

Here, on the stone slab at the north end of the room lies the body of Flail the Great — a famous priest of Thyr — who was killed on a great holy quest. On either side of the corpse is a small altar covered with a square of pure silk on top of which is an *everburning candle* (similar to an *everburning torch*).

The three other caskets in the room hold his followers, their names lost in time. The two tapestries depict Flail teaching Bannor to be a Paladin, and Flail and Bannor together with sword and staff raised in full splendor.

This room is covered with a *hallow* spell.

Sanctifying a Person as a Justicar of Muir: Flail was one of the few persons who in life knew the ritual to ordain a worthy candidate as a Justicar (see the **Appendix**).

If a *resurrection* spell is cast on the corpse of Flail, he rises as a spirit and completes the ritual necessary to sanctify a person as a Justicar and casts *holy word,* presuming the candidate is worthy to receive ordination. He may also set some task in the form of a *quest* upon the candidate. Once ordination is complete, he offers his blessing to the new Justicar and returns to his rest. There is no limit to the number of Justicars he will ordain, though each request requires a separate *resurrection* spell to be cast on Flail.

Obtaining Knowledge from Flail: If *resurrection* is cast on Flail as detailed above, characters may ask Flail a question in lieu of asking him to ordain a Justicar. He answers the questions of lawful good-aligned characters, though he may require some small quest. This could be a means for the characters to gain information regarding Abysthor and the monolith on the lower levels. Flail answers only six such questions in this fashion.

Secret Door: The secret door is *invisible,* requiring *true sight* or some other form of magic to locate. It, too, is sealed with a *forbiddance* spell and can be opened only by one of pure faith speaking the name "Flail."

Experience: Interaction with the ghost of Flail can earn quite a bit of XP for the party. Use your discretion. This tomb should not be troubled or desecrated in any way by any good-aligned character. Absent a quest or some other deific justification, any good-aligned character disturbing these sarcophagi or their contents loses 1,000 XP. Any lawful good–aligned character loses 2,000 XP and must do *atonement* prior to advancing in level.

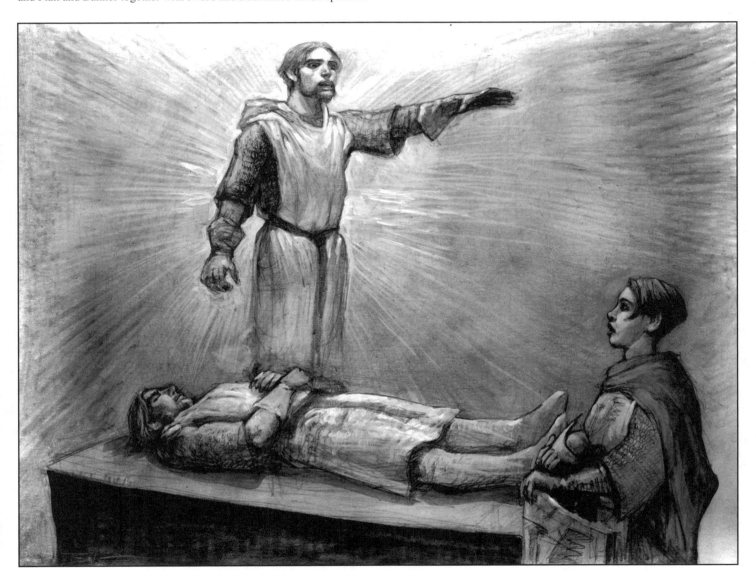

5. The Hall of Glory

This room is filled with fourteen stone sarcophagi (see **Standard Features**) that contain the corpses of valiant warriors who have fallen in the service of Thyr and Muir. PCs can make a DC 22 Knowledge (history or religion) check to recognize the names of these lesser knights of legend. GMs are free to create these names as befits their campaign. The last sarcophagus, undistinguished from the rest, is the final resting place of Eric the Paladin.

Each corpse wears a suit of masterwork chainmail and bears a masterwork shield and a *+1 keen longsword*. Each wears a circlet of silver worth 50 gp.

This room is under the effects of a *hallow* spell.

The Tomb of Eric the Paladin: This tomb contains the remains of Eric the Paladin. He is armed and armored as detailed above with one exception: also within the tomb is his magical lance. The lance is a *+3 holy heavy lance*. The *lance* cannot be removed from these chambers without the permission of Flail (see **Area 4**, above). If it is removed without Flail's permission, the lance becomes simply a *+1 lance*.

Rat Tunnel: A small rat tunnel, dug by dire rats, opens into this room from the cavern to the south. The tunnel is very small and passable only by Small characters wiggling on their stomachs.

Experience: Absent a quest or some other deific justification, any good-aligned character disturbing these sarcophagi or their contents loses 500 XP. Any lawful good–aligned character loses 1,000 XP, must do *atonement* prior to advancing in level and is *quested* to return any items taken.

6. Inner Tomb

Here, behind the secret door, rests Flail's parents — their bodies preserved in stone sarcophagi. This room, like **Areas 4** and **5**, is covered by a *hallow* spell.

Experience: Any good-aligned character disturbing these sarcophagi or their contents loses 1,000 XP.

7. Inner Shrine

Here, on the north and south walls respectively, are statues of Thyr and Muir, and on the east wall is a small shrine and basin of holy water. Good spells are cast here at +2 caster level.

Experience: Any good-aligned character disturbing this shrine loses 1,000 XP.

8. The Corridor of Stalactites (CR Varies, 0–7)

This corridor is, as its name implies, full of stalactites. It is the playground for the psionic chokers at **8A** and **B**. There is a 1–8 on 1d20 chance that **1d4 psionic chokers** are here. The openings that lead to **8A** and **B** are 30 feet off the ground, and the ceiling height is 35 feet. The stalactites hang down about 15 to 20 feet.

PSIONIC CHOKERS   **CR 3**
XP 800
hp 16 (see **Level 2A, Area 6**)

8A. Lair (CR Varies, 5–8)
There are **1d4+1 psionic chokers** here.

PSIONIC CHOKER   **CR 3**
XP 800
hp 16 (see **Level 2A, Area 6**)

Treasure: In the north end of the cave is a pile of treasure containing

3,507 sp, 2,411 gp, twelve gems worth 50 gp each, a *+1 flaming long sword* and a suit of *+2 full plate*.

8B. The Little Lair (CR Varies, 0–5)
There is a 1–10 on 1d20 that **1d2 psionic chokers** are here.

PSIONIC CHOKERS   **CR 3**
XP 800
hp 16 (see **Level 2A, Area 6**)

9. The Big and Wet Fungus Cave

This big cavern has several large columns and a large, glassy pool of water fed ever so slowly by water dripping from the ceiling. The walls and floor are covered with fungus of various shapes and sizes, from mold to mushrooms. There are no piercers in this room, though there are **6 shriekers** of various sizes within the room (marked by blue dots on the map). Light within 30 feet and movement within 10 feet sets them off. When this occurs there is a 1–15 on 1d20 chance of an immediate wandering monster other than mobats for each round of shrieking until one appears.

SHRIEKERS (6)   **CR —**
XP — (*Pathfinder Roleplaying Game Core Rulebook,* "Hazards")
This human-sized purple mushroom emits a piercing sound that lasts for 1d3 rounds whenever there is movement or a light source within 10 feet. This shriek makes it impossible to hear any other sound within 50 feet. The sound attracts nearby creatures that are disposed to investigate. Some creatures that live near shriekers learn that this noise means there is food or an intruder nearby.

10. The Lair of the Basilisk Family (CR 5)

This cavern area always contains **1 basilisk.** There is another, though he is encountered only as a wandering monster. If the wandering basilisk has not been killed before the party kills the basilisk in this room, he comes to help his mate in 2d4+5 rounds.

BASILISK   **CR 5**
XP 1,600
hp 52 (*Pathfinder Roleplaying Game Bestiary* "Basilisk")

Treasure: The fat section of the southern spur of this cave holds their treasure: 6,914 sp, 21,396 gp, twelve gems worth 50 gp each, four gems worth 200 gp each, two pieces of jewelry worth 100 gp each and a 2,000 gp crown inlaid with gems, a *ring of freedom of movement*, a scroll of 2 divine spells (*divination* and *prayer*, CL 7th) and a *belt of giant strength +2*.

11. Worked Cavern (CR 7)

The east wall of this cavern has been worked and a door placed in it. The door contains a thin sheet of lead within it to contain the *teleport* ability of the demon at **Area 14**, if released. The door is trapped with a *stinking cloud* trap. Further, the bands of the door are covered with *explosive runes* that are triggered if read.

Locked and Trapped Iron-Bound Wooden Door: 2 in. thick; hardness 8; hp 30; Break DC 30; Disable Device DC 25.

STINKING CLOUD TRAP   **CR 4**
XP 1,200
Type magical; **Perception** DC 28; **Disable Device** DC 28

Trigger spell; **Reset** none

Effect spell effect (*stinking cloud*, CL 6th, nausea, DC 14 Fortitude save negates); multiple targets (all targets in 20-ft. radius)

EXPLOSIVE RUNES TRAP   CR 6
XP 2,400
Type magical; **Perception** DC 28; **Disable Device** DC 28

Trigger spell; **Reset** none
Effect spell effect (*fire trap*, CL 10th, 1d4+10 fire, DC reading rune, no save, DC 15 Reflex save for half); multiple targets (all targets within 10 ft.)

12. The Old Wizard's Lair

There used to be quite a bit of magical equipment here, but Balcoth and Natasha have taken all of it. There are now only various broken instruments and paraphernalia in various states of disrepair.

Note: Areas 12, 13 and 14 are encompassed by a lead box worked into the stone of the place so that the demon cannot *teleport* too far away. This lead lining interferes with *teleportation* and other types of magical transportation.

13. The Secret Door and Inner Chamber (CR 8)

Natasha and Balcoth, in haste not to disturb the statue at **Area 14**, never discovered the secret door to this room, and thus it is undisturbed.

Secret Door: Unlike the standard secret doors in the dungeon, this one is opened by stepping twice on a loose tile directly in front of the door, which causes it to slide up into the ceiling.

The room beyond is a library, which holds 75% of all 1st-level spells, 45% of all 2nd-level spells, 25% of all 3rd-level spells and 10% of all 4th-level arcane spells form the *Pathfinder Roleplaying Game Core Rulebook* (plus any others the GM wants to place here specifically). The spells are contained in a total of thirty-eight volumes. Each volume has a page of *explosive runes* and is trapped with a *fire trap*.

EXPLOSIVE RUNES TRAP   CR 6
XP 2,400
Type magical; **Perception** DC 28; **Disable Device** DC 28

Trigger spell; **Reset** none
Effect spell effect (*explosive runes*, 6d6 damage to one reading rune, no save, DC 15 Reflex save for half); multiple targets (all targets within 10 ft.)

FIRE TRAP   CR 5
XP 1,600
Type magical; **Perception** DC 29; **Disable Device** DC 29

Trigger spell; **Reset** none
Effect spell effect (*fire trap*, CL 10th, 1d4+10 fire, DC 16 Reflex save half damage); multiple targets (all within 5 ft.)

14. The Statue (CR 9)

This circular room is very dangerous. Within it is a statue of **Zraaln the vrock.** His name is carved minutely in the base of the statue in an ancient tongue. The room itself faintly exudes evil, and if a force of good or powerful magic enters the room, the statue animates. It also animates if its name is read on the base of the statue. This demon was summoned and imprisoned here as a servant by the mage that previously occupied this area. The mage disappeared, lost on another plane, though his servant remains.

ZRAALN THE VROCK   CR 9
XP 6,400
hp 112 (*Pathfinder Roleplaying Game Bestiary* "Demon, Vrock")

15. Broken Ground (CR 3)

Here, the ground is newly unearthed as if digging or burrowing has recently taken place. When here, there is a 1–5 on 1d20 chance of encountering an **ankheg**. If someone walks on the ground, an ankheg appears in 1d8+4 rounds.

ANKHEG   CR 3
XP 800
hp 28 (*Pathfinder Roleplaying Game Bestiary* "Ankheg")

16. Sinkhole Above (CR Varies, 0–4)

These areas contain small crevasses in the ceiling that link to the outside. They cannot be traveled by creatures of larger than Tiny. There is a 1–4 on 1d20 chance that there are **2d4 stirges** here.

STIRGES   CR 1/2
XP 200
hp 5 (*Pathfinder Roleplaying Game Bestiary* "Stirge")

Level 4: The New Temple of Orcus

This level is the home of the new temple of Orcus, founded by Koraashag, from the dungeon of Rappan Athuk. A vision from his dark god commanded Koraashag to search for a "pit of the abyss" and there build a new temple. Finding the pit at **Area 14** and the chamber to the north, Koraashag carried out the wishes of his demonic master and built this temple. From here, he hopes to discover the Black Monolith and harness its power and lead an assault against the surface dwellers.

The more senior priests live in the complex proper. Most acolytes and visitors live in the outer caverns, where slaves and sacrifices are kept in a large pen. The priests employ zombies and font skeletons to do menial labor and act as guards. A gang of ogres serves as more formidable guards. Aside from the named priests on this level and any others detailed on other levels, there are a total of 9 priests, 14 lesser priests and 22 acolytes of Orcus on this level. There are a total of 10 zombie guards, 20 zombie servants and 20 font skeletons, as well as 6 ghouls, in addition to the gang of 9 ogres. Many of these creatures are encountered as wandering monsters. In addition, undead from other levels of the dungeon could be here for their own evil purpose, such as the shadows or Draeligor the wight from **Level 1**, or the ghouls or ghast from **Level 2**.

Ordinarily, the denizens of this level go about their normal daily routine: sacrificing slaves, whipping underlings, creating and controlling undead, plotting secret evils and taking part in worship at the whim of the more powerful priests. There is no set schedule of worship or sacrifice, nor are there set times where the various occupants can be found in certain locations. The level is, on the whole, quite chaotic — lorded over by the evil will of Koraashag.

Cries of pain from torture, sacrifice or "discipline" are not uncommon on this level.

ACOLYTE OF ORCUS CR 2
XP 600
hp 23 (see **Level 4, Area 1**)

FONT SKELETONS CR 1
XP 400
hp 11 (see the **Appendix**)

LESSER PRIESTS OF ORCUS CR 4
XP 1,200
hp 55 (see **Area 2**)

ZOMBIE GUARDS CR 1/2
XP 200
hp 12 (see **Area 1**)

ZOMBIE SERVANTS CR 1/2
XP 200
hp 12 (see **Area 3**)

1. Entrance Chamber (CR Varies, 2–5)

This carved chamber is illuminated by the glow of several smoky torches. The air here is thick and foul. There are always at least **3 zombie**

Level 4: The New Temple of Orcus

Difficulty Level: 8 (16 at the temple)
Entrances: Stairs from the demon door on the Entrance Level, **Area 10**; stairs from **Level 2, Area 25**.
Exits: Crevasse above **Level 5, Area 24A**; pit ledge leading to a passage to the Under Realms from **Area 14**.
Wandering Monsters: Most monsters on this level are priests or their undead servants. Check for wandering monsters once every 10 minutes by rolling 1d20 on the following table:

ROLL 1D20	RESULT
1–4	**1d3 acolytes of Orcus**, 50% chance accompanied by **1d6 font skeletons**
5–6	**1d3 lesser priests of Orcus**, 50% chance accompanied by **1d6 font skeletons**
7	**1d4 zombie guards**
8–10	**1d6 font skeletons**
11	**Major priest** (either **Staurauth, Mazarbul, Koraashag** or **Tavik** — if he is present), accompanied by **1d2 ogre guards** (see **Area 13**, below) and **1d4 lesser priests**, 50% chance also accompanied by **1d8 font skeletons** or **zombie guards**
12–14	**1d8 zombie servants**
14–16	The PCs hear a shriek or cry of intense pain.
17–20	No encounter

Standard Features: This level is composed of cavernous areas and areas of worked stone. The caverns are all huge, filled with tall columns and wickedly sharp stalactites and stalagmites. The worked areas are all of carved stone, shaped by magic and evil. All the hallways and rooms bear demonic images as well as workings of the wand of Orcus. The images are grotesque, wholly evil and randomly placed. The air is thick and foul. All areas are lit by sputtering torches or by coal-filled braziers that give off a hellish glow.
Continuous Effects: The entire level is under the effects of a modified *widened unhallow* spell, emanating from the statue of Orcus in **Area 12**. This specialized spell effect, a gift from Orcus, is used to ensure his followers have a secure base in the war against Good.

guards here, standing watch. Since nothing ever comes this way except priests from the surface, they are not very alert (–2 circumstance penalty). There is also a 1–5 on 1d20 chance that there are **1d3 acolytes of Orcus** here. Two large tapestries — one depicting Orcus standing with his skull-tipped wand and one depicting Orcus surrounded by hordes of demons and undead — hang on the north and south walls.

ZOMBIE GUARDS (3)   CR 1/2
XP 200
Male human zombie (*Pathfinder Roleplaying Game Bestiary* "Zombie, Medium")
NE Medium undead
Init +0; **Senses** darkvision 60 ft.; **Perception** +0

AC 12, touch 10, flat-footed 12 (+2 natural)
hp 12 (2d8 plus 3)
Fort +0; **Ref** +0; **Will** +3
DR 5/slashing; **Immune** undead traits

Speed 30 ft.
Melee heavy mace +4 (1d8+3) or slam +4 (1d6+4)

Str 17, **Dex** 10, **Con** —, **Int** —, **Wis** 10, **Cha** 10
Base Atk +1; **CMB** +4; **CMD** 14
Feats Toughness
SQ staggered

Gear heavy mace

Staggered (Ex) Zombies have poor reflexes and can only perform a single move action or standard action each round. A zombie can move up to its speed and attack in the same round as a charge action.

ACOLYTE OF ORCUS   CR 2
XP 600
Male human disciple of Orcus 3 (see the **Appendix**)
CE Medium humanoid (human)
Init –1; **Senses** darkvision 60 ft.; **Perception** +2
Aura evil

AC 16, touch 9, flat-footed 16 (+6 armor, –1 Dex, +1 shield)
hp 17 (3d8 plus 3)
Fort +3; **Ref** +0; **Will** +7

Speed 20 ft.
Melee heavy mace +4 (1d8+1)
Special Attacks channel negative energy 3/day (DC 11, 2d6)
Spells Prepared (CL 3rd; melee touch +3, ranged touch +1):
2nd—*bull's strength* (DC 14), *ghoul touch*ᴰ (DC 14), *hold person* (DC 14)
1st—*bane* (DC 13), *doom* (DC 13), *hide from undead* (DC 13), *protection from good*ᴰ (DC 15)

0 (at will)—*bleed* (DC 12), *create water*, *guidance*,
resistance
D Domain spell **Domain** Undead*

Str 12, **Dex** 8, **Con** 11, **Int** 9, **Wis** 15, **Cha** 10
Base Atk +2; **CMB** +3; **CMD** 12
Feats Blind-Fight, Command Undead[B], Iron Will, Toughness,
Weapon Focus (heavy mace)
Skills Heal +7, Knowledge (history) +3, Knowledge (religion)
+5, Linguistics+3, Spellcraft +7
Languages Abyssal, Common
SQ see in darkness, death's kiss (1 round, 3/day), undead
lord's proxy, variant channeler (undeath#)
Combat Gear 3 vials unholy water, 3 flasks of oil; **Other Gear**
chainmail, light steel shield, heavy mace, flint and steel,
wooden unholy symbol of Orcus
Pathfinder Roleplaying Game Advanced Player's Guide
Pathfinder Roleplaying Game Ultimate Magic

Fooling the Guards: Because the zombie guards are beaten and
dominated so cruelly by the priests of Orcus, they do not look directly at
anyone appearing to be a priest. Thus, PCs gain a +2 bonus when trying to
fool the zombies if disguised in evil priest garb. This bonus does not apply
to any acolytes present. Anyone attempting to pass must show an unholy
symbol of Orcus, regardless of any Disguise check. The zombies attack
anyone not doing so.

Tactics: The zombie guards immediately cry out with a roar if the area
is entered by anyone not identified as an evil priest (or someone on official
business). See the sidebar "**Alerting the Temple**" for more details. The
zombie guards immediately attack, as do any acolytes present.

Alerting the Temple

If anyone raises an alarm, there is a strong chance it is ignored
by all but those in adjacent rooms, as cries of terror and pain are
not uncommon on this level. In addition, since the level is mostly
unorganized, response to any alarm is sporadic and haphazard,
until one of the more powerful priests is alerted, at which time his
superior intellect allows for more ordered response.

Normally, cries of alarm are met by **1d2 lesser priests**, **1d4
acolytes** and **1d3 font skeletons**, if nearby (check adjoining room
keys). A few rounds later **1d3 zombie** guards come lumbering
along. Priests, however, are smart enough to send at least one of
their number to alert others in the temple.

Once the more senior priests learn of intruders, they send
several ogres (from **Area 13**) and more undead to deal with the
disturbance as well as a number of priests, lesser priests and
acolytes. Koraashag and the head priests join in any encounter
with intruders. They use all magic at their disposal.

If sorely pressed, they retreat to the cave outside the temple
(**Area 12**) and then to the temple itself (**Area 15**), where they
amass their forces against any final onslaught.

If there is an intrusion into the temple and the intruders retreat,
undead guards are doubled at all entrances (**Areas 1** and **7**) and **2 lesser
priests** are stationed at each location as well, along with an ogre.

2. Lesser Priests' Chambers (CR 7)

These spartan chambers are the bed chambers for **3 lesser priests of
Orcus.** There is a 1–5 on 1d20 chance for each priest that they are present.
If they are not present, they are attending service in **Area 15** or are on
some errand. The rooms have cots and small chests, with effects including
daggers, robes, small unholy symbols of Orcus and small idols.

LESSER PRIESTS OF ORCUS (3) CR 4
XP 1,200
Male human disciple of Orcus 5 (see the **Appendix**)
CE Medium humanoid (human)
Init +2; **Senses** darkvision 60 ft.; **Perception** +6
Aura evil

AC 20, touch 12, flat-footed 18 (+6 armor, +2 Dex, +2 shield)
hp 55 (5d8+15 plus 5)
Fort +7; **Ref** +3; **Will** +7

Speed 20 ft.
Melee +1 unholy morningstar +8 (1d8+4)
Special Attacks channel negative energy 8/day (3d6, DC 15)
Spells Prepared (CL 5th; melee touch +6, ranged touch +5):
3rd—*animate dead*[D], *bestow curse* (DC 16), *blindness/
deafness* (DC 16)
2nd—*bull's strength*, *ghoul touch*[D] (DC 15), *hold person* (DC
15), *silence* (DC 15)
1st—*bane* (DC 14), *cause fear* (DC 14), *command* (DC 14),
cure light wounds, *protection from good*[D]
0 (at will)—*detect magic*, *guidance*, *light*, *resistance*
D Domain spell **Domain** Undead*

Str 16, **Dex** 14, **Con** 16, **Int** 16, **Wis** 17, **Cha** 16
Base Atk +3; **CMB** +6; **CMD** 18
Feats Combat Casting, Command Undead (DC 15),
Extra Channel, Selective Channeling, Weapon Focus
(morningstar)
Skills Appraise +7, Diplomacy +7, Heal +11, Knowledge
(arcana) +11, Knowledge (dungeoneering) +4, Knowledge
(engineering) +4, Knowledge (history) +7, Knowledge
(planes) +7, Knowledge (religion) +11, Perception +6, Sense
Motive +7, Spellcraft +11, Stealth –4
Languages Abyssal, Common, Goblin, Undercommon
SQ death's kiss (2 rounds, 6/day), see in darkness, undead
lord's proxy, variant channeling (undeath#)
Gear masterwork chainmail, heavy steel shield, +1 unholy
morningstar, wooden unholy symbol of Orcus, 2 vials of
unholy water

See in Darkness (Ex) The holiest of rites to Orcus are
performed in total darkness. At 1st level the Disciple of
Orcus gains darkvision 60 ft. The range increases to 90 ft. at
6th level. At 8th level the Disciple of Orcus can also see in
magical darkness. If the Disciple of Orcus already possesses
darkvision its range increases by +30 ft. at 1st and 6th levels.
Undead Lord's Proxy (Su) Undead recognize the Disciple of
Orcus as a conduit to the Demon Lord. At 3rd level Disciples
add +2 to the DC to resist channeled energy when used to
command undead.
Undeath Variant Channeling (Su) Heal—This works like a
standard channel (not halved). Harm—The healing effect
is enhanced (+50%) for undead creatures and those with
negative energy affinity.
Pathfinder Roleplaying Game Advanced Player's Guide
#Pathfinder Roleplaying Game Ultimate Magic*

3. Minor Hall (CR Varies, 4+)

This hall contains several tables and cots. There are always at
least **2d4 acolytes of Orcus** present here. **Mazarbul**, the priest in
charge of the acolytes, is also generally present here unless he is
in the main temple area or on an errand (GM's discretion). A large
tapestry depicting Orcus in his Palace of Bones adorns the west wall.
There is a 1–4 on 1d20 chance that either some **zombie servants** or
font skeletons are here doing menial tasks — cleaning, serving and
so on.

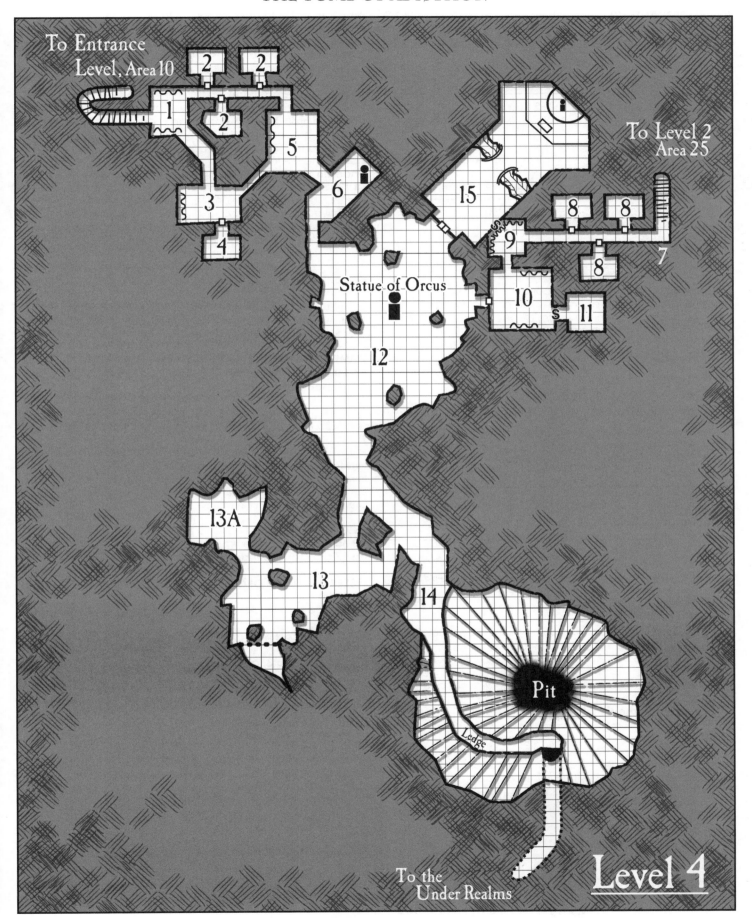

To Entrance
Level, Area 10

To Level 2
Area 25

Statue of Orcus

To the
Under Realms

Level 4

ZOMBIE SERVANTS (2)   CR 1/2
XP 200
Male human zombie (*Pathfinder Roleplaying Game Bestiary*
("Zombie, Medium"))
NE Medium undead
Init +0; **Senses** darkvision 60 ft.; **Perception** +0

AC 12, touch 10, flat-footed 12 (+2 natural)
hp 12 (2d8 plus 3)
Fort +0; **Ref** +0; **Will** +3
DR 5/slashing; **Immune** undead traits

Speed 30 ft.
Melee dagger +4 (1d4+3/19–20) or slam +4 (1d6+4)

Str 17, **Dex** 10, **Con** —, **Int** —, **Wis** 10, **Cha** 10
Base Atk +1; **CMB** +4; **CMD** 14
Feats Toughness
SQ staggered
Gear stained leather serving smock, dagger

Staggered (Ex) Zombies have poor reflexes and can only perform a single move action or standard action each round. A zombie can move up to its speed and attack in the same round as a charge action.

ACOLYTE OF ORCUS   CR 2
XP 600
hp 17 (see **Level 4, Area 1**)

MAZARBUL, MASTER OF ACOLYTES   CR 5
XP 1,600
Male human disciple of Orcus 6 (see the **Appendix**)
CE Medium humanoid (human)
Init −1; **Senses** darkvision 90 ft.; **Perception** +6
Aura evil

AC 18, touch 9, flat-footed 18 (+7 armor, −1 Dex, +2 shield)
hp 39 (6d8+6 plus 6)
Fort +6; **Ref** +1; **Will** +11

Speed 20 ft. (30 ft. base)
Melee +1 unholy heavy mace +8 (1d8+3)
Special Attacks channel negative energy 6/day (3d6, DC 14)
Spells Prepared (CL 6th; melee touch +6)
3rd—*animate dead*D, *blindness/deafness* (DC 17), *invisibility purge, prayer*
2nd—*align weapon, bear's endurance, ghoul touch*D (DC 16), *hold person* (DC 16), *spiritual weapon*
1st—*bane* (DC 15, x2), *cause fear*D (DC 17), *entropic shield, obscuring mist*
0 (at will)—*bleed* (DC 14), *detect magic, detect poison, guidance*
D Domain spell **Domain** Undead*

Str 14, **Dex** 8, **Con** 12, **Int** 10, **Wis** 18, **Cha** 13
Base Atk +4; **CMB** +6; **CMD** 15
Feats Command Undead^B (DC 14), Extra Channel, Iron Will, Toughness, Weapon Focus (heavy mace)
Skills Heal +8, Knowledge (arcana) +4, Knowledge (planes) +6, Knowledge (religion) +9, Linguistics +5, Perception +6, Spellcraft +6
Languages Abyssal, Common, Orc
SQ death's kiss (3 rounds, 4/day), see in darkness, undead lord's proxy, variant channeler (undeath#)
Combat Gear 2 *potions of cure serious wounds, potion of invisibility*; **Other Gear** +1 breastplate, masterwork heavy steel shield, +1 unholy heavy mace, cloak of resistance +1, unholy symbol of Orcus, prayer book, a fine black robe

emblazoned with the symbol of Orcus, 18 gp

See in Darkness (Ex) The holiest of rites to Orcus are performed in total darkness. At 1st level the Disciple of Orcus gains darkvision 60 ft. The range increases to 90 ft. at 6th level. At 8th level the Disciple of Orcus can also see in magical darkness. If the Disciple of Orcus already possesses darkvision its range increases by +30 ft. at 1st and 6th levels.
Undead Lord's Proxy (Su) Undead recognize the Disciple of Orcus as a conduit to the Demon Lord. At 3rd level Disciples add +2 to the DC to resist channeled energy when used to command undead.
Undeath Variant Channeling (Su) *Heal*—This works like a standard channel (not halved). *Harm*—The healing effect is enhanced (+50%) for undead creatures and those with negative energy affinity.
Pathfinder Roleplaying Game Advanced Player's Guide
#*Pathfinder Roleplaying Game Ultimate Magic*

4. Storage Chamber (CR 1)

This room contains barrels of water and foodstuff as well as timber and building tools. There is a small brick enclosure here in which food can be cooked. There are **2 zombie servants** here.

ZOMBIE SERVANTS (2)   CR 1/2
XP 200
hp 12 (see **Area 3**, above)

5. Gathering Hall (CR Varies, 6+)

This gathering hall holds many tables and chairs. The priests gather here for meals of vile rat porridge. It simmers in a cauldron in the northeast corner of the room. A large tapestry depicting the Wand of Orcus covers the west wall. There are always **1d4 lesser priests, 2d4 acolytes** and **1d6 zombie servants** here at any time.

ACOLYTE OF ORCUS   CR 2
XP 600
hp 17 (see **Level 4, Area 1**)

LESSER PRIESTS OF ORCUS   CR 4
XP 1,200
hp 55 (see **Level 4, Area 2**)

ZOMBIE SERVANTS   CR 1/2
XP 200
hp 12 (see **Area 3**, above)

6. "Hall of Tortures" (CR Varies, 0–5)

This room is filled with frescoes detailing torture and death — to train the acolytes with a vision of the abyss and the hell that awaits them. A plaster statue of Orcus stands in one corner. There is a 1–5 on 1d20 chance that there are **1d3 acolytes** here.

ACOLYTE OF ORCUS   CR 2
XP 600
hp 17 (see **Level 4, Area 1**)

7. Entrance Corridor (CR 5)

The stairs from Level 2 end here in this corridor. There are always **3 zombie guards** and **2 font skeletons** stationed here around the corner from the stairs. They act as do the guards at **Area 1**. The skeletons, however, cannot be fooled by a disguise.

ZOMBIE GUARDS (3)   **CR 1/2**
XP 200
hp 12 (see **Area 1**, above)

FONT SKELETONS (2)   **CR 1**
XP 400
hp 11 (see the **Font Skeleton** sidebar in the **Entrance Level** chapter)

8. Priest Quarters (CR Varies, 0–6)

These spartan rooms are similar to those occupied by the lesser priests (see **Area 2**, above). They each house **2 priests of Orcus**. There is a 1–5 on 1d20 chance for each priest that they are present. If they are not present, they are attending service in **Area 15** or are on some errand. The rooms have cots and small chests, with effects including daggers, robes, small unholy symbols of Orcus and small idols.

PRIESTS OF ORCUS (2)   **CR 5**
XP 1,600
Male human disciple of Orcus 6 (see the **Appendix**)
CE Medium humanoid (human)
Init –1; **Senses** darkvision 90 ft.; **Perception** +6
Aura evil

AC 18, touch 9, flat-footed 18 (+7 armor, –1 Dex, +2 shield)
hp 39 (6d8+6 plus 6)
Fort +6; **Ref** +1; **Will** +11

Speed 20 ft.
Melee mwk heavy mace +8 (1d8+3)
Special Attacks channel negative energy 6/day (3d6, DC 14)
Spells Prepared (CL 6th; melee touch +6)
3rd—*animate dead*ᴰ, *blindness/deafness* (DC 17), *invisibility purge*, *prayer*
2nd—*align weapon*, *bear's endurance*, *ghoul touch*ᴰ (DC 16), *hold person* (DC 16), *spiritual weapon*
1st—*bane* (DC 15) x2, *cause fear*ᴰ (DC 17), *entropic shield*, *obscuring mist*
0 (at will)—*bleed* (DC 14), *detect magic*, *detect poison*, *guidance*
ᴰ Domain spell **Domain** Undead*

Str 14, **Dex** 8, **Con** 12, **Int** 10, **Wis** 18, **Cha** 13
Base Atk +4; **CMB** +6; **CMD** 15
Feats Command Undeadᴮ (DC 14), Extra Channel, Iron Will, Toughness, Weapon Focus (heavy mace)
Skills Heal +8, Knowledge (arcana) +4, Knowledge (planes) +6, Knowledge (religion) +9, Linguistics +5, Perception +6, Spellcraft +6
Languages Abyssal, Common, Orc
SQ death's kiss (3 round, 4/day), see in darkness, undead lord's proxy, variant channeler (undeath#)
Combat Gear 2 *potions of cure serious wounds*, *potion of invisibility*; **Other Gear** +1 breastplate, masterwork heavy steel shield, mwk heavy mace, *cloak of resistance +1*, unholy symbol of Orcus, 18 gp

See in Darkness **(Ex)** The holiest of rites to Orcus are performed in total darkness. At 1st level the Disciple of Orcus gains darkvision 60 ft. The range increases to 90 ft. at 6th level. At 8th level the Disciple of Orcus can also see in magical darkness. If the Disciple of Orcus already possesses darkvision its range increases by +30 ft. at 1st and 6th levels.
Undead Lord's Proxy (Su) Undead recognize the Disciple of Orcus as a conduit to the Demon Lord. At 3rd level Disciples add +2 to the DC to resist channeled energy when used to command undead.
Undeath Variant Channeling (Su) *Heal*—This works like a standard channel (not halved). *Harm*—The healing effect is enhanced (+50%) for undead creatures and those with negative energy affinity.
Pathfinder Roleplaying Game Advanced Player's Guide
#Pathfinder Roleplaying Game Ultimate Magic*

9. Foyer

This small room contains a number of hooks on which hang ceremonial robes and other ceremonial items, such as daggers and incense burners. A tapestry depicting Orcus accepting sacrifices adorns the west and north wall, to either side of the secret door that leads to **Area 15**. The door itself is covered with a tapestry depicting the demonic skull of Orcus. This tapestry may be moved aside, allowing access to the secret door behind. A low, brass brazier filled with glowing coals sheds evil light here.

Secret Door: The secret door can be opened only by speaking the phrase "Our Horned Father" in Abyssal.

10. Hall of Study (CR Varies, 5+)

This hall contains several tables and several racks of books as well as a small statue of Orcus. A tapestry on the north wall depicts the destruction of a white marble temple by black-robed priests of Orcus, while a tapestry on the south wall depicts priests raising hordes of undead while Orcus looks on approvingly. There are always **1d3 priests of Orcus** here studying and praying to their evil god. There is also a 1–8 on 1d20 chance that there are **1d3 lesser priests** and the same chance that there are **1d4 zombie servants**.

PRIESTS OF ORCUS   **CR 5**
XP 1,600
hp 39 (see **Level 4, Area 8**)

LESSER PRIESTS OF ORCUS   **CR 4**
XP 1,200
hp 55 (see **Level 4, Area 2**)

ZOMBIE SERVANTS   **CR 1/2**
XP 200
hp 12 (see **Area 3**, above)

Tomes: The books present are all written in Abyssal and deal with the worship of Orcus and other minor demons. They could have some value to sages, wizards or other evil priests. They could also convey some information on banishing demons. There is no market value for such rare tracts. The GM should use his or her discretion in determining a value for them.

Secret Door: The door to **Area 11**, Koraashag's chamber, is locked (Disable Device DC 30) and trapped. The door is covered with a permanent *invisibility purge*, meaning that any invisible creatures passing into the chamber are revealed. In addition, on the lintel above the door on the east side of the door are traced three *glyphs of warding*. They inflict blast damage to any person other than Koraahsag who opens the door. All three glyphs discharge at once.

127

Note: Persons approaching from the west cannot see the *glyphs* since they are carved on the east side of the door, and thus cannot disarm them from that side.

TRIPLE GLYPHS OF WARDING (BLAST) TRAP · CR 5
XP 1,600
Type magical; **Perception** DC 28; **Disable Device** DC 28

Trigger spell; **Reset** none
Effect spell effect (*glyph of warding [blast]* x3, 10th-level cleric, 5d8 fire, DC 15 Reflex save half damage); multiple targets (all targets within 5 ft.). The *glyph* may be identified (with *read magic*) without triggering it with a successful DC 13 Spellcraft check.
Note: Because all three *glyphs* go off at once, treat this as three CR 5 traps for XP purposes.

11. Koraashag's Chamber (CR 10)

This chamber is more opulent than the spartan chambers of the other priests. Velvet hangings and tapestries — carried here from Rappan Athuk on the backs of slaves — cover the wall. A large bed and chest as well as a small desk and chair fill the room. The tapestries depict Orcus in his most demonic visage with Koraashag at his right hand. Various personal effects and unholy items litter the room.

Though this is Koraashag's bed chamber, and he is frequently here when he is not in the temple at **Area 15**, it is not his most private sanctuary. That sanctuary is located high in a cave on **Level 5**, at **Areas 26–27A**.

Koraashag's statistics are provided at **Area 15**.

Treasure: The bedding is of finest quality (worth 500 gp). The chest in the room is locked and ingeniously trapped. The chest's lock is exquisitely crafted and worth over 500 gp if it can be removed without being destroyed, though the key for it must also be available (it is kept on Koraashag's person). It would take a master craftsman weeks of study to create a key to fit the lock. The chest has a **poison needle trap**, but that trap is meant to be detected. If the poison needle trap is detected and disabled, this actually triggers the **second trap** (unless that second trap is also detected and disabled, which is nearly impossible without the key to the chest). This second trap is bypassed only by use of the lock's key (or by a rogue with otherworldly skills). Additionally, within the lid of the trap is a **vial of burnt othur fumes** that is released if the chest is broken with force. Inside the locked and trapped chest are silks and other finery (worth 500 gp) as well as 31,000 gp and seventy-eight gems of value from 10 to 100 gp each (GM to determine). Also within the chest is a scroll of 4 divine spells (CL 18th; *contingency, word of recall, heal* and *unholy word*). Koraashag treasures this scroll and does not carry it on his person, nor would he use it in combat.

Locked and Trapped Wooden Chest: 1 in. thick; hardness 5; hp 10; Break DC 18; Disable Device DC 30.

POISON NEEDLE TRAP · CR 1
XP 400
Type mechanical; **Perception** DC 20; **Disable Device** DC 20

Trigger touch; **Reset** manual
Effect attack +8 ranged (1 plus greenblood oil poison); disabling this trap triggers the *slay living* trap

SLAY LIVING TRAP · CR 6
XP 2,400
Type magical; Perception DC 30; Disable Device DC 30

Trigger spell; **Reset** none
Effect spell effect (*slay living*, +8 ranged touch, 12th-level cleric, 12d6+12 damage, DC 17 Fort save for only 3d6+12 damage)

BURNT OTHUR FUMES TRAP · CR 10
XP 9,600
Type mechanical; **Perception** DC 25 (cannot be detected without opening the chest); **Disable Device** DC 20

Trigger location; **Reset** none
Effect poison gas (burnt othur fumes); never miss; onset delay (1 round); multiple targets (all targets in a 5-ft.-by-5-ft. area)

12. Cavern of Orcus and Bronze Portals (CR Varies, 5–12)

This great cavern serves as the outer chamber of the temple of Orcus. The cavern reaches 100 feet in height. The ceiling of the cavern is filled with stalactites. Several large pillars formed of joined stalactites and stalagmites give the cavern a grand and ominous feel. The cavern itself is dominated by a huge statue of the demon prince standing upright and holding his wand above his head, his batlike wings fully spread. This statue was shaped from the black rock of the chamber by Koraashag using *stone shape*. Surrounding the statue, which towers some 30 feet tall, are a number of bronze braziers filled with coals that give off a hellish glow. Behind the statue are the great brass portals to the temple itself. In front of the statue is a rough black pit filled with bones of sacrifices.

This cavern is a hub of activity and is the common area of the temple, the carved areas reserved for the more important priests and for temple functions. The cavern itself is occupied mostly by acolytes. There are **2d8 acolytes** here at any time. The acolytes make their individual camps randomly around the statue, where they are constantly in devotion. There are always **1d8 zombie servants** here as well as **1d4 zombie guards**. There is also a 1–6 on 1d20 chance that there are **1d3 lesser priests** here, either disciplining the acolytes or conducting their own secret business. There is a 1–5 on 1d20 chance that there are **1d6 font skeletons** present and the same chance that there are **1d3 ghouls** present, in various parts of the cavern. There is also a 1–4 on 1d20 chance that **1d2 ogres** are in the cavern, either coming or going from their lair at 13 to the temple at 15.

On very rare occasion (GM to determine), a small group of pilgrims either from another temple of Orcus or from some other chaotic evil deity are here visiting the temple. They make their camp near the great statue of Orcus.

ACOLYTE OF ORCUS · CR 2
XP 600
hp 17 (see **Level 4, Area 1**)

LESSER PRIESTS OF ORCUS · CR 4
XP 1,200
hp 55 (see **Level 4, Area 2**)

ZOMBIE GUARDS · CR 1/2
XP 200
hp 12 (see **Area 1**, above)

ZOMBIE SERVANTS · CR 1/2
XP 200
hp 12 (see **Area 3**, above)

FONT SKELETONS · CR 1
XP 400
hp 11 (see the **Font Skeleton** sidebar in the **Entrance Level** chapter)

GHOULS · CR 1
XP 400
hp 13 (*Pathfinder Roleplaying Game Bestiary* "Ghoul")

OGRES CR 2
XP 600
Male ogre warrior 1 (*Pathfinder Roleplaying Game Bestiary* "Ogre")
CE Large humanoid (giant)
Init –1; **Senses** darkvision 60 ft., low-light vision; **Perception** +5

AC 17, touch 8, flat-footed 17 (+4 armor, –1 Dex, +5 natural, –1 size)
hp 34 (1d10+2 plus 4d8+8 plus 6)
Fort +8; **Ref** +0; **Will** +3

Speed 30 ft.
Melee greataxe +8 (3d6+7/×3)
Space 10 ft.; **Reach** 10 ft.

Str 21, **Dex** 8, **Con** 15, **Int** 6, **Wis** 10, **Cha** 7
Base Atk +4; **CMB** +10; **CMD** 19
Feats Intimidating Prowess, Iron Will, Toughness
Skills Acrobatics –4, Climb +7, Escape Artist –4, Intimidate +7, Perception +5, Stealth –8, Swim +2
Languages Giant
Gear hide armor, greataxe, sack with a human skull and a hunk of uncooked meat, 3d20 gp, 2d20 sp.

Tactics: The occupants of this cavern do not expect any strangers. Thus, anyone entering this cavern is attacked immediately, though the occupants are momentarily unprepared and taken off guard by the presence of such unexpected intruders.

13. Far Cavern (CR Varies, 3–8)

This tall cavern is the home of a band of ogres, enlisted by Koraashag to the service of Orcus. They are fanatically loyal to the demon god and to Koraashag. They serve as guards to the temple. Between them, they have five suits of half-plate and take turns wearing the suits as their shift of guard duty begins. There is always **1 ogre guard** here with **1d3 ogres**. There are always **1d3 zombie guards** here as well. On a 1–4 on 1d20 there are also **1d4 acolytes** here. There are a total of 11 ogres, though there are no more than 4 here at any time. Two ogres are always at **Area 15**, wearing two of the five sets of half-plate, while 2 more ogres are always at **Area 14**, wearing two more of the five sets of half-plate. A fifth is always here, wearing the final suit of half-plate and guarding the slave pen (see below). The other ogres present are either eating or sleeping while off duty.

OGRE GUARD IN HALF-PLATE CR 3
XP 800
Male ogre fighter 1 (*Pathfinder Roleplaying Game Bestiary* "Ogre")
CE Large humanoid (giant)
Init –1; **Senses** darkvision 60 ft., low-light vision; **Perception** +5

AC 21, touch 8, flat-footed 21 (+8 armor, –1 Dex, +5 natural, –1 size)
hp 34 (1d10+2 plus 4d8+8 plus 6)
Fort +8; **Ref** +0; **Will** +3

Speed 30 ft.
Melee greataxe +8 (3d6+7/×3)
Space 10 ft.; **Reach** 10 ft.

Str 21, **Dex** 8, **Con** 15, **Int** 6, **Wis** 10, **Cha** 7
Base Atk +4; **CMB** +10; **CMD** 19
Feats Intimidating Prowess, Iron Will, Power Attack, Toughness
Skills Acrobatics –8, Climb +3, Escape Artist –8, Intimidate +7, Perception +5, Stealth –12

Languages Giant
Gear half-plate, greataxe, sack with a human skull and a hunk of uncooked meat, 3d20 gp, 2d20 sp.

OGRES CR 3
XP 800
hp 34 (see **Level 4, Area 12**)

ZOMBIE GUARDS CR 1/2
XP 200
hp 12 (see **Area 1**, above)

ACOLYTE OF ORCUS CR 2
XP 600
hp 17 (see **Level 4, Area 1**)

Slave Pen: The southern spur of the cavern is walled off with stout wooden posts, into which is set a barred wooden gate. This pen holds humanoids captured in the Under Realms or purchased from orc or gnoll raiding bands from the surface. These creatures are to be sacrifices to Orcus. At least one such creature is sacrificed every day. There are currently 2d10 humanoids from the surface (from pillaged villages or farms) and 1d10 humanoids from the Under Realms (gnomes or others captured by slavers and sold to the priests here). The gate is barred with a heavy wooden log, easily lifted by the ogres.

Wooden Slave Pen: 4 in. thick posts; hardness 5; hp 40; Break DC 23; DC 16 Str check to lift bar; up to three creatures on the outside of the gate can add their Str bonus to the check; creatures within the pen take –2 on the check).

SLAVES (3d10) CR 1/3
XP 135
hp 1–6 each (commoners of various humanoid races)

13A. Pool Cavern (CR 0–6)

The pool in this low cavern contains brackish water. It must be boiled to be consumed (except by the ogres, who drink it as it is) or the drinker is subject to filth fever (*save* Fort DC 12; *onset* 1d3 days; *frequency* 1/day; *effect* 1d3 Dex damage and 1d3 Con damage; *cure* 2 consecutive saves).

There is a 1–5 on 1d20 chance that there are **1d3 zombie servants** here fetching water for the priests. There is a similar chance that **1d2 ogres** are here, drinking or bathing in the water.

ZOMBIE SERVANTS CR 1/2
XP 200
hp 12 (see **Area 3**, above)

OGRES CR 3
XP 800
hp 30 (see **Area 13**, above)

14. Stinking Pit (CR 5)

This cavern passage ends in a ledge that spirals down the inside of an abyss of unknown depths, leading to a cave mouth that leads to a passage to the Under Realms. The abyss is bottomless. Anyone falling into it is forever lost unless he or she has magical aid. The abyss itself emits foul smokes and vapors. All except ogres (who are used to such smells) passing through this room are afflicted as per a permanent *stinking cloud* spell (Fort save DC 18). The effect cannot be magically resisted or dispelled, though a save is allowed as per the spell. There are always **2 ogre guards in half-plate** here, guarding the entrance to the chambers to the north. They are stationed at the location of the number "**14**" on the map. The footing on the ledge that spirals into the abyss is treacherous; it is less than a foot wide and is slippery, thus it requires a DC 12 Acrobatics check for any activity other than careful walking.

OGRE GUARD IN HALF-PLATE (2)   CR 3
XP 800
hp 30 (see **Area 13**, above)

Passage to the Under Realms: The cave opening at the bottom of the spiraling ledge leads to a passage that connects with the labyrinthine web of passages that make up the Under Realms. The path eventually leads to a secret passage that links up with the lower levels of the famous dungeon of **Rappan Athuk**, though such a trek would require many weeks and great danger.

15. Temple of Orcus (CR Varies, 12+)

Beyond the heavy brass portals lies the Temple of Orcus, built by Koraashag at the direction of his demonic deity. The temple chamber is split by a large crevasse, which opens up to **Level 5** far below. The portion of the temple beyond the crevasse sits some 20 feet above the portion of the room south of the crevasse. The ceiling of the temple is over 50 feet high. The crevasse is spanned by a thick bridge of solid black stone. A row of glowing braziers line either side of the crevasse, filling the chamber with a hellish glow. Black candles of a most unholy aspect stand in long candleholders along either wall and flicker with a faint and evil light. Obscene censers issue forth foul smokes.

The portion north of the crevasse is dominated by a gold-plated and jewel-encrusted statue of a seated Orcus, his wand upraised in one hand and the other hand outstretched with an open palm facing upward, on which is set the heart and entrails of many sacrifices. Before the statue and on the same raised platform is an altar of black stone, stained even deeper with the crimson blood of hundreds of sacrifices. A large bronze brazier, full of burning coals, stands to either side of the statue of the demon prince.

Normally during rituals or functions, acolytes and servants remain in the lower portion of the temple below the chasm while the lesser priests and priests gather directly before the altar. The senior priests such as Koraashag (or any others with names) stand on the raised platform by the altar (thus benefiting from the *unholy aura* generated by the statue).

Magical Protections: The entire room is under the effect of an *unhallow* spell, as well as *invisibility purge* and *bless* (for followers of Orcus).

The Upper Platform: In addition to the spell effects above, all persons on the raised platform with the statue of Orcus are under an *unholy aura* spell.

The Crevasse and Bridge: The crevasse opens above **Level 5, Area 24A**. Anyone falling into the crack falls 50 feet through stone before reaching the ceiling of **Level 5, Area 24A**, and then falls 100 feet more to the cavern floor below — a total of 150 feet!

CREVASSE (150 FEET DEEP) CR 3
XP 800
Type mechanical; **Perception** DC —; **Disable Device** DC —

Trigger location, **Reset** none
Effect 150-ft.-deep pit (15d6 falling damage); DC 20 Reflex avoids

The Statue of Orcus: This hideous statue is covered in nearly 3,000 gp worth of gold plate and encrusted with one hundred gems worth 100 gp each. All are *cursed* and afflict anyone removing them with a *bestow curse* spell. In addition, the statue radiates *unholy aura* as detailed above.

The Shimmering Portal: Together, when the above priests chant for 1 hour in an obscene ritual and sacrifice a living humanoid, they can contact Orcus directly in his Palace of Bones in the Abyss through a shimmering portal that appears in the middle of the temple. He will speak with the gathering as per the *divination* spell. Using another variant of this ritual, the priests can communicate with each other through this shimmering portal over far distances.

Occupants: Normally present in the temple are **Koraashag, the High Priest**, 2 ogre guards in half-plate, 2 priests of Orcus, 2 lesser priests of Orcus, 2d6 acolytes of Orcus, 1d6 zombie guards, 1d6 zombie servants and 1d6 font skeletons. There are also always **1d4 shadows** present. There may be more acolytes and lesser priests if a major service or sacrifice is taking place, in addition to ghouls or visitors from other levels of the dungeon. Also, **Staurauth** (see **Level 2A, Area 14**) can be found here in the main temple during important rituals. Finally, **Tavik** — the evil priest from *The Crucible of Freya* — will also be here if he was driven off but not defeated by the PCs in that adventure. If present, Tavik has been severely reprimanded by Korashaag for his failures regarding the ruined keep (see *The Crucible of Freya* for more details), though he has gained 2 levels of experience.

ACOLYTE OF ORCUS CR 2
XP 600
hp 17 (see **Level 4, Area 1**)

LESSER PRIESTS OF ORCUS CR 4
XP 1,200
hp 55 (see **Level 4, Area 2**)

PRIESTS OF ORCUS CR 5
XP 1,600
hp 39 (see **Level 4, Area 8**)

OGRE GUARD IN HALF-PLATE (2) CR 3
XP 800
hp 30 (see **Area 13**, above)

ZOMBIE GUARDS CR 1/2
XP 200
hp 12 (see **Area 1**, above)

ZOMBIE SERVANTS CR 1/2
XP 200
hp 12 (see **Area 3**, above)

SHADOWS CR 3
XP 800
hp 19 (*Pathfinder Roleplaying Game Bestiary* "Shadow")

FONT SKELETONS CR 1
XP 400
hp 11 (see the **Font Skeleton** sidebar in the **Entrance Level** chapter)

TAVIK CR 3
XP 800
Male half-orc cleric of Orcus 4
CE Medium humanoid (human, orc)
Init +1; **Senses** darkvision 60 ft.; **Perception** +3
Aura evil

AC 19, touch 11, flat-footed 18 (+6 armor, +1 Dex, +2 shield)
hp 29 (4d8+4)
Fort +5; **Ref** +2; **Will** +6
Defensive Abilities ferocity

Speed 20 ft.
Melee +1 unholy heavy mace +8 (1d8+4)
Special Attacks channel negative energy 4/day (2d6, DC 13), destructive smite (+2, 5/day)
Domain Spell-Like Abilities (CL 4th; melee touch +6):
5/day—*bleeding touch* (2 rounds)
Spells Prepared (CL 4th; melee touch +6, ranged touch +4):
2nd—*bull's strength, death knell*D, (DC 14), *hold person* (DC 14, x2)
1st—*bane* (DC 13), *cause fear*D (DC 13), *doom* (DC 13), *protection from good, silence*
0 (at will)—*bleed* (DC 12), *guidance, resistance, virtue*
D Domain Spell **Domains** Death, Destruction

Str 16, **Dex** 12, **Con** 12, **Int** 12, **Wis** 15, **Cha** 12
Base Atk +3; **CMB** +6; **CMD** 17
Feats Power Attack, Weapon Focus (heavy mace)
Skills Acrobatics –4 (–8 jump), Climb –2, Diplomacy +7, Heal +6, Intimidate +6, Knowledge (religion) +8, Perception +3, Sense Motive +6, Spellcraft +5, Stealth –4, Survival +4
Languages Abyssal, Common, Orc
Combat Gear *potion of cure serious wounds*; **Other Gear** masterwork chainmail, masterwork heavy steel shield, +1 unholy heavy mace, restorative ointment, 6 vials unholy water, holy symbol of Orcus

KORAASHAG, THE HIGH PRIEST OF ORCUS CR 9
XP 6,400
Male orc disciple of Orcus 10 (see the **Appendix**)
CE Medium humanoid (orc)
Init +5; **Senses** darkvision 120 ft.; **Perception** +8
Aura evil

AC 22, touch 11, flat-footed 22 (+8 armor, +1 deflection, +1 Dex, +2 shield)
hp 88 (10d8+30 plus 10)
Fort +10; **Ref** +4; **Will** +13
Defensive Abilities ferocity
Weakness light sensitivity

Speed 20 ft.
Melee +1 keen unholy spiked heavy mace +12/+7 (1d8+5/19–20)
Special Attacks channel negative energy 6/day (5d6, DC 18), touch of darkness 10/day
Spells Prepared (CL 10th; melee touch +11, ranged touch +8):
5th—*slay living*D (DC 19), *spell resistance, true seeing*
4th—*cure critical wounds* x2, *death ward, enervation*D (DC 18), *freedom of movement*
3rd—*animate dead*D, *bestow curse* (DC 17), *deeper darkness, dispel magic, prayer*
2nd—*aid, death knell* (DC 16), *ghoul touch*D (DC 16), *hold person* (DC 16, x2), *silence* (DC 16)
1st—*bane* (DC 15), *cause fear*D (DC 15), *command* (DC 15), *cure light wounds* x2, *divine favor*
0 (at will)—*bleed* (DC 14), *detect magic, light, read magic*

Str 18, **Dex** 12, **Con** 17, **Int** 15, **Wis** 19, **Cha** 17
Base Atk +7; **CMB** +11 (+13 to sunder); **CMD** 23 (25 vs. sunder)
Feats Combat Casting, Command Undead (DC 18), Improved Initiative, Improved Sunder, Iron Will, Power Attack
Skills Heal +8, Intimidate +4, Knowledge (arcana) +8, Knowledge (history) +7, Knowledge (planes) +11, Knowledge (religion) +15, Perception +8, Sense Motive +10, Spellcraft +15, Stealth –4
Languages Abyssal, Common, Orc, Undercommon
SQ death's kiss (5 rounds, 7/day), undead lord's proxy, variant channeling (undeath#)
Combat Gear 2 *potions of cure serious wounds, ring of spectral hand* (with 20 charges, see **Appendix**), eight vials of unholy water; **Other Gear** *+2 breastplate,* heavy steel shield, *+1 keen,* unholy spiked heavy mace, *ring of protection +1,* a *cloak of the demon* (see **Appendix**), an iron unholy symbol of Orcus, black robes emblazoned with the symbol of Orcus, and the key to the chest at **Area 11**.

See in Darkness (Ex) The holiest of rites to Orcus are performed in total darkness. At 1st level the Disciple of Orcus gains darkvision 60 ft. The range increases to 90 ft. at 6th level. At 8th level the Disciple of Orcus can also see in magical darkness. If the Disciple of Orcus already possesses darkvision its range increases by +30 ft. at 1st and 6th levels.
Touch of Darkness (Su): At 9th level, once per day per level, the Disciple may make a melee touch attack to deal 1d4+1 points of Strength damage to a target (Fortitude save for half damage). If the target is reduced to 0 Strength or less, they die, and rise as a shadow under the control of the Disciple one round later. The Disciple may have one controlled shadow per two Disciple levels. This is equivalent to a 5th level spell. The save DC is Wisdom-based.
Undead Lord's Proxy (Su) Undead recognize the Disciple of Orcus as a conduit to the Demon Lord. At 3rd level Disciples add +2 to the DC to resist channeled energy when used to command undead.
Undeath Variant Channeling (Su) Heal—This works like a standard channel (not halved). Harm—The healing effect is enhanced (+50%) for undead creatures and those with negative energy affinity.
Pathfinder Roleplaying Game Advanced Player's Guide

Tactics: Once attacked, Koraashag immediately uses his *cloak* and attempts to summon a **vrock** (named **Z'veerikrrol**). He sends the ogres to attack the party. He commands the priests to attack the party also. Koraashag himself remains back on the raised platform (remaining under the protection of the *unholy aura*) and use his *spectral hand ring* to use his touch of darkness ability on intruders as well as *enervation* and *slay living*. If attacked by a mage, he most likely casts *spell immunity* either to *fireball, magic missile* or whatever other area of effect spell the mage used on the acolytes below. If engaged in melee, Koraashag relishes using his touch of darkness ability after softening up his foe with a few channel negative energy blasts and blows from his *mace*. If the going gets tough for Koraashag, he *teleports* down into the crevasse and then uses his wings to fly down to **Level 5, Area 26**, where he retreats to his hidden underground shrine. Remember, too, that Koraashag is under a modified *refuge* spell that transports him to **Level 5, Area 27A** if his hit points are reduced to 10 or fewer. Any other senior priests (except Tavik) also remain on the raised platform, using their spell abilities and receiving the protection of the *unholy aura*. The ogres attack with directness and the demons use their *teleport* ability to keep the party confused. They enjoy using magic or force to knock PCs into the chasm. The priests use their spells such as *bull's strength* on themselves, *command* and *hold person* on fighters and *silence* on any spellcasters before wading into combat. They attack with melee weapons to soften up their foes before using their death touch power. The priests and the demons attempt to throw any *held* intruders into the crevasse. If someone is thrown into the crevasse, Koraashag teleports and flies down to make sure he or she is dead, takes any valuable items and then returns to the fray. Zombies and skeletons attack mindlessly. If Tavik is present, he attacks the party with reckless abandon, hoping to have his revenge on the PCs and to regain his stature in the eyes of Koraashag.

Note: Koraashag, by the blessing of Orcus, has had a *refuge* spell placed on him. If ever he is reduced to 10 hit points or fewer, he is brought immediately to **Level 5, Area 27A**, where he uses the healing available to him there. A lengthy and unholy ritual allowed Koraashag to be imbued with this ability.

Level 5: The Great Cavern and the Temple of the Frog

The tsathar — a vile subterranean race that worships the demon frog god, Tsathogga — control this level of the dungeon. Several huge caverns dominate the level; one includes an underground lake that is lorded over by the tsathar's main temple — the Temple of the Frog. In the lake and in the temple's breeding pits, the tsathar breed hundreds of loathsome, monstrous frogs that they let free to roam the level. A chasm in the ceiling of a cavern connects a portion of this level to the Temple of Orcus on **Level 4**, above.

Aside from Lokaug, the High Priest of Tsathogga, and any others detailed on other levels, there are a total of 14 frog-priests, 28 filth-priests, 42 supplicants and 38 tsathar scourges in total on this level. In addition, there are over 200 normal tsathar on this level.

Any party that attempts to take this level head-on is doomed. Stealth has to be the order of the day, as wiping out a whole colony of these creatures under unfavorable conditions is nigh impossible. If some tsathar are found dead or are missing, the rest blame the priests of Orcus for the trouble and do not even think it possible that an adventuring party is at work. At the GM's discretion, it is even possible that the PCs could open up hostilities between the tsathar and the priests of Orcus, using the two separate forces to wipe each other out. It is unlikely that the PCs can form an alliance with the inhuman tsathar, though creative use of *alter self* and *tongues* spells may allow some chance.

Standard Features: The entire level (except for **Areas 26** and **27**) consists of stone caverns. The walls are always wet and slippery, due to the presence of the underground lake. The entire level seems to be covered with a coating of slime — though it does not extend to areas numbered **19** or higher. Climb checks in the slime-filled areas (**Areas 1–18**) are at –4, and no running or combat is allowed without a DC 8 Reflex save every round such activity is attempted. Failure results in the character slipping and falling. All denizens of this level are immune to this check, since they live in the slime. The lake itself glows with a faint, foul green phosphorescence, and the large idol of Tsathogga at **Area 4**, which dominates the main cavern, radiates a faint, sickly green light.

Fungus covers most surfaces on this level: 20% of the fungus is edible, while 10% is poisonous (Fortitude save DC 16 or take 1d6 Con/1d6 Con). A DC 20 Knowledge (dungeoneering or nature) or Survival check allows PCs to determine which are edible. (Gnomes and other underground creatures gain a +2 bonus to their checks.)

POISONOUS FUNGUS: ingested; *save* Fortitude DC 16; *onset* 10 min; *frequency* 1/min for 5 min; *effect* 1d6 Con; *cure* 1 save.

Continuous Effects: A majority of this level (**Areas 2–14**) radiates *unhallow* due to the effect of the evil temple. *Detect evil* spells and paladin abilities fail to function in these portions of this level. The entire area registers as evil — such is the power of the idol of Tsathogga at **Area 4**.

GIANT FROGS   **CR 1**
XP 400
hp 15 (*Pathfinder Roleplaying Game Bestiary* "Frog, Giant")

Level 5: The Great Cavern and the Temple of the Frog

Difficulty Level: 10.
Entrances: Stairs from **Level 1**; crevasse from **Level 4**.
Exits: Hidden stairs **to Level 5A**, stairs **to Level 6**.
Wandering Monsters: The tsathar and their foul frogs very densely populate the huge caverns of this level. Every 15 minutes, or every time the party makes significant noise or light, roll 1d20 on the following table:

ROLL 1D20	RESULT
1–3	**1d6 giant frogs**
4	**1d6 giant poisonous frogs**
5	**Tsathar hunting party** (1 tsathar filth-priest, 4 tsathar and 4 giant frogs, searching the level for food or heading to Level 6 to eat dire rats)
6	A group of **tsathar pilgrims** (1 tsathar filth-priest, 2 tsathar supplicants and 1d6 tsathar, visiting the temple from the Under Realms, exploring the environs)
7	**1d2 killer frogs** that have gotten free from the breeding pits; there is a 1–8 on 1d20 chance that **1d6 tsathar scourges** arrive 1d6 rounds later to recapture the rogue frogs
8	**Tsathar training mission** (1 tsathar filth-priest, 1 tsathar scourge, 1 killer frog and 2 tsathar)
9	**Tsathar patrol** (1 tsathar scourge, 4 tsathar, 1 killer frog and 2 giant frogs)
10–12	Group of **1d6 tsathar** traveling the caverns for their own purposes
13	The **behir** from Level 6 (see **Level 6, Area 10** for details; only encountered in **Areas 15–17**; otherwise no encounter)
14–20	No encounter

KILLER FROGS   **CR 1**
XP 400
hp 6 (*The Tome of Horrors Complete* 671)

TSATHAR   **CR 2**
XP 600
hp 13 (*The Tome of Horrors Complete* 616)

TSATHAR FILTH-PRIEST   **CR 7**
XP 3,200
hp 62 (see **Area 4**)

Level 5

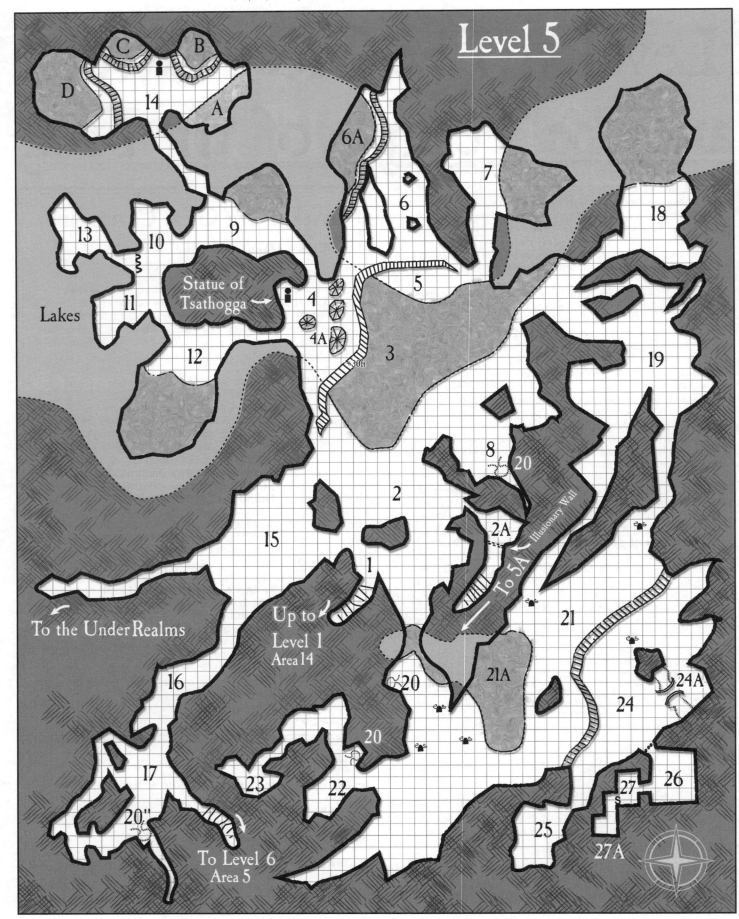

C

B

D

A

i

14

6A

7

18

13

10

9

6

5

11

Lakes

Statue of
Tsathogga

i

4

4A

12

3

19

8

20

2

2A

To 5A

Illusionary Wall

15

1

To the Under Realms

Up to
Level 1
Area 14

20

21

21A

24A

16

20

24

17

27

26

20"

22

23

25

To Level 6
Area 5

27A

1. Stairs from Level 1

The walls and floors of this area are slime and fungus covered, in part due to the heat and humidity associated with the entirety of this level and in part due to the cultivation of such things by the local inhabitants. Molds and mushrooms sprout from every crack and crevice. A faint glow can be seen coming from **Area 4**, across the fetid water of the lake (**Area 3**). Its green-shaded light casts eerie shadows over the whole cavern.

PCs that hide and observe the area from this location are relatively unmolested (unless attacked by wandering monsters). From this entrance location, they can observe the goings on in **Areas 2, 3, 4** and **15** due to the ever-present greenish light from **Area 4**. Because these stairs are almost never used, Stealth checks in the area of the stairs are at +2.

2. Great Cavern

This cavern has a vaulted ceiling reaching 100 feet into the darkness above. In the north side of the cavern is a large, fetid lake smelling of swamp water and decay. Water drips from the ceiling in thick, gooey droplets, occasionally dripping on some creature below. Pale green light emanates from the idol at **Area 4**, creating vast areas of shadow (+10 on Stealth checks) and allowing vision to a range of 200 feet. The raised platform and statue in **Area 4** can be seen as dim outlines in the distance. As this area is heavily traveled, an immediate wandering monster check should be made as soon as the (relative) safety of **Area 1** is left.

The passage to the south from **Area 1** is dark and is bisected by water from the small pool at **Area 21A**.

2A. Side Room and Hidden Stairs

Upon first glance, this is a normal empty, small side cave. It is unremarkable. The south wall, however, hides stairs to **Level 5A** — the location of the monolith and the major secrets of this dungeon.

Hidden Stairs: Long ago, before the coming of the Temple of the Frog and before the founding of the burial halls, when the chambers containing *earth blood* were warded, this chamber was seen as the entrance chamber to the caves that led to the *earth blood* (**Level 5A**). The stairs to **Level 5A** were warded by a complex ritual cast by the high priests of the earth god, resulting in a strange and divine *improved illusory wall*. The section of wall indicated on the map with dashed lines is that wall. It does not radiate magic and cannot be detected in that fashion. It appears to be a wall even during *scrying*, as if under the effects of a *screen* spell. Even those physically interacting with the wall cannot normally detect it as an illusion. Unless disbelieved (see below), the wall remains real. Objects strike it and bounce off.

Detecting the Wall: The wall can be detected only if successfully disbelieved. Disbelief, however, requires more than some speculative guess or random search. To allow a disbelief roll (DC 25 Will save), the viewer must have some tangible reason why he or she believes that a passage extends from this room. For example, if the characters were led to this location by a spell such as *find the path* or some other similar spell and thus have a belief that the path continues on past this cave, or if they see someone who knows the wall is an illusion pass through the wall, they may qualify to make a save to disbelieve. Similarly, speaking with the spirit of Flail, reading Koraashag's journal or capturing and successfully interrogating Lokaug or one of the frog-priests (though neither Lokaug nor the frog-priests reveal this information unless magically compelled, even on threat of death or torture) about the location of the Black Monolith leads to this cave and allows an opportunity to disbelieve the wall. Unless these conditions or similar conditions are met, the wall cannot be detected. Even *true seeing* or a *ring of x-ray vision* does not reveal the wall. The bottom line is this: random search — regardless of the magic used — does not reveal the wall. To earn a disbelief roll, the person must *know* that a passage leads from this room. A person gets only one roll to disbelieve. If failed, he or she can never pass through the *illusory wall*.

3. The Underground Lake of Filth (CR Varies, 6–10)

This lake contains foul, desecrated water fit only for swamp dwellers and other disease-ridden beasts. Bacteria in the lake give off a faint phosphorescent light, creating the look of an evil-looking, algae-filled swimming pool. The lake and bacteria give off a foul smell of sulfur and rotting organic material, creating a *stinking cloud* effect within 15 feet of the shore (DC 12 Fortitude save or affected as per spell). This lake covers much of this level, extending off the map edge to both the northeast and northwest. To the northeast, the lake eventually exits these caverns under the lakeshore of Crystal Lake (located on the **Wilderness Map**). Swimming to the outside requires some magical means of breathing underwater, as it is too far a swim to make without such means. This lake is used by the tsathar to house their many foul frogs. The lake is full of giant frogs of all sizes — both poisonous and nonpoisonous. The special frogs, such as killer

frogs, do not live here. Any non-frog or non-tsathar swimming in the lake is immediately attacked by **2d6 giant frogs**, **1d3 giant dire frogs**, and **1d3 giant poisonous frogs** — it is like a pond of piranha. They do not eat each other, unless one is wounded (see below). The shores of the lake are thick with mud and filth. Movement along the shores is at 1/2 speed due to the suction and slippery conditions created by this mud.

GIANT FROGS	CR 1

XP 400
hp 15 (*Pathfinder Roleplaying Game Bestiary* "Frog, Giant")

GIANT DIRE FROGS	CR 3

XP 800
hp 50 (*The Tome of Horrors Complete* 670)

GIANT POISONOUS FROG	CR 3

XP 800
N Large animal
(*Pathfinder Roleplaying Game Bestiary* "Frog, Dire")
Init +6; Senses low-light vision, scent; Perception +6

AC 19, touch 11, flat-footed 17 (+2 Dex, +8 natural, –1 size)
hp 50 (4d8+28)
Fort +11; **Ref** +8; **Will** +2

Speed 40 ft., swim 40 ft.
Melee bite +8 (1d8+6 plus grab and poison) or tongue +8 touch (grab)
Space 10 ft.; **Reach** 10 ft. (20 ft. with tongue)
Special Attacks pull (tongue, 10 feet), swallow whole (1d8+6 bludgeoning damage, AC 12, 2 hp), tongue

Str 23, **Dex** 15, **Con** 24, **Int** 1, **Wis** 12, **Cha** 10
Base Atk +3; **CMB** +10 (+14 to grapple); **CMD** 22 (26 vs. trip)
Feats Improved Initiative, Lightning Reflexes
Skills Acrobatics +11 (+15 jumping), Perception +6, Stealth +2, Swim +14; **Racial Modifiers** +4 Acrobatics (+8 jumping), +4 Stealth

Poison (Ex) Injury—bite; *save* Fort DC 19; *frequency* 1/round for 6 rounds; *effect* 1d2 Con damage; *cure* 1 save. The save DC is Constitution-based

Feeding: Because there are so many frogs (literally hundreds fill the lake), the priests catch a number (about ten to fifteen) each day, gut them and toss them into the pits at **Area 4**. This is a daily ritual. The frogs eat the ones that have been killed in this manner. Thus, because they do not eat each other unless fed by the priests as described, the frog population has the strange capacity to sustain its own booming population.

Traveling beneath Other Chambers: Note that the lake runs beneath many of the rooms in the northwest portion of the level. The lake — when beneath other chambers — is either fully submerged or has a ceiling of only a foot or two above the level of the water. No meaningful transportation can be had across the surface of the lake when not exposed in a larger chamber.

GM Note: Players coating themselves with mud and slimy water loses 10 points of Charisma to non-tsathar while coated. However, they also become invisible to the giant frogs on this level for 1d10+10 minutes after coating themselves with muck, as they are rendered "kindred spirits" by their stench. Likewise, the frogs do not notice *invisible* or hiding characters for 1d20+30 minutes after coating themselves, as the smell of fresh meat is overwhelmed by the stench of the muck.

4. The Temple of the Frog (CR 12)

This is the outer entrance to the Temple of the Frog. There is a huge statue of Tsathogga here, in his form of a hugely fat, grotesque humanoid toad with great fangs and huge talons attached to each of his six legs. The statue stands (or rather squats) 40 feet tall. The statue of Tsathogga is made of a foul green stone from the plane of Tarterus. It feels like some type of alien soapstone.

This place is very busy at all times. There are always at least **1d4 tsathar filth-priests, 2d6 tsathar supplicants** and **2d8 normal tsathar** here, taking turns bringing up slime and filth from the shores of the lake and rubbing it over the surface of the idol, while the priests and supplicants cast *curse water* and gesticulate in random worship of their uncaring god. These tsathar are quite occupied by their work and are at –5 on their Perception checks to notice intruders.

In addition to the priests, supplicants and normal tsathar, there are occasionally groups coming and going along the path from **Area 4** to **Area 15** and on to the Under Realms. This temple — though far from the nearest population of tsathar — is a site of major importance to this race. It is not uncommon for tsathar merchants or pilgrims to trek to this shrine, nor is it uncommon for traders or priests to leave from this shrine accompanied by several of the foul frogs bred here — particularly the killer frogs — and several tsathar scourges.

TSATHAR   **CR 2**
XP 600
hp 13 (*The Tome of Horrors Complete* 616)

Unhallow **and** *Dispel Good:* The area radiates evil because it is under the effects of an *unhallow* spell, as detailed above. In addition, all areas within 50 feet of the statue are under the effects of *dispel good*. If intruders attack this temple area, two of the acolytes flee to **Area 12** to get aid.

TSATHAR FILTH-PRIEST   **CR 7**
XP 3,200
Male tsathar filth-priest cleric 5 (*The Tome of Horrors Complete* 616, see the **Appendix**)
CE Medium monstrous humanoid (aquatic)
Init +3; **Senses** darkvision 90 ft., scent; **Perception** +7
Aura evil

AC 17, touch 13, flat-footed 14 (+3 Dex, +4 natural)
hp 62 (2d10+6 plus 5d8+15 plus 5)
Fort +7; **Ref** +7; **Will** +13
Resist cold 10
Weakness light blindness

Speed 30 ft., swim 30 ft.
Melee *+1 keen sickle* +9 (1d6+4/19–20) or bite +3 (1d4+1) and 2 claws +3 (1d6+1)
Special Attacks channel negative energy 5/day (3d6, DC 14), destructive smite 7/day (+2)
Spell-Like Abilities (CL 5th)
1/day—*summon hydrodaemon* (4th level, 40% success)
Domain Spell-Like Abilities (CL 5th; melee touch +8, ranged touch +8):
7/day—*icicle*
Spells Prepared (CL 5th; melee touch +8, ranged touch +8):
3rd—*rage*^D, *prayer*, *blindness/deafness* (DC 17)
2nd—*bull's strength*, *hold person* (DC 16), *fog cloud*^D, *dread bolt*^# (DC 16)
1st—*divine favor*, *shield of faith*, *bane* (DC 15), *protection from good*, *obscuring mist*^D
0 (at will)—*resistance*, *virtue*, *create water*, *detect magic*
D Domain Spell **Domain** Destruction, Water

Str 16, **Dex** 17, **Con** 16, **Int** 14, **Wis** 18, **Cha** 11
Base Atk +5; **CMB** +8; **CMD** 21
Feats Channel Smite^B, Extra Channel, Improved Channel, Iron Will, Skill Focus (Knowledge [religion]), Skill Focus (Perception)
Skills Acrobatics +4 (+28 high jumping, +16 long jumping), Climb +7, Escape Artist +16, Handle Animal +5, Intimidate +6, Knowledge (arcana) +8, Knowledge (dungeoneering) +4, Knowledge (nature) +3, Knowledge (planes) +8, Knowledge (religion) +15, Perception +7, Sense Motive +8, Spellcraft +9, Stealth +7, Survival +8, Swim +15; **Racial Modifiers** +14 Acrobatics when long jumping or +24 Acrobatics when high jumping, +12 Escape Artist
Languages Abyssal, Aquan, Common, Tsathar
SQ amphibious, frog god's proxy, implant, slimy, summon hydrodaemon
Combat Gear potion of cure light wounds, wand of contagion, 2 vials of foul water^&; **Other Gear** +1 studded leather armor, +1 light wooden shield, +1 keen sickle, unholy symbol of Tsathogga

Frog God's Proxy (Su): All batrachian beings recognize the Filth-Priest as a conduit to the Frog God. At 3rd level Filth-Priests add a +4 bonus to Handle Animal checks made when dealing with frogs, toads, and any frog-like animal. The Filth-Priest further gains a +2 bonus to Diplomacy when dealing with frog-like outsiders (hydrodaemons, greruor demons, hezrous demons, etc.)

Implant (Ex) Tsathar are sexless, reproducing by injecting eggs into living hosts. An egg can be implanted only into a helpless host creature. The host must be of Small size or larger. Giant frogs, bred for this very purpose, are the most common host. Implanting an egg requires one minute to perform.

Accompanying the egg is an anaesthetizing poison that causes the host to fall unconscious for the two-week gestation period of the egg unless the host succeeds on a DC 20 Fortitude saving throw; this save DC includes a +8 racial bonus. If the save succeeds, the host remains conscious, but is violently ill (-10 penalty on attack rolls, saving throws, ability checks, and skill checks) 24 hours before the eggs hatch. When the eggs mature, the young tsathar emerges from the host, killing it in the process.

A *remove disease* spell rids the victim any implanted eggs. A DC 20 Heal check can be attempted to surgically extract an egg from a host. If the check fails, the healer can try again, but each attempt (successful or not) deals 1d6 points of damage to the patient.

Leap (Ex) Tsathar are incredible jumpers, able to leap up to 30 feet horizontally or 10 feet vertically. They have a +14 racial bonus on horizontal jumps, or +24 on vertical jumps, and they do not need to make a 10-foot minimum running start before jumping to avoid doubling the jumping DCs. Tsathar can always take 10 when making an Acrobatics check to jump.

When a tsathar begins its round by jumping next to an opponent it can make a full attack in the same round. A tsathar wearing medium or heavy armor or carrying a medium or heavy load cannot use this ability.

Summon Hydrodaemon (Sp) A tsathar with at least five levels of cleric can, once per day, attempt to summon a hydrodaemon (q.v.) with a 40% chance of success. This ability is the equivalent of a 4th-level spell.

Slimy (Ex) Because tsathar continuously cover themselves with muck and slime, they are difficult to grapple. Webs, magic or otherwise, do not affect tsathar, and they usually can wriggle free from most other forms of confinement. This grants them a +12 racial bonus to their CMD to escape grapples, and to their Escape Artist checks.
^#*Pathfinder Roleplaying Game Ultimate Magic*
^&see ***Rappan Athuk*** for more details

TSATHAR SUPPLICANTS   **CR 3**
XP 800
Male or Female tsathar cleric 1 (*The Tome of Horrors Complete* 616)
CE Medium monstrous humanoid (aquatic)

Init +2; **Senses** darkvision 90 ft., scent; **Perception** +4
Aura evil

AC 16, touch 12, flat-footed 14 (+2 Dex, +4 natural)
hp 20 (2d10+2 plus 1d8+1 plus 1)
Fort +3; **Ref** +5; **Will** +6
Weakness light blindness

Speed 30 ft., swim 30 ft.
Melee sickle +4 (1d6+2) or bite +4 (1d4+1) and 2 claws +4 (1d6+1)
Special Attacks channel negative energy 6/day (1d6, DC 11), destructive smite 4/day (+1)
Domain Spell-Like Abilities (CL 1st; ranged touch +4):
4/day—*icicle*
Spells Prepared (CL 1st; melee touch +4, ranged touch +4):
1st—*bane* (DC 12), *divine favor*, *obscuring mist*D
0 (at will)—*create water*, *detect magic*, *resistance*
D Domain Spell **Domain** Destruction, Water

Str 14, **Dex** 14, **Con** 12, **Int** 12, **Wis** 13, **Cha** 12
Base Atk +2; CMB +4; CMD 16
Feats Extra Channel, Skill Focus (Knowledge [religion]), Skill Focus (Perception)
Skills Acrobatics +2 (+26 high jumping, +14 long jumping), Escape Artist +15, Handle Animal +5, Intimidate +5, Knowledge (arcana) +5, Knowledge (nature) +2, Knowledge (religion) +9, Perception +4, Sense Motive +5, Spellcraft +6, Stealth +6, Survival +5, Swim +14; **Racial Modifiers** +14 Acrobatics when long jumping or +24 Acrobatics when high jumping, +12 Escape Artist
Languages Abyssal, Common, Tsathar
SQ amphibious, implant, slimy
Combat Gear 2 vials of foul water&; **Other Gear** studded leather armor, light wooden shield, sickle, stone unholy symbol of Tsathogga

---

Implant (Ex) Tsathar are sexless, reproducing by injecting eggs into living hosts. An egg can be implanted only into a helpless host creature. The host must be of Small size or larger. Giant frogs, bred for this very purpose, are the most common host. Implanting an egg requires one minute to perform.

Accompanying the egg is an anaesthetizing poison that causes the host to fall unconscious for the two-week gestation period of the egg unless the host succeeds on a DC 20 Fortitude saving throw; this save DC includes a +8 racial bonus. If the save succeeds, the host remains conscious, but is violently ill (-10 penalty on attack rolls, saving throws, ability checks, and skill checks) 24 hours before the eggs hatch. When the eggs mature, the young tsathar emerges from the host, killing it in the process.

A *remove disease* spell rids the victim any implanted eggs. A DC 20 Heal check can be attempted to surgically extract an egg from a host. If the check fails, the healer can try again, but each attempt (successful or not) deals 1d6 points of damage to the patient.

Leap (Ex) Tsathar are incredible jumpers, able to leap up to 30 feet horizontally or 10 feet vertically. They have a +14 racial bonus on horizontal jumps, or +24 on vertical jumps, and they do not need to make a 10-foot minimum running start before jumping to avoid doubling the jumping DCs. Tsathar can always take 10 when making an Acrobatics check to jump.

When a tsathar begins its round by jumping next to an opponent it can make a full attack in the same round. A tsathar wearing medium or heavy armor or carrying a medium or heavy load cannot use this ability.

Slimy (Ex) Because tsathar continuously cover themselves with muck and slime, they are difficult to grapple. Webs, magic or otherwise, do not affect tsathar, and they usually can wriggle free from most other forms of confinement. This grants them a +12 racial bonus to their CMD to escape grapples, and to their Escape Artist checks.
&see *Rappan Athuk* for more details

4A. The Pits (CR Varies, 7–12)

On the plateau of the temple in front of the statue itself are a number of pits that descend down into the lake that runs below. This is where sacrificed frogs (see above) are tossed to feed the frogs in the lake. Any other non-tsathar sacrifices (such as captured PCs) are also thrown into these pits to be eaten by the frogs. The frogs are trained that they can eat anything thrown into these pits — even their own kind or tsathar if they fall into the pits by mistake. There are **3d6 giant dire frogs** and **1d6 giant poisonous frogs** within the vicinity of each pit.

GIANT DIRE FROGS   CR 3
XP 800
hp 50 (*The Tome of Horrors Complete* 670)

GIANT POISONOUS FROGS   CR 2
XP 600
hp 15 (see **Area 3**)

5. Shore of Filth (CR Varies, 6–11)

This shore of the lake for some reason is particularly caked with filth, as if all the excrement of the frogs and tsathar collects here. The tsathar use this as a waste area. They cart the waste up the ramp to **Area 4**, where priests and others spread the filth on their foul idol, mimicking how Tsathogga lives in his plane of slime. There are always **2d6 normal tsathar** here as well as **2d6 giant poisonous dire frogs,** lounging in the filth.

TSATHAR   CR 2
XP 600
hp 13 (*The Tome of Horrors Complete* 616)

GIANT POISONOUS FROGS   CR 2
XP 600
hp 15 (see **Area 3**)

6. Tsathar Living Area (CR 14)

Both wings of this cave and its attendant portion of the lake are the dwelling place of all non-priest tsathar. There are approximately **60 tsathar** here, along with an equal number of noncombatant children. They swim in the portion of the lake at **Area 6A**. They have no treasure. If faced by a powerful opponent, the noncombatants flee to the edge of the lake, while the 60 male tsathar fight. Combat in this area draws all priests and frogs from **Areas 4** and **9–13** within minutes of first blood being drawn. Anyone attempting to end the tsathar threat here is in real trouble.

TSATHAR   CR 2
XP 600
hp 13 (*The Tome of Horrors Complete* 616)

6A. Pool (CR Varies, 6–10)

The tsathar use this pool for "recreation." It lies at the foot of a ledge some 20 feet below **Area 6**. The pool is about 20 feet deep in this area. Since it links to the lake at **Area 4**, it contains **giant frogs** and **giant dire frogs,** as detailed at **Area 3**, above. This pool is not used for breeding.

GIANT FROGS   CR 1
XP 400
hp 15 (*Pathfinder Roleplaying Game Bestiary*)

GIANT DIRE FROGS   CR 3
XP 800
hp 50 (*The Tome of Horrors Complete* 670)

GIANT POISONOUS FROGS   CR 2
XP 600
hp 15 (see **Area 3**)

7. Breeding Den (CR Varies, 8–14)

This room is used to breed the frogs that the tsathar use to reproduce — which they do by implanting into a frog an egg that grows and hatches (see the description of the tsathar in the **Appendix** for more details). There are **4d10 giant dire frogs** and **2d6 tsathar** here at all times.

GIANT DIRE FROGS   CR 3
XP 800
hp 50 (*The Tome of Horrors Complete* 670)

TSATHAR   CR 2
XP 600
hp 13 (*The Tome of Horrors Complete* 616)

8. Fungus Garden (CR Varies, 0–8)

This area is another location where the tsathar have carted some of their filth. They use it to grow mushrooms and other fungi. Behind the fungus garden is the sinkhole (**Area 20**). There are usually (50%) **2d4 tsathar** here at any time harvesting various fungi.

TSATHAR   CR 2
XP 600
hp 13 (*The Tome of Horrors Complete* 616)

9. Inner Breeding Pits (CR 14)

This pool is used to breed the giant poisonous dire frogs. There are currently **24 giant poisonous frogs** being trained here. They take special handling — though not as much as the killer frogs. **3 filth-priests**, **5 tsathar supplicants** and **8 tsathar scourges** oversee the breeding of these particular frogs.

GIANT POISONOUS FROGS — CR 2
XP 600
hp 15 (see **Area 3**)

TSATHAR SCOURGES — CR 3
XP 800
hp 33 (*The Tome of Horrors Complete* 617)

TSATHAR FILTH-PRIEST — CR 7
XP 3,200
hp 62 (see **Area 4**)

TSATHAR SUPPLICANTS — CR 3
XP 800
hp 20 (see **Area 4**)

10. Priests' Quarters (CR Varies, 11–16)

The priests and supplicants of Tsathogga sleep here. There are 6 frog-priests, 15 filth-priests and 30 supplicants in total, and there are **1d4 frog-priests**, **2d6 filth-priests** and **2d8 supplicants** here at any time. Tsathogga is a chaotic and uncaring god, so there is no rigorous hierarchy as for sleeping arrangements, though priests do not usually share living space with non-priests. They have no treasure, though each possesses a small soapstone statue of Tsathogga.

TSATHAR FILTH-PRIEST — CR 7
XP 3,200
hp 62 (see **Area 4**)

TSATHAR SUPPLICANTS — CR 3
XP 800
hp 20 (see **Area 4**)

TSATHAR FROG-PRIEST — CR 9
XP 6,400
Male or Female tsathar filth-priest cleric 7 (*The Tome of Horrors Complete* 616; see the **Appendix**)
CE Medium monstrous humanoid (aquatic)
Init +3; **Senses** darkvision 90 ft., scent; **Perception** +13
Aura evil

AC 25, touch 16, flat-footed 21 (+5 armor, +2 deflection, +3 Dex, +1 dodge, +4 natural)
hp 80 (2d10+6 plus 7d8+21 plus 7)
Fort +10; **Ref** +8; **Will** +12
Resist cold 10
Weakness light blindness

Speed 20 ft., swim 30 ft.
Melee *+1 wounding sickle* +10/+5 (1d6+3) or bite +4 (1d4+1) and 2 claws +4 (1d6+1)
Special Attacks channel negative energy 7/day (4d6, DC 15), destructive smite 7/day (+3)
Spell-Like Abilities (CL 7th)
1/day—*summon hydrodaemon* (4th level, 40% success)
Domain Spell-Like Abilities (CL 7th; ranged touch +10): 7/day—*icicle*
Spells Prepared (CL 7th; melee touch +9, ranged touch +10):
4th—*blessing of fervor** (DC 18), *inflict critical wounds*D (DC 18), *plague carrier* (DC 18)
3rd—*bestow curse* (DC 17), *dispel magic*, *prayer*, *rage*D
2nd—*disfiguring touch*# (DC 16), *hold person* (DC 16), *resist energy*, *shatter*D (DC 16), *silence* (DC 16)
1st—*bane* (DC 15), *divine favor*, *doom* (DC 15), *obscuring*

*mist*D, *ray of sickening* (DC 15), *shield of faith*
0 (at will)—*bleed* (DC 14), *create water*, *detect magic*, *resistance*
D Domain Spell **Domain** Destruction, Water

Str 15, **Dex** 17, **Con** 16, **Int** 12, **Wis** 19, **Cha** 14
Base Atk +7; **CMB** +9; **CMD** 25
Feats Combat Casting, Dodge, Extra Channel, Great Fortitude, Skill Focus (Knowledge [religion]), Skill Focus (Perception)
Skills Acrobatics +4 (+28 high jumping, +16 long jumping, +0 jump), Climb +0, Escape Artist +14, Fly +1, Handle Animal +8, Intimidate +6, Knowledge (arcana) +5, Knowledge (nature) +2, Knowledge (religion) +13, Perception +13, Ride +1, Sense Motive +8, Spellcraft +8, Stealth +5, Survival +8, Swim +16;
Racial Modifiers +14 Acrobatics when long jumping or +24 Acrobatics when high jumping, +12 Escape Artist
Languages Abyssal, Common, Tsathar
SQ amphibious, implant, slimy, summon hydrodaemon
Combat Gear *potion of barkskin +3, potion of cure moderate wounds, wand of unholy blight,* 2 vials foul water&; **Other Gear** *+1 hide armor of light fortification, +1 wounding sickle, ring of protection +2,* stone unholy symbol of Tsathogga

Implant (Ex) Tsathar are sexless, reproducing by injecting eggs into living hosts. An egg can be implanted only into a helpless host creature. The host must be of Small size or larger. Giant frogs, bred for this very purpose, are the most common host. Implanting an egg requires one minute to perform.

Accompanying the egg is an anaesthetizing poison that causes the host to fall unconscious for the two-week gestation period of the egg unless the host succeeds on a DC 20 Fortitude saving throw; this save DC includes a +8 racial bonus. If the save succeeds, the host remains conscious, but is violently ill (-10 penalty on attack rolls,

saving throws, ability checks, and skill checks) 24 hours before the eggs hatch. When the eggs mature, the young tsathar emerges from the host, killing it in the process.

A *remove disease* spell rids the victim any implanted eggs. A DC 20 Heal check can be attempted to surgically extract an egg from a host. If the check fails, the healer can try again, but each attempt (successful or not) deals 1d6 points of damage to the patient.

Leap (Ex) Tsathar are incredible jumpers, able to leap up to 30 feet horizontally or 10 feet vertically. They have a +14 racial bonus on horizontal jumps, or +24 on vertical jumps, and they do not need to make a 10-foot minimum running start before jumping to avoid doubling the jumping DCs. Tsathar can always take 10 when making an Acrobatics check to jump.

When a tsathar begins its round by jumping next to an opponent it can make a full attack in the same round. A tsathar wearing medium or heavy armor or carrying a medium or heavy load cannot use this ability.

Summon Hydrodaemon (Sp) A tsathar with at least five levels of cleric can, once per day, attempt to summon a hydrodaemon (q.v.) with a 40% chance of success. This ability is the equivalent of a 4th-level spell.

Slimy (Ex) Because tsathar continuously cover themselves with muck and slime, they are difficult to grapple. Webs, magic or otherwise, do not affect tsathar, and they usually can wriggle free from most other forms of confinement. This grants them a +12 racial bonus to their CMD to escape grapples, and to their Escape Artist checks.

*Pathfinder Roleplaying Game Advanced Player's Guide
#Pathfinder Roleplaying Game Ultimate Magic
&see **Rappan Athuk** for more details*

11. Scourge Quarters (CR Varies, 7–12)

This area is the bed-down locale for the specially trained tsathar scourges. These creatures oversee the training of the special killer frogs and act as bodyguards for the priests. There are 20 scourges present on this level, and there are **2d4 tsathar scourges** present in this room at any time. Likewise, due to the intense training required for the killer frogs, each scourge is accompanied by **1d2 advanced giant killer frogs** while in this room. The scourges actually sleep with the beasts to build loyalty and trust with the creatures. They have no treasure, but wear a set of crossed iron bars, indicating their status as scourges, pinned into their chests.

TSATHAR SCOURGES	CR 3
XP 800	
hp 33 (*The Tome of Horrors Complete* 617)	

ADVANCED GIANT KILLER FROGS	CR 3
XP 800	

N Medium animal
(*The Tome of Horrors Complete* 671; see the **Appendix**)
Init +2; **Senses** low-light vision, scent; **Perception** +5

AC 18, touch 11, flat-footed 17 (+1 Dex, +7 natural)
hp 10 (1d8+6)
Fort +8; **Ref** +4; **Will** +0

Speed 10 ft., swim 30 ft.
Melee 2 claws +5 (1d6+5 plus grab), bite +5 (1d6+5)
Special Attacks rake (2 claws +5, 1d6+5)

Str 20, **Dex** 15, **Con** 22, **Int** 2, **Wis** 13, **Cha** 10

Base Atk +0; **CMB** +5 (+9 to grapple); **CMD** 17 (21 vs. trip)
Feats Improved Natural Attack (claw)
Skills Acrobatics +6 (+10 jumping), Perception +5, Stealth +6, Swim +13; **Racial Modifiers** +4 Acrobatics (+8 jumping), +4 Stealth

12. Priest Breeding Pits (CR Varies, 11–15)

This pond is where the priest class reproduces with a select group of frogs and humanoids. Priests that implant eggs into giant dire frogs normally result in tsathar capable of becoming scourges. To create new priests, however, tradition dictates that those must come from eggs implanted into intelligent humanoids. In addition to the paralyzed frogs present here carrying eggs of future scourges, there are a number of paralyzed intelligent humanoids here — humans or other races captured from the surface, or gnomes, troglodytes, drow or other Under Realms races either captured or purchased as slaves for the purpose of breeding priests. Tsathar enjoy using troglodytes to breed their priests, since the two races are enemies (though Lokaug is attempting to form an "alliance" with them).

Aside from the paralyzed hosts mentioned above, there are **1d4 frog-priests** and **1d6 filth-priests** here at all times, attended by **1d8 giant poisonous frogs**. There are always at least **2 scourges** and **2 advanced giant killer frogs** here protecting the priest breeding pits. Note that supplicants are not allowed the privilege of breeding priests and must spawn with common tsathar until they achieve higher level. The pond itself contains over fifty embryonic priest-caste tsathar set to hatch over a period of one to six months and nearly double that number of scourge-caste tsathar. Unless they are destroyed, a great number of priestly tsathar will soon populate this area. Destruction of the nest (relatively easy to do using poison or a similar spell) nets the party a 2,000 XP bonus story award. The pond is shallow (less than 3 feet deep) and has similar properties to the lake at **Area 3**.

GIANT POISONOUS FROGS	CR 2
XP 600	
hp 15 (see **Area 3**)	

ADVANCED GIANT KILLER FROGS (2)	CR 3
XP 800	
hp 10 (see **Area 11**)	

TSATHAR SCOURGES (2)	CR 3
XP 800	
hp 33 (*The Tome of Horrors Complete* 617)	

TSATHAR FROG-PRIEST	CR 9
XP 6,400	
hp 80 (see **Area 10**)	

TSATHAR FILTH-PRIEST	CR 7
XP 3,200	
hp 62 (see **Area 4**)	

13. Lokaug's Chamber (CR 20)

This is the lair of **Lokaug, the Most Foul High Priest of Tsathogga**. He rules with malice, on whim and caprice. He is loathsome and evil, wicked and cruel. Unlike his tsathar followers, Lokaug not only hoards treasure, but also uses it if it can aid him in combat.

Four frog-priests share the chamber with him, as do **3 abyssal giant dire frogs**. Also present is an emissary from another Under Realms race: **C'kusi**, a **troglodyte monitor**, and his **6 troglodyte**

servants. The monitor is here to establish relations between his race and the tsathar in a mutual war against the drow, though the tsathar are normally enemies of the troglodytes. In fact, this is a grand treachery planned by Lokaug. He intends to dupe the troglodytes into cooperating with him and then secretly destroy them. He plans to call on them to assault the priests of Orcus and then attack them once they have expended their warriors against the evil temple.

ABYSSAL GIANT DIRE FROGS (3)   CR 4
XP 1,200

hp 58 (*The Tome of Horrors Complete* 295)

TROGLODYTE SERVANTS (6)   CR 1
XP 400

Male or female troglodytes (*Pathfinder Roleplaying Game Bestiary* "Troglodyte")
CE Medium humanoid (reptilian)
Init +0; **Senses** darkvision 90 ft.; **Perception** +3
Aura stench (30 feet, 10 rounds, DC 13)

AC 16, touch 10, flat-footed 16 (+6 natural)
hp 13 (2d8+4)
Fort +7; **Ref** +0; **Will** +2

Speed 30 ft.
Melee club +2 (1d6+1) or bite +2 (1d4+1) and 2 claws +2 (1d4+1)

Ranged javelin −2 (1d6+1)

Str 12, **Dex** 10, **Con** 14, **Int** 10, **Wis** 15, **Cha** 12
Base Atk +1; **CMB** +2; **CMD** 12
Feats Great Fortitude
Skills Knowledge (religion) +1, Perception +3, Stealth +6 (+10 in rocky areas); **Racial Modifiers** +4 Stealth in rocky areas
Languages Draconic
Gear club, 3 javelins, leather body harness, bag of 87 gp, wooden holy symbol of Tsathogga

TSATHAR FROG-PRIESTS (4)   CR 9
XP 6,400

hp 80 (see **Area 10**)

LOKAUG, MOST FOUL PRIEST OF TSATHOGGA   CR 20
XP 307,200

Male tsathar filth-priest cleric 11/mystic theurge 2/sorcerer 5 (see the **Appendix**)
CE Medium monstrous humanoid (aquatic)
Init +6; **Senses** darkvision 90 ft., scent; **Perception** +16
Aura evil

AC 28, touch 16, flat-footed 25 (+5 armor, +3 deflection, +2 Dex, +1 dodge, +4 natural, +3 shield)
hp 165 (2d10+6 plus 11d8+33 plus 2d6+6 plus 5d6+15 plus 31)
Fort +16, **Ref** +14, **Will** +26; −2 penalty vs. fire effects, +2

resistance bonus vs. water planar foe's effects
Defensive Abilities slimy; **Resist** cold 10; **SR** 18
Weakness light blindness

Speed 30 ft., swim 30 ft.
Melee +1 keen unholy wounding morningstar +18/+13/+8 (1d8+5/19–20) or bite +17 (1d4+4) and 2 claws +17 (1d6+4)
Special Attacks channel negative energy 9/day (6d6, DC 21), destructive aura (30 ft., +5 damage, 11 rounds/day), destructive smite 8/day (+5), touch of filth 11/day (DC 25)
Spell-Like Abilities (CL 11th)
1/day—summon greruor demon (6th level, 60% success), summon hydrodaemon (4th level, 40% success)
Bloodline Spell-Like Abilities (CL 11th; melee touch +17):
7/day—dehydrating touch (1d6+2 non-lethal)
Domain Spell-Like Abilities (CL 11th; ranged touch +15):
8/day—icicle (1d6+5)
Spells Known (CL 7th; melee touch +17, ranged touch +15):
3rd (5/day)—dispel magic, rain of frogs#
2nd (7/day)—bull's strength, invisibility, mirror image, slipstream*B (DC 16)
1st (7/day)—expeditious retreat, hydraulic push*B, mage armor, magic missile, ray of enfeeblement (DC 15), shield
0 (at will)—bleed (DC 14), detect poison, drench (DC 14), mage hand, message, read magic, touch of fatigue (DC 14)
Bloodline Aquatic*
Spells Prepared (CL 13th; melee touch +17, ranged touch +15):
7th—disintegrateD (DC 22), word of chaos
6th—blade barrier (DC 21), harm (DC 21), harmD (DC 21),
5th—break enchantment (DC 20), greater command (DC 20), ice stormD, major curse (DC 20), righteous might
4th—aura of doom (DC 19), blessing of fervor, control waterD, cure critical wounds, divine power, spell immunity
3rd—bestow curse (DC 18), blindness/deafness (DC 18), contagion (DC 18), cure serious wounds, protection from energy, rageD
2nd— augury, eagle's splendor, hold person (DC 17), resist energy, shatterD (DC 17), spiritual weapon
1st—bane (DC 16), command (DC 16), cure light wounds, divine favor, doom (DC 16), obscuring mistD, protection from good
0 (at will)—detect magic, guidance, read magic, resistance
D Domain Spell **Domains** Destruction, Water

Str 19, **Dex** 14, **Con** 17, **Int** 20, **Wis** 20, **Cha** 18
Base Atk +13; **CMB** +17; **CMD** 33
Feats Channel SmiteB, Dodge, Eschew Materials, Extra Channel, Improved Channel, Improved Initiative, Iron Will, Leadership (24), Multiattack, Selective Channeling, Skill Focus (Perception), Step Up, Toughness
Skills Acrobatics +9 (+33 high jumping, +23 long jumping), Climb +11, Craft (alchemy) +13, Diplomacy +10, Escape Artist +19, Handle Animal +10, Intimidate +20, Knowledge (arcana) +18, Knowledge (dungeoneering) +13, Knowledge (history) +13, Knowledge (local) +10, Knowledge (nature) +12, Knowledge (planes) +20, Knowledge (religion) +28, Linguistics +10, Perception +16, Sense Motive +15, Spellcraft +18, Stealth +1, Swim +24, Use Magic Device +21; **Racial Modifiers** +12 Escape Artist, +14 Acrobatics when long jumping or +24 when high jumping
Languages Abyssal, Aklo, Aquan, Celestial, Common, Draconic, Terran, Tsathar, Undercommon
SQ amphibious, combined spells (1st), frog god's proxy, implant
Combat Gear pearl of power (3rd and 6th), potion of cure moderate wounds, potion of cure serious wounds, potion of haste, potion of neutralize poison, potion of lesser restoration, ring of elemental command (water), robe of the

archmagi (black), staff of swarming insects, wand of acid arrow, wand of shatter, wand of summon monster III; **Other Gear** +2 studded leather armor, absorbing shield, +1 keen unholy wounding morningstar, ioun stone (lavender and green ellipsoid), ioun stone (pale lavender ellipsoid), ioun stone (pearly white spindle), mirror of mental prowess, ring of protection +3, "soapstone" unholy symbol of Tsathogga

---

The Frog God's Proxy (Su) All batrachian beings recognize the Filth-Priest as a conduit to the Frog God. At 3rd level Filth-Priests add a +4 bonus to Handle Animal checks made when dealing with frogs, toads, and any frog-like animal. The Filth-Priest further gains a +2 bonus to Diplomacy when dealing with frog-like outsiders (hydrodaemons, greruor demons, hezrous demons, etc.)
Implant (Ex) Tsathar are sexless, reproducing by injecting eggs into living hosts. An egg can be implanted only into a helpless host creature. The host must be of Small size or larger. Giant frogs, bred for this very purpose, are the most common host. Implanting an egg requires one minute to perform.

Accompanying the egg is an anaesthetizing poison that causes the host to fall unconscious for the two-week gestation period of the egg unless the host succeeds on a DC 20 Fortitude saving throw; this save DC includes a +8 racial bonus. If the save succeeds, the host remains conscious, but is violently ill (-10 penalty on attack rolls, saving throws, ability checks, and skill checks) 24 hours before the eggs hatch. When the eggs mature, the young tsathar emerges from the host, killing it in the process.

A remove disease spell rids the victim any implanted eggs. A DC 20 Heal check can be attempted to surgically extract an egg from a host. If the check fails, the healer can try again, but each attempt (successful or not) deals 1d6 points of damage to the patient.
Leap (Ex) Tsathar are incredible jumpers, able to leap up to 30 feet horizontally or 10 feet vertically. They have a +14 racial bonus on horizontal jumps, or +24 on vertical jumps, and they do not need to make a 10-foot minimum running start before jumping to avoid doubling the jumping DCs. Tsathar can always take 10 when making an Acrobatics check to jump.

When a tsathar begins its round by jumping next to an opponent it can make a full attack in the same round. A tsathar wearing medium or heavy armor or carrying a medium or heavy load cannot use this ability.
Summon Greruor Demon (Sp) At 11th level, once per day the Filth-Priest of Tsathogga may attempt to summon 1 greruor demon with a 60% chance of success. The demon is under no compulsion to obey the summoner, but is not immediately hostile. This ability is the equivalent of a 6th-level spell.
Summon Hydrodaemon (Sp) A tsathar with at least five levels of cleric can, once per day, attempt to summon a hydrodaemon (q.v.) with a 40% chance of success. This ability is the equivalent of a 4th-level spell.
Slimy (Ex) Because tsathar continuously cover themselves with muck and slime, they are difficult to grapple. Webs, magic or otherwise, do not affect tsathar, and they usually can wriggle free from most other forms of confinement. This grants them a +12 racial bonus to their CMD to escape grapples, and to their Escape Artist checks.
Touch of Filth (Su) At 9th level, once per day per level, the Filth-Priest may make a melee touch attack to deal 1d4 points of Charisma damage to a target (Fortitude save for half damage). If the target is reduced to 0 Charisma or less, they die, dissolving into a pile of retch and filth. The save DC is Wisdom-based.

Pathfinder Roleplaying Game Advanced Player's Guide
#*Pathfinder Roleplaying Game Ultimate Magic*

C'KUSI, TROGLODYTE CONSUL CR 15
XP 51,200
Male troglodyte cleric 5/monk 10 (*Pathfinder Roleplaying Game* "Troglodyte")
LE Medium humanoid (reptilian)
Init +2; **Senses** darkvision 90 ft.; **Perception** +12
Aura evil, stench (30 feet, 10 rounds, DC 13)

AC 26, touch 20, flat-footed 23 (+2 Dex, +1 dodge, +3 monk, +6 natural, +4 Wis)
hp 130 (17d8+34 plus 27)
Fort +18; **Ref** +10; **Will** +16; +2 vs. enchantment effects
Defensive Abilities evasion, improved evasion; **Immune** disease

---

Speed 65 ft.
Melee bite +13 (1d4+2) and 2 claw +13 (1d4+2) or unarmed strike +13/+8/+3 (1d10+2)
Special Attacks channel negative energy 2/day (3d6, DC 11), destructive smite 8/day (+2), flurry of blows +8/+8/+3/+3, ki strike (cold iron/silver, lawful, magic), stunning fist 11/day (DC 23; stun, fatigue, sicken)
Domain Spell-Like Abilities (CL 5th; melee +13):
8/day—*bleeding touch* (2 rounds)
Spells Prepared (CL 5th; melee +13, ranged +13):
3rd—*animate dead, blindness/deafness* (DC 18), *protection from energy, rage*D
2nd—*bear's endurance, hold person* (DC 17), *owl's wisdom, shatter*D (DC 17)
1st—*cause fear* (DC 16), *divine favor, doom* (DC 16), *protection from good, shield of faith, true strike*D
0 (at will)—*bleed* (DC 15), *detect poison, guidance, resistance*
D Domain Spell **Domain** Destruction, Water

Str 14, **Dex** 15, **Con** 14, **Int** 10, **Wis** 21, **Cha** 9
Base Atk +11; **CMB** +16 (+18 to trip); **CMD** 33 (35 vs. trip)
Feats Alertness, Athletic, Blind-Fight, Combat Reflexes, Deflect Arrows, Dodge, Fleet, Great Fortitude, Improved Trip, Improved Unarmed Strike, Mobility, Spring Attack, Toughness
Skills Acrobatics +15 (+27 jump, +25 to jump), Climb +12, Diplomacy +3, Escape Artist +10, Intimidate +3, Knowledge (dungeoneering) +5, Knowledge (planes) +6, Knowledge (religion) +10, Perception +12, Sense Motive +12, Sleight of Hand +5, Stealth +12 (+16 in rocky areas), Survival +10, Swim +12; **Racial Modifiers** +4 Stealth in rocky areas
Languages Draconic
SQ fast movement (+30 ft.), high jump, ki defense, ki pool, maneuver training, purity of body, slow fall 50 ft., wholeness of body
Combat Gear *potion of barkskin +5, potion of cure serious wounds, potion of fly, potion of gaseous form, potion of invisibility, potion of nondetection, potion of lesser restoration;* **Other Gear** stone holy symbol of Tsathogga

Lokaug and the Tsathar's Tactics: Lokaug is a cruel and wickedly evil creature of unearthly intelligence. As a high priest he lords over the tsathar with the knowledge that he is far more powerful and deserving of rulership than they. He has no rival to his authority, nor would he allow one to develop. When melee ensues, he prefers to send his powerful subjects into combat and watch from a distance as he uses his formidable magical might. He prefers to begin with his spells (*blindness, disintegrate, word of chaos* to start) and follow up with swarms from his *staff* or charges form his *wands*.

The tsathar he commands — even the most powerful — mean little to him. In his mind they are all his servants, and their duties include dying for

him. Despite his aloof demeanor, he is an amazingly capable combatant, and if the opportunity presents itself, he wades in with glee. He enjoys wading into combat with his *sickle*, casting *righteous might* and *harm*. Once he learns he is up against stiff competition, however, he withdraws; if pressed severely or damaged seriously he flees to his *mirror* and to his home plane.

The tsathar priests, in the presence of their priest-king, fight to the death without question and sacrifice their lives to save his. They cast spells (*bull's strength, divine favor, command* or *prayer* being favorites) or use their *wands of command* and then engage foes in melee, ordering the frogs to do the same. The abyssal frogs attack at Lokaug's command, though if he flees they attempt to follow him through the *mirror.*

C'kusi's Tactics: He does not fight in a combat with PCs unless he is attacked or if there are any elves present in the party (whom he considers drow spies). If combat is going against Lokaug, C'kusi flees the chamber and retreats to **Area 15** to await the final outcome of the fight. If Lokaug is killed or flees through his *mirror*, C'kusi retreats into the Under Realms, never to be seen again.

Note: Lokaug is not meant to be killed. This is a horribly difficult encounter — even for **Frog God Games**.

Treasure: Lokaug has stashed the remains of several adventurers and priests of Orcus piled in disordered heaps around his lair. This room contains the following:

22 suits of full plate armor, in various states of repair.

14 shields, in a condition similar to the armor, though one is *a +2 heavy steel shield.*

11 silver unholy symbols of Orcus; 2 holy symbols of Muir and 1 holy symbol of Hecate.

A large pile of rotting leather armor, backpacks and miscellany, containing filth, rotting foodstuff, rancid wineskins and a cloak of fame.

12 longswords, 14 heavy maces, 3 light crossbows and a *+3 greatsword of dancing.*

A locked chest containing 2,200 gp, and three *scrolls of 1 spell (time stop, freedom* and *sunburst,* respectively).

A small coffer containing four *potions (levitation, heroism, cure serious wounds, delay poison).* This coffer has a secret compartment (Perception DC 25) containing a *ring of x-ray vision.*

A large pile of coins containing 23,416 sp and 11,997 cp, 22 gems (determine value randomly) and four pieces of jewelry (determine value randomly).

In addition, hidden behind a curtain in his room, Loakug has a *mirror of mental prowess.* He uses this mirror to transport himself back and forth between here and his home plane of Tarterus.

14. Inner Breeding Pits and Training Grounds (CR Varies, 13–14)

This is the area in which the tsathar scourges train the lethal killer frogs used by the tsathar legions in battle. Anyone other than a tsathar priest or scourge that enters this area is immediately attacked by the **28 advanced giant killer frogs** that inhabit **pond D** (see below). Only scourges and frog-priests (not filth-priests or supplicants) can command the killer frogs. Someone must restrain killer frogs with *command* powers or they kill the nearest living thing they see. This room contains **2d6 tsathar scourges** at any given time.

A huge statue of the frog god is present in the center of the back wall of this cave. This statue grants all followers of Tsathogga a +2 morale bonus on all dice rolls (like a double-strength *prayer* spell). The statue itself is composed of the same weird soapstone material as the statue at **Area 4**. This material seems to be slowly degrading and leaching into the

water. The effect of the degradation of this stone is that it infuses a bit of Tsathogga's power into these frogs, turning them into the killer variety. The water here is poisonous to mammals, and anyone drinking from the ponds must succeed on a DC 12 Fortitude save or take 1d4 points of Str, Con and Dex damage. There are four breeding pits here. Each contains killer frogs in various states of maturity.

TSATHAR SCOURGES   **CR 3**
XP 800
hp 33 (*The Tome of Horrors Complete* 617)

ADVANCED GIANT KILLER FROGS (28)   **CR 3**
XP 800
hp 10 (see **Area 11**)

Pits A through D (CR 12)

These are the breeding pits. **Pit A** holds **11 "normal" giant frogs**. **Pit B** holds **12 first-generation killer frogs** (as per killer frogs). **Pit C** holds **14 second-generation killer frogs**. These are then impregnated and their offspring are housed in **Pit D**, where they grow to become advanced giant killer frogs. Killer frogs never eat each other unless commanded to do so. There is no treasure in this room.

KILLER FROGS (26)   **CR 1**
XP 400
hp 6 (*The Tome of Horrors Complete* 671)

GIANT FROGS (11)   **CR 1**
XP 400
hp 15 (*Pathfinder Roleplaying Game Bestiary* "Frog, Giant")

15. Large Cavern

This cavern is empty but for the coming and going of tsathar headed to **Level 6** to hunt dire rats. Also, there is a 1 on 1d20 chance that a group of merchants or pilgrims is coming or going through this room from the Under Realms. Pilgrims and merchants are primarily tsathar, though they do not need to be. They could be drow or troglodyte or even duergar — though duergar hate the tsathar. The exact nature of these travelers, as well as the areas present nearby in the Under Realms, is left up to the GM.

16. Phosphorescent Cavern (CR Varies, 0–5)

This cavern contains a massive quantity of an edible phosphorescent orange fungi. Some tsathar gather it. Dire rats love it. There is a 75% chance that **3d6 dire rats** are present at any given time. As they are busy eating the fungus, there is only a 10% chance that they molest intruders unless harassed.

DIRE RATS   CR 1/3
XP 135
hp 5 (*Pathfinder Roleplaying Game Bestiary* "Rat, Dire")

17. Exit to Level 6 (CR Varies, 0–5)

There is a 50% chance that **3d6 dire rats** are here, heading toward **Area 16** to eat the orange fungi, which they love. They are 50% likely to ignore intruders, as they quickly pass by in search of the orange fungus. The stairs down to **Level 6** appear extraordinarily old and worn, plus they are scratched as if by large claws, with divots fully 2 inches deep (the behir from the level below).

DIRE RATS   CR 1/3
XP 135
hp 5 (*Pathfinder Roleplaying Game Bestiary* "Rat, Dire")

18. Frog Pond (CR Varies, 7–11)

This pond is not currently used for breeding or reproduction. There is a 25% chance that **1d6 tsathar** are here for purposes of their own. They flee if approached. This pond is occupied by **2d4 giant dire frogs** and their lesser cousins, **3d6 giant frogs.**

GIANT FROGS   CR 1
XP 400
hp 15 (*Pathfinder Roleplaying Game Bestiary* "Frog, Giant")

TSATHAR   CR 2
XP 600
hp 13 (*The Tome of Horrors Complete* 617)

GIANT DIRE FROGS   CR 3
XP 800
hp 50 (*The Tome of Horrors Complete* 670)

19. The Bat Cave (CR 12)

The ceiling of this cavern is even higher than that of the cavern at **Area 2** (over 120 feet!). Up in the stalactite-ridden ceiling is a small cave that houses a batch of **24 mobats.** They have learned to avoid groups of tsathar but are not averse to attacking lone tsathar or frogs. If the PCs attempt to hide in this cave, the tsathar avoid them (not liking to tempt the bats). The bats likewise do not attack any creature if in a group of six or more, unless that creature strays more than 50 feet from his mates, in which case 1d6 bats swarm the creature. Noise and combat from this area are ignored by other local denizens, as they know of the bats and just figure someone was dumb enough to get in trouble.

MOBATS (24)   CR 3
XP 800
hp 34 (*The Tome of Horrors Complete* 53)

20. Sinkholes

This area marks the numerous sinkholes on this level. Each is a slippery, funnel-like passage that eventually narrows and becomes too small to traverse. The slippery slides carry persons falling into them down and wedge them in. It is nearly impossible to escape without assistance. PCs attempting to move in the area marked as a sinkhole must make a DC 12 Reflex save. If they fail, they have slipped into the sinkhole and become inextricably stuck or lost. They starve to death unless removed by magic.

21. The Border Cavern (CR Varies, 17+)

This cavern acts as the border zone for the uneasy truce that the priests of Orcus have with the tsathar. No tsathar will pass into this cavern willingly, keeping north of here and out of **Area 19.** The ceiling in this cavern is high (80 feet), and numerous bats and rats are present. It, too, is filled with stalactites and stalagmites as well as huge columns that stretch from floor to ceiling. Water drips ominously. A large ledge runs the length of the east side of the cavern. It is sheer and slippery, even though the room is not covered with the slime in the other caverns. The ledge (**Area 24**) is some 50 feet above the ground level of the main cavern and requires a DC 20 Climb check to ascend. This room contains the only source of drinkable water — drinkable by non-tsathar, that is — on this level. Hence, bats and rats of both normal and dire varieties densely populate it. There are **12 dire bats** here, they attack only small parties, preferring easy meat to prey that fights back. They behave in every way like the mobats in **Area 19** but do not approach the ground anywhere near the sinkhole exit area leading to **Area 2.** There are also **3d6 dire rats** here at all times.

DIRE BATS (12)   CR 2
XP 600
hp 22 (*Pathfinder Roleplaying Game Bestiary* "Bat, Dire")

DIRE RATS   CR 1/3
XP 135
hp 5 (*Pathfinder Roleplaying Game Bestiary* "Rat, Dire")

Roper Guards: A total of **6 ropers** guard the various entrances to this cavern. The ropers attack any creature other than a priest of Orcus (whom they serve) that approaches within 60 feet of their location. They hide in waiting until they can attack using their strands, slowly pulling trapped creatures into their toothy maws. The ropers act as a wonderful deterrent to tsathar intrusion into the southern caves (**Areas 21–27**).

ROPERS (6)   CR 12
XP 19,200
hp 162 (*Pathfinder Roleplaying Game Bestiary* "Roper")

21A. Small Pool

This pool is not connected to the lake, and its source is pure surface water, thus it is fit to drink. No frogs inhabit it. Bats, rats and other life drink here. It is fed by an underground spring.

22. Cavern of Death

This cave floor contains the battered remains of dozens of human and humanoid skeletons, hacked to bits and broken into many pieces. It looks like something even continued beating on the remains after they were dead, as there are random body parts (identifiable by similar armor design) up to 40 feet away from the corresponding torsos. Nothing of value remains in this area.

23. Cave of Dargeleth, The Bleeding Horror (CR 11)

This cave is the home of Dargeleth — once a famed dwarf warrior, now an undead servant of the *axe of blood.* He came to these caves through the tunnel to the Under Realms at **Area 15.** He skirted the temple at **Area 4** by heading past **Area 1** and to the large cave at **Area 21.** There he fought a group of frog-priests. He was sorely pressed and fed the axe one final time — leading to his death and his current fate. This cave is his base. For some

unknown reason he seldom strays from it. He keeps the bodies of those he kills at **Area 22**. He is maddened by the scent (that only he can smell) of the *earth blood* on **Level 5A**, though he cannot pass the wall at **Area 2A**.

DARGELETH, THE BLEEDING HORROR   CR 11
XP 12,800
Male bleeding horror dwarf warrior 10 (The Tome of Horrors Complete 703)
N Medium undead (augmented humanoid, dwarf)
Init +2; **Senses** darkvision 60 ft.; **Perception** +2
Aura horrific appearance (DC 12)

AC 33, touch 14, flat-footed 31 (+10 armor, +2 deflection, +1 Dex, +1 dodge, +5 natural, +4 shield)
hp 90 (10d10+30 plus 10)
Fort +11; **Ref** +5; **Will** +3; +2 vs. poison, spells, and spell-like abilities
Defensive Abilities channel resistance +4, defensive training; **DR** 15/magic; **SR** 22

Speed 20 ft.
Melee *axe of blood* +15/+10 (1d8+4/19–20/x3) or 2 claws +8 (1d6+1)
Special Attacks blood consumption (DC 12), create spawn, hatred
Spell-Like Abilities (CL 8th):
3/day—*bloodstorm* (see **Sidebar**)

Str 16, **Dex** 15, **Con** 16, **Int** 12, **Wis** 10, **Cha** 14
Base Atk +10; **CMB** +13; **CMD** 27 (27 vs. bull rush, 27 vs. trip)

Feats Cleave, Dodge, Mobility, Power Attack, Toughness, Weapon Focus (battleaxe)
Skills Appraise +4, Climb +7, Craft (armor) +4, Disable Device +1, Handle Animal +10, Intimidate +3, Perception +2 (+4 to notice unusual stonework, such as traps and hidden doors in stone walls or floors), Ride +3, Stealth –4
Languages Common, Dwarven, Giant
SQ find target, greed, hardy, slow and steady, stability, stonecunning +2
Gear *+1 full plate, +2 heavy steel shield, axe of blood*

Bloodstorm (Sp) Bleeding horrors can cast *bloodstorm* up to three times per day as an 8th–level sorcerer.
Blood Consumption (Su) When a bleeding horror successfully hits a living opponent with a claw attack, it heals a number of hit points equal to the damage dealt. However, it can't gain more than the subject's Bleeding Horror current hit points + the subject's Constitution score, which is enough to kill the subject. A bleeding horror can't gain more hit points than the maximum hit points allowed by its Hit Dice. For example, a 12-HD bleeding horror may not have more than 144 hit points.

If a bleeding horror hits an opponent with both claw attacks in a single round, that opponent suffers catastrophic blood expulsion, taking 1d4+2 points of Constitution damage. A successful Fortitude save reduces the damage by half. For each point of Constitution damage dealt, a bleeding horror gains 5 temporary hit points.
Create Spawn (Ex) Any creature slain by the blood consumption attack of a bleeding horror becomes a

Bloodstorm

School evocation [fear]; **Level** sorcerer/wizard 3
Casting Time 1 standard action
Components V, S, M (a small vial of blood)
Range medium (100 ft. + 10 ft./level)
Area cylinder (10 ft. radius, 40 ft. high)
Duration 1 round/level
Saving Throw see text; **Spell Resistance** yes

This spell summons a whirlwind of blood that envelops the entire area of effect and has several effects on those caught within it. First, those in the area must make a Reflex save or be blinded by the swirling blood while they remain within the whirlwind and for 2d6 rounds after leaving it. Second, all attacks within the area have a –4 penalty to attack rolls, including ranged attacks fired into it. Third the blood deals 1d4 points of acid damage per round of exposure to the whirlwind. Finally, any caught within it must make a Will save or become frightened if 8 HD or more or panicked if less than 8 HD.

bleeding horror in 1d4 minutes under the command of its creator.

Find Target (Sp) If the *axe of blood* is taken from a bleeding horror before the creature is destroyed, it can find it unerringly, as though guided by *discern location*.

Horrific Appearance (Su) A living creature within 60 feet that views a bleeding horror must succeed on a Fortitude save or take 1d6 points of Strength damage. This damage cannot reduce a victim's Strength below 0, but anyone reduced to Strength 0 is helpless. Creatures affected by this power or those that successfully save against it cannot be affected again by the same bleeding horror's horrific appearance for one day.

24. Plateau

This ledge rises 50 feet above the main cavern floor below. There is no tsathar slime present in this area. The floor of the plateau is covered with fungus and rockfalls. In the back half of the area, the ceiling rises an additional 100 feet above the floor of the plateau.

24A. Crevasse Above

High in the ceiling, some 100 feet above, is a crevasse that leads to the main temple of Orcus on **Level 4**. A hellish glow from the braziers of the temple above radiates through the crevasse. A bridge spans the crevasse above on **Level 4**, which can be seen from below on a successful DC 25 Perception check. Koraashag, the evil priest of Orcus who runs the temple above, has a *cloak of the demon* that allows him to access his hidden retreat here. Far up on the wall (some 75 feet above the floor of the cavern) is an *illusory wall* covering the entrance to **Area 26**. Beneath the crevasse, on the floor of the cavern lie a number of twisted skeletons, picked clean by the scavengers of the dungeon — the remains of those who have fallen into the crevasse on **Level 4, Area 15**.

25. Empty Cave (CR Varies, 0–4)

There is a 25% chance of encountering **2d6 dire rats** here; otherwise, this cavern is empty. Rocks and fungi are ever present.

DIRE RATS CR 1/3
XP 135
hp 5 (*Pathfinder Roleplaying Game Bestiary* "Rat, Dire")

26. Hidden Shrine (CR 9)

This area is usually unguarded, though if he has not been previously slain, or if he escaped, Koraashag is here 30% of the time. The secret door to this area is not really a door. It is instead a permanent *illusory wall*, hiding a 5-foot-diameter passage leading into **Area 26**. Only careful feeling along the wall, 75 feet above the plateau floor, will find it. The entrance chamber contains a small shrine to Orcus consisting of a small brazier, a 3-foot-tall ivory statue of Orcus with red-ruby eyes (grants a *prayer* effect to followers of Orcus within 60 feet) and a small set of sacrificial instruments (bowl, knife, etc.). This is Koraashag's retreat, where he comes in times of danger or when he wants privacy. The entrance to this room is **trapped**. Anyone not of chaotic evil alignment entering the chamber is greeted by a most unfortunate surprise: a **vrock demon** is *summoned* in to the room and attacks all present!

SUMMON MONSTER VII TRAP CR 9
XP 6,400
Type magical; **Perception** DC 32; **Disable Device** DC 32

Trigger spell; **Reset** none; **Bypass** alignment (chaotic-evil)
Effect spell effect (*summon monster VII*, CL 15th, summons **1 vrock**)

VROCK
hp 112 (*Pathfinder Roleplaying Game Bestiary* "Demon, Vrock")

27. Bed Chamber (CR 4)

This room contains a slightly more plush setting (including a bed, a desk and candles) than does **Area 26**. There is a trapped secret door connecting to **Area 27A** on the west wall. A large unholy symbol of Orcus made of solid gold is nailed to the wall above the bed. The gold and gems in this symbol are worth over 5,000 gp if melted down and sold. The desk is locked (Disable Device DC 20) and contains Koraashag's notes about the Black Monolith (**Level 5A**) and how he suspects that it is a great power for evil, possibly an item that will open a gate between the abyss and this plane. There is a letter in the desk that names his superior in Bard's Gate (Sartorious, an evil priest, posing as an acolyte of Myr in that city!) and tells him to continue his investigations and report back as details become available. It is obvious that the priests of Orcus have a great interest in the monolith; this alone should make the players wonder about letting them find it. The second drawer in the desk is unlocked and contains several *potions*: *invisibility, nondetection, cure serious wounds* (x2), and *haste*. This room contains a **trapped secret door**.

Secret Door: 2 in. thick; hardness 10; hp 80; Break DC 30; Perception DC 25

SYMBOL OF STRIFE TRAP CR 10
XP 9,600
Type magical; **Perception** DC 34, **Disable Device** DC 34

Trigger spell; **Reset** none
Effect spell effect (opening the door triggers a *symbol of strife* spell in **Area 27**; DC 28 Will save negates)

27A. Secret Room and Teleportal

This room contains a two-way teleportal pentagram inscribed on the floor, which can be activated by speaking the name of Koraashag's fell god Orcus. Once activated, a shimmering portal is opened, linking this room with the main temple of Orcus in the dungeon of Rappan Athuk (see *Rappan Athuk* for more details). Communication can thus be had between both locations. Spells cannot be cast through the portal, however.

Anyone stepping through the portal is taken from one location to the other, though only one creature may pass through the portal per round. By speaking a command word, Koraashag or any of the high priests can cause the teleportal to close behind them and break the link, rendering it useless. Koraashag is required to make periodic reports to his superiors in Rappan Athuk regarding his progress. If the temple in this dungeon is destroyed and Koraashag is forced to flee for his life, he comes to this chamber, gathers all he can carry and passes through the portal, speaking the word and closing the portal behind him permanently.

Treasure: Hanging on the wall are two *wands*: *restoration* (22 charges, CL 9th) and *unholy blight* (32 charges, CL 9th). In a small, unlocked chest are 6 *potions of cure serious wounds*.

Note: Koraashag, by the blessing of Orcus, has set this room as his sanctuary for a modified *refuge* spell that has been placed on him. If he is ever reduced to 10 hit points or fewer, he is brought immediately to this room, where he uses the healing available to him here. A lengthy and unholy ritual allowed Koraashag to be imbued with this ability.

Level 5A: Tomb, Blood and Stone

This level holds the three secrets of the dungeon: the Tomb of Abysthor, the Chamber of Earth's Blood and the Black Monolith. The secret of the Tomb of Abysthor is that it is empty. Abysthor is trapped in the Black Monolith. Before his imprisonment, he took steps to seal the Chamber of Earth's Blood, crafting the seal at **Area 8**. The key to this seal lies in his tomb. Lokaug, the High Priest of Tsathogga, seeks the power of the Black Monolith. He was thwarted by Abysthor, who discovered the monolith first and used the power of the *earth blood* to seal the monolith and the Chamber of Earth's Blood as well. Lokaug keeps some of his priests and "watch-frogs" on this level to make sure the priests of Orcus, or other powers in the dungeon, do not enter this area. The priests of Orcus know of the monolith (though not its exact location), though they have not yet attempted to seek it out because of its proximity to Lokaug and the priests of Tsathogga.

1. Entrance

These stairs lead down from the secret entrance to this level on **Level 5**. Once the stairs are descended, the bizarre nature of this level becomes apparent. Anyone here realizes immediately that this is no normal cavern complex. The walls seem to breathe, and the floor seems to be covered in a fine, uniform, sandy material, each grain perfectly rounded and clear, as if made of little balls of glass. The stones of the walls radiate magic, and all divination spells, while functional, give the caster a strange, uneasy feeling for their duration.

Since this area is at the end of a secret entrance, no guards are waiting to ambush the PCs when they arrive. In fact, in rather un-**Frog God Games** fashion, there is a high probability that once the party arrives on this level, it will be able to surprise the evil priests at **Area 2**. The local priests have grown lethargic due to the lack of intruders on this level and can be easily spotted (DC 12 Perception check) camping and lounging at **Area 2**. The priests have a –6 penalty on their Perception checks.

2. Watch Point (CR 12)

Lokaug stationed **1 frog-priest, 1 filth-priest, 2 tsathar scourges** and **4 advanced giant poisonous killer frogs** here to make sure the priests of Orcus do not invade this area of the dungeon. Lokaug and the priests have been so far thwarted by the enchantments at **Area 4** and the seal on **Area 8** and do not know how to get past the maze at **Area 5**. The filth-priests and several other tsathar enter the transporter periodically to try to find a path to the monolith, which they know lies beyond. None returns.

These priests have set up a relatively comfortable campsite at this location. They are bored with sentry duty and have grown fairly careless (a fact that will get them sacrificed and fed to the frogs on **Level 5** soon enough!). There are several comfortable bed areas, a small fire area, complete with a large stash of coal (40 pounds), three large kegs of ale and several boxes of dry foodstuff.

ADVANCED GIANT POISONOUS KILLER FROGS (4)   CR 4
XP 1,200
XP 800
N Large animal
(*Pathfinder Roleplaying Game Bestiary* "Frog, Dire")
Init +6; **Senses** low-light vision, scent; **Perception** +6

AC 19, touch 11, flat-footed 17 (+4 Dex, +10 natural, –1 size)
hp 52 (4d8+36)
Fort +13; **Ref** +10; **Will** +4

Speed 40 ft., swim 40 ft.
Melee bite +10 (1d8+8 plus grab and poison) or tongue +10 touch (grab)
Space 10 ft.; **Reach** 10 ft. (20 ft. with tongue)
Special Attacks pull (tongue, 10 feet), swallow whole (1d8+8 bludgeoning damage, AC 12, 2 hp), tongue

Str 27, **Dex** 19, **Con** 28, **Int** 1, **Wis** 16, **Cha** 14
Base Atk +3; **CMB** +12 (+16 to grapple); **CMD** 24 (28 vs. trip)
Feats Improved Initiative, Lightning Reflexes
Skills Acrobatics +13 (+17 jumping), Perception +6, Stealth +4, Swim +16; **Racial Modifiers** +4 Acrobatics (+8 jumping), +4 Stealth

Poison (Ex) Injury—bite; *save* Fort DC 21; *frequency* 1/round for 6 rounds; *effect* 1d2 Con damage; *cure* 1 save. The save DC is Constitution-based.

TSATHAR SCOURGES (2)   CR 3
XP 800
hp 33 (*The Tome of Horrors Complete* 617)

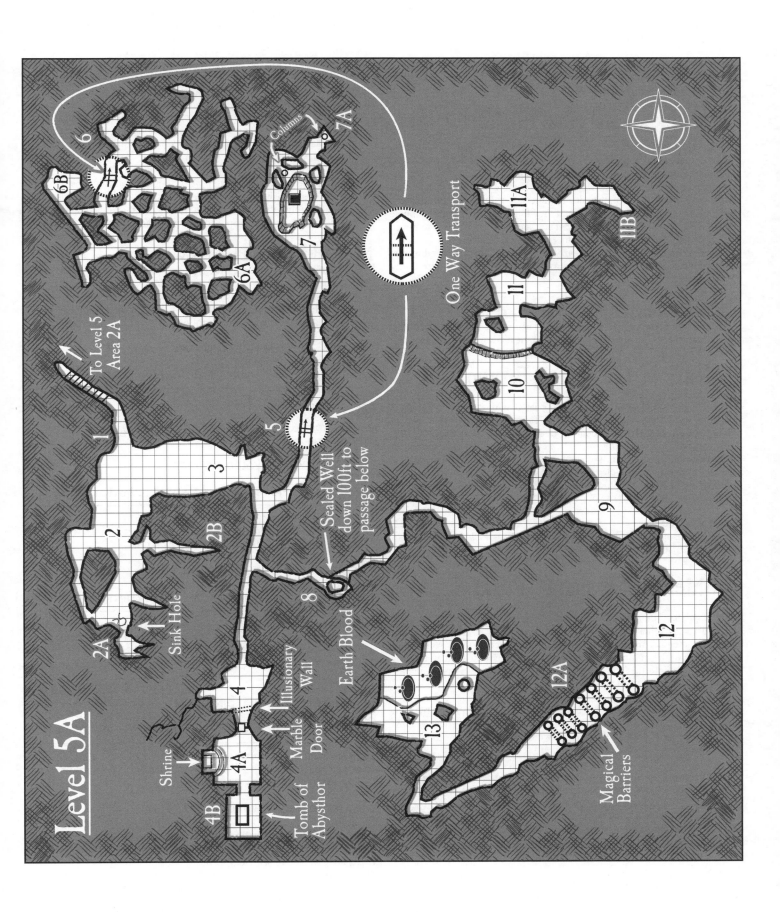

Level 5A

6
6B
6A
7A
Columns
7
One Way Transport
11A
11B
11
To Level 5
Area 2A
10
1
3
5
Sealed Well
down 100ft to
passage below
2
2B
9
8
Sink Hole
Earth Blood
2A
12
4
Illusionary
Wall
12A
Shrine
4A
Marble
Door
13
Magical
Barriers
4B
Tomb of
Abysthor

TSATHAR FROG-PRIEST CR 9
XP 6,400
hp 80 (see **Level 5, Area 10**)

TSATHAR FILTH-PRIEST CR 7
XP 3,200
hp 62 (see **Level 5, Area 4**)

2A. Small Cave and Priest Lair (CR Varies, 0–8)

This cave lies on the opposite side of a sinkhole. Attempting to cross the sinkhole requires either a successful jump (no problem for tsathar) or some other magical means. Because the passage through which they must jump is so narrow, there is a –2 circumstance modifier to the jump roll. Failing that, they must make a DC 12 Reflex save. If they fail, they slip into the sinkhole and become inextricably stuck or lost. They starve to death unless removed by magic. The tsathar at **Area 2** use this sinkhole as a latrine.

The frog priest makes this room his personal lair, not minding the smell of the hole. There is a 1–4 on 1d20 chance that he is here rather than at **Area 2**.

2B. Small Shrine (CR Varies, 0–8)

The priests at **Area 2** have placed a small soapstone statue of Tsathogga here. There is a 1–4 on 1d20 chance that **1 priest** from **Area 2** is here.

3. Walls of Glistening Brown (CR 2)

The walls of this passage nexus are coated with several inches of a glistening brown material. The priests of Tsathogga secured this area by placing a huge **brown mold** coating over the walls, floors and ceiling. They bypass the mold using *resist elements* spells. A 50-foot section of the passage has been liberally coated with the mold, and cold damage is assessed each 10 feet traveled. The mold can be killed by magical cold, requiring 50 hp to destroy the colony or 25 hp of cold damage to make a path to either **Area 4** or **Area 5**.

BROWN MOLD CR 2
XP 600 (*Pathfinder Roleplaying Game Core Rulebook*, "Environment")

4. Shielded Cavern (CR 12)

On approach, this cavern appears nondescript in every way. It is identical to the other cavern passages on this level and looks like just another dead end. This is far from the truth, however, as this cavern hides the entrance to the Tomb of Abysthor and a holy temple dedicated to the goddess Myr. Note that the entrance to this chamber is warded against lawful good-aligned characters (see below).

GM Note: This cavern is the entranceway to the Tomb of Abysthor. Strangely, it is filled with wards against both evil and good. The GM must familiarize himself with all the various wards on this room prior to entry by the characters.

Background: Abysthor built these chambers (**4A** and **4B**) using spells and magic. Once he built his tomb at **Area 4B** and set off to disable the Black Monolith, Abysthor warded the rooms against intrusion by evil forces. He placed the *hallow* and *forbiddance* spells on the area. He placed a *symbol of death* and other wards on the marble door he created. Then, as is the tradition of the priests of Muir, he covered the door with an *illusory wall*, using a divine ritual that simulates the arcane spell. Abysthor, however, did not return.

Lokaug, having encountered Abysthor previously and driven him back, had long been tracking the good priest. A group of tsathar saw Abysthor travel through the *illusory wall* at **Level 5, Area 2A** and down to these chambers. Lokaug and his minions used this information to bypass that wall and descend to this level. Lokaug discovered this chamber and sensed that it was the lair of Abysthor. At Lokaug's direction, a frog-priest used a *true sight* scroll to scan the chamber. The priest reported seeing the marble door but was immediately slain when he observed the *symbol of death*. This confirmed Lokaug's suspicion. Unwilling to subject himself to such power, Lokaug instead filled **Area 4** with evil wards against good in the attempt to prevent other powers of good (or even Abysthor himself) from entering the area. He placed the *forbiddance* on the entrance to the room. He placed ten *greater glyphs of warding* within the room itself and he placed an *unhallow* on the portion of the room not covered by the *illusory wall*.

Thus, the area is double warded: Abysthor warded it against evil, and outside of those wards Lokaug warded it against good. The wards placed by Lokaug will therefore be addressed first, since they must be penetrated before the illusory wall and door to **Areas 4A** and **4B** can be reached.

Magical Wards Placed by Lokaug

Forbiddance on the Entrance: Lokaug placed a *forbiddance* on the entrance passage to **Area 4**.

Glyphs: In **Area 4** proper, Lokaug has placed ten *greater glyphs of warding*. These glyphs include the following:

GREATER GLYPH OF WARDING TRAP CR 8
XP 4,800
Type magical; **Perception** DC 30; **Disable Device** DC 30

Trigger spell; **Reset** none
Effect spell effect (*greater glyph of warding* [*flame strike*], 11d6 damage, DC 20 Ref half, CL 11th); multiple targets (all creatures in a 10-foot radius)

GREATER GLYPH OF WARDING TRAP CR 7
XP 3,200
Type magical; **Perception** DC 31; **Disable Device** DC 31

Trigger spell; **Reset** none
Effect spell effect (*greater glyph of warding* [*antilife shell*], CL 11th); covers the entire corridor to **Area 4A**

GREATER GLYPH OF WARDING TRAP CR 6
XP 2,400
Type magical; **Perception** DC 31; **Disable Device** DC 31

Trigger spell; **Reset** none
Effect spell effect (*greater glyph of warding* [*mass inflict moderate wounds*], 2d8+10 damage, DC 20 Will half, CL 11th); multiple targets (11 creatures, no two of which can be more than 30 ft. apart)

GREATER GLYPH OF WARDING TRAP CR 7
XP 3,200
Type magical; **Perception** DC 31; **Disable Device** DC 31

Trigger spell; **Reset** none
Effect spell effect (*greater glyph of warding* [*symbol of fear*], DC 21 Will, CL 11th)

GREATER GLYPH OF WARDING TRAPS (6) CR 6
XP 2,400
Type magical; **Perception** DC 31; **Disable Device** DC 31

Trigger spell; **Reset** none
Effect spell effect (*greater glyph of warding* [*blast*], 5d8 fire damage, DC 21 Ref for half, CL 11th); multiple targets (all creatures within 5 ft. of the *glyph*)

Unhallow: In addition, though he could not dispel the permanent *hallow* effect, Lokaug placed *unhallow* in the portion of **Area 4** not covered by the *illusory wall*.

Magical Wards Placed by Abysthor

Illusory Wall: This wall requires an act of active disbelief to bypass. A DC 17 Will save may be made to bypass the wall. Otherwise it remains "real" in the minds of those attempting to pass through it and may not be crossed. If other individuals "help" by walking through it, for example, the save may be retried. See Illusions in the *Pathfinder Roleplaying Game Core Rulebook* and the *illusory wall* spell description for more details.

The Marble Door: This huge door is made of 4-inch-thick stone and resists all attempts to open it. It can be opened only by great force, unless a lawful good creature tries to open it, in which case it slides open easily.

Symbol **Trapped Door of Silver-Encrusted White Marble:** 4 in. thick; hardness 8; hp 100; Break DC 45; damage reduction 10/magic; spell resistance 18.

SYMBOL OF DEATH TRAP   **CR 9**
XP 6,400
Type magic; **Perception** DC 33; **Disable Device** DC 33

Trigger visual; **Reset** none
Effect spell effect (*symbol of death*, DC 28 Fortitude save or die, CL 16th); multiple targets (All Chaotic Evil characters passing through the door and all within a 60-foot radius viewing the symbol (up to 150 hp worth of creatures)

Hallow and *Forbiddance:* The whole area beyond the illusory wall is under the effects of *hallow* and *forbiddance*. Originally, the whole room was covered with a *hallow*, but Lokaug was able to dispel that using foul magic. He could not, however, dispel the *hallow* effect beyond the *illusory wall*.

4A. Shrine to Thyr

This simple stone room is a humble shrine to Thyr. It is carved of plain stone. The raised alcove to the north contains a plain altar of white marble and a small statue of Thyr the Lawgiver.

Hallow and *Forbiddance:* This room is the source of the *hallow* and *forbiddance* spells cast by Abysthor. The *hallow* and *forbiddance* spells cannot be dispelled in this area, as they were cast in conjunction with *earth blood* Abysthor found in **Area 13**, which makes the spells permanent.

4B. The Tomb of Abysthor

Here, in a simple stone sarcophagus, lies the prepared tomb of Abysthor, the last high priest of Thyr. The tomb, however, is empty of any corpse. Abysthor prepared this chamber as his final resting place and then set off for his last task: destroying the Black Monolith. He never returned. In the tomb, *invisible* and detectable only by *true seeing* cast by a lawful good cleric or paladin, are a key and a note.

The Key: The key is the magical key that opens the great seal at **Area 8**.

The Note: The note reads:
Praise to Thyr and greetings to one more worthy than I! Should I fail to return, this key opens the great seal I have created. Seek the chamber of the earth's blood. Use the power you find there as Thyr commands. I pray, Brother, that you do not fail as I have. May Thyr watch over you.
                                                                —Abysthor."

5. Transporter to the Maze

This area is a seamless transporter to the Maze at **Area 6**. Persons looking down the passage to **Area 5** do not see beyond to **Area 7**. Rather, they see and enter the passages as depicted in the maze at **Area 6**. Unless this is bypassed, GMs should simply treat their map as seamlessly joining between the transporter on the map at **Area 5** and the transporter marked on the map at **Area 6**. Except, of course, that they cannot return (as detailed in **Area 6**, below). The PCs should have no idea they are being transported.

Detecting the Transporter: Though they have no external clue to do so, characters checking detect strong *conjuration* magic in the area of the transporter. This transporter acts as an unmarked *gate* spell cast at 20th level of ability. No save is allowed for this transporter. Once the *gate* is activated, Pandora is sent to the Maze from the Celestial Realms, acting as if she were under the effects of a *planar ally* spell.

Bypassing the Transporter: Only a person possessing *earth blood* can pass the transporter without being taken to **Area 6**. The extreme magic and antimagic effects of *earth blood* disrupt the transporter, allowing a person possessing it to travel to **Area 7**.

6. The Maze

For many unfortunate priests of Tsathogga, this area was a one-way trip. The *gate* ward guarding the Black Monolith is a one-way trip to a maze that exists in its own demiplane. The origin of this demiplane is a mystery. Perhaps the gods of good intervened long ago and erected it here as a barrier to prevent access to the Black Monolith. Maybe the great holy man Abysthor, empowered by those gods, created the Maze himself (see the *create demiplane* spells in the *Pathfinder Roleplaying Games Ultimate Magic* resource). No one knows for certain.

It is possible that anyone transported here is doomed, for only the bravest and wisest adventurers may survive being teleported to the Maze. The maze itself is very simple, though it seems to lead nowhere. The only exit is the answer to a puzzle, which is presented only to those deemed worthy of it by the celestial sphinx Pandora.

The Maze

The Maze is a mysterious demiplane that serves as a barrier to the Black Monolith. It has the following planar traits (see the *Pathfinder Roleplaying Game GameMastery Guide* for more information on **Planar Traits**).

Normal Gravity: The effects of gravity in the Maze are as they function on the Material Plane.
Normal Time: Time flows normally within the Maze.
Finite Shape: The demiplane of the Maze comprises only the Maze and nothing else.
Alterable Morphic: The physical reality of the Maze is similar to that of the Material Plane.
Strongly Lawful Good-Aligned: A –2 circumstance penalty applies on all Intelligence-, Wisdom-, and Charisma-based checks made by all creatures not of the plane's alignment. The penalties for the moral and ethical components of the alignment trait stack. (So a chaotic evil spellcaster suffers a –4 penalty).
Impeded Magic: The spells and spell-like abilities of evil divine spellcasters is impeded in the Maze. To cast an impeded spell, the caster must make a concentration check (DC 20 + the level of the spell). If the check fails, the spell does not function but is still lost as a prepared spell or spell slot. If the check succeeds, the spell functions normally.

6A. Pandora's Puzzles (CR 9)

This is the domain of **Pandora, a lawful good celestial sphinx** that lives in the maze, guarding this area for Abysthor. Pandora was *geased* to guard the Maze until one worthy of passing to the Black Monolith could answer her riddles. Abysthor defined worthy as one of good alignment, preferably a priest or a paladin. All evil-aligned visitors were to be slain or left to starve. Hence, priests of Tsathogga who have ended up in the maze have never been able to exit, for Pandora was also entrusted with the only means of exiting this dead-end trap. Because of her dedication to Abysthor's cause, the Gods have granted her a few additional powers to help her carry out her task. Among these are the ability to cast *symbol of death* once a week. She is automatically called to the Maze when the *gate ward* is activated.

Bones and old, rusted chain and plate armor lie strewn about the area around the Maze, the remains of dozens of frog-priests and dire frogs who made it this far, only to perish. Pandora is an ancient creature, having lived for thousands of years. If the PCs attack her, or if they fail to successfully answer her riddles, her task cannot be completed and she returns to the Celestial Realms — likely leaving the PCs to starve to death. When the characters first encounter Pandora, she is sitting statue-still on a long, flat dais. She calmly asks them if they have come at the behest of Orcus. If they say no, she asks if they are instead friends of the frog god. An affirmative answer to either question causes her to cast *symbol of death* and disappears back to the Celestial Realms. Negative answers to both questions causes her to smile and tell them that they may be worthy of completing the task that Abysthor bade her do so many years ago. If they are good aligned, she then asks them three riddles; if they solve all three, they (and she) will be released from this imprisonment (see below). If they fail, she sighs, returns to her home plane. Similarly, if the PCs are not good-aligned, she does the same. The riddles she asks are as follows:

"I never was, am always to be,
No one ever saw me, nor ever will
And yet I am the confidence of all
To live and breathe on this terrestrial ball."

Answer: "Tomorrow"

If this riddle is solved, Pandora smiles and states that she is happy that the PCs are so wise, and things may need to be a little tougher. She converses with them in a friendly manner and passes some time just talking. Finally, after a few minutes have passed, she asks them the second riddle:

"The beginning of eternity
The end of space and time
The beginning of every end
And the end of every place"

Answer: "The letter E"

If the PCs successfully solves the second riddle, Pandora becomes excited and giggles, telling them how brave and wise they are and how she has been long awaiting their arrival. She speaks of an androsphinx whom she misses and how she cannot wait to see him again. She also explains that she will give the party several vials she was told to guard, and that only with these vials can *earth blood* be contained. She explains that to reach the Black Monolith, one must carry a vial of *earth blood*. This, she explains, will allow them to bypass the transporter and allow passage into the chamber beyond. Her mood finally takes a more serious tone, as she takes a deep breath and asks her final riddle:

"I count time in circles
I have no voice
But my limbs allow me to whisper in the wind"

Answer: "A tree"

If the party answers this final riddle successfully, Pandora laughs, smiles and returns to the Celestial Realms, her task completed at long last. On the dais, she leaves behind a fine crystal rod and twelve vials of solid *living rock* — a magical metal that creates an *antimagic* aura over a small area (e.g., inside the vials). These vials are worth 1,000 gp each to a dwarven smith or wizard, though a greater use would be to fill them with *earth blood*, as they are the only material capable of containing it safely. The crystal rod allows the reverse *teleportal* to be activated, depositing the PCs back in the hallway (**Area 5**).

Note: Three example riddles are supplied here, though the GM may use others if these are thought to be too hard or too easy.

PANDORA, THE CELESTIAL SPHINX   **CR 9**
XP 6,400
LG Large magical beast
(*Pathfinder Roleplaying Game Bestiary* "Sphinx"; see the **Appendix**)
Init +5; **Senses** darkvision 60 ft., low-light vision; **Perception** +21

AC 21, touch 10, flat-footed 20 (+1 Dex, +11 natural, −1 size)
hp 102 (12d10+36)
Fort +11; **Ref** +9; **Will** +10
DR 10/evil; **Resist** acid 15, cold 15, electricity 15; **SR** 14

Speed 40 ft., fly 60 ft. (poor)
Melee 2 claws +17 (2d6+6/19–20)
Space 10 ft.; **Reach** 5 ft.
Special Attacks pounce, rake (2 claws +17, 2d6+6), smite evil 1/day (+4 to attack rolls and +12 damage bonus against evil foes)
Spell-Like Abilities (CL 12th; melee +17, ranged +12):
Constant—*comprehend languages, detect magic, read magic, see invisibility*
3/day—*clairaudience/clairvoyance*
1/day—*dispel magic, locate object, remove curse, legend lore*
1/week—*symbol of death* (DC 22); symbol lasts for 1 week maximum

Str 22, **Dex** 13, **Con** 16, **Int** 18, **Wis** 19, **Cha** 19
Base Atk +12; **CMB** +19; **CMD** 30 (34 vs. trip)
Feats Alertness, Combat Casting, Hover, Improved Critical (claw), Improved Initiative, Iron Will
Skills Bluff +14 , Diplomacy +14 , Fly +7 , Intimidate +14 , Knowledge (history) +6 , Knowledge (religion) +6 , Perception +21 , Sense Motive +19 , Spellcraft +12
Languages Common, Draconic, Sphinx
Gear Twelve vials of *living rock*, a crystal rod (all items are in the Celestial Realms and cannot be recovered unless retrieved on that plane).

6B. Shimmering Silver Portal

The portal here is the size of a door and looks like it is made of liquid mercury. This is the transporter back through the transporter and can be activated only by touching the crystal rod from **Area 6A** (possessed by Pandora) to the surface of the portal. When this is done, the shimmering surface disappears for 20 seconds, revealing a corridor beyond (**Area 5**). During this time, anyone stepping through the surface is released to **Area 5**. A creature who passes through the portal at any time that the mirrored surface is present must succeed on a DC 25 Reflex save or be irreversibly crystallized into ice. Success indicates a creature is quick enough to pull himself or herself back out before being crystallized. Failure means death. Persons passing through the portal exit at **Area 5**, heading west.

7. The Black Monolith (CR Varies, see below)

This room contains a vast sinkhole, fully 40 feet deep, with steep walls plummeting down into the darkness. Within this hole is a large stone

THE TOMB OF ABYSTHOR

monolith, composed of pure, black stone. The monolith is covered with undecipherable writings and alien symbols. No means of opening or affecting the monolith are obvious, though the southwest side of the stone contains a 2-inch diameter hole, a perfect fit for the crystal shard from **Area 7A**.

Black Monolith: 400 hp; hardness 20; **DR** 20/epic; **SR** 50; Break DC impossible; can be opened only by the shard at **Area 7A**.

Background of the Monolith: The Black Monolith is an ancient construct from before the God's War and functions as a planar gate to the Abyss. The monolith itself is a moveable instrument of the gods of evil, and it has been set in a number of locations prior to being placed here. If it is activated, a *gate* opens that no mortal can close, providing free access for all the demonic armies to invade this plane. Obviously, both the priests of Tsathogga and Orcus would desire to open the planar gate.

When Abysthor learned of the monolith he immediately sought to find a way to destroy it, or failing that, to seal it forever. Essentially, the only way to destroy the monolith is by a willing sacrifice of life energy from a lawful good being (detailed below). The ritual to perform this feat was learned long ago by Abysthor, who burned the ancient text after he memorized its lessons (for it also contained the ritual to open the gate). A copy of this text is also in the possession of a high priest of Orcus living under cover as a lord in Bard's Gate. Abysthor located the monolith by using *earth blood* to bypass the maze, warding the maze with Pandora. He entered the monolith but he failed to complete the ritual, as he himself lacked the power needed to succeed. This act left him drained of all divine power and incapable of returning from within the monolith. Abysthor is now trapped within. The monolith has kept Abysthor neutralized, unable to contact Muir and recover his spells and abilities.

Currently, the priests of Tsathogga know where the monolith is, though they do not know how to get at it or the ritual to use it. The priests of Orcus know how to use it but not where it is. Luckily, since both groups appear unwilling to cooperate, both will continue to be unable to find or operate the monolith for some time.

Entering the Monolith: If the shard from **Area 7A** is used as the key to this hole, a one-way *phase door* opens and allows egress inside for ten rounds. The shard then teleports back to its resting place in **Area 7A**.

Inside the Monolith: The inside of the monolith is 20 feet square (larger than its exterior dimensions), with a flat shelf resting about 4 feet off the floor. On this shelf are twelve pairs of holes into which one may place his hands. Anyone inside the monolith cannot leave under their own power (see the freeing conditions, below). No divine powers may be regained within (from the Good gods), but hit points heal normally, and the air is breathable. Inside the monolith is the high priest **Abysthor**.

Destroying the Monolith or Opening the Gate: If enough people place their hands in the holes, and the proper ritual is performed, all individuals whose hands are in the holes immediately begin to lose life levels. The lost levels come from the highest level character first (e.g., Abysthor loses all his levels before the PCs finally lose 2 if they are successful at destruction of the monolith) unless the persons with their hands in the holes make an agreement otherwise. Abysthor insists that he sacrifice his levels (20 of them) before any of the PCs.

There are enough hand holes for twelve individuals to participate. There is no possible way to recover these lost levels. When a total of 22 Lawful Good levels are sacrificed, the monolith is destroyed, crumbling to dust in but a single minute. If 21 Chaotic Evil levels are sacrificed, the planar gate opens and the horrors of the Abyss are unleashed upon the world. Abysthor explains this to the party and will allow them to participate only if they are willing.

Options: Three scenarios can now occur. First, the PCs can "do the right thing" and sacrifice the 2 levels needed (in addition to those of Abysthor) to complete the ritual and destroy the monolith. This is the best outcome, and each PC participating receives a permanent +2 bonus to their Wisdom score as a blessing from Thyr and Muir. The party also may recover Abysthor's personal magic items. A second possible scenario is that the PCs are unwilling (or unable, if none are Lawful Good) to complete the ritual. If this is the case, Abysthor frees everyone from the monolith by sacrificing one of his levels and waits here, protecting the monolith from the priests of the evil gods. This in turn leads to the third scenario. Six months hence, a massive

contingent of Orcus's minions arrives and, barring intervention before that time by the players, defeats Abysthor and activates the planar gate. The land area around the Stoneheart Mountain Dungeon then becomes filled with demonic hosts, and all the local area is essentially wiped from the map. It is only a matter of time before the priests of Orcus discover the *earth blood* cavern, and the party should be able to make this decision without much brainpower. Success at destruction of the Black Monolith also nets the PCs a story award of 5,000 XP each.

ABYSTHOR   **CR 19**
XP 204,800
Male human cleric 16/paladin 4
LG Medium humanoid (human)
Init +1; **Perception** +17
Aura lawful

AC 11, touch 11, flat-footed 10 (+1 Dex)
hp 143 (16d8+16 plus 4d10+4 plus 16)
Fort +20; **Ref** +12; **Will** +24
Immune disease, fear

Speed 30 ft.
Melee +3 *disruption holy heavy mace* +20/+15/+10/+5 (1d8+4)
Cleric Spells Prepared (CL 16th): none
Paladin Spells Prepared (CL 1st): none
D Domain spell **Domains** Healing, Protection

Str 12, **Dex** 12, **Con** 12, **Int** 20, **Wis** 21, **Cha** 20

Base Atk +16; **CMB** +17; **CMD** 28
Feats Alignment Channel (Evil), Channel Smite, Combat Casting, Endurance, Extra Channel, Extra Lay on Hands, Fearless Aura#, Improved Channel, Selective Channeling, Turn Undead (DC 25), Word of Healing#
Skills Appraise +10, Craft (stonemasonry) +13, Diplomacy +22, Heal +20, Knowledge (arcana) +28, Knowledge (dungeoneering) +10, Knowledge (history) +14, Knowledge (planes) +13, Knowledge (religion) +28, Linguistics +10, Perception +17, Profession (miner) +20, Ride +5, Sense Motive +20, Spellcraft +28, Survival +10, Swim +1 (+5 to resist nonlethal damage from exhaustion), Use Magic Device +10
Languages Abyssal, Celestial, Common
Combat Gear *rod of absorption* (50 spell levels), *staff of life*; **Other Gear** *+3 disrupting holy heavy mace, ring of sustenance, stone horse* (destrier)
#*Pathfinder Roleplaying Game Ultimate Magic*

7A. The Lost Shard

This small cavern at the bottom of a deep depression contains a large column in 4 feet of water. At the bottom of the water is 2 feet of mud. Hidden in the mud behind the column is the crystal shard described in **Area 7**. This shard is the key to opening the Black Monolith and freeing Abysthor. Only careful searching of this area reveals its presence (DC 25 Perception). The crystal shard is of purest black and is at once clear and opaque, glowing with an unearthly green inner light.

8. The Great Seal and the Well

In the center of this hallway is a great mithral seal, fully 10 feet wide and inscribed with runes and wards against evil. This well goes straight down some 120 feet to the passage below. Abysthor crafted the seal of mithral and placed it on the opening to the well in the floor of the room above. It is warded with *forbiddance* (good) so no evil creatures can pass. Good-aligned creatures may remove the seal (it weighs 300 pounds) using conventional means (levers, lifting) if they have the key from Abysthor's tomb at **Area 4**. Note that the seal cannot be opened by any other method. It has 150 hit points, hardness 15, spell resistance 30 and damage reduction 10/magic. It is not possible to tunnel through the surrounding earth with magic due to the nature of the ground here (see **Standard Features**, above).

Abysthor's seal isn't the only ward on this well. There is some magic in the middle of the shaft going down that prohibits passage. Anyone using magical means of descent will be sorely disappointed. At the 60-foot mark in the well shaft is a seam of *antimagic*, caused by the presence of *earth blood* in this area. Anyone passing this point is struck by *dispel magic* with a CL 20. Falling 60 feet causes 6d6 points of damage to any that land on the stone surface below.

9. Cavern

This cavern contains a high, vaulted ceiling and is wrought with wild-colored streaks of minerals and glowing, shimmering veins of strange metal. The GM should describe in vivid detail the bright colored veins of yellow, silver, green and red. Any dwarves in the party are immediately struck with great joy at the mineralogical wonders in this room. Mining this room would result in the recovery of over 30,000 gp in strange, rare ores and metals. It also would bring down the wrath of the geon and his minions (see **Area 10**) and would take several months by a trained mining crew.

10. Chamber of The Stone Guardian (CR 9)

This area is the lair of an ancient creature bound here by the gods of the earth to guard the chamber of *earth blood* against intrusion by unworthy

mortals. Left as a defender is a **geon**. A **host of elder xorn** are allied with him, drawn here by the elemental power of the *earth blood*. The rare metals and minerals of these caverns serve as a steady food supply of tasty treats for these critters.

The geon and elder xorn are prohibited by the earth god from entering the *earth blood* cavern, though they enjoy devouring traces of the *earth blood* from the surrounding stone.

The geon stands in this central chamber. The xorn roam the caverns at will (**Areas 11, 11A** and **11B**). The geon remains still unless the area to the east (**Area 11**) is approached. It then animates. The geon has an unpronounceable name but is initially friendly.

If he is attacked, he calls his friends (the elder xorn) and animates boulders. The geon speaks a broken form of Common and can communicate with the party. The geon asks the PCs why they are here and what they want. He forbids them from taking any of the rare earth metals and strange jewels present in the chamber, as this is holy ground for earth creatures such as him, and it would be an act of desecration to have mortal creatures disturb the walls of these caverns. Only if the players explain with great detail that they must obtain *earth blood* from **Area 13** will he listen. He has no problem letting them try to do this, knowing full well the effect it will have on them. The geon sees this as a test of the worthiness of the party to be here in the first place. If they are destroyed by the *earth blood* (as he expects they will be), no matter. If, on the other hand, they are not (if they have obtained the *living rock* vials from the sphinx), the geon decides that the players are blessed by the earth god himself and that they should be allowed free range in his domain. He explains that the xorn are allied with him but that he cannot fully control them; that they may require payment from the party for passage in their areas.

He also realizes that they must first pass through the "wall of many colors" as he calls it (**Area 12A**). If a DC 21 Diplomacy check is made while asking him about the walls, he suggests a trade. If the PCs give him all their metal armor, he offers them a way to pass through the wall. What the geon gives in place of the armor are a series of four crystals; one red (ruby), one yellow (topaz), one green (emerald) and one deep violet (a garnet). Each crystal is worth 500 gp but is also enchanted to remove the corresponding color of the *prismatic wall* at **Area 12A** (one use only). The remaining layers must be removed normally. The geon feeds the armor to the xorn, so once the deal is made, it is a permanent trade.

If a second DC 21 Diplomacy check is made, the geon tells the characters a story. The story tells of a strange human that came here long ago and bathed in the blood of the earth. The geon decided that this creature was indeed blessed by the earth gods and gave him a crystal shard that was related to a strange black stone that was found long ago. He has no idea what the shard is for but wishes to have it returned to him. If they will agree to do so, he promises a block of solid mithral (weighs 80 pounds; can make two suits of human-size armor) as a reward. The crystal shard is of purest black, he explains, and is at once clear and opaque, glowing with an unearthly inner light (this is the shard that allows the Black Monolith to be opened and can be found in **Area 7A**).

GM Note: The geon is neither evil nor malicious. Humans and their ilk are like bugs to him. He is old and wise and relates to the players in an almost fatherly tone. He really considers humankind, and all the other "new" races to be far beneath him. One exception to this is that all dwarves make Charisma-based skill checks at a +4 bonus when dealing with this creature, due to their affinity with rock and stone.

GEON   **CR 9**
XP 6,400
hp 92 (*The Tome of Horrors Complete* 312)

11. The Lesser Guardians (CR 16)

This cavern contains a nest of **6 elder xorn** who associate with the geon in **Area 10**. The walls, floor and ceiling are similar to that in **Area 9**, with a total value of 20,000 gp. If the party enters this room having harmed the geon in any way, the xorn attack at once. If the characters passed the geon without incident, one xorn confronts them and demands that they pay tribute for their passage. This tribute can consist of all of their precious metals or of one suit of metal armor; their choice. If they do not pay tribute, they may not pass. If they continue or ignore the xorn, they are attacked by the whole group. An exception to this is that if the party has agreed to recover the crystal shard for the geon, it is left alone and the xorn never even make an appearance.

ADVANCED GIANT XORN (6)
XP 12,800

CR 11

N Large outsider (earth, extraplanar)
(*Pathfinder Roleplaying Games Bestiary* "Xorn"; see the **Appendix**)
Init +1; **Senses** all-around vision, darkvision 60 ft., tremorsense 60 ft.; **Perception** +19

AC 25, touch 14, flat-footed 24 (+1 Dex, +15 natural, −1 size)
hp 145 (10d10+80 plus 10)
Fort +11; **Ref** +8; **Will** +9
DR 5/bludgeoning; **Immune** cold, fire, flanking; **Resist** electricity 10

Speed 20 ft., burrow 20 ft.; earth glide
Melee bite +18 (5d6+9), 3 claws +18 (1d6+3)
Space 10 ft.; **Reach** 10 ft.

Str 29, **Dex** 12, **Con** 26, **Int** 14, **Wis** 15, **Cha** 14
Base Atk +10; **CMB** +20; **CMD** 31 (33 vs. trip)
Feats Awesome Blow, Cleave, Improved Bull Rush, Power Attack, Toughness

Skills Appraise +15, Intimidate +15, Knowledge (dungeoneering) +15, Knowledge (planes) +15, Perception +19, Sense Motive +15, Stealth +10, Survival +15; **Racial Modifiers** +4 Perception
Languages Common, Terran

All-Around Vision (Ex) A xorn sees in all directions at the same time, giving it a +4 racial bonus on Perception checks. A xorn cannot be flanked.
Earth Glide (Ex) A xorn can glide through any sort of natural earth or stone as easily as a fish swims through water. Its burrowing leaves no sign of its passage nor hint at its presence to creatures that don't possess tremorsense. A move earth spell cast on an area containing a xorn moves the xorn back 30 feet, stunning the creature for 1 round unless it succeeds on a DC 15 Fortitude save.

11A. The Planar Gate

The back wall of this cave seems to roil and ooze as if made from quicksand that somehow stands vertical along the wall. This wall is in reality a planar gate to the Plane of Earth. Any creatures transported there cannot breathe and must retreat through the gate or suffocate (see the *Pathfinder Roleplaying Game Core Rulebook*, "**Environment,** Suffocation"). The plane itself has the consistency of a heavy sandstorm. This gate is used by the geon and the xorn to "visit home" when they want to. It also allows for replacement guardians to access this area if they are slain.

11B. The Metal Cave

This entire cave is covered in veins of metallic ore of high content. There are raw veins of copper, iron and mithral throughout the cave on the floors and ceiling. Rubble from the rock matrix material is strewn across the floor, making passage difficult (all movement is at 1/4 normal). Were this area to be mined, over ten tons of copper, sixty tons of high-grade iron, and one ton of mithral could be extracted over a long period of time. Hidden under the rubble are three large pieces of mithral, each weighing about 80 pounds. It is from here that the geon retrieves the reward for the party that brings the shard from **Area 7**.

12. Warning Chamber

Inscribed on the floor in alien runic script is a dire warning, written in the magical tongue of earth elementals — Terran. Reading this script without knowing that language requires a *read magic* spell or a DC 25 Linguistics check. The inscription reads:

Beware all that would pass the walls of light
For beyond lies the seeping wound of the Earth
Flee mortal, before the blood of the gods consumes you
For to reach for immortality is to tempt the very forces of creation
And the end of the beginning is close at hand

12A. Barriers of Light (CR 8)

Between each of the seven columns set in the wall courses colored electricity. The layers in order from south to north are the red, orange, yellow, green, blue, indigo and violet layers of a *prismatic wall* (see *Pathfinder Roleplaying Game Core Rulebook* for the details of this spell). Anyone passing through the layers takes damage as per the spell of the same name. The walls may be lowered by the proper counterspell, or the red, yellow, green and violet layers can instead be removed with the crystals given to the party by the geon in **Area 10**. The remaining layers must still be dealt with normally (see the spell). The save DC for the effects of the walls is 32. Again, the *prismatic walls* cannot be circumvented by burrowing around because of the qualities of the rock on this level (see **Standard Features**, above).

13. The Chamber of Earth Blood (CR 10)

This chamber contains a pool of steaming, bubbling, thick red goo known as *earth blood*. It is a strange elemental substance believed to be the very essence of the god of the earth himself. This material is a source of unspeakable power. Why it is present here is a secret long forgotten even by the oldest of sages. The pool is 10 feet deep and has fissures leading deep into the crust of the earth. This material has highly magical *and* antimagical properties. It radiates immense levels of abjuration and transmutation magic Merely casting a *detect magic* spell on the material gives spellcasters headaches from the power radiated.

Effects of touching the material vary. For some it is a blessing, for others, certain death. Any inorganic material touching *earth blood* is immediately consumed on an elemental level and is considered lost forever. The only exception to this is *living rock*, a material so resistant it is also believed to be part of the earth god's bones. In addition, this pool was blessed by the earth god so that it could hold the *earth blood*, though that blessing is lost if any of the stone is removed from this chamber. Immersion of living material (such as PCs) that contacts the *earth blood* requires a DC 28 Fortitude save. Failure indicates death. Success has variable effects as follows.

1D100	EFFECT
01–20	Subject gains a natural armor bonus of +4. This stacks with any current natural armor bonus the subject already possesses.
21–30	Adjust ability scores as follows: Str +2, Con +2, Dex –2.
31–40	Subject gains **SR** 12, but if an arcane spellcaster, loses the ability to cast one spell of each level (one slot of each level for sorcerers).
41–50	Subject gains **DR** 5/magic.
51–60	Subject gains the effects of a permanent *stoneskin* spell as skin becomes rock; however, divine *cure* spells from any source no longer work on subject (although *mending* acts as *cure light wounds*, and *make whole* as a *cure serious wounds*. Watch out for *transmute rock to mud*!)
61–70	Roll again on this table; only effect lasts for seven days if otherwise permanent, or is permanent if otherwise temporary.
71–80	Subject gains a Str bonus of +8 and a Dex penalty of –4. The effects last for 1 month.
81–90	Subject gains **SR** 22 temporarily; however, arcane spellcasters lose all ability to cast spells. This effect lasts for one month.
91–96	Roll twice on this table, rerolling duplicates.
97–00	Subject is turned into a **greater earth elemental** and becomes an NPC.

The main purpose and use of this material in this adventure is to free Abysthor. A vial full of *earth blood* allows the party to bypass the transporter at **Area 5** and to access the Black Monolith in **Area 7**. Once the party has this material, it can be certain that the end of the adventure, one way or another, is near. Those who risk otherwise touching the *earth blood* can gain the bonuses above.

In addition, *earth blood* can be used to make spells permanent if it is used as a material component of the spell or to affect items that are ordinarily impervious to magic.

GM Note: It requires *living rock* vials (normally obtained only from the Plane of Earth, but rare even there) to remove the *earth blood* from this chamber. You should not allow PCs to remove more than one or two vials of this liquid from this room (other than those needed to free Abysthor).

Level 6: The Deep Caverns

The initial builders of this complex never found this level. Its main significance is that it serves as a way to reach **Level 5** from the upper levels — **Level 2A** in particular. The priests of Orcus, who have access to **Level 2A**, are beginning to explore this level as a means of reaching the Black Monolith (see **Level 5A**). This level also has several exits to the surface that open up some miles distant in the surrounding mountains and woods. The main creature on this level is the behir, as well as a lich who has not yet been located by the priests of Orcus.

DIRE RATS CR 1/3
XP 135
hp 5 (*Pathfinder Roleplaying Game Bestiary* "Rat, Dire")

FONT SKELETONS CR 1
XP 400
hp 11 (see the **Appendix**)

LESSER PRIESTS OF ORCUS CR 4
XP 1,200
hp 55 (see **Level 4, Area 2**)

PRIESTS OF ORCUS CR 5
XP 1,600
hp 39 (see **Level 4, Area 8**)

PSIONIC CHOKERS CR 3
XP 800
hp 16 (see **Level 2A, Area 6**)

SPIDERS, GIANT CR 1
XP 400
hp 16 (*Pathfinder Roleplaying Game Bestiary* "Spider, Giant")

Level 6: The Deep Caverns

Difficulty Level: 7 (unless you encounter the lich).
Entrances/Exits: Stairs from **Level 2A** and from **Level 5**.
Wandering Monsters: Several monsters roam this level. Check every 30 minutes by rolling 1d20:

ROLL 1D20	RESULT
1–2	2d6 dire rats
3	1d6 psionic chokers
4	1d4 giant spiders
5	A **priests of Orcus** scouting party (1 priest of Orcus, 3 lesser priests of Orcus and 6 font skeletons, scouting the level)
6	The **behir** (see **Area 10**)
7	1d4 wererats (see **Areas 4B** and **13**)
8–20	No encounter

Standard Features: Except for the passages at **Area 6**, all of the cavern passages are rather small — no more than 6 feet high. They also are covered with strange claw marks at all heights (from the behir). Alert PCs (DC 10 Knowledge [dungeoneering or nature] check) notice a surprising lack of stalactites in all the passages and chambers (except for **Area 6** and beyond), as they have been broken away by the behir slithering down the passages.

1. Level Entrance

The small set of stairs from **Level 2A** leads to this long, narrow cave passage. The ceiling is very low (6 feet), and even Medium creatures feel constricted. All actions within this passage receive a –2 circumstance penalty.

1A. Boxed Lunch (CR 3)

This room is the lair of a single rogue **psionic choker.** This male beast was driven out of the main lair (**Area 6**) by the dominant male living there. This beast hides in a small cubbyhole 10 feet above the floor, only appearing if fewer than three PCs enter. Also in the room is a cache of food and water, left here by the priests of Orcus. Three large boxes of preserved rations (a total of forty-man-days) and two 10-gallon casks of water (stagnant but drinkable) are placed against the far north corner of the cave.

PSIONIC CHOKER CR 3
XP 800
hp 16 (see **Level 2A, Area 6**)

2. The Shape of Things to Come

This room contains the remains of seven acolytes of Orcus who met a violent end at the claws of the behir. Blood and gore cover the room, and bits of armor, torn by the claws of the behir, are scattered across the chamber. The combat seems recent and the bodies are charred with electricity and huge claw and bite marks — an omen of things to come. One large stain in the shape of a bolt of lightning traces down the hall to the west, scarring the stones of the wall. Most of the acolytes' gear is destroyed; however, one suit of masterwork full plate remains intact, etched by the electricity of the behir but otherwise intact.

3. Flowstone Cavern

This cavern is devoid of monsters and treasure. It is vacant except for a very strange geologic feature in the west portion of the room. A huge iridescent plug of flowstone has emerged from the ground below the cave, partially blocking passage to the east with a 12-foot-high, blue-green hunk of stone. The stone contains embedded layers of bright blue and bright green sections. It is very weird looking, though neither valuable nor dangerous in any way.

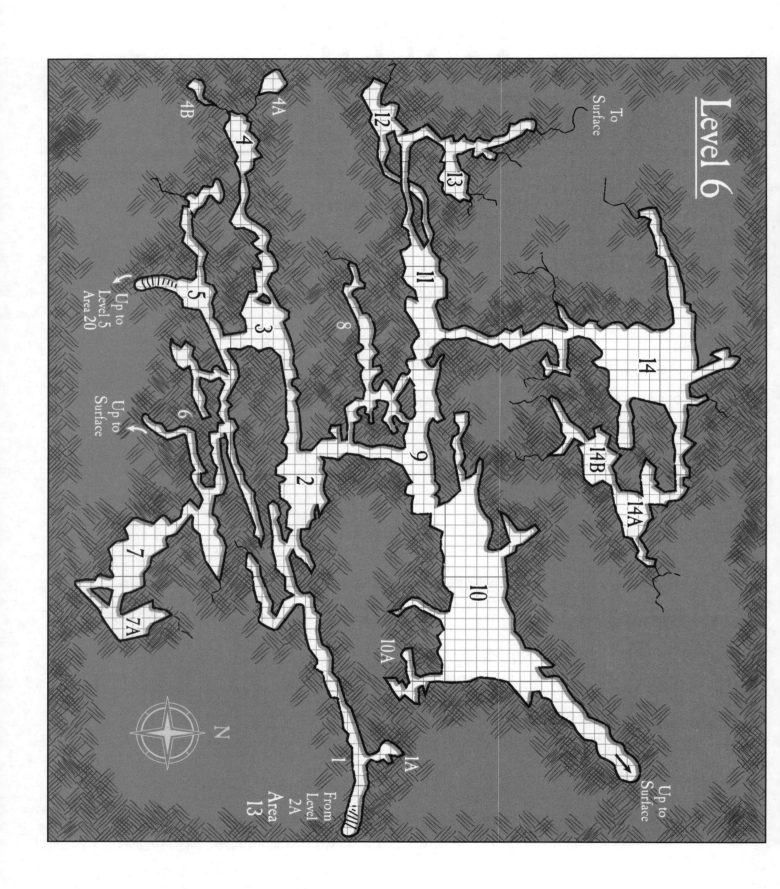

Level 6

To Surface

12

13

4B

4A

4

5

Up to Level 5 Area 20

3

Up to Surface

6

8

11

14

2

9

14B

14A

7

7A

10

10A

N

1

1A

From Level 2A Area 13

Up to Surface

4. Rat Cavern (CR 5+)

This cavern is literally filled to the brim with rats of all shapes and sizes. Two huge nests are found down the largest two rat tunnels leading from the cave. Each minute spent here draws the attack of **1 rat swarm** and **1d6 dire rats**. There are a total of 200 normal rats and 42 dire rats in this cave. Once 3 rat swarms and 12 dire rats are killed, the rest retreat to **Areas 4A** and **4B**.

DIRE RATS	CR 1/3

XP 135
hp 5 (*Pathfinder Roleplaying Game Bestiary* "Rat, Dire")

RAT SWARM	CR 2

XP 600
hp 16 (*Pathfinder Roleplaying Game Bestiary* "Rat, Swarm")

4A. Rat Lair (CR 5)

This room contains a nesting area for the rats in **Area 4**. Torn cloth, fungus and other materials reside in eight fluffy piles strewn about the room. An additional **10 dire rats** and **36 baby dire rats** (treat as non-combatant) are in this cavern. This nest also contains a bunch of shiny baubles (not valuable) in the form of rock chips, bones, bits of metal and pieces of glass.

DIRE RATS (10)	CR 1/3

XP 135
hp 5 (*Pathfinder Roleplaying Game Bestiary* "Rat, Dire")

4B. Queen Rat (CR 11)

This rat lair appears much as the lair in **Area 4A**. It varies in two major ways. The first is that in addition to the **8 dire rats** and **22 (non-combatant) baby dire rats** living in the nesting material, there are also **6 wererats** hiding here in dire rat form. These wererats pretend to scurry away from any intruders, only to attack from behind by surprise. The **wererat leader** is a large, light gray specimen named **Marala**, a 7th-level rogue.

Tactics: Marala avoids combat with any armored individuals, preferring to wait until she can attack lightly armored foes by surprise. She then retreats into **Area 4** and uses her magic *horn*. She quaffs her *potions* and enters melee, attempting to slay all spellcasters. If cornered, she offers information about **Area 14** if the PCs release her. She knows that there is a long-lost crypt there and that a tomb of an ancient king is somewhere in the cavern. The remaining wererats are also cowards, preferring to let the rats who serve them bear the brunt of any combat. They attempt to strike fast then run.

Treasure: Hidden in one of the nests, in addition to useless yet shiny baubles as in **Area 4A**, are two *ioun stones* (dusty rose and dark blue).

DIRE RATS (8)	CR 1/3

XP 135
hp 5 (*Pathfinder Roleplaying Game Bestiary* "Rat, Dire")

WERERATS (5)	CR 2

XP 600
hp 18/20 (*Pathfinder Roleplaying Game Bestiary* "Lycanthrope, Wererat")

MARALA	CR 7

XP 3,200
Male human natural dire wererat rogue 7 (*Pathfinder Roleplaying Game Bestiary* "Lycanthrope, Wererat")
LE Medium humanoid hybrid form (human, shapechanger)
Init +3; **Senses** low-light vision, scent; **Perception** +12

AC 17, touch 14, flat-footed 13 (+3 armor, +3 Dex, +1 dodge)

hp 53 (7d8+21)
Fort +4; **Ref** +8; **Will** +2
Defensive Abilities evasion, trap sense, uncanny dodge

Speed 30 ft.
Melee mwk rapier +9 (1d6/18–20)
Ranged light crossbow +8 (1d8/19–20)
Special Attacks curse of lycanthropy (DC 15), sneak attack +4d6

Str 10, **Dex** 17, **Con** 14, **Int** 14, **Wis** 10, **Cha** 6
Base Atk +5; **CMB** +5; **CMD** 19
Feats Alertness, Dodge, Mobility, Spring Attack, Weapon Finesse[B]
Skills Acrobatics +13, Appraise +10, Bluff +5, Climb +5, Diplomacy –2 (+2 to change attitude vs. animals related to lycanthropic form), Disable Device +11, Disguise +4, Escape Artist +9, Intimidate +3, Knowledge (local) +7, Linguistics +8, Perception +12 (+15 to locate traps), Sense Motive +12, Sleight of Hand +13, Stealth +13, Survival +5, Swim +5, Use Magic Device +8
Languages Aklo, Common, Dwarven, Goblin, Orc, Undercommon
SQ change forms, lycanthropic empathy, rogue talents (fast stealth, ledge walker), trapfinding +3
Combat Gear *horn of valhalla* (silver), *potion of cure serious wounds, potion of heroism, potion of invisibility*, 2 vials deathblade poison; **Other Gear** masterwork studded leather armor, masterwork rapier, light crossbow, 20 bolts, masterwork thieves tools

Curse of Lycanthropy (Su) A natural lycanthrope's bite attack in animal or hybrid form infects a humanoid target with lycanthropy (Fortitude DC 15 negates). If the victim's size is not within one size category of the lycanthrope, this ability has no effect.
Disease (Ex) *Filth fever*: Bite—injury; *save* Fort DC 14; *onset* 1d3 days; *frequency* 1/day; *effect* 1d3 Dex damage and 1d3 Con damage; *cure* 2 consecutive saves. The save DC is Constitution-based.
Lycanthropic Empathy (Ex) In any form, natural lycanthropes can communicate and empathize with animals related to their animal form. They can use Diplomacy to alter such an animal's attitude, and when so doing gain a +4 racial bonus on the check. Afflicted lycanthropes only gain this ability in animal or hybrid form.

5. Stairs to Level 5 (CR 10)

This area contains stairs leading up to **Level 5**. The priests of Orcus want to guard this passage against intrusion by the priests of Tsathogga, and they don't want the priests of Tsathogga to know they are here looking for a back door entrance to the Black Monolith. To this end, the priests of Orcus have placed several *glyphs of warding* along the stairway. These *glyphs* are hidden along the stairs at 10-foot intervals (five *glyphs* total).

GLYPH OF WARDING TRAPS (5)	CR 4 or 6

XP 1,200 or 2,400
Type magical; **Perception** DC 28; **Disable Device** DC 28

Trigger spell; **Reset** none
Effect spell effect (*glyph of warding*, CL 8th, effect varies, see below); multiple targets (all targets within 5 ft.); may be identified (with *read magic*) without triggering it with a successful DC 13 Spellcraft check.
Sound burst in a 10-foot radius, cast at CL 8th, **CR 4**.
Blast (sonic) in a 5-foot radius, CL 8th (4d8 damage), **CR 6**.

Blast (acid) in a 5-foot radius, CL 8th (4d8 damage), **CR 6**.
Blast (cold) in a 5-foot radius, CL 8th (4d8 damage), **CR 6**.
Bestow curse in a 10-foot radius, CL 8th (–4 on saves), **CR 4**.

6. Psionic Choker Maze (CR 3–8)

This batch of twisty passages is different from the passages on the rest of the level: the ceiling is some 20 feet above and festooned with stalactites. Broken and chewed bones litter the floor of these tunnels. One passage leads outside of the dungeon into a small cave that eventually leads to a small, forested area on the surface. The PCs may attempt a DC 20 Survival check to notice the absence of bats and rats in these caves.

This is a psionic choker playground. There are always **1d6 psionic chokers** here. The lair of the psionic chokers is in **Area 7**. These creatures guard this area viciously, and other denizens of this level have learned to avoid these caves.

PSIONIC CHOKERS   CR 3
XP 800
hp 16 (see **Level 2A, Area 6**)

Tactics: Psionic chokers always attack with their psionic assault prior to melee. If pressed, they retreat to their lair — **Area 7**.

7. Psionic Choker Lair (CR 9)

This room serves as the lair of the psionic chokers that inhabit this level (excluding the rogue male in **Area 1A**). All the psionic chokers here are female, except for the dominant male, and immature specimens. There are **7 psionic chokers** here waiting for the PCs. Like **Area 6**, these caves have 20-foot-high ceilings and are congested with stalactites and stalagmites. All creatures in these caves are assumed to have concealment at distances greater than 20 feet, and all movement is at 1/2 normal rates due to the clutter on the floor.

PSIONIC CHOKERS (7)   CR 3
XP 800
hp 16 (see **Level 2A, Area 6**)

Tactics: When **Area 7** is first entered, all adult psionic chokers present attack using their psionic assault (this ignores concealment penalties). They melee felled opponents, scurrying away if approached by an un-stunned foe.

7A. Psionic Choker Den (CR 10)

This room contains the nesting area of the psionic chokers. The dominant male and dominant female psionic choker keep nest here. Scattered all over the floor are the remains of various creatures, felled by the pack attacks of the psionic chokers. The baby psionic chokers cling like little monkeys from the roof. There are **2 dominant (advanced) psionic chokers** (the dominant male and female), **8 psionic chokers**, and **7 young psionic chokers** here.

Tactics: These creatures are very pack oriented and fight until slain. Cavern height and concealment rules apply as in **Area 7**. The baby psionic chokers do not attack an un-stunned opponent, but they swarm a felled opponent like a pack of piranhas.

Treasure: Buried in the piles of bones and litter (DC 28 Perception check) is a strange magic item, lost long ago—the *Shard of Hel* (see the **Appendix** for more details).

PSIONIC CHOKERS (8)   CR 3
XP 800
hp 16 (see **Level 2A, Area 6**)

ADVANCED PSIONIC CHOKERS (2)   CR 4
XP 1,200
CE Small aberration
(*Pathfinder Roleplaying Game Bestiary* "Choker"; see the **Appendix**)
Init +8; **Senses** darkvision 60 ft.; **Perception** +3

AC 21, touch 15, flat-footed 17 (+4 Dex, +6 natural, +1 size)
hp 22 (3d8+9)
Fort +4; **Ref** +5; **Will** +6

Speed 20 ft., climb 10 ft.
Melee 2 tentacles +8 (1d4+5 plus grab)
Space 5 ft.; **Reach** 10 ft.
Special Attacks constrict (1d4+5), grab (Large), psionic assault, strangle

Str 20, **Dex** 18, **Con** 17, **Int** 8, **Wis** 17, **Cha** 18
Base Atk +2; **CMB** +6 (+10 to grapple); **CMD** 20
Feats Improved Initiative, Skill Focus (Stealth)
Skills Acrobatics +10, Climb +17, Stealth +15
Languages Undercommon
SQ quickness

Environment any underground
Organization solitary, pair, or clutch (3–8)
Treasure standard

Quickness (Su) A choker is supernaturally quick. It can take an extra move action during its turn each round.
Strangle (Ex) Chokers have an unerring talent for seizing their victims by the neck. A creature that is grappled by a choker cannot speak or cast spells with verbal components.
Psionic Assault (Su) At will as a standard action, a psionic choker can unleash a stunning blast in a 15 ft. cone. Any creature within the area of effect must succeed at a DC 15 Will save or be stunned for 1d3 rounds. An opponent that succeeds on the saving throw is immune to that same creature's psionic assault for 24 hours. Psionic chokers are immune to this ability.

YOUNG PSIONIC CHOKERS (8)   CR 1
XP 400
CE Tiny aberration
(*Pathfinder Roleplaying Game Bestiary* "Choker"; see the **Appendix**)
Init +5; **Senses** darkvision 60 ft.; **Perception** +1

AC 18, touch 17, flat-footed 13 (+5 Dex, +1 natural, +2 size)
hp 3 (1d8–1)
Fort –1; **Ref** +5; **Will** +2

Speed 20 ft., climb 10 ft.
Melee 2 tentacles +1 (1d3–1 plus grab)
Space 2 1/2 ft.; **Reach** 5 ft.
Special Attacks constrict (1d3–1), grab (Medium), psionic assault (5 ft., DC 11), strangle

Str 8, **Dex** 20, **Con** 9, **Int** 4, **Wis** 10, **Cha** 12
Base Atk +0; **CMB** +3 (+7 to grapple); **CMD** 12
Feats Skill Focus (Stealth)
Skills Climb +11, Stealth +16
Languages Undercommon
SQ quickness

Psionic Assault (Su) A young psionic choker's psionic attack fills only one 5 ft. square.

8. Side Cavern (CR 4)

This cave is largely ignored by all intelligent denizens. This wing of the caverns has a 40-foot ceiling covered in stalactites. A large, bubbling water spring gurgles at the end of the cave, making strange echoing sounds that pervade throughout this area. Even the behir gives this one a wide berth. This is due to the huge patch of **green slime** living in the back 40 feet of the cave. For each round spent in this area, there is a 25% chance of the slime dropping from above. It requires 60 points of damage to completely eradicate the slime, though a path may be cleared with considerably fewer.

GREEN SLIME   **CR 4**
XP 1,200 (*Pathfinder Roleplaying Game Core Rulebook* "Environment")

9. Low Cavern

This broad cavern is only 6 feet high. The behir (see **Area 10**) can slither through here with little trouble, though again there are telltale claw marks and notable scorch marks from electricity. There is a mysterious absence of stalactites.

10. Behir Lair (CR 8)

This is the lair of the **behir**. He is big and hungry. He leaves the psionic chokers alone because a group of them hit him with a batch of psionic assaults once and almost did him in — though he fried a good number of them. He hunts only their stragglers. The room also has a large opening that leads to a long, steep passage to the surface, exiting several miles from the dungeon in the surrounding mountains. The behir normally heads to the mountains to hunt, preferring roc eggs that he finds there to the dire rats in these caves. He also sometimes slithers up to **Level 5**, where he hunts the monstrous frogs bred in the pits, though the passage from **Area 2** to **Area 3** is a bit of squeeze for him. The behir has no treasure.

Tactics: This behir is old and wise. As such, he preferentially targets anyone in metal armor with his breath before closing in to eat less labor intensive (no peeling required), light-armored foes. He retreats up the exit tunnel at full speed if reduced to fewer than 30 hp.

BEHIR   **CR 8**
XP 4,800
hp 105 (*Pathfinder Roleplaying Game Bestiary* "Behir")

10A. Side Cavern

The passage to this cavern is too small for the behir to fit into under most circumstances. Several years ago a female behir (who was a more petite version of the behir in this room) came here and laid a clutch of eggs. They will hatch in six months. That alone is an interesting treasure. Also here is the corpse of a rogue who snuck in while the behir was away. The behir returned and smelled the rogue but didn't want to blast him with electricity because he didn't want to fry his own eggs. So the rogue — afraid to leave — tried to wait out the behir. The behir waited, too. But the rogue starved to death first.

Treasure: The body of the rogue wears leather armor, and a rusty but usable masterwork short sword lies nearby. On one finger of the corpse is a *ring of water walking*. A pack nearby contains three oil flasks, a lamp, 50 feet of hemp rope, one vial of acid and 22 gp.

11. The Spring

This small cavern contains little of interest. It does contain a 20-foot-diameter clean, clear pool of water, fed and drained by an underground spring. Many of the local denizens get their water here. When this cavern is first entered, a roll on the wandering monster table is appropriate.

12. The Tainted Pool (CR 1–6)

This cavern contains a pool of water similar to that in **Area 11**. The water in this pool appears to be clean and clear, as does the pool in **Area 11**; however, the water is tainted with virulent bacteria. Anyone drinking from this pool must make a DC 18 Fortitude save or suffer the effects of *filth fever.* Rats frequent this room as well. At any given time, **3d6 normal rats** are present and may attack.

RATS	CR 1/4

XP 100
hp 4 (*Pathfinder Roleplaying Game Bestiary* "Familiar, Rat")

13. The Wererat Nest (CR 7)

This room contains a nest of **5 wererats**. These beasts serve Marala and act as guardians for her secret exit to the surface. These critters hide here in rat form, only attacking if they have a clear chance for an ambush (like a camping party). Otherwise, they watch and wait, following anyone who enters this way until an ambush becomes possible. They will not participate in a stand-up fight. They have no treasure.

WERERATS (5)	CR 2

XP 600
hp 18/20 (*Pathfinder Roleplaying Game Bestiary* "Lycanthrope, Wererat")

14. Another Bad Omen

This large cavern has several notable features, the most prominent of which is the series of ancient hieroglyphic stories and curses inscribed on its walls. Virtually every surface of the walls is covered in strange pictograms, weird symbols and ancient writing. Reading these writings requires a DC 30 Linguistics check. Success reveals that this cavern contains the hidden tomb of the long-dead sorcerer-king Gremag (now a lich) from a civilization lost for over ten thousand years. Marala has deciphered some of the writings and read enough of the evil wards and curses described to leave this place in peace.

14A. The Minions of Gremag (CR 12)

This area is carved with bas-relief frescoes of warriors dressed in ancient garb. Ten warriors are depicted in the scenes, all wearing old-style armor and carrying bone and copper weapons, with feathered headdresses and ivory collars. There is no apparent entrance to **Area 14B**, though carved on the wall at the real entrance is an inlaid image of a gate. This gate image is a clue to the real entrance into **Area 14B**. If the tomb of Gremag is to be accessed, the stones themselves must be painstakingly disassembled. Men with mining tools (the wall is 6 feet thick) can easily do this over a period of several days. Unfortunately, as soon as a stone begins to fall, the stone-encased spirits of the guardians awaken as **10 mummies** and claw through the stone to assault intruders. There is no treasure here.

MUMMIES (10)	CR 5

XP 1,600
hp 60 (*Pathfinder Roleplaying Game Bestiary* "Mummy")

Tactics: The mummies attack without hesitation, *geased* in life to protect their lord after death. They do not pursue out of **Area 14**.

14B. Gremag's Lair (CR 20)

This is the tomb and final resting place of the ancient sorcerer-king **Gremag**. It is hidden behind 6 feet of solid brick, covered with the painting of the gate described in **Area 14A**. The chamber itself is similar to **Areas 14** and **14A** in that its walls are covered with strange hieroglyphs and writings. In the center of the room is a large open crypt. If the PCs dig the area open, Gremag is waiting for them.

GREMAG THE LICH	CR 20

XP 307,200
Male human lich druid 6/mystic theurge 9/sorcerer 4 (*Pathfinder Roleplaying Game Bestiary* "Lich")
NE Medium undead (augmented humanoid, human)
Init +2; **Senses** darkvision 120 ft.; **Perception** +13
Aura fear (60-ft. radius, DC 24)

AC 17, touch 12, flat-footed 15 (+2 Dex, +5 natural)
hp 185 (6d8+30 plus 9d6+45 plus 4d6+20 plus 6)
Fort +14, **Ref** +8, **Will** +19; +4 vs. spell-like and supernatural abilities of Fey and against effects that target plants,
Defensive Abilities channel resistance +4; **DR** 15/bludgeoning and magic; **Immune** cold, electricity, mind-affecting, polymorph, undead traits

Speed 30 ft.
Melee touch (1d8+9 plus paralyzing touch)
Special Attacks paralyzing touch (DC 28)
Domain Spell-Like Abilities (CL 15th; ranged touch +12): 8/day—acid dart, tremor (CMB 9)
Arcane Spells Known (CL 13th; melee touch +10, ranged touch +12):
6th (4/day)—disintegrate (DC 21), summon monster VI
5th (7/day)—magic jar (DC 20), teleport, waves of fatigue
4th (7/day)—greater invisibility, phantasmal killer (DC 19), stoneskin, stone shape
3rd (7/day)—fly, hostile levitation** (DC 18), tongues, vampiric touch
2nd (7/day)—mirror image, see invisibility, spectral hand, touch of idiocy, web (DC 17)
1st (8/day)—corrosive touch# (DC 16), expeditious excavation*B (DC 16), magic missile, protection from good, shield, ray of enfeeblement (DC 16)
0 (at will)—acid splash, arcane mark, bleed (DC 15), detect magic, mage hand, message, open/close (DC 15), read magic, touch of fatigue (DC 15)
Bloodlines Deep Earth*
Divine Spells Prepared (CL 15th; melee touch +10, ranged touch +12):
8th—earthquake (DC 23), repel metal or stone
7th—creeping doom (DC 22), elemental body IV, true seeing

6th—*antilife shell, greater dispel magic, hungry pit** (DC 21), *tar pool*** (DC 21)
5th—*baleful polymorph* (DC 20, x2), *transmute mud to rock* (DC 20, x2), *unhallow* (DC 20), *wall of stone* (DC 20)
4th—*dispel magic, echolocation#, freedom of movement, obsidian flow***(DC 19), *rusting grasp, spike stones* (DC 19)
3rd—*burrow#* (DC 18), *meld into stone* x2, *spike growth* (DC 18), *spiked pit*D (DC 18), *stone shape*
2nd—*chill metal* (DC 17), *create pit*D (DC 17), *fog cloud, heat metal* (DC 17), *soften earth and stone, stone call*
1st—*faerie fire, magic stone*D, *obscuring mist* x2, *ray of sickening#* (DC 16), *speak with animals, stone fist*
0 (at will)—*detect magic, mending, read magic, resistance*
D Domain Spell **Domains** Caves*

Str 10, **Dex** 14, **Con** —, **Int** 16, **Wis** 21, **Cha** 21
Base Atk +10; **CMB** +10; **CMD** 22
Feats Ability Focus (negative energy touch attack), Bouncing Spell*, Combat Casting, Deepsight, Echoing Spell#, Elemental Spell* (acid), Eschew Materials^B, Improved Ability Focus& (negative energy touch attack), Persistent Spell*, Quicken Spell, Resistance to Positive Energy& x2
Skills Craft (alchemy) +18, Craft (gemcutting) +14, Diplomacy +17, Heal +19, Intimidate +20, Knowledge (arcana) +18, Knowledge (nature) +18, Knowledge (religion) +18, Perception +13 (+15 to notice unusual stonework, such as traps and hidden doors in stone walls or floors), Sense Motive +20, Spellcraft +17, Stealth +10, Survival +20, Use Magic Device +18; **Racial Modifiers** +8 Perception, +8 Sense Motive, +8 Stealth
Languages Aklo, Common, Druidic, Sylvan, Terran
SQ combined spells (5th), nature bond abilities (caves), rejuvenation, resist nature's lure, stonecunning +2, trackless step, wild empathy (+11), wild shape (2/day; animal, elemental), woodland stride
Combat Gear wand of confusion; **Other Gear** portable hole, tattered robes, a gold crown (2,200 gp), a platinum ring with large ruby (15,000 gp)

Fear Aura (Su) Creatures of less than 5 HD in a 60-foot radius that look at a lich must succeed on a Will save or become frightened. Creatures with 5 HD or more must succeed at a Will save or be shaken for a number of rounds equal to the lich's Hit Dice. A creature that successfully saves cannot be affected again by the same lich's fear aura for 24 hours. This is a mind-affecting *fear* effect. The save is Charisma-based.
Paralyzing Touch (Su) Any living creature a lich hits with its touch attack must succeed on a Fortitude save or be permanently paralyzed. *Remove paralysis* or any spell that can remove a curse can free the victim (with a DC equal to the lich's save DC). The effect cannot be dispelled. Anyone paralyzed by a lich seems dead, though a DC 20 Perception check or a DC 15 Heal check reveals that the victim is still alive. The save is Charisma-based.
Rejuvenation (Su) When a lich is destroyed, its phylactery (which is generally hidden by the lich in a safe place far from where it chooses to dwell) immediately begins to rebuild the undead spellcaster's body nearby. This process takes 1d10 days—if the body is destroyed before that time passes, the phylactery merely starts the process anew. After this time passes, the lich wakens fully healed (albeit without any gear it left behind on its old body), usually with a burning need for revenge against those who previously destroyed it.
The most common form of phylactery is a sealed metal box containing strips of parchment on which magical phrases have been transcribed. The box is Tiny and has 40 hit points, hardness 20, and a break DC of 40.
Other forms of phylacteries can exist, such as rings, amulets, or similar items.
*Pathfinder Roleplaying Game Advanced Player's Guide
**Pathfinder Roleplaying Game Ultimate Combat
#Pathfinder Roleplaying Game Ultimate Magic
&see **Rappan Athuk** for more details

Tactics: Gremag takes no prisoners if anyone disturbs his tomb, and begins his attack as soon as anyone breaks through the outer wall. He casts *stoneskin* immediately, followed by an *unhallow, greater invisibility* and *protection from good*. After his protective spells are in place, the gloves come off. He makes liberal use of *summon monster VI* to keep melee fighters at bay, *spike stones* and *fog cloud* to confuse and split the party, and *antilife shell* to keep the living away from him. Should the lich be angered by a continued assault, he uses *waves of fatigue, magic jar, repel metal or stone, hungry pit*, and *tar pool* to harass the PCs. Should he somehow feel threatened, he unleashes repeated *disintegrate* spells against wizards, *phantasmal killers* against fighters, saving *creeping doom* for any clerics he can see. Gremag does not surrender or retreat, but he may parley if a DC 30 Diplomacy check is made (+5 bonus if the Diplomacy check is made by a druid). Gremag does not pursue out of his lair, instead resealing his tomb with a series of *stone shape* and *mud to rock* spells.

Treasure: Hidden amongst the writings and pictograms is a *portable hole* that can be found on a successful DC 30 Perception check. The hole contains an *iron flask* (which contains a **vrock**), 4,100 gp and an ancient statue, made from mithral, of a swan in flight over a pond of lotus leaves. The statue is valued at 13,000 gp.

Appendix

New Classes

Disciple of Orcus (Archetype)

The Disciple of Orcus has dedicated their life from their first pious moments to serving the Demon Lord of the Undead. They instruct the secret cabals in the teachings of Orcus and also work to raise the undead army that will someday rise up to destroy the world. The disciples of Rappan Athuk differ theologically from the disciples of Tsar, and will attack the later more often than not.

Death Domain: The disciple of Orcus must choose the Death domain (or the Undead subdomain from the *Advanced Player's Guide,* if available in the campaign). They gain no second domain or domain powers. In all other respects, this works like and replaces the standard cleric's domain ability.

Variant Channeler: When the Disciple of Orcus channels energy it is modified by the undeath variant from *Ultimate Magic.*

***See in Darkness* (Ex):** The holiest of rites to Orcus are performed in total darkness. At 1st level the Disciple of Orcus gains darkvision 60 ft. The range increases to 90 ft. at 6th level. At 8th level the Disciple of Orcus can also see in magical darkness. If the Disciple of Orcus already possesses darkvision its range increases by +30 ft. at 1st and 6th levels.

Bonus Feat (Ex): At 1st level the Disciple of Orcus gains Command Undead as a bonus feat.

Undead Lord's Proxy (Su): Undead recognize the Disciple of Orcus as a conduit to the Demon Lord. At 3rd level Disciples add +2 to the DC to resist channeled energy when used to command undead.

Touch of Darkness (Su): At 9th level, once per day per level, the Disciple may make a melee touch attack to deal 1d4+1 points of Strength damage to a target (Fortitude save for half damage). If the target is reduced to 0 Strength or less, they die, and rise as a shadow under the control of the Disciple one round later. The Disciple may have one controlled shadow per two Disciple levels. This is equivalent to a 5th level spell. The save DC is Wisdom-based.

Undead Creation Mastery (Su): At 11th level when the Disciple of Orcus creates undead (either through the spell or other means) they gain a +4 bonus to their caster level when determining what type of undead they can create. Undead the Disciple of Orcus creates are immediately under their control as per *control undead.*

Reprinted from *Rappan Athuk* by **Frog God Games**

Filth-Priest of Tsathogga (Archetype)

The Filth-Priests of Tsathogga has dedicated their life from their first moments in the slime infused muck to serving the Demon Frog God. They tend the secret breeding grounds of the various killer frogs species the tsathar set upon humankind and also work to raise the batrachian army that will someday rise up to destroy the world. The Filth-Priests are a highly zealous group, and will kill and devour clerics of other faiths, especially those of the goodly races.

Domains: The Fifth-Priests of Tsathogga must choose the Destruction and Water domains, exemplifying the stagnant sludge the Demon Frog lives in.

Bonus Feat (Ex): At 1st level the Filth-Priest gains Channel Smite as a bonus feat.

The Frog God's Proxy (Su): All batrachian beings recognize the Filth-Priest as a conduit to the Frog God. At 3rd level Filth-Priests add a +4 bonus to Handle Animal checks made when dealing with frogs, toads, and any frog-like animal. The Filth-Priest further gains a +2 bonus to Diplomacy when dealing with frog-like outsiders (hydrodaemons, greruor demons, hezrous demons, etc.)

Touch of Filth (Su): At 9th level, once per day per level, the Filth-Priest may make a melee touch attack to deal 1d4 points of Charisma damage to a target (Fortitude save for half damage). If the target is reduced to 0 Charisma or less, they die, dissolving into a pile of retch and filth. The save DC is Wisdom-based.

Summon Greruor Demon (Sp): At 11th level, once per day the Filth-Priest of Tsathogga may attempt to summon 1 greruor demon with a 60% chance of success. The demon is under no compulsion to obey the summoner, but is not immediately hostile. This ability is the equivalent of a 6th-level spell.

Justicar (Prestige Class)

A Justicar of Muir is the living embodiment of the first and most important of the triune virtues of Muir—Truth. As an embodiment of truth, and in keeping with the strictness of Muir, a Justicar of Muir must follow an extremely strict moral code beyond that required of a common paladin. The benefit of this purity and stricture is awe-inspiring—eventually allowing the Justicar of Muir to become an avatar of Muir herself.

Role: Justicars of Muir are the elite paladins in the worship of Muir. While there may be many paladins of Muir, there can never be more than 13 Justicars of Muir alive at any one time. The leader of the Justicars of Muir is known as the Grandmaster. The grandmaster must be a Justicar of at least 8th level.

Alignment: Lawful Good
Hit Die: d10

Requirements

To qualify to become a Justicar, a character must fulfill all the following criteria.

Base Attack Bonus: +8
Class: A Justicar must have at least 3 paladin levels and may not be an ex-paladin. In addition, the PC must have taken their last level as a paladin prior to becoming a Justicar. Thus, a person who takes 3 levels of paladin and then 7 levels of cleric cannot be a Justicar, though a person who has taken 7 levels of cleric and then 3 levels of paladin could be a Justicar.
Deity: Muir
Quest: A Justicar-to-be must complete an arduous quest of some significance to Muir to demonstrate his worth to Muir before he may be ordained (see below).
Skills: Diplomacy 2 ranks, Knowledge (religion) 8 ranks, Sense Motive 2 ranks.

Class Skills

The Justicar's class skills (and the key ability for each skill) are Craft (Int), Diplomacy (Cha), Handle Animal (Cha), Heal (Wis), Knowledge (nobility) (Int), Knowledge (religion) (Int), Profession (Wis), Ride (Dex), Sense Motive (Wis), and Spellcraft (Int). Bluff, Disguise, Intimidate, Sleight of Hand and Stealth are prohibited skills.

Skill Ranks per level: 2 + Int modifier.

Class Features

All the following are Class Features of the Justicar prestige class.
Armor and Weapon Proficiencies: Justicar's gain proficiency in the bastard sword as an exotic weapon per the feat Exotic Weapon Proficiency

(bastard sword).

Spells per Day: When a Justicar of Muir level is gained, the character gains new spells per day as if he had also gained a level in any one spellcasting class he belonged to before he added the prestige class. He does not, however, gain other benefits a character of that class would have gained, except for additional spells per day, spells known (if he is a spontaneous caster), and an increased effective level of spellcasting. If a character had more than one spellcasting class before becoming a Justicar, he must decide to which class he adds the new spell level for purposes of determining spells per day.

Resist Illusions (Su): A Justicar gains a +4 divine bonus on Will saves against illusion magic. In addition, Justicars are allowed to save to disbelieve illusions without having to interact with the illusion, even if that is normally required to disbelieve the illusion.

Zone of Truth (Sp): Once per day for every three Justicar levels, a Justicar can cast the spell *zone of truth* as a spell-like ability. The ability functions as if cast by a caster of a level equal to the Justicar's total character level.

Enemy of Evil (Su): A Justicar gains a +2 divine bonus to attack and damage rolls against evil-aligned undead and outsiders.

Celestial Companion (Su): A Justicar gains a celestial falcon—the holy animal of Muir—as a companion per the druid animal companion rules (see "Druid" in Chapter 3 of the *Pathfinder Roleplaying Game Core Rulebook*).

Starting Statistics: Size Small; **Speed** 10 ft., fly 80 ft. (average); **AC** +1 natural armor; **Attack** bite (1d4), 2 talons (1d4); **Ability Scores** Str 10, Dex 17, Con 12, Int 2, Wis 14, Cha 10; **Special Attacks** smite evil 1/day as a swift action (adds Cha bonus to attack rolls and damage bonus equal to HD against evil foes; smite persists until the target is dead or the celestial falcon rests); **Special Qualities** darkvision 60 ft., low-light vision, DR and energy resistance per *Pathfinder Roleplaying Game Bestiary* "Celestial Creature", SR equal to class level +5

4th-Level Advancement: Ability Scores Str +2, Con +2.

Discern Lies (Su): At 2nd level, a Justicar can *discern lies* as the spell once per day and an additional time per day for every 3 Justicar levels thereafter (2 at 5th, 3 at 8th). The ability functions as if cast by a caster of a level equal to the Justicar's total character level.

Shield of Truth (Su): Beginning at 3rd level, a Justicar can invoke Muir's shield of truth once per day. Invoking this ability either enhances the Justicar's current shield or temporarily creates a supernatural shield for the Justicar to use. The shield has the following abilities: +2 divine bonus (if the shield is created, this is the only armor benefit it provides) and becomes a *blinding shield* (see the "Magic Items" section in Chapter 15 of the *Pathfinder Roleplaying Game Core Rulebook*), except the blinding effect only affects evil creatures. In addition, the shield radiates the effects of a *prayer* spell for its duration. This ability lasts for 30 minutes. Shield of truth cannot be used in combination with either sword of courage or armor of honor until the Justicar gains the avatar ability.

Mark of Justice (Su): Beginning at 4th level, the Justicar gains the ability to pass holy judgment on others once per day and place a *mark of justice* on persons so judged as the spell (but as a standard action). The ability functions

as if cast by a caster of a level equal to the Justicar's total character level.

Immunity to Illusions (Su): Beginning at 5th level, a Justicar is immune to all illusions. A Justicar notes the presence of illusions but recognizes them for what they are and disbelieves them immediately and automatically.

Sword of Courage (Su): Beginning at 6th level, a Justicar can invoke Muir's sword of courage once per day. Invoking this ability either enhances the Justicar's current sword or temporarily creates a supernatural magical bastard sword for the Justicar to use. The sword gains a +2 divine bonus to attack and damage rolls. The sword also becomes a *holy* weapon (see the "Magic Items" section in Chapter 15 of the *Pathfinder Roleplaying Game Core Rulebook*) for its duration. In addition, the sword radiates *remove fear* in a 30-foot radius for its duration (caster level equal to the Justicar's total character level). The ability lasts for 30 minutes. Sword of courage cannot be used in combination with either shield of truth or armor of honor until the Justicar gains the avatar ability.

Scourge of Evil (Su): At 6th level, a Justicar gains an additional +1 divine bonus to attack and damage rolls and doubles the normal critical threat range against all evil-aligned creatures (of all types). This ability stacks with the enemy of evil ability and the Improved Critical feat or *keen* weapon quality if the Justicar has these as well.

True Seeing (Su): Beginning at 7th level, a Justicar can use *true seeing* as the spell, once per day. The ability functions as if cast by a caster of a level equal to the Justicar's total character level.

Armor of Honor (Su): Beginning at 8th level, a Justicar can invoke Muir's armor of honor once per day. Invoking this ability either enhances the Justicar's current armor or temporarily creates a suit of magical chainmail around the Justicar. The armor gains a +2 divine bonus to AC. The armor also has the qualities of *moderate fortification, invulnerability,* and *spell resistance (15)* (see the "Magic Items" section in Chapter 15 of the *Pathfinder Roleplaying Game Core Rulebook*) for its duration. This ability lasts for 30 minutes. Armor of honor cannot be used in combination with either shield of truth or sword of courage until the Justicar gains the avatar ability.

Holy Word (Su): Beginning at 9th level, a Justicar can speak a *holy word* as the spell once per day. The ability functions as if cast by a caster of a level equal to the Justicar's total character level.

Avatar (Su): At 10th level, a Justicar can use shield of truth, sword of courage, and armor of honor at the same time up to once per week. When all three powers are invoked at the same time it seems as if a spectral figure of Muir herself overlaps the body of the Justicar and mimics his every movement. In combat against evil creatures the figure of Muir becomes even more apparent. In addition to allowing all three powers to operate in unison, when a Justicar becomes an Avatar of Muir he is treated as if under the effects of a *greater heroism* spell (caster level equal to the Justicar's total character level) for the duration of the ability. The avatar ability lasts only so long as all three abilities—shield of truth, sword of courage, and armor of honor—are in effect at the same time.

Demonbane (Su): At 10th level, a Justicar becomes an evil-killing machine. His critical threat range is doubled against evil undead and outsiders. This ability stacks with both the scourge of evil ability (see above) and the Improved Critical feat or *keen* weapon quality if the Justicar has these as well.

LEVEL	ATTACK BONUS	FORT SAVE	REF SAVE	WILL SAVE	SPECIAL	SPELLS
1	+1	+1	+0	+2	Resist Illusions, Zone of Truth, Enemy of Evil, Celestial Companion	+1 lvl of existing class
2	+2	+2	+0	+3	Discern Lies	+1 lvl of existing class
3	+3	+2	+1	+3	Shield of Truth	+1 lvl of existing class
4	+4	+3	+1	+4	Mark of Justice	+1 lvl of existing class
5	+5	+3	+1	+4	Immunity to Illusions	+1 lvl of existing class
6	+6	+4	+2	+5	Sword of Courage, Scourge of Evil	+1 lvl of existing class
7	+7	+4	+2	+5	True Seeing	+1 lvl of existing class
8	+8	+5	+2	+6	Armor of Honor	+1 lvl of existing class
9	+9	+5	+3	+6	Holy Word	+1 lvl of existing class
10	+10	+6	+3	+7	Avatar, Demon-bane	+1 lvl of existing class

The Gods: New Spells and Domains

Freya, Goddess of Love and Fertility

Alignment: Neutral Good
Domains: Animal, Good, Healing, War
Symbol: Blood-red upraised sword on a white background
Garb: White wool robes with an upraised sword and hand in red.
Favored Weapons: Longsword, longbow
Form of Worship and Holidays: Regular worship and fasting on the eve before known battle or before confirmation or promotion of the ranks of the faithful.
Typical Worshipers: Human females

Freya is a lesser goddess of love and fertility. Freya is also the leader of a great band of women warriors — known as Valkyries on some planes of existence. Freya represents fertility in all its forms. On this plane, Freya represents the cycle of death and rebirth. She is a goddess of the coming harvest, as well as of sexuality and procreation. Her beast is the falcon, though she is fond of the winter wolf and the hind. She appears most frequently to her worshipers as a beautiful human woman dressed in robes and a cloak of winter-wolf fur, though she occasionally appears as a hunter in leather armor with sword and bow or as a warrior in shining mail with a glowing sword. She can take the form of a falcon — or any other bird — at will, as well as that of a huge winter wolf.

Muir, Goddess of Virtue and Paladins

Alignment: Lawful Good
Domains: Law, Good, Protection, War
Symbol: Blood-red upraised sword on a white background
Garb: White wool robes with an upraised sword and hand in red.
Favored Weapon: Longsword or bastard sword
Form of Worship and Holidays: Regular worship and fasting on the eve before known battle or before confirmation or promotion of the ranks of the faithful.
Typical Worshippers: Humans and paladins

Muir is the sister of Thyr. While he represents law and peace, she represents the martial valor necessary to make that peace a reality. As such, she is the goddess of paladins. She is often depicted as a dark-tressed maiden warrior in shining mail with an upraised (often bloodstained) sword. She is noble and single-minded of purpose. The tenets of her worship include honor, truth, and courage. A great order of paladins known as the Justicars are sworn to her service. Muir expects self-sacrifice, humility, and charity as well as unswerving loyalty. Her standards are extreme and she quickly turns her back on any who fail to live up to them. Those who maintain her standards, however, may become Justicars, an order of paladins imbued with even greater holiness. Her symbol is a blood-red uplifted sword on a white background, symbolizing her endless fight against evil. Her worshipers must be lawful good. The falcon is her sacred animal. She is the tireless foe of all evil creatures and undead, demons, and devils in particular are her sworn enemy.

Narrah, the Lady of the Moon

Alignment: Neutral
Domains: Darkness, Protection, Travel
Symbol: An upturned crescent moon
Garb: Dark robes, midnight blue cloaks
Favored Weapon: Sickle
Form of Worship and Holidays: Regular worship and fasting on the full moon. Eclipses and other astrological events are sacred.
Typical Worshippers: Humans, druids, lycanthropes, oracles

A lesser-known goddess, Narrah is the Lady of the Moon, and is worshipped by star-gazers, lycanthropes, and lovers. She is neither good nor evil, light nor dark. She represents neutrality is its most natural form. She is the moonlight in the dark, she is the push and pull of the tides, and she is the navigation point when one is lost. Actively worshipped by druids, she imparts the secrets of the universe under the cover of night.

Orcus, Demon

Demon-Lord of the Undead
Alignment: Chaotic Evil
Domains: Chaos, Evil, Death, Destruction
Symbol: Wand of Orcus
Garb: Black cowl and robe ensemble
Favored Weapons: Ornamental Heavy Mace (spiked or skull-tipped)
Form of Worship and Holidays: Day of the Dead (Late Fall), Nights of blood red and horned moons. Worship usually involves grave robbery and the animation and conscription of the newly dead to the forces of evil.
Typical Worshippers: Monsters, Undead and Evil Humanoids

Though a demon prince, Orcus is worshipped as a deity. He is the lord of all the undead and resides in the Abyss in his Palace of Bones. Evil and wonton destruction are his only goals. He is most often depicted as a bloated, board-headed, bat-winged monstrosity with cloven-hoofed goat legs. He wields a skull-tipped wand that reported slays any living thing it touches.

St. Abysthor, the Warden

Alignment: Lawful Good
Domains: Law, Good, Protection
Symbol: White shield on a black background
Garb: White wool robes trimmed with black.
Favored Weapon: Heavy Mace
Form of Worship and Holidays: Prayers for protection and guidance before duties.
Typical Worshippers: Paladins and sentries

Abysthor is a new member of the divinity, having just recently ascended with the help of some stalwart adventurers. Rewarded for years of faithful service, and his steadfast guardianship of the Black Monolith from the forces of evil marshaling against him, Thyr, the God of Law and Justice, elevated him to sainthood. Now an even more tireless foe of Evil, St. Abysthor is the patron of those who guard or seek to close portals to the Lower Planes.

St. Abysthor has a particular enmity for worshippers of Orcus and Tsathogga, as he kept those forces at bay for many years, blocking their access to a particularly weak gate to the Abyss. Had St. Abysthor failed in his guardianship, the entire world may well have been overrun by demonic forces.

St. Abysthor is currently only active in the Stoneheart Valley region, and may render some form of assistance to worshippers of Thyr or Muir, should they beseech him for aid, especially against the forces of Orcus or Tsathogga.

168

Thyr, God of Law and Justice

Alignment: Lawful Good
Domains: Good, Healing, Law, Knowledge, Protection
Symbol: Silver cross on a white field
Garb: White robes trimmed with silver, purple or gold — the colors of kingship
Favored Weapons: Light or Heavy Mace
Form of Worship and Holidays: Last day of every month, on the last holy day of every year is set-aside for non-royalty to have their grievances heard.
Typical Worshippers: Humans, Royalty

Thyr is the god of wise and just rule. He is normally depicted as a wizened king seated on a great throne holding a rod of kingship in one hand and a chalice of peace in the other. His principles are justice, order and peace. He represents proper and traditional rule and as such was once worshiped (at least in name) by all human royalty. He is the embodiment of the enlightened human caste system where each person has a fairly determined role in a lawful society intended to create the greatest good for the greatest number. His symbol is a silver cross on a white field, symbolizing the upturned cross-haft of his sister's sword, which he thrust into the earth to end the gods' war. Upon seeing the blood of so many gods shed, Thyr foreswore the use of swords and his priests, for this reason, may not use bladed weapons. Many favor reinforced rods, similar to light maces, modeled after Thyr's own rod of kingship. The noble eagle and lion are his sacred creatures.

Tsathogga, Demon Frog God

Alignment: Chaotic Evil
Domains: Chaos, Destruction, Evil, Water
Symbol: Likeness of the Frog God, carved in soapstone
Garb: Green and violet robes, if any
Favored Weapon: Any that slash, cut, and are wickedly curved, as well as, ropes or nets
Form of Worship and Holidays: Too gruesome and perverse to describe even by Our standards!
Typical Worshippers: Aberrations, tsathar, sentient frogs, evil water monsters, The Violet Brotherhood

This foul frog-demon cares less about the machinations of men and power than he does about obliterating light and life with slow, oozing sickness and decay. He is the vicious dark evil bubbling up from beneath the surface, the foul corruption at the heart of the earth. Making his home on the plane of Tarterus at the mouth of the vast swamp of filth deposited by the River Styx as it flows out of the Abyss, Tsathogga's main form is a colossally bloated humanoid frog with spindly, elongated limbs and fingers. His corpulent body exudes all manner of foul humors and fluids that leak into the vile swamp in which he lies. He has positioned himself so that all of the slime and filth from the River Styx feeds into his gaping, toothy maw. He never moves and rarely speaks other than to emit an unintelligible shrieking. Tsathogga commands a host of evil creatures — notably evil aberrations and his own vile frog race, the tsathar. Thousands of fawning tsathar servants continuously bathe his body in fetid slime from the evil swamp, awaiting the divine bliss of being randomly devoured by him. His hatred of light and lack of human worshippers (though there are a few notable exceptions) mean that he is little known to surface races. He has had few organized centers of worship and no standardized holy symbol — each worshipper choosing its own way to best depict his deific vileness. Occasionally, tsathar priests of Tsathogga on Tarterus sculpt a small likeness of him out of foul chunks of solid waste from the Styx that harden into a vile green substance similar to soapstone when taken from that plane. Such items are prized as holy relics.

New Cleric Domain
Vermin Domain

Granted Powers: At 1st level, you gain a +4 divine bonus to saves against poison and can cast *detect poison* 2/day.

Vermin Domain Spells: 1st—*spider climb*; 2nd—*summon swarm*; 3rd—*poison*; 4th—*giant vermin*; 5th—*insect plague*; 6th—*web*; 7th—*creeping doom*; 8th—*summon monster VIII* (monstrous abyssal vermin or demon only); 9th—*summon monster IX* (monstrous abyssal vermin or demon only)

New Spells
Chant

School conjuration (creation); **Level:** cleric 2, paladin 2
Components V, S, DF
Casting Time 1 standard action
Range 40 ft.
Area all allies and foes within a 40-ft. burst centered on you
Duration concentration; maximum 5 min./level (see below)
Saving Throw none; **Spell Resistance** no

As long as you chant, you bring special favor upon your allies and bring disfavor to your enemies. You and your allies gain a +1 luck bonus on attack rolls, weapon damage rolls, saves, and skill checks while your foes take a –1 penalty on such rolls.

You must chant in a clear voice. Any interruption in your chanting, such as a failed concentration check, a *silence* spell or speaking or casting another spell, ends this spell. As an exception to the general rule, the effects of this spell stack with those of a *prayer* spell if cast by a cleric of your alignment and who worships the same deity as you.

New Items

Potion of foul water

This non-magical concoction renders 1,000 cubic feet of water undrinkable and immediately desecrates a font of holy water. **Price** 60 gp Originally appeared in ***Rappan Athuk***.

New Magic Items

Weapon Special Ability: Striking

Price +2 bonus
Aura moderate transmutation; **CL** 7th; **Weight** —

DESCRIPTION
This weapon's enhancement bonus to damage may be increased by +3, 2/day, and by +6, 1/day. This effect lasts for one attack, and for that attack the weapon acts as a weapon of its raised enhancement. This ability can only be added to bludgeoning weapons.

CONSTRUCTION
Requirements Craft Magic Arms and Armor, *greater magic weapon*; **Cost** +2 bonus.

Ring of Spectral Hand

Aura moderate necromancy; **CL** 7th
Slot ring; **Price** 30,000 gp; **Weight** —

DESCRIPTION
This ring is charged with the spell *spectral hand* and allows the user to cast that spell. The ring may be activated as a swift action, allowing a spell to be cast the same round the ring is activated. All other effects are as per the spell, except that the *hand* may also render any other touch-delivered effects available to the wearer, including an evil priest's death touch special ability. The ring normally has up to 30 charges. When expended the ring is worthless. It cannot be recharged.

CONSTRUCTION
Requirements Forge Ring, *spectral hand*; **Cost** 15,000 gp

Minor Artifacts

The Axe of Blood
Aura strong necromancy; **CL** 20th
Slot none; **Weight** 6 lb.

DESCRIPTION
Wielded until recently by the famous dwarf fighter Rhezenuduk, legend holds that the *axe of blood* was lost on a quest to another plane of existence. The axe itself is rather nondescript, made of dull iron. Only the large, strange rune carved into the side of the double-bladed head gives any immediate indication that the axe may be more than it seems. The rune is a *rune of lesser life stealing*, carved on it long ago by a sect of evil sorcerers. This is, in fact, the only remaining copy of that particular rune, thus making the axe a valuable

item for that reason alone. Further inspection reveals another strange characteristic: the entire length of the axe's long haft of dark wood is wrapped in a thick leather thong that has been stained black from years of being soaked in blood and is sticky to the touch. When held, the axe feels strangely heavy but well balanced, and it possesses a keenly sharp blade.

At first blush, the axe appears to be no more than a *keen battleaxe*. Until activated, the axe is just a *keen battleaxe*. The wielder must consult *legend lore* or some other similar source of information to learn the ritual required to feed the axe. Despite the gruesome ritual required to power the axe, the weapon is not evil but is instead neutral. Bound inside it is a rather savage earth spirit.

The axe draws power from its wielder in order to become a mighty magic weapon. Each day, the wielder of the axe can choose to "feed" the axe, sacrificing some of his blood in a strange ritual. This ritual takes 30 minutes and must be done at dawn.

Using the axe, the wielder opens a wound on his person (dealing 1d6 points of damage) and feeds the axe with his own blood. In this ritual, the wielder sacrifices Constitution to the axe. For each point of Constitution sacrificed, the wielder gains a +1 bonus on attack rolls and weapon damage rolls (maximum of +5 on each) with the axe. Constitution points sacrificed to the axe cannot be healed magically, but heal at the rate of 1 point per day. Similarly, the damage caused by the opening of the wound may not be healed by any means until the sacrificed Constitution is regained. Note that the axe retains its *keen* quality when powered.

If the axe is powered to an amount less than the full +5 during the morning ritual and the wielder subsequently wishes that day to power the axe further, he may again wound himself (a full-round action dealing 1d6 points of damage) to sacrifice additional Constitution. In this instance where such a "second feeding" is done, the wielder must sacrifice 2 points of Constitution per additional +1 on attack rolls and weapon damage rolls (up to the same maximum of +5).

There is a chance that the Constitution sacrificed to the axe is lost permanently. If the wielder always skips a day in between powering the axe and always powers the axe with the morning ritual, there is no chance of permanent loss. If, however, the axe is fed on consecutive days or powered in a second feeding, there is a 1% chance plus a 1% cumulative chance per consecutive day the axe is powered that Constitution sacrificed to the axe on that day is actually permanent ability drain. This check must be made for each point of Constitution sacrificed to the axe that day.

If reduced to Con 0 as a result of feeding the axe, the wielder becomes a bleeding horror (see **The Tome of Horrors Complete** 703 for more details).

Note: An undead creature can use its Charisma ability score to power the axe. Charisma damage heals at the rate of 1 point per day. An undead that reduces its Cha to 0 is destroyed.

DESTRUCTION
If a wielder of the axe with the lawful or chaotic subtype and 20 or more Hit Dice willingly uses it to reduce himself to Constitution 0, the axe is destroyed and the slain wielder does not rise as a bleeding horror.
Reprinted from **The Tome of Horrors Complete**

Cloak of the Demon
Aura strong conjuration; **CL** 20th
Slot shoulders; **Weight** 2 lb.

This cloak appears as a heavy cloak of black leather or some other thick fabric. It possesses great magical powers.

When unfolded fully and spread wide, which may be done up to two times per day, the cloak is revealed to be a pair of demon wings. Unfolding the wings in this fashion grants the wearer the innate abilities of a vrock demon.

Fly (speed 50 ft. per round, average maneuverability)

Spell-like Abilities (CL 12th)

1/day—*greater teleport, heroism, mirror image, telekinesis,* summon (Level 3, vrock 35%)

Stunning screech as a vrock (see the *Pathfinder Roleplaying Game Bestiary* "Vrock:)

The wearer counts as a vrock for purposes of the *dance of ruin,* but the wearer does not gain the ability to release spores.

DR 10/good

SR 20

Immune electricity and poison

Resist acid 10, cold 10, and fire 10

Telepathy (Sp) The ability to communicate telepathically with any creature within 100 feet that has language. These abilities last for 15 minutes. It is an inanely evil act to don the *cloak of demons,* and its powers only function for those of Evil alignment.

DESTRUCTION

If the cloak is soaked in a holy water bath for 24 hours, it disintegrates. The holy water is spoiled, and becomes unholy water that cannot be re-consecrated.

The Shard of Hel

Aura strong abjuration (evil); **CL** 20th

Slot none; **Weight** 1 lb.

DESCRIPTION

Appearing as a large icicle or sliver of quartz, the *Shard of Hel* is a holy artifact to those who follow the fell goddess. The *shard* confers complete immunity to all diseases and an SR of 15 on anyone who carries it. It also grants the bearer +1 caster level for purposes of spell effects for all evil spells if the bearer is a follower of Hel (this is in addition to the power granted under the Evil domain).

The *shard* has one drawback: any priests of Hel who find this item in the possession of a non-priest of Hel will do everything in their power to slay and sacrifice the bearer as a heretic. If the *shard* is brought within 100 feet of a cleric of Hel of 5th level or higher, that priest can make a DC 8 Wisdom check to feel the presence of the *shard.* The *shard* also slowly turns the bearer neutral evil. Each full moon, the bearer must make a DC 20 Will save or move one step closer to neutral evil — first moving along the good/evil axis to evil and then along the law/chaos axis, if necessary.

DESTRUCTION

If the *shard* can be held in a ray of sunshine (or *daylight*) by a priest of Freya of 12th level or higher for 24 hours, the shard melts away into nothingness.

Valkyria

Aura strong abjuration (good); **CL** 20th

Slot none; **Weight** 15 lbs.

DESCRIPTION

This *+1 longsword* appears to be little more than a ceremonial sword or possibly a druidic weapon of some type. Its handle of horn makes it appear unsuitable for true combat, and it is encased in a rustic, unadorned reinforced leather scabbard. However, once the blade is drawn, it is clear that this sword is of exquisite workmanship. The length of the blade is traced with finely etched runes of an unknown design. There is an ethereal quality to the sword that those looking at it cannot comprehend. Once gripped, the horn handle fits the wielder's hand better than any weapon ever held, and the blade glows with a warm, low light in the presence of any priestess of Freya or in any area holy to Freya. The horn handle was crafted from a stag sacred to the goddess and sacrificed to her.

This sword was, in fact, crafted on another plane and used at one time by one of Freya's Valkyries. When taken to any of the outer planes, the sword becomes a *+3 longsword.* Any good-aligned character holding the weapon sees a vision of the goddess Freya, differing in intensity based on her Wisdom and Charisma scores. If the wielder's Wisdom and Charisma scores are 14 or above, the vision of the goddess is incredibly strong, and the goddess greets the wielder and invites her to worship her as one of her clerics. If the wielder is good-aligned but does not have sufficient scores, she simply feels the goddess' presence. If the wielder does in fact become a priestess of Freya, the sword grants additional power. Once per week, the wielder can contact the Valkyrie who was the previous owner of this sword. This contact is treated as a *commune* spell, but allows the wielder to ask only one question.

DESTRUCTION

If the sword is placed upon an unholy alter, and a *desecrate* spell is cast directly on it, it loses all magical powers.

New Monsters

Choker, Psionic

This hunched-over wretch has long, pliable arms like tentacles capped with five wide, spiny claws.

CHOKER, PSIONIC   **CR 3**
XP 800
CE Small aberration (*Pathfinder Roleplaying Game Bestiary* "Choker")
Init +6; **Senses** darkvision 60 ft.; **Perception** +1

AC 17, touch 13, flat-footed 15 (+2 Dex, +4 natural, +1 size)
hp 16 (3d8+3)
Fort +2; **Ref** +3; **Will** +4

Speed 20 ft., climb 10 ft.
Melee 2 tentacles +6 (1d4+3 plus grab)
Space 5 ft.; **Reach** 10 ft.
Special Attacks constrict (1d4+3), grab (Large), psionic assault, strangle

Str 16, **Dex** 14, **Con** 13, **Int** 4, **Wis** 13, **Cha** 14
Base Atk +2; **CMB** +4 (+8 to grapple); **CMD** 16
Feats Improved Initiative, Skill Focus (Stealth)
Skills Climb +16, Stealth +13
Languages Undercommon
SQ quickness

Environment any underground
Organization solitary, pair, or clutch (3–8)
Treasure standard

Quickness (Su) A choker is supernaturally quick. It can take an extra move action during its turn each round.
Strangle (Ex) Chokers have an unerring talent for seizing their victims by the neck. A creature that is grappled by a choker cannot speak or cast spells with verbal components.
Psionic Assault (Su) At will as a standard action, a psionic choker can unleash a stunning blast in a 15 ft. cone. Any creature within the area of effect must succeed at a DC 15 Will save or be stunned for 1d3 rounds. An opponent that succeeds on the saving throw is immune to that same creature's psionic assault for 24 hours. Psionic chokers are immune to this ability.

CHOKER, ADVANCED PSIONIC   **CR 4**
XP 1,200
CE Small aberration (*Pathfinder Roleplaying Game Bestiary* "Choker")
Init +8; **Senses** darkvision 60 ft.; **Perception** +3

AC 21, touch 15, flat-footed 17 (+4 Dex, +6 natural, +1 size)
hp 22 (3d8+9)
Fort +4; **Ref** +5; **Will** +6

Speed 20 ft., climb 10 ft.
Melee 2 tentacles +8 (1d4+5 plus grab)
Space 5 ft.; **Reach** 10 ft.
Special Attacks constrict (1d4+5), grab (Large), psionic assault, strangle

Str 20, **Dex** 18, **Con** 17, **Int** 8, **Wis** 17, **Cha** 18
Base Atk +2; **CMB** +6 (+10 to grapple); **CMD** 20
Feats Improved Initiative, Skill Focus (Stealth)

Skills Acrobatics +10, Climb +17, Stealth +15
Languages Undercommon
SQ quickness

Environment any underground
Organization solitary, pair, or clutch (3–8)
Treasure standard

Quickness (Su) A choker is supernaturally quick. It can take an extra move action during its turn each round.
Strangle (Ex) Chokers have an unerring talent for seizing their victims by the neck. A creature that is grappled by a choker cannot speak or cast spells with verbal components.
Psionic Assault (Su) At will as a standard action, a psionic choker can unleash a stunning blast in a 15 ft. cone. Any creature within the area of effect must succeed at a DC 15 Will save or be stunned for 1d3 rounds. An opponent that succeeds on the saving throw is immune to that same creature's psionic assault for 24 hours. Psionic chokers are immune to this ability.

CHOKER, YOUNG PSIONIC   **CR 1**
XP 400
CE Tiny aberration (*Pathfinder Roleplaying Game Bestiary* "Choker")
Init +5; **Senses** darkvision 60 ft.; **Perception** +1

AC 18, touch 17, flat-footed 13 (+5 Dex, +1 natural, +2 size)
hp 3 (1d8–1)
Fort –1; **Ref** +5; **Will** +2

Speed 20 ft., climb 10 ft.
Melee 2 tentacles +1 (1d3–1 plus grab)
Space 2 1/2 ft.; **Reach** 5 ft.
Special Attacks constrict (1d3–1), grab (Medium), psionic assault (5 ft., DC 11), strangle

Str 8, **Dex** 20, **Con** 9, **Int** 4, **Wis** 10, **Cha** 12
Base Atk +0; **CMB** +3 (+7 to grapple); **CMD** 12
Feats Skill Focus (Stealth)
Skills Climb +11, Stealth +16
Languages Undercommon
SQ quickness

Environment any underground
Organization solitary, pair, or clutch (3–8)
Treasure standard

Psionic Assault (Su) A young psionic choker's psionic attack fills only one 5 ft. square.

A psionic choker is a variant choker (see the *Pathfinder Roleplaying Game Bestiary* "Choker") that has developed the ability to emit a punishing blast of psionic energy. Aside from this unusual ability, they are like normal chokers in their habits, environment, and social structure.

Font Skeleton

This skeleton is armed with a dinged longsword and a battered wooden shield. It is slick with fresh blood, and leaves bloody footprints as it shambles along.

FONT SKELETON   **CR 1**
XP 400
NE Medium undead
Init +5; **Senses** darkvision 60 ft.; **Perception** +0

AC 15, touch 11, flat-footed 14 (+1 Dex, +3 natural, +1 shield)

hp 15 (2d8+2)
Fort +1; Ref +1; Will +3
Defensive Abilities channel resistance +4; DR 5/bludgeoning;
Immune cold, undead traits

Speed 30 ft.
Melee longsword +2 (1d8+1) or 2 claws +2 (1d4+1)

Str 12, Dex 12, Con —, Int —, Wis 10, Cha 12
Base Atk +1; CMB +2; CMD 13
Feats Improved Initiative[B]
Combat Gear longsword, light wooden shield
SQ increased hp

Increased hp (Sp) All font skeletons created in the Font of Bones receive the effects of an *desecrate* spell, which grants them +2 hp per level.

Font skeletons are created by the Font of Bones, a corrupted artifact of great power, in the burial halls of Thyr and Muir. These skeletons are covered in red stains from the blood within the font from which they are spawned. Their eyes glow with a fiendish light. They normally wield longswords and use shields, as these are the weapons of the goddess of paladins and these skeletons exist as mockeries of the followers of that deity.

Frog, Advanced Giant Killer

A frog, roughly the size of a hound, advances with murderous intent in is slimy eyeballs.

FROG, ADVANCED GIANT KILLER CR 3
XP 800
N Medium animal (*The Tome of Horrors Complete* 671)
Init +2; Senses low-light vision, scent; Perception +5

AC 18, touch 11, flat-footed 17 (+1 Dex, +7 natural)
hp 10 (1d8+6)
Fort +8; Ref +4; Will +0

Speed 10 ft., swim 30 ft.
Melee 2 claws +5 (1d6+5 plus grab), bite +5 (1d6+5)
Special Attacks rake (2 claws +5, 1d6+5)

Str 20, Dex 15, Con 22, Int 2, Wis 13, Cha 10
Base Atk +0; CMB +5 (+9 to grapple); CMD 17 (21 vs. trip)
Feats Improved Natural Attack (claw)
Skills Acrobatics +6 (+10 jumping) , Perception +5 , Stealth +6 , Swim +13 ; Racial Modifiers +4 Acrobatics (+8 jumping), +4 Stealth

Environment temperate or warm land, aquatic, and underground
Organization pack (2–5), cluster (4–7), or swarm (3–18)
Treasure none

Killer frogs are similar to their dire cousins, except that they stand partially erect and use their front claws as well as their bite. Killer frogs are created by an evil mutation of dire frogs through a practice thought to be known only to the worshipers of Tsathogga. Killer frogs, being more humanoid in appearance, do not have adhesive tongues.

Ghast

A feral, degenerate humanoid with rough and dirty skin, as though it just crawled form a grave. A horrible stench emanates all around it.

GHAST (ADVANCED GHOUL) CR 2
XP 600
CE Medium undead (*Pathfinder Roleplaying Game Bestiary* "Ghoul")
Init +4; Senses darkvision 60 ft.; Perception +7
Aura stench (10-foot radius, Fort DC 15 negates, sickened for 1d6+4 minutes)

AC 18, touch 14, flat-footed 14 (+4 Dex, +4 natural)
hp 17 (2d8+8)
Fort +4; Ref +4; Will +7
Defensive Abilities channel resistance +2; Immune undead traits

Speed 30 ft.
Melee bite +5 (1d6+3) and 2 claws +5 (1d6+3 plus paralysis)
Special Attacks paralysis (1d4+1 rounds, DC 15, elves are *not* immune to this effect)

Str 17, Dex 19, Con —, Int 17, Wis 18, Cha 18
Base Atk +1; CMB +4; CMD 18
Feats Weapon Finesse
Skills Acrobatics +6, Climb +8, Intimidate +9, Perception +9, Sense Motive +9, Stealth +9, Swim +5
Languages Common

Disease (Su) Ghoul Fever: Bite—injury; *save* Fort DC 15 ; *onset* 1 day; *frequency* 1/day; *effect* 1d3 Con and 1d3 Dex damage; *cure* 2 consecutive saves. The save DC is Charisma-based. A humanoid who dies of ghoul fever rises as a ghoul at the next midnight. A humanoid who becomes a ghoul in this way retains none of the abilities it possessed in life. It is not under the control of any other ghouls, but it hungers for the flesh of the living and behaves like a normal ghoul in all respects. A humanoid of 4 Hit Dice or more rises as a ghast.

Gynosphinx, Celestial

The head and torso of a beautiful human woman rests upon the body of a great luminous cat, with golden eagle wings.

GYNOSPHINX, CELESTIAL CR 9
XP 6,400
LG Large magical beast (*Pathfinder Roleplaying Game Bestiary* "Gynosphinx")
Init +5; Senses darkvision 60 ft., low-light vision; Perception +21

AC 21, touch 10, flat-footed 20 (+1 Dex, +11 natural, −1 size)
hp 102 (12d10+36)
Fort +11; Ref +9; Will +10
DR 10/evil; Resist acid 15, cold 15, electricity 15; SR 14

Speed 40 ft., fly 60 ft. (poor)
Melee 2 claws +17 (2d6+6/19–20)
Space 10 ft.; Reach 5 ft.
Special Attacks pounce, rake (2 claws +17, 2d6+6), smite evil 1/day (+4 to attack rolls and +12 damage bonus against evil foes; smite persists until target is dead or the sphinx rests)
Spell-Like Abilities (CL 12th)
Constant—*comprehend languages, detect magic, read*

magic, see invisibility
3/day—*clairaudience/clairvoyance*
1/day—*dispel magic, locate object, remove curse, legend lore*
1/week—*symbol of death* (DC 22); symbol lasts for 1 week maximum

---

Str 22, **Dex** 13, **Con** 16, **Int** 18, **Wis** 19, **Cha** 19
Base Atk +12; **CMB** +19; **CMD** 30 (34 vs. trip)
Feats Alertness, Combat Casting, Hover, Improved Critical (claw), Improved Initiative, Iron Will
Skills Bluff +14, Diplomacy +14, Fly +7, Intimidate +14, Knowledge (history) +6, Knowledge (religion) +6, Perception +21, Sense Motive +19, Spellcraft +12
Languages Common, Draconic, Sphinx

Xorn, Elder

This squat beast is as wide as it is tall. Strangely symmetrical, it has three arms, three legs, three eyes, and one huge mouth.

XORN, ELDER (ADVANCED GIANT)   CR 11
XP 12,800
N Large outsider (earth, extraplanar) (*Pathfinder Roleplaying Games Bestiary* "Xorn")
Init +1; **Senses** all-around vision, darkvision 60 ft., tremorsense 60 ft.; **Perception** +19

AC 25, touch 14, flat-footed 24 (+1 Dex, +15 natural, −1 size)
hp 145 (10d10+80 plus 10)
Fort +11; **Ref** +8; **Will** +9
DR 5/bludgeoning; **Immune** cold, fire, flanking; **Resist** electricity 10

Speed 20 ft., burrow 20 ft.; earth glide
Melee bite +18 (5d6+9), 3 claws +18 (1d6+3)
Space 10 ft.; **Reach** 10 ft.

Str 29, **Dex** 12, **Con** 26, **Int** 14, **Wis** 15, **Cha** 14
Base Atk +10; **CMB** +20; **CMD** 31 (33 vs. trip)
Feats Awesome Blow, Cleave, Improved Bull Rush, Power Attack, Toughness
Skills Appraise +15, Intimidate +15, Knowledge (dungeoneering) +15, Knowledge (planes) +15, Perception +19, Sense Motive +15, Stealth +10, Survival +15; **Racial Modifiers** +4 Perception
Languages Common, Terran

All-Around Vision (Ex) A xorn sees in all directions at the same time, giving it a +4 racial bonus on Perception checks. A xorn cannot be flanked.
Earth Glide (Ex) A xorn can glide through any sort of natural earth or stone as easily as a fish swims through water. Its burrowing leaves no sign of its passage nor hint at its presence to creatures that don't possess tremorsense. A *move earth* spell cast on an area containing a xorn moves the xorn back 30 feet, stunning the creature for 1 round unless it succeeds on a DC 15 Fortitude save.

Elder xorns are wise members of their species who often act as gurus and advisors to lesser xorns. They are also known to serve powerful creatures native to the Plane of Earth.

Pre-Generated Characters

CORIAN CR 1/2
XP 200
Male human sorcerer 1
CG Medium humanoid (human)
Init +1; **Perception** +1

AC 13, touch 11, flat-footed 12 (+2 armor, +1 Dex)
hp 11 (1d6+1 plus 4)
Fort +1; **Ref** +1; **Will** +3

Speed 20 ft.
Melee dagger +0 (1d4/19–20) or morningstar +0 (1d8)
Ranged light crossbow +1 (1d8/19–20)
Spells Known (CL 1st; melee touch +0, ranged touch +1):
1st (4/day)—*mage armor, magic missile*
0 (at will)—*detect magic, disrupt undead, light, read magic*
Bloodline Arcane

Str 10, **Dex** 13, **Con** 13, **Int** 15, **Wis** 13, **Cha** 17
Base Atk +0; **CMB** +0; **CMD** 11
Feats Armor Proficiency (light), Eschew Materials[B], Toughness[B]
Skills Craft (alchemy) +6, Knowledge (arcana) +6, Sense Motive +2, Spellcraft +6, Use Magic Device +7
Languages Common, Draconic, Elven
SQ arcane bond (light crossbow), metamagic adept
Gear leather armor, light crossbow, 20 bolts, dagger, morningstar, backpack, bedroll, map case, flint and steel, ink (1 oz. vial, black), inkpen, 5 sheets of parchment, 8 days rations, small sack, 5 torches

Background: You have lived all your life with your uncle, a mage in the city of Reme. Your parents died when you were a very young child and your uncle has never bothered to hide the insinuation that you were somehow responsible for the fire that took your mother's and father's lives. Your uncle, seeing little other use for you, put you to work as an apprentice. Your innate knack for magic led your uncle to begin teaching you the arcane principles of wizardry. As a student, however, you were an utter failure. You could never seem to grasp the use of all the rote memorization forced on you by your uncle. Why did a mage need to learn such things, you wondered, when all one needed to do was imagine the desired effect and it happened? Despite your stubbornness, you learned the basics of spellcraft—though your instincts still rebelled against the formalism of your uncle's methods.

Finally, in a fit of anger over your lack of interest in your studies, your uncle released you from your apprenticeship. This suited you just fine, for you recently discovered a strange amulet that you were interested in learning more about…

GALDAR CR 1/2
XP 200
Male human cleric of Vanitthu 1
LG Medium humanoid (human)
Init +6; **Perception** +3
Aura good

AC 19, touch 12, flat-footed 17 (+5 armor, +2 Dex, +2 shield)
hp 11 (1d8+2 plus 1)
Fort +5; **Ref** +3; **Will** +6

Speed 20 ft.

Melee morningstar +3 (1d8+3)
Ranged heavy crossbow +2 (1d10/19–20)
Special Attacks channel positive energy 4/day (DC 11, 1d6), spontaneous casting (cure spells)
Spell-Like Abilities (CL 1st):
6/day—*battle rage* (+1 damage), *resistant touch*
Spells Prepared (CL 1st; melee touch +3, ranged touch +2):
1st—*bless, magic weapon*[D], *protection from evil*
0 (at will)—*guidance, light, resistance*
D Domain spell; **Domains** Protection, War

Str 16, **Dex** 14, **Con** 14, **Int** 12, **Wis** 16, **Cha** 12
Base Atk +0; **CMB** +3; **CMD** 15
Feats Improved Initiative[B], Turn Undead (DC 11)
Skills Diplomacy +5, Heal +7, Knowledge (religion) +5, Spellcraft +5
Languages Celestial, Common
Gear scale mail, heavy wooden shield, heavy crossbow, 20 bolts, morningstar, backpack, flint and steel, hooded lantern, 5 pints of oil, sack, holy symbol of Vanitthu, spell component pouch, 5 days rations, waterskin.

Channel Positive Energy (Su) A good cleric can channel positive energy to heal the living and injure the undead; an evil cleric can channel negative energy to injure the living and heal the undead.
Spontaneous Casting The cleric can convert stored spells into cure or inflict spells.
Turn Undead Your channel energy can make undead flee.

Background: You are a cleric of Vanitthu, the god of the steadfast guard. Following divine law is your all-encompassing mission in life, regardless of whether the result is for good or evil. It is enough that the law of your deity commands an action. While an acolyte at the temple of Vanitthu in Reme, you received a divine vision instructing you to seek out a man named Corian who you were instructed had an amulet in his possession. You were commanded by your god to follow that amulet wherever it might lead. You have found Corian at an inn called the Starving Stirge and you have agreed to travel with him — so long as he retains possession of the amulet.

BANNOR CR 1/2
XP 200
Male human paladin of Muir 1
LG Medium humanoid (human)
Init +2; **Perception** +3
Aura good

AC 19, touch 12, flat-footed 17 (+5 armor, +2 Dex, +2 shield)
hp 13 (1d10+2 plus 1)
Fort +4; **Ref** +2; **Will** +4

Speed 20 ft.
Melee longsword +4 (1d8+3/19–20) or heavy mace +4 (1d8+3)
Special Attacks smite evil 1/day (+3 attack and AC/ +1 damage)
Spell-Like Abilities (CL 1st):
At will—*detect evil*

Str 17, **Dex** 14, **Con** 14, **Int** 12, **Wis** 14, **Cha** 16

Base Atk +1; **CMB** +4; **CMD** 16
Feats Combat Reflexes^B, Power Attack
Skills Diplomacy +7, Heal +6, Knowledge (religion) +5, Perception +3
Languages Celestial, Common
SQ code of conduct
Combat Gear scale mail, heavy steel shield, longsword, heavy mace, backpack, bedroll, flint and steel, wooden holy symbol of Muir, 50 ft. rope, sack, 5 torches, 5 days rations, waterskin

---

Aura of Good (Ex) The paladin has an Aura of Good with power equal to her class level.

Background: As a young child, you were abandoned at a monastery of Mitra. Your physical gifts led you to serve as a squire to the holy order of knights. However, almost one year ago, while sweeping the stables, you were struck by an overpowering vision of Muir, a long-forgotten Goddess of Valor. A lesser deity, worship of Muir has all but died out. Her temples are few and most are in ruin or long abandoned by all but a handful of dedicated followers. The revelation of your vision was met with scorn by the brother knights. "Why would Muir appear at a monastery of Mitra to a stable boy," they asked. Yet in your heart you knew the truth of your vision. You asked for and were granted permission to leave the order. The brother knights gave you your armor and your trusty longsword. Though they advised that it would be better to stay in the service of Mitra, you set out alone to do the will of Muir. Your travels brought you to Reme. There, you stopped for supplies and came across Corian's notice at the Starving Stirge. You agreed to follow Corian's path, as it leads towards Fairhill and Bard's Gate where it is said there is still a temple of Muir.

PHELPS   CR 1/2
XP 200
Male human rogue 1
CN Medium humanoid (human)
Init +3; **Perception** +7

AC 16, touch 14, flat-footed 12 (+2 armor, +3 Dex, +1 dodge)
hp 10 (1d8+2)
Fort +2; **Ref** +5; **Will** +3

Speed 20 ft.
Melee rapier +3 (1d6/18–20)
Ranged sling +3 (1d4)
Special Attacks sneak attack +1d6

Str 11, **Dex** 16, **Con** 14, **Int** 14, **Wis** 16, **Cha** 12
Base Atk +0; **CMB** +0; **CMD** 14
Feats Dodge^B, Weapon Finesse
Skills Acrobatics +7, Climb +4, Disable Device +8, Disguise +5, Escape Artist +7, Knowledge (local) +6, Linguistics +6, Perception +7 (+8 locate traps), Sense Motive +7, Sleight of Hand +7, Stealth +7, Use Magic Device +5
Languages Common, Draconic, Elven, Undercommon
SQ trapfinding +1
Gear leather armor, rapier, sling, 5 sling bullets, backpack, flint and steel, grappling hook, hammer, 6 pitons, 50 ft. silk rope, sack, thieves' tools, 3 days rations, waterskin, 36 gp

---

Trapfinding +1 to find and disable traps.

Background: Slender and nimble, you are a jack-of-all-trades. You were born a street urchin and during your youth learned to live through hard experience. Desiring to escape your gutter life, you indentured yourself to a rich merchant where you learned the customs that accompany wealth. You now move comfortably in either world—the alleyway or the noble's court. Certain "unfortunate situations" which you are reluctant to

discuss in detail have made you desperate to leave Reme. When you read Corian's posting at the Starving Stirge promising gold and adventure, you decided that maybe a little adventuring "vacation" from Reme was exactly what you were looking for. Besides, Grenish would never bother sending assassins into the wilderness over a few little gems…or so you hope.

BELFLIN   CR 1/2
XP 200
Male elf ranger 1
CG Medium humanoid (elf)
Init +4; **Senses** low-light vision; **Perception** +8

AC 17, touch 14, flat-footed 13 (+3 armor, +4 Dex)
hp 11 (1d10+1)
Fort +3; **Ref** +6; **Will** +2; +2 vs. enchantments
Immune sleep

Speed 30 ft.
Melee longsword +2 (1d8+3/19–20) and short sword +2 (1d6+1/19–20) or longsword +4 (1d8+3/19–20)
Ranged longbow +5 (1d8/x3)
Special Attacks favored enemy (giants +2)

Str 16, **Dex** 18, **Con** 13, **Int** 12, **Wis** 14, **Cha** 12
Base Atk +1; **CMB** +4; **CMD** 18
Feats Two-Weapon Fighting
Skills Acrobatics +3, Climb +6, Handle Animal +5, Knowledge (geography) +5, Knowledge (nature) +5, Linguistics +2, Perception +8, Stealth +7, Survival +6 (+7 tracking), Swim +2
Languages Common, Elven, Giant, Sylvan
SQ elven magic, track +1, wild empathy +2
Gear studded leather armor, longsword, short sword, longbow, 20 arrows, backpack, bedroll, flint and steel, 50 ft. rope, sack, 5 torches, 5 days rations, 2 waterskins.

Elven Immunities +2 save bonus vs. Enchantments.
Elven Magic +2 racial bonus on caster checks to overcome spell resistance. +2 to Spellcraft checks to determine the properties of a magic item.
Enemies: Humanoids (Giant) (Ex) +4 to rolls vs. humanoids (giant).
Track (Ex) +1 to Survival checks to track.
Wild Empathy (Ex) Improve the attitude of an animal, as if using Diplomacy.

Background: As most of your race and profession, you are a loner. Yet you are even more reserved than most. Quiet and grim, you prefer the silence of the woodlands to the din of the city. Those few who know you learn that beneath your gloomy exterior lies a noble heart—a person whose word is his bond. Those who do not know you find you to be a pessimist, seeing doom and ill fortune in all paths. Your dark demeanor is not surprising, given that you are the sole survivor of a troll raid on your elven village. You have pledged your life to seek out these foul creatures and slay them wherever they may lurk without quarter. Stopping in Reme only to acquire some needed equipment, you noticed Corian's post in the Starving Stirge. Intrigued, and against your better judgment, you approached the young sorcerer. Sensing a kindred spirit, you agreed to travel with him wherever the road may take you.

HELMAN   CR 1/2
XP 200
Male halfling rogue 1
CG Small humanoid (halfling)
Init +5; **Perception** +7

AC 20, touch 17, flat-footed 14 (+3 armor, +5 Dex, +1 dodge, +1 size)
hp 9 (1d8+1)
Fort +2; **Ref** +8; **Will** +2; +5 vs. fear

Defensive Abilities bravery +1

Speed 20 ft.
Melee dagger +3 (1d3+2/19–20) or short sword +3 (1d4+2/19–20)
Special Attacks sneak attack +1d6

Str 14, **Dex** 20, **Con** 13, **Int** 14, **Wis** 13, **Cha** 14
Base Atk +0; **CMB** +1; **CMD** 17
Feats Dodge
Skills Acrobatics +10, Appraise +6, Bluff +6, Climb +7, Disable Device +9, Escape Artist +8, Perception +7 (+8 locate traps), Sense Motive +5, Sleight of Hand +8, Stealth +12, Swim +1
Languages Common, Elven, Halfling, Orc
SQ trapfinding +1
Gear studded leather, dagger, short sword, backpack, thieves' tools, 2 days rations

Fearless +2 morale bonus vs. fear saves.
Sneak Attack +1d6 damage if you flank your target or your target is flat-footed.
Trapfinding +1 to find and disable traps.

Background: The youngest of twenty-three brothers and sisters, you were always overlooked and forgotten. You did not help matters in that regard for you learned at a young age the skills of coming and going unobserved. With twenty-three siblings, that was not an easy task. You decided on your thirty-first birthday to set out on your own. It was weeks before your brothers and sisters even noticed you were gone. Fascinated all your life with tales of the city, you set out for Reme—the great port city to the north of your homeland. Your curiosity coupled with your nimble fingers and knack for disappearing at just the right time caught the attention of a band of thieves in Reme and soon enough you were a cutpurse of some renown. But you enjoyed your profession more for the thrill of the theft than for the greed of the haul and you quickly ran afoul of your employers who were none too keen on your cavalier disregard for keeping an accurate accounting of your night's takes. As you have always done before, you gave them the slip as well. While laying low at the Starving Stirge, you noticed Corian's post and decided then and there that a life of adventure was just the thing for you—particularly a life of adventuring that would take you away from Reme…at least until you decide on something better to do.

KREL   CR 1/2
XP 200
Male half-orc barbarian 1
N Medium humanoid (orc)
Init +2; **Senses** darkvision 60 ft.; **Perception** +4

AC 16, touch 12, flat-footed 14 (+4 armor, +2 Dex)
hp 16 (1d12+3 plus 1)
Fort +5; **Ref** +2; **Will** +0
Defensive Abilities ferocity

Speed 40 ft.
Melee greatsword +5 (2d6+6/19–20)
Special Attacks rage (7 rounds/day)

Str 18, **Dex** 14, **Con** 17, **Int** 6, **Wis** 11, **Cha** 10
Base Atk +1; **CMB** +5; **CMD** 17
Feats Power Attack
Skills Climb +2, Intimidate +2, Perception +4, Survival +4, Swim +2
Languages Common, Orc
SQ fast movement, orc blood, weapon familiarity
Gear chain shirt, greatsword, backpack, bedroll, 5 days rations, 2 waterskins

Fast Movement (Ex) +10 feet to speed, unless heavily loaded.

Orc Ferocity 1/day, when brought below 0 HP but not killed, you can fight on for 1 more round as if disabled. The next round, unless brought to at least 0 HP, you immediately fall unconscious and begin dying.
Rage (7 rounds/day) (Ex) +4 Str, +4 Con, +2 to Will saves, –2 to AC when enraged.

Background: The unwanted progeny from an orc raid on your village in the frozen north, you were despised by your father, who showed mercy on you at your mother's request by selling you into slavery rather than killing you at birth. For the last ten years you have served as a galley slave and rowed, chained to an oar, on various ships as they sailed the length and breadth of the known world. For all of your life as a slave you suffered cruel beatings for being a half-breed and you learned to hate that part of yourself—the part you feel is responsible for your miserable lot in life. Yet, even as you learned to despise your orc half, you found that it gave you strength and an animal rage that you have slowly learned to control. On your most recent voyage, the ship's captain released you from your chains and made you a member of the crew after you aided the ship in repelling a pirate attack. At landfall in Reme, the captain made you a free man.

With but a few coins to your name, a chainmail shirt given to you by the captain and the greatsword you liberated from a dead pirate, you sought out a pub as far from the docks as possible—desiring to make a new life for yourself. You made your way to the Starving Stirge where you met Corian. He greeted you as a friend. For the first time in your life a person saw you not as a half-breed but as an equal. You agreed at that moment to follow Corian anywhere. You are fiercely loyal to him.

DREBB   CR 1/2
XP 200
Male dwarf fighter 1
NG Medium humanoid (dwarf)
Init +2; **Senses** darkvision 60 ft.; **Perception** +1

AC 19, touch 12, flat-footed 17 (+5 armor, +2 Dex, +2 shield)
hp 13 (1d10+3)
Fort +5; **Ref** +2; **Will** +0; +2 vs. poisons, spells, and spell-like abilities
Defensive Abilities defensive training

Speed 20 ft.
Melee dwarven waraxe +6 (1d10+4/x3)
Ranged heavy crossbow +3 (1d10/19–20)
Special Attacks hatred

Str 18, **Dex** 14, **Con** 16, **Int** 15, **Wis** 11, **Cha** 11
Base Atk +1; **CMB** +5; **CMD** 17 (19 vs. bull rush and trip)
Feats Power Attack[B], Weapon Focus (dwarven waraxe)
Skills Appraise +3 (+5 nonmagical metals or gemstones), Perception +1 (+3 unusual stonework), Sense Motive +1, Stealth –3, Swim +2
Languages Common, Dwarven, Giant, Goblin
SQ slow and steady, stability, stonecunning
Gear scale mail, heavy steel shield, dwarven waraxe, heavy crossbow, 10 bolts, backpack, 50 ft rope, grappling hook, 5 days rations, waterskin

Slow and Steady Your base speed is never modified by encumbrance.
Stability +4 to avoid being bull rushed or tripped while standing.
Stonecunning +2 bonus to Perception vs. unusual stonework. Free check within 10 feet.

Background: Falsely accused of leaving your post during an orc raid by a superior with a grudge against you, you were expelled from your homeland and dis-owned by your family. Travelling down the coast road from your homeland in the north, you sought to put your shame behind you and prove your worth by a life of adventure. You dream every day of returning to your homeland, your reputation established, ousting the coward who stained your good name and being accepted by your father. Because the dwarf who falsely accused you was from a noble family, and thus his accusation was not questioned, you have no love for those of wealth and power. You see them as weaklings who cannot match their words with deeds. Finding yourself in Reme at the end of the coast road, you took a room at the Starving Stirge. There, you read Corian's note and decided that joining with Corian would lead you to glory and fame. And redemption.

CEDRIC CR 1/2
XP 200
Male half-elf druid 1
N Medium humanoid (elf)
Init +4; **Senses** low-light vision; **Perception** +9

AC 16, touch 14, flat-footed 12 (+2 armor, +4 Dex)
hp 9 (1d8+1)
Fort +3; **Ref** +4; **Will** +5; +2 vs. enchantments
Immune sleep

Speed 30 ft.
Melee scimitar +2 (1d6+2/18–20) or shortspear +2 (1d6+2)
Ranged sling +4 (1d4+2)
Spell-like Abilities (CL 1st):
6/day—*storm burst* (1d6 nonlethal)
Spells Prepared (CL 1st; melee touch +2, ranged touch +4):
1st—*cure light wounds, obscuring mist*ᴰ, *speak with animals*
0 (at will)—*detect poison, purify food and drink, resistance*
D Domain spell; **Domain** Weather

Str 14, **Dex** 18, **Con** 13, **Int** 14, **Wis** 17, **Cha** 12
Base Atk +0; **CMB** +2; **CMD** 16
Feats Skill Focus (Knowledge [nature])ᴮ, Spell Focus (conjuration)
Skills Diplomacy +2, Handle Animal +5, Heal +7, Knowledge (nature) +11, Perception +9, Survival +9, Swim +6
Languages Common, Druidic, Elven, Orc, Sylvan
SQ elf blood, nature bond (Weather domain), nature sense, wild empathy +2
Combat Gear *potion of cure light wounds*; **Other Gear** leather armor, scimitar, shortspear, sling, 10 bullets, wooden holy symbol, spell component pouch, belt pouch, backpack, 50 ft. rope, 4 days rations, waterskin

Spontaneous Casting The Druid can convert stored spells into Summon Nature's Ally spells.
Wild Empathy (Ex) Improve the attitude of an animal, as if using Diplomacy.

Background: You are a follower of the dryad Ossyniria. You reside in her grove in a forest near Bard's Gate with you fellow druids. You, however, are the only non-elf. You do not know your parents. Your human half has led you to have a fascination of human civilization. Following the end of your apprenticeship, you requested Ossyniria to allow you to leave the grove and observe men and their cities. Seeing the honesty of your request, she granted your wish. You have since wandered along the Tradeway from Bard's Gate to Reme. There, at the Starving Stirge, you met Corian. You had been away from the grove for some time and longed to return. When Corian asked for your aid you agreed to travel with him on your way back to Bard's Gate and the grove that is your home.

FLARIAN CR 1/2
XP 200
Male elf bard 1
CG Medium humanoid (elf)
Init +3; **Senses** low-light vision; **Perception** +5

AC 16, touch 13, flat-footed 13 (+3 armor, +3 Dex)

hp 9 (1d8+1)
Fort +1; **Ref** +5; **Will** +1; +2 vs. enchantments
Immune sleep

Speed 30 ft.
Melee rapier +1 (1d6+1/18–20) or dagger +1 (1d4+1/19–20)
Ranged shortbow +3 (1d6/x3)
Special Attacks bardic performance 7 rounds/day (countersong, distraction, *fascinate*, inspire courage +1)
Spells Known (CL 1st; melee touch +1, ranged touch +3):
1st (2/day)—*comprehend languages, ventriloquism* (DC 14)
0 (at will)—*detect magic, flare* (DC 13), *ghost sound* (DC 13), *summon instrument*

Str 13, **Dex** 16, **Con** 12, **Int** 13, **Wis** 8, **Cha** 16
Base Atk +0; **CMB** +1; **CMD** 14
Feats Skill Focus (Perform [string])
Skills Acrobatics +2, Diplomacy +7, Knowledge (history) +6, Knowledge (local) +6, Knowledge (nobility) +6, Linguistics +5, Perception +5, Perform (string) +12, Spellcraft +5 (+7 identify magic item properties), Stealth +2
Languages Common, Elven, Gnome, Goblin
SQ bardic knowledge +1, elven magic
Gear studded leather, rapier, dagger, shortbow, 20 arrows, backpack, bedroll, masterwork harp, 50 ft. silk rope, 3 days rations, waterskin.

Bardic Knowledge (Ex) Add + 1 to all Knowledge skill checks.
Bardic Performance: Countersong (Su) Counter magical effects that depend on sound.
Bardic Performance: Distraction (Su) Counter magical effects that depend on sight.
Bardic Performance: Fascinate (Su) One or more creatures becomes fascinated with you.
Bardic Performance: Inspire Courage (Su) Morale bonus on some saving throws, attack and damage rolls.

Background: Few of your race leave the confines of your forest realm. You, however, have long been drawn to humans, who live their short lives with a passion that you feel your race lacks. You wish to travel on to the legendary city of Bard's Gate, there to learn the songs of legend. Recently, while performing at the Starving Stirge in Reme, you met an engaging human named Corian. He told you of a strange amulet he possessed. He did not know its history, though his veiled comments made you believe there was an epic story behind it. He told you he wished to unlock its secret and asked you to travel with him. You agreed, believing you might learn the tale of the amulet and thereafter compose a song of its history.

FARKLE HURP CR 1/2
XP 200
Male gnome fighter 1
NG Small humanoid (gnome)
Init +2; **Senses** low-light vision; **Perception** +4

AC 17, touch 13, flat-footed 15 (+4 armor, +2 Dex, +1 size)
hp 17 (1d10+4 plus 3)
Fort +6; **Ref** +2; **Will** +1; +2 vs. illusions
Defensive Abilities defensive training

Speed 20 ft.
Melee warhammer +5 (1d6+2/x3)
Ranged light crossbow +4 (1d6/19–20)
Special Attacks hatred
Spell-like Abilities (CL 1st)
1/day—*dancing lights, ghost sound** (DC 11), *prestidigitation, speak with animals*
*Illusion spell

Str 15, **Dex** 14, **Con** 18, **Int** 16, **Wis** 12, **Cha** 11

Base Atk +1; **CMB** +2; **CMD** 14
Feats Toughness, Weapon Focus (warhammer)[B]
Skills Acrobatics +1, Craft (alchemy) +9, Escape Artist +1, Perception +4, Stealth +5, Survival +5
Languages Common, Dwarven, Gnome, Goblin, Orc, Sylvan
SQ gnome magic
Gear chain shirt, warhammer, light crossbow, 10 bolts, backpack, bedroll, 5 days rations, waterskin

---

Gnome Magic +1 to the save DC of all illusions spells you cast.
Illusion Resistance +2 racial bonus to saves against illusions.

Background: As a youth, a band of orcs raided your home cave in the Under Realms. Many of your brethren were slaughtered and a great gem—an heirloom of your clan—was stolen. At the time, you were a student of illusion magic. You left those studies because they seemed to offer little practical means of revenge. Instead, you began the study of the ways of the warrior.

Setting off on your own, you left your underground home to take revenge on the orcs. However, fate has not brought you the vengeance you seek. You have not located the marauding orc band, nor heard word of the whereabouts of the missing gem. You still carry with you the orcs' token, taken from their fallen chief: a poorly worked medallion bearing the image of a red severed arm over two crossed axes. You also plan one day to resume your study of illusion magic, perhaps to allow you to infiltrate the vile orcs when you find them.

Intrigued by Corian's post in the Starving Stirge, you have agreed to join his company. Hopefully, his powers will be able to aid you in finding the orcs responsible for the slaughter of your relatives.

DRINNIN   CR 1/2
XP 200
Male human monk 1
LN Medium humanoid (human)
Init +3; **Perception** +7

AC 17, touch 17, flat-footed 13 (+3 Dex, +1 dodge, +3 Wis)
hp 10 (1d8+2)
Fort +4; **Ref** +5; **Will** +5

Speed 30 ft.
Melee quarterstaff +4 (1d6+6) or unarmed strike +4 (1d6+6)
Special Attacks flurry of blows +3/+3 (1d6+4), stunning fist 1/day (DC 13)

Str 18, **Dex** 16, **Con** 15, **Int** 11, **Wis** 16, **Cha** 9
Base Atk +0; **CMB** +4 (+6 to grapple); **CMD** 21 (23 vs. grapple)
Feats Dodge[B], Improved Grapple[B], Improved Unarmed Strike[B], Mobility, Stunning Fist[B]
Skills Acrobatics +7, Escape Artist +7, Perception +7, Sense Motive +7, Sleight of Hand +4, Stealth +7
Languages Common
Gear quarterstaff

Stunning Fist (Ex) At 1st level, the monk gains Stunning Fist as a bonus feat, even if he does not meet the prerequisites.

Background: You were sent by your master from the Monastery of the Standing Stone to retrieve for him a fine ruby. He provided you with a purse of coins and sent you on your way to Reme. He did not explain his purpose, other than to caution you that material possessions often cloud those on the path of truth. Not one to question your master you dutifully traveled to Reme and traded your coins for a brilliant ruby. As you passed through an alleyway within the city, near a tavern called the Starving Stirge, you were set upon by thugs. They apparently were unfamiliar with the uses to which a stout staff may be put in combat. You provided them their education. A likeable fellow named Corian emerged from the tavern and offered you his assistance. When you explained you were unhurt and had an errand requiring your attention he explained he was seeking companions to uncover a mystery. When he mentioned he would be traveling to Fairhill—back towards the Monastery of the Standing Stone—you agreed to accompany him.

The Eamonvale Incursion

The Long-lost prequel and sequel to the infamous and best-selling Grey Citadel. This one never got published, and is available here for the first time. One of the long-lost Necromancer Games books for sale in all its original glory as a real book!

Adventures in the Valley of the River Eamon

Hard times have fallen on the frontier realm of Eamonvale. Economic hardship, inexplicable kidnappings, strange politics, raids by feral elves and rising brigand activity on the Trade Road combine to spell trouble for the people of the valley. Can the heroes sort fact from fiction and unearth the connections before uncertainty gives way to fear and panic?

Far worse things than dragons draw their shadows over Eamonvale.

The Eamonvale Incursion is a mini-campaign of urban investigation and wilderness exploration designed for 4 or more characters of at least 7th level. Finding the connections between recent disturbances takes the heroes from the bustling market town of Broadwater to the sleepy rural village of Fagan's Hollow, from the boggy wasteland of the Bleak to the shaded depths of the Elfwood, and into the hearts and minds of the people whose whole world is Eamonvale. Expanding on the setting of the author's first book The Grey Citadel (but fully useable without it), The Eamonvale Incursion features challenging parallel plot threads, a richly developed setting, vibrant NPCs and numerous secondary plot hooks to foster ongoing adventures in Eamonvale.

FORMATS V3.5

Page Count: 226 - Authors: Nate Paul - Retail: $29.99 for pdf or $34.99 for pdf and perfect bound softcover.

Demonheart

The Lost Necromancer Books...ready to print but never printed! This is one of the 3 books that never made the trip back from China...available for the first time as a print book.

Darkness in the Heart of the Forest

Generations ago, a fearful battle between raged in the depths of the Westwood. An entire tribe of forest elves gave up its very existence to turn back the rising tide of evil. Despite their noble sacrifice, a fragment of evil remained, and has now begun to awaken, drawing allies both old and new and transforming the Westwood into a place of fear and darkness.

Ancient Wrongs To be Righted

Today, the past lies forgotten and a settlement of innocent humans has sprung up near the old battleground. Little do the inhabitants of Tanner's Green suspect that a remnant of the old enemy has returned, and that its followers plot their downfall. Creatures of unspeakable evil lurk in the dark shadows of the forest, and only a small band of adventurers can find and stop them before the enemy rises once more.
Demonheart is mini-campaign for 3-5 player characters, beginning at levels 6-8 and rising to levels 10-12, with adventures that range from intrigue in the town of Tanner's Green to a life-or-death contest in the court of the king of the dark fey, all leading to a final confrontation with the ancient enemy.
Terror grows with each beat of the Demonheart. Can the adventurers stop it in time?

FORMATS V3.5

Page Count: 98 - Authors: Anthony Pryor - Retail: $14.99 for pdf or $21.99 for pdf and perfect bound softcover.

Hex Crawl Chronicles

By John Stater

FROG GOD
GAMES

This series provide a sub-setting in your own campaign world. They populate the world, and allow you to let your players explore that world, rather than just "travel 20 days" to the dungeon. Written by John Stater of NOD fame, each of these supplements details an area with a specific theme. Monster and NPC statistics are provided for each encounter area detailed.

Available now for Pathfinder and Swords & Wizardry at
www.talesofthefroggod.com

FROG GOD
GAMES

the northlands saga

By Kenneth Spencer

Now available at
www.talesofthefroggod.com

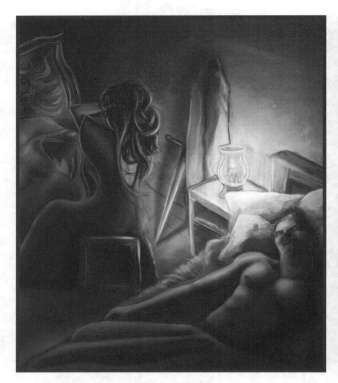

The Tome of Horrors Complete
— Unlimited Edition —

Trapped within this tome one may find beasts from the dawn of role-playing games to fresh meat many have never seen before. Converted for both the Pathfinder Roleplaying Game and Swords & Wizardry rules we are proud to bring you the monster book that will **eat** your other monster books!

Pathfinder Unlimeted Edition $109.99
Swords & Wizardry Edition $99.99

Tome of Adventure Design

Frog God Games is proud to present to you a comprehensive guidebook for designing your own fantasty adventures. In this volume Matt Finch presents advice and tables on topics ranging from villainous motives to monster design to dungeon creation.

Whether you're a veteran game master or a total beginner at the fine art of creating adventures, you will find that the Tome of Adventure Design is an invaluable resource when it's time to prepare for the game. Whatever you need for your adventure, you'll find ideas and table for it in this book.

Available Now! $42.00

Don't miss out! Order these Tomes and more at the Frog God Games website!
www.talesofthefroggod.com

Ursined, Sealed, & Delivered

By Dennis Sustare

One of the One Night Stands series, Ursined, Sealed and Delivered is a newly written adventure module, but it's a truly unique window into the early days of the game. The module is written by Dennis Sustare, the designer and author of the original Druid class that has become a key character class in virtually every fantasy game ever written since 1978. I've done almost no editing of Dennis's text, although the tournament format has been shifted around to be more easily used during play. The result is that you are about to read an adventure that's a direct window into the imagination of one of the great figures of fantasy gaming. Any typographical errors or glitches in the "flow" of the adventure are the responsibility of the editor, and all the high-adventurous moments of this fast-moving, gripping adventure are to the credit of the author.

Available now for Pathfinder and Swords & Wizardry at www.talesofthefroggod.com

FROG GOD GAMES

Now available at
www.talesofthefroggod.com